STI.

Joe Donnelly, currently writing for the *Sunday Mail*, has worked for various newspapers and travelled extensively. In 1991 he was awarded Scottish Reporter of the Year for his investigative writing on child abuse cases, and for the feature that resulted from his being the first on the scene after the Shotts Prison riot. He is the author of three previous chillers, *Bane*, *Stone* and *The Shee*, and his latest book, *Shrike*, will be published by Century in 1994. Joe Donnelly lives in Dumbarton with his family.

STILL LIFE

Joe Donnelly

ARROW

Published by Arrow Books in 1994

1 3 5 7 9 10 8 6 4 2

Copyright © Joe Donnelly 1993

The right of Joe Donnelly to be identified as the
author of this work has been asserted by him in accordance
with the Copyright, Designs and Patents Act, 1988.

First published by Century in 1993

Arrow Books Limited
Random House, 20 Vauxhall Bridge Road, London SW1V 2SA

Random House Australia (Pty) Limited
20 Alfred Street, Milsons Point, Sydney
New South Wales 2061, Australia

Random House New Zealand Limited
18 Poland Road, Glenfield
Auckland 10, New Zealand

Random House South Africa (Pty) Limited
PO Box 337, Bergvlei, South Africa

Random House UK Limited Reg. No. 954009

A CIP catalogue record for this book
is available from the British Library

ISBN 0 09 910391 5

Printed and bound in Germany by
Elsnerdruck, Berlin

For Vivienne Schuster, who can work magic.

1

FUTURE

He could hear his own heartbeat. He could feel it pounding fast, *too fast* in his chest. It was the only thing he knew was real.

And *Christ* it hurt.

Martin Thornton held on to the pain in his heart. It ripped and twisted inside with every hammer blow, as if it was going to explode. He tried to slow down his savage, frantic breathing, but that didn't work. His heart kept banging against his ribs and the pain flooded over him in wave after wave.

The darkness was absolute. It crowded in on him, and behind the darkness shapes loomed in, twisting, changing shapes that had no form. He screwed his eyes shut against them, against the pain, and felt himself begin to fade out again. He was falling down that well, tumbling dizzily away from the hurt. The darkness raced away, a nightmare express train screaming into the beyond, and colours spangled and danced in behind his eyelids.

He was losing it again, and that was the worst of all. He couldn't hold on to the pain any more. It faded away from him in slow, pounding pulses that dulled down with every beat. Then he was back in nightmare country again, though he knew this was no dream.

He felt himself twist inside out as all other sensation shattered and then he was *there*. He bellowed in fear and the staccato sound of his voice echoed from tree to tree and faded into the distance.

Twisted hands reached for him and took him by the head and arms and feet. Faces from a nightmare – this living nightmare – snarled at him. He flinched away (*though he knew they were not real*) but was powerless to stop them. He struggled and screamed while they ripped and tore at him, twisting his limbs, digging claws into his skin, tearing him apart.

He smelled moist earth and rot. He smelled his own blood. He heard the mad cackle of their laughter and the shivering scrape of their horny fingers. He saw their grotesque bark-like faces shift and *change*.

Something gave, quite painlessly. A gnarled hand brought a mess of red wetness up before his horrified eyes and he knew it was a part of himself. An inhuman face leaned over him and a waft of decay and corruption engulfed him. He felt himself lifted up and then slammed down on the mouldering forest floor. Hard hands forced him through the leaf litter into damp earth. He sensed it against his skin, slick and slimy, until all but his head and shoulders remained.

Then the shapes that had ripped and torn him moved back, silently. They stood in a circle around him, staring with wooden eyes in creased, lumpy faces. They raised their hands and he saw their bodies elongate, stretching upwards. The arms lengthened, spread. Fingers grew and branched. Moss raced up cross-hatched flanks and still the terrible lifeless eyes riveted him.

Beneath the ground sensation flooded into his broken body. He felt blood flow out and cold wetness ooze in.

He tried to breathe, but no breath came. He strained to drag himself out of the damp earth, but he could not make his arms move beyond a spasmodic twitch. Below his waist, he felt a crawling on his skin, a movement where his legs were, where they should be. Something moved, and he realised it was *himself*. He felt his toes curl and stretch, probing the earth. The hairs of his legs twisted and lengthened, burrowing into the soil. His arm moved in front of him with a hellish *creaking* sound and he saw the fingers twist and curl, knuckles popping out from brown, wrinkled skin. He tried to bring it close to his face, but his arm disobeyed him.

And down below, he felt the pores draw in the water that lay underneath the surface. It swelled into him, rising up his knotted veins, drawing ever higher in a cold, turbid ooze.

He tried to call out, to shout, and his throat constricted raspingly. No sound came.

His arms stretched ever upwards, fingers splaying, branching. He felt the *green* of the forest all around him, and a shiver ran through his rooted feet. He felt it vibrate upwards to flutter the branches overhead as the moisture pulsed upwards. And all around was the boom *boom* BOOM of the pulse of the trees.

Wooden eyes blindly stared him down and he sensed the silent watching of the other shapes that had planted themselves in the clearing. His roots merged with theirs and the pulse went on and on and on.

The living heart of the forest beat through him and a wind caught his outstretched hands and swayed them with the rest of the treetops. He was trapped, helpless against the terrible force of this place where life quickened in the very earth, dragging him into itself, becoming one with the terrible soul of the green wood.

The deep boom of life flowed and ebbed in waves, forcing itself into him, making him become part of it. The cold surged and a monstrous pressure drove it up through him, overwhelming him with its power.

The wind strengthened and shook him, bending him this way and that, twisting and turning so that he felt his whole length cry out as the strain ripped cell from cell. Great cracks appeared where thick barky skin tore and green spurted out. His rigid body gave before the wind and the booming pounded up through him in a series of violent, irresistible blows.

Now he felt the snap in a shock wave that blasted up and down in an instant of destruction. A sense that was not pain, but of devastating *damage* shuddered through him. A roaring noise ripped out through the forest and he was falling, tumbling, crashing his way downwards. Branch-arms broke and snapped. Root-feet stretched and tore asunder. Tree-trunks wrenched and split and the ground came up to meet him with dizzy speed. There was another shock of awful force as he hit and rolled, deadened by the enormity of the blow. Sensation faded out, leaving him oblivious to everything but the incessant pounding that shivered the ground in deep rolling waves.

And suddenly Martin Thornton was back again.

His searing lungs scooped in air from the darkness. His heart was still thudding fast, too fast, but the pain was easing now. He rolled over the crest of it, breathed out again, then in, gasping hard, letting the oxygen flood into him.

He tried to move, but that was still impossible. The darkness held him in its grip, but at least be was back, out of *there*, out of the awful other world of the hallucination.

His heart slowed a little more, and the pain abated slowly, a

3

sluggish pool draining out, giving him a chance to *think* again. Martin Thornton tried to move again and this time his arm flopped languidly. Pins and needles jangled up and down between his forearm and wrist, but at least there was *something*, some feeling other than the pain under his ribs. He raised his head an inch and it jarred back onto the hard surface. The deeper darkness surged in again and he panicked, thinking he might lose consciousness again, and that was the *last* thing he wanted.

The numb itch ran up and across his shoulders then rippled down the length of him. The return of sensation, *any sensation*, sent hope leaping. He tried the arm again and this time, lazily, torpidly, it did his bidding. It was too dark to see, but finally his fingers, leaden arm tingling all the while, brushed against his cheek.

They felt just like fingers. Stiff and sluggish, but *human*. And as they were coming back to life, so was his memory. It was hazy, fuzzy. Shadowed. Yet, something was stirring, an image wavered then winked out. A thought fleeted in, elusive, then vanished before caught. His mental grasp was as numb as his fingers, but slowly, the pins and needles in his head would ease off too. *He hoped*.

The room was pitch-black, but it smelled old and musty. He was lying, he realised, on a hard, stone floor. He could hear something rustling, but his hearing was distorted by the still-fast pounding in his ears. Finally, he tried to raise his head again. A sharp pain flared in his neck, but not enough to make him give up. He rolled onto his side and managed to get an elbow between himself and the cold stone. His left hand reached out as he blindly probed the dark and touched a wall, damp and slick under his fingers.

He raised himself to his knees, swaying dizzily with the effort, and at last got to his feet. He lifted his head slowly, unsure of the height of the ceiling. There was a rasping sound from a few yards away and he stiffened instantly, holding himself tight and still. The noise was not repeated. Very carefully he felt his way along the wall, which now streamed moisture. The spongy surface was cool and wet. His fingertips oozed into the slick coating as if probing rotted flesh, and he felt nausea squeeze inside him.

There was something he had to do.

He knew there was something he had to do. Very urgently. A matter of great importance. A matter of *life and death*.

Yet his befuddled, panicked, *sickened* mind was trapped in thick sludge, struggling to get out, trying not to drown. There was something he had to do, and for the life of him he couldn't remember what.

He stumbled blindly along the wall, and finally he reached a corner. It seemed he'd come a long way, hands slithering on the poisonous toadstool surface. The junction was running with water, or slime, and he had to fight down his disgust, keep his fingers on the wall, to feel his way further. Ten steps, maybe twenty steps in the darkness, with the images swooping in on him, flitting from shadow to shadow and just beyond his grasp.

Then his knuckles struck a doorhandle.

Relief bubbled up like a spring. He breathed in and the jangled jumbled thoughts began to untangle themselves.

Just at that moment, somewhere in the east, a flash of lightning sparked outside. The sizzling orange speared through the cob-webbed and dusty hatch window of the basement of a house at the edge of a forest. The dark scattered.

Martin Thornton turned to the window and the light hit him straight in the eyes. He screwed them up against the flickering glare and blinked back sudden tears. In a moment his spinning vision cleared. He looked down at his hand, gripped tight on the old doorknob and grunted in alarm.

The wood of the door was crawling with fungus. Flanges of dripping Jew's Ear writhed on rotten oak panels. Black clusters of Witch's Butter, like diseased brains, crawled on the frames. Threadlike hyphae stretched and spread spidery webs, visibly multiplying from the rubbery growths, probing the air and then, finding a space on the wood, wormed their way into the surface where yet more of the crawling toadstools swelled into life.

Martin stood and watched while the light increased and the thunderstorm walked in the valley. His out-of-step thoughts finally got themselves in order, then memories too marched in, quick step, one image on the heels of another. He knew what it was he had to do.

'I have to get out of here,' he said aloud. It was the first time he had spoken since—*how long?* His words were swallowed by the glistening, heaving, tapestry of swelling fungus. Outside, the thunder hammered across the sky.

The living decay oozed over the doorknob, slug-like and somehow *alive*. Martin Thornton dragged his eyes away from it and turned round. Now that his eyes had got used to the gloomy light from the small hatch window, he saw shelves stacked against the far wall, heavy wooden shelves on which bottles and glass flasks, dust-covered and weirdly threatening, were crowded together. In the corner furthest from the window, where his fingers had probed the amphibious skin that covered the walls, an old spinning wheel, its wool bobbin dangling like a hanged man, stood on four lathe-turned legs, a stiff shadowy horse.

Movement caught his eye and he swivelled to face the shelves again. The bottles clinked against each other as if a tremor had run through the room. He took three slow steps towards them and saw that within each flask and demijohn liquids were bubbling and frothing. A sudden loud *pop* almost stopped his heart and the cork cap of one glass jar ricocheted off one of the low beams with a solid thump. Martin ignored that movement. His eyes were nailed on the jar from which green, slug-like tentacles were now looping over the neck and probing, tentatively, yet with a horrible *gelid* purpose. Slimy fingers slowly waved, stretched and blindly sought. One of them, slipped, almost casually, round the neck of another glass bottle, flexed, and the container spun to the floor. There was no crash of shattering glass, only a dull crack as the bottle broke and from it scattered a brown wave which flowed with the distant sound of a riptide on shingle.

Martin made to walk over the scattering of seed, away from those *unreal* tentacles, when the seeds themselves started to move. His foot was just about to come down when his muscles froze in a jolt of paralysis.

The seeds had started to *move*. There were thousands of them, each the size of a sunflower kernel. In a single nightmare *flick* the mass of them started to crawl with the dizzy speed of cockroaches, on tiny hair-like, pistoning legs.

'Oh for God's sake,' he said, though he wasn't aware of it. He twisted his body so that his foot came down on the floor, away from the mass of scuttling insectile seed-cases. It caught half a dozen outrunners, though, cracking their papery shells. He could feeling them squirm under his shoe.

'No, no, no, no,' he said aloud, almost groaning, shaking his head to deny what his eyes were showing him. He *knew* it was not real. This was the same as the hallucinations. *She* had given him something. Put it in his drink. Blown it into his nose. The mad bitch had fed him something that had blasted his mind right out of his skull into a nightmare country. He was no longer in *there*, but whatever she had given him must still be working.

'Damned *witch*,' he mouthed and the useless fury in his words made him feel just a little bit better. 'Out of here,' he said again. Into the fresh air, the light of day. To *do* whatever it was that he knew he had to do.

He scrunched across the creeping carpet of insectile seeds that he told himself *were not there*. He ignored the wavering tendrils of slimy, luminescent green that now stretched a yard or more from the jar's neck. He closed his eyes to the bubbling, *living* motion in the bottles and jars, squirming to be born from their translucent vitreous wombs. He made his hand – and his mind – reject the clammy, pulsating toadstools growing in an obscene rubbery mass on the door and all over the doorknob.

He knew *it did not exist.*

Martin Thornton gripped the knob as hard as he could with both hands, until his fingers finally squelched through the growth and found the brass underneath. He dropped his right shoulder, raising his left to twist the handle clockwise. There was a dull click and he pulled back, throwing his full weight into dragging the door open. The strands and threads of mould stretched like toffee, ripped and then gave as the door swung wide. Dry air flooded in and Martin heaved himself out. To the left was a wall festooned with old-fashioned iron coathooks. He turned right towards the bottom of a narrow wooden staircase leading up to a green door. The treads creaked as he lumbered up as fast as he could make himself go. At the top, he barged into the door which opened without hesitation and he spilled headlong into a dim hallway, taking a crack on the knee and landing on all fours.

Bright flashes of pain heliographed up his leg and he grunted with the effort of not crying out. Again momentary tears pricked his eyes and he forced them back. His vision swam loopily and everything swelled out of focus before shrinking back to clarity. He was heaving himself up when a low growl shuddered the hallway. He stopped in mid push and saw something black uncurl from the shadows. At first he thought it was a cat, and in that instant a memory came barging back at him, though he didn't have time to grab it and think.

The shape unfolded in a fluid ebony slither and snaked towards him, hurtling down the hallway. He saw a mouth gape and the growl became a roar. He saw muscular, furry legs jerk with lightning speed and heard claws plough furrows in the polished floor. It was no cat. It was a sinuous monstrosity, a roaring, glaring, *fast* creature that bulleted the length of the hallway with the serpentine motions of a stoat.

Sheer fright saved him.

He tried to push himself backwards, but his arms wouldn't move. He simply slipped. He saw muscles bulge, noticed a froth of saliva whip back from a gaping mouth, caught the flash of jagged spiked teeth and, just as the nightmare on legs leapt to take him in the throat, he tumbled face down onto the boards. There was an *express train* of a roar a foot above his head and out of the corner of one eye he saw a black shape sail over him. Even then, something whipped down from that moving mass, something so incredibly quick it was just a blur, and sliced an eight-inch groove in his back. Blood spurted and streamed down his sides, down his arms and legs. Without even thinking, he tried to crawl, but the slippery red under his hands and knees gave him no purchase. He was crawling, but going nowhere. There was a thump somewhere behind him, hard and loud enough to make the walls shake, and the roaring cut off instantly.

Martin Thornton's hand slipped in his own blood and he fell again, but this time the momentum carried him forward far enough for his hands and knees to reach a part of the floor that wasn't soaked frictionless. Down there, in the cellar, the thing that had come at him, the hellish nightmare that had uncoiled and come roaring at him, was snarling and spitting its rage. He could hear it banging and thumping its way upstairs and he knew it was coming for him. He made it to the end of the hallway, to the old carved coatstand that stood by the heavy door, and grabbed the first thing that came to hand. It was a black umbrella.

He whirled, naked and bleeding, screwed up so tight that he was beyond fear. He was in that place a cornered rat reaches when the terrier closes in for the kill and there is no way out. He was a man, naked and alone and trapped, clutching an old black umbrella in a death grip, powered now completely by instinct that did not allow rational thought. There was no chance of flight. The chemicals in him, the *animal* in him, dictated *fight*.

Muscles moved of their own accord. He launched himself wildly from the wall back the way he had stumbled, the black point of the umbrella before him, ready to meet head on the monster, ready to shove the spike into its mad eye. He slipped on his own blood and slammed against the doorpost which conveniently prevented his headlong sprawl down and into the jaws of the thing that was thumping its way up.

His eyes, wide with feral *rage-fear*, flicked right, left and down, scanning the whole stairwell in a second. There was nothing on there. Something moved to the left of the cellar door. A long black body, thumping against the wall. A head with a blunt snout swivelled this way and that, a snarling, caterwauling. The thing was hanging on the wall, legs *(how many legs?)* scrabbling on the wooden panels.

From its back, staining the black, shaggy coat with runnels of scarlet, four old iron coathooks shoved their way out of the matted fur, puckering the skin up into jagged tents. The thing was impaled. It screamed and lashed its head from side to side as he watched, still shaking, at the top of the stairs, until the jerking stopped and the scream became a howl, then a shuddering moan, then silence.

Martin Thornton felt the muscles of his legs give way and he slid down the doorpost until his backside was on the floor.

Down there, on the coathooks, the thing that had waited to kill him was withering fast on the wall, shrivelling into itself, deflating as it decayed.

Some time later, he didn't know just how long, though it must only have been moments, Martin Thornton seemed to jerk back to life again, like a man whose thoughts had been far away and was startled back to reality, though *unreality* would have been a better description of what was really the case.

He had to go. He had to get out of there. Because someone would surely die if he didn't.

PRESENT

It was late spring. The air was still and the sun shone down in a tranquil blue sky beyond the Dumbuie Hills which formed the northwest wall of Linnvale glen. Up on its flanks the Corrie Linn, a natural lake scooped from the soft shale and held in by the hard sandstone, collected water from the tumbling streams, swollen from recent rains. The Linn kept it a while before letting it brim over the falls to become the Corrie River, which in turn pounded its way down past Linnvale village, frothed white under the bridge and then plunged, after a couple of tight turns, down into the shade of Fasach Wood. It emerged some miles later on the flat valley basin, cold and dark, to meander its willow-avenue path and empty itself into Loch Corran.

From the slopes of the Dumbuie Hills, in the hour before sunset, the village looked like a toytown. In the far distance, the blue of the loch beyond the main road would turn purple. Hill farms with whitewashed walls formed pale rectangles against the deeper purpling of the heather, and the sheep even smaller blobs. Down the slope, where the hills which bounded the glen on almost four sides lost height and swept towards the basin, the spread of Fasach Wood in the early evening light would take on a deeper green and the shadows within it darken to black.

Fasach Wood was old and it was dark under the crowded beeches and oaks. It was a forest of shadows and the whispering rustle of wind in high leaves, the creak of branch upon trunk. Night fell in Fasach Wood before the rest of the sleepy glen.

It seemed a dead place, but in its depths there was life. Oh, there was life.

On this late spring day, the first fine day of the year, there was noise in Fasach Wood. Down at its south edge, where the River Corrie sluggishly crept out from under the trees, two pyramids of green stood close together on the flat slope at the bottom of a long-fallow field. Most of it was covered in thistles which had not reached their full summer height. The two green canvas tents huddled beside a willow tree whose gnarled and tangled roots looped into the water like siphons.

10

Angie Clark emerged on hands and knees, shoving back the flap and rising to her feet. Danny Grindlay followed, tucking his shirt into his black leathers and, finally, pulling up his zip. His hair was long and caught in a greasy ponytail. There was a tattoo on his shoulder that looked like a squint dagger. The knuckles on his right hand read EVIL if read from the receiving end, though the letters were turned backwards, a testament to Danny's lack of foresight when he painstakingly designed his personal tattoo. Angie was thin and had long black tangled hair with that dead lacklustre texture of the recently dyed. Her black, silver-studded leather jacket was a smaller version of the one Danny Grindlay had slung across his shoulder.

Over to the upstream side, beyond the edge of the trees, a low roaring sound came echoing out from the shadows.

'What's going on in there?' Danny asked, fishing his cigarettes from a pocket. He lit one, took a drag and passed it to the girl.

The roaring got suddenly louder, a ratchety, jarring noise that broke up and came together again as it ricocheted from the tree-trunks. There was movement in the shadows and something big and black launched itself towards them.

The powerful black motorbike crashed through the thistles, its heavy-treaded rear wheel kicking up a spray of dirt. It skidded to a halt, the rear-end slewing round in a half circle.

'Brilliant.' Mick O'Dell grinned. 'There's some great tracks in there. It's like moto-cross.'

'Aye and you'll bring every hick in the valley down on us.'

'Aw, come on, Danny. Lighten up. We can get right through to the other side. There's nobody about.'

The girl behind the rider was wearing a shiny black helmet. Her hands were clamped around his waist. From under the visor, she gave the other two a slow smile.

'Come on. Let's have a bit of fun, eh? Me and Mick'll race you through to the top end. There's a good place near the river to pitch the tents. Unless you're too tired after your exercise, that is.'

Norma Wardlaw gave Danny a broad wink, which he missed because of the reflection on the visor.

Angie Clark looked at him. He seemed to consider it.

'Aye, all right. We'd better move on out of here anyway.'

Mick jacked his bike up and he and Norma clambered off. They collapsed the small tents and rolled them up with practised ease, tying their bags to the carriers behind the pillions. There were two light rectangles on the grass where it had been flattened under groundsheets. Danny Grindlay poured a pan of water onto the dying embers of their small fire. Steam billowed briefly on the hot circle of stones, then faded.

'Right,' he said. 'Let's get going.'

Mick swung his leg over the saddle, flicked his wrist to make his bike roar throatily, then let the machine slew forward, leaving a half-moon brown scar on the turf. Norma clung behind him as he angled the machine straight into the trees. Danny and Angie were only yards behind as they dashed into Fasach Wood.

The trees rang with the clatter of engines. The big treads sent up sprays of dead leaves as they roared down the narrow hardpacked tracks that led straight into the heart of the forest. Tree-trunks whizzed past, blurred in peripheral vision. They came to an old stone dyke where the toppled stones were covered in thick moss. The path they'd taken went straight on through to where the trees crowded more densely, the branches above so thick that most of the daylight was cut out.

Mick pulled to a halt a little way along the track. Ahead of them, when the roar of powerful engines died, they could hear the sound of the river. They angled the bikes under a spreading beech tree beside a small stream which trickled and murmured between mossy banks.

'Not a bad place,' Mick said. 'They can't see us from the road.'

'It's a bit dark in here,' Angie said, looking around.

'You scared of the dark?' Norma smirked.

Angie ignored her. She looked around the glade. The trees stood thick and massive and ancient. Great beeches and oaks, gnarled Scots pines with red bark and trails of amber resin running like slow candlewax down their flanks. And beyond there was a stand of huge ferns, almost like trees, with wide fronded leaves sprouting in bunches from the top of bare stems. The air was thick and humid.

'The river's down that way.' Mick pointed down a straight track where the earth was bare from the passage of feet or hooves or whatever came down to this shady part of the woods.

Danny gave Angie a nod and the two of them strolled off. They passed the big ferns and pushed their way under the thick succulent leaves of some forest plant. Up above, previously-silent insects fluttered on papery wings, whirring unseen through the heavy air. There was a sweet smell of pollen that caught the back of the lungs, and underneath it a whiff of decay. It reminded Danny of a greengrocer's midden in the summer.

Angie took off her jacket and put her arm around his waist, digging her hand into the hip pocket of his jeans. Mick and Norma watched them stroll off.

'Never gets enough,' he said.

'Her neither. Thinks she invented it.'

'Probably did,' Mick said, chuckling. The pair of them waited until the others were out of sight before they got off the bike. 'Will I put the tent up?' he asked, raising his eyebrows. She caught the look in his eye.

'We don't need the tent yet. It's dry here.' She walked forward, put her arms round his waist and raised her face to his.

Down the track, Danny and Angie came to the river. It moved slow and sluggish between banks that were a tangle of snake-like willow roots. Black whorls flared on the surface as if unseen things were moving below it.

'Like the Amazon here,' Angie said. 'Creepy.'

Danny walked downstream a little way to where a wide beech with smooth grey bark stood massive not far from the water's edge. She followed him, keeping close, a city girl nervous in the country. Danny sat on one of the roots that muscled out from the base and took a lock-knife from his pocket.

'Look at that. Not a mark on it,' he said, running his fingers over the trunk. 'Seems a shame to waste it.' The point of the blade dug in through the surface till it hit hard wood. Sap swelled and ran down the steel as he worked it upwards, hand screwing back and forth until he had cut a straight vertical line. He cut a curve to complete his first initial, then quickly carved the second, in letters about four inches tall.

'Not bad,' he said, standing back to look at his handiwork. Angie stayed close. Her eyes were raised to the overhanging canopy where leaves rustled and small things moved in the shadows. Danny leaned back to his task and cut her initials below his.

13

'How's that?' he asked her. Angie looked round, momentarily distracted from her growing sense of unease. She saw the initials together and smiled. 'Put a heart round them,' she said. 'Show me you mean it.' Danny grinned back and winked at her. 'Only if you mean it,' Angie said, tossing her hair back, almost coquettishly. He turned to the tree. She saw the point drive into the trunk and winkle out the wood until the stylised shape surrounded the letters, pure white against the dark grey bark.

'That'll stand for a hundred years,' Danny said.

'Just like yourself,' Angie said with a knowing smile, feeling a warm glow inside her that banished her unease. She was pleased he'd done it for her. She bent down to where he was leaning, half-seated on the root, and kissed him full on the mouth.

Danny deftly closed the lock-knife and shoved it into his pocket. He raised his arm and pulled her down to his level, turning her as he did so. She allowed herself to be lowered onto the thick carpet of leaves, still clamped to Danny while his other hand instinctively came sliding up over her ribs. She gave a little sigh that was almost a moan and felt the surge well up hot again. Danny heaved himself on top of her and his weight pressed her deeper into the leaves. Something hard pushed up against her spine and she shifted, trying to get comfortable. She opened her eyes and froze.

It took Danny twenty seconds to realise that her response had stopped, and that she had gone completely rigid. He opened his eyes, saw her staring to the side, and pulled his head back.

'What's up?' he asked. She opened her mouth to speak and he turned, following her gaze.

The side of the tree was pouring red from the heart he had carved in the bark.

The thick scarlet bubbled up in strong pulses, filled the deep gash he'd cut, then spilled out in a steady flow. The whole side of the tree was slathered in it, awash with red. Something caught in the back of his throat and he almost choked on the thick metallic tang that wafted towards him.

'It's *blood*.' Angie said. 'It's bleeding.' Danny shoved himself up, more perplexed than concerned.

'Naw. It can't be . . .'

He never finished the sentence. It all happened so fast that for an instant Angie didn't even understand *what* had happened. One second he was lying on top of her and the next he was twenty feet above her. There had been a jolt. Danny had grunted, and then he had just heaved into the air.

Angie blinked. He seemed to be *flying* upwards, hands outstretched, legs spreadeagled. She opened her mouth and then she heard his hoarse scream.

Suddenly it *clicked* inside her head. Her mind had refused to take it in despite what her eyes had told her. There had been a slow movement just behind Danny when he'd started to speak. Something had grabbed him with the speed of a striking snake and had plucked him from the ground.

She jerked up and Danny screamed her name, hoarse and desperately loud from up above her where the leaves shivered in the wind.

'Angie. *Angie!*'

He made a little coughing sound and then he screamed again. She sat there, frozen in fright, head arched back and eyes locked on the scene above her head. Something else lashed out, hidden by the dense foliage. She saw his leg jerk and he squirmed desperately against whatever held him. His hands tore at something on his chest, but she couldn't see what it was, for the whole mass of branches was shaking and bending as he struggled. All her staring eyes could make out was his shape high above her. Her ears were ringing with his frantic cry.

The scream died instantly. Up there, something *flexed*. There was a rustling sound, then a dull crack. Danny disappeared into the high leaves. At least half of him was dragged upwards. The other half, still kicking and dancing in mid air, was pulled in towards the tree in a violent jerk.

She heard the spatter of rain on the leaves at her feet. Scarlet roses blossomed instantly. Something wet splashed onto her hand and she snatched it back in horror. Angie's mouth opened so far the bones in her cheeks creaked painfully, but no sound came out. Her lungs simply refused to work. Her hands flew to her black hair and her nails dug into her scalp, but still she couldn't scream. She crouched, frozen for a few minutes, eyes wide and staring, and then a movement right ahead punched its way through to her stunned brain. Angie jerked straight. Her throat opened. Something blurring fast shot out from an oak-tree close to the beech. She

15

stumbled backwards and this time her screaming mechanism worked just fine. She let out such a howl of terror that it could have been heard from the edge of Fasach Wood, had there been anybody there. She stumbled back, fell, hauled herself to her feet and took two steps. Something clenched on her ankle and hauled her backwards. The girl's fingernails clawed in the ground, raking up handfuls of leaves. She was jabbering incoherently as the panic swamped her.

The girl was dragged through the brambles and wild roses across the dell and then Angie was lifted up off the ground. Something grabbed at her with hard, rasping fingers, pinioned her thrashing legs and arms, pulling them in opposite directions. She felt a terrible wrench in her shoulder and another at her pelvis as limbs were forced beyond their capacity.

As she was drawn up from the ground she saw a movement just ahead. Mick O'Dell had come running into the clearing, with Norma on his heels. He stood there open-mouthed, his face just a pale blur far down from where Angie struggled like a fly in a web.

She tried to call to him, but all she could manage was a shrill shriek. Down below her waist something *gave*. Mick turned, dragged Norma away and over her terror she felt a jolt of hatred which lasted only long enough for the pain to come ramming up from her hips. Everything went black.

Mick O'Dell came racing through the trees towards where they'd parked the bike. Behind him, dragged in his grip, Norma Wardlaw was wailing like a fire siren. They got to the tent, crashed right over it. Mick jumped onto the saddle, pulling Norma onto the pillion. Around them the forest seemed to be *alive* with motion. He kicked the pedal hard. It coughed, sputtered and died. Norma screeched in his ear. He twisted the throttle, kicked down again with all his weight and the engine roared. He slammed the clutch and the bike reared up, kicking a fountain of leaves. The front wheel came down and he jerked the handlebars. The bike spun away from the tree and he shot out of the clearing. Norma was screeching hysterically in his ear, but he ignored it. His only thought was to get *out*.

Mick aimed the bike along the track, heading for the tumble-down wall. He could see it in the distance. He twisted the handle and the machine almost took off again, ramming its way though overhanging ivy and crushing ferns and brambles which ripped and clawed at them as they crashed along the path.

Then something snatched down from above. Danny ducked. He felt the jolt as Norma was hauled from the bike. There was a frantic tug at his waist as her hands tried to claw for him, then she was gone. Over the roar of the engine he could hear her scream pierce the air as if got higher – from the ground – behind him. He didn't stop; didn't turn. Mick saw the break in the wall and zoomed towards it, wheels kicking up a back-wave of leaves. He was twenty yards from it, going faster than he would ever have dared in the close confines of the forests. He was getting away. He was almost there. He was . . .

He was riding through the air.

The ground had disappeared. A long shape darted out from the tree and snatched the bike, heaving it up from the track. Mick didn't even see what it was. He felt himself thrown forward. There was a wrench on both arms as his hands automatically clamped on the grips, then he was tumbling through the air. In a flash of jumbled vision he saw the black bike soar away, hauled upwards. He tried to grab on to branches whipping past him, failed, and soared on. He broke through the overhanging leaves, flying towards an enormous forked trunk. The thick foliage slowed him down, but still he hit above the fork with such a thump that his breath was socked out. His face smacked into the hard wood and his nose burst like a ripe peach.

Mick O'Dell grunted, vision spinning, less than half conscious. He was folded over a thick branch which angled out from the trunk twenty feet up from the ground. His arm was snagged on something, twisted awkwardly, and a shrill bite of pain grated in his elbow joint. Mick moaned and a stream of snot and blood welled down from his nose. He tried to move, but the glassy pain in his elbow shrieked at him and he froze.

His vision came back into sharp focus. All around him the green leaves were shivering in the breeze.

Without warning, something squeezed at him with such force that all he could manage was a reflexive gulp. He tried to pull away from the pressure but underneath him something *flexed*. Monstrous pain slammed into his ribs. They popped like fire-crackers in three short, muffled cracks. The monumental pressure

17

slammed him from both sides. Mick O'Dell felt the ribs on his left give then something stabbed deep inside him. There was a fountain of hurt, a great frantic gusher of agony. A grinding sound crunched at his pelvis and the unbelievable pain erupted in white heat. He could not escape it, could not move.

Mick's blood flowed in rivers down the trunk of the tree. His bulging eyes never saw it. They were fixed straight ahead of him. The last thing he saw was the dancing of young green leaves as they shivered in the breeze. The vision winked out.

PAST

They had come to the edge of the forest on a moonlit night.

There was no sound except for the soft rustle of feet on the grass until they came to the dike that encircled the wood, then they passed through on the dark path, walking by the full moon, shadowed figures, taking slow measured steps.

They had stopped at the cup stone and had stood in a circle, waiting. The air tensed with expectancy.

The child was brought forward, held between two black-cloaked figures. On the other side of the stone a voice began a slow chant and then all of the circle joined in. The girl, dark-haired and shivering despite the moist warmth in the air, said nothing. Her eyes were wide, but she looked blind and compliant. One of the figures lifted her to sit on the stone and then gently drew her back, so that her small frame lay across it, head dangling down one side, feet on the other. Her white hands trailed on the earth.

The chanting grew stronger. Overhead, the moon slid across the velvet sky. A hand brought out a small sachet and sprinkled a powder over the child. The moonbeams caught the motes and made them dance silver. The chant died and the air grew tense again.

Above the child two hands rose up. Polished stone glinted, then flashed a silvery arc. A sound like an apple crunched under stone filled the glade and was swallowed by the dense foliage. The child made no noise, except for a startled gasp. Her dark eyes flew open and her mouth yawned in a silent scream. Her body jerked and both hands shot up to scrabble at the centre of her chest. The fingers hooked on the long stone blade, slipping on the blood which pulsed out and onto her pale skin. Thin legs kicked, tried to run, but gained no purchase in the still forest air.

Around her the figures were silent. The girl's head turned, mouth still agape, young, wide eyes suddenly filled with a devastating wisdom. They swivelled and took in the shapes around her, mute appeal searing their shadowed faces. The figures did not move. Finally the girl's hands stopped their jittery clawing at the blade. She shivered, as if a dread cold wind had blown through her, then she sighed and her breath came in a hoarse rattle. Still none of them moved. The shivering stopped slowly and the girl jerked twice then was still.

Blood flowed into the cup and drained on the rings carved on the flat top of the stone, spiralling outwards in a night-black stream to pour into the runnels which channelled it to feed the dry earth.

Underfoot, a slow, sonorous pulse started to beat.

The moon had moved across the sky by the time all the five ringstones had been fed. It now blazed its light down into the clearing where the tree stood, massive and bare, a giant of the forest. The cloaked figures stood around it, while before it the moonlight glazed the pale skin of the young woman who stood facing the hoary old trunk. The beat of the earth could be heard here, in the heart of the forest, and felt in powerful rhythmic vibrations.

The woman stood, arms raised, delicate frame matching the colossal reach of the tree. There was movement and a *twist* in the air. A shadow blotted out the moonlight and tension rippled through the hooded figures. In the shadow *something* had *arrived*.

On the dead branches, leaves began to uncurl. Flowers, shot with moonbeams, blossomed and from their luminescent depths golden fruits swelled with life, each of them pulsing light of its own to counter the silver glow of the full moon.

The circle of cloaked figures were reaching for the magical fruits, even as the trunk swelled darkly and split with a wrench down its centre. It creaked open, revealing hollow black depths which no light could penetrate.

A voice chanted and the darkness welled out from the fissure, taking almost solid shape as it reached to envelop the girl. The shadow rolled around her, dimming her pale, naked form. It smothered her and then she was blotted from sight.

The blackness curled and roiled, a moving night-*shade*, while the fruits swelled to golden globes shining with their own light.

19

The cloaked figures plucked them from the drooping branches while the darkness from within the tree receded, shrinking back to the hollow.

There was a grinding noise and the edges of the fissure clamped seamlessly with a final, grinding rasp. The young woman was *gone*.

The black-cloaked figures took their rewards and made their way back along the paths, over the wall, and out into the valley. In fields where men had toiled since beyond spoken memory, new life burgeoned with sudden vigour.

2

Caitlin Brook was running. Running for the joy of it. She *flashed* along the path that snaked between the trees, and it was *wonderful*.

The blood was singing, sizzling in her veins. She could hear the pulse and ebb of it behind her ears, warm and alive. Her breath was fast and even and the air she drew in was scented with pollen and the green of the forest. Above her head, the canopy of spreading beech and lime and oak let in dazzling flashes of high summer sun.

She ran like the wind, like a roe fawn along the tracks the deer used. All around her, the forest was alive with the buzzing of insects high in the shaded leaves. Ahead of her, to the right, the stream murmured to itself as it tumbled over the rocks in the shallows and sang to itself as it cascaded into the deep dark pool. Her hair, the colour of a chestnut fresh from its spiked shell, streamed in her wake, a mane of fire. Perspiration sheened her back and arms and the air blew it dry in her passing, leaving her skin tingling and cool while inside all was heat and motion.

She jinked past the hoary trunk of a massive oak, so close the beards of moss caressed her flank. Ahead of her, the stream became a river and changed its song. She could hear it over the hum of insects and the rhythmic crackle underfoot. It called out its roar as the water tumbled between the big rocks at the falls where the valley narrowed to a cleft. Before the falls there was a wide shallow pool. She skirted a stand of ash saplings without breaking step. She could see the water now sending sun-sparkles back to her as it chuckled on the shallows before roaring into the black pot-hole in the defile.

Diamonds of water fountained up, catching their own rainbows as Caitlin splashed her way, laughed her way, across the stream. Her delight pealed through the trees, echoing from trunk to trunk, silver bells in a summer wood. It seemed the forest laughed with her. Up high, a squirrel chittered its encouragement. Down by the

21

water a wren warbled quicksilver song. On her left now, a solitary ray through the thick green ceiling caught a trout leaping for a fly. Its scales were jewels flashing incandescent before trading the light for the dark pool.

Caitlin ran on, holding the laughter into herself, though it sang in the blood that surged in her veins. The path followed the defile, high on its steep slope where the oak gave way to tall pines and the swooping limbs of larch. There the sunlight was strong enough to let her shadow flicker on their mottled trunks. Then down again, taking the slope in giant strides, she ran to the bank of the river that meandered in the flat forest deeps. Here she had never run before. This was a part of the forest she had never seen, but the pathway was wide and clear. She followed it, keeping the unknown trees to her left and the familiar forest on her right until, ahead, she could see the track fork. One side led down into the more shadowed depths where the tall trees stood so close together that their leaves merged in a green blanket. That way no squirrels snickered or chittered, no pigeons burbled, no bees hummed.

Closer came the fork with every smooth stride. It was tempting to take the low road. She would, she knew she would. But this time the sunshine beckoned her. She could feel the counter pull of the dark, shaded place and felt the tide of it within her, a strong tug on her that was hard to resist. But this was a time for running. She did not want to stop to explore, not yet, not *this* day. She made herself stay on the right-hand path, though she felt a twinge of regret. But then the motion took over and she ran on, keeping always to the right side, towards the sunlight at the edge of the forest. Behind her shadows loomed, but she ignored them and ran onwards towards the day.

The trees flickered past, though more spread out. She was on the home track, breath still even and fast, the smile spread wide on her face, eyes sparkling with the delight of it. Then she was out on the road, on the smooth black. She pounded along, feet slapping the surface in even thuds. She rounded the corner, catching sight of her cottage. The gate swung open at her touch, squealing on its hinge, then whacked back behind her as she loped on the flagstone path between the lobelias and alyssum, catching their scent in her passing.

Caitlin was slowing now, powering down. She reached the

corner of the cottage and passed the trailing green strings of Virginia creeper that tumbled down from the guttering. Here, for the first time, she faltered, breaking her stride from a canter to a fast walk, to a slow walk, almost to a standstill.

Something was waiting for her. Something expected her.

She knew it and froze.

Her breath, until now easy and effortless, caught and stuttered. *Something in the garden* there, behind the house, out of sight. She took a step backwards, stopped, then brought her foot silently forward again.

Fear clenched in her belly. Her legs didn't seem to want to move, but something made them go one slow, hesitant, fearful step at a time.

She came to the edge of the building where the roof sloped down to meet the south-east wall. Here it was like the deep part of the forest, cool shade. Here no bees buzzed, no chaffinches chirped. A black beetle scuttled across the flagstones and straggly, sun-starved weeds poked weakly through dark earth. Caitlin shivered as a breeze brought gooseflesh trickling across her skin.

She took a deep, faltering breath, then a step. She could see the light green of the sunlit back lawn. A second step and the alarm bells in her head shrieked at her to turn and run and never stop. A third step took her round the corner and she saw it.

Her heart fell like a stone and hit with a thud. The world spun. The ground tilted this way and that. Freezing sickness looped up inside her.

It sat there on the grass. Alien. Mindless. Cold.

It sensed her and beckoned her, drawing her towards it like a malevolent spider. Its spindly, hard frame gleamed harshly under the high summer sun.

Come now, it whispered in her mind. *You belong with me, forever.*

She shook her head, denying the scrapy voice. But it sat there, pulling her towards it with a force she could not deny.

No, no, no! she tried to say, but her throat locked over the words.

She could not resist the inevitability of it. She had no strength to refuse the awful pull. She reached where it sat and its arms were opened to her. It dragged her down into its hard, jealous embrace.

She was trapped, caught, imprisoned. She went down into its embrace and knew with cold certainty that she would be there forever.

Caitlin woke with a wail of fear and despair ready to blurt from her lips. She started forward, eyes staring unfocused at the vision in her dream, recoiling from its impact.

A shiver shook her, helping to dispel the blank despair. She was cold. The sun had moved behind the tall cypress trees at the far end of the garden. The dream jangled and danced behind her eyes like a leering gargoyle with a sick, malevolent grin on its face. It had its fun with her and danced away, leaving her drained and empty. The world focused around her and she sat back in the chair, feeling it rock with the motion. Awful dejection clamped cold hands down on her.

The run was over. Now *it* had her helpless in its arms and would *never* let her go.

A tear, the latest of many, sparked and stung in her eye, and she wiped it away with a quick scrape of her finger.

She shook her head, still slugged from sleep and the aftermath of the dream, shaking it away, everything, the despair, the hopelessness. She turned to the easel that stood like a capital *A* on the short grass. Using both hands on the wheels, she manoeuvred her chair, a silvery, spindly thing, towards it. There, on the canvas, with the colours blocked in confident strokes, was a view of the pool above the Corrie Bridge; the water was in spate, tumbling down between the boulders, the way it had last been in late spring. Beyond the river, there was a stand of silver birch which seemed to shimmer on the canvas and behind them, the bulk of the forest dark and shadowed as a backdrop.

The thick woods showed in many of the paintings she'd done since she'd come to live in Linnvale. They were a permanent feature of the secluded glen, a deep and shadowed reminder of the ancient woods which had covered all of the land to the west of Loch Corran.

She'd never been in the forest, though she'd often had a notion to explore its cool depths. But the edges were as close as she could venture. Her wheelchair would not get twenty feet beyond the forest edge before getting snagged on a branch or a bramble runner.

Caitlin would never run there under the high canopy. Caitlin would never run again. *Not ever.*

'*Hello!*'

The voice, a man's voice, came from out of sight beyond the corner of the cottage, just where, in the dream, Caitlin had stopped, tremulously apprehensive, getting ready to be *afraid*.

Her attention snapped away from the picture on the canvas. She turned her head towards the sound; the sun flared on the waves of red as her hair swung with the motion.

'*Anybody there?*' the voice came again, a little louder. She craned forward, leaning an arm on the seat. A man came into view, sauntering round the edge of the building. He stood there for a moment, half-hidden in the shade from the clematis that tumbled in a green cataract from the wall.

Caitlin raised a hand over her eyes to ward off the slanting rays of the sun which pierced the trees, but still couldn't make out the stranger.

'Hi. Can I come in?'

Then she recognised him. Memories came swooping in on her on night-black wings; powerful memories that swamped her in an instant of awful bleakness. She shoved them away, shivering as she did so.

'You *are* in,' she said flatly.

'I knocked on the door, but there was no reply.'

'At least your mother taught you something,' she said, hearing the cold welcome in her voice. It was uncharacteristic and instantly she regretted it, fought it down, the way she had done the bitter memories.

He walked out into the light, almost shyly. Martin Thornton was tall and slim-built. He was wearing a well broken-in leather jerkin, faded jeans and a pair of scuffed walking shoes. In one hand he held a bunch of flowers, tight colourful buds peeking out above crumpled tissue, in the other a bottle of wine, its shape moulded in wrapping.

'Oh, it's you. I didn't recognise you at first.' It was a small lie, not even a complete lie, but there was nothing else for it. It wasn't *his* fault that his very presence brought back everything she had been running from, in her dreams, in her *mind*. It wasn't *his* fault that he had been there, the first thing she had *seen* when her eyes had opened.

He came on through the vivid stramash of flowerbeds, following the flagged paths and onto the green, with a little half smile that said he hoped he would be welcome but thought he might not. He reached where she sat beside the easel and in one casual movement sat himself down on the short grass, putting himself just below her eye-level and almost directly in front of her so that she wouldn't have to lean or strain. Few people knew enough to do that and she instinctively gave him an extra plus point, again regretting the coolness of her reception.

'Hi, how have you been?' he asked amiably.

'Terrific,' she said, then changed her mind. 'No, not terrific. Good days and bad days. Some better than others.'

He gave a little nod. No '*I understand*', no '*I know how you feel*'. Nobody understood. Nobody knew how she felt. Nobody *could*. In the little silence that followed, she gave him another plus. It wasn't that she didn't like him. It was just that he brought everything back in that huge swamping wave. Full-colour wrap-around action replay. With sound. She could do without that, especially in the wake of the dream.

'Here, I brought you something,' he said, holding up the bunch of flowers in such a way that they were right in her lap. She only had to open her hands and take them. The scent of freesia perfumed the air. He looked around and waved a hand to encompass the garden. 'Though I didn't know you had plenty of your own. It's lovely here.'

She was about to thank him when he held up the wrapped bottle, though keeping it in his territory.

'And I brought some wine too. I thought I could cadge a bite. Haven't eaten all day,' he said disarmingly.

'So nothing's changed, I see.'

'Not a bit. We rough tough hacks live on whisky and bad news,' he said, and grinned.

'And you're only good for your expenses,' she said, unable to help smiling back. The memories were receding, the dream was just a grey shadow evaporating under the sun.

27

'There you have me. Encapsulated my whole rotten profession in one snappy headline.'

'How did you find me?' Caitlin surprised him.

'Contacts,' he said, knocking a finger to his nose in exaggerated conspiracy.

'The only contacts you ever had were taxi drivers, drunks and barmen.'

'And you. *You* told me.'

'That's not true. Only a couple of people knew I was moving here, and they promised not to tell a soul.'

'Ah, but you told me a while back about staying with your grandparents when you were young. You said you always wanted to go back. I couldn't remember the name of the place. I racked my brains, but it's one of those places you can never remember.'

'It's hard enough to find when you do,' she allowed.

'That's true. But then one of our stringers came up with a story about a row over some holiday chalets, and the name just sprang back into my head. I'd tried the union and your lawyer. They wouldn't say a thing. And the hospital didn't want to know me. But once I got here, Alex Stirling told me. He knows everybody for forty miles in every direction.'

'That's because the nosy bugger reads all the mail before putting it through the letter boxes. I'll kill him,' Caitlin said vehemently, though he thought she wasn't really annoyed.

'Anyway I asked him if he knew Caitlin Brook and he said "Everybody knows the painter." Said you were a hot-rodder. He even showed me where you stayed and here I am. I didn't know you were an artist.' Martin shoved himself on his backside closer to where she sat and looked up at the canvas. 'That's very good.'

'I sell a few in Levenford, through a friend of mine who runs a shop. And once or twice I get a buyer from Glasgow or Edinburgh looking for landscapes. It keeps the wolves from the door. I also teach a bit at the school in Craigard.'

'I thought you did all right with Criminal Injuries Compensation.'

'*All right?*' she snorted. 'They don't have a clue. They just have no idea what it is exactly I have lost. They can't begin to realise what this has done to the quality of my life.' The words came out tight and sour. 'They even tried to say that I had *contributed* to this.' She thumped the arm of the wheelchair hard enough to rock it from side to side. 'In the end I got enough to pay for this place and nothing left over. It needs some work to make it liveable – I mean liveable for someone like me – but it's home, and it's out of the way, and I don't have to put up with people staring at me and treating me as if I'm mentally defective instead of someone whose legs just don't work.'

He nodded again, not commenting, just letting her know that he was listening. She let out a long sigh, clearing out the anger.

'Tell me where the glasses are and I'll open this,' he said, nodding to the bottle.

She seemed to think about it for a moment then lifted a hand to point to the back door of the cottage, half hidden in a curtain of yellow roses.

'The kitchen's just in there. Glasses are in the cupboard next to the sink. Ice in the fridge if it's white wine.'

Martin got to his feet and followed her directions. She watched him amble the short distance to the door and incline his head to negotiate the low lintel and disappear from view. It had been more than a year since she'd seen him and he seemed a bit thinner, maybe even a little hesitant. She wondered why he was here.

Caitlin came right to the point when he came back out with the ice chinking in two tall glasses of the universal filling station variety.

'Two reasons,' he said after taking a large sip and letting it swill around before swallowing. 'I'm doing a piece on the despoliation of this beautiful valley. At least that's what the old biddies in the preservation group are claiming.' He turned and favoured her with a big smile that took ten years off him. 'That's the excuse anyway. It gives me a few days here if I can wangle it, and I can think of plenty of worse places to be, I have to tell you. I can knock up a story on that with my eyes shut.'

'If that's the excuse, what's the real reason?' Caitlin said. The wine was cool, just dry enough not to be sweet. Perfect for a summer's afternoon.

'I came to see you. I've got a guilty conscience.'

'What about?'

'And I've got something for you,' he said, ignoring the question.

'You gave me the flowers. And the wine.'

29

'But there's something else,' he said. He reached into his jacket and drew out a white, slightly creased envelope that looked as if it had been in the jacket for a few days, maybe even a few weeks.

'Before I give you this, I want to ask you to let me do another story.'

Caitlin stopped in mid-sip and brought the glass down from her mouth.

'No,' she said. It was emphatic.

'Seriously, I do want to do another piece.'

'You can want all you like. But no. I've had enough of all that. I just want to get on with my life. I don't want photographers hanging about outside and I don't want people pointing everywhere I go. Not that I go anywhere. But no thanks.'

Martin shrugged. 'We'll talk about it later. Here,' he said, holding out the crumpled envelope. 'This is yours. That's why I've been trying to find you.'

'What is it?'

'Open it and see.'

Caitlin got a thumbnail under the flap and ripped it open. She frowned as she drew out the piece of paper. It was a cheque. She held it up, the frown deepening, then dropped her hand to her lap.

'I told you. I don't want you to write a story.'

'So?'

'I don't want this money.'

'That's got nothing to do with anything. I won it. Look at the thing. It's not from the newspaper. The *News* never pays that much anyway. It's from me.'

'But why?'

'Guilty conscience.'

'A thousand pounds is a lot of guilt. What the hell have you done?'

'It's more what I haven't done. Anyway, I won the damned thing. Two grand. I reckoned at least half of it was yours.'

'How did you come to that conclusion?' Caitlin said, waving the cheque about as if looking for a place to put it down and get rid of it.

'I got a trophy as well and you can have that if you like. Reporter of the Year award. All very big deal. The Editor is like a dog with two tails, as they say. I'm back in his good books again.'

'But what's that got to do with me?'

'I won it for *your* story. They had me up at the big lunch and I had to go up and shake hands with some chinless nonentity who thinks he runs the country and who I didn't vote for. They gave me a nice cheque though. All very jolly until I started thinking about it. You know what it's like in newspapers. Yesterday's news is only used to wrap fish and chips. You're only as good as your next story. That's why I haven't seen you in more than a year.'

'I did wonder what had happened. It was nice of you to come to the hospital. And your stories *were* good. I kept the cuttings. But I still don't understand.'

'Two things. I should have followed the story up, kept in touch, but I didn't.' He stopped and this time he took a long swallow of his wine. 'And I felt a bit of a shit raking in all that money for just doing my job. I just happened to be there at the time, and that was only because I'd been a bad boy and I was sent out on all the crappy stuff. You could say I was in the right place at the right time – for winning awards, that is – but the idea of getting a reward for it sort of stuck in my throat. It wasn't my story. It was *your* story. I mean, nothing happened to *me*. I just wrote about it. And what did you get? A Humane Society medal and your marching orders.'

'More like my wheeling orders,' Caitlin said. He turned towards her and their eyes met and suddenly, quite simultaneously, they both burst into laughter.

'Wheelies then,' Martin said when he got his voice back. He looked up again at her and saw the sun glint on her burnished hair and caught the sparkle of a tear – *was it the laughter*? – in her eye, and saw something in her that he had never quite realised before.

'Anyway, here we are. I've got a couple of days to do a story on the chalets that have started this range war, and you're going to give me dinner, or I'll take you out and we can blow some of that money. And then you can tell me what's been happening with you and I'll try to persuade you to let me do the story. The final one.'

'I told you, I don't want a story,' Caitlin said. The sparkle had fled and she held the cheque out towards him. 'And you can forget about bribery.'

'I only said I'll *try*. The money has nothing to do with it. That's the truth and I don't lie. I decided to split it with you the night I got it. It's got nothing to do with anything else.'

'But a *thousand*. It's a hell of a lot of money.'

'That's what my father said.'

'Did you tell him you were giving me this?'

'No. He got the other half. He's retired and he's been talking about getting a boat to go fishing. He put up a hell of a fight about it, but he's out this week looking at outboards. Anyway, I owed him it. He wanted me to be a carpenter like him, but he went ahead and let me get into newspapers, though he never saw it as a *real* job.'

'But this is a lot of money, Martin. I can't take it.'

'Oh, come on. Easy come, easy go. I would only drink it, and I've been trying to leave off the booze for the past year. The hard stuff anyway. You're doing me a favour.' He looked up at her and favoured her with his best foot-in-the-door boyish smile. 'So what's for dinner then?'

He had sat at the kitchen table while she worked, watching as she awkwardly manoeuvred her chair. She seemed unconcerned, though it was plain the kitchen was not designed for someone in a moving seat. When they had come inside from the garden, he had let her lead, not holding the chair, or shoving it like a pram the way some people did, even when she had to jump the little front wheels over the doorstep and bump down the small step into the small hallway. As soon as he was in the kitchen, he had sat himself down as quickly as possible, so she wouldn't have to crane up to speak to him. She had asked him where he'd learned that and he'd told her about the boy he'd met in one of the hospitals in the north side of Glasgow. The way he spoke of the youngster told her he'd been moved by the contact.

'He wasn't put together properly,' Martin had said. 'Born with a big head and withered legs. Somebody had got him a CB radio to keep in touch with the world and he was full of American truckers slang. Saw himself as Burt Reynolds. He gave me a shot in his chair and laughed himself silly because I couldn't steer the thing. He told me he hated people thinking he was a moron just because his body didn't work. Then, a couple of weeks later, I had some people down at the *News*. They'd won the special Olympic games and when they arrived at the office I tried to give Rob Robertson a hand with his chair. He'd won a gold in the discus and he nearly took my head off for helping him.'

'What did he say?' Caitlin asked.

'He told me I was a patronising bastard, except his choice of words was *really* choice.'

'And he was right.'

'Of course he was right, but it wasn't deliberate on my part. I told him so. I said it would do him more good if he would explain it to me instead of being such a bad-tempered shit. I just didn't like being embarrassed because of good intentions. Anyway we went for a drink later and he got pissed and I had to help him get into a taxi, but before that he told me what it's like to be in a wheelchair. It's something you don't think about, then when you do it's something you don't forget.'

Caitlin made a salad, sending Martin out to the garden on several forays for lettuce and spring onions and peas which were swelling their pods. She heaped his plate with greens and told him it was good for him. He poured another two glasses of wine, almost killing the bottle, then told her he'd another one in the car, in case they needed it. They did.

While they were eating, she asked what he meant when he said he'd been a bad boy, sent on all the crappy stories.

Martin laughed. 'It was the horse that did it.'

'What do you mean?'

'We stole a horse,' Martin said matter-of-factly.

'You did *what*?'

He grinned across the salad bowl. 'That's what the Editor said when he found out. It was Davy O'Neil and myself. I think you met him, the photographer?'

'Yes. He took some pictures in the hospital.'

'That's the one. We were up north on a story about tenants being evicted by one of the big landowners, another chinless wonder with an Eton accent. Anyway, our car broke down in the middle of nowhere and we were dying for more drink after an afternoon with the crofters. They just don't know when to stop pouring. So there's this horse in a field and Davy said we should maybe ride it back to the hotel. It seemed like a good idea at the time, seeing we were both a bit smashed, and we got the horse across to the fence and climbed up on its back. It didn't seem to mind. It took us about three miles to the hotel and Davy only fell off three times. But when we got there, we couldn't stop the

33

damned thing. It went clopping right inside with the two of us on its back. Which would have been all right, except for one thing.'

'What was that?' Caitlin asked, giggling girlishly at the picture he conjured in her mind.

'It dropped a ton of steaming manure on the brand-new carpet. We were back in the office the next day when the boss took the call. I couldn't have written a better script.' Martin shoved himself back from the table and mimicked a man talking on the telephone. 'They stole a *what*?! Yes. Yes. I understand. It did *what*? On the *carpet*?!'

By this time Caitlin was laughing so hard the tears were running down her cheeks.

'So that was it for the two of us. We'd been working on special investigations for about a year. We'd had a couple of scrapes and the boss thought we needed a lesson. He put us both on the cut-and-slash run.'

'What's that?'

'Driving about the city on a Friday and Saturday night with the radio tuned – quite illegally – to the police band. You pick up the messages and head for where the action is. Mostly it's lowlife stuff. But that's how I got to meet you, though I wish I hadn't.'

'Oh, that's nice,' Caitlin said, though lightly enough to convey no offence.

'No. I mean, I wish I had met you under different circumstances,' Martin said and, despite the wine they'd drunk, he sounded completely sober.

A silence fell between them then spread out to surround them, heavy in the warm air of the kitchen. Finally Caitlin sighed. She put her hands on to the arms of the wheelchair.

'Me too,' she said.

4

In the silence the memory came swooping back to him unbidden, unwanted. He recoiled from it, hating its smothering power.

The same memory had shivered Martin Thornton on the night that he'd pushed the boat out and bought the drink for all-comers in the Horseshoe Bar that sat cheek by jowl with the front door of the *News* office. It had come on him like a gatecrasher, killing the mood of the party, and he had been unable to get rid of it.

Oh, that memory had hit him once or twice before, *plenty of times before*, in the small hours of the night, or maybe the dark of morning when he couldn't sleep for seeing again that black-rag plummet. But on the night of the award ceremony the elation fled in the flick of an eye when the vision came roaring back.

Blame the horse. Blame the pile of shit on the carpet. Blame O'Neil for being a madman, a *persuasive* madman who thought it would be just a huge laugh to hitch a ride back to the hotel. Blame whoever he liked, Martin could only accuse himself for knowing *something* and not being smart enough to know that he knew, or quick enough to do anything about it.

Down in the Horeshoe, known to every newsman as the *Dunny* for its resemblance, like every other newspaper pub, to a refuse tip, the night had been rolling along and the drink had flowed. Martin had put up the funds behind the bar and all-comers were making a manly effort to empty the gantry. His trophy, a glass plaque with his name and the award engraved on the surface, glinted from a safe position on a high shelf. Almost everyone was getting monumentally drunk. Colleagues from his own newspaper basked in his reflected glory. Opposition friends and rivals dropped by for a free drink and some ribaldry. The Editor had clapped him on the back and given a spiel that was expansive and congratulatory. He seemed to have forgotten that he'd told Thornton and O'Neil they'd be lucky if they ever saw their names in print again. On this night, Martin was a credit to his newspaper, to newspapers in general, to the art of journalism.

And suddenly he had felt like a complete fraud.

It was then that the memory had come swooping down on a dark thermal to settle its weight on his shoulders. Around him was the raucous laughter of men getting well drunk. Within him the gloom deepened and he was back *there* again.

It had been a cold night, one of those bitter November nights when the sky is clear in the east and thick clouds are bubbling up in the firth of Clyde, promising snow but getting set to break the promise and deliver freezing drizzle. You get many nights like this in the west of Scotland. They are no fun.

Thornton and O'Neil were in the radio car on the west side of the city, what would be considered the fashionable end where boutiques jostled for space with little restaurants with fashionably obscure names and initials in their titles. Down at the casualty admissions in the infirmary, fashion flew out of the window. Cut-and-slash run was no misnomer. Friday night on the town was a testament to man's baser instincts and the national shame of the Scotsman's inability to hold either his drink or his temper.

The night porter gave them the rundown. A drunk who had broken a leg after losing an argument with a taxi. The driver was in a corner gesticulating with the police while a nurse, who looked as if it was past her bedtime, swabbed his flattened nose, evidence of a violent connection with his steering wheel. There was a girl, sobbing quietly as she clung to her boyfriend. He seemed too drunk to feel the stanley-knife slash down his cheek and would probably wear it as a badge in a week's time. An overdose case had clattered by on a trolley, heading for crash ward and maybe eternity. Life and death on a Friday night. Nothing to write home about. Nothing to *write* about at all.

Back in the car they'd picked up the flash on the radio. Martin missed the call code but Dave O'Neil heard enough to nudge him hard in the ribs.

'Sounds like a shoot-out. Springfield. Let's go.'

Martin slammed in the gear, reversed out of the tight space in the outside car park and rolled the jeep through the gates. They headed towards the centre, then up onto the loop road to take them to the north side of the city.

The radio crackled again. Martin caught the word '*hostage*' and put his foot down. Even then, two white police cars flashed past in a wink of blue light, sirens wailing like banshees in the night. There were more police cars there when they got to the bleak huddle of tenements at the edge of the sprawling housing scheme. Martin had been here before, many a time, none of them pleasurable occasions. This part of the city was an argument for the death sentence for city planners. Social work had given up on this spot. It looked as though God had turned his back on it too. Here and there smashed windows like eyeless sockets glared emptily. The only colour was in four-lettered words spray-painted on every vertical surface, promoting or denying the infallibility of the Pope, the monarchy, or whichever teen-gang happened to have the upper hand at the moment.

Martin pulled the car up behind the flashing lights of the police cars which sat in a wagon-train semicircle on a vacant piece of ground. Beyond them, kept back with some difficulty by a few uniformed patrolmen, were the usual crowd of folk gawping.

'What's happening?' Martin asked the nearest policeman while Dave O'Neil footered with his camera equipment. Martin flashed his press card, though the big sergeant recognised him and nodded hello.

'Some nutter holed up in there,' he said, nodding to the Soviet-style barrack of concrete. 'Got a shotgun. Fired twice so far.'

'Anybody hurt?'

'Not yet, but he's going to be a bastard to get out of there.' The policeman pointed up to the third floor. 'Only way in is up those stairs and along the balcony walk. Anybody goes along there and he's a dead man. There's no phone either, so this is going to be a loudspeaker job. That's going to take all night. Bang goes my supper.'

He laughed rueful resignation and Martin went along with it. So far it would make a few paragraphs, maybe more later as long as the gunslinger didn't stay holed up all night. He went back to the car and phoned some words to copy as a holder and passed a message to the newsdesk that he was sticking with it just in case.

A half-hour passed with no response from the darkened third window up. A superintendent with plenty of silver on his shoulders and a bullhorn in his hand bawled: 'Donald Leggat. Is there anyone besides yourself in the house?' Obviously they'd got the creep's name from somewhere.

The rising wind whipped at the words as they bounced tinnily from wall to wall. Donald Leggat, whoever he was, sat tight.

Half an hour on and both Martin and Davy could have done with a serious drink. They had a flask of coffee between them and were sheltering from the wind and drizzle against the car. Another police vehicle raced up and out poured more uniforms, two women and two men. They came walking quickly towards the superintendent. Martin raised the coffee to his lips as they passed by and the headlights of the car caught the red hair of the slim girl in the lead. She turned her head and he got a glimpse of her profile, a straight, almost pert nose and a strong feminine chin. The plain uniform and the little hat did nothing to diminish her striking looks, seen in the white beam. Martin's eyes lazily followed the girl as she marched past, feet crunching on roughcast gravel.

'Arrest me any time,' O'Neil whispered from close by. 'With handcuffs.'

'Remember, you're still on remand, horsethief. Anyway, she's not on the force. She's a cop-angel.'

'What's that?'

'Don't you read your papers? They've got them in all the housing schemes. She's a nurse teamed up with the police for emergencies. Wife beatings. Child abuse, that sort of thing.'

'For her I'd go to jail.'

'And probably will,' Martin said, easing himself off the car and sauntering towards the police huddle. He couldn't make out too much of what was being said, but he picked up the odd word and filled the rest in for himself. The police thought there might be a woman in the house. Possibly a baby, though there hadn't been a sound. Firearms were to be used only as a last resort. The young woman nodded and turned from the group, her face composed as if concentrating. She scraped past Martin as if unaware of his presence, then turned, apologetically.

'Sorry, my fault,' she said and gave him a small smile. The lights caught her green eyes, making them flare startling emerald for a second and Martin felt a jolt like a jab in his belly. Her face turned, the light went out and she was gone, moving quickly towards the entrance to the block. Martin took a step backwards. It was as if something had sparked between them as soon as their eyes had locked, and there was no reason, *absolutely no reason*, why that should have happened. He followed her with his eyes until the darkness of the entrance swallowed her up. He shook his head and walked back to the car.

'Get her number then?' O'Neil asked with a smirk. Martin shot him a look but said nothing. He was still wrong-footed by the contact with the girl.

A scream tore the air, knifed through the wind, high pitched and suddenly *frantic*, a woman's scream.

A spotlight swivelled on gimbals and raked its beam across the dismal facade. There was no movement, but there came the crash of breaking glass and immediately the huge boom of a twelve-bore. Shot slammed into the lead police car and its window collapsed milkily. Pellets rapped and on the roof of the car, not the way they do in films, but with a flat sound of hard hail. Somebody yelled from the crowd. O'Neil blurted "*Shit!*" through a mouthful of coffee and the superintendent bawled at everybody to take cover.

From up there a coarse voice shouted down: '*Get to fuck, you bunch of swines.*'

'Donald Leggat!' the brass bulled up at him. 'There is no need to be alarmed.'

'Alarmed? I'm shitting myself,' O'Neil bawled, then started to giggle.

'Please put the gun down,' the chief continued as evenly as his voice would allow. 'We have no wish to harm you.'

'*Piss off, bastards,*' the voice yelled back. Everybody could hear the tension twisted up in it. The woman's scream came again, closely followed by a baby's frightened wail. 'Shut your mouths, both of youse, or you'll get it as well.' The woman and child continued screeching. The gun roared, everybody ducked and the sound was cut off instantly.

'Oh, for God's sake,' Martin heard the big sergeant say. 'The madman's killed them.'

The superintendent was frantically speaking into the radio when the woman's voice came again.

'Donny. Put it down! Please, Donny.'

'I fucking told you to shut your mouth, you stupid cow. Just shut your face while you've still got one.'

Despite the tone, a sigh of relief swept round the crowd. He hadn't shot her, whoever *she* was.

39

Behind the car, protected from the wind and the sleet *and* the gunshots, Martin was mentally preparing his words for the final edition. Easy. Bit of drama, a few gunshots, a man arrested. A few quotes from the police. A bit of shock, horror and drama to satisfy their tabloid mentality and then down for a drink.

There was a rumpus along the balcony. Martin was in the act of swallowing his last mouthful of coffee when it happened, but that wasn't what made him choke.

Something flashed behind his eyes and slammed into his brain. It came so hard and fast that he was physically rocked backward with the force of it. A sound like alarm sirens was clamouring in his ears, a huge *panicky* noise. In an instant he was engulfed, *flooded* with a terrible sense of danger. He staggered back from the car, a hand held up to his temple, and the vision flooded into him.

He saw the long balcony walkway. A door slammed open, noise echoing loud. A shape tumbling out. A woman. Something in her arms. Fear stretching her mouth wide.

Panic *sizzled* through him. He tried to speak but no words came. The woman was running. Someone was waiting, hands outstretched. He could hear words, all jumbled up, garbled in his head.

The long barrel of a gun came nosing out of the door. It turned towards the woman. She tripped, fell headlong. The bundle came tumbling through the air. The gun swung round, and the double muzzles expanded, over and under, a black figure eight. He sensed turning, running, instant fear screwed up inside and then the thunder of the gun. The searing burn on his back and a blow like a kick. Flipping end over end, clutching something small. The whole world spun and Martin spun with it, fetching up hard against the car, sucking in cold air.

'What the hell's wrong with you?' O'Neil shouted in his ear, but he never heard the words.

He felt the sickening swoop, the pain, then the vision flicked out. It was as if someone had switched off a light inside his head. It was simply gone. He was *released*.

He stood in the drizzle, breathing hard, and then the blood simply drained out of his face.

'Oh *Christ*,' he mouthed, though no words came out.

O'Neil stood, hands on the car, completely perplexed as

Martin Thornton turned and started to run towards the entrance. Up above, on the balcony, somebody was shouting. There was a clatter of a door almost thrown off its hinges and slamming against a wall. Somebody bawled '*Watch out!*' and a yammering, unintelligible high-pitched babbling followed, but Martin Thornton heard nothing. All he knew was that he had to get there, he had to stop her. His feet skidded on the mud and gravel, splashing through the puddles, all the time knowing that he was too late.

Twenty yards from the close-mouth he looked up and saw the black form tumble and twist in the air. It happened in that graceful slow motion of high panic, when the intensity of the moment is so complete that normal time ceases to exist.

The roar of the shotgun was slamming itself between the concrete facades of the buildings in a bombardment of noise. Martin got four steps further, *willing* himself to get between the ground and the falling form. His legs made huge, treacle-slow strides, his feet hitting the ground with dull, prolonged impacts. He saw her hair flash in the light, unravelled from its tight roll, a falling firebrand. Another two steps and her pale face flashed in a strobe-effect as it turned in the beams of the spotlights.

She hit the wall with such a sickening thud that Martin felt everything inside him turn to slush. He heard the bones break with a sound of wood snapping, but worse than that, *oh, much worse*, was the cry that was forced out of her when she hit. It wasn't a human sound at all. It sounded like *death*.

Some sounds are keys to the hidden corners of the mind. The noise the girl had made when she hit the ground, half gasp, half groan, all dreadful *hurt*, yanked a picture from nowhere and shoved it into Martin Thornton's mind. He'd only been six years old when he'd first gone into the slaughterhouse that sat on the edge of the River Leven. He couldn't remember why, maybe to deliver something from Mrs Bain, the farmer's wife, some errand that meant a hot penny in a small boy's pocket. Whatever the reason, he had wandered in to the smell of the *shambles*. Hot, steaming flesh, channels running with rivers of steaming blood. Cows *baying* in the sheds as they smelt death on the warm air. Great slabs of animals, half-cows, whole pigs, skinned sheep with only their black heads to show what kind of animal they were, hung down from hooks thrust through their hamstrings. Slithery gobbets, gall bladders, fluke-ridden livers, pieces of intestine lay limp on the hard stone floor. The young Martin Thornton, the one who could already chisel and cut a mitred joint in oak at his father's worktable, had turned the corner just as big brawny Sid McCann had brought the gun up to the beast's head. There was a sharp crack like a gun shot and the animal was *dead*. Its eyes rolled and its feet scrabbled at the floor in an instinct to escape, but the sensation of pure *deadness* came off it in waves. The pin, he later found out, had drilled a hole through its brain to the spinal cord and killed it in a fraction of a second. It was only the spastic jerk of freed nerves that made the hooves scrabble and clatter on the floor. Life had gone. That big black *Aberdeen Angus* collapsed to the stone like a monster puppet whose strings had been cut. When it hit, it made that noise, not like any cow or any animal. It was a sound thrust from its throat by the force of the fall.

That was the sound the policewoman had made and that was the noise that shook Martin Thornton out of the party mood that night in the Horseshoe Bar when all around was drink and laughter. He sat at the bar, alone in a cocoon of remembrance. That noise, that half-gasp, had pierced the hubbub and socked him with its monumental *meaning*.

What was Caitlin Brook doing now?

Was she celebrating? Was she having a *good time*?

It had come crowding in on him when he least expected it. The noise she'd made; the *flop* of her body.

Behind him had been panic and anger. His memory played it back. Somebody was bawling to somebody else to get that *bloody fool* out of there and he didn't even realise it was directed at him. He had skidded to a halt, going down hard and tearing the knee out of his cavalry twills.

The baby was still clutched in her arms. It wasn't even crying. That was the strangest thing of all. Its eyes were open and it just lay there, on the uniform, as if it was in a cot. The young nurse's hat was off to one side, lying upside down in a puddle. He had thrown himself down on the ground. The girl was *shaking*, and that was scariest of all. Her eyes were open and her body was twitching as though someone had sent fifty-thousand volts through it. Every nerve in her body seemed to be dancing to a tune of its own and the image of the dead Aberdeen Angus came back again. It too had scrabbled and jittered, galvanised with death.

He'd leaned over her and stared into her eyes. Then she'd blinked, a miraculous small movement that was so horribly *normal*. A great tear formed in her eye and spilled down her cheek. Her mouth opened and no noise came out. She tried again and this time she managed to croak.

'Please. Please help me.' She stared at him with such intensity he could feel it burn into him. It was as if all her being, her whole *life*, was focused on him. 'Oh, please,' she croaked again.

Then her eyes rolled up in their sockets and the fever light in them just seemed to blink out.

Somebody grabbed him and hauled him backwards. Martin slipped and fell on his backside and the constable flung himself to the ground exactly as Martin had done all those interminable seconds ago. The young officer leaned over her and took hold of her shoulder.

'Caitlin. Kate. Are you all right? Come on Kate, *speak* to me!'

From somewhere behind, up high, came two sharp cracks, unmistakably gunfire, but Martin didn't hear them. He scrambled forward on his knees and grasped the policeman's trouser band, heaving him back off the girl.

'What the fu—' the young officer grunted.

'Keep your hands off her, you bloody idiot. Don't touch her.

'You don't—'

'She's broken her back, for God's sake. You'll kill her.'

Martin shoved in beside her, almost shouldering the young man away. All around were running feet. There was noise upstairs, the clatter of something metal falling on concrete. The bullhorn. He leaned over the girl, pressed by the crowd of blue serge legs that surrounded them now. She opened her eyes again and the fever light was back. They sparkled wetly in the flickering lights of the cars and police flashers. They swivelled and fixed on him and locked into his brain again.

He didn't know whether it was a convulsive shudder, or whether she had made a little nod.

But he heard her tiny whisper.

She said: '*Thank you*.'

5

Something moved in the trees. It was like a shadow flicking between the tall trunks that stood guard beside the stream. Ben Haldane caught the faint motion in the corner of his eye and whipped round, almost losing his footing on the smooth stones.

'What was that?' he said, almost to himself. Beside him, Dorothy, younger than he was by eighteen months, but so like her brother, with the same brown wavy hair and a faceful of freckles, there was no mistaking the connection. Dorothy was seven-and-a-half years old. Ben, at nine, more than a head taller, had the authority that older brothers acquire naturally, without question.

'*Shhhh*!' he said, holding a finger up to his lips and motioning her to silence with his left hand, flapping it up and down quickly.

'What *is* it?' Dorothy insisted, ignoring his non-verbal instructions.

'I saw something. Over there.' He pointed into the edge of the trees. She followed his direction and peered between the soaring trunks. They stood silent and huge, giants at the forest margin. The sunlight dappled up from the stream and spangled them with dots and whorls of light, but the reflections from the clear water could not penetrate the gloom behind the outrunners. Beyond the spread of the nearest trees, Fasach Wood was gloom for as far as the eye could see.

'I think it's a deer,' Ben said, still whispering. 'I saw it move.'

'I didn't see anything.'

'Well, I did,' Ben affirmed bossily, his voice rising back to normal tone.

'Well, I can't see anything now, smartypants.' Dorothy had a long, thin ash branch in her hand, taller than she was. She was waving it over the sparkling flow of the stream and brought it down in an arc to splash the surface. Silver droplets laced upwards like diamonds. Below the ripples, the dark bodies of small trout fled for the safety of the big rocks.

'*Something* was there.' Ben kept looking into the trees. 'Maybe it wasn't a deer. Maybe it was a bear. Or even a wolf.'

'Silly. You don't get wolves here.'

'That's what you think,' Ben said, making a manly effort to keep his voice serious and his face straight. 'There's all sorts of wild things in the woods. The wolves are the worst. They come out when you're not looking and get you.'

'Oh don't, Ben. That's scary,' Dorothy said, wide eyes flicking between him and the trees.

'And they like girls best. 'Cos they're small and tasty,' Ben said, his face now breaking into an evil grin. He stuck out his tongue, dog-like, as far as it would go and panted convincingly lupine. Dorothy edged towards him nervously.

Suddenly he lunged his head forward at her, opening his mouth wide and snapping it closed only inches from her face, and making a snarling noise as he did so.

Dorothy let out a little squeal and jerked back, losing her footing on the water-worn rock. For a second her arms windmilled and then she lost balance and landed in the shallows. More diamonds fountained in the sunlight as she squealed again, thrashing her hands hard down on the gravel to shove herself up to her feet again.

On the bank Ben hooted with laughter as he watched her struggle, then realised *he* could be in trouble for making her fall into the stream. His sister managed to get her balance and came clambering towards him, water pouring from her soaked jeans. Her tiny red canvas shoes slapped wetly on the stones.

'That was your fault. I'm telling mum.'

'It's only water,' Ben defended himself. 'It'll dry in a minute.'

'You shouldn't have done it. You're just a bully. *I'm telling!*' She stamped her foot on the stone for emphasis, but it was wet and slipped on the smooth surface and she lost her balance again. Arms grabbed air and she was tumbling backwards when Ben reached forward and caught her before she fell into a deeper part of the stream. He pulled her back to where the shingle formed a wide border between the water and the trees.

'Look, I didn't let you fall that time,' Ben said earnestly. 'That's us quits, okay?'

She looked up at him, knowing she had a lever on him, but she couldn't stay angry with Ben. Not for long.

'Oh, all right. But don't go scaring me again. It's not fair.'

'I won't. Scout's honour.'

'You're not in the Scouts.'

'Well, cross my heart and hope to die.'

She shrugged.

'Deal?' He held out his hand. She took it. His grip encompassed her little fingers.

'Deal,' she said. Ben kept his grip on her hand and pulled her towards him. He gave her his biggest grin and with his free hand he ruffled her hair in brotherly fashion.

'You're a pal, Dorrie,' he said.

They had been playing down at the stream all morning. It was their favourite place. Their house, the small farmstead, stood at the end of the lane which snaked up from the village and over the flat, wide bridge. Way in the distance, they could hear the buzz of the chainsaw as their father sliced the trees that he'd cut the previous winter in preparation for the foundations of the new houses he wanted to build. The saw hummed lazily, its sound muted by the warm summer air, filtered through the trees and hedges that hid this part of the stream from the open fields. Here, where the big trees crowded onto the water, could be anywhere at all for a small boy and his sister. In the first days of the summer holidays it had been their desert island, their mountain fastness, their pirate lair. The long holiday stretched ahead of them into infinity, in the wonderfully elastic timescale that only the very young live in.

Ben had woken with the sun streaming into his room, making the insides of his eyelids glow pink. He'd yawned, stretched and then bounced out of bed like a startled cat, instantly awake, immediately *alive*. He'd gone into Dorrie's room and shaken his sister until her eyes had opened sleepily. He'd kept it up as she tried to turn over to press her face into the pillow, attempting to *stay* asleep. Her efforts under the onslaught of a nine-year-old racing to greet the day were futile. He was already halfway through his plate of rice krispies when she toddled downstairs, hair tousled, knuckles of both hands grinding her eyes.

'Come on, slowcoach,' Duncan Haldane had called up to her.

He scraped his chair back on the stone floor and went across to the foot of the steps. He held both his big hands up and said: 'Jump.'

Dorothy drew her hands down from her eyes, favoured him with a wide, sleepy grin and launched herself into the air from six steps up. Her father's hands saddled her armpits, strong and safe. He swung her up in a high arc, letting her light weight feather across the room. He sailed her round, her little feet kicking the air, and sat her on her seat.

'Right, milady,' he said, putting on the plummy voice of one of the puppets in a TV series the kids liked to watch. 'Breakfast is served.'

Dorothy looked up and gave him another broad smile, though now her eyes were sparkling, fully awake.

'Oh thank you, Parker,' she said in accented English. 'That will be all.'

Duncan laughed aloud and his big hand came down and vigorously rubbed her back. She could feel his strong fingers span her narrow shoulders and she wriggled under the hot friction in delight until it became too much.

'Daddeee! That tickles,' she piped.

'Yes, milady,' he said, leathery face still creased with the grin. 'Come on now, eat up. I want the two of you to help me roll some logs.'

'Really, Dad?' Ben lost interest in his cereal. 'Can we help you cut them up too?'

' 'Fraid not, son. I have to use the chainsaw today to get some clearing-up done. Two many chips and skelfs flying around, and I don't want to be tripping over you two when I'm at it. Last thing I need is sliced children.'

Ben's face fell. He wanted to get his hands on the big cutter. He'd watched his father, goggles hiding his eyes, standing in a spray of sawdust while the blade bit into the trunks like a hot knife in butter. That was *man's* work. But he could see there was no arguing the point.

'Anyway, it's summer. You two should be out there enjoying yourselves while you've still got time. You'll miss it when you get to my age.'

Ben didn't quite believe he'd ever be that age, or that big, or that strong.

Rose Haldane came into the kitchen. She had her hair pinned back girlishly behind her ears and she wore one of Duncan's big shirts, tied into a knot over her hip.

'Hi, Mum,' Ben and Dorothy welcomed in unison.

'Morning, babies.' Rose turned and flicked up a stray strand of hair that had fallen over her eyes. Duncan eyed her appreciatively. She had that feminine countryside sturdiness that is more pretty than elegant. She looked casually comfortable in a scuffed and faded pair of jeans.

He gave her a low whistle and the kids looked at each other and giggled.

'You do more for that shirt than I ever did,' he volunteered.

'Maybe so, but it's the only clean one in the house. When you get those chalets built and sold, I want a new washing machine.'

'Think *big*, woman. When that's all done, you'll have a new *house*.'

'A washing machine would do fine for now,' she said. Rose came across to sit beside them. Duncan poured her a cup of tea, while she turned to the children.

'Right, you two. Try to stay clean today. And dry.' She swung to Duncan. 'And you too. You're worse than that pair.'

'That's because I'm a hardworking man.'

'Well, try to stay a *clean* one as well, otherwise I won't even have *this* shirt to wear.'

'If that's an offer, I'm going out to get really filthy,' he said, giving her an exaggerated nudge.

Rose reached across and slapped him lightly on the shoulder.

'Go on, get out of here, or I'll never get a thing done.'

Duncan had manhandled the big yellow saw out of the shed at the corner of the now-empty pigpen. There was still a swine-smell about the place though the last of the litter had gone months before. He toted the machine across the edge of the grassy slope that butted onto the garden and looked down at the tangle of trunks and branches. Another week and it would be cleared and ready for the digger.

His family had farmed this valley for more than three hundred years; possibly twice that. He had inherited it from old Angus Haldane in the year Ben had been born, and had been set to spend the rest of his life on the land.

Some hope.

The valley had gone sour on him so quickly it was as if the earth itself had turned against him.

The croft had made a living. Duncan and Rose were never going to be rich, but he was a good husbander, a natural farmer. They'd a few sheep up on the hill and some cattle on the low field where the stream turned and dived into the forest. The pigs hadn't quite brought home the bacon, but Rose had worked a miracle in the smokehouse to bring them extra cash from the bigger towns and even the market down at Levenford. The land had been fertile and, bounded on three sides by hills, it should have stayed that way. Duncan had gone in for organic farming, for the premium he could command at the market, and it had been a good idea at the time, for the land *had* been good. It didn't need a mess of ICI chemicals, and the savings he would make, when added to the top price he'd get for his produce, widened the margin from subsistence to a good living.

Then the valley had gone sour.

First the sheep had come down with scrapie, despite the fact they'd been dipped only a month before. The whole herd had been slaughtered by brown-coats from the Department of Agriculture. The insurance hadn't been enough to replace it and anyway there was no point in doing that until the ground was given the all clear and that could take more than a year. There were times he felt he'd been farming Gruinard Island, up in the north west, where they'd experimented with anthrax during the war. The island was still blighted and Duncan's slopes had gone the same way.

The small herd of Jerseys, his pride and joy, some of the best milkers from Lochend to Craigard up the length of Loch Corran, had broken out of their field. He'd spent a bad autumn week putting up new wire on that stretch, ripping his hands to shreds to make sure the cattle stayed out of the trees. Then during the spring a big blow had tumbled a tall beech tree across the fence and the Jerseys had wandered into the edge of the forest, where they'd all gorged themselves on yew leaves and died within hours, bawling their pain to the grey spring sky.

The previous summer the potato crop had been a joke. The shaws had stood tall and strong until August, when they had gone rusty and fallen under their own weight, like straw in a gale. What tubers had grown were not worth keeping.

It had been a catalogue of disaster, one thing after another. Something similar had happened to Bill Aitken who farmed the east of the valley beyond the edge of the Fasach woods which sat in the hollow of the glen. Nobody knew exactly what had happened. Some said his cattle had drunk polluted water, maybe from a broken septic tank. Whatever it was, he had lost his whole herd of beef. He'd sold up and moved down to Levenford to work in a factory.

Duncan Haldane had decided not to work in a factory. He wanted to stay in the glen where he'd been raised. He racked his brains all winter for a way to haul them out of the financial quicksand that was dragging the family under. The answer had come to him one night when he'd awoken in a panic, his hands clenched so tightly into fists that his nails were digging red crescents in the skin of his palms. The worry of the prolonged catastrophe had brought on many such nights. He'd gone downstairs and sat, flicking through a magazine, and the picture had jumped straight out at him. It showed cabins on the west coast, little log houses with pitched roofs set in a line along the banks of some loch. He looked at the houses and then the rental prices and when Rose had come down in the early morning she'd found him slumped over the table with a diagram of their land spread out underneath him. She'd shaken him awake and he'd come to dozily and then he'd given her a smile the like of which she hadn't seen in the past six months.

'Rosie, girl, I think we're saved.'

That had been more than a year ago. Now he bent his back, taking the weight of the saw in both hands. The torque of the spinning chain-blade twisted the machine clockwise in his hand, bucking with a deadly life of its own, and he had to lock both elbow joints to keep it straight. He lowered it onto the beech trunk that lay angled into the air, elephant-grey and nearly two yards wide. The thought came to him of that other mighty beech that had crumpled his new-built fence and let his herd escape to die. This one he had cut himself, his regret at killing something monstrous and old conflicting with the pleasure of getting something *done*. He recalled that other forest-edge monster, with its great trailing arms and the huge fan of root and red earth hauled out of the ground in an arch. There had been something odd about the tree, he remembered, something *out of place* about its position, but in the panic of the lowing, *dying* herd, the thought had fled from his mind.

Now, as he worked, in a spray of sawdust that spat out from the dead trunk, the memory of the huge tree sprawled and broken on his land came back to him. There *had* been something strange about it. He couldn't recall what it had been. The clattering buzz of the saw changed note as the blade bit through the bark and into the hard wood and the picture flicked from his mind as he braced himself to concentrate.

Down at the stream, Dorothy was wringing her socks out, though it was a pointless task. Her sodden jeans were draining into her shoes and seemed set to drip for some time, but she fastidiously squeezed every last drop of moisture from her white ankle socks and hoped her mother wouldn't notice they'd been wet.

She was no longer angry with Ben. The two of them were too close to be anything but best friends, despite the fact that there were a few children their age in Linnvale. Some of the young mothers had organised a summerplay for them, with hill rambles and day trips, and there was a special picnic organised for the end of the holiday which all the small children were looking forward to. But on the first few days out of school, Ben and Dorothy were content to play together in their valley down at the stream.

Whilst Dorothy missed the animals, even the smelly pigs, there was no end of things to do. Ben was the brains behind their games, on account of his eighteen-month seniority and because he was good at thinking up new adventures. As always, Dorrie was first mate to his captain, navigator to his pilot, but she didn't care. It had always been that way.

They followed the edge of the stream as it twisted and turned in the flat basin of the valley, always edged by the trees that eventually became Fasach Wood where some of the men went hunting for woodcock and pheasant in the winter. Their father had always cautioned them to stay out of the thick forest, which covered the entire bowl of the lower glen, because the river Corrie, into which their stream fed, got deep and fast down there.

He had said that beyond the tarn, the Haldane Tarn, named for their farm and their family, the water swept into deep ravines filled with pot-holes and could sweep you away in a second flat.

The way he described it made Dorothy shiver. She could imagine what being swept away *in a second flat* would be like; tumbling and rolling in the bubbling water, dashed against the rocks and then later, a *long time later*, being found washed up on the edge of wide Loch Corran. They did not go into the forest. The tarn at the boundary of the coppice where the plantation merged with the real woods was the limit when Ben wanted to fish for the big brown trout. Beyond that was mystery, dark and shadowed by the immense trees; the far side of her world.

They had played hide-and-seek and Dorothy's jeans had dried quickly under the hot summer sun, although her little red sneakers were still damp and squishy. It didn't matter, because Ben too had slipped on a stone and had drenched himself up to his knees, so if there was any blame to be dished out, they could share it and that was much easier. Far behind them, the buzz of the saw had softened down to a dragonfly drone. Ben was lying on a flat quartz rock which sparkled in the direct sunlight, both his hands groping underneath.

'What have you got?'

'A trout, I think. It feels like a whopper.'

Dorothy nimbly leapt from stone to stone, never missing her step, until she stood beside him, waving her arms for balance. Ben was head down, concentrating, a lick of hair trailing in the water. Then his hands moved. She could see the muscles ripple in his skinny arms and then he hauled himself up. The silver flickered in his hands, a burn trout twisting madly for freedom. His left hand was clamped over its head and gills to prevent it slipping forwards or back and he let out a whoop of glee.

'What a beauty. What a *monster!*' he yelled. He clambered across to the far bank, with his sister following like a brown shadow.

'Let me see. Is it a biggie?'

'It's a *giant*,' he crowed. 'At least a *salmon*.'

He opened his right hand and she saw his wrist being twisted this way and that by the trout's muscular thrashings, much in the way that their father's brawny arms strained against the torque of the saw. It was a big fish in his small hands, maybe a foot long and fat, a fighting fish of fast water. Its colours rainbowed iridescence and she could see its jaws gulp for water.

'Can we keep it?'

'You bet,' Ben affirmed with great pride. 'And I'm going to catch enough for all of us.'

He searched the bank for a moment until he found a thin honeysuckle creeper which he pulled away from its twist around the bole of a sapling. With a quick movement the boy stripped the leaves, pulling the tendril through one closed hand, and then, with equal sleight, threaded the runner through the trout's gills. It hung there, silver and sightless, mouth agape.

'Come on, Dorrie, let's catch another.'

She followed her brother on the smooth, water-worn stones to the bend in the stream where the water had carved out ledges under a steep stone bank. Beyond that, the stream took its dive into Fasach Wood. Ben let Dorothy hold the fish while he explored under the ledges and rocks, following the flow of the water. In a few moments the sound of the chainsaw faded out and they were in the shade of the trees.

6

They lay side by side on the dry moss under the sweep of a tree. Her head lay on his chest, fair hair curling under his chin. Both of them were drowsy in the afterglow.

The sun slanted down through the branches to dapple the forest floor, picking out the bluebells and forest primroses in spots of brilliant colour.

'We'll have to get back soon,' Betty MacKinnon said. Norrie Ritchie mumbled sleepily.

She smiled and nudged him awake.

'Come on, lazybones. We'll have to go. Somebody might come.'

He shook his head. 'Nobody comes down here. It's all right.'

'But if I don't get back, he'll wonder where I am. It's too close to home.'

'Nah. He never thinks of anything but business. He's got me working all hours. I'll have to look for another job, and then I'm taking you with me, out of this place.'

She looked up and smiled.

'Only if you can keep me in the manner I've got accustomed to,' she said, drawing her fingers slowly up the length of his bare leg. Beside them, their clothes lay in a heap.

'You know I always do my best,' he said, a little smugly. Norrie Ritchie was a good ten years younger than his employer's wife, though the age difference was not apparent. Betty was tall and slim and had mischievous sparkling blue eyes.

They had met at the stile overlooking the valley and taken the path down the field, staying close to the hedge for cover, towards Fasach Wood on a warm afternoon. Their affair had been going on since the New Year when old Donnie MacKinnon had thrown a party. She had passed Norrie on the stairs and had casually slipped her arm around his waist and given him an unmistakable smile. From that crackling moment they had spent every possible moment together, difficult in such a tight, close-knit village as Linnvale.

They had strolled arm in arm under the trees, each aware of the other's desire, every touch electric. They had clambered over the tumbledown dyke and found a sheltered place under the tree where the moss was a thick dry carpet. They had made love urgently to the sound of bees buzzing in the high canopy and wood-pigeons cooing in the forest shadows. Then they had lain in each other's arms, the sweat cooling on their hot bodies.

Finally Norrie stirred and sat up. Betty kept her hand on his thigh and he could feel the heat of her touch. It made him want to start over again. He kissed her and she responded; then, after a while, she began to pull away.

'Come on, greedy. Save it for another time.'

'I'll try,' he said. He turned away from her towards his clothes and she lay back again, eyes closed.

'Hey, that's a nice one,' he said.

'Which one?' she said, eyes lowered to her own breasts. She was grinning mischievously.

'This flower. Look.'

She opened her eyes and slowly sat up. He was craning up to a plant that draped from the tree under which they'd made love. It spread a cluster of blood-red flowers, each petal as big as a butterfly wing, each bloom saucer-sized.

'Oh, it *is* lovely,' she said. She knelt, got to her feet and came over beside him.

'Never seen anything like that. You'll have to pick a bunch for me. I'll tell Donnie I've a secret admirer.'

'Not secret for long,' he replied. 'We'll have to do it soon.'

She smiled, then reached upwards towards the flower. He heard her sniff lightly, then she gave a little cough.

Norrie Ritchie was reaching for his clothes when she coughed again. He turned back and saw her move forward, face still pressed against the flower.

He was about to turn away when she made a little gurgling sound and her whole body jerked.

'What's . . .?' he started to say.

Betty MacKinnon let out a strangled wail and he moved towards her. Then his whole body went rigid.

The blood-red petals were clamped tight on her face. The cup-shaped flower had closed over her nose and mouth as if it had been glued there. She made another noise and her body spasmed again, pulling backwards. Her hand came up and grabbed the thick stem and heaved. In that instant, he could see the smooth muscles on her arm tense with the effort, but neither flower nor stem gave.

The strangled sound came again and her feet drummed on the moss. Norrie scrambled towards her and got his hand on the plant. It felt rubbery and somehow *alive*. His fingers clenched on it and one of the stems twisted round his wrist.

At that moment, Norrie Ritchie did not think he was in any danger. He didn't think anything. He pulled his wrist towards himself and the plant pulled back.

Confused, he tugged again and the creeper vine with its beautiful flowers jerked against him.

He looked at it, bewildered, unable to comprehend what was happening, while beside him Betty MacKinnon's slim body was writhing and jerking, her face still clamped inside the flowerhead.

He stared at the plant and then he saw the flower nearest him open its petals, then slowly, and somehow very *menacingly*, close them again.

'What . . .?' he began to say again, but the words were cut off when the plant *flexed* and pulled him upwards with a jerk. He tumbled, off balance, and swung headlong into a tangled mass of the plant. Something wet and leathery closed over his face. His vision went red and when he tried to breathe, no air came. He attempted to call out, but all he managed was a muffled grunt.

A sickly smell invaded his nose and liquid filled his mouth. He felt his feet lift off the ground.

Then his entire body spasmed as whatever he had tasted seeped in through the skin of his tongue and cheeks, oozed into his nerves and surged into his brain.

Sudden intense pain razored him from head to foot.

Inside his head, Norrie Ritchie screamed in agony, but no sound was heard in the forest, except for the spasmodic thrashings of the two naked bodies.

The noise took a long while to stop. When it did, a kind of silence returned to Fasach Wood. In the low branches of the spreading tree under which Norrie and Betty had lain, there were small, almost imperceptible movements twitching the plant with the blood-red flowers. It spread slowly, air-roots and runners seeking purchase, shoots seeking nourishment. As daylight began to fail, the plant had spread and grown into two elongated patches covered with scarlet blossoms, hanging from the thick boughs.

From a certain angle, the flower patches might have formed the outline of a hanging man and a spreadeagled woman, though no one saw them, and by this time there was nothing left of the two people who had come down to the woods.

Of Norrie Ritchie and Betty MacKinnon, nothing was ever heard again.

7

'It doesn't get better,' Caitlin said. Martin looked at her, keeping his expression still.

She reached awkwardly and took a sip of her wine. The second bottle was almost finished and the remains of their salad lay limp in a glass bowl. He watched her movements, got the impression she was moving slowly to keep herself from moving fast.

'Nobody knows what it's like.' She shook her head, confirming the world's ignorance, and her hair moved like molten copper. 'And the worst thing is knowing it goes on forever.'

'I read somewhere about nerve regeneration. They seem to think they might be able to manage that.'

'And that's something I can't think of.' She brought him up short, but without anger. All the anger was inside her. He could feel it struggling to get out. 'If I think of that, if I think of a cure, then I start to *hope*. I can't afford that.'

'I don't understand,' Martin said, honestly.

'Didn't expect you to, but at least you make an effort,' Caitlin said softly, then smiled at him. He felt the warmth.

'They told me all about this in physio and in the other kind of therapy. I have to accept what I am. I have to tell myself every morning that I'll be stuck in this chair for the rest of my life. If I start to think of cures and nerve regeneration, then I can't accept this.'

She slammed the heel of her hand down on the wheelchair's arm for emphasis. The chair rocked with the motion.

'And if I don't accept this, I will go completely mad. There is no fairy with a magic wand. There is no spell. No witch's brew.'

Martin sat back, letting her continue if she would, not wishing to push it.

'It's amazing the things you take for granted. It's not just the walking. Not even the running, though I miss that like crazy.'

'I know. You told me. I looked out the marathon pictures. You turned in a good time.'

'And I would have done better, too. I loved pushing myself to the limit. Now I have to push *this* damned thing. You don't realise how much you have to learn just to make one of these move. At first I thought it was a joke. I kept going round in circles. I bet you never think about ramps in shops, and how the hell you're going to manoeuvre into a bathroom. Nobody does until something like this happens and you realise the world is built for walkers and runners.'

'What do you miss most?' Martin asked.

'You'd never believe it.'

'Try me.'

'Maybe sometime. Not now. But I do miss dancing. I can't do a strip-the-willow in this thing. I miss control and balance. And I miss not being the right *height* for anything. Look at this place.'

Martin looked round at the old-fashioned kitchen.

'All the shelves are too high. I have to get somebody in to fix this place up so I can use it properly. Dougie Scott up at Craigard said he'd come and do it, but I've waited a month.'

'It's not a big job. I can fix it up if you want,' Martin volunteered.

'What do you mean?'

'It's only woodwork. It would have been my trade if I hadn't joined the yellow press. I give my father a hand now and again.'

'You. A *carpenter*?'

'It'll be something to fall back on when I get thrown out of newspapers. Or when I quit the rat race altogether. But you'll have to let me have a try in the wheelchair, to get the idea of what you need.'

'Are you serious?' Caitlin asked. The look on her face told him she expected some punchline.

'Sure. Why not. I reckon two days at the most. Take the bases off the units. Drop the sink. Lower the wall cupboards. Maybe a ramp at the back door to save you killing yourself on the step.'

'Ah, I've got it. This is another bribe.'

'No. And the first one wasn't either. You will either let me do a story, or you won't. I'd rather do it, because I hate leaving things unfinished, but it's not the end of the world.'

'But why should you?' Caitlin asked.

'Why not?'

'There's more to it than that.'

'I suppose there is.' He nodded, but said nothing more. He reached and poured the remaining wine into their glasses, getting the measures just about even.

'Tell me then,' she demanded.

'It goes back to that night.' He paused. Caitlin looked at him directly, eyebrows raised in question.

'The night I broke my back. Let's not skirt around it. It *happened*.'

He nodded again, put in his place.

'You ever wonder why I came to see you in hospital?'

'For a story.'

'More than that.'

'Oh, you fancied my helpless body?'

'I can't deny that,' he said. 'I've always been a sucker for redheads. But it was more than that . . .' He paused again, as if searching for the word. 'I *saw* it,' he said simply.

'Saw what?'

'I saw it happen, *before* it happened.'

Caitlin looked at him directly, puzzled. 'You've lost me.'

'I saw you fall before you did . . . Look, I've only told one other person about this, and nothing like that ever happened to me before, but I got a premonition, or a *déjà-vu* experience or something. Anyway, whatever it was, I got this ringing in my ears, like somebody stuck two electrodes on my head and switched on the current. I can't explain it properly, but it was as if every nerve in my body was up and dancing and then I *saw* it. That's why I got to you first and managed to pull that idiot away when he tried to pick you up.'

'I remember that. I was so scared,' Caitlin said. Her eyes showed she was back *there*. Back *then*.

'Me too. I remembered you walking past and giving your legs the once-over.'

'Last chance for everybody, eh?' Caitlin gave a little rueful laugh.

'Then this thing hit me inside my head and I *saw* it. The gun came out of the door, the woman was running, then she fell. I saw the hands reach out for the baby and then there was this sensation of pain, but it wasn't in *me*. I could just sense it. Then I saw you go over and I started running to warn you.'

He stopped and put his glass down with a faint clink. 'I wasn't fast enough. I thought I could catch you. I'm sorry. To tell you the truth, I've been sorry ever since.'

Caitlin stared at him levelly, straight in the eye, for at least half a minute. There was no expression on her face. Finally, her lips curved in a small smile.

'Is this another line? You expect me to believe that?'

'Not really,' Martin said. He realised he'd been holding his breath all the time she'd been staring at him. He let it out slowly.

'I can hardly believe it myself. I've been trying to puzzle it out, but I can't get an answer to it.'

'You're trying to tell me you had a premonition of me getting shot?'

He nodded.

'I don't believe you.'

'Fair enough.'

She stared at him again as if trying to see into him, see *through* him. He didn't react.

'Okay then. You saw it, describe what happened.'

'I'll tell you some of it. You tell me the rest.'

'We'll see.' She put her hands on the chair arms and pushed her body back, waiting.

'The woman came out, running. She had a sort of cardigan on. It was flapping. She had the baby out, holding it out in both hands.' Martin demonstrated the action, holding out his hands, as if in offering. 'She was saying something. Screaming, I think. I couldn't hear those words, but somebody beside you told you to get back and you said you had to get it. Then the woman was down and the baby was in the air and you caught it. You turned, back towards the exit where the others were, and you got hit in the back.'

'Everybody knows that,' Caitlin said dully, her eyes cloaked with memory.

'When you went over the balcony you were thinking about the baby. When you started to fall, you were twisting, so you wouldn't land on it and kill it. That's why you hit the wall on your back. Then, when your eyes opened, you were thinking of someone else. A woman. Fair hair, maybe grey hair. I think it was your mother.'

Caitlin looked at him again and this time her face was slack. Tears welled up in her eyes and brimmed over, trailing down her cheeks. Martin was transfixed by the change in her expression, reading the emotions written there.

'My mother,' she finally said in a soft, faltering voice. Then she burst into tears. Her whole body shook with the force of them. Martin was taken aback. He didn't know what to do. Finally, unable to watch her crying, he moved across to where she sat and bent down to put his arm round her shoulder. He patted her back idiotically, but it made *him* feel a little better. He felt her body shaking against his in jerky little movements. After a while the crying stopped. Quite naturally, she turned her face into him, into the curve of his neck. He could feel the wetness of her tears on his skin and the trails of autumn-fire hair against his cheek. He held her there till the shaking too subsided.

A few minutes later he gradually loosened his arms and she slowly pulled herself away. Both of them felt awkward, she for crying, he for witnessing her discomfort.

'I'm sorry about that. I try to avoid that sort of thing.' She took a handkerchief from her shirt pocket and wiped her nose. She sounded snuffly, childlike.

'Oh, don't worry about it. At least you girls *can* do it. Us guys aren't allowed.'

She looked at him and favoured him with a watery smile.

'It's just that the mindbenders don't prepare you for this kind of thing. *The sudden flashback.* The physios can teach you to get around and keep your muscles in good order. I've an exerciser in there to keep my legs in shape, though why I bother I don't know. It's part of the ritual; to keep yourself *alive*. But the flashbacks, they come at any time. Like today, when you walked round the side of the house. That's why I was a bit grumpy. I know you came to the hospital a lot, and I do appreciate that, but when I saw you it all came crowding back.'

'Well, I'm sorry for that,' Martin ventured.

'Oh don't be. It's not your fault. Not anybody's fault, except that mad bastard with the gun. It's only . . .' She stopped, searching for the word. 'It's hard to explain. I should count my blessings, really.'

Martin gave a short bark of a laugh. 'Oh, sure you should.'

'No. Really. It could have been worse. The shot could have killed me, but it didn't, because it was light stuff, birdshot or something, and the barrel was shortened, so I didn't get the full load. When I went over the balcony and hit that wall, I could have broken my neck.'

'Would that have been worse?'

'Sure. The lower the break, the better it is. I could have been in an iron lung for the rest of my life. At least I can move my arms. With this chair I'm developing biceps like a shot-putter.' She gave a little chuckle at that, flexing them. 'I had a bad break on one of my lumbar vertebrae. It's almost a complete lesion, which means the spinal cord was nearly cut in two. I've lost all motor and sensory function. I was a bit unlucky with the shot. Two pellets are still lodged against the sacral bone nerves. That's the part which controls all those embarrassing functions. Sometimes the inflammation there causes me a lot of embarrassment, I don't mind telling you.'

'I don't mind either. Whatever you feel all right about telling,' Martin said.

'Depends on the day. I get moody. Swing up and down. Anyway, they had to put a brace in there to hold the bones because they were pretty well crushed. Of course, relationships are out of the question.'

'Why's that?' Martin asked. 'Plenty of people in wheelchairs are married.'

'When I say relationships, I'm talking about the one-to-one kind. Like . . . you know . . .'

'Oh.' Martin felt uncomfortable again, as if he was prying to the centre, peering where he shouldn't look.

'Yes: oh. When I say I'm dead from the hips down, I mean exactly that.'

Martin didn't know what to say to that. Instead he took another direction.

'When I got to you, you were shivering all over. You didn't look as if you were paralysed, but I *knew* you were hurt. That's why I stopped that fellow from moving you.'

'Saved my life, probably. I'm grateful for it. I was conscious then. I *remember*. That's one of the odd things about this. You get some muscle spasms later. Makes you think the doctors are wrong

63

and that you're getting better. At least I did, even though they told me to expect it. They've trailed off now, but I still get the jumps in my legs. It's quite strange to watch, but I can't feel a thing.'

'When did you start getting used to it?'

'Don't kid yourself about that, Martin,' Caitlin said very definitely, eyes fixed levelly on his. 'You *never* get used to it. I still dream that I'm running. I feel my whole body in motion. Sometimes I just don't want to wake up to this. That's the truth.'

The starkness of her words was chilling. Martin could feel the clench of despair behind them. Again he had nothing to say in reply. He was relieved when, after a moment of silence, she tossed her head, using the movement to swing her hair back from her face.

'Anyway, enough of this. What about you? Whose side are you on in the range war?'

'Oh, I'm supposed to be impartial as a judge. I don't know. I'm all for conservation. I can understand why people don't like development in a place like this.'

'Me too. But I know Duncan Haldane. He's a decent man. He's had some bad luck. The Linnvale Preservation Society are making all the noises. I think they were the Women's Rural Institute before they got militant. All flower arranging and coffee mornings.'

'But now they're organised?'

'So I gather. I've only been here a few months. They haven't asked me to join.'

'And would you?'

'I'm a bit like you. I don't want the valley covered in chalets, but I think a couple of log cabins on Duncan's land won't matter much to anybody. He owns the north edge of the forest, and where he's building isn't even visible from the village or the Linn Road. I think they should leave him in peace and let him earn a living.'

'I'll talk to him tomorrow. I've got a room at the Corrie Hotel for tonight.'

'How long are you staying?'

'As long as it takes,' Martin said, smiling. 'As long as I can screw expenses out of them. Maybe I can stretch it for a couple of days. The best thing about that award was being reconciled with the Editor. He thinks I'm a hero. It'll cost him.'

He shoved back his chair on the tiled floor, reaching behind him to unsling his jacket from the back.

'I suppose I'd better go up and meet some locals,' he said.

'I'm told the food's good at the Douglas Arms.'

'That's a relief. It's the only place in twenty miles. Maybe I can take you up there?'

'Another bribe?'

'Sure. What else?'

She laughed at that, hair swinging with the motion.

'All right. You're on.'

8

The buzz of the chain saw teeth biting into the fallen beech tree had faded and died when they had followed the bend in the stream. The water tumbled over the stones, crystal-clear and cold as snow, despite the heat of the summer. It had come down from the heights of Dumbuie Hill towering head and shoulders above the rest of the mountains enclosing the glen. From there it had pooled in the black depths of the Corrie Linn before pouring out in the cataract that fell a straight sixty feet to the series of pot-holes worn smooth by winter torrents. Now, just inside the edge of the forest, the water shot back the rays of the sun that managed to pierce the spreading canopy of oak and beech and ash, sending spears of white light to catch the motes of pollen and the clouds of tiny insects dancing in the still air.

Dorrie hunkered down on a round, moss-covered rock while her brother lay on a flat stone, arms plunged up beyond his elbows, feeling in the crevices for the slippery touch of a trout. Already his jeans were smeared with algae and mud from the stream bank. His head was down, nose almost touching the surface, brow furrowed with concentration.

'Anything yet?' Dorrie was lightly splashing the water with the slender rowan wand he'd been using to poke into ledges that were too deep to reach.

'Nah. Just wee ones.'

Ben raised himself from the stone and used his hands to wipe cold water from each sturdy arm. The droplets spattered like rain on the stream. He looked across to where she was sitting, then turned on the rock, eyes scanning downstream.

'There's some good places down there.' He pointed to where the water raced between granite boulders then slowed to flow into wide flat pools. From where he stood, he could see the dappling of small fish rising for nymphs, spreading silver rings on the placid surface, shadowed by tall trees.

'We're not supposed to go that far,' Dorrie called back, hesitantly.

'Oh, come on. It's not far. I need more fish.'

His sister held up the one he'd already caught, swinging it by the twiny runner.

'This one is enough.'

'But there's bigger ones,' he said, determined.

Before she could respond and put barriers in his way, he turned and skipped from stone to stone, following the flow. She watched as he reached the narrow defile, standing with each foot on a smooth granite lump, then he jumped forward and disappeared. It was as if the forest had swallowed him up. She sat there for a moment, unsure. Dorrie was torn between wanting to go back up into the sunlight and following her brother. She waited, hoping to see him reappear between the stones, even to catch sight of him below the defile, but there was no movement. Up above, an eddy of wind caught the tops of the tall trees and a low sigh ran through Fasach Wood. The running water mumbled and muttered in response as, up in the leaves, the insects hummed. Although she knew Ben was only a few yards away, beyond the tumbling falls, she felt completely alone.

Somewhere, beyond her vision, a woodpecker rapped a sudden hollow staccato, startling her. Again the solitude crowded in on the small girl and she took two steps downstream. Maybe they *shouldn't* be so far down the valley, but she *definitely* didn't want to be there alone. She jumped onto a stone that jutted from the water near the crevice and skittered in pursuit of her brother, using the narrow stick to balance. In her other hand the trout flopped wetly.

She stood at the lip of the narrow falls, peering down the shadowed glen, much as Ben had done only moments before.

He wasn't there.

She swept her eyes left and right, puzzled. There was no sign of him. The stream flowed straight for twenty yards through two wide, shallow pools, then turned to the left at a high shale bank that had been undercut by heavy flows in the past. She held her breath, listening, but there was no sound except the muttered conversation of running water.

Dorrie hesitated again and the solitude tugged at her. She was not scared yet, not quite *afraid*. But little whispers of apprehension were telling her *don't go down there, don't go by yourself*.

She shook her head, denying the insistent voices, and jumped down to the flat bank on the far side. She moved quickly towards the turn, feet rustling through the low fern clusters. She reached the angle and had to lean against the tall bank for balance to peer round. The stream ambled through a series of jinks and twists so that she could only see the water in the places where it doubled back into her line of vision. There was still no sign of Ben.

The little knot of apprehension swelled. The forest had gone quiet.

She called out: '*Ben, where are you?*'

She expected to hear him call back, annoyed at his little sister's shout. She shouted again, her voice reedy and high.

'Bernard Haldane! Ben! I can't *see* you!'

As if the insects and birds had fled from her cry, the silence deepened.

Dorrie moved along past the high bank, walking as quickly as she could on the slippery stones, using the flat ones to crisscross the water where she could. Twice her foot slipped and she went into the stream up to her knees, soaking her jeans again. Round the left bend, then the right. She cut across a low hollow where the stream meandered around a point, thinking she would save time and distance. She climbed the sloping bank where the big beech roots clung like grey, muscular arms, then she was over the lip and down the other side. The leaf litter crackled under her feet, last year's canopy now a dry rustling russet carpet. She slipped on the steep slope and the honeysuckle thong snapped as her arms pinwheeled for balance. The dead fish spun away from her and flopped into a tangle of dogweed.

'Damn!' The word slipped out of her mouth before she knew it. Dorrie wasn't allowed to say that, and a whole list of other words besides, no matter that her father peppered his adult conversations with them all the time.

Her momentum carried her down the incline, past the dogweed cluster, and she couldn't stop herself. Her little legs pattered on the leaves as she tried to slow herself down and keep from falling. Then, as the slope levelled out, she tripped on a root and sprawled headlong, almost burying herself in the thick leaf mould. She bounced, landed on her back and the breath was slammed out of her chest. She lay dazed for several seconds while the world spun dizzily. The trunks of the trees wavered in and out of vision as tears smarted her eyes. She blinked rapidly to clear them and her breath came back painfully in staggering whoops.

Slowly Dorrie hauled herself to her feet, disorientated. She was at the base of a small, dark hollow overhung by the spreading branches of the big trees. She blinked fresh tears away, ignoring the one that spilled out and down her muddied cheek. The fish was gone. She'd dropped her rowan stick. She looked around the hollow then started to climb out. It was difficult because the leaves slid from under her feet and she slipped back one step for every two forward. Using her hands, though, digging her fingers into the earth for purchase, she finally got to the lip of the depression again and made her way carefully down the other side towards where she thought the stream was.

She could hear the water, but the sound echoed from the tall trunks of the trees and was muffled. She got about fifty yards deeper into the gloom of Fasach Wood before she realised she must be going in the wrong direction.

There were no tracks here. No well-worn ruts scraped by booted feet. No narrow passages formed by deer or blundering sheep. She changed direction, heading to the right, where the sound of the stream seemed loudest, and stumbled through the thick ferns and tangles of honeysuckle that twined around the ash saplings reaching for the light. The further she went, the taller the ferns and briars seemed to become. The sound of the stream got suddenly fainter and once again she could hear insects in the high canopy. They sounded *louder* here. Wings whirred as dragonflies banked in aerial combat. She heard beetles skittering on bark and scraping through the undergrowth. Then suddenly she was aware of the *smell* of the forest, green and damp, resin and sap. And underneath and overall, the smell of decay and rot. The forest smelled both dead and alive at the same time.

Dorrie stopped, listening for the sound of the stream, but she could no longer hear it. The apprehension that had been winding up inside her now was tight and singing like a wire.

'Ben!' she called out again. 'Bernard, where *are* you?'

She took a step forward, unsure of which way to go, then another two to the left.

Tall trunks stood all around her, great giants that seemed to bar her progress. The fickle wind stirred the thin branches and they scraped against each other, high, incomprehensible voices.

'*Ben!*' she cried out again and it was more like a scream.

Ben was in trouble, and he knew it. The prospect of being kept in the next couple of days, maybe even for a week of the summer holidays, loomed large and heavy like a thunderstorm over the glen.

No matter how he explained it, it would be *his* fault. He could hear his father's voice, angry and disappointed, telling him he should have *known better*. He was the *big brother*. He'd been *trusted* to look after his sister. The impending pleasure of going home with a stringful of fat trout had evaporated fifteen minutes after jumping down from the rocks at the low falls. Dorothy had been sitting on a stone and he'd told her to come on. It was only a little bit downstream. The fish had been dappling the water, big ones, he just *knew*.

He'd waited a minute, then he'd had to go for a pee. It had come on him suddenly, probably because he'd been lying face down on the rocks, belly pressed against the hard surface. He'd cut away from the stream – because everybody knew you never pissed in the water – and angled into the trees, to go along with directive number two: boys don't piss in front of girls, not even sisters.

Well out of sight of the brook, he'd watched with the fascination all boys have as he made a water-pattern, a figure of eight, on the dry leaves. When he'd finished he zipped himself up and nonchalantly made his way back to the stream.

Dorrie evidently hadn't followed him down beyond the rocks. He didn't notice the splash marks on the dry stones a few yards downstream where she'd lost her balance and soaked her foot. He craned up at the low falls to where she'd been sitting, but there was no sign of her. That's when he began to think he might be in trouble.

'We're not supposed to go that far,' she'd said. Now she'd gone home and their father would know they'd been down beyond the Haldane Mill Dam.

'*You don't go down into those trees.*' That's what he'd said, sitting with his elbows on the kitchen table, brown arms hard and knotted as wood. '*You could get lost in there and we'd never find you. And that Corrie could sweep you away quick as a blink.*'

The Corrie didn't look that fearsome to Ben, though he knew a couple of youngsters had drowned in it one autumn before he'd been born. He wasn't scared of it, but he *was* scared of feeling his father's hardworking hand working on his backside. It didn't happen often, but when it did it gave you something to think about, that was for certain.

Ben stood up and looked upstream to the turn where they'd come down into the trees. It was brighter up there beyond the fringe. The sun still caught the water. He took a couple of steps in that direction, then hesitated, typically boyish, debating with himself whether to be hanged for a sheep as a lamb. He was in trouble anyway, nothing surer. How much would depend on how far Dorothy had said they'd gone, and she might not even be sure of the distance. There were big fish down there in the pools, he knew. He turned and took a couple of steps backwards. If he went home with a string of trout, there was a possibility that the prize would take the bite out of the punishment. He stopped again, undecided, wanting to go further downstream, then he realised that Dorrie couldn't have gone far. He could run and catch her up before she got to the farmhouse. Maybe he could even persuade her to say nothing. He nodded to himself, quite impressed with his reasoning. He ran up the bank towards the dogleg turn in the stream.

Just then, he heard his sister call out.

'Ben, where *are* you?'

He skidded to a stop. The sound of the water and the slight soughing of the breeze had almost smothered his sister's cry. He turned, unsure whether her call had come from up or down the valley, then it came again, clearer, more urgent, but damped down, as if it had come a long way through the trees.

'Dorrie,' he shouted back and heard his own words ricochet from the trees, fragmented, bouncing back at him in little echoes.

'*Bernard, where are you?*'

This time there was no mistaking the direction. Ben retraced his steps at a run, springing up onto the two rocks at the head of the little falls, then nimbly leaping over the water to the shingle on the far side. The trees thickened around him as his feet pattered on the deer track that paralleled the water. He followed the zigzags of the river, using the stones where he could. A couple of times he called out her name and thought he heard her voice reply, though he couldn't be sure.

The more he ran, the darker the forest got. The trunks became thicker and more gnarled, the spreading canopy more dense. Beyond the series of twists the river plummeted into a ravine overgrown with scrubby juniper and festooned with thick ropes of honeysuckle straggling up from the damp moss. These falls dropped into a series of deep black pot-holes where the murmur of the water became a roar of constant thunder. The sound of the torrent was funnelled back up the ravine, drowning out every other noise.

Ben held onto a snaky root and leaned out over the falls to see if there was a way to get down to the lower level. There was none. Dorrie *couldn't* have come this way, he thought. But then, *what if she had*?

Cold fingers took a grip on his belly and squeezed slowly. He imagined his sister scrambling down here, *looking for him*, reaching the edge of the falls. Here the rocks were covered in damp moss and algae. He pictured her trying to stop, arms windmilling, feet slipping, body crashing down into the black pool, and tried to suppress the cold bubble of panic. Down there, the Corrie could swallow you *'quick as a blink'*.

Ben held the twisted root in a death grip and swung himself over the cataract, leaning out as far as he could, peering into the depths of the pool. The surface of the water wavered and shifted, throwing back shadows and reflections of the dark branches overhead. He thought he saw a movement and the cold hand clamped over his heart, sending ice into his veins. Then the light shifted again and he saw nothing there.

'Dorrie,' he called out. *'Dorothy!'* This time the trees did little to smother his cry. He heard his own voice over the rush of water, smacking and jarring from the tall trunks out into the woods. He hauled in his breath again and screwed himself up for the big shout.

'Dorothy!' he bawled.

72

And the root gave way.

He heard a noise like a growl as the stringy growth first ripped out of the ground, pulled by his weight, then tore in two. In the corner of his eye he saw the white, fibre-torn end pull away from the rest of the stem, pale against the dark earth. His whole body lurched to one side. Instinctively, reflexively, his free hand swung round, lunging for a tangle of rootlets knotted on the steep slope. His nails scrabbled at them, one of them tearing to the quick in the futile grab. He felt himself twist in mid air then suddenly plummet into the water.

The cold of it took his breath away. The world spun as he was tossed in the turbulence under the falls, head up one instant and tumbled upside-down the next. And all the time his lungs were crying out for air.

The icy watery darkness closed in on him as he felt his vision start to fade. His legs jerked in a spasm of panic and his arms flailed. One hand touched something slick that *moved* with a muscular flex against his clawing fingers and a dread worse than the fear of drowning ripped through him. His mouth opened, his lungs began to suck and then his head broke the surface and instead of cold river-water flooding inside him he gasped cool air through his rasped throat.

Ben managed to draw in two breaths. On the third he screamed for help but, as he did so, he slipped under the water again and the words came out all bubbly and distorted. He could hear them loud and echoing in his ears, as if he was inside a watery bell. Something nudged at his leg, something hard and wriggly that *shivered* along his calf and then was gone. An explosion of *fright* kicked him in the belly and this time he did scream. The yell reverberated all around him, spanging off the smooth sunken stones. Then his chest heaved and the dark water poured into him in a suffocating deluge. Everything went black as Ben's senses went into instant overload. He felt his *self* fading out, tumbling down a deep, dark well. Then his hands hit something hard and his fingers hooked around it in a spastic grip. His arms, which seemed to be working without any instructions from his brain, hauled and he came head and shoulders out of the pool, nails dug into the waterlogged tree trunk that angled into the water.

Something inside his chest jerked and the water he swallowed came vomiting out. It came down his nose and out of his mouth and he coughed, gasping as his lungs emptied themselves. Even then he did not stop, because there was something in the water, something that had *shivered* across his leg. Even though he was still gasping for breath, like the trout he had caught not half an hour before, the terror of something down in the depths, a big fish, a huge eel, a ravenous pike, was enough to drive him, scrabbling for purchase, right out of the water and on to the damp rocks. He lay there, heaving air into himself, gagging the remains of the water from his aching lungs, exhausted.

It was several minutes before he could move. Finally he turned himself over, feeling his wet clothes drag at him, and managed to get an elbow under his side to force himself up far enough to sit. Tears blinded him and his ribs hitched jerkily. He used the back of his hand to clear his vision and, when he had done so, looked at the pool. It was black as death down there. Away from the turbulence, right below the cataract, the water moved slowly, still waters running very deep. As he watched, there was a swirl in the water, as if something big and fast had surged up from the bottom and turned just below the surface. He got a flash of black shadow, then it was gone. But it had been fast. And it had been *big*.

He backed away from the water. He tripped over a root, stopped himself from falling and then turned and ran between the trees. In a matter of seconds the roar of the river faded to a murmur, then a whisper, then nothing.

Ben ran on until he came to a low, tumbledown dyke of stones and passed through a caved-in break in the old barrier. He stopped, gasping for breath, holding his ribs as he bent over. The pounding in his ears subsided a little and he stood up. This was a part of the forest he'd never seen before. When he took off from the river, from the thing that had nudged at his leg and made a sinister swirl in the water, he hadn't paused to think of which direction he was going. He had just run, like a frightened fallow buck. Now he was in a dark glade. The trees crowded in on him, tall and shadowed. The moist, damp smell of decay was all around him. He turned around in a circle and it was as if the world spun. Everywhere he looked there were tree trunks. They marched on and on, old and hoary and solid.

And *silent*.

The forest was *different*. Ben did not know why, but the thought had come with abrupt certainty. The air smelled *old* somehow. From nearby, a woodpecker rapped on a rotten log and the sound was like a sudden hammering, too loud in the stillness of the forest. Up above, he heard the racket of dragonfly wings, razoring against each other. Something moved at the edge of his vision and he spun, alarmed. The movement stopped. All around him the leaf carpet was rustling with creeping, *crawling* life.

Suddenly Ben was very alone and very lost. He was also so very scared he thought he was going to be sick.

Worse than that, his little sister was also alone here in the shadowed forest. He had brought her here, where you could wander for days, so they said, and *never* find your way out again.

A shiver ran through him at the thought of Dorrie tripping and stumbling in the undergrowth, crying, scared, unable to get home. Thoughts of punishment had long since fled. He was now scared for himself, and even more scared for Dorrie. If it hadn't been for him, she would be playing safely up at the sunny stream. Guilt and fear bathed him in a cold flow. Finally he bit them both back. Hesitantly, he walked out of the glade and went to look for her.

Dorothy felt she had been walking for hours, with no conception of time or direction. Occasionally she came across a track worn by animals and followed it until it crossed another or forked to right or left. The paths were better than the undergrowth which caught and snagged. Already she had a rip in her shirt and a gash at the knee of her jeans. Both canvas shoes were covered in grime and burrs were hooked into her hair.

She was beyond tears. It seemed there were none left. Instead, every now and again a little dry, hiccuping sob would escape her. Even this she tried to suppress, because for some time now, since she'd taken the path through the breach in the old dry-stone wall, since she'd first smelled the powerful forest odour, she'd had the feeling that she was not quite *alone*.

The forest felt *alive*. She could hear it in the rustle of the leaves and the buzzing of the unseen insects and the occasional startling call of some bird. The further she walked, the more foreign, the more *alien*, the forest seemed to become. She could not find the river. Its sound had *gone*, as if it had plunged underground and disappeared into a secret depth. If she could find the water, she knew instinctively, she could follow it back and get home again. She was about to move on, up the low rise that was the same as the other rises she'd scrambled up, when she heard a call far off in the woods.

She halted in mid-stride, frozen in the act of taking the step. Then, very slowly, she put her foot down on the leaves, trying to make them crackle as little as possible, holding her breath in case the sound came again and she missed it. She waited and heard nothing except for the muted scuttlings and small invisible movements. Eventually she began to move again, slowly, one step at a time, until she reached the top of the rise.

Then the call came a second time, faint, muted, distant. Unmistakable.

'Dorrie.'

It was Ben, calling her name.

Warm relief soared inside her. The panic fled. She waited a second or two more, then heard him again. There was urgency in his voice and she tried to pinpoint where he was, but the trees muffled the direction.

She made a decision, turned and scampered back down the slope shouting his name at the top of her voice as she did so. She slipped halfway down, tumbled, rolled and bounced to her feet with the wonderful accidental timing that small children are sometimes blessed with, and kept running.

'Ben! *Bernard!*'

'Dorrie! Is that *you*?' he shouted back and she had tó smother a chuckle. Even at the age of seven and a half, she realised how ridiculous his question was. Of course it was *her*. Who *else* was lost in Fasach Wood?

'It's me, Ben. Over here.'

'Where?'

'Here!'

'*Where?*'

It could have gone on for a long time. Dorrie kept running, jinking between the trees, dodging the overhanging branches of the oaks and beeches that trailed down arms with long scraggy wooden fingers. Thorns tugged at her and tightly rolled woodland ferns snatched at her shoes, but she didn't stop. She could hear him now, much louder, much *closer*.

'Over here, Ben.'

'I'm coming,' he replied, though she still couldn't see him. As she ran, she didn't notice that the trees were now much closer. The air was dank and *wet*. The trunks were festooned with moss and there were different *kinds* of plants. There were strange growths with broad, umbrella-shaped leaves. Giant hairy stalks flourished, spreading yellowish leaves like rotting rhubarb. Instead of ash and rowan saplings, odd plants like thick grasses reached upwards towards the canopy. All of this passed her by, unnoticed in the blur as Dorrie ran for her brother.

Ben was somewhere up ahead. She could sense it now. She could hear his blundering progress though the undergrowth. Twigs snapped under his feet. Bark rasped as his shoes scraped against them. Dorrie breasted the rise of yet another hollow, flew over the ridge and down the other side. She reached the flat when Ben came whizzing out from the right and almost knocked her off her feet. He managed to skid to a halt, holding on to her for fear she would fall and for fear he would lose sight of her again.

Then the two of them simply burst into tears. Dorrie held on to her brother and he held her up in his stronger arms and the tears of relief and fear and *love* for each other ran down their cheeks.

After a little while, Ben drew his arm away and sheepishly wiped his eyes clear. Dorothy's face was still buried in his chest and he could feel the little shivery spasms of her sobs.

'Hey. It's okay now. Come on, Dorrie, don't cry.'

She mumbled something into his shirt.

'I know. But you're not lost now, are you?'

She shook her head against him and he gave her a very brotherly hug and finally she pulled away from him a little. She looked up and he saw the streaks under her eyes where the tears had trickled through the grime. He used the thumb of his free hand to wipe away the moisture but only succeeded in making the smudges worse.

'Hey. You look like a panda,' he said, trying to be light.

She looked up at him and saw the half-smile.

'You're worse. You were crying,' she accused.

'No I wasn't,' he retorted, embarrassed. 'I was coughing.'

'Yeah? Well, why are your eyes all red? And why are you all wet?'

Relieved at the change of subject, he told her: 'I fell in a pool. I thought you'd gone over the falls and I was hanging onto a root. I got the fright of my life.'

'You could have *drowned*.'

'Nah. I can swim like a fish.' As he said it, the image of the swirl in the water came back to him and he shivered.

'You'll catch your *death* of cold,' she said, sounding just like her mother.

'I know. We'd better get home.'

'Which way is it?'

'I think it's that way,' Ben said, pointing the way he was facing. He didn't know *which* direction they should travel, but he didn't want Dorrie to know that. He knew she'd been badly scared, even worse than him. He didn't want her frightened again. If she thought *he* was confident, she'd feel better. And anyway, he'd got her into this. It was his job to get her out. He was the *big brother*.

Ben took Dorrie's hand and held it tightly in his.

'Now don't get lost again,' he said, smiling. She gave him a playful punch and they walked out of the hollow, hand in hand.

In half an hour, Ben still didn't know where they were.

He was certain of one thing only.

The forest had become very strange indeed.

9

Caitlin watched from the window as Martin Thornton walked down the pathway between the borders of alyssum and lobelias. He had his jacket slung over his shoulder and a hand in the pocket of his jeans. He walked nonchalantly, as if he had nowhere special to go on this early summer afternoon. He got to his old, well-dented Land-Rover and hauled himself in, turning as he did to look at the window. She pulled her face away from the pane, leaning to get behind the lace curtain, unaware that he'd been on too many stories and knocked on too many doors to have missed the movement. He looked away as if he'd seen nothing, twisted the key and put the jeep into reverse. When the sound of the engine disappeared beyond the tall hedge, Caitlin let out a small sigh.

She was perplexed. She didn't know why he had suddenly turned up in her back garden with a bottle of wine in one hand, a cheque in his pocket, a thousand pounds made out to her, '*a/c payee only – not negotiable*', signed with a barely legible flourish. That cheque had wrong-footed her. It wasn't just the amount, but the *reason* for it too. It had the ring of truth. But then again, he *was* a reporter. When he had told her about how he'd felt about the award, it had *sounded* true, the way his face had gone impassive, completely flat, as if he was telling a story about somebody else and not himself. Maybe she just *wanted* it to be true, not for the money, though, God knew, she could use every penny right now.

It was just that she'd been cast adrift. When the thick nerves in her spine had snapped on the low wall, the strings that held her life together had been cut just as neatly. Everything had changed, she most of all.

Then he'd walked round under the shade of the hanging Virginia creeper into the sunlight and all of it – *all of it* – had come looping and rolling back to her in an instant of dreadful clarity, a black squall within her, stirring up the fear and despair that she'd shoved down under the surface.

Yet when they'd talked, she'd *talked*. She'd opened herself up without realising it and he'd just sat there and listened to it all, hardly saying a word, taking it all in.

'Damn,' she now hissed just under her breath. If he wanted a story, he *had* one now. Once the words had started, they just wouldn't stop. She'd spilled it all. *God*, she'd even told him about going to the *bathroom*. Caitlin felt herself redden. Maybe it had been the wine, she told herself, though she knew it wasn't. It was having somebody to talk to. Somebody who had been *there*.

There. *Then.*

When her whole life had plunged to shatter on the hard concrete.

What was more, what was even more confusing and shivering strange, he'd said he'd seen it *before* it had happened.

Caitlin wheeled herself back from the window, thoughts whirling around inside, unbidden, uncaught.

How could he have known what went through her mind?

Martin steered the old Land-Rover through the narrow entrance to the Douglas Arms car park and reversed into a wide space, backing up until the bumper scraped against the tall privet hedge.

The girl on reception led him upstairs to a small and surprisingly modern back room in the old, ivy-draped inn. She told him he could have dinner any time after seven and breakfast in his room if he wanted. He nodded thanks, and she gave him a pleasant smile. When she'd gone he unrolled his shirts from the overnight bag and hung them up in the small wardrobe. He stood for ten minutes under the shower, turning the handle all the way to the right until the broad rose threw the water out in a scalding jet. When he had finished, he changed into a fresh shirt, slung his jerkin over his shoulder and sauntered down the narrow staircase to find the bar. There was a lounge which would have been comfortable had there been anybody in there, but there wasn't and its emptiness made it dark and forbidding. Martin went through another door and found a small dining room with half a dozen laid-out tables. The bar itself was at the end of a narrow corridor that led to an old stone annexe. He reached for the door handle, hearing muted voices beyond.

Alec Stirling was perched on a stool at the far end, both elbows on the polished surface. He was talking to a couple of other fellows who were lounging against the adjacent corner, nursing pints of dark beer. The three of them looked up as he walked in, ducking his head in the low doorway to avoid the lintel.

'Hey, boss,' the postman called over, shoving his thick-lensed glasses up the bridge of his nose.

'Hello, Scoop. What're you for?'

Alec lowered a lanky leg and edged his postman's bag away with the round high-capped toe of his workshoes, clearing a space.

'Seeing it's after five, I'll have another beer.'

The girl behind the bar was the same one who'd been on reception. She poured two pints and then, on Martin's insistence, doubled the order for the two other men.

Martin allowed himself a man-sized swallow, before putting his half-empty glass back on the deck.

Alec turned to his companions. 'This is the bloke I was telling you about. Martin Thornton.'

He reached across and shook hands with each of them. They had big, farmers' hands and strong, horny grips.

'Robbie Wallace and Jock Weir Dunbar. Jock's with the gas plant and Robbie drives for Aitkenbar.'

Martin raised an eyebrow in question.

'That's the farm supplies depot. It's like ICI up there.' He turned to the local men. 'Martin's the reporter. Come to do a story on the range war.'

'If there is one. And there had better be a good reason for dragging me up this hole in the wall.'

'Course there is. Never let you down yet, have I?'

Martin didn't answer. Alec Stirling was a good enough stringer. As postman he was welcome in every house all down the lochside and he had a natural nosiness and an ear for a story that made him worth keeping sweet with regular tip-off payments. Apart from that, Martin liked the man. He was tall and gangly and had the relaxed air of somebody who was at ease with himself and his life. He also had the kind of mischievous sense of humour that Martin appreciated in an often funless world.

'Well, have I ever let you down?'

'Not this month,' Martin finally conceded, and the other two grinned.

'I thought I'd come up and have a look anyway, just to make sure you haven't lost your touch.'

'Course I haven't. It's a goodie. It's got the whole valley split right down the middle.'

'Yes, but is it a story?'

'Oh aye!' Robbie Wallace piped up in a surprisingly high voice for such a big man. 'Everybody's talking about it up here.'

Martin looked at Alec. 'Well, Scoop, will everybody be talking about it everywhere else?'

'You just speak to folk here and work it out. If it doesn't make a page lead at least, I'll get you a bottle of your favourite malt. If it does, I want top whack.'

'And you'll get it. Except I'm off the whisky. It was killing me.'

'I know. You told me. Good news for the kidneys though. Yours were like saddlebags last time I saw you. Anyway, enough of your problems,' Alec said, throwing the other two a wink. 'I've lined up a couple of people to speak to.'

The postman rapped his empty glass on the bar. In a couple of seconds the girl came through from the lobby and started pouring again. She laid out beers for all four of them. Martin hadn't even got halfway down his pint, but the other three glasses were empty. She looked at Alec Stirling, but he just cocked his head in Martin's direction. Finally, the coin dropped. Martin fished his hand back in his pocket and brought out a crumple of notes.

Alec took a large swallow. 'Thanks, boss,' he said.

By seven o'clock the postman was three-quarters drunk. Martin had stuck to the second beer, sipping it very slowly, though, in all honesty, he really felt like a drink. Robbie Wallace was beginning to slur his words but Jock, who had shoulders like an ox and had listened to the conversation quietly all night with hardly a word said, looked as if he could pour another gallon down his throat and never feel it. By this time the bar had filled to overflowing with farm labourers and workmen from all over the valley. Martin was introduced to each in turn then promptly forgot their names, but he did get an impression of how the story was going. None of the men he spoke to gave much of a damn about how many log cabins Duncan Haldane planned to build on his forty acres of hill, nor the extra section of trees he planned to cut down to make room for them.

'It's the bloody women,' a tall, skinny man with a bobbing Adam's apple announced loudly. 'They got a bee in their bonnets. It's all the fault of that daft cow Garvie. The old biddies get a touch of colour back in their hair and she's got them all joining Greenpeace.'

'Garvie? Who's that?' Martin asked.

Alec Stirling was about to reply when one of the other men chimed in. 'Not just a hair rinse. There's some men here been seen down at her place. I reckon they're trying to get some more lead in their pencils.'

There was a loud burst of laughter in the crowded bar.

'What a bunch of jessies, listening to women's teetle-tattle,' Alec rejoined.

'Who're you calling a jessie?' somebody growled from beyond the corner of the bar. Alec and Martin looked over to where a stout, red-faced man with a flat cap was holding up the bar. 'You want to come round here and say that again?'

'Settle yourself down, Ernie,' Jock Weir said quietly, but loud enough to make the words stick. The man with the florid, beefy face squinted meanly at him, but held his peace. Jock outweighed him by nearly a hundredweight.

Alec looked away and when Martin raised an eyebrow in question, the postman said: 'Bad man in drink, yon fellow. They'll throw him out in a minute and we'll all get a bit of peace.'

'Who was the woman you were talking about?'

'Sheila Garvie?' Alec asked. 'Her grandmother lived here-abouts for eighty years 'til she died this last winter. Sheila came back and they started up the Linnvale Association. The women, that is. They're all for saving the lentil and patching the ozone layer and Duncan Haldane's chainsaw's got their camiknickers in a twist. They don't want him to cut down any trees and they've got a real downer on log cabins. Worried about the old Caledonia Forest, they are, though I'll give you ten to one there's damn few of them ever been down in Fasach Wood.'

Alec took a long pull on his beer, wiped his mouth and started to grin.

'And there's damn few of them I'd take down there myself, and that's saying plenty. Though the minister's wife, she's a good-looking big thing.'

'Where do I find her?'

'In the minister's house. Why, are you interested?'

'Not her, daft bugger. This Sheila Garvie.'

'Oh, she's down at the old millhouse.'

'Will she talk to me?'

'God knows. She doesn't talk to me, and I'm delivering parcels to her place nearly every morning. She's a funny old bitch, that's for certain.'

'What's this about hair colour?'

'Oh, just women's blethering. They say she gives the women pills and potions and whatnot. Old Molly Carr from the school and a couple of the biddies in the Association have changed their hair colour. Gone darker. There's a whisper she can fix up women whose men have the miseries in bed. Satisfaction guaranteed, that's the story. Load of shite, if you ask me.'

'What does she do?'

'A botanist or something like that. Who knows? Who cares?'

'I'll speak to her tomorrow.'

'I'd speak to the minister's wife. She's the committee boss. Gail Dean. We call her Howling Gail 'cause she's red-hot at the choir singing. Like I said, good-looking big woman. She'll tell you everything you want to know.'

It was still bright, a warm summer evening with the sun just sinking towards the gap in the ridge of the Dumbuie peaks to the west. Martin left Alec Stirling and the rest of the men roistering and went into the small restaurant for a surprisingly fine meal of trout in a sauce he couldn't identify and sprinkled with fresh herbs that left a lingering aftertaste. After a couple of cups of coffee he decided on a stroll to walk off the dinner.

Linnvale proper huddled itself around the Corrie River which came tumbling from the Linn, a glacier-gouged natural reservoir high up on the slopes. The village was not large but remained busy despite its relative isolation. There was only one road in to the broad glen, the Linn Road, of course, unless you counted the high track of Hill Road that went over the pass between the peaks of the Ardbeg and Dumbuie Hills. That way took you nowhere except for a few outlying crofts and sheep farms and then down a tortuous serpentine road that ended in Glen Douglas, where the Ministry of Defence had tunnelled into the hard rock to store an

Armageddon's worth of tactical and strategic hardware. Martin had done stories on the Glen Douglas dump before, so he was familiar with the territory on the other side of the hills. Linnvale itself was one place on the map he'd never been. There had never been reason before, though he must have passed the Linn Road turn-off while driving along the shores of Loch Corran a thousand times.

'Pretty enough place,' he said aloud as he stood on the bridge, watching the tumbling water. The valley was like a wide bowl, carved thousands of years ago, like the Corrie Linn, from old red sandstone by the marching glaciers of the last Ice Age. It was surrounded on three sides by hills which sheltered it from the west and north winds, while on the east there was a lower series of slopes which hid the whole glen from view from the lochside. It was a broad valley, but gave the impression of being closed off from the rest of the world, which in effect, despite the telephone lines and the single road, it was. As he stood facing upstream, where the water tumbled white over a series of falls, Linnvale village stood on his right, a motley collection of old stone houses and narrow roads branching off the main one. There was a church hall and a church with a low, heavily built four-cornered tower. The hotel was at the south end while there was another bar on the opposite side. The houses petered out within a couple of hundred yards, but for all that there were others, single or double, dotted sporadically beyond the village. Beyond them were farms and then, up on the slopes, the usual mat of sitka spruce Forestry Commission vandalism marching in serried bottle-green ranks to the tree line up on the high slopes.

To his left the river took a series of twists. There were more houses downstream, including Caitlin's place. He could just make out the shadow of the millhouse, huddled against the mass of the forest that covered the floor of the valley, a riot of green summer leaves, blanketing the basin for the three miles that flanked the Linn Road to Loch Corran.

Linnvale was the kind of valley that people dreamed of retiring to. Quiet, isolated, but not too far from civilisation. There would be some good fishing in the river, some fine shooting on those hills, and you could get used to the rough-and-ready company of the hotel's bar any day of the week.

Martin looked across to the farmland where Duncan Haldane planned to build his log cabins. In fact, he couldn't see the place clearly from his position on the bridge. There was a tarmac track leading off from the main road, but it took a left sweep behind the leading edge of the trees and he couldn't quite picture how the cabins would look. Martin understood how the locals wouldn't want ten thousand summer folk crowding into their glen for the only three months they had any chance of decent weather. Having said that, though, a few log cabins and some trees cut from those thousands, all out of sight of the village, wouldn't turn this into Disney World. He remembered Caitlin – and Alec Stirling – explaining that the houses would get the farmer out of some sort of financial quagmire. The man hadn't had too much luck of late.

Martin looked down into the turbulent water once more, just in time to catch the glint of a big fish, a salmon, most likely. The fishing here *would* be good.

It only took ten minutes to get to the Haldane Farm from the bridge. He stopped to close the gate, a lesson he'd never forgotten from childhood, and noticed that he could just see Caitlin's house across the stream from where he stood. The gate clanged shut and he turned up the winding path towards the small farmhouse.

A small woman with dark hair cut in a bob was backing out of the door with a yellow basket filled with washing. When he said hello she gave a visible start and the pile of shirts and towels started to slide groundwards. Martin reached forward and steadied the linen.

'Sorry about that,' he said, taking the basket from her in both hands.

'And so you should be, scaring the daylights out of me like that.'

She looked up at him, blue eyes in a round, pleasant face. There was no anger in her expression.

'I thought I'd better say something before you bumped into me. That would have been worse.'

'You'd probably have got the back of my hand.'

'Good old highland hospitality,' Martin threw back lightly and the woman gave him a smile in return.

'Anyway, can I help you? Are you lost or what?'

'No. I'm looking for Mr Haldane.'

'Right place. I'm Rose Haldane. Duncan's gone out to fetch the kids. Can I help you?'

Martin told her who he was and why he had come and he saw her expression tighten a little, shading to wariness.

'I think you'd better speak to Duncan about that. He might not want to say anything. Things are still getting themselves sorted out.'

'So I heard.'

'I can't see it making much of a newspaper story, though.'

'I don't know either. But I always talk to folk to find out for myself. Sometimes there's no story, and sometimes there is.'

She looked at him directly. He was still standing with the washing basket up against his chest.

'It's nobody's business but ours.'

'I never take one side of a story, but other folk have made it *their* business.'

'*Aye*, they have that. After the year that Duncan's had, that's the last thing he needs.'

She stopped and cocked her head to the side, as if considering.

'Oh, you'd better come in anyway. Duncan won't be ten minutes. Put that down on the kitchen table and I'll fill the kettle.'

Martin followed her into a wide kitchen that branched off into a dining area. He dumped the basket on a broad deal table and looked around. The place was well lit, surprising in a farmhouse. It was kitted out like a modern kitchen, done in light hardwoods, but Martin recognised a craftsman's touch. He went across to where the stove nestled at the cul-de-sac end of a long breakfasting bar and ran his hand along the surface. It was smooth and dry, one broad piece of wood from a wide trunk. The grain was tight and so smoothly polished that it refracted the light, seeming to swirl into itself as he passed.

'Beech,' he said, appreciatively. He raised his hands to the glass-fronted cupboards above. 'And elm too. Somebody's done a marvellous piece of work here.'

'Duncan and his uncle put this together for me a couple of years ago. You know about woodwork?'

'Raised with it. My father's a carpenter. If your husband could build kitchens like this he'd make a fortune.'

She laughed. 'That's option number two. Let's see how we get on with the cabins.'

'He'll be building them himself?'

'Him and Uncle John.'

'They'll be pretty good then. For sale or rent?'

'Why do you want to know? Is this for your newspaper?'

'No,' Martin said, and now he laughed. 'I might want to buy one of them. If they're anything like this,' he said, running his hand along the velvet wood surface.

'He'll do a good job. He always does.'

Martin nodded. Rose Haldane turned to the stove and lifted the kettle off. She made tea and brought it to the table, setting a plate of biscuits between them.

'He shouldn't be long. The kids were supposed to be back an hour ago. You know what they're like.'

'I know what *I* was like. Summer holidays went on forever. I spent my time up the hills fishing and catching rabbits. The days lasted for weeks and I was always getting my backside tanned for coming home late.'

'Those two will be lucky if they don't. Duncan's been cutting up a tree all day. He won't be happy at missing his supper. This might not be a good time to talk to him.'

Martin looked at her, taking the hint.

'Oh, I can come back tomorrow.'

'Tomorrow might not be a good time either. He's fair fed up with people trying to stop him making a living. Things have been bad enough this past year without folk poking their noses in where it doesn't belong. They'd see the kids starve.'

'Bad as that?'

'Worse. You'd think it was a high-rise hotel we were building, instead of a few wee wooden houses. Look at the other side of the valley. You've got Aitkenbar Farm Supplies. Nobody bothers about them building concrete sheds. And the distillery at the far side of Linnvale. If that closed down half the men here would be out of work. MacKinnon's expanded his calor-gas store to three acres along the hill road where the old quarry used to be. Nobody turned a hair about that. It's because they're big business, and Duncan is just one farmer trying to make ends meet.'

'What's all this about the forest?'

'Oh, it's just the old biddies who never cared about trees before. They've got experts to say it's part of the old Caledonia Forest that needs to be preserved. That's a laugh. Half of them have never *been* in the woods,' Rose said with a trace of bitterness in her voice. 'They don't understand that Duncan's grandfather planted the trees that are to come down. The forest only came as far as the stream before, but old Hamish put a coppice on the low bank for fencewood near on a hundred years ago, so there's nothing ancient about that. Duncan's only taking back what's his, and the land's good for nothing else. He's got a clean title to the timber and there's nothing to stop him, no matter what they say.'

Martin waited until the silence lengthened.

'So why are they getting all worked up about it?'

'God knows, for we surely don't,' Rose said.

10

Duncan Haldane had told Rose not to worry, but now *he* was worried.

He'd worked solidly all afternoon, cutting the roundels from the fallen beech, great slabs of good seasoned wood which would cut into fine planks. Despite the protectors he'd worn, the sound of the chain saw still crackled in his ears long after he'd shut the thing off, and his forearms were still tight and knotted with the grip he'd held on it to stop it bucking on the grain. They'd be stiff and sore in the morning but, as he looked at his handiwork, a series of sawdust piles and the massive trunk cut into sections, he felt as if he'd done a good day's work.

'Supper in half an hour,' Rose called out from the corner of the house.

Duncan nodded and wiped the beads of sweat from his forehead, leaving streaks down his forearm.

'Not much left of that,' Rose said, smiling across the distance.

'Be nothing left once I hitch up the tractor. We'll have a better view as well, and a few bob. This stuff's worth a hundred a foot, and wait until I clear those oaks on the bottom end.'

'Oh, give yourself a break, man,' Rose ordered. 'And when you get your breath back, give Ben and Dorrie a shout, would you? It's nearly seven.'

He nodded again, feeling the work-tightness ease out of his back and shoulders. Duncan shoved the jagged chain saw blade into the fork of a large branch and let it dangle there. It was safe enough to leave it lying around until the morning. Few people came up the path to the farm. No one who did would steal from Duncan Haldane.

The children had gone down the slope towards the stream earlier in the afternoon, when the sun had been much higher than it was now. Duncan wiped the fine smear of sawdust from the face of his old watch and checked the time. They should have been back an hour ago. He walked round the segments of sawn trunk and looked down into the valley. There was no sign of them, but that was no surprise. It was summertime. School was over, the valley a place for kids to wander. He'd been born and brought up here. He recalled summer days when his father would let him off from farm work and he'd been like a young red buck, running up and down the hills, scooping trout from the burn and swimming in the Mill Lade. *His* father had never known where the young Duncan would be from one minute to the next, and history was only repeating itself. Ben knew he had to look after his little sister and he was a responsible boy. They'd be around somewhere, playing hide-and-seek, or Robin Hood or whatever.

He got to the edge of the short field just before it took its swoop down the steep embankment to the stream.

He put two fingers in his mouth and whistled a piercing call, three short and one long, the distinctive family whistle that he'd run to when he was small and his father had run to, ragged-arsed and tackety-booted, in the wintry days of the depression.

Duncan stood for a minute, head to the side, listening for the reply. There was no wind, and little sound save the murmur of the stream below and the far-off call of a curlew up on the hill. Ben's return whistle did not come, but that meant nothing. A loud whistle could carry for miles on the flat land or on the hillside, but if the children were down at the water, or beyond the coppice, they'd hear nothing. Duncan shrugged and started off along the edge of the dip to where the stream turned in a series of serpentine meanders before plunging down into Fasach Wood.

A quarter of a mile from the farmhouse, the sheep track took him up the slope to where a drystane dyke separated his land from the edge of the moor on the Douglas Hills where the ferns stood high as a man and the arable land gave way to scrub and bracken. From here he had a vantage over most of the glen. Rose was out in the garden hanging the washing. Off on the far side, the Ardbeg Distillery chimney was trailing a plume of white steam into the still air. One of Donnie MacKinnon's three calor-gas tankers was trundling up the Linn Road after its run round the lochside. A smudge of white on the hill near the Corrie Linn told him old Hector Ritchie was taking a wedge of his flock down to the pens for the market. A few hundred yards up the hill to his left, he could see the pile of larch trunks he'd cut for the walls of the cabins.

They were stacked up in a great pile where they'd been weathering over the winter. They'd be seasoned by now. Duncan looked forward to the day when he'd be able to haul them from the bearing logs and drag them down the hill to the flat. He wanted to see those cabins take shape.

To his right the expanse of Fasach Wood spread down the length of the valley in a thick blanket. He whistled again, hearing the shrill note come back to him a full twenty seconds later, bouncing from the flat, fan-shaped cliff on Dumbuie. It was the only answer.

Duncan shook his head, beginning to get annoyed with Ben. Underneath the annoyance there was a tickle of unease.

Folk in the village, a mile away, would have heard his whistle and identified it, the way he knew every other farmer's call in the glen. Ben should have heard it and replied, unless . . .

Duncan turned to the right and looked down on the tops of the trees at the edge of the wood below.

'No,' he said aloud into the still air, shaking his head again. Ben wouldn't have gone into the forest, not with Dorrie. He'd been told a *million* times.

Still a buzz of apprehension tickled at the back of his head.

'They'll be down playing at the stream,' he said to himself. 'And I'll toe the bugger's arse when I find him.'

He shoved himself off the drystane dyke and followed a sheep track down the slope, following the contours as the flocks had done for years. Duncan got to the stream and looked up and down the gully. There was no sign of anyone. They couldn't be upstream because he could see the meandering water all along the track. He turned to look downstream where the water took a sharp turn to the left and ran straight into the woods.

Something gave his stomach a soft, insistent *twist*.

'If he's gone in there, he won't sit down tomorrow,' he muttered, trying to ignore the twist, trying to get *angry* instead of worried.

'Ben! Dorothy!' he called out, his deep voice booming down the narrow defile and breaking up on the tree-trunks. A wood-pigeon cooed back.

Two strides on the boulders took him across the stream and he walked steadily down to the turn, eyes taking in everything. Down a few yards, a thin sapling wand stuck up between two stones. He reached it and bent to pick it up. It was a rowan stick. The end was frayed, thin bark hanging off in strips, and immediately Duncan knew that Ben *had* been here. Anybody who had grown up in Linnvale would have recognised a branch that had been used to poke and prod in the crevices under stones to flush out trout. He felt the end, then smelled it. It was freshly cut that day, the sap still sweet and green. He threw the stick down on the stones and walked downstream further, round the bend where the water tumbled between the big moraine boulders. Something white caught his eye. He turned towards it and his heart made a double leap.

The little ankle sock was lying flat out on a stone.

Duncan lowered himself to his haunches, holding his breath. He looked at the thing for a minute without moving, reluctant to touch it. Off to the right, lying on another stone, was its twin. Finally he reached out and picked the first one up. There was only the faintest trace of dampness on the sock top where it had dangled over the edge of the stone, in the shadow. The rest of it was bone-dry.

It must have been lying there for hours.

Duncan's stomach twisted involuntarily again as the muscles clenched.

They could only be in Fasach Wood.

And they had been there for hours.

Duncan slowly raised himself to his feet. His eyes followed the flow of the water to where the stream disappeared abruptly into the trees. He took a deep breath to stop the clenching feeling beneath his ribs and then started walking, taking big purposeful strides. In half a minute, the forest swallowed him up.

Dorrie had been crying softly for some time. Ben was very scared, *shaky* scared, but he couldn't let his sister see it.

The forest had become very strange, a frightening place of shadows and unfamiliar, *alien* sounds. It seemed they had walked for a long time, mostly hand in hand, sometimes clambering between rough thick stems that soared towards the canopy of leaves high above, sometimes crawling through thick shrubbery that crowded like rubbery rhododendrons in massed thickets. And everywhere the trees reached for the hidden sky.

At the edge of the forest there had been tall limes and oaks and beeches, some of them hundreds of years old. Here, in the dark strange place, Ben couldn't identify the trees. All he knew was that they were massive and gnarled. Plants grew on their mossed, scarred trunks. Lesser trees sprouted from the crooks of forked branches. There was a smell of rot and decay, the kind of odour that would suddenly assault the nose when the wind blew from the compost heap on a hot morning, the kind of smell that choked the throat when a dead sheep in the gorse gave up its gases on a stifling afternoon. Here the smell was thick and cloying, a wet, dripping kind of stench, as much wild growth as putrefaction.

'Where *are* we?' Dorrie sobbed.

'We're going home,' Ben said as confidently as he could, trying to keep the *shake* out of his own voice, trying to be brave for her.

'But we're *lost*!'

'No, we're nearly there,' he lied, giving her hand a strong squeeze to convince her of the truth of it.

They came through another tangle where the honeysuckle creepers, thick as hawsers, coiled like snakes in constricting loops round strangled saplings. Ben hauled Dorrie behind him and came into a clearing. He could hear the river now and headed for the welcome sound. They crossed the wide glade where the massive pillars of the tree trunks stood like guardians reaching knotted, muscular arms to the green ceiling. Underfoot, last year's leaf litter was piled on the detritus of preceding decades. In places it was feet deep and they crunched and crackled their way through the springy, russet carpet. The boy and his sister had reached the far side when they heard the voice.

'What was that?' Dorrie asked sharply and Ben stopped, his whole body tense, listening.

'I heard something too.'

They held their breaths, and then the voice came again, disembodied, carrying through the glade from the shadows beyond. Somebody was singing, a low chant, too far away for the words to make any sense.

'It's a woman!'

'Shhh!' said Ben, holding a finger to his lips.

They crept forward, stepping past the nearest of the tall, twisted trunks. Ben stood on something that gave liquidly under his feet. He looked down and saw a huge toadstool, fully half a yard across, slimy scarlet cap dotted with poisonous-looking yellow spots. His foot had punctured the clammy skin. It oozed a viscid juice. He shuddered, scraped his foot against a mossy root and walked on, hauling his sister behind him. Another monstrous fungus, this one knee high, trembled as they passed. The warty, swollen toadstools were like nothing either of them had ever seen. The thought of touching one of them made Ben's skin crawl. They had the look of disease about them. They exuded an eerie deadliness.

The low chant came to them again from beyond. There was something about the sound that made Ben bite down his instincts to shout for help. It was an adult voice and, in Linnvale, adults were people who would help. Grown-ups knew where they were and what to do. But for some reason that he could not explain, Ben wasn't *sure*. Not here, not in the woods where nothing was as it should be. Even at the age of nine, he knew there was something badly *wrong* with today, with *this place*.

There was a small incline at the far end of the glade, rising to just above head height. They scrambled up it and, before them, the river meandered in a wide loop.

Yet the river too was *different*. It was wide and sluggish, as if it had gathered waters from much further than the valley itself. On its far bank, willows trailed their skeletal fingers into the water, almost hiding the tangle of snakelike roots. Here and there, great iridescent dragonflies droned in squadrons, wings rattling as they banked. Out of the corner of his eye, Ben saw something flash from the water. He heard a snap as jaws closed, but when he turned there was only a spreading ripple on the dark surface.

Further downstream a series of large, moss-covered flat stones formed a stepway across the flow. He realised then that it wasn't the far bank he'd seen. It was a low island in the middle of the river. The voice was coming from over there, now a steady chant, repeating the same words over and over again.

He heaved himself to his feet, holding Dorrie close to him. She had stopped snuffling and he put his arm around her shoulder, squeezing tight, letting her know, in that one movement, that she had to be very quiet.

There was somebody across there. He stood on tiptoe, using the root of a tree to gain a few extra inches.

Across there, on the island, he could see one huge tree standing alone. In front of it stood a woman, her hands held high above her head. Ben couldn't make out who it was, but then another movement caught his attention and his eyes flicked towards it. There were three other figures standing off to the right and, hidden from view, he suspected there were more. They were all kneeling, facing the massive dead tree whose bare, dry and broken branches reached up in an angry plea to the sky.

'What are they doing?' Dorrie asked.

'I don't know. They look like loonies to me.'

'Are we going across there?' .

Ben waited a minute before he answered.

'I don't think so, Dorrie. I don't like it.'

'Why not? They'll know the way home.'

'I just don't like it, Dorrie.'

'But we have to get *home*!' Dorothy wailed, her voice rising alarmingly high.

Across there the figures turned towards them. Ben felt his stomach sink like a stone though he didn't know exactly why.

The woman turned slowly. The hood on her purple coat shadowed her face. One of the others said something in a low voice; then, without warning, something shot from the willows on the far side, something black that moved with blurring speed and hit the water with such a splash that Ben and Dorrie jumped back, startled.

Instantly Ben got a flash of memory from a nature programme he'd seen on television before the summer holidays. The picture had stayed with him for several nights after he'd watched an immense crocodile launch itself up from a river pool and snap its jaws closed on a wildebeest with such shocking speed the animal didn't have time to move. Even more shocking to the nine-year-old boy was how the huge reptile had simply turned its head and thrown the big animal into the water. In less than a second there had been nothing on the surface but ripples to show that there had been a monster and a live animal that was now dead.

The thing had shot from the willows and into the river just like that crocodile had done. And now Ben could see a peculiar hump in the water like a bow wave as something big powered, submerged, towards them.

A little cry of fear escaped Dorrie's lips and was instantly cut off as her brother grabbed her hand and simply jerked her off the lip of the rise, dragging her down the slope and across the glade. They ran to the far edge of the circle of trees and plunged on through the tangle of scraggy undergrowth, forcing themselves through while twigs and small jagged thorns snatched and scratched at them. Ben hooked the upright stem of a stunted sapling and swung his sister round before she ran smack into another trunk looming in front of them. He let himself go, almost losing his balance, and smashed into one of the big toadstools. There was a wet *rip* and the mottled surface burst asunder as his foot went through the moist skin of the flat crown. Immediately something spurted up and slathered him with a viscous fluid. There was an overwhelming reek and he felt his throat tighten against the gagging sensation that blurted up from his throat.

Ahead of them the stand of huge fungus growths crowded together amphibiously. Behind, they could hear something crashing through the undergrowth, far enough away to be faint, close enough to be terrifying.

Ben pulled Dorrie along, unaware of her incessant wail. He shoved his way through the crowd of toadstools, his own flesh recoiling from the slithery touch of their decaying skins. He pushed at one with his free hand, feeling the surface give under the pressure as if his fingers would crunch right through into the yellow poison inside. Instead, the rubbery growth bent away from him with the sound of a balloon being twisted and swung back as he passed. He held Dorothy close to him. A movement ahead caught his eye and he saw one of the umbrella-shaped growths swell quickly, its domed cap everting upwards from convex to concave and showing an accordion of bright orange gills. The movement happened so smoothly and naturally that Ben did not consciously react to it, but he was not operating on a conscious level. His whole *self* now functioned on pure flight instinct as the most primitive *animal* part of his brain fizzed and sparked its urgent commands. His eyes saw the motion. At any other time he would have stood in wonder, fascinated, perhaps a little repelled. This time his body *threw* itself away as a mighty surge of *alarm* shrieked through him.

Even as he moved, even as he still heard the crackle of pursuit behind, his eyes were locked on the toadstool that now pulsed, sending shivers along the origami striations of its gills. Without warning they flexed and, with a sound like tearing cloth, burst asunder.

Silver stars exploded into the air.

It was as if a Guy Fawkes Night rocket had detonated right in front of his eyes. Bright dots of light shot out all around from the shredded remnants of the growth.

Something cold landed on his bare arm. He was in the act of turning his head and raising his hand when Dorrie screamed, high and piercing and terribly *loud*. Ben whirled round and saw one of the bright dots, trailing a fine silver thread behind it, on her cheek. Dorrie's free hand snatched at her face, a fast, cat's paw blur. The bright silvery thing came away and fell to the ground. A bright red, feverish blotch marked the skin just under her eye.

The ice-cold sensation on Ben's bare arm twisted itself inside out and flared into white heat. A strangled gasp coughed out through clenched teeth and instant tears sparked in his eyes. Something else touched his shoulder and stroked numbness into his skin. He snatched at it the way Dorrie had done, unable to reach the pain on his arm, unable to make his fingers loosen their grip on his sister's tiny hand. He felt a tugging sensation as his fingernail snicked on a hard bud that felt like a tick burrowing through the surface and then a small wrench just as the fire blossomed. The heat flashed and then faded. The thread trail caught in his finger and burned a line across his knuckles, then it snapped and the pain died. All around, the frighteningly *pretty* silver spores were arcing out from the ruin of the exploded toadstool, while other bulbous growths in the stand of fungus were stretching and swelling in a grotesque and menacing ballet.

They charged on. Without thinking, as he passed a gnarled pine, Ben reached out and scraped his arm across the rough surface in a savage rasp. A different *real* pain hissed there, but the dreadful acid burn was gone.

All of this happened in mere seconds as Ben's heightened awareness expanded to distort time. He was aware, on that exalted instinctive level, of *everything* around him. His senses stretched out before and behind and above. He could hear

Dorrie's panicked breath coming in short feverish gasps. He could hear the crash of saplings and juniper branches from behind. Far away there was the muted roar of the river, tumbling through rocks, way ahead, in the direction he knew he must go. The silver-tinsel explosion of the toadstool spores were points of light, whipping past him to land on trees and leaves. Where they hit they seemed to burn and burrow while the trailing threads grew taut and swelled like webbing. All around was the smell of *poison*, thick and yellow in the air.

They twisted and swerved, intuitively jinking left and right to avoid those burning tendrils that were beginning to form a skein net stretching between the trees where the spores had hit. Dorrie slipped on moss on an incline where a trickle of water had made a damp runnel and Ben barely managed to keep his feet. He hauled at her, feeling the muscles in his shoulder shriek as they twisted, and she came up, pulled off her feet and onto the flat. She had stopped sobbing now. All her breath was used up in the effort of moving fast, little feet pattering beside her brother's. They were both lacquered with mud.

They scrambled past a big oak with trailing branches and a hairy trunk that looked a thousand years old and Ben grabbed one of the straggly branches to whip both of them round onto a rough track, the first they had seen since they got lost in the forest.

He felt his body swing to the right, Dorrie a counterweight in his grip. Way to the left something heavy and dun-coloured, with antlers like jagged scoops, turned its head and was gone. Above it, on a low, rotted branch, an owl as big as an eagle blinked a yellow eye and then froze into a moss-covered stump.

And the branch that Ben grabbed twisted in his hand and pulled away from the oak tree with a creak that was not wooden at all.

Dorothy tumbled into the dead leaves. Ben followed, crashing on top of her, one hand clenched around her fingers and the other unable to let go its hold of the thing that was not a branch.

The children bounced and rolled. Dorrie was up first, then Ben, dizzy with shock, right at her heels. In his hand, the skeletal arm he had pulled from the tree ended in fingers hooked like claws, long brown skin-covered bones stiff in the act of grasping.

Dorrie turned. She got a blurred glimpse of what Ben gripped in his hand, but he jerked it away with a cry of disgust before it could

99

even register. The skin of his hand crawled, still feeling the shape of what it had held. Ben reached again for Dorrie and pulled her close. He turned and sheer terror froze him to stone.

The skull glared at him.

The black holes of its sockets looked right into his soul. Its mouth was opened in a scream. White teeth poked up from blackened, rotted gums. There was a flash of red from inside one of the gaping eye-holes that focused demonic hatred at them, then a big centipede wormed its way, scaly and shiny, out of the hole and down the rutted cheek.

Ben felt his mouth work but no sound came out. Little silvery sparks, like the malignant spores, whirled in front of his eyes. Then Dorrie twitched beside him. She was about to turn round and see the nightmare face. That was enough to unlock Ben's mind from the horror that had his mind clenched in a death grip. His eyes took in the mouldering corpse hanging between the two trees. The head was slumped forward, right down on the chest, and the jaw, gaping impossibly because it had sprung out of its socket, was lolling on the washboard ridge of ribs. The legs, incredibly long and skinny, with every bone delineated, were trailing down to a few inches above the ground. One booted foot had fallen off into a clump of ferns. Mould covered the black leather. Something slimy crawled over it.

Yet worse than all that, so much terribly worse that Ben felt the big scream machine wind itself up inside him, were the arms that suspended the skeleton. They were stretched out on either side in a grotesque crucifixion. But there were *no nails*, no *ropes* holding the thing aloft. The hands were not visible. The arms, pulled taut on either side, ended at the wrists on the roughened surface of the tree. Ben saw a swelling on the bark above and below the join, like the kind of growth he'd seen on old trees when they had grown round and swallowed up a piece of fence wire that had drawn too tight.

It looked as if the tree had opened up and swallowed those hands, keeping this thing, whoever it was, *whatever it was*, suspended and dead in the middle of the forest.

The forest got him the forest got him the forest got him.

His thoughts ricocheted around inside him, out of control.

They were in the forest. And it had tried to get them too.

It was still trying to get them.

Ben felt the scream begin to break through. The horror of it was too much. His brain was high and hot and sparking in all directions, way beyond overload. Something had to give way or his head would burn out.

Dorrie's head turned. Her breath hitched and then she screeched so loud and so high that Ben was almost thrown sideways. Immediately his own unborn scream died and a switch inside him diverted the pressure from deep down and threw it out towards her.

He grabbed her again before she had any more than a fleeting glimpse of the horror snared within the tree-trunk. He clamped her face in against his shoulder, his own eyes still riveted on the screaming dead face, lodged in the fork where one thick limb joined the trunk. The head was oddly *squashed* where it had been gripped by irresistible pressure. Ben could see what the pressure had been. The limb was twisted up on itself like a real arm that had flexed and gripped. The skull bones had been squeezed between it and the hard wood of the trunk. One eye socket was forced almost on top of the other. The teeth had meshed together. It was a skull, but so distorted it did not look like a human skull.

Oh Jeez, it got him too. Ben's thought flashed just behind his eyes.

He took a step backward, pulling Dorrie with him. She squirmed in his grasp.

He turned away from the apparition, inadvertently pointing them back in the direction they had come. Something sleek, black and blindingly *quick* came out of the undergrowth on the far side of the glade. Ben only got a flash of movement. It came bulleting out from a thicket and dived straight into the thick carpet of leaves. Ben got a rerun of the sight at the swampy river's edge. He stood transfixed while the leaves exploded upwards in a bore-wave as the thing ploughed towards them, more terrible because it was unseen, its threat magnified by the fundamental impossibility of it. The hump in the brown and russet leaves swelled, then, mysteriously – incredibly – it stopped.

Both of them stood, transfixed, fear-locked.

Then, behind them, off to the right, someone called Dorrie's name.

The far-away voice came booming through the trees and a sudden bubble of relief swelled inside Ben's heaving chest. He felt Dorrie pull towards him and he clasped her tight, unable to look at her, eyes still fixed on the mound of leaves which hid the blurring thing that had chased them.

'Dorothy! *Bernard*!'

Their father's voice, now a little closer, rolled through the glade, deep and urgent and strong.

'Dad, we're here!' Ben called back without turning his head. He could hear his own voice, unnaturally high, bounce and break up and scatter itself in the dark wood.

Holding Dorrie tight, Ben took a step backwards, then another. He heard his feet scrape in the leaves. He had to pull Dorrie along with him, as though her legs had lost their strength, given up their ability to move, to flee. Still, she came with him, while he kept his eyes staring blinkless at the heap of leaves under which crouched – *ready to spring* – the unseen creature.

'I'm coming,' Duncan Haldane's call told them, closer, yet still distant.

Ben took another step backwards and felt his heel hit against a gnarled root. His attention was diverted for a moment as he tried to keep his balance and his eyes flickered downwards, off the mound of leaves. Then the heap exploded into the air in a blizzard of brown and red, as if a bomb had gone off in the middle of the glade.

The tornado of dead leaves whirled upwards in a cone. The noise of the rustling scraped against Ben's ears like fingers scratching on his skull. He got his balance and managed another step backwards, holding Dorrie's face tight, against his chest, while he stared at the maelstrom in the middle of the flat patch of ground overhung by big trees. The leaves whirled, spread apart in their flurry, then were drawn in together again. They gathered under an impossible gravity, coalesced and began to form into a shape.

'Dorrie! *Ben!*' Their father's shout came again. Ben didn't hear it, his eyes wide, staring at the apparition.

The flurry stopped. A man-shaped thing stood there in the middle of the patch.

It was a man-shaped thing made of *dead leaves*.

It stood there, leaf legs planted apart, rust arms akimbo, gold-bronze chest thrust forward, raggedy head pulled back.

Everything in the forest went still. The air between Ben and the leaf-man sparked with unbearable tension as he stared at the figure. Its expressionless, papery face held him in some sort of thrall.

Then it *moved*. The head came down with a dry rustling *scraping* sound and the hands came off the hips. It slowly lifted one clumpy *shapeless* foot from the rest of the litter and one crumpled, dead oak leaf tumbled off. The foot came down with an unearthly crackle, loud in the exquisite silence. It took another step and the *threat* of the motion was a palpable force that Ben could feel inside his skin.

The third step, a slow, crackling motion, was enough to unlock his paralysis. Still holding his sister tight he swivelled away and ran. Dorrie banged against his hip and he loosened his hughold and grasped her by the wrist. He saw her head turn and he jerked her arm so that she was whipped back towards him. Even on the soaring wave of fear, he didn't want his sister to see *that*. The leaf-creature pursued them, the susurrus whispering of its progress a dry and vicious chuckle scraping on his raw nerves.

They found the path again, a yard-wide, well-trodden track. Up ahead Duncan Haldane called out and Ben got a glimpse of a shape moving between the tree-trunks. Off to the left the sound of the river came suddenly loud, but not loud enough to drown out the dreadful rustling of the appalling thing made of leaves that was striding, every step like a brush fire, like dry gorse sparking, at their backs.

'Daddy! *Daddy, please!*' Dorrie broke the spell.

'Over here!' Duncan Haldane called out.

Ben saw him run towards them. He flicked a glance behind him and saw the thing, the *leaf-thing*, close behind them. His heart kicked like an angry horse behind his breastbone. The glance, a mere flash, encapsulated the moment as if he'd stared for hours, searing the image in his brain. The leafy head had taken a shape, there were holes and shadows where eyes should have been, and in the centre of them two dead acorns shone dully. There was another gaping hole where a mouth now yawned, fringed by thorns and wide as a tunnel. The arms were now stretched out towards them, sycamore fingers and beech nails, to grab at them.

'Daddy! *Daddy! Help!*' he bawled at the top of his voice.

Duncan Haldane hadn't gone far into the woods when he'd heard a screech from down beyond the turn in the river, below the point where the stream fed into the deep, fast-flowing water.

He'd already decided there was an odds-on chance that Ben and Dorothy might have gone beyond where they had been told many a time *not* to go and he could feel the irritation turn to the kind of anger well known to any father who's been disobeyed. He'd already decided that if Ben had taken Dorrie into Fasach Wood there would be no dinner for him tonight, and plenty of work for him in the morning to make him remember.

Fasach Wood was old and dark and spread its dense cloak over five miles of the lower glen. There were a few deer and the odd polecat and wildcat, but nothing to worry about, not like the old days when there would have been bears and wolves and wild boar rooting about. But there was the river, deep and fast, with sheer wet walls and deep pot-holes that could hide a couple of small children for weeks. Both of them could swim, but that didn't mean they could swim in the Corrie when it was fast and cold and dark.

There were other dangers, too. Bob McCourt, the gamekeeper from the Douglas estate which had borders on the south side of the forest, had scared off many a poacher from the river and the trees. In Fasach Wood, there was always a tinker taking rabbits and deer. Last summer a crowd of ne'er-do-wells in three beat-up vans housing their dirty families and scabby-headed children had been rousted from the south side where they'd set up camp.

Duncan Haldane didn't let his kids into the wood because you never knew who was there, and whoever *was* there wasn't anybody he'd like his kids to meet on their own. Yes, Ben was going to get his little arse spanked hard enough to make him remember that for a long time to come. Duncan felt his anger grow hot.

Then he'd heard the squeal, like a puppy whose tail has been nipped in a door, and instantly he knew it was Dorrie. How he knew he could never have said, but that high, involuntary screech, coming from deep down in the wooded valley, shivered some nerve within him on the deepest level of parental instinct.

The worry fled and a big *scare* flooded into him. The tiny cry talked to him loud and clear. It said *fear*.

Duncan Haldane took off alongside the river on the worn track then veered to the left in the direction of the sound, bawling the kids' names. In his mind's eye he saw visions of some stranger, some loner in the forest, holding his children, *touching* them, *hurting* them. He felt the anger change direction away from Ben and turn itself into black fury at whoever it was who had made Dorrie cry like that.

He ducked between two trees and, without stopping, bent to snatch up a heavy stick that had fallen down from one of the trees. It wasn't straight, but it was hard and felt weightily good in his hands. He called out their names again and ploughed on, ignoring the thorns and runners that snagged him, as Ben had done on his flight from the thing at the river's edge.

'Dad, we're here,' Ben called back. Duncan heard the tightness in his voice although his son's reply sounded very far away, as if somehow close but in another place. But he did not pause to figure out that impossible idea. He only speeded up, battering his way though the juniper and honeysuckle and stunted rowans, using the stick as a heavy club.

He shouted again, hoping his voice would scare whatever had scared *them* into taking flight.

He veered sharply towards the sound and, in the distance, caught a brief flash of white, a flicker far off in the trees. The glimpse spurred him on. A stitch flared in his side, but he didn't even register the knife of pain. All he could think of was that his children were in danger. He was angry enough to kill.

He got another fifty yards and Dorothy screeched again: '*Daddy, please!*' The pain of the cry drilled down the nerves of his spine.

He got past the stand of beech trees and plunged down the slope into the thick part of the forest, crunching over last winter's dead leaves. He leapt a dip, landed lightly for a man of his size, then took another flier over the gnarled roots of a massive tree. There he looked up and saw them coming towards him just beyond the old fallen dyke. Ben was struggling with Dorrie, holding her tight. Beyond them, hidden by a thick scrub of woody holly bushes, a dark shadow flitted.

Duncan saw Ben let Dorrie go and his heart sank, then it kicked back up again when he saw him reach to grab her hand and heave her along behind him, her little legs taking huge strides.

She screamed again: '*Help us!*'

Without being aware of it, Duncan Haldane changed the position of the club in his hands, left hand clenched on the thinner end, right-hand fingers gripping further up the shaft, close to the thick gnarled wood where the branch had been joined to some tree. He covered the last fifty yards in what felt like three strides. Ben saw him coming and swerved towards him, dragging Dorrie in his wake. Duncan saw the pale terror on his son's face and his anger exploded inside. It was as if he was carried up on a wave of pure heat. Everything in him seemed to swell with a huge pressure. He didn't stop to clasp them to him as he would have done at any other time. Instead he launched himself past the small children, almost knocking them over in the process, and crashed through the holly-stand to where he could see the shadow of the *bastard* who was chasing his children.

He broke through and saw something dark fall to the ground. A branch caught his boot and he rolled an almost perfect somersault, landing so heavily on his backside that his teeth snapped together with a loud click. Without stopping to think, he was on his feet and he scrambled, now shouting incoherently, towards where the shape had dived into the leaves.

There was no one there, though that didn't register on Duncan Haldane's overheated brain for several seconds. He had seen the shadow dive into the leaves so that's what he did too. There was no rational thought, just the anger. It took him over, suffused him with such fury that his only instinct was to strike.

He raised the club in his hands and battered it down on the mound of leaves. He hefted it again and used all his force to smash it on the heap. He beat and battered at a useless pile of leaf litter until the thick stick snapped in his hands. By this time leaves were scattered all around, on him, on the overhanging branches, on the bushes.

Finally he stopped, exhausted. The anger drained out of him, leaving him breathless and shaking in its aftermath.

He'd seen a shape. *Something* had moved behind the bushes. He'd been *sure* there was something *there*.

Duncan stood, chest heaving, eyes flicking from side to side, getting his breath back. He was confused, bewildered, but then he turned and saw Dorrie and Ben standing white-faced where their skin showed beneath the spattering of mud and grime. They were looking at him as if he was some sort of god, a knight in armour. He walked quickly towards them, bent and scooped them both up in his arms and held them almost tight enough to crack their ribs.

11

Martin Thornton heard some of it afterwards, though nobody could tell for certain what really happened.

He'd been sitting with Rose Haldane, committed now by courtesy to wait with her as the minutes stretched to nearly an hour. She'd been getting agitated. She tried to hide it, but to him it was obvious in the nervous glances at the old clock on the wall, and the way she kept lifting her cup and putting it down again. They'd had some more tea and she'd gone to the oven and turned it off. Martin made small talk, told her a couple of his milder newspaper anecdotes and the minutes dragged on.

It was close to eight and the shadows were lengthening when Duncan Haldane came pounding on the door. Rose gave a start, dropped a cup, then caught it on reflex halfway to the floor. She almost ran to the door. Her husband, tall enough for his head to almost scrape the lintel, had a child in the crook of each arm. The little girl was asleep. The boy was awake, tired, but his face had that pinched, dull look of somebody who has come through the wars. Martin Thornton had seen the look. The American vets called it the 'thousand-yard stare', the aftermath of shock overload.

'In the bloody woods. Somebody chased them,' he heard Duncan Haldane say. Rose was reaching for the little girl, instinctively grasping for her.

'Saw something. Can't say what it was, if it was anything,' Duncan went on. Martin could hear the crack in his voice as the man relived his own fright, the deadly *dread* of a parent whose children have been in danger.

He was still sitting at the table, though he had shoved his chair back, unsure whether to sit through this family moment. Duncan Haldane turned sideways and saw him.

'Who are you?' he demanded.

'I'm . . .' Martin began to say. What *did* you say to a worried father who'd just found his children in the forest after they'd been scared out of their wits by some unknown pursuer?

'His name's Mr Thornton. From the newspaper,' Rose put in for him. 'He wants to talk to you about the planning thing.'

'Well, that can wait.' Haldane eyed the reporter up and down. The hostility in his voice and stance were all due to his panic, but Martin didn't know that. He felt very uncomfortable. An invader.

'We need Doctor Gregor up here. They've had one hell of a shock and they're cut to bits. Dorrie's got something on her face. Looks like a sting.'

All the words came out in a rush. Clearly Duncan Haldane was wound up and jangling.

Martin took the opportunity to jump in.

'I'll phone him, if you like.'

'Phone's out, man. Cut off six months ago.' The words came out in a snap.

'Well. My car's outside. Tell me where to go. I can even take the children.'

'No. They stay here.'

'Fine. Give me directions. I'll fetch him.'

Rose told him where to go. The doctor lived at the top end of Linnvale, in a fairly large stone house that overlooked most of the valley. A grey-haired, soft-spoken woman answered the door after three rings, then directed Martin to the greenhouse.

Dr Gregor was a tall, angular man who managed to look well groomed in an old pair of dungarees and gardening boots. He wore a pair of half-moon glasses, over which he peered, making him look slightly aggressive, which in fact he was not. He came out of the greenhouse with a terracotta plant-pot in which a single small plant rooted. It bore a perfect mother-of-pearl rose bloom that spangled the warm rays of late sunlight from water-droplets on its petals.

'Look at that. First prize in any show,' he said without introduction. 'You a flower man?'

'Can't say I am. But it's nice. Pretty.'

'Damned perfection.' He jerked his head in the direction of the house and walked on, bearing the rose like a trophy. Martin followed him into the house. 'What can I do for you, young fellow?'

'Duncan Haldane asked me to come and fetch you.'

'Oh, did he now?'

'It's his children. They got lost in the trees. They're pretty shook up.'

109

'Shaken up.'

'Yes. And cut. The wee girl's got some sort of bite on her face. They've had a hell of a fright.'

'And did Duncan tell you I've been retired for ten years?'

That stopped Martin in his tracks.

'No. He didn't mention. He just said to get you up to the farm.'

'They're all the same, you know. I've been in this village for forty years. They refuse to believe that I'm drawing my pension. Got a perfectly good health centre down at Lochend and a top-class hospital at Levenford. Any time somebody gets a hangnail, they send for Doctor Gregor.' He peered furiously over the top of his glasses. 'Fortunately for them, it makes my day,' he said, and then he let out a chuckle. 'All right, Mr . . .?'

'Thornton.'

'Friend of the family?'

'No, just passing by.'

'Lucky for Duncan. Hasn't had a phone in the place for months. Ran out of money.'

Dr Gregor came out of the house with an old, tattered bag and eased himself into the passenger seat. He was still wearing the dungarees and green boots, but he'd put on a fore-and-aft hat that made him look somehow more professional. They got to the Haldane farm five minutes later.

Rose Haldane hurried them both inside. The doctor went upstairs with her while Martin Thornton hung back in the kitchen. A few minutes later he heard heavy footsteps on the stairs. Duncan Haldane came in and sat down heavily at the table.

He looked Martin up and down again, but this time there was no hostility. The man looked strained. Finally he held out a big hand. Martin shook it.

'Thanks for getting the doctor.'

'He says he's retired.'

'Sure he is, but he's still the doctor.'

'How are they?' Martin asked, nodding in the direction of the stairs.

'Scratched to bits. The wee one's nearly hysterical. They've had a bad scare.'

'So have you, by the looks of it.'

'Damn right. I thought I saw something in the bushes. Went after it but there was nothing there. They say a man chased them. I couldn't say. Probably my imagination. You think the worst when you hear the kids bawling like banshees.'

'They'll be all right?'

'I reckon so. Don't like that bite on Dorrie's face. Ben's got something on his hand. He said it was a mushroom or a toadstool. And he said he saw skeletons down there. Probably jumping at shadows. It's pretty dark in Fasach Wood.'

Martin let him go on.

'They say they found an island in the river. I don't know where they got that idea. I've been through those woods since I was a boy. There never was an island in the Corrie between the old Mill dam and the Loch. Ben said there were people in cloaks or somesuch and then an animal came running after them.'

'You think they might have eaten mushrooms?'

Duncan Haldane caught his drift immediately. 'No, Ben's not that daft. They could have imagined it all. Hell, *I* probably imagined seeing something. I just heard them yelling and saw them running. I *assumed* they were being chased.'

A few minutes later Dr Gregor came down the stairs with Rose.

'Nothing to worry about. They've had a bad scare. The cuts are only superficial. I've cleaned them up, and those stings, whatever they are, I've put some antihistamine cream on. I think it's some kind of nettle they've reacted to, but it's not spreading. A good night's rest will see them all right.'

'Thank you, Doctor Gregor, and thanks for coming,' Rose said.

'Always a pleasure. Makes me feel wanted,' he said. He reached out his hand and gave her arm a little squeeze.

Dr Gregor declined a lift back to his house. It was still a fine night, with a white, full moon just rising in the east, and he said he'd rather walk. Martin offered twice, but the old fellow shook his head. He strode off down the farm road, lanky legs eating up the yards, swinging his bag jauntily.

'I'll put the kettle back on,' Rose said. 'Dinner's ruined.'

Duncan just nodded. Martin pushed his chair back.

'I'll get back to the hotel. Maybe I can drop in tomorrow when things are less hectic.'

'No, stay and have a cup, man. Thanks for getting the doctor for us.'

'You don't look as if you're in the mood for it.'

'Keep my mind off the kids,' Haldane insisted.

Once he got talking, Duncan Haldane didn't stop. Rose poured them two steaming mugs and left them to it. She went upstairs to the children's bedroom and came down twenty minutes later to say they were both sound asleep.

The story was much as Martin had heard it. Duncan Haldane had fallen on hard times. Making the farm pay, after a series of disasters, was an impossibility. All he wanted was to use the timber from the high spruce plantation to build a few Finnish-style log cabins and either rent them out or sell them if he had to.

'The Preservation Society took it into their heads that a few cabins would blight the landscape. I've had planners and councillors crawling all over me. It's cost a fortune fighting them and I'm running out of money. What I've got left I need for building and hiring a couple of men. If I don't, I'll have to leave here. They object to me cutting down the coppice but I need that timber for collateral. It's all good oak and beech. And anyway, my grandfather planted every one of those trees. It's not part of the wildwood.'

He put his mug down on the table, almost hard enough to splash the remains of the tea over the lip.

'Nobody is going to run me out of this glen. My family have been here for hundreds of years. Most of them that's against me are incomers. White settlers. I'll see them in hell.'

Duncan was a likeable big fellow. Martin could see the tension mount in him as he talked, but he knew that was partly the result of the scare he'd got down in the forest. His big shoulders were tight and they moved slightly from side to side as he spoke, as if he was keeping a hard rein on himself.

'They say it's to preserve the old forest. What do they know? Those trees, from the old Mill dam up to here, are all mine. The forest proper starts below the dam, where there's an old dyke that used to mark the boundary. My grandfather planted the upper coppice and the rest are just chance trees where the forest has encroached on my land. Squirrels plant acorns and beech nuts and before you know it Fasach Wood has crept up to your door.'

'Why are they so dead set against it?' Martin asked.

'Christ alone knows. They never turned a hair when Aitkenbar opened up the farm supply store. And Donnie MacKinnon's propane-gas depot is hardly what you could call rustic. But they all want hot fires in the winter at the turn of a switch and big business beats all. That road down yonder's humming with tankers every day and nobody gives a tuppeny damn.'

'What's the importance of the forest?'

'The society say it's one of the last remnants of the old Caledonia Forest. Used to stretch from the borders all across the highlands. There's one or two bits of it left. Maybe the middle of Fasach Wood *is* part of it, I don't know. But the rest definitely *isn't*. The old woods were all pine and fir and oak. In there you get everything from sycamore to beech and lime. They're not native to these parts. I know my trees.'

'And your wood. You've done a good job here. Good beechwood, that.'

'Thanks. Do a bit of DIY yourself?'

'Dad was a carpenter. A *cabinetmaker*. I still keep my hand in. Something to fall back on when I've had enough of this game.'

Duncan Haldane smiled and the tension just seemed to drain out of his face. He was not handsome, but he had a big, craggy, homely face that had its own appeal.

'And when would that be?'

'Any day now. It's getting to that stage.'

'So, are you going to write a story?'

'I don't know, to be honest. I have to speak to the other side.'

'They want to take this to the Scottish Office. Trying to get the secretary of state to step in.'

'It's unlikely they'll get that.'

'I don't know. They've been pretty determined. I don't know what happened down there in the woods tonight. I can't say if the kids *imagined* it or not, though I thought for a minute I saw something. Anyway, I wouldn't put it past those old biddies to put a scare into the wee ones just to get at me.'

'I haven't met them yet,' Martin said, non-committally. He thought Duncan Haldane's remark showed more than a trace of paranoia, but he let it go.

Martin slid the mug across the table and pushed his chair back.

'Thanks for the tea, and the chat.'

'Any time. I appreciate your help anyway.'

Martin told him he would speak to a few folk the following day and get back to the farmer if he needed anything more. To himself he thought there was no real story here: a storm in a teacup.

Perhaps there might be a bit of colour, but at the end of the day it was only one man who wanted to cut down some trees and build some cabins and his neighbours objected. So far he was on Duncan Haldane's side. He sympathised with his plight and couldn't see what difference it would make.

'All the difference in the *world*,' Gail Dean said the following morning. The minister's wife was a well-groomed, handsome woman with short, neatly cut fair hair. Martin estimated her at somewhere in her forties, though which end of that decade he couldn't guess.

'*Somebody* has to make a stand. I'm sorry it's Duncan who is involved. The poor man's had a very difficult year. But our action is not just for us. It's the tip of the iceberg, the thin end of the wedge.' Gail Dean talked quickly in short sentences. Martin sat opposite her in the comfortable drawing room of the manse. The minister, the Reverend John Dean, whom he'd never met, was visiting a parishioner down in Levenford General.

'You look at Loch Fescail, just a few miles over the hill. It's a complete ruin with all the trees cut down and chalets littering the hillside.'

Martin knew about Loch Fescail. A local farmer had made the place into a holiday camp, leaving the few folk who lived in the nearby village seething at the loss of their privacy. It had been well documented in all of the papers.

'This is part of Scotland's heritage. It's important to the whole country. If we allow this to go ahead, then we could see developments encroach all over the glen. It would completely ruin the character of the place.'

'What about the Aitkenbar site and the gas storage plant?'

'The committee wasn't formed when they were built. And anyway, they're not in the forest. It's a different matter entirely.'

They talked for an hour or so. Martin liked the woman. She was forthright, plied him with tea and biscuits and, later, insisted on him having a small sherry. It was sweet but none the worse for that.

When he left the manse in mid-morning, Martin had decided there wasn't much to justify a story. It was just a small-town row. There were a thousand of them going on every day. It wouldn't make a major piece. He went back to the hotel where he'd spent the night and checked out. He toyed with the idea of taking a turn up to the Haldane farm, but thought better of it. Instead he went past the turnoff and along the flat to Caitlin Brook's house. He stopped the Land-Rover, letting the engine idle for a moment or two, undecided. She was nowhere to be seen and he presumed she'd be out in the back garden, painting in the soft morning sunshine. He didn't get out. Instead, he drove along the Linn Road which snaked past Fasach Wood, the winding way to the lochside where it joined the main route south and east towards the city.

Professionally it had been an unproductive day and a half. Personally, however, he was glad he'd taken the notion to visit Linnvale and meet Caitlin Brook again. There was something about the girl that appealed to him. In the year and a half since her fall, he'd thought about her from time to time and wondered. Most of those times he'd wondered about the strange *prescience* he'd got before her catastrophic swoop from the balcony.

Back at the office there were a dozen call messages stuck on the spike on his desk, a remnant from the days when newspapermen used actual paper and typewriters instead of the keyboards and screens which had sprouted like weeds throughout the trade.

He checked in with the news editor, told him he'd write a few paragraphs, fielded a couple of uninteresting ideas dreamed up by deskbound executives trying to justify their existence, and then he got on the phone.

Andrew Toye answered on the fourth ring. He sounded distracted, but Martin knew that was nothing new. It was a mixture of other-worldly absent-mindedness and childlike enthusiasm. Martin liked the man, one of the few academics he had much time for.

'I've got some pictures for you,' Andrew told him after a few seconds silence.

'Paintings, photos or what?'

'Photographs. It's a case of poltergeist activity. Alleged activity, that is.'

'Pull the other one,' Martin said, laughing.

'No. I'm serious. Not a poltergeist *proper*. I don't believe there actually *is* such a thing. But I do have some very interesting shots which suggest some sort of paranormal activity. They're quite sensational, as a matter of fact,' he said blandly.

Had it been anybody else, Martin would have hung up, but Andrew Toye had what he described as the best job at Glasgow University. Maybe it *was* an honorary title, but he was the only professor of Paranormal Studies north of the border. It allowed him to indulge his hobby and debunk fraudsters, and all in the line of research. Also he was a natural journophile. He liked newspapermen and Martin in particular. Indeed, Andrew Toye was the only other person who knew about Martin Thornton's vision of Caitlin Brook.

'There's often a rational explanation for this kind of thing,' Toye had explained over a few beers in a quiet pub round the corner from the University.

Andrew Toye loved his beer. A small, wispy man with no co-ordination of any kind, none of his clothes matched and you had to protect your drink closely or lose it to one of his flailing arms. However, inside his head, the professor was very well co-ordinated indeed. He had a phenomenal memory for facts, dates and places. Martin had told him about his déjà-vu, thinking his friend might explain it.

'There have been many claims made for telepathy. I haven't seen it proved yet. But tel-*empathy* is a different matter. There have been dozens – *hundreds* – of documented cases of that kind of thing. People getting visions of friends and family at the same time as they die hundreds of miles away. It's more common than you'd imagine. There was a lot of research done after the Aberfan disaster. Many people had dreams about that coal heap sliding down on the school and killing the children. The Flixborough explosion was another case in point. There was a well-reported case of someone who had contacted a newspaper and described the whole thing *before* it actually happened.'

'All right. Let's say it *can* happen. Why *me*?'

'I don't know the mechanism. It could be to do with the stress of the situation. Dark night. Gunfire. Danger. The young lady was in a pretty stressful state. There must have been something that made you empathise with her.'

'I liked her legs. Does that count?'

Andrew laughed. 'Who knows? Were they that good?'

'They're no bloody good now, that's for sure,' Martin said drily.

Now, back at the office, Martin listened to Andrew Toye tell him he had photographs of a possible poltergeist haunting in, of all places, a high-rise flat in a rundown part of the city. If that was true, it certainly *was* news. He knew the professor did not actually believe in poltergeists, but when he heard that a sound-activated camera had been set up an the eighth floor of a tower block in Glasgow and that *something* had been caught on film, then that could be a story.

They met up at the University on Gilmorehill. To get to Andrew's office Martin had to climb three flights of the old worn stone stairs then negotiate a narrow, dark corridor; Mystic Wing, the professor called it. On his old, polished door, his official title Professor of Celtic Studies was engraved on an old brass plate which had the fluorescent patina of age. Below it, on a neat new plastic panel, Martin read: Department of Paranormal Phenomena.

Andrew eventually answered the door and ushered him in. The old leathertop desk was a clutter of papers. Books lined the walls and stacked themselves up in almost every available space. Andrew had to take an armful from a chair before Martin could sit down.

'I tried to get you yesterday, but they said you were out.'

'I was checking something out. Didn't come to anything.'

'Pity. You could have been there.'

'Where?'

'Where we got the pictures. I didn't have much time to set it up. We only got the call the day before.'

Martin held his hands up. 'Slow down, Andy. I'm missing half of this. Can we start at the beginning?'

'Oh. Of course. Want a cup of tea?'

Martin shook his head.

'I got a call from the parish priest, because he doesn't want to get involved in any of this, and anyway, the family aren't part of his flock. They only called him in because they've seen too many films. Why do they always call in catholic priests, I wonder? Why not Jehovah's Witnesses?'

'People spend all their time trying to keep them *out* of their homes, not inviting them *in*.'

Andrew laughed. 'I expect you're right. Anyway, he told us the family were frightened of something in the house. He thought I might be able to help. Told him I was delighted to, of course.'

He fished around in a bulging drawer and drew out a thick manilla envelope.

'We came up with this,' he said, sliding it across the clutter on the desk. Two other thick wads of paper cascaded onto the floor. The professor ignored them.

The pictures were very clear. Pin sharp.

At first Martin's eyes couldn't resolve anything in them. He turned them over, one by one, and then it hit him. They showed two girls high in the air above an unmade bed. The camera had caught everything in its flash. One in pyjamas, the other wearing a singlet and a pair of pants. Their mouths were open, but it was impossible to tell from their expressions whether they were laughing or *screaming*.

'What's this? Some sort of trampoline shot?'

'You would think so, at first glance. The pictures are in reverse order. The camera had a sound cell. It was set to flash at any noise louder than a whisper. We've got six shots of the girls sleeping. They snored or coughed. We can match the prints up in sequence to the sound tape. Now look at the sequence from there.' He reached across and shuffled through the photographs. 'There. There's a spike on the tape. A noise like a cough. Shot one. The next is only half a second further on and the rest are on fast drive, shooting at three frames every second. You'll see what I'm getting at.'

Martin saw. The last of the startling series showed the girls asleep in a double bed. Martin flicked back. The girls were lying flat. Next frame the covers were thrown into the air, though there was no obvious sign of any movement from either girl. The third frame showed the girls themselves in the air above the bed, maybe a whole yard up from the mattress. After that the motordrive caught them, at three frames a second, turning in the air and falling back onto the bed in a curious stop-motion replay.

'You'll notice that there seems to be no muscular movement between the children lying prostrate and them being in the air. There is only half a second's difference between the frames, which doesn't give them both an awful lot of time to get ready to leap into the air simultaneously.'

'So what's happening?'

'That's what I have to try to find out. The girls' parents are worried silly about all this. They tell me it's been going on for about six weeks. They can't get to sleep a night and neither, apparently, can the girls, although they don't seem half as upset as their parents do.'

'Is that all there is to it?'

'The family certainly don't take that attitude,' Andrew said with mild reproof.

'No, I mean, does anything else happen?'

'All the action is in the girls' bedroom. Things get thrown about, clothes taken from the wardrobe and scattered on the floor, books fly around. The light goes on and off by itself.'

'I've seen that happen,' Martin said.

'Oh. Where?'

'In *Poltergeist*. The movie. Great special effects.'

Andrew looked blankly at him for several seconds. 'Haven't seen that one.'

'You should. It's right up your street. Turns out it's ghosts from a cemetery that cause all the problems.'

'Well, there's no cemetery here. It's eight floors up.'

'Don't take it so literally, Andy. It just *reminded* me of the film.' Martin shrugged a half-apology. 'So what do you think, then?'

'I'm not certain. The family are convinced it's a poltergeist. I'm not quite sure. I know it's only a tiny time lag, but I'd like to see what happened in that half second between the frames. There could be some kind of paranormal activity. This kind of thing almost always involves early teenage children, mainly girls entering puberty or in some kind of trauma. Some of them seem to display a degree of telekinesis – things get *moved*.'

'But in this case?'

'I don't see any evidence to show that they actually jumped. It *looks* as if they were just catapulted into the air. I'll have to do some more tests. I'm getting the loan of an infra-red camera and I have other equipment to line up. It should be fun. Want to come along?'

'Wouldn't miss it. How about the family? Won't they mind?'

'No. I told them I was going to tell you about it. You'll probably have to drop some cash their way, but that's up to you.'

'No problem.' He lifted up the batch of photographs. 'Can I use these?'

'Of course,' Andrew said.

As Martin was leaving, the professor turned to him. 'By the way, you haven't had any more interludes yourself, have you?'

'Not since then.'

'Peculiar one, that,' Andrew mused. 'Did you ever tell the girl about it?'

'Strange you should ask. I told her only the day before yesterday. She didn't believe a word of it.'

Andrew laughed. 'Don't worry about it. I'm the world's biggest cynic and *I* believe you.'

'I'll sleep well for that,' Martin said and Andrew laughed again.

12

Caitlin Brook did not sleep well that night. She had faithfully done her exercises on the pulleys, slipping her feet into the holds and then hauling them alternately into the air. There was no sensation of motion, or of touch, but the movement helped the flow of circulation and went a long way to prevent her leg muscles wasting away. Already her calves and thighs were painfully thin from lack of use. She had lain on the low bench pumping with her arms. The balance was changing. She knew her arms and shoulders were getting stronger every day, to compensate for the loss of power in her legs. At times she thought the pulley exercises were a waste of time, but the physiotherapist had stressed their importance as soon as she had got out of bed in hospital.

'You might not feel them, and they may seem useless to you, but they're still *part* of you.'

Caitlin knew they were still part of her, but sometimes, breathless and exhausted from the exertion, she resented them. Sometimes she *hated* them.

And at night she dreamed she ran.

She awoke in a lather of sweat, gasping for breath while the remnants of the fragmented dream faded. She tried to catch the pieces but they slipped away, dodging her grasp, leaving her dismayed and empty. Her body, the parts she could *feel*, was tingling. Nerves jumped and skittered under her skin. Down her back she could feel the skin pucker and crawl coldly as it often did when she was awake as the messages from her brain to her legs were interrupted at the broken junction and tried to find currency, radiating in waves of interference, random instructions, confused yet *urgent*.

She had come awake suddenly and in the blurry, *scary* aftermath she had tried to sit up as she had done all her life, but of course she couldn't use her legs as counterweights or levers. Her back ached with the strain before she got her elbows underneath her and used them to push herself up. She awkwardly got herself to the edge of the bed and sat there, slouched against the pillows that leaned on the headboard, waiting for her lungs to slow. There was a pressure in her bladder which meant a slow journey to the bathroom at the far end of the hall, but Caitlin was grateful for that discomfort, a small mercy. For the first three months, there had been no sensation there. Even now, on distressing occasions, her damaged spine played tricks on her, taking her by surprise. The shotgun pellet was still lodged in there, irritating the nerve lining, causing it to swell from time to time. Another millimetre and she would have been utterly incontinent. At least now she could choose to wheel herself to the bathroom.

In her dream she had been running again, down the forest trail, the place she had never been but saw only in the startling visions of sleep. She had woken, she knew, before she returned to face the metal monster, the rack that opened its arms to her and held her down. *Another small mercy.*

She pushed against the pillows to force herself upright, and with her free hand she swept the fiery copper curls away from her face, shaking her head as she did so, and Martin Thornton inexplicably flashed into her thoughts. He hadn't come back, although she'd half-expected he would, maybe even half-*hoped* he would.

She lowered herself gingerly into the wheelchair and made it to the bathroom. Using only her arms to get her whole body around made everything an effort. She bore with it, feeling ungainly and lumpy, trying to ignore her own awkwardness and feelings of inadequacy. It was fifteen minutes before she was back in bed again and able to think about anything else but the exertion of moving.

Caitlin lay back on the pillows with the bedside light casting a glow in the corner. As soon as Martin had turned the corner, the old bitterness had come rushing in like a black tide. Of course, she told herself, it wasn't his fault, but he had been there, he had seen her fall, and the sight of him brought the moment back with terrible clarity.

His visit had been a puzzle. The cheque still stood on the low mantelpiece. He'd refused to take it back, so it stood there like an ornament, a token. She still hadn't decided whether to keep it or not. There was more than a hint of bribery in the amount of money. There was something roguish about Martin Thornton, and she surprised herself by finding that attractive.

Yet there was something else. Behind the easy chat there was a spark of sincerity in the man. He'd told her he wanted to do a story and she'd refused and he'd brought back that awful memory again. Yet when he'd gone, the house had felt empty, and when he hadn't turned up after seeing Duncan Haldane, she'd felt a twinge of regret.

She thought back to his explanation of what he'd seen that night and couldn't make up her mind. It was ridiculous, of course, preposterous. But Martin Thornton had told her the story in such a flat, straightforward way, that it was clear *he* believed it.

Caitlin smiled to herself. 'Must be getting back to normal,' she said aloud in the quiet room. She reached behind her to even out the pillows and stretched awkwardly to switch the light off. She lay back in the darkness, head turned towards the window. The curtains weren't closed over and the moon was rising behind the trees. Somewhere an owl shrieked and another one responded with a low, feral hoot from far off in the forest. The tops of the trees were stirred by a night breeze. Backlit by the full moon, their silhouettes looked like beckoning hands.

Caitlin closed her eyes and fell asleep. If she ran again that night, she did not remember in the morning.

Duncan and Rose Haldane got little sleep at all.

On the night that Duncan had come up the lane with his children in his arms, Doctor Gregor had given both of them a tablet apiece which he said would help them sleep. All next day, both Dorrie and Ben had hung around the house looking listless and wary. They didn't seem to have the energy for games. Rose and Duncan played it gently. After the scare of the children being lost in the woods, neither of them wanted to bring the fright back by interrogating them.

At breakfast, the mark on Dorrie's face was still red and angry, but it had shrunk to a hot point. It wasn't spreading, so couldn't be poisonous and if Doctor Gregor had said it would go away, then that was fine. There was nothing Duncan knew of in the trees that was strong enough to do much damage. Maybe the adders up on the hill, but they kept to the high heather and bracken. Ben was still covered in scratches and abrasions and his shirt was consigned to the ragbag, but even the scratches and cuts were *normal* looking, the kind any youngster might get playing in the scrubby undergrowth. Duncan recalled coming home many a time in his own childhood to a clout on the ear for getting himself into such a mess. That was always the way of it with boys.

The big farmer sat at the end of the table and watched the two of them taking their shredded wheat, eating quietly, heads down over their plates, with none of the usual boisterous, high-summer, early-morning spirit. Rose watched him watching them, saw his concern and said nothing.

At nine o'clock Duncan was back outside ripping up the blow-downs. He worked for an hour, much as he had done on the day before, and Ben came out with a cup of tea and some biscuits. Duncan didn't hear him coming over the roar of the cutter and gave himself a fright when the small boy suddenly appeared by his side. Ben handed over the big mug and the saucer of biscuits. Duncan took a hot sip and sat himself down on a thick smooth branch. He reached over and clasped a big hand on his son's shoulder. The boy looked pinched and nervous.

'Take a break with the old man,' Duncan said gently, pulling Ben towards him.

The boy sat down beside him, very small, staying close. Duncan moved so his arm could hold Ben in a hug.

'Got a bit of a scare yesterday.'

Ben nodded.

'All of us. And your mum. And not much fun for you and Dorrie.'

Ben shook his head. He hadn't said a word.

'Not a good place, the woods. Not down below the Mill Dam. You know that now, don't you?'

'Yes, Dad,' Ben said at last in a very small voice.

'Now I'm not giving you a bad time, for you've learned that lesson for certain, and I don't think you'll do that again in a hurry.'

'I won't, Dad,' Ben blurted with surprising vigour. 'I'm never going in those trees again. *Not ever*.'

He looked up at his father and Duncan could see the scared determination in his son's face.

'Good idea, boy. Good idea.' Duncan reached and took another sip of his cooling tea. He held the mug for Ben to take a slurp, a small sharing between father and son.

'Remember yesterday, you said you were being chased?'

'It was the *leaf man*.'

'The what?'

'It was made of leaves. I saw it, Dad, *honest*. We were down at the river . There's an island there. There were people at a big tree and one of them saw us. Then something came into the water after us and I pulled Dorrie away and we ran and ran.'

Ben's words came tripping and tumbling in a torrent. Duncan could see his son looking backwards, remembering, though exactly *what* the boy was recalling, he wasn't certain.

'We went past the mushrooms. They were *big*, Dad. Big and horrible. They all swelled up and they burst and some of it got on Dorrie and on my hand. And then the leaves started to bunch up together and there was a man made of all the leaves. He was brown and crackly and he *scraped* when he moved. And Dad, he was going to get us if you hadn't been there.'

Duncan's own mind flicked back a day to when he was running towards the children. He had seen the flicker of their faces behind the undergrowth and then they had come into view, Ben hauling Dorrie so hard her feet hardly touched the ground. Behind them – had it been a trick of the shade? Had there been something? He remembered roaring, though he couldn't recall the words, if there were any. He had run past the children and crashed through the scrub at the movement, the shadow. And there had been nothing there. Only the leaf-litter mounds, the kind that filled every glade in the wood. He was about to speak when Ben blurted out.

'And there were skeletons, Dad. There were skeletons in the trees.'

'Skeletons, son?' Duncan asked softly, not wanting to put Ben off.

'Yes, Dad. I thought it was a branch hanging down and I held on to it when I was running and it came away and it *wasn't a branch*.'

Ben's voice soared up the register.

'It's all right Ben, boy. Take it easy, eh?' Duncan squeezed his son tight, trying to impart as much comfort as he could. Ben made a little sob. A big tear sparkled in his eye and then rolled down his cheek.

'It wasn't a branch. It was an arm. I *saw* it. And there was a skeleton hanging out of a tree. It was all brown and horrible. And . . . and . . . Dad . . . the *trees got them*. It was the trees!'

Ben burst into tears. Duncan could feel his small body spasm with the force of the sobs and he held on, keeping his son tight by his side. He waited until they began to subside. It took a long time.

Finally, when Ben's sobs were reduced to loud sniffles, Duncan looked down at him again.

'You didn't eat anything that was growing in there, did you, son?'

Ben said nothing. Duncan continued, coaxing.

'Like berries or anything? Or maybe that wild rhubarb that grows beside the stream?'

'No, Dad.' Ben sniffed. 'We didn't eat anything.'

'You didn't touch mushrooms and put your fingers in your mouth?'

'We didn't see any mushrooms. Except the big ones that burst on us.'

'And did you swallow any?'

'I don't think so.' Ben shook his head. All the time his father watched him and saw that occasionally the boy's eyes would flick over to the left, towards the slope that led down to the stream and to the forest. Duncan saw his eyes go still and then swerve away, as if negating what he had seen. The boy didn't want to look at the trees. He didn't want to *think* about them.

'You sure?'

'Yes,' Ben said, then gave a little hiccup. 'I don't remember eating anything.'

'And Dorrie?'

'Not while I was with her. We got mixed up. I thought she'd gone home and she thought I was in the woods. I didn't mean it, Dad. Really I didn't. I went looking for her and she was looking for me. Then we got lost, and . . . and . . . and it's *different* down there. There's *things* in the trees.'

'Aye, son. And yon forest goes on a long way. A man could get himself lost in there.'

Duncan hefted Ben up and sat him on his knee. The boy was growing fast, but he was still light enough to swing. Ben put his head against his father's chest and the snuffling subsided.

'You've had a fright, that's for sure, eh?'

Duncan had listened to the two of them babbling in fear when he carried them up the valley towards the farmhouse. He couldn't make head nor tail of it then, when the pair were almost hysterical with fright. Even now it wasn't easy, but like every father faced with an incredible tale from a small child, he rationalised it.

They'd obviously gone down into Fasach Wood and got themselves lost. They'd been scared. They'd seen something and worked themselves up into a lather about it, much as he had done when he'd heard them screaming in the woods. Maybe a deer, or one of the sheep that had got through the fence and into the trees. Maybe they'd eaten something. There were a few things growing down there that *were* poisonous. Giant hogweed by the river. Some of the toadstools that grew under the beech trees were as toxic as they looked. There was laburnum growing even down by the valley with pods full of seeds that looked like peas and could kill a child.

Probably the wind or their feet had stirred up the leaves and they'd imagined they were being chased. Maybe they saw an otter diving into the river. The skeletons? Now that, Duncan told himself, was a puzzle. Maybe the carcass of some dog strung up by the gamekeeper Bob McCourt. *Maybe.*

The children had imaginations, like any other kids. They could see a shadow and a shape and in a state of panic they could make anything of it. That's what Duncan Haldane told himself. Ben and Dorrie had had a scare. They were fine now. They were home and they were safe. He didn't have to worry about them getting lost in Fasach Wood again. Despite that, Duncan Haldane decided that in a day or two, when the wood-ripping was done, he'd take a turn down into the trees and have a look for himself.

It was late when Ben Haldane woke up. He knew it was late because it was dark outside and there was a silver of moonshine on the windowpane. He had woken up from a dream in which he was running through the trees. He'd been running for his *life*. His breath was high and tight and there were flickering dark shadows all around, keeping pace with him as he passed the trunks, dodging and ducking, trying to get away. He held Dorrie's arm by

126

the wrist, hauling her along, terrified in case what was behind them would get her, yet unable to drag her in front of him. The dream wound itself up inside him like a mad clock. He ran, bursting with panic, unable to cry his fear, while behind him came the scuttery crackle of the *leaf man*. He could hear the rustle whisper of the dry-leaf feet, the soughing of dead breath and cold laughter.

He ran and ran, dodging and turning, and everywhere he ran there would be a tree barring his path. It was as if the trees were deliberately planting themselves in his way, walking on thick roots to try to trap him.

He brushed past a tall beech, a grey shadow in the darkness, and felt it *move*. It twisted and he could hear the screech of the bark rending. From the corner of an eye he saw a thick branch, elephant-grey and warted, *flex* and reach downwards. His mouth opened and he tried to scream but no words came out. And anyway there was no one to hear it in the deep dream forest but the terrible dry leaf man and the deadly trees with corpses in their gnarled branches.

Ben got to a clearing and hauled Dorrie across it, scared to turn round, knowing that dry and rustling hands were reaching scrapy fingers for them. He instinctively grasped a branch to swing himself around another obstacle and he felt the branch quiver like muscle and he let it go in terror. He spun and Dorrie spun with him, only it wasn't Dorrie. The wrist he held was thin and hard and dirty-brown. Clawed fingers held open in a frozen grab were spider-thin. The nails were black as night. At the shoulder a skull with black eyeholes. A washboard rib-cage dragged the ground and bony legs trailed behind, light as Dorrie, foul as rot.

Ben looked down and saw the fingers twitch and hook themselves in to his arm. The nails caught on his skin and started to squeeze like the claws of a big insect. With his right hand he tore the thing away, peeling away his own flesh with it. Then the glade erupted into a maelstrom of leaves. He whirled and the leaf man was reaching for him with a hand made of dry bracken and twigs and leaves.

Ben awoke with the scream still locked in his throat.

He was sitting up in his bed and his whole body was shaking. The dream was still there, emblazoned on the forefront of his mind. He saw in the darkness the cracked and mottled head in front of him, the holly-spine teeth, the oak-apple eyes, and he could still hear the death-rattle voice calling to him in words that scraped on the inside of his skull.

It took him several seconds to realise that he was *not* in the forest. He was here, at home. He was safe.

Yet his mind was still yammering at him, yelling '*Danger! Danger! Danger!*'

He sat there, quivering, afraid to move. The room was dark and shadowed. Through the wall he could hear the muffled sound of his father snoring, a sound which would normally have been a comfort, but now sent shivers of alarm through him. What if he couldn't wake his father. What if he screamed and nobody came?

Ben turned to the window where the moon silvered the glass. Outside, the sky was cobalt blue, shading to black. A low wind moaned under the rafters and riffled the slates on the roof in an eerie rattle. Tentatively Ben got out of bed, still shivering. He wanted to go next door and crawl in between his mum and dad, the way he used to do when he was really small. Part of him knew that his father wouldn't mind, not tonight, not after the talk they'd had today. But the gulf between being a baby and being nine years old was enormous. He was the second man of the house. Something held him back. He turned from the door and moved back towards the bed, past the window. As he did so the light wind gusted more strongly and through the glass he saw the tops of the trees shiver and wave at him, black hands in the night. He felt his belly clench and every nerve in him jumped. Despite the startle, he could not help himself. His feet seemed to move of their own volition as he walked barefoot towards the window.

Outside, the moonlight limned the great beech branches from the massive blow-down. It caught on the sections that his father had cut. Beyond, down the slope, the stream was a trail of silver, a beautiful ribbon of light. On the far side of the stream the forest spread like a black blanket, untouched by the moonlight. The blackness stretched on forever, shade upon shade.

The wind gusted again, quite strongly, and Ben clearly heard, over the rattle of the slates, the squeal of branches bending. It sounded alien, *animal,* alive with threat.

There was a movement at the edge of the trees. Ben's eyes

flicked towards it and the movement stopped. There was a small tree at the edge of the stream. Maybe the wind had caught the leaves. Another movement in peripheral vision made him turn his head to the field closer to the left, next to the dry-stone dyke. Another tree, maybe an oak, was swaying in the breeze. A similar motion right in front of the house, near the sawn-off sections of the fallen beech, made him jerk his attention that way. Then his eyes swept back to the first tree, standing by the bank of the stream opposite the wall of vegetation that marked the edge of the forest.

His heart leapt so hard it was like a pain in his chest.

'No,' Ben tried to say, but all that came out was a dry whisper.

The tree was on *this* side of the silver stream. When he'd seen the movement it had been on the *far* side.

And then it came to him, why the motion had been so unexpected. He knew the whole section of the valley from the village bridge to the turn of the stream. There was no tree in the low pasture at all. There was grass and a few scrubby thistles, but no tree. Not on *either* side of the brook. He felt his breath catch and suddenly the need for oxygen made his head spin. He looked down towards where the blow-down lay in pieces, its exposed roots still standing like a fan. The other tree was there, closer to the main trunk. Beside it a small sapling shivered in the breeze.

Neither of them had been there before.

'No,' Ben tried to say again, with as little success as before. His jaw worked. No sound came out. It was just like in his dream. His father was snoring next door and Ben could not wake him. He couldn't even *move*.

The wind suddenly shrieked under the rafters and sang through the now-useless telephone wires that swung from the corner of the house to the pole near the gate.

In front of the house the trees were waving and beckoning, but worse, *oh much worse,* he could see movement there in the root-shadows. He could see trunks bend and flex. There was a blur of fast motion down in the pasture, a cloud of something that billowed out from the crowding trunks. It looked like a tornado, a black dust-devil, like the kind you saw when the straw was whipped round in a circle by the northwest wind when it shrieked round by the barn.

Thick, fast-moving, it came in a straight line towards the

129

farmhouse, then stopped travelling but kept swirling fiercely in a blur of circular motion on the short grass a stone's throw from where Ben, muscle-locked, nerve-frozen, watched.

Then the turning cloud crystallised. It happened so quickly that even Ben, his whole attention *nailed* on the commotion, didn't see it happen.

All he knew was that one minute there was a dust-devil storm of debris and the next the leaf man was standing in front of the house.

His heart took another jolt and he felt the blood drain from his head. The room spun around him and the window pane wavered in and out of vision. His hands instinctively clamped on the sill to steady himself. He couldn't blink. He couldn't move. He couldn't yell. Every part of him was frozen and fixed on the terrifying vision down there on the short grass.

The leaf man stood there, a ghastly apparition in the night. It stood with its feet planted apart, a raggedy horror from which dead leaves and twigs were tugged and torn by the wind. It lifted its hands as if to reach up for him and then it laughed.

It laughed like the wind in an autumn forest. It laughed like the scuttering of insects under dead wood. It laughed like wasps chewing the rafters up in the loft.

It laughed at Ben Haldane.

That was enough to snap the taut spring. Ben's whole body gave a jerk away from the window and his scream echoed through the house.

'Jesus Christ'! his father bellowed. There were footsteps outside the door. The handle rattled as it turned, failed to catch and turned again. The door slammed open and his father, dressed only in pyjama bottoms, came bounding in.

Ben was on the floor, cowering under the window sill, his whole body shaking. Duncan Haldane reached for him and scooped him up in one easy motion. He could *feel* his son's heartbeat against him. The boy was vacant-eyed and his mouth wide open and dribbling. Duncan Haldane turned towards the bed. His son had obviously had a nightmare. As he turned, he thought he saw a motion out there on the low pasture, a figure like a man. He whirled quickly, but the figure was gone. There was only a cloud of leaves blown by the freshening wind down towards the stream. As he turned away, the movement of the wind through the trees next to the blow-down hardly registered in his mind.

He sat himself on the bed and held Ben tight until his fright passed. Rose had come in by this time and reached for the boy. They held him between them and finally the shivering stopped.

It was several long minutes before Ben could speak. When he did, he could only say the same phrase over and over again.

'The leaf man.'

Down in Fasach Wood Bob McCourt heard the whispering wind and ignored it. He was close to the south end of the spreading forest, near where the River Corrie emerged in a cascade of moonlit water to meander smoothly down to Loch Corran. Douglas Estate had the fishing rights to the east side of the Corrie and organised a shooting syndicate for the well-heeled on the hills and at the edge of the woods. There were plenty of roe deer at the south end, red deer up on the hills along with the grouse and, down in the valley, pheasants from the pens that Bob McCourt kept well-stocked. He was a conscientious gamekeeper, and that's why he was inside Fasach Wood, instead of home in his bed or up at the Douglas Arms enjoying a dram and a beer chaser. He was on his own, though he'd rather have had young Jimmy McGregor with him. Bob was a stocky man, wide-shouldered and short-legged and strong as an ox. Jimmy was twenty years his junior, keen as mustard and head and shoulders taller than his boss. He was the classic poacher turned gamekeeper, as Bob himself had been. Despite his youth, Jimmy was tough as old boots and a good man to have beside you in a scrap with the tinkers who would gut the river of every salmon quick as a blink. Unfortunately Jimmy was down at Lochend at the cinema with his girlfriend. Bob had allowed him the night off, so that was why he was walking slowly into the edge of the trees on his own.

He didn't expect much trouble tonight. There hadn't been a drop of rain in the past fortnight, which was rare enough in itself, but that meant there would be few salmon hurrying up from the loch. The next spate would bring a run of big ones and Bob would take a couple for himself while guarding the rest for Douglas Estates. He was conscientious, but no saint.

He settled back against the bole of a tree, cupping his hand round his cigarette so the pinpoint of light wouldn't show. He wasn't worried about the smell of smoke, because from where he sat he could see anything that moved into the forest along the edge of the river. The bomber's moon in the clear sky would silhouette any movement and, anyhow, the wind was eddying towards him to carry the smoke into the deep part of the woods. The breeze picked up, shivering the tops of the trees, but down below the canopy there was hardly a breath.

It was a warm night and the midges were ferocious. Swarms of the tiny insects were coming off the water in droves, murderous little things that would get into your ears and under your eyelids and they felt as if they had teeth like tigers. The mosquitoes were fewer, but worse. They came singly, announced only by the eye- watering buzz of their frantic wings. You normally heard them after they'd got a bellyful of your blood. Bob had slapped them off his face five or six times since he started and he knew he would look like a warthog in the morning. The only trouble with this job was the summertime stake-outs: he was allergic to mosquito bites. The cigarette was defence against them; the smoke tended to keep them away.

It was unlikely there would be any bother tonight, but if there was he would give any potential poachers a real scare. He kept his twelve-bore over and under close to his side and sat, shifting his weight to get comfortable, and pulled his fore-and-aft hat over his eyes. A close observer might have failed to spot him in the darkness.

Bob had seen the footprints in the clay beside the Corrie, and further upstream he'd found an ash sapling stripped of its leaves and side shoots into a pole maybe fifteen feet long. The end was ragged and scraped, a typical prod for fish under rocks. The poachers would scare the salmon from under ledges and chivvy them downstream into a net strung across the flow. They could catch a dozen in a night and that was a dozen less for the upper-crust fly-fishers who paid a fortune for a few days on the beat. The stick could have been left by one of the lads from the village. Bob turned a blind eye to the boys taking a fish or two. They weren't greedy and the folk of the glen, in his and everybody else's opinion – except those of the estate manager and the law – believed they had a right to take fish from their river.

But there were tinkers and poachers from Glasgow who would fill a van with fish, given half a chance. They would use home-made bombs of weedkiller and sugar in paint tins to float fish to the surface in pools, or cyanide which took all the oxygen out of the water and suffocated them. He'd seen whole stretches of river poisoned that way and knew it took years for the stocks to recover. The poisons some of the bastards used killed every living thing for miles. The only benefit was, he thought, slapping his face again and feeling the crunch of an insect belly split under his fingers, that they also killed the mosquitoes. It was a small mercy.

It was past midnight when the first movement alerted him. Bob was surprised to find himself almost dozing off despite the midges, but the flicker of motion ahead brought him wide awake. Over the murmuring of the water he heard a low voice and an equally low reply, though he couldn't make out the words.

Very slowly he reached beside him for the gun and brought it up, keeping it in the shadow of the tree lest the movement give him away. With his left hand he checked for the big flashlight that dangled from his webbing belt. In the shadows, he grinned to himself.

There were two of them. They came, backlit by the moon, right into the trees, hands in pockets, heads down. There at the edge of the woods there was still enough light to see by. They kept close to the river, talking in muted tones. Bob didn't recognise them as they furtively passed within twenty yards of where he crouched by the tree. He let them get further. They weren't expecting any trouble because they made little effort to move really quietly. They didn't sound like professionals, which was good, because that meant they wouldn't put up much of a fight.

They passed Bob and went deeper into the forest, following the Corrie upstream. One of them had a sack over his shoulder, perhaps a net. Whatever it was, he'd have it before the morning, plus any fish he let them take out. He suppressed a chuckle as he thought of letting them do the hard work for his benefit. And there would be a bonus from the estate when he hauled the two of them up to the house and called the police down from Craigard to make an arrest.

He gave them a few minutes and then began to follow them. He knew every inch of the bank of the river and could trail them quickly and silently. Sooner or later, most likely sooner, they'd stop at one of the pools and fix their net and then he'd scare the living daylights out of them.

About five hundred yards up from where the river tumbled out into the open the two figures reached a series of deep pools carved from the stone by the force of the water where the fish crowd in the depths gathering strength for their leap upstream. The lowest and shallowest is the Priest's Hole, fed by the run-off from the next one upstream, by far the deepest and known in the glen, for as long as anybody could remember, as the Witch's Cauldron. It was aptly named. The bore of the water had sculpted out a massive hole in the hard rock over thousands of years. It was maybe twenty yards across and the water was so deep it was black as ink. Trees crowded round letting hardly a beam of the bright moon through. Where the odd sliver of light hit the water, it reflected back in sapphire flashes. The sides of the pool were slimed and slippery. Upstream they were overhung with clinging ivy. Down at the lip there was a narrow channel where the water cascaded into the Priest's Hole. The only sound was the tumble of the falls, a deep booming thunder that reverberated back from the overhanging trees. If Bob McCourt had wanted to poach fish, this was the place he would have chosen. This was the place the two dark figures had chosen.

Bob picked a position, huddled among the roots of a giant sycamore where they looped out of the ground in a tangled twist. From there he could see everything, despite the gloom. His eyes, more accustomed to the darkness than those of the poachers because of the long wait in the trees, picked up every flash of light from the water. He could make out the two shapes standing near the head of the pool, heads close together, the waterfall roar drowning out every sound. From where he sat, he had the advantage. They had nowhere to go except past him, unless they wanted to try to climb the falls or take a gamble on the ivy taking their weight on the smooth rock. Neither seemed a likely option.

The figures moved downstream towards him. The bag went down on a rock and one of them drew out the roll of net. It was simple, much like a tennis net. There were ropes at each corner and these were looped around protruding roots on either side. One of them got a couple of rounded stones and weighted the bottom of the net just ahead of the smooth runnel where the water flowed out. Everything was set.

Watching from only five yards away, still as stone, Bob McCourt wondered what the next step would be. The poachers hadn't cut any big branches to sweep the depths for fish and drive them into the net. He wondered about cyanide and had almost decided to make a move there and then to prevent a stretch of the river being poisoned. He decided to hold back for a few minutes more – and then it happened.

One of the men reached into the bag. Bob saw his arm jerk and there was a tiny metallic tinkle, then a snap. The man's arm moved in a lazy arc. Something hit the water with a splash that was drowned by the waterfall. The two figures moved quickly away from the water to stand beside a tree.

The explosion happened less than twenty seconds later with such force that the ground shivered. For an instant the water went flat as ice, as if it had suddenly solidified. Over the sound of the waterfall there was a deep muffled *thud*, like a dull shock in the small bones of the ear. The water did not erupt. A froth of bubbles boiled in the centre of the pool and, when they had burst, a grey vapour floated upwards and was quickly dispersed.

'Bloody hand grenade,' Bob McCourt said aloud, though even *he* didn't hear the words.

Apart from the froth on the surface, that was it. It was as simple and as quick – and virtually noiseless – as that. Down in the depths, thirty feet below the surface, the shock wave would have slammed out from the explosion, smacked against the smooth pool walls and reverberated back to the centre again, diminishing as it went. A hundred yards from the pool, the noise would hardly have been heard.

Bob kept still for another few seconds and then saw the stretched net quiver as the first fish floated into it. Four more in quick succession shook the net violently and the ropes went taut as they took the strain, the nylon netting bulging downstream as it filled. The figures reappeared from cover and made their way quickly to the runnel. One, slightly taller than the other, crossed the narrow channel and untied the ropes on the far side, keeping them tight as he came back across. The other did the same, only yards from where Bob sat.

'Fuckin' brilliant,' the nearest one called out. 'Good on, the Territorials. Feel the *weight* of that net.'

Bob smiled. He could see there were more than a dozen fish in there, stunned or dead but all unmarked. They were big ones too, by the looks of it. And he knew where the hand grenade had come from. Most likely one of the poachers was a part-time soldier practising night manoeuvres. He'd see how he reacted to an ambush.

The gamekeeper let them haul the net onto the bank and watched as they tied it up into a bag of fish. They slung it, grunting, between them and started moving downstream at the edge of the trees.

Bob stood up and flicked the switch on his flashlight. The beam stabbed the night and caught the leading man straight in the face. The fellow let out a wail of fright and Bob laughed.

'Oh Jesus Christ, my *eyes*.'

His hands flew to his face and he dropped the end of the net. The other man was suddenly thrown off-balance as the heavy bag of fish swung down and hit him on the knees with a solid thump. The momentum swept his legs from underneath him and he tumbled to the bank, landing with an audible whoosh of breath on top of the pile.

'Bastard! I'm *blind*!' his partner bawled. Bob kept the six-cell light pinned on his face.

The other poacher scrambled to his feet, cursing loudly and eloquently. He took two steps forward, trying to clamber over the net-load of fish, slipped on the scales and went crashing down again with a yelp. By an amazing stroke of luck his face missed all the rocks. His chin connected with one of the few pockets of gravel which saved him from fracturing his skull on hard granite, but even then his teeth clicked shut on his tongue and nearly cut it in half. Now incoherent with fright, anger and pain and stunned by the fall, he groped to his knees, got to his feet and then slipped on a smooth rock. His arms pinwheeled for balance. Bob flicked the torch beam towards him and saw the man hugging air as he did a slow topple backwards. He went straight into the water with a spectacular splash. As his feet disappeared below the surface, Bob laughed again. The poachers' expedition had become pure farce.

He swung the beam around and pinioned the other man in light.

He stood there, crouched, holding his hand up in front of his face.

'Get that light off me, you cretin,' he growled.

'Now, now, lad. That's no way to talk. Want to try it again.'

'You're blinding me.'

'Don't worry about it. I know the way out of here.'

The man's other hand came up from his baggy jacket pocket. The other hand came down with surprising speed and Bob saw a finger hook out.

'Right,' the stranger shouted. 'Don't move or I pull the pin.'

Bob didn't move.

'I don't suppose you can see this,' he said, making sure the beam stayed on the other man's face. He risked a glance to the left and saw the other man haul himself out of the water on the far side of the runnel. 'I've got a twelve-bore pointing straight at your crotch. Make one move to cock that thing and I'll de-cock you, get the picture? So let's not be a silly boy, eh? If that pin comes out, you won't have time to throw it. Think about it.'

The man paused, half-crouched, his finger still hooked in the ring, eyes turned away from the light.

'Throw it, Fergie. Kill the bastard.' The voice came from the other side of the river. Bob kept the torch beam on the nearest man's face. Without warning he swung the gun to the left and squeezed the trigger. In the close confines of the hollow the thunder of the hy-max shells was deafening. The shot hit the edge of the pool only yards from where the soaked man was standing. The water erupted with the force of it and sent a huge spray of water into the air.

'Shit. He's off his fuckin' head.' The man yelled in a voice so high it was almost a scream.

Bob swivelled the barrel back just in time to see the nearest man leap sideways behind the big sycamore. Over to the left the second man's feet crunched gravel and he disappeared into the trees.

'Hold it,' Bob shouted. Something came clanking down onto the rocks, then he too jumped to the side. He got about fifteen yards into the trees and threw himself behind another trunk, keeping his face well down in the dead leaves.

The explosion wasn't what he expected. The shotgun was louder. There was a loud crack like a firework and a ripping sound followed on its heels. For the space of twenty yards around the explosion there was a noise like rainfall. Bob lifted his head from where it was pressed into the mulch and felt the droplets hit him in the face. One sniff told him it wasn't rainfall at all. It was small pieces of fresh fish that had been blasted to salmon paté by the grenade.

'Damn,' he said to himself. 'What a waste!'

He heaved himself to his feet and found his gun a full ten feet from where he'd been sprawled. Out in the trees he could hear the crashing footsteps of the poacher on his side of the Corrie. The man was making no pretence. He was running away at full tilt, through the dark forest. A thump and a muffled groan testified to the fact that his night vision hadn't returned. The crashing, lumbering footsteps continued, dwindling with distance, as the man headed into the trees, in the opposite direction from which he'd come. The other fellow had disappeared into the darkness. The roar of the waterfall hid his direction.

Bob picked the gun up and stood for a moment, wondering what to do. The poachers must have had a car and he debated heading downstream out of the trees to find what would most likely be a beat-up transit van parked in the hedge at the side of the road. Eventually, he knew, the men would find their way out of the trees and head back to their wheels. He was certain they wouldn't try to walk away. The Linn Road was miles from anywhere.

On reflection, though, it wouldn't be much of a problem to find the fellow who was barging through the undergrowth. Bob knew the forest better than anybody and the poacher was making enough noise to be heard from fifty yards away, despite the muting effect of the trees. And he would be leaving a trail a child could follow. Bob decided to catch him. The thought of another grenade didn't worry him. It was unlikely a poacher would carry three. Even if he was a part-time soldier, nobody would need that many to clean out a salmon pool. Despite that, he switched the flashlight off and waited a few minutes to let his eyes grow accustomed to the gloom. Here and there a shaft of moonlight cut through the thick foliage, vertical bars of silver catching the motes of pollen and dust and the fluttering wings of tree-moths.

Bob took a breath, cursed himself for letting both men go so easily, and started to follow. Ahead there was another yell as the fleeing man took another collision and the gamekeeper smirked to himself. By the time he caught up, the other man might have killed himself, or at least broken a leg.

He walked steadily, avoiding the tangles of straggly juniper and the bramble runners that snaked out like jagged ropes to snare his boots. Overhead, glimpsed in a beam of moonlight, an owl flicked silent wings and was gone into the shadows. A mosquito whined by his ear and he managed to slap it on his cheek before it sunk its bloodsucking nozzle into him. They were moving away from the river. Beyond the tangles and down a slope, the water-roar shut itself off and the forest became quiet save for the rattling of high branches stirred by the falling wind. Ahead, the poacher's progress was easily heard. The man was not used to the country, no matter what he knew about salmon. His best bet, Bob knew, would have been to find a fallen log and lie under it, until dawn if need be. Running around in Fasach Wood was no job for a city boy, no matter how many TA hand grenades you had in your pockets. The gamekeeper almost sauntered along, thinking about how he was going to kick the living shit out of the poacher before he hauled him out of the woods and up to the estate house. The temptation to whistle while he walked was hard to fight down.

13

In the past five minutes Fergie McGhee had run through as many emotions as he knew he possessed.

He'd enjoyed the thrill of nervous tension as he and Malky Miller had crept into the forest beside the river. He'd experienced a surge of pleasure when the grenade had worked. (Fergie was not in the territorials, but he knew a few folk who were. He drank in the same dingy city bar as they did. You could buy anything there.) He had felt a twist of glee when the net had started to bulge under the weight of fish and he counted them in. There were at least a dozen big fish, easily worth a few hundred under the counter in any hotel. Easy pickings for a summer stroll in the country, even if the midges were biting something fierce. He wondered how the country bumpkins put up with the little flying terrors. If he'd seen Bob McCourt's face he'd have known they didn't put up with them too well at all.

Then the light stabbed his eyes and the pain jabbed like hot knives. Instant tears blinded him and dazzling orange and purple lights danced under his eyelids.

Equally instant fear almost made his bowels void themselves. It was touch and go, and the small damp patch on the front of his trousers showed that more than fear had spurted.

Hot on the heels of the fear came the anger. That was an instinctive thing. He'd heard stories of what gamekeepers did to poachers before they were handed over to the police, and with his record of previous convictions that would mean a two-year stretch in Drumbain Jail, and two years beating the Drum was not a prospect to be relished.

The man with the light, whoever the bastard was, told him the gun was pointed at his groin and Fergie felt everything down there cringe and try to climb for cover. He'd never felt so exposed in his life. Then Malky shouted, the man swung the gun away and Fergie made his move. As he ducked away from the water the nerves down his spine had been wound taut like banjo strings waiting for the twelve-bore to roar again. The grenade had gone off first.

Now he was blundering through the forest, heading God alone knew where, but at least he'd got away. Twice in the past minute he'd barked his shin on fallen logs. He could feel a trickle of blood run down the inside of his jeans. Another twice he'd slammed into unseen tree-trunks. The first collision had flattened his nose which was bleeding quite freely down onto his mouth and chin. The second time he had caught the tree with a shoulder and knocked himself to the ground.

It is fair to say that Fergie McGhee was not having a fun night, but at least, he told himself, he was getting away, and he would heal. And then, he swore, he'd come back to this one-horse town and find the maniac with the shotgun and make him sorry he'd ever met Fergus McGhee.

He blundered on, hands outstretched, to avoid barging into trees, skinning his knuckles painfully in the process. Somewhere to the right some animal screeched like a woman and his heart leapt into his throat. He had no idea what kind of animals lived in a place like this and he didn't want to meet anything that sounded like that.

Fergie McGhee heard a noise to the left. *Running water.* He veered towards it, crashing through bracken and brambles and feeling his jeans tear in a dozen places. In twenty paces he reached the side of the river. He paused for a moment, turning his head this way and that. A short distance downstream, the river was nipped in by two brackets of rock. Spanning them was a huge tree-trunk, grey in the moonlight, that had blown down across the water to form a natural bridge. The trunk was at least six feet wide and he could cross it easily. He debated doubling back and following the flow of the water down to the edge of the forest but there was always the possibility of running smack into the man with the shotgun who might be less than happy about having a grenade thrown at him. The thought of those double barrels pointing at his groin made Fergie's mind up for him. There was enough light from the moon here, where the tree-branches failed to meet over the river, for him to find his way across the old deadfall. The bark was dry and rough and wide as a path. At the far end, the trunk forked several times into thick limbs for him to step down onto the far bank. Beyond the dead branches there was a tangle of willowherb and cow parsley – though Fergie didn't know what the hell it was and cared even less – that crackled as he passed through. Then there were some trees trailing low branches which he ducked and found himself in a moonlit clearing and, beyond the next stand of close-packed trees, a wider glade where a massive tree stood alone.

As he made his way forwards a black shape came out of the shadows and touched him on the shoulder. Everything below his belt loosened and threatened to fertilise the forest floor.

'Oh, Jesus,' Fergie groaned.

'Shut the hell up, *eejit*,' a voice told him urgently.

'Malky. Oh my . . . You daft bugger. You scared the *keich* out of me.' Fergie's heart was trying to hammer its way out of his ribs.

'Sshhh!' his pal urged. 'Did you lose him?'

'Aye. I just kept runnin'.'

'Was there just one of him?'

'Never saw anybody else.'

'Good. What next?'

'Get the fuck out of here.'

'Aye, but which way?'

'We should stay on this side. How'd you get across?'

'The stream's shallow up at the top of the pot-holes. Heard you coming like a herd of elephants. I thought it was that nutter with the gun. Nearly shit myself.'

'*You* nearly . . . ?' Fergie hissed, trying to keep his voice down. 'When you touched me I nearly had a heart attack.'

Malky giggled.

'There's nothin' funny about it.'

'But we got away,' Malky said, still chortling. 'We can come back another time. This place could make us a fortune.'

'Aye, but first we have to get out of here.'

Malky jerked his head back. 'C'mon. Let's go.'

Fergie McGhee followed. The two of them moved slowly forward through the small clearing and started to pick their way through the close-packed trees.

Malky stopped and held up a hand. He was just a black shadow in the gloom and Fergie almost bumped into him.

'What is it?' he whispered.

'I saw something. Out there.' He pointed ahead to the wider clearing where the massive tree stood alone reaching for the moon. Fergie peered forwards. There was a movement, close to the base of the tree. There was someone there but, in the dim light and at that distance, neither man could make out much shape.

'Is it him?'

'Nobody else in this bloody place, is there?'

They backed away and turned to retrace their steps, Fergie taking the lead. Then something reached down from the trees and grabbed Malky Miller by the head.

It happened so smoothly and silently that he didn't have a chance to cry out. A small surprised grunt escaped him and that was all. An enormous pressure gripped his skull and he was swung right off the forest floor. His feet kicked frantically at the air and a huge pain blossomed in his neck.

Fergie McGhee beckoned to his friend to hurry up. He scuttled on about ten paces, trying to be as silent he could, before he stopped beside a tree and scanned ahead.

'Nobody there. Come on,' he whispered.

There was no response.

Fergie glanced back, expecting Malky to be at his shoulder. He was only mildly surprised to see that he wasn't.

He stood up, eyes sweeping the ground right and left, when a jittery dark movement at head height caught his eye. He peered into the gloom of the branches and picked out Malky's feet kicking in the air.

'Come on,' he hissed. 'Stop fartin' around.'

Malky made no response. The other man walked back the ten paces and reached up to grab his friend's ankle.

'We got no time for climbin' trees, arsehole.'

His fingers clutched Malky's ankle and, as they did, Fergie felt a weird *shivering* running through the other man's leg. He pulled tentatively and the leg kicked in a sudden spasm, sending a jolt through his arm.

'What in Chr—?' Fergie started to ask, when the movement in the branches let a shaft of moonlight in.

The lower half of Malky's face was contorted with agony, distorted with pressure. He could see the mouth wide open and a trickle of something that in the weird light looked black and oily,

143

but which Fergie knew with sudden freezing certainty was blood. His own mouth opened wide and he felt his stomach clench violently. Hot bile flooded his throat.

Malky was suspended by his head, his temples gripped in what looked like a hand.

A noise like a cough came out of the hanging man's mouth, then a blob of blood spattered to the ground. The moonlight glistened on a black bubble expanding from one nostril. Then something dark snaked out and looped around whatever was gripping Malky's head.

Fergie was still holding onto his friend's ankle. There was a low *crack* and then a shower of blood came raining down on him. The shadows moved again and *flexed,* and there was another crack and the whole of Malky's head imploded. The body went into a dreadful jittering spasm. The crazy, dangling legs kicked out, then went dreadfully limp. The sound of blood dripping onto the leaves was like heavy rain.

Fergie stood transfixed, still holding onto the ankle despite the urgent orders from his brain telling him to let it go. His mouth was wide open and his head was shaking from side to side as he tried to negate what he'd seen.

Blood dripped onto his head and shoulders. It had a warm metallic smell of old pennies. Above him, a black shadow moved and he felt a tug as Malky's body was drawn upwards, his fingers still clenched around the dead ankle. His arm was drawn straight, then he was pulled onto the tips of his toes. It was only when his consciousness realised that *he too* was about to be pulled up into that tree that some sort of reality smacked into his brain.

Whatever was up there in the tree had caught Malky by the head and it had killed *him*.

Belatedly, Fergie realised that the movement up there *was* the tree, the branches themselves, twisting and flexing.

Fergie understood what his brain was telling him but he couldn't believe it.

The branches were moving. Up *there* Malky's feet were slowly disappearing, hauled inch by inch into the thick canopy of broad, black leaves, and the twisting of *living wood* made a sound like saw teeth on Fergie's backbone.

'Oh,' he said, and it came out in a low moan. He backed away very slowly, unable to take his eyes off the disappearing boots.

He fetched up against another tree, almost tripping on the thick roots. He put a hand out to steady himself and felt *movement* under the bark. For an instant his fright was so intense that his vision faded to a blur and in that moment he had the dreadful notion, the nightmare idea, that he would faint.

Fergie McGhee took off like a hurdler. He leapt through the stand of cow parsley and willowherb, demolishing a man-sized track. Something snagged his boots and he almost fell headlong. He went down on one knee then came up running. He made it to the big deadfall across the river and scampered up the thick limbs like a monkey, then raced across the wide trunk like a sprinter. He skidded to a semi-stop just before the root-fan that spread ten feet above the ground and launched himself into the bracken on the far bank. Bramble runners hooked his jacket and jeans and he dragged himself out of their clutches. A little clear corner of his mind wished he'd never wasted that second hand grenade. He wished he'd brought a whole box of them.

Bob McCourt heard the crashing and blundering of the poacher as he tried to make his escape and followed at his own pace, knowing he could find the man easily. He probed deeper into the woods, where the trees crowded together tightly, covering about five hundred yards. Then, suddenly, the noise stopped.

The gamekeeper brought himself up sharply. He thought of the grenades and a small flutter of unease ran through him. Bob reckoned the chances of a third one were slim, but slim was far from *certain*. The man had stopped, that meant he was *waiting*. And if he was waiting, well, Bob didn't want to walk into an ambush. He stood there, keeping his body as close to a tree as possible, while he thought it out. Then, very slowly, he moved off to the right, making hardly a sound as he went.

The man up ahead would be down behind something, looking back the way he'd come. If he didn't have a grenade, he'd have a stout branch or a rock, anything he could lay his hands on to batter a gamekeeper's skull. The stakes in poaching were high. The sentences were heavy and Drumbain Jail was no holiday camp.

Bob had an advantage. He could move quickly and quietly and he knew the woodland. From the sound of the water, muffled now as he veered away, he could tell he was maybe a hundred yards from the river. Another hundred yards ahead, beyond a couple of dips, was the old moss-covered line of boulders that marked the ancient dry-stone dyke which was the original forest boundary before the turn of the century. Inside there, Fasach Wood hadn't been touched for generations. Beyond the wall the forest took a dip into a depression that was almost a mile wide and where the trees were so dense that the red deer avoided the place. Over the years Bob had found a few big bucks which had wandered in after the winter rut and got their spreading antlers caught in the tangles of crowded trees. They'd starved to death.

It took only five minutes, moving swiftly from tree to tree, to reach the dyke, a good distance north of where he'd last heard the noise of the running man. He'd heard nothing since, so he knew the poacher had not doubled back. The man didn't know how to walk in the forest. Bob clambered agilely over the line of boulders. They were big and furred with dank moss. He went down the other side of the four-foot mound on his backside, listening all the time and keeping one arm stretched ahead. Here it was pitch dark. The crowded trees excluded the moonbeams. The sound of the river was gone. All was quiet.

He squeezed himself between two trunks, almost losing a button off his jacket, and skirted a scraggy holly that snagged insistently at him. Something buzzed his ear and he shook his head irritably. He planned to go a further hundred yards just to be sure, down a dip and up the other side, over tangled roots that, in the dark, felt like stone serpents, before he started to veer left again.

Then, somewhere in front of him, he heard a noise, a small metallic *snick* that made him remember the grenade. Very slowly he moved his head, looking for a log under which he could roll in a hurry. Here, in this part, there were no logs. All the trees crowded upright, almost within a man's arm-span of each other. Their branches formed a black roof over his head.

He heard the metal *tink* again, twice in quick succession. Every nerve alert, he carefully moved forward. The forest here was unfamiliar, *strangely unfamiliar*, even in the darkness. When he'd come over the wall, he'd walked through a clump of big mushrooms that broke wetly under his feet. Right beside him there was a monstrous one, growing almost to his knees. Even in the dark he got an impression of wet sheen, of mottled skin. He passed it by, every footstep now carefully planted so as to *squeeze* the leaves underfoot, not crunch them. Here, however, most of the leaves were wet and mouldy. His foot sank several inches into the detritus before his weight found a solid underbase.

He rounded a tree, keeping his eyes firmly ahead where the space between the trunks was pitch blackness. He knew that in this light he could see nothing in front of him, but his peripheral vision, more suited to the dark, would catch any motion on either side as he moved forward.

Something caught his eye and he stopped again, not turning his head, but merely widening his eyes further. Very carefully he eased the gun barrel round to point in the direction of the motion. It stopped. There was nothing there, nothing except another big toadstool.

Bob let out his breath slowly. Mushrooms and toadstools couldn't harm him. Even so, he was struck by the strange growth. He'd never seen anything that size in all his years as a keeper. Even the big puffballs that grew on the south side only managed to swell to a foot or so across before they burst. These ugly things were huge. He could imagine a pixie sitting on one of them. A *big* pixie.

Bob sniffed and noticed a dank, almost fetid, smell about the place. The air was still, but it carried a whiff of corruption on it, a sweetness that tickled the throat, a slight bitterness that scraped the lining of the nose. And the insects here were more numerous. Something flicked past his ear with a hum rather than a whine. Up above, something even bigger rattled by on papery wings. Some insect tapped out a morse message on a dry branch.

His attention still focused ahead, Bob thought: 'This place is odd.'

He scraped past a juniper bush and again he heard the tinny noise. His heart gave a little leap, but he thought, calmly, if somebody was hiding, he wouldn't want to make a noise that would give his position away. It must be something else, maybe a tin can left by some tinkers, or even picnickers in the wood. He pressed forward and came into a little space where the trees crowded less densely. The noise came from the right and he turned slowly. It came from about head height and he carefully eased towards the source.

Chink, chink. Right beside his ear. He swivelled his head an inch at a time and then his eye caught a small glimmer. Hanging from the branches was a metal chain. Whatever tiny breath of wind that sneaked through the forest was moving it slightly, causing the links to hit against each other.

Bob McCourt let out a slow sigh of relief. Now he could get back to the main job of finding the hidden man. He reached out and pulled at the chain. It was caught on something further up. He pulled harder and Bob's whole body gave a start of alarm as something big and dark swung towards him.

'What the—?' he said, almost aloud.

Then the smell hit him and immediately his throat spasmed in a gag. The foul stench was thick in the still air, a cloud of putrescence that enveloped him.

Without thinking, he reached to his belt for the flashlight. His thumb found the button and a bright cone of light caught the thing that swung towards him, dangling from the branches.

An involuntary cry forced its way out of his mouth before he clenched it off.

The dreadful rotten corpse pendulumed slowly, hanging upside down. Its dead eyes were pits in white circles of bone. Its teeth, long and narrow, were black where they joined the jaw. Straggles of long matted hair trailed down from the fleshless skull.

The stench was awful. Bob felt his gullet open and close, then something twisted in his belly and he lost everything from lunch onwards. He stood there for a minute, head down, the hand holding the torch clenched against his midriff as the spasms lessened.

The hidden poacher almost forgotten, Bob straightened up and knuckled involuntary tears from his eyes. His vision cleared and as he brought the hand down from his face the flashlight flicked in a fast arc, giving him a subliminal flicker of another horror.

There was another body, on the next tree. He held the torch as steady as he could, though the beam wavered from side to side, and suddenly he wished he had never come out to catch the poachers. The corpse was imprisoned *within* the tree. It was as though the trunk had opened and then clamped around the dead face. Only the front of a horribly *squashed* skull protruded from the bark. On either side skeletal arms reached out in supplication.

148

'Oh, God,' Bob heard himself say. 'Oh, sweet fucking Je—'

Already he was backing off. Eyes riveted to the apparition, he took several shuffling steps straight back until he bumped into something solid. For an instant he had a vision of a tree opening up and swallowing *him* and he jerked away. He stood, gulping for breath, the stench still clogging his nostrils and the taste of bile hot and rasping at the back of his throat. Then the world sparked into shards of light. Bob reeled, dazed and fighting to retain consciousness. He didn't even pause to consider what had hit him with enough force to smack his head against the trunk. All he could feel was a terrible pain and waves of black nausea looping up from his empty stomach. He staggered forward, stumbling from side to side, unaware of what was happening, fists still clenched on his gun. He got to the dry-stone wall; he managed to get over the top and started to roll. His death-grip on the gun-stock loosened. The twelve-bore went flying into the night. It spun away into the darkness with Bob tumbling afterwards, mind still whirling. He landed against a fallen log, bounced, went over it and there was a huge flash. Something hit him in the leg with such force it almost tore it from his body. A vast pain burgeoned just below his groin, then everything faded away.

What hit Bob McCourt was Fergie McGhee. The gamekeeper hadn't even heard the man coming, so fixed was his attention on the corpses in the trees. The poacher was running blindly through the forest and, by some miracle, had missed every tree on his mad dash from the deadfall on the river and the terrible thing that had happened to Malky Miller beyond it. Fergie's mind was just one vast blank need to run. Instinct had taken over completely. There was no conscious thought. Only the picture of Malky's head splitting like an egg, and the dreadful expression on his contorted face.

Fergie had forgotten all about the gamekeeper. Frankly, he was in no position to give a damn. He was in a forest where the trees *moved* and he wanted out of there. He wanted out of there more than anything in the world and if he got away from these trees he intended to keep on running through open country and never set his foot inside a forest again.

He'd come blundering full-tilt along a natural pathway between the trees and had smacked into Bob McCourt. He hadn't even seen the flashlight. The force of the collision had slammed the other man back into a tree. Though he'd almost wrenched his arm out of its socket Fergie ran on blindly, not knowing where he was going. His route took him parallel to the wall as he jinked between trunks, leapt over rotten deadfalls and crashed through thickets. His face was scratched and his clothes were torn yet still he kept going. Then, in his panic, Fergie darted in another direction, back the way he had come, into the densest part of the forest.

The terrified poacher stumbled down into a hollow and slithered up the far side, holding on to gnarled roots to heave himself over the edge, all the time fearful that one of the roots would twist in his hand and make a snatch for him. Something razored out of the air on helicopter wings and spanged against his face, causing him to yelp in fright. Ahead there was a little dell where a few shafts of moonlight pierced to the forest floor and he made for that. As he ran pell-mell he failed to see a twist of honeysuckle rope that looped from one low branch to another. He ran into it and the thing writhed around his neck like a snake. His momentum carried him on and the impetus swung his feet away from him. He gasped once and the vine simply clenched. One hand reflexively jerked towards his neck. There was a snap and a terrible wrench of pain as his head was forced back. The tendrils, knotted and woody, tightened around his throat.

Fergie McGhee was vaguely aware of another snap as a neck tendon was wrenched off its bone. Fire sizzled at the base of his skull and then there was nothing at all.

The body twitched in a macabre dance for more than a minute and then all was still. A big insect swooped down from the overhanging branches and landed on the dead man's face. A long proboscis unrolled, flexed and then probed for the trickle of blood from his ear.

Bob McCourt came round groggily on the far side of the wall. For a moment he imagined he'd gone to sleep and rolled over on top of the campfire. He'd been out camping in the forest with the rest of the boys and . . .

Reality swooped in on him. The dazed dream evaporated. He was lying in Fasach Wood. His leg was a huge sea of hurt. What had happened?

Bob tried to remember. He had a vague recollection of falling. Falling from where? The memory wouldn't come. Another memory looped in. His gun. It had spun away. There had been the flash and the roar and his leg . . .

Christ, his leg hurt.

He reached down and felt a pulpy wet mass.

'I've been shot,' he murmured to himself. 'I've been *shot*.'

How it had happened he couldn't recall. He didn't even remember being slammed against the tree and staggering dazed and almost unconscious for fifty yards towards the wall.

He pulled himself up to a sitting position, face screwed up as rivers of lava ran up and down his thigh. The flashlight on its lanyard lay beside him. He switched it on and aimed the beam at his leg. The mess gave him a terrible fright. Blood soaked him from groin to ankle. He could even see where it pulsed slowly from a gaping wound a hand's span from his crotch. The flesh was ragged and torn to tatters.

'Oh, *shite!*' It was the best he could come up with.

His vision wavered again and Bob realised he was going to die unless he did something. He didn't know how long he had been lying there and how much blood he had lost, but already he felt a creeping lethargy steal coldly over him. Using enormous effort, he dug his hands into his poacher's pockets and rummaged around among penknife and cartridges until he found the braided steel rabbit snare. He managed to snake the thin flexible wire around his leg and cinched it tight. The brass ring at the loop join locked the noose in place. Bob gritted his teeth and threw his weight on it, feeling the wire bite into the puckered and torn skin. The pain flared blindingly but he kept hauling until the flesh was crimped in like an hourglass. He slumped back breathless, sparks flashing in front of his eyes, and gave himself a few moments before angling the beam onto his tattered thigh. The pulse of blood was gone, which was good. But he was going to have to *move*. If he didn't get to a hospital, he was going to die, and damned soon.

With a vast effort, Bob McCourt hauled himself to his feet and stumbled away up the slope. Every few steps he got dizzy and had to rest, but something inside spurred him on. He had to get out of Fasach Wood. If he stayed here, he would die. He focused his mind on that one aim and dragged himself, yard after exhausting yard.

It took him more than an hour to traverse the half a mile to the edge of the forest, using a broken branch as a crutch, and another twenty minutes to cross the fields and get to the road where he'd parked his jeep. By this time the first pink tinges of dawn were colouring the peaks of the Douglas Hills.

He made it across a five-barred gate then his strength gave out. Bob flopped to the ground and lay still.

Alec Stirling found him an hour after that lying beside the road. The postman came trundling down in his van, as he did every morning, and passed Bob's jeep. He craned round in his seat to wave to the gamekeeper, but there was no one in the vehicle. Alec turned the corner and saw the body lying beside the gate. He jammed his foot on the brake so hard he almost put the little van into a spin.

Bob McCourt was barely alive. Alec could feel a flicker of pulse at the man's neck and, without further ado, he lugged him into the back of the van. He didn't care how many letters were soaked in blood. Bob was a *friend*. The postman made it to Lochend in record time. The van had never, in all its fifteen years, travelled beyond sixty miles an hour. Alex made it do ninety and hardly braked on the bends. All the time he was yelling at Bob to hold on and not die. Bob had come round a little, but was not completely conscious. In the last mile before Lochend, he started screaming in the back of the van.

'The trees . . . oh my Christ . . . the trees.'

Alec Stirling didn't care what he said, as long as he stayed alive until he got him to Lochend. He got his package there in record – and highly illegal – time. The keeper was rushed into emergency, where the nurses started filling his collapsing veins with plasma. They worked on him for eight solid hours, at the end of which Bob McCourt was barely alive.

By the time the operation was over, everybody in Linnvale knew that Bob McCourt had been shot, though nobody knew any of the whys and wherefores. Alec Stirling had got his priorities right. He got Bob to hospital and then carried out his next major task.

He phoned Martin Thornton, like any good stringer would do.

14

Caitlin Brook was building up speed on the level road that led to the lower bridge over the Corrie. The afternoon sun was high and hot on her cheek and, though the wind had died at dawn, her thin blouse ruffled with the breeze of her own making. The wheels hissed smoothly on the dry road as she moved, elbows now resting on the padded arms, one finger just touching the brake lever.

There was no traffic on the Linn Road and, even if there were, she had become a familiar sight by now. The occasional farmer in his tractor, Alec Stirling in his van, anybody in Linnvale would give her right of way on the flat stretch. Even Donnie MacKinnon's bowser drivers, hauling their tankers up from the Lochside road, would slow down with a grind of gears and a sharp cough of air brakes when they saw Caitlin on the move.

Nobody offered to help any more. One of the benefits of small village life is that everybody quickly finds out what's wanted and leaves it at that. Caitlin didn't like to be pushed like a baby in a pram.

She came this way every day, rain or sun, though she preferred the hot dry weather. From her house to the village there was a slight gradient which meant an effort, but was good for her muscle tone. Down past her house, heading to the bend that swept the road alongside the forest and down to the Loch, it was almost flat, but the momentum on the upper slope carried her almost quarter of a mile in an exhilarating run.

She'd heard about Bob McCourt from Jean Fintry, who ran the corner shop and stocked everything a village would need and more besides. There were few shops left like it, which Caitlin thought was a pity. Jean, who was in her fifties, had always been a jolly, plump, grey-haired woman. In the past few weeks, Caitlin noticed, she'd been tinting her hair and doing it well. It was gradually shading back to black, but so slowly and evenly that the change almost looked natural. The shopkeeper had also lost a lot of weight. She looked years younger.

'Morning, dear,' she'd called out in her normal fashion when Caitlin had swung the door open. The little bell on the catch at the lintel had tinkled merrily.

Caitlin smiled up at her and Jean beamed back, her face a picture of robust country humour.

'Great morning for a run in your hot rod,' she said and Caitlin laughed. Jean never called it a wheelchair. It was a racer, or a bogey or a hot rod. Occasionally, when she let gravity swoop her down the hill, Caitlin could think of it that way too. 'What a night we've had, eh?'

'What's that?'

'Oh, you won't have heard. Bob McCourt, you know the Douglas ghillie?'

Caitlin allowed that she knew him. There were few in the glen she didn't know by now.

'He's in the infirmary. Got shot in the leg last night. Touch and go it was, and still is, so I hear.'

'What happened?'

'Nobody knows for sure. Big Eck Stirling found him at the side of the road down beyond the Lee Brae. Covered in blood he was, poor soul. Had a terrible wound in his leg, so Eck says. He ran him to the hospital fast as he could.'

'Who did it?'

'They think maybe he fell and his gun went off, though that's not like Bob. He's always been a canny bugger. Tommy Dunbar said he thought he heard some noise down in the woods last night. It could have been poachers, but who knows. They'll have to wait until Bob can tell them, and he's still in the intensive care. Doctor Gregor took Rhona down there early this morning. His wife is watching the wee ones.'

Caitlin made the usual noises, although she didn't really know the gamekeeper well. She'd seen him pass on the road and he always gave her a cheery wave from his jeep.

'And then Dr Gregor was called out to the Haldane place the other night,' Jean continued with her news bulletin. 'They say the wee boy and girl got hurt down in the woods. Got bit by something, so the story goes.'

'Are they all right?' Caitlin asked. She knew the Haldane family well. She often saw the children playing in the field on the other side of the stream which meandered past her garden and occasionally Ben and Dorrie would cross over to her side and have a lemonade with her as she sat painting. She liked them both and was fond of Duncan and Rose Haldane who, despite the problems they'd had over the past year, were good neighbours.

'Aye, seems so. A few scratches and scrapes.'

'And what bit them?'

'Oh, I don't know. A wasp or something. Came out in big lumps. But they're fine now. Got a bit of a scare, I shouldn't wonder, but Duncan should know better than to let them play in the woods. I never let any of mine in there when they were wee. But that man, he's so stubborn. Look at the trees he's planning to cut down.' Jean frowned and shook her head.

Caitlin smiled again. She'd forgotten that Jean Fintry was in the Preservation Society along with the minister's wife and half the women of the village. She was smiling because the thought struck her that Jean and the others were so concerned to save the forest, but she suspected the woman wouldn't set foot in the place.

She bought fresh milk, butter and bread and placed an order for some groceries which Jean's teenage son would deliver later in the day, then wheeled herself out of the shop, using her weight and balance to flip the small front wheels over the low wooden step at the door. She turned right on the main road and rumbled over a cobbly patch, feeling her teeth chatter with the vibration and then manoeuvred, with some small effort, into the tearoom. The place was alive with the buzz of conversation. In Linnvale the Glen Tearoom, run by Meg Balfron, was more of a meeting place than the church annexe or the community hall, and even rivalled the bar at the Douglas Arms. It was very twee, with doilies and delicate cups and little silver tiered platters with fresh scones and fancies in pyramids, but it was, for most part, the centre of the village.

When Caitlin swung the door wide enough to take her wheelchair, the conversation died for a strange moment, then a familiar voice called out: 'Over here, my dear. Come on, Molly, make room for young Caitlin.'

A chair scraped back, a cup chinked on a saucer and the buzz of conversation switched on again as if it had never stopped. Caitlin wound round one small table where four women sat together, elbows on the tablecloth, cups raised to their mouths. They all seemed to be speaking at once.

Gail Dean, the minister's wife, who was also chairman of the Society and had a seat on the community council, called to Meg Balfron for another cup and she moved her seat sideways to let the younger woman join the group.

'I heard about Bob McCourt,' Caitlin said. Beside her Molly Carr, who was one of the two teachers in the little primary school up the hill road, made a disappointed face.

'You should come here *first* instead of getting the news from Jean next door. What's the point of knowing the gossip if somebody always beats you to it?'

Everybody laughed. Caitlin glanced around the table. Here were the stalwarts of the community. Agnes Gillon was the wife of perhaps the most successful farmer in the glen. She'd had her own troubles, Caitlin knew. Once you lived for a while in a place like this, everybody's family history was slowly unravelled. Only a few years ago her sister-in-law had shot both herself and her crippled son down on their farm at Ardmhor, not ten miles away over the hills. It had been a tragedy that had made all the newspapers at the time, before the even bigger tragedy that had happened in that village.

Fiona Herron lived in a big house next to the manse. She was a widow, whose husband had been something big in legal circles in Glasgow and had left her very well found after his heart attack. Despite the arthritis that gnawed at her hands and warped her fingers into angry-looking misjointed hooks, she was a robust woman who had thrown herself into community work since the week she'd been widowed. Caitlin knew her daughter Susan who came along to help with the youngsters in the Summerplay classes.

Gail Dean, however, was the one they all deferred to. She was a delightful woman, tall and well-groomed. Her friendly face had been pretty in its time and was now what the men would call *handsome*. She had clear skin and near-perfect teeth and a good word and a ready smile for everyone. Her hair, which had been fair in her youth, had gone prematurely silver and was cut in a short, wavy, almost girlish style. Caitlin noticed that Gail too was bowing to the years. Among the silver, she noticed threads of gold catching the light that spangled through the waved translucent glass window. Everybody thought Gail, or Howling Gail, as she was affectionately known because of her singing in the church choir, would have made a great mother, and everybody knew that it was a great sorrow to the minister's wife that she and John were unable to have children. She bore that sadness bravely and treated the whole village and surrounding farm families as her own.

'You're right. Jean told me, but she didn't know too much,' Caitlin admitted, giving the women an opening. 'I only heard he was shot in the leg.'

'Well, Alec Stirling deserves a medal for what he did,' Agnes said. 'He found him nearly dead with his leg nearly taken off.' Agnes paused and for a second she'd a faraway look in her eye. The rest of the group knew that if anybody knew what sort of damage a shotgun could do, *she* did. The only person who knew even more was Caitlin Brook. 'He saw Bob's Land-Rover parked at the edge of the road and was looking out for him. Everybody knows Alec is a nosy big so-and-so, but if he wasn't poor Bob would have been dead by now.'

'Does anybody know what happened?'

'Everybody *thinks* they know,' Gail said. 'But until the police get a chance to talk to Bob, it's anybody's guess.'

'I heard something down in the woods last night. It woke me up.' Everybody turned to Caitlin. 'I thought it was thunder, but there was no rain.'

'That was probably the gun going off. It can carry for miles. In August you can't get a minute's peace for the shooters up on the hills.'

'No. I don't think it was that. I know what a shotgun sounds like.'

There was a small silence that stretched on for a few moments, then Gail reached out a hand and placed it on top of hers.

'Of course you do, my dear.'

'Oh, don't be embarrassed. I didn't mean that at all,' Caitlin said. 'I wasn't even thinking about that.' She smiled to show them she meant it. In fact, the connection between shotguns and her own injury hadn't crossed her mind at that moment.

'Jimmy McGregor said Bob was taking a look down at the Corrie,' Fiona resumed the flow. 'He thought somebody might have been after the salmon. Jimmy's in a dreadful state. He took a

157

night off and went to the pictures with his Alison. He's saying it wouldn't have happened if he'd been there with Bob.'

'Might have been worse,' Molly Carr said. 'It could have been *him* too.'

'What's happening now?'

'The sergeant from Craigard took a couple of men along by the Corrie this morning,' Fiona said. 'Nobody's heard anything since. He's not from Linnvale, so he wouldn't say anything. We'll have to wait until Alec Stirling comes back with the mail. If anybody can find out, he can.'

'I heard there was some trouble up at the Haldane place,' Caitlin volunteered.

'Not enough, if you ask me,' Molly said drily. Gail slapped her down firmly.

'Now, Molly, there's no bad in Duncan Haldane. We might disagree with what he's doing, but we wouldn't wish any trouble on him and his family.'

Well said, Caitlin thought.

Gail turned to her. 'He's had a lot of trouble, you know. That's what's made him decide to build those cabins and cut down the trees on his side of the wood. If things had been better for him he wouldn't be doing it. I feel quite strongly about the whole thing. If you have a way of life that's good then you should make an effort to protect it and that's what we're doing. Maybe we can recruit you?'

'I don't know enough about it. I'm too new here.'

'Nonsense, girl, you were raised here, weren't you?'

'Summers and Easters, yes,' Caitlin agreed.

'I knew your grandparents. We all did. Fine people. Old Morag Brook would have been with us, you know.'

'Yes, probably. She was an old battle-axe at times,' Caitlin said fondly. 'But I can't make up my mind. I don't fancy the idea of the whole valley being built over, but I sympathise with a man trying to earn a living.'

'Despoiling the place,' Molly put in. Gail held up a placatory hand.

'Let's not lose tempers on a nice morning like this. We still have a chance with the secretary of state. After that we can decide what else to do. We have to go through the proper channels.' Molly

Carr narrowed her eyes and sipped her tea. Caitlin got the impression that Molly would go through *any* channels to get her own way. 'Anyway, I understand young Ben and little Dorothy are fine. They only got a fright. Everybody knows it's dangerous down in Fasach Wood. They should keep out of there.'

That was the second time in less than half an hour that Caitlin had heard that. Of all the people in Linnvale, she was the only one who *couldn't* go into the forest because the trails were rough and narrow and she'd never get her wheelchair along them. She wondered, briefly, what was so special about that belt of trees to get people so worked up. And she wondered why people said it was *dangerous* to go down there. She had never heard that phrase used before. Now she had heard it twice.

The conversation meandered on, changing direction, hopping from subject to subject. At about ten o'clock Caitlin wheeled herself back from the table. She left some money on the doily – despite protests from the other four – and eased herself out of the door. The other women watched her go. She reached back to swing the door closed and saw Gail give her a friendly wave. Molly Carr was looking less cheery.

Caitlin rumbled over the cobbles once more with the bag of provisions balanced on her lap. A shadow loomed beside her.

'Hey, Kate, I was speaking to a friend of yours today.'

She stopped her wheelchair and turned, squinting against the sun.

Big Alec Stirling was standing on the pavement, his wide mailsack slung from a shoulder. His eyes crinkled over the glasses that had slipped down his nose as he favoured her with his customary grin.

'Oh?'

'Aye. Martin Thornton, your reporter fellow. Wasn't he down at your place the other day with a bottle of wine? I was hoping there was a wee romance on-going. Nice bloke, Martin. Pays well too.'

The penny dropped.

'Ah. You took Bob to the hospital and then phoned the newspaper.'

'Well, at least I went to the hospital first,' Alex said quite candidly. 'If it was somebody I didn't know, I might have called him *before* I went.'

Caitlin laughed out loud.

'At least you're honest. I just don't know why you didn't become a reporter yourself.'

'What, and join that rat race?' Alec shook his head as if the thought was preposterous. 'I tried it after I left school. I joined the *Craigard Herald* and left after a week. All they wanted me to do was cover coffee mornings.' He arched his back and stretched, shifting the weight of the mailbag. 'No. I've got it made here. This job's fine for me. No stress and no strain and a cup of tea at every door. And any stories I get I just phone them in. It's the life.'

'I'll bet. A cup of tea and more besides.'

'Any rumours to that effect are just calumnies on my character,' Alec said, shoving the glasses back up his nose with his middle finger, but he was laughing as he did it. You just couldn't offend him. Everybody knew that the tall affable postman was welcome in more than a few crofts on his mailround. They said he could talk the hind legs off a donkey, and Caitlin believed it.

'Here, I've got news for you. I'll tell you first before the old biddies get a hold of it and tear it to shreds.' Alec looked around, almost furtively, then hunkered down beside the wheelchair. Caitlin was grateful for no longer having to screw her eyes against the direct sunlight and twist her neck awkwardly.

'They found his gun down near the river. The stock was broken where it had hit a rock and they found the place where Bob was when he was shot. It was covered in blood.' Alec paused.

Caitlin nodded.

'They reckon he took a tumble and his gun went off by accident.'

'And is he all right?'

'No. He's in pretty bad shape, but better than he was this morning. I thought I'd a corpse on my hands.'

'They say if it wasn't for you, he'd have died.'

'That's true enough. If I ever drive that fast again, I'll lock myself up. That's not good for my wee van, you know. I don't think it's recovered yet.' Alec laughed. Caitlin went along with it. She could see he was trying to deflect the compliment.

'Oh, and another thing nobody knows yet. They found a catch net at the Witch's Cauldron, so there must have been poachers about, even if they don't think they shot Bob, and Bob's not telling

160

anybody yet, though he was yelling his head off this morning. Talking rubbish too. The odd thing was that the net was all torn up and it was covered in bits of fish. That's a real puzzle for Sergeant Adams. But then, everything's a puzzle to that big useless eejit.'

Alec grinned again, having imparted his news. 'Anyway, what about the romance then?'

'What romance?'

'You and my pal Mister Thornton.'

'Sorry to disappoint you. No romance.'

'That's a shame. I thought I might have a scoop. I've my reputation to think of.'

'Well, don't go spreading rumours. Your Mr Thornton only wanted a story from me.'

'And what would that be?' Alec asked, eyebrows raised. Caitlin laughed out loud.

'You're incorrigible.'

'I hope that isn't a serious complaint?' Alec asked, face all innocence.

'No, pest. I'm not giving you any ammunition. He only wanted to do a follow-up on something he did before.'

'Thought so. I read that piece. Good story.'

'Maybe for the newspaper. Maybe for Mr Thornton.'

'Oh, I didn't mean—'

'No. I know you didn't, so don't worry about it. Anyway there is no romance. And if I hear any rumours to the contrary, I'll know who started them.'

'Would I ever?' Big Alec was all innocence again.

'Too true you would,' Caitlin said, with as much mock severity as she could muster. She failed miserably. 'Now, if you'd step aside and let a young lady go about on her business?'

The pair of them laughed. Caitlin shoved on the wheels and Alec stood up to let her pass. She moved a few yards then stopped and deftly swung the chair around. Alec had turned away to go on up the street.

'By the way. I think you *should* get a medal,' she called out.

He flashed her another cheerful grin.

'Does that mean the hero gets a kiss?'

'Some other time, you old rogue.'

'Not so old, ginger,' he shot back, laughing. Caitlin snorted and tossed her head as she spun the wheelchair. The sun caught her russet waves and flashed gold and copper. Then she was gone down the slope towards her cottage.

After lunch, when the sun was high over the birch trees that bordered the far end of her garden, Caitlin sat at her easel. She painted for a couple of hours and, while not dissatisfied with the result, she was surprised by it. She'd taken sketches of the scene along by the old bridge near the millhouse the day before, where the tall larch trees at the edge of the wood gave way to firs and, beyond, a mix of dark oaks. The light sketches were only for reference, just to get the shapes and the angles. She'd marked in shadow where the sun slanted through the edging foliage, casting slants of shade which contrasted with the upright lodgepole trunks.

In the garden she'd blocked in colour, using light washes of beige and grey to get the feel of it, then started fining out the shades of leaves, from the blue-grey of the conifers to the strong oak greens and the bright limes on the edge. There was a nice gradation of colour following the lines of shadow that gave a balance that appealed to her. At times like this her hand moved almost of its own volition while her mind soared away in every direction.

She thought again of waking the previous night, cold with perspiration and shivering with that peculiar, unwelcome anxiety that clenched her from time to time. The dreams were coming more frequently and, while at first they were *good*, their endings, with the terrible fear and despair, were quite shocking. Running dreams she could cope with. She was *free* for a brief moment. But she could not train her subconscious to accept the wheelchair. In her dreams she felt herself drawn back to the *monster*, a hideous, angular metal trap with jaws that were gaping to spring closed on her. The deep part of Caitlin's mind, the part that contained her *self*, rejected it and fought against it and she woke up with tears on her cheeks and cold perspiration on her brow.

She wondered where she ran in those dreams. It was Fasach Wood, she knew, but why she sped through there, legs pumping, lungs hauling, she did *not* understand. Even as a child, when she played here during the summer holidays, the thick forest was a place she had been warned to keep away from. The river, she recalled, was deep and fast and far down beyond the road there were no pathways. A child could get lost and wander for a long time.

In the dreams she raced along pathways that were wide and hard and seemed to be *going* somewhere. They joined other paths which seemed important, feeding in from the sides like highway junctions, solid, well-trodden pathways from *other* places.

Her thoughts tumbled on and her hand moved by itself.

Martin Thornton. His face spun into her mind unbidden.

She was not sure of Martin Thornton. She recalled again that she had expected him to drop in before he went back to Glasgow, and remembered her mild disappointment when he hadn't. Had it been *mild*? Caitlin told herself that it had been. He meant nothing to her.

No. That was wrong. He *did* mean something to her. He had been there, and he had tried to protect her, because somehow he had *known* how badly she was injured. She wasn't sure of the tale he had told her, wasn't quite convinced it wasn't some reporter's trick, despite the sincerity in his voice.

She had read his piece in the newspaper that very morning. It wasn't a major piece, on the inside, just before the centre pages and TV listings. He had talked not in terms of a *range war*, which other folk had done, but had given a fair and balanced view of the situation. He had mentioned Duncan Haldane's troubles and the fact that he was a man trying to earn a living. He had spoken about the beauty of the glen and the concern of the folk living there to preserve it. Gail Dean had a sizeable quote as did Duncan Haldane. At the end of the story, she had the impression that Thornton sympathised more with Haldane, but he had been careful to walk the tightrope without falling into newspaper bias. It was a thoughtful piece. Not a story to win awards, but honest enough.

Caitlin wondered why he hadn't come back again. She had decided to return the cheque after he'd gone, but now she wasn't sure. He didn't seem to care about it. Was it a bribe? Was he trying to *buy* a story? Caitlin didn't know. She rather wished she did. He was pretty good-looking in a *normal* sort of way; slim, but not skinny, with short brown hair and quite piercing blue eyes. Best of all, she conceded, he had two creases on his cheeks, laughter lines that deepened when he smiled. That meant he laughed a lot. Caitlin liked that in a man.

The day before, when she'd been sketching, she had been doodling in charcoal on a spare sheet. She'd started off just testing shades and thicknesses. One of the circles she'd drawn became the deep curve of a horse's jaw and she had done a fast, stylised picture of the animal galloping. Horses were a favourite of hers. She drew the petals of a rose and then a face. It had started out as just a shape, but as she filled in the features and shades her hand had automatically formed curves of eyebrows. The charcoal had lined in a strong chin and a half smile on the mouth. It had been Martin Thornton. Caitlin had shaken her head in annoyance and had reached to scrunch the sheet of paper into a ball, but she'd stopped herself halfway through the motion. She'd looked at it for a long moment, then slipped it into a folder where she kept the other sketches. It hadn't been a bad likeness. The eyes were right. She thought about it and shook her head.

'I'm not getting into this,' she told herself. 'He only wants a story,' she insisted. Yet she had been displeased when he failed to show up. It wasn't that she fancied him, she mentally asserted. Oh, but he was the first decent-looking human being she'd spoken to in a long time. A girl in a wheelchair, she didn't see too many of them. And if she did, damned few looked back.

Somewhere off beyond the murmuring stream a cock pheasant proclaimed its territory with the sound of tortured metal and Caitlin came back to the present. She looked at the scene on the board. She'd been painting for half an hour with only part of her mind on the picture. Now that her whole attention was on the colours, she was taken aback.

It was *good*. Surprisingly good.

Yet it was also strange. She had caught the tall, straight trunks, with the edging of moss on their north sides and the sunlight shooting through to slant oblique shadows. Beyond them, where the broad leaves should have been thickening, she had painted more of a clearing, quite distant, but clearly visible. For some reason the delicate strokes had washed an atmosphere of summer in between the trees, hazing the view down as if the air was full of pollen, giving it an odd, almost misty-gold effect. In the foreground, she had used russet and sepia and strong tones to pick out the leaves on the forest floor. Some of them, done with mere dabs of the brush-tip, were swirling up as if a breeze had caught them, tumbling into the air in a will-o'-the-wisp. Way beyond, where the forest thinned out, there was a shape in the haze, another tree, hardly seen, standing by itself. She had to look closely to make it out. Even then she wasn't quite sure. The shape was only a shade within a shade, almost a trick of the light, a trick of her *brush*.

She checked her light sketch again, the first one she'd done. There, where in her painting the forest thinned out, the sketch showed it thick and dark and gloomy. What she had come up with, with only a part of her mind on the scene, looked just *right*. It balanced the whole picture. She sat back, admiring her work.

This was the best painting she had done in a while, and she hadn't even realised she was painting it. She checked her watch. It was not long after two in the afternoon. She'd only been painting for a couple of hours and she had *never* done anything like this in less than two days. Caitlin leaned forward again, seeing the brush strokes on the tumbling leaves. She certainly couldn't recall paying as much attention to detail as these had obviously needed. She could almost make out the individual veins on the dead foliage, though she knew that must have been a lucky accidental scrape of the fine hairs at the tip of her brush. Over on the right third there was an owl on a branch. She looked closely at it and realised it was only the broken-off stump of a limb. There was a similar stump in the sketch, but the painted one, at first glance, could have been a big tawny owl, perfectly camouflaged. Caitlin smiled to herself. If she had painted in an owl without noticing it, she *would* have been concerned.

She hoisted the board off the easel and put it carefully in a holder so that she could carry it into the house, edging it into the frame lest she smudge the paint. She was always worried about damaging the surface and having to start over again, but she knew that if she left the picture on the easel on a summer afternoon, it would soon be covered in tiny dead fruitflies. She spent a few minutes cleaning her brushes in spirit and then blew into the bristles to separate them and put them in her box. The paints stacked into an old square leather satchel. She carried the lot into the house, making three trips to finish the job. Then she made herself a cup of tea.

In her living room, sipping the hot drink, she glanced at the painting again. It was curious how she'd made a space between the trees to let the viewer see deep into the forest. Oh, she'd done many landscapes of the countryside in the glen and they sold well in the gallery down at Levenford, and in them, like many another artist, she'd moved a tree here and there, or redesigned a rock face on the Dumbuie Hills. Even a couple of times she'd changed the course of the stream that tumbled down from the Corrie Linn. That had all been deliberate. In this picture, it had been accidental. She had wanted to draw the forest as it *was*, yet she had painted something else. And that hint of a massive tree far off in the depths – she could not recall the strokes that had planted the shade there, off-centre, but in such a position that other lines drew the eye to it in the depths.

'It's good, though,' she said aloud. 'It's damned good.'

Caitlin finished her tea and then went out again, but instead of going up to her place in the shade of the silver birch, she wheeled herself round the corner and down the slabbed pathway and out of the front gate. It shut behind her with a squeal of old hinges and a snap of the catch. The air smelled of alyssum and pink honeysuckle. There was not a breath of wind and she could feel the heat of the sun welcome on her shoulders.

Instead of turning left towards the village, she went right, following the road round the shallow curve where the tall larches marched up the slope towards the verge. She found the place where she had pulled off onto the grass to sketch, where the alyssum smell gave way to the sweet scent of the bluebells that carpeted the down-slope in a smoky haze that shaded to grey with distance. Wood sorrel and white helleborine nodded gently, even in the still air, as if agreeing with the day.

Caitlin stopped and looked down into the trees. Yes. She had caught it. The lines were the same, the colours matched. She felt a thrill of pride in her work. Yet down there, beyond the larches and firs, the oaks and gnarled elms crowded in on each other. There were no spaces between them and their leaves formed a thick, dark canopy, impenetrable and shadowed. Strangely, her own picture, the one she had painted while her thoughts were off in different places, looked *right*.

She smiled to herself, unconcerned.

'Maybe I should sign them *Constable*,' she murmured into the scented summer air.

She backed out from the short grass, listening carefully for any traffic, and on to the road again. Further along there was a flat bridge which had crenellated bays where she sometimes sat, listening to the water, and occasionally getting a delightful spray from the waterfall beneath. She turned the chair and headed in that direction, humming to herself, feeling better than she had in days.

She was building up speed on the level road that led to the lower bridge over the Corrie. The sun was high, and hot on her cheek and though the wind had died at dawn, her thin blouse ruffled with the breeze of her own making. The wheels hissed smoothly on the dry road as she moved, elbows now resting on the padded arms, one finger just touching the brake.

15

It happened with such shocking speed that Caitlin didn't have a chance.

She was trundling along, happy in her thoughts, when a flurry of leaves tumbled out from the edge of the trees, whirling together with a languid, circular motion. It didn't even strike her that there was not a breath of wind. It happened lazily at first, so easily she wasn't aware that anything *was* happening. The maelstrom of leaves rustled their way across the smooth tarmac with a dry susurration and then blew into the hedgerow on the other side. As Caitlin passed, she could hear the rustle as they snicked against the tight and tangled hawthorn stems. She kept her finger on the brake, just letting the wheels whirr on the road metal, easily steering herself on the left side.

Behind her a sharp crash, like branches snapping, startled her out of her thoughts. Then came a low growl, so deep and vicious it seemed to shudder through her bones. She gave a little gasp and tried to turn, but the confines of the chair prevented her. Just at the edge of her vision, something squat and black and appallingly *fast* launched itself towards her.

Caitlin felt her whole *self* cringe in dread. A small cry that was pure fright escaped her. The monstrous, throaty growl came again and she felt the vibration shiver down between her shoulder-blades. Then there was an enormous jolt as something hit her wheelchair with such force that her head was snapped back in a violent whiplash.

In that second she didn't have time to think or even react. A huge wave of panic suddenly swamped her completely.

The wheelchair was thrown forward. There was a tight high ringing in her ears and a searing burn of wrenched muscle just above her shoulders as she too was catapulted in rebound with a jerk almost violent enough to throw her out of the chair. Instinctively her hands grasped the arms before she landed on the road. Behind, the roaring sound shattered the air and Caitlin cried out again. She heard dull footfalls thump the ground in quick succession and an accompanying harsh scrape, like a dog's claws on the road, but louder, bigger. *Much bigger.*

Pure terror seized her. She was suddenly *flooded* with fear for her life. Despite the searing pain in her neck and just under her jaws, all her attention was riveted on what she couldn't see, behind her. It had just been a black blur, moving with liquid speed. The guttural, gurgling roar it had snarled was *huge*, like a tiger, a *vast* hunting tiger, and it had attacked her.

She heard saliva rattle in its throat as it drew breath for another thunderous growl and her whole body tensed, expecting it to spring at her, to fix its jaws on her exposed head. *To tear her to pieces.*

The scrape of claws on the road came loud and fast behind her, a feral nightmare scrabble. The nerves above the break at the bottom of her spine twitched with the tension of expectation. She squealed again, a high, pathetic and helpless sound, but this time she was prepared for the violence of the blow. Her whole body was rigid and that saved her neck from whiplashing back to strike the upright edge of the wheelchair. The wheels bounced and she shot forward, even faster, straight across the low bridge and on to the rougher tarmac on the lower side. Here there was a hill which curved as it sank, paralleling the forest on the right. The sounds of vicious pursuit kept pace as the chair picked up speed, hurtling down the hill, wobbling from verge to verge. Caitlin heard the growl begin again and she envisaged a huge black beast, a gaping maw, and she cried out in fear.

The hedgerow on the left whipped by in a flurry of green and the wheels kicked up small stones and gravel. The scutter of clawed feet receded behind her and a wave of relief looped up within her. She was *beating* it. She was *outracing the thing*. Hope flared inside her as she tried to steady the wheelchair. The road swooped in a steep gradient and Caitlin, imprisoned in her own juggernaut, swooped with it. She swerved close to the side of the road and a bramble runner, notched with sawtooth barbs, snatched at her summer blouse and left a line of red razored on her arm. A broken branch of a rowan, jutting out from the hedgerow, snagged her flowing hair, giving it a violent tug. Then she was in the middle of the road, hurtling out of control.

169

The speed was frightening. It wasn't as numbingly terrifying as the thought of the black, blurring animal that had attacked her and thrown the chair forward. Now she realised she was going *too fast*. The beast, the big dog or *whatever* it was, had vanished. There was no sound of it.

Ahead the road took another twist, this time to the left. Caitlin grabbed the short brake and hauled back on it.

Nothing happened.

The wheelchair and its prisoner sped on.

She yelled without even knowing and jerked back on the brake again. The wheelchair did not even slow. She risked a glance down and saw that the lever assembly and its big pads were clogged with a wad of dry leaves. The lever was jammed open. The brake wouldn't work.

The edge of the forest was dead ahead. Big oaks there formed a barrier, old and gnarled and terribly *rough*. In an instant flash she saw herself crashing into one of them, *crushing* herself into one of them. She saw her head smash and her bones break and a wail of pure desperation leapt out from her. She tried to steer into the corner, holding her weight right over the left arm, and the right wheel came up. The whole contraption wobbled as she tried to skid it round the turn, trying to judge how far she could lean without toppling.

Then, from behind and to the left, the *thing* shot out in an ebony streak. She got a glimpse of a gaping pink mouth, a flash of spiked teeth and a glistening, fluid sheen of black. She jerked back with a scream and the right wheel came down *hard* on the road. The front wheels skittered and jumped. She lost control and the wheelchair veered right across the road. By a miracle, she shot between two oaks. A tangled branch hooked her hair and pulled out a long strand from her scalp. The wheels demolished a swathe of nodding bluebells and Caitlin was plummeting out of control between the hoary trunks.

The land dropped in a steep swoop down the side of the valley. She held on with a desperate grip, teeth rattling against each other, now so terrified her mind was a blank. The wheelchair bounced and turned left and right. It hit a raised lip and flew two feet into the air. Caitlin's stomach seemed to drop as she rose, then tried to leap into her mouth as she fell. The wheelchair smacked the

170

ground with a crashing thump which jerked her neck violently to the side, then it hit a moss-covered log and she was thrown out at enormous speed.

The chair bounced off and away and Caitlin sailed through the air, body twisting and turning. Her whole mind was numb. All she was aware of was the dizzy looping sensation. Green and brown whirled bewilderingly around her. The side of the valley here was so steep that she crashed through the branches of a tree rooted further down the slope. Instinctively her hands grabbed at the leaves and twigs but her fingers only succeeded in tearing the leaves away.

A branch swiped her face so hard it felt as if she'd been ripped to the bone. There was a roaring in her ears, as if her heart were beating inside her head. She came plummeting forward and hit a long horizontal bough, which caught her low down on her back. The sudden bolt of pain was indescribable. The blow was such a stunner that the whole world went black. Caitlin was flipped over the thick branch, flopping like a puppet whose strings have been cut, then fell straight down through a tangle of overhanging leaves.

She hit the water with enough force to send a fountain twenty feet in the air.

The shock of it knocked out what breath was left in her lungs and she plunged deep into the pool.

Her eyes opened and she saw a dark shimmering world around her. She did not even realise she was in the water. She lifted an arm and saw it float, pale and wavery, in front of her eyes. A far-off part of her mind assumed she was dead and, in that little corner, she wondered dreamily why being dead was so sore. The pain soared up from her back on slow bellows of fire, reaching white heat, then easing down to an unbearable burn. She tried to breathe and found she could not. Something cold forced its way down her throat and tried to freeze out the pain, but it kept on burning there like a blowtorch.

Consciousness swam back again with the slowness of daydream. She replayed her tumble through the trees and heard the triumphant thunderous growl behind her. Then, suddenly, she was *drowning*.

She was drowning in the river.

Dread propelled her to the surface. She fought with her arms

171

while her brain sent urgent messages to her dead legs to kick out. The cold flooded into her and her lungs tried to cough it out, but they couldn't. An eternity later, her head broke the surface. Blinding stars were dancing crazily in front of her eyes. She coughed again and this time a gout of water shot into the air. Her searing lungs hauled in air and then went into a spasm of racking splutters. She whooped desperate breaths in between the spasms, frantically trying to keep her head above the water. The current carried her down to the edge of the pool where large, smooth rocks formed a narrow neck. She was shoved against one and reached out to grasp it.

Caitlin's fingers slipped off the damp surface and she slid under once more. She fought her way up again and clawed at the rock like a thing possessed, tried to hug it with her arms but she could find no purchase. The stone was water smooth and coated with river slime. There was no purchase for her. There was no way out.

The realisation hit her with a shock that was deeper than the cold of the river water.

I'm going to die here.

The words formed in her mind and the idea of it, the *certainty* of it, blazed on the forefront of her brain.

Her hands couldn't keep her afloat and they could not haul her out of the river. Her legs were dragging and useless, their dead weight pulling her down into the depths.

I'm going to die.

She saw herself as if she was standing some distance away, as if perhaps she was floating above the *drowning* Caitlin. It came very clear and very sharp and in full detail.

She saw fingers scrabble and claw at the rock and the exhaustion of her body slow down their movements. She pictured her head sliding, at last, below the surface and then she saw that other Caitlin Brook, that *dead* Caitlin Brook, tumbling slowly in the current, red hair trailing out in a copper fan, her face a pale moon dappled by the sunlight through the ripples.

'*No!*' she gasped, and swallowed another mouthful of water. It came out again in a desperate splutter. Using all her strength, she turned herself around and hauled against the current.

I will not die here!

The command came driving in at her from that other corner of her mind where the will to live burned blue and hot.

She heaved at the water, pulling herself away from the rock, aiming her whole being at the shallows next to the falls where a gravel bank sloped gently into the pool. It was perhaps forty feet away. It looked like forty miles.

She grunted with the effort, gasped with the exertion. Her arms moved like pistons as she dragged herself upstream against the almost irresistible force of the river. She made one yard, fought for another, won a third.

She was beating it, beating the river. She shut her mind to everything but the enormous effort of fighting upstream, using only her hands, trying to ignore the deadly drag of her feet and legs trailing behind her. Caitlin's shoulders screamed agony, her arms pleaded with her to stop. She gained another two yards and reached a fierce current that swirled away from the bank. It forced her back the distance she'd won. Despair tried to force her under and she fought that too. Her breath was coming out in jagged little pants and her lungs felt as if they were on fire. She clawed her way forward, reclaiming the few yards and almost made it, then her arms simply stopped working.

Her right hand reached forward and she felt the muscles flex for the huge effort of pulling it back under the surface, when it gave up on her. It flopped underneath her body. She tried to order it to move, but it refused. Her left arm sagged too. Her head started to sink and, just before it slipped under the water, she saw the far bank, grey and glistening, recede. She tried to lift her head and it refused to come up. A tendril of her hair snaked across her mouth and was sucked in when her lungs hauled for breath. Her chest heaved twice and then even the effort of coughing was too much.

Caitlin's strength was gone. She had nothing left to give. She floated backwards in the pool, her body tumbling slowly just under the surface. She saw dark, then light, then dark again. The darkness grew thick. It grew black. Then there was nothing at all.

It was dark for a long time. There was no sensation of pain, no feeling at all, no fear. She was content. She was not body, only mind. She had no name, she had no thoughts. She was, but she was not. It was dark for a long time. Then there was light, just a faint light, far away. She did not want the light. She turned her self away

173

but it kept turning her back again, drawing her with a nagging insistence. It came closer, expanding as it did so, swelling up to swallow her and she wanted only the dark and . . .

The light *exploded* in on her and Caitlin Brook wailed as the pain surged back.

'Hush now, girl,' a voice came from nowhere. 'Hush now. You've been hurt, but you'll be fine soon.'

The voice came closer. Caitlin couldn't open her eyes. She felt that if she did, her eyes would melt with the terrible pain. She felt her mouth open so wide her jaw muscles creaked.

'You'll be better soon. The pain will go,' the soothing, gentle voice said. She felt a hand slip under her head and slowly draw her upwards. There was a sensation on her lips and then a coldness that flowed like ice down her throat, instantly snuffing out the fire raging in there. She gulped and coughed, but the hand still cupped her head and more liquid came. She felt her head being lowered down again and then the pain began to subside. It seemed to take a long time, but gradually it diminished, faded away and was gone.

Caitlin Brook finally fell asleep.

And in her dreams she tumbled, helpless in her wheelchair, through a terrible forest with a beast of hell growling behind her, breathing fire.

16

Only one elevator was working in the grandly-named Lord Kelvin Court. It was lofty, but it was not a court. It was twenty storeys of concrete punctuated by small windows and laddered with tiny balconies where the residents had a couple of square yards to hang their washing, enjoy a quite spectacular view over the city and right down the river Clyde, or drop things onto unsuspecting passers-by and the ambulance and firemen who were called on a regular basis.

Martin Thornton had been here – or places just like it – often enough to know the ropes. Andrew Toye was an academic to whom housing schemes like Blackhale were foreign, dangerous, and slightly exotic. Social workers and reformers called it *Bleak-Hell*. The police called it *Black-Hole*. The folk who lived there called it *The Sump*. They were all correct. It was not a wholesome place. It was a corral for the poor and underprivileged. Everybody who lived there wanted to live somewhere else. Unfortunately, around the city, there are too many places just like that.

Andy Toye drove his new car right up to the front entrance where the local talent had shown artistic promise with colours from paint-spray cans and none at all with either grammar or spelling or originality.

'Not here,' Martin advised. He pointed to a tarmac square that stretched fifty yards from the building. 'Take it down the far end.'

'Why?'

'I'll show you in a minute.'

Andy reversed the car and drove it to the corner where the tarmac gave on to a patch of hard earth denuded of grass. The deep footprints in the caked dirt showed that the last time it had rained, it had been a quagmire. They got out and Andy opened the boot. Martin helped him with some of the equipment. It was awkward, but not heavy. It was almost ten at night, still light, though the sky was shading to red in the west.

They carried the boxes past two old cars. One was down on its haunches, the other stilted on bricks, and then onto the concrete slabs that formed a base around the tower block. Martin stopped and indicated with a nod of his head.

'That's why,' he said. The concrete was pitted and dented. Shards of black bakelite and small leaves of metal were scattered all around.

'They use cars for target practice. That's a car battery there. They throw them off the top and they hit like bombs.'

'Isn't that dangerous?'

Martin laughed. 'It's bloody lethal, Andy.'

'So why don't they stop it?'

'The only way to stop it is to tear these monstrosities down and give folk decent places to stay. And jobs, and good schools.'

'But they could *kill* somebody.'

'I think that's the idea,' Martin said as he shouldered the door open. It was heavy and the panes of wire-strengthened glass were starred by the impact of thrown objects.

'I parked there last week,' Andy said.

'Well, I hope you're insured. You were lucky. They don't like cars that actually move. New shiny ones they just *hate*.' The lift door opened grudgingly. Inside it smelled of cats and piss.

'But why?'

'Because this is Auschwitz without the gas chambers. One in eight of them has a job, and it won't be a good job. Didn't you see the needles out there in the grass? One in five of the kids putting something into a vein. These people have been dumped here because they have no value to anybody. Nobody wants them, so they're left to fester.'

'I didn't know you felt so strongly,' Andy said as the elevator jolted upwards.

'That's the trouble. Nobody does feel strongly. And the folk here don't feel anything but anger. It's the new slum. In the old days, folk were poor, but they didn't know any better. Here everybody has a television and bugger-all else. They can see how the other half live. They *know* they're screwed.'

His thoughts jumped to Linnvale, that sleepy hollow where the air was clean and the only signs were on farm gates. It was a place where people would fight to preserve their way of life. He couldn't blame Caitlin Brook for hiding herself there.

'What about the people who get the car batteries on their heads?' Andy asked, eyes wide behind the bulbous lenses.

'It hasn't happened yet. Keep your fingers crossed.' Martin gave him a rueful smile. The professor was an innocent abroad.

They reached a dirty green door. The bell didn't work. Martin knocked. Betty Reid was a small woman with a pinched face and matt black hair with greying roots showing through. She wore a mud-brown cardigan that was obviously her husband's. The sleeves were rolled up into thick cuffs.

She invited both of them in through the narrow lobby and into the small living room. As high rise flats go, it was clean, yet crowded. A television flickered in the corner opposite a glass-fronted cabinet filled with Spanish dolls. Her husband was watching a sports programme.

'Martin Thornton, George Reid. And here's Christine and Kim. You've seen their pictures.'

Martin reached to shake hands all round. George Reid was almost as small as his wife, balding, and with a resigned look on his face. The girls were pretty, Kim about ten years old with a tousled head of fair hair, Christine, a couple of years older, with startling black Irish eyes and straight raven hair pulled back into a pony tail.

'Anything last night, George?' Andrew asked airily. 'No disturbances?'

The small man shook his head. He looked as if he hadn't had a good night's sleep in weeks.

'No, but we kept waiting up for it. This is driving us round the bend. Betty here's on Valium and the girls are nervous wrecks.'

Martin thought the girls looked fine. The parents looked at the end of their tether.

He sat down with his notebook and started asking questions and taking a few notes, while Andrew fixed up the equipment in the girls' room. He screwed a video camera onto a tripod. A trail of wires led back down the hallway into the living room where the professor fixed up a small monitor.

The story was much as Andrew had told Martin when he'd shown him the peculiar pictures. Two months ago the Reids had begun hearing a tapping on the walls. At first they had blamed the neighbours and their belief had led to a couple of stairhead arguments. But then the tapping had become a banging, mostly in the girls' room, always at night. Then there were the ornaments which had moved position by morning. Young Kim said she had seen shadows moving in the room at night and, when she put the light on, her collection of cuddly toys were jammed along the curtain rail. Finally, in the last fortnight, the girls themselves had become the focus of whatever disturbance was affecting the house.

As George and Betty lay sleepless in the room next door, they would hear screams and come running through to find Christine and Kim lying on the floor. Records would be scattered all over the threadbare carpet. The blankets would be rumpled and twisted and draped over the wardrobe and the small easy chair that sat in a corner.

'We called in that priest. They're the ones who can fix this kind of thing,' George Reid said. 'But he didn't believe us. He told us to speak to the professor here. It's been nearly every night this past fortnight. We're run ragged. We have to get out of here.'

Martin nodded, taking notes in shorthand, automatically translating the man's glottal Glasgow dialect into plain English.

'And what do you think's causing it?'

'I dunno. It's like something out of one of those films. You just don't know what's going to happen next.'

At about ten-thirty the girls were packed off to bed. George and Betty went to theirs about half an hour later. For the next two hours Martin and Andrew sat together, talking in very hushed tones as the sky darkened finally to black.

Andrew had been unable to get the infra-red equipment he wanted for this stake-in, but the video camera was on long play, which gave them three hours of continuous filming. At one o'clock he reached and flicked a switch on one of the wires and the monitor came to life. The picture lacked sharpness. Even with the low-light compensation, the room was fuzzy and grey. There was no real colour. Martin could make out the two shapes on the one bed and beside them the truncated cone of a bedside light. On the chair, a teddy bear's eyes caught a stray beam from somewhere and gleamed wickedly into the lens. The sound quality was good though. They could hear the deep, even breathing as the girls slept. At one point one of them – it sounded like Kim – mumbled in her sleep, snuffled and then turned over.

178

'What do you think?' Martin asked.

'I don't know. Nothing might happen tonight.'

'If it did, what would cause it?'

'That's something that has puzzled me ever since I was ten years old. They talk about poltergeists, but I don't believe in them. I don't really believe in anything, as a matter of fact. I've told you before. I'm what you'd call a *sceptic*.'

'So why do you get involved in this?'

'Just because I don't believe in it doesn't make it any less fascinating. This is just a sideline for me, but getting paid for your hobby is the best job in the world. I study the life and times of people long since gone. You know, the one thing they all had in common was a belief in the supernatural. The Celts believed in all sorts of things. They thought there were spirits in everything. They believed that people could be taken over by spirits, but they didn't worry about it. It was a bit of a privilege. They had a good relationship with their magic. They *all* believed in it and, for them, maybe it worked. Now people don't believe, but everybody has a sneaky fear at the back of their minds.'

'I don't believe in anything, ghosts, poltergeists, the lot.'

'So why are you here?'

'For the story, of course.'

'Ah, that's what you say. But if you didn't think something strange might be happening, you wouldn't be here at all. You're just like me. You *want* some proof,' Andrew challenged him.

'Maybe so,' Martin conceded.

'And look at last year, with that girl. What was her name again?'

'Caitlin Brook.'

'Now, how do you explain that?'

'I don't know. How do you explain it?'

'Me, I'm looking for explanations. I keep an open mind.'

Andrew stopped and turned to Martin, a mere shadow in the darkened room. 'Did you say you were speaking to her again?'

'Yes. Coincidence really. I picked up a story in Linnvale. That's way up the Loch Corran road, about ten miles north of Levenford.'

'I've heard of it,' Andrew said.

'Well, I hadn't, though I must have passed it a thousand times. It's in the middle of nowhere.'

179

'No,' Andrew said, and Martin heard his shadow chuckle. 'It's in the *centre* of nowhere.'

'How do you mean?'

'Ah, you pragmatic reporters. You never read anything but headlines and bylines. Have you never read Friel's *Ley Lines*?'

'No, what is it? A poetry book? A train-spotter's manual?'

Andrew gave an exasperated sigh.

'It's the definitive work on force lines. Power conduits in the earth. The Celtic druids had them mapped out all over these islands. All their stone circles and *cromlechs* were built where they intersected. They even built towns on the lines.'

'Yes, but what *were* they?'

'They were like power-lines under the ground, maybe a bit like rivers of force linking one place to another. You can imagine it like the lines of magnetism in the earth's crust, only the force was supernatural. Maybe that's the wrong word. The old Celts didn't believe in the supernatural. They thought *everything*, even the paranormal, was just a part of life. They had a nice way of looking at things.'

Martin shook his head. 'I can't remember how this started.'

'We were talking about your episode last year. You were talking to the Book girl.'

'Brook,' Martin corrected.

'Yes. Her. Well, she lives in Linnvale and I told you I'd read about it in Friel. It was one of the centres of the *ley lines*. Like a crossroads. Way back a few thousand years ago they used to have a big festival there. Druids came from all over. Even as late as the seventeenth century it was an important centre, till the Presbyterians put a stop to it. Drowned a few folk testing for witches.'

'Sounds like our own legal system,' Martin said drily. 'And these *ley lines*, what were they for?'

'Some folk still believe in them today. They were like the low roads. You'll have heard the song . . .'

'You take the high road and I'll take the low road?'

'That's the one. The low road was to the underworld. There was power on the ley lines which followed those roads. And at the major junctions, the earth power was concentrated. Now Linnvale gets a special mention in Friel because all the roads end there. The highland line comes down over the pass. There's another that bisects the three islands on the Loch and cuts across the Ardoch hills, and there are three others coming east, west and south. It's a bit like a five-pointed star radiating out from the one spot. The Celts thought this was heap big magic.'

'Sounds like heap big crap,' Martin said. Andrew chuckled.

'I didn't say I *believed* it. I just said that some folk did. Still do.'

'You're nothing but a charlatan, Andy. You should lose your tenure.'

'Ha, there's no force on earth can do that to me,' Andrew said, and laughed again. 'I'm—'

The monitor flickered, the picture vanished and the screen showed a series of jagged flashes. The quiet breathing from the speaker suddenly became a loud hiss of static.

'What's that?' Martin asked.

'Wheesht, man,' the professor hushed him, holding up a forestalling hand. He fiddled with a control. The screen still flickered and flashed. Thin bands of bright white rolled upwards in quick succession. 'I think maybe a lead's come loose,' he said. He moved back from the low screen on his hands and knees. 'Maybe I should—'

The screen went blank, there was a *tick* and the picture came back on. The scene was the same, except Christine, lying on the right as the camera faced, was now on her back. A pale arm hung out of the bed, palm up. Andrew scanned the picture.

'Everything's just the same,' he said. Martin peered at the screen, checking the dim scene against his own memory. He scanned quickly, taking in the lines of shadow, the white shapes. The chair was still there and the teddy bear's black beady eyes still caught that ray of light and sparked with mindless life.

'Must have been interference,' Andrew said.

Martin sat back against the sofa. He could have used a drink, but neither of them had brought a bottle. He closed his eyes and Caitlin Brook's face swam up from nowhere. He thought of meeting her again and recalled how the *vision* he'd experienced had flicked across his memory. He had planned to go back and see her, but he'd just driven on. He didn't know why.

There was something *special* about her. It wasn't just her fine, heart-shaped face or her startling green eyes or her even more startling flaming mane of hair. There was a straightforward honesty about her that he warmed to. He'd promised her he'd fix up her kitchen and at that moment he made a mental note to arrange for a few days' leave. It had been months since he'd used his father's tools and it would do him the world of good to get away from the city and get his hands dirty working with wood again.

Andrew coughed quietly in the darkness and Martin's attention came back to what they were doing. He turned his head, eyes sweeping past the monitor screen, and he *froze*.

Something *moved*.

It happened so slowly that at first he didn't believe it had happened.

Andrew saw him stiffen. 'What's up?'

Martin raised his hand towards the screen, pointing at the surface.

'I thought I—' He shook his head slowly. 'No. It was nothing.'

Andrew followed the direction of the pointing finger and peered myopically. The blue light reflected distorted in the thick lenses. 'I don't see anything.'

The two of them watched for a few seconds. The pale arm hanging out of the sheets twitched slowly, then the fingers, wide open, almost in supplication, closed very slowly into a fist. Both Martin and the professor followed the pale motion.

Then the teddy bear moved.

It just twisted forward. Its eyes glinted, then it tumbled from the chair.

'What the—?' Andrew said under his breath.

The screen flickered and then flashed wavy, distorted and jagged lines. The speakers simultaneously spat and hissed with a crackly roar that filled the room.

'Good God *damn*!' Andrew said out loud.

He reached across and turned the knob to the left and the hissing subsided to a low sizzle.

'Did you *see* that?' Martin asked. His voice sounded shaky. The strange image of a harmless cuddly toy moving a few inches on that screen had imprinted itself on a part of his mind he did not know existed. There had been something *dreadful* in that inexplicable movement, something black and completely *wrong*.

'I saw something move,' Andrew said.

'It was the bloody teddy bear. It came off the chair.'

'Probably balanced wrongly.'

Martin replayed the image in his mind. The thing had *moved*. It *hadn't suddenly slipped or lost balance. It had moved towards the camera.*

Andrew was still fiddling with the controls and Martin could only see his shape, surrounded by the corona from the flickering monitor. 'Damned machine. Must be the wiring.'

Just then there was a noise from the girls' room. Martin heard a faint, high cry, then a loud crash. Immediately the two girls started screaming. The flickering on the screen rolled upwards in two fast flashes and then the picture returned.

It lasted only for three or four seconds, but in that time Martin and the professor saw the girls in the air *above* their bed. Their bodies rise to within a couple of feet of the ceiling, the smaller of the two almost upside down, feet higher than her head, while her sister was almost horizontal. The upward flight ended and, as they started to fall, the screen went completely blank and silent.

'What's happening?'

'Same as last time.' Andrew threw himself towards the monitor and started fiddling again, while his left hand pounded the flat top. 'I hope we're getting all that.'

Martin watched. He didn't know what was happening in the next room, but the small part of his mind, the little secret compartment that is in everyone's mind, had now opened, after lying closed all the years since childhood. In there was the bogeyman. In there was the thing with green scaly fingers that would grab your toes if you let them dangle out of the bed on a winter's night. In there were all the irrational fears of the unexplained and the shadowy that all children have to some degree and lock away as they get older and pass beyond the magical, sometimes frightening years when Santa Claus exists, and elves and dragons and *things* lurk under the bed.

The hard-bitten, seen-it-all journalist found himself shaken. His heart was pounding and his breath came in short gasps. The irrational had opened up the childhood compartment in his mind with such a wrench that for a moment he was too stunned to move.

They heard an almighty crash from the next room and then the girls were yelling at the tops of their voices. From the other room,

Martin heard Betty Reid yammering, high and frantic, and her husband's sleepy bawl, asking her what the hell was the matter.

The crash unfroze him. Andrew turned from the screen just as Martin headed for the door. He yanked it open and stepped into the narrow hallway, with Andrew right on his heels. He stopped at the door to the girls' room. The pair of them were screeching, high and startlingly clear. Up above somebody pounded on the floor and, while the words couldn't be made out, the sentiment was clear. He reached for the handle and stopped. Sudden beads of cold sweat sprung out on his forehead. He forced his hand forward, grasped the handle, pulled it down and shoved. The door stuck.

'Oh shit,' he muttered. He'd already seen this movie.

He shoved again and the door sprung open. There was a rushing sound, as if all the air was being sucked out of the room, like a big engine winding down. It tickled a sympathetic vibration in Martin's teeth. Then and later, Martin would never be able to say for sure if he actually heard it, or whether it was just the blood rushing in his ears. There was a flat metallic *bong* sound from the corner, as if a bedspring had just given way. The girls were spreadeagled, each facing different directions. They were whimpering. The smaller one's nightdress was rucked up round her armpits. The light from the hallway caught her skinny buttocks. Her sister had both hands jammed against her mouth and she looked as if she was shivering with cold. Her dark eyes were fixed on Martin as he walked into the room on shaky legs. The window was wide open and the camcorder was lying on the floor, its tripod legs splayed drunkenly. The chair had toppled onto its side. All the bedclothes were strewn around the room, as if blown off by a sudden gale.

Andrew Toye touched the reporter gently on the shoulder and Martin visibly *jumped*.

'Let me see,' he said, brushing past the other man, just as George and Betty Reid came bustling out of their own room, jamming themselves against the doorposts in unconscious farce. Their faces displayed no comic humour.

'Kim! Tina!' Betty bawled. Her hair had two big rollers stuck on the front, one blue and one pink. They bounced up and down as she came scooting along in her bare feet, shoving past both men.

The distraught mother quickly pulled down her daughter's nightdress then gathered the two of them into her arms. Christine's eyes were huge and dark, almost luminous.

'There, there,' Betty said, trying to pat each of them on the back. Her eldest daughter, who was actually a few inches taller than her mother, didn't seem to notice. She looked as if she was in a dream. Her face was pale and still, except for the small motion of her head caused by her mother's petting. She didn't blink.

Martin stood there, feeling shaken. A nerve at the back of his knee twitched and jittered all on its own. He drew his eyes away from the girl's unfocused gaze and looked at the window. It was one of the safety kind you get in high-rise blocks, designed to prevent children falling out. It was open about six inches, the bottom of the frame jutting out about six inches or so. It moved slowly on the pivot of its hinges. Both handles were in the up position, which meant they had been opened. He remembered Andrew had closed them firmly after setting up the equipment.

'Damn it,' the small professor was saying to himself while examining the fallen camera. 'We should have waited for the infra-red. Even a temperature reading would have helped.'

The room was cold, though Martin couldn't tell if it was because the window was open. Certainly there was no wind, not now, though it did look as if a gale had shrieked in and whirled round the room. He turned back toward the scene on the bed. George Reid was hovering at the end of the double divan, obviously fretting, seemingly incapable of reaching out to his daughters.

The older daughter was still as a statue, her fine features carved from marble. Her huge eyes reflected back the light and she did not blink once. Beside her, little Kim was sniffling and snuffling, her hands shaking. Martin felt unnerved and out of place. He turned to go back into the living room when the girl spoke.

'She's drowning,' she said in a flat voice.

Martin turned. It was an odd, *unreal* moment. The girl had spoken to *him*. How he knew that, he did not understand. She was kneeling on the bed, clamped in her little mother's embrace, eyes lustrous and wide and staring as if she was somehow *blind*, or looking at something infinitely distant.

'*She's drowning*,' the girl said again in that flat, ethereal voice.

'She's in the water and she can't swim. Her legs won't move and she's drowning.'

The girl absently pushed her mother away and her hands started to crawl slowly in the air, making lethargic swimming movements. Still her eyes gazed far into the distance.

Her mouth opened as if she was about to speak again, but all that came out was a hoarse, almost frantic gasping sound, and then she coughed raspingly. Even then her huge eyes did not blink.

The arms kept up their motion and everybody watched. There was a sudden stillness in the room.

'A brook. A river. A tree. A willow. She's drowning. She can't breathe and the water is cold. The willow will take her, but she is still dying.'

'Christine. *Tina!'*

The girl did not seem to notice her mother's anguish. She was talking to Martin Thornton, and he did not know why. It was as if invisible webs had threaded themselves between her eyes and his. The black irises were swallowing him up.

'There's still life. Still life. Life and death. Life in death.'

The girl's mouth closed and she froze to marble again. Martin felt his own jaw drop. She gave a little moan, more of a mewling cry, almost kittenish, and then her hands came down together and grabbed at her abdomen.

'Oh,' the girl said, very softly. Her eyes rolled upwards and she slumped back onto the pillow. Everybody in the room, except for little Kim who was still hugged into her mother, saw the spreading stain on the front of the girl's nightdress.

Andrew picked up the camcorder, flicked the tripod legs closed and moved towards the door. He took hold of Martin's arm and pulled him away. The reporter followed him without a word.

17

She swam slowly up to the surface. The pain had faded to a slow pulse that waxed and waned with the slow beat of her heart. It came in dull, regular waves, not in fiery stabs.

There were hands on her back, soft and strong and smooth. Caitlin tried lazily to come completely awake, but it took too much effort. She hovered there, between exhausted sleep and wakefulness, below the surface membrane. It was like being in the womb.

A voice was saying words, but it sounded faint and far away and she couldn't make sense of them nor had the will to want to. She felt herself floating upwards towards wakefulness and then a slow darkness spread over her, pulling her back down into a warm oblivion.

And she dreamed.

She dreamed she was moving through the forest. Not running, just *moving*, floating her way between the trees. The light from above flickered and flashed through the leaves, dappling her with its gleaming as she moved down the hill. She was *flying*. Ahead of her the tree spread its branches to catch her, to stop her flight, but she slipped through its grasp and she was no longer soaring. She was *falling*. She tried to call out, but no cry came. She plunged down and down and down, through the green, afraid and voiceless, and then she was in the water. The cold knifed through the warmth and into her soul. It carried her downstream and she was drowning again. She heard a voice cry out in denial.

'No, *no, no!*'

Caitlin woke with every nerve shivering. She cried out again and her words were muffled by the soft pillow.

Behind her a woman's voice told her everything was all right. She didn't know where she was. Hands were on her shoulders, smoothly drawing themselves across her skin. She could feel their soft texture gentle on her skin and strong as they pushed themselves into her muscles.

There was pain there. A dull throbbing pain that gnawed right down her back to the place where it burned fiercely.

'You'll be fine, my dear. You've been hurt, but you're getting better.'

Caitlin shifted her head on the pillow. She didn't know where she was. She recalled the terrible flight as she careered down the hill with the black beast roaring behind her and the awful plummeting swoop through the trees into the water. She remembered fighting the current, desperately willing herself upstream and cursing her crippled legs. Then she remembered *dying*.

Yet she was not dead. She was alive. Her throat was sore and her shoulders were thudding with pain and down on her back, where the surgeons had pinned her together with titanium to hold her crushed bones, there was a seething cauldron of hurt.

'You're a lucky girl,' the woman's voice said. 'You nearly *drowned* in the river. But where there's hope, there's still life yet.'

Caitlin tried to turn herself over, but as soon as she moved, agony lanced down her spine. The hand came again on her shoulder and insistently pushed her back down into the softness.

'I've given you something for the hurt, young lady,' the unseen woman told her. 'Be patient, it should only take a few minutes. Oh, your back was in a proper mess. And you've hurt it before, I see.'

'I think I need a doctor,' Caitlin finally found the strength to say. 'I think my back's broken again.'

It felt as if it was. The symptoms were there. The last time, the *first* time, she'd come awake and everything above her pelvis was jittering. And she could feel her legs jump and dance of their own volition. That was just the messages her nerves were telling her, and they were getting it all wrong. She could feel her legs twitch and writhe, but there was no movement there. It had taken weeks for the sensations to die away, but her legs had never moved since. Now she was getting the same sensations. The notion of movement in her legs was at once wonderful and hateful. She knew it was a lie.

'No, girl. You've hurt it again, stretched a few muscles, I shouldn't wonder, but there's no break. I would know.'

'Are you a doctor?'

'Only in a way, but that's neither here nor there. How is your pain?'

188

Caitlin stopped to think. Miraculously it was fading rapidly. 'I think it's getting better.'

'Good. I thought so. You'll be able to turn over in a minute or two. You had a bad night last night. Bad dreams. And, oh, I've never seen bruises like that in years. Not since the MacFarlane was caught up in the corner of his byre by a big brown bull. He was like a tartan plaid when the reeve pulled him out, but that was long ago, when I was just little. Even my grandmother couldn't fix him up. But you'll be fine. As good as new.'

'I'll never be good as new,' Caitlin said, her voice muffled by the pillow.

'What was that? Oh, you young folk. Always a despair, aren't you?'

The woman was trying to scold her, but she had a soft, gentle voice. It was Scottish, but her vowels were rich and finely enunciated. The hands continued to move on her skin, massaging deep below the surface. With every movement the pain lessened. It was as if the fingers and palms were *drawing it* out of her. Caitlin breathed in and caught a scent. It was sweet, yet there was an afterscent of spice in it.

'What's that stuff?'

'Oh, it's just a lotion that's good for drawing pain. Good for the skin too. You've more scratches to you than a cat's paw, my girl, but don't you worry. None of them are deep and they'll be gone by the morning.'

'Where am I?'

'You're in my house, silly girl.' The hands drew away. 'There you are. You can try turning round now and, if it's too much, just say so. No need to run before you can walk.'

Caitlin thought it was an odd thing to say. Obviously the woman didn't know about her legs. Around her, people rarely spoke of walking. They never talked of running. She managed to get an elbow underneath her ribs and shoved herself up and round. There was a brief twist of pain in her neck which died immediately. She turned around, very slowly and stiffly, and felt as if every bone and muscle creaked and ground together. Eyes screwed tight shut with concentration, Caitlin pushed herself backwards until she rested against the pillow and let herself gingerly ease back. Then she opened her eyes.

189

Sitting on the side of the bed, a white-haired woman was smiling at her.

'Now hello to yourself,' the woman said, favouring her with a bright smile. Eyes, so dark they were almost black, twinkled at her.

'I'm Sheila Garvie.'

Caitlin reached forward and was surprised that her hand moved easily. She remembered trying to make her arms move, desperately *willing* them to move.

The older woman took her hand in a firm grip.

'And you're Caitlin Brook, I believe. We've never met before, but I'm glad we have now.'

'Me too. I don't understand. I was in the water. I was going *under*.'

'You were indeed, Caitlin. Can I call you that?'

'Of course. Everybody does.'

'Good name. It means *seedling*. It suits you. Like a rowan seedling, red in the autumn.'

Caitlin smiled, taking the compliment. She looked Sheila Garvie up and down. Despite the white hair which was pulled into a chic roll, she couldn't guess how old the woman was. Fifty? Sixty? It was difficult to say. There wasn't a line on her face, except for one or two laughter crinkles around those gleaming, lustrous eyes. And when she smiled, her teeth were white and even. In her youth, she must have been a rare beauty. Even now, despite her obvious maturity, Caitlin thought she was one of the most stunning women she had ever seen.

'I never come this far down the lane. The hill is too steep for me. I've never seen you before up in the village.'

'I don't go up every day. Too busy most of the time. But I've seen you whizzing along in that machine of yours. Sometimes I envy your speed.'

Caitlin laughed at that. *Nobody* ever told her they envied her speed. 'I thought I knew everybody in the glen. But I don't get around much either. I think I've heard your name before.'

'That'll be from Gail Dean, or Jill Gregor, no doubt.'

Caitlin looked around. She was in a wide, old-fashioned bed in an upstairs room. She knew it was upstairs by the slope of the ceiling. Outside, some sort of creeper or ivy dangled over the window. There were pictures on the walls, old, faded prints, maybe even oils. On a dresser at the side of the bed there were glass containers with different coloured liquids.

'How did I get here?'

'Oh, I got you here. You were like a drowned rat. I was down on the river path and I heard this almighty splash. I thought the bank had fallen in, the way it sometimes does up the stream after a heavy rain. I got to the pool and there was nothing to be seen. It was lucky for you that you've such fire in your hair, or I'd have missed you. That's what caught my eye, that lovely autumn hair of yours.'

Sheila Garvie reached forward and stroked at the curls. A flicker of unease crossed Caitlin's mind, but the woman was smiling gently, in a motherly sort of way. There was no threat here.

'I don't understand how you got me up here. I mean, all on your own.'

'Oh, you find strength when it's needed, my dear.'

'You mean, you carried me?'

'Like a fireman does. I'm afraid I wasn't very gentle with you. And you were a ton weight, with all that water dripping from you. I think it was very close. Touch and go. You were blue when I got you out of the water. Ruined a good pair of boots in the process, and a fine set of moleskins.'

'Oh. I'm sorry.'

'Only joking with you, girl. They've dried by now. None the worse for a soaking.'

'I don't remember getting out of the water.'

'No. You were close to gone. Have you always been lucky?'

Caitlin thought about it. At times in the past, when she was getting used to the wheelchair, she thought she must be the unluckiest girl alive. But she'd only broken her back. The fall could have snuffed her out in an instant. She shrugged. 'That stuff you gave me. What is it? Morphine?'

'Oh no. I don't prescribe. It was just something from the flowers. Look there. There's lavender and primrose and eye-bright. And the one at the end, that's valerian. Good for relaxing sore muscles. All from the flowers. Best healers on earth, they are.'

Sheila Garvie gave her another smile and stood up. She was quite tall and slimly elegant. 'Try to get some rest now and, if the pain comes back, you let me know. I think it's gone though.'

Caitlin nodded sleepily.

'If you smell anything, it'll be me cooking breakfast. Think you can eat?'

The girl shook her head.

Sheila smiled again, eyes twinkling. 'You wait half an hour and tell me again.'

She turned and went out, closing the door behind her. Caitlin heard her light footfalls on the stairs. She lay back and felt herself relax. The pain was gone now. Completely gone.

18

It was three o'clock in the morning when Martin Thornton and Andrew Toye came rattling down from the tenth floor in the smelly elevator carrying the video equipment in cardboard boxes. The lift lurched to a juddering halt and the doors slammed open, the noise echoing loud from the graffiti-daubed walls. A faint tinge of orange pastelled the sky to the east, presaging an early dawn. The air was cool and had a touch of city damp about it. The four tower blocks, Blackhale's row of grey sentinels, reared dark and threatening. Neither of them had spoken since leaving the Reid home.

They turned the corner and walked by the flank of the block, feet crunching on the shards of bakelite, then angled onto the bitumen, past the two derelict cars. They were halfway to Andrew's Ford estate when Martin stopped.

'We've got a problem,' he said.

'Hm?' Andrew was away in a world of his own.

'Look at the state of that!' Martin nodded, indicating ahead.

The car's door was lying wide open.

Andrew's eyes opened wide behind the thick lenses. His mouth sagged open. In any other circumstance it would have been comical. His jaw worked up and down silently for several seconds.

'My *car*!' he finally managed to blurt.

They walked the final forty yards and Martin dumped his box on the ground. The wheels were gone. The car had been jacked up and then laid down again on four short pillars made from loose bricks. He turned and looked at the other cars they'd passed. The one which had been up on bricks was now hunkered down to the same level as its rusting mate. The thieves hadn't gone far to look.

They'd even re-cycled the bricks. Martin wondered how often these red oblongs had been used to strip cars down to rusting shells. He now knew why the car park was empty.

Andrew put his carton next to Martin's. He stood up, holding his hands out to indicate his complete disbelief. This kind of thing just did not happen down at Gilmore Street where the professors parked their cars under the shade of the trees by the University.

'Bloody *hell*!' he exploded. He reached forward and thumped the roof. His car teetered and there was a crunch of crumbling brick. For a second Martin thought the whole thing was going to slide off and crash to the ground, but the estate car only rocked a little and then was still.

'What'll we do?' Andrew asked. He looked like a fish out of water. This was only his second incursion to the no man's land which was Blackhale. The reporter had been here before. He knew the people. Andrew felt helpless and angry.

'First thing is to organise something to get your car out of here. If you leave it for another day, they'll strip everything.'

'But look at that. They've taken my stereo. And my speakers. That cost a fortune.'

'Yes, but look on the bright side. They've left the doors and the seats. And the steering wheel.'

'They wouldn't take that, would they?'

Martin shook his head incredulously. He felt sorry for his friend. Andrew was one of the more friendly professors in the stuffy atmosphere at the old university next to the River Kelvin. He had liked the little *fey* fellow on first sight. Finding the car up on bricks and with the sound system ripped out had taken his mind off the scene in the Reid house. All the way down in the elevator, he couldn't shake the memory of the girl sitting up in bed, talking in that flat voice. It had sent a shiver through him. Try as he might, he couldn't close that compartment inside his mind that had opened up and loosed the bogeymen from childhood. Now, however, he had something to think about. Something *normal*, although the professor certainly didn't see it that way.

He leant forward and gave the car a light shake, checking its balance. He bent and looked underneath. It was pretty firmly bedded; no chance of falling down onto its axle. Andrew fidgeted, feeling helpless, which in fact he was. He knew less about cars than he did about Blackhale. Martin got in and leaned across to free the bonnet catch. There was a clunk, and the front lifted half an inch. He got out again, fiddled under the lid, sprung the lock and lifted the bonnet high.

'You're in luck. You still have the engine, and the gearbox. Have you got the keys?'

'What do we need them for? The car's open.'

'Oh, just give them here,' Martin said, with a touch of exasperation. 'I want to see if it'll start.'

'But we can't go without wheels.'

'Trust me, Andy. We can't go if the engine won't. I don't know what they've stripped.'

The professor fished the keys from his trouser pocket and handed them, jangling, to Martin. The engine coughed and started at the first turn.

'All right. Put the stuff in the boot and get in the car. I've got to make a call, if I can find a phone that works.'

'I'll come with you.'

'Only if you want to lose the University's equipment,' Martin said, pointing to the boxes.

'But there's nobody around,' Andrew protested.

Martin laughed. He pointed up at the first tower block.

'There's two thousand people in that one. There'll be half a dozen watching us right now. Think about it, Andrew. Up here, everybody sees everything, and nobody sees anything. There's hardly forty people in there who've got day jobs. So it doesn't matter to most of them whether it's day or night.'

He swivelled and gestured to the next block, maybe two hundred yards away. Three figures were standing at the entrance, not going anywhere, just standing together in a huddle.

'Those guys could have taken your stereo. If they did, they'll have sold it. Shot themselves up with something and now they might be looking for more easy money. You stay and guard the gear.'

'But what if they come back?' Martin could hear the apprehension in his voice. Andrew was well out of familiar territory.

'Here,' he said, springing the catch on the boot. He dumped the boxes inside and came back out again with a tyre jack. 'Get in the car and close the doors and lock them. They won't come while you're here. If they do, they'll have to break in. If they do that, get out and beat the shit out of them with this.'

Andrew looked as if he didn't believe what he was hearing.

'Remember,' Martin went on, with an odd smile on his face. 'Always go for the biggest one first.'

He waited until the professor got into the car and heard the clunk of the locks going down. Andrew turned around, his face, pressed against the window, a picture of miserable apprehension. It took half an hour to find a phone box with a receiver that actually worked. In fact it was the first kiosk with a receiver. The other three had been empty, except for a few trailing wires. None of them had any glass in the frames. Martin had thought of calling the AA for a tow truck and then remembered it would be difficult to tow a car with no wheels. He then called the newspaper office and asked to be put through to the editorial driver who would be on shift until four in the morning.

Rab Anderson was a bear of a man. The telephone did little to diminish the raucous laughter when Martin explained what had happened.

'A new Ford Sierra where? Are you off your head or what?' Martin waited for another gale of laughter to subside. 'Hey. I thought you were a professional. You must be losing your touch.' Rab started spluttering again. Martin gritted his teeth.

'Yes. Funny, isn't it? Meanwhile I'm stuck here in a phone box with the west wind blowing up my arse, and giving you a belly laugh.'

'No offence, big man,' Rab said. He called everybody that, despite the fact that he towered over most.

'Listen, Rab. I need a set of Sierra wheels in a hurry.'

'What? At this time of the morning?'

'If I don't get them, there won't be a car to fit them on.'

'I see what you mean. I was brought up near there. You're lucky there's anything left.'

'What about the garage?'

'We don't keep wheels,' Rab said. There was a pause. 'Oh. Yes. Yon Willie Brown's motor's in for a service.'

Martin breathed a sigh of relief. All the assistant editors got company cars. It was a contentious issue because they all had desk jobs, while the reporters, the ones who actually drove to stories, used their own cars. The good news was that the company provided them with Ford Sierras.

'I'll only need them for a couple of hours,' Martin said. 'It'd be a big favour.'

'It'll cost you.'

'I'm not daft, Rab.'

'Okay, big man. I'll be up in half an hour. Be there.'

'Nowhere else to go,' Martin said, hanging up.

He pulled his collar up against the early morning air and shoved his hands deep in his pockets. By the time he got back to the car, there were a few people about, moving quietly, on their own, or in groups of two or three. Blackhale was beginning to stir.

Andrew was sitting in the driver's seat, head flicking from side to side. When Martin rapped on the window, the little professor jumped and his hand came up, tightly gripping the tyre lever.

When he recognised Martin an expression of relief washed over his face.

'Where have you *been*?'

'Long-distance phone call,' Martin said lightly.

'Why on earth were you phoning long distance?'

'Not phoning. Walking long distance. To find the bloody phone.'

Andrew shot him a querulous look. 'What's happening?'

'We're fixed. A friend of mine is bringing wheels. It's a short-term loan. You'll have to get a new set first thing.'

They sat in the car and the sky lightened. A group of youths came by, wearing bright jackets and baseball hats. They came close to the car, then saw the two men sitting inside. One of them pointed at the bricks and they all laughed and moved on.

'It's not funny,' Andrew complained.

Their conversation turned to the night in the Reid house. Andrew, despite what had happened to the car, instantly became animated.

'I don't know what's on the tape. I'm just hoping the monitor was faulty. But I wish we'd had the infra-red stuff. It would have picked up everything.'

'It was *weird*,' Martin said.

'There's probably an explanation.'

'Yes. The house is haunted.'

'Now, you don't really believe that,' Andrew said, in charge of the situation once more.

'It shook me, I can tell you. I don't know why.'

'And that girl. The things she was saying. What was that about?'

Andrew shrugged. 'Talking in her sleep.'

'The whole place was a mess. It looked as if a whirlwind had hit it.'

'Yes. But did you notice the girl's . . . um . . .'

'The blood?'

'Yes. That's quite common apparently. Many of these occurrences centre on young girls just passing through puberty. Best theory is that it's some kind of telekinesis brought on by hormonal changes. Not really supernatural, but *natural*. Like a burst of mental activity that moves things around.'

'You believe that?'

'I believe that the human brain is a lot more powerful than people realise. We only use about a tenth of our thinking power. If we had access to the rest, if we could really *use* it, who knows? We could move mountains, probably.'

Rab Anderson arrived fifteen minutes later while Andrew was still expounding enthusiastically. A sleek, black Bentley appeared behind the Sierra, slowed to a crawl and stopped silently.

Andrew's eyes flicked to the wing-mirror and he gave a visible start.

'There's a car behind us,' he said in a hushed voice.

Martin twisted in his seat. Big Rab got out of the car.

'Oh, for God's sake,' Martin said, laughing.

'What is it?' Andrew asked quickly.

Martin ignored him and opened the door, stepping out and turning to face the other man.

'What's this? Travelling in style?'

'It was the only one with space for the wheels and the pneumatic jack,' Rab said. His stood with his hands on his hips, barrel-chested and with iron-grey hair cut into a crew cut.

'But the Editor's car . . .' Martin said.

'If I get caught I'll be out on my ear, so let's make this quick so I can get it back to the office before anybody notices.'

Martin chuckled and Rab gave another bellow of laughter. Even if he was caught, it was unlikely anybody would have the nerve to sack him. Martin introduced Andrew, who automatically stuck out his hand and felt it enveloped in a huge horny mitt. The crudely-worked tattoo on the driver's knuckles did little to instil confidence.

It took them ten minutes to fit the wheels on and tighten the bolts. Rab heaved the jack out of the Bentley's boot and pumped it up until it connected with the frame. The Ford lifted a couple of inches and the big man swept his foot under the front. The pillars of bricks tumbled to the tarmac. He did the same at the back and lowered the Sierra to the ground.

'Right, let's get this show on the road,' Rab said. He turned towards the Bentley, then stopped.

'Hey, prof,' he bawled across. 'Follow me down to Clyde Street. There's a wee man who'll do you a set of wheels and tyres for less than a ton. Brand-new.'

'Are they hot?' Martin asked.

'Of course they're fucking hot.'

Martin looked at Andrew, who stared at him over the rims. A small, conspiratorial smile twisted the academic's mouth. 'Oh, why not. They're probably mine anyway.'

Martin clapped him on the back and returned the grin.

By ten in the morning, they pulled up outside Andrew's rooms on Gilmour Avenue, close to the bridge over the River Kelvin in the University quarter of the west end of the city.

Martin was ravenously hungry. The professor fired up the kettle and made two mugs of coffee, which they drank while the smell of grilling bacon wafted from the kitchen.

'What a night,' Andrew said. 'I'll have to write this all up today.'

'I don't know if I'll be able to use it yet,' Martin said. 'I'll see how the pictures turn out. I've a reputation for getting facts. I just don't have a clue what the facts are here.'

'Well, just write what happened,' Andrew called from the kitchen. He came though with two plates piled high with bacon sandwiches.

Martin didn't give him a chance to lay them on the low table. He grabbed the nearest one and stuffed it into his mouth. It was the best thing he'd tasted in weeks. He swallowed a huge mouthful and washed it down with hot, sweet coffee.

'But I don't know *what* happened,' he said when he was able to speak.

'Just write what you saw.'

'I don't know what the hell I *saw*.'

'Let's finish this and check the tape.' They ate silently for fifteen minutes.

Andrew was fastidiously washing the plates when Martin took the keys and went down to the car. He unlocked the boot and swung the lid high, reaching in for the box with the camcorder.

His fingers touched something furry and his hand jerked back reflexively. He twisted his body, shifting the carton to peer behind it.

His heart leapt into his throat and quivered there like a startled mouse.

The little brown teddy bear was lying on its back. Its beady obsidian eyes glittered up at him.

'Oh my—' Martin mouthed, almost silently. His heart was beating like a triphammer and his breath refused to come. The harmless little furry toy was so utterly *alien*, so preposterously *menacing*, that Martin couldn't draw his eyes away from it.

He stood there for a stretched-out minute, unable to move. His mind zoomed back to the scene in the darkened room when the movement on the screen had made his head whip round.

The teddy bear *had moved*.

It had very slowly changed position, then it had tumbled off the chair, as if it had jumped towards the camera, or as if it had been *pushed* by an invisible hand.

Martin got his breath back and stood up, finally unlocking his eyes from its mindless stare.

Martin remembered putting the boxes into the boot. He had turned and given Andrew the tyre lever. There had been nothing in there except an old waterproof coat.

How had it got in there?

He didn't know. He didn't really *want* to know. Last night he had seen something that his mind couldn't break down into facts and figures. He'd seen something that he couldn't explain, and it had shaken him for some reason that he did not understand.

The box was still in the boot. He bent quickly and hoisted it out, turning to put it on the dry pavement. He straightened. The little bear still lay there, motionless, unblinking. Martin hesitated for a moment, then reached in and grabbed the thing, hooking it out. His fingers gripped the soft artificial fur and he felt the body squeeze in his grip in a strange, almost *living* way. He spun, twisted his body and hurled the thing away from him. It soared into the air, tumbling over and over as it flew in an arc over the low blossoms of a decorative cherry tree, and then fell fast. It hit the grey waters of the River Kelvin with a small, inaudible splash, bobbed twice as the current carried it downstream and then it sank from view.

Martin could still feel the texture of the fake fur on his hand and automatically rubbed his palm on the side of his cords. He gave a small shiver. The river surface rippled and then the ripples were gone. He did not see the little teddy bear again. He didn't want to think of what he would do if its head broke above the surface and turned and lanced him with those button eyes.

No, he did not want to think about that *at all*.

Finally he slammed the bonnet down and picked up the carton. He hefted it under an arm and carried it up the stairs. If Andrew noticed anything in his expression, any paleness on his face, he didn't mention it.

The professor set up his own television set, connected the leads and switched the camera to playback.

It was a waste of time. There was nothing on the tape but snow. It looked as if someone had drawn a magnet over the cassette and wiped everything.

'What would do that?' Martin asked.

'It's either a fault in the camera, or an electromagnetic pulse.'

'Where do they come from?'

'Well, you get them from nuclear explosions, but we can rule that out. A big spark from a generator could do it, but I don't think that happened.'

'So what's the explanation?'

'I think the girl might have been responsible,' Andrew said. 'Damn, the physics department could have loaned me an oscillator that would have picked up any energy in the room. I didn't even have a temperature gauge.' Andrew looked furious and disappointed all at once.

'We can go back again,' Martin said, though inside himself he knew that he never wanted to go back to that flat in the tower block again. He was still trying – and failing – to close the door into childhood that last night's happenings had slammed open.

'I suppose we could,' Andrew said miserably.

The two of them stood looking at each other, both glum-faced. Each had his own reasons.

Duncan Haldane turned the envelope over in his hand. It was a large buff-coloured thing with black, official printing on it. His name was typed on a white sticker. The reverse bore the legend: 'The Scottish Office, St Andrew's House, Edinburgh.'

He'd had it in his hands for ten minutes and hadn't opened it yet.

Alec Stirling sat on the chair, elbows on the kitchen table, mailbag lying abandoned on the floor. He was nursing a cup of tea.

'Howling Gail got one this morning,' he volunteered. Duncan's attention was riveted on the envelope.

'Huh?' he said absently.

'Gail Dean, the minister's wife. She got one too. I hung about to see if she'd open it, but she took it inside. Maybe it's good news.'

'Maybe. If it isn't, I'm buggered. I can say goodbye to this place.'

'You'll never know unless you open it. And remember what my mate said in his story. The Secretary of State hardly ever gets involved in one-off issues. It's your land and your trees, and you're only building a few cabins, out of sight of the village. I reckon you're right in there.'

Duncan lifted his head and looked at Alec. His expression was worried. The postman could sense the turmoil and tension.

'Ach, go on. Open the bloody thing.'

Out in the back they could hear Rose talking to the children. Any minute now she would come in and see the envelope and then there would be no delay. Rose was forthright and straight. She would demand that they open it right away, even if just to see who they'd have to fight next.

'Oh, to hell with it,' Duncan said, resigned. He reached across to the breakfast bar and hefted a long breadknife. His big hands held it delicately while he surgically slit the top of the envelope. He peered inside. There were several sheets of white paper. He paused for a moment or two, then dived his big, calloused hand inside and drew them out.

'What's it say, Dunc?'

'Give me a chance, man,' the big farmer rumbled miserably.

He scanned the sheets quickly. Alec could see his lips move as he read. He flicked to the next page, then the third, then back to the first, which he read slowly. His expression was fixed.

'Okay? What's the news?' Alec was a study in impatience.

Duncan let the pages slide to the table. He brought both his hands up and cupped his big head in them and let out an enormous sigh. Alec thought he could see his shoulders shaking.

'Aw, hell, Duncan,' he said. 'I'm sorry.'

The big man sat like that for a few long moments, head in hands, as if he'd all the weight of the world on his shoulders, then he lifted his face up and bawled: 'Rose! *Rosie!*'

His wife came bustling in through the back door.

'What's the matter?' she said as she came in. Then she saw Alec and said hello.

'We've got it, girl!'

'What's that?'

'We've won,' the big man shouted. His voice rumbled hugely around the kitchen. 'Look. It's all here. They're not going for the inquiry. The Scottish Office don't want to know.'

'Oh . . . oh, Duncan,' Rose almost wailed. Duncan grabbed her in a bear hug, lifting his wife right off the ground. Alec gave them their moment, peering over the top of his glasses.

'Does that mean—?'

'Yes,' Duncan interrupted. 'We go ahead. We're back in business.'

Then Rose suddenly burst into tears. It was as if a pent-up floodgate had suddenly sprung open. She bawled, completely unrestrained, while Duncan held her tight against him. Alec looked away.

The children appeared at the back door. Dorothy looked up at her parents, bewildered. Ben looked concerned.

'What's wrong, mum?' he asked. Rose continued crying and snuffling into her husband's chest.

'It's all right, son, she's happy,' Duncan said, a huge grin splitting his face.

Ben looked at Dorothy and gave her the look that children do when faced with the inexplicable vagaries of adult behaviour. He shrugged and the two of them went back out into the garden.

Unable to help himself, Alec read the letter. As soon as he got home he telephoned Martin Thornton to give him the news.

When he came out of his house and down the winding lane to the main street that cut along the front of Linnvale, he sauntered past the big picture window that fronted Meg Balfron's tearoom and coffee shop. As he expected, every seat round the big table at the far corner was filled. The women had gathered. He stood in the sunlight, nonchalantly lighting a cigarette without realising he was running the flame over the cork filter, while sneaking a peek inside. Gail Dean was holding up three pages. Her face was quite impassive, but she did not look happy. Molly Carr, opposite her, was saying something. Alec couldn't hear a word, but the expression told him everything. Her eyebrows were knitted in an angry frown and the corners of her mouth were turned down as she talked. She was *furious*.

Alec tittered to himself, enjoying the scene. One of the women, it looked like Meg Balfron, was gesticulating. One long finger with a red nail came down like a spear and stabbed at the papers. Molly snatched them up and brandished them, her thin face pinched and sour, which was nothing particularly new for the schoolteacher. They were getting quite heated in there.

Alec took a big drag on his cigarette and coughed as the acrid fumes caught his throat. He pulled the thing from his mouth, looked at it in disgust and threw it on the ground. The heel of his big black postman's shoes ground it onto the pavement. He selected another one from his packet and made sure he got the right end. He drew in again and sucked smoke into his lungs and blew it out contentedly.

Inside, it looked as if a hen fight was going on. Through the glass, Alec could hear high voices. They all seemed to be talking at once. Gail Dean leaned forward to say something. She didn't look angry, but even through the glass and at the distance from where Alec stood, he thought she looked *worried*. She was shaking her head while, opposite her, Molly Carr was talking quickly, her fist tight, with one finger pointing forward and jabbing aggressively at the air. Molly's thin, lank hair swung back and forth in time to the movements.

Alec laughed to himself again. He liked Duncan Haldane, and he didn't give much of a damn about a few trees and a couple of cabins. It wasn't as if anybody was going to be able to see them anyway. And the trees in the Haldanes' lower pasture, they'd been planted as a coppice by the farmer's grandfather. Duncan had inherited the trees as he'd inherited the farm. They were hardly part of the great Caledonia Forest if they'd been planted by hand, now, were they?

The postman had lived in the glen all his life. He loved the place as much as anybody. As a boy he'd gone up the Dumbuie Hills to trap rabbits, and he'd taken his fair share of running salmon from the Corrie, and that was in the days when Old Leitch was the gamekeeper and what a bad bastard of a ghillie he'd been. He'd taken a deer or two out of Fasach Wood in the autumn. The last thing he wanted was for the glen to be turned into a holiday camp.

Experience and a sharp mind told him that there was no chance of that. The place was greenbelt. Donnie MacKinnon had got the go-ahead for his calor-gas store because hardly anybody used peat any more in these parts and there was enough of a demand. Even then, he'd had to surround the plant with spruce trees to keep it hidden from view, so as not to spoil any of the scenery. Aitkenbar had started up his farm-supplies depot without any problem, because it was an agricultural business, and all he'd done was convert his barns and farmyard. There was no planning problem there and, anyway, the ground wasn't too good in the valley any more. Down in the Douglas Arms there were old pictures on the walls. This had been a place where the Glasgow Boys from the art school had liked to come in summer seasons to paint their landscapes. Their oils and watercolours had shown the farms as healthy and rich. There were scenes that could have come from a Constable painting. Loaded haycarts and overfilled grain wagons. There were paintings, now old and faded, showing round-faced farmers driving herds of fat black Angus bulls down to the market at Craigard. There was one stunning oil that showed the valley from up on Dumbuie, looking southeast towards the Loch, over Fasach Wood. That was Alec's favourite picture. It showed the glen as it had been a few generations back. Many of the houses were still there, though a couple of hedgerows had gone as the farmers tried to maximise the yield in the face of ever-poorer crops, and Fasach Wood had been smaller then. The Haldane plantation hadn't been seeded. You could see right down to the Mill lade below the farm, glimmering in the afternoon light, and there, at the lower end, the old millhouse, one of the three that had been working when the Glen was fertile and productive. You could see the old drystane dyke at the edge of the trees. That was now deep in the forest. Then it had been a line of grey boulders. Now, Alec recalled, though he hadn't been in the woods for a year or two now, it was a jumble of green, moss-covered boulders.

The glen hadn't changed that much, and Duncan Haldane's chain saw and his few log cabins wouldn't change anything. The big farmer had been smart enough to understand the homesteading sections of the planning act. He had the right to build on his own land on places where buildings, the old shepherd's quarters, had been before. And if he could make a living at it, where the farming had failed him, then Alec wished him all the best.

He took another drag of his cigarette and turned round to take a glance at the scene in Meg's tearoom. Hands were still gesticulating, voices were still yammering all at once. The women of the Preservation Society were getting themselves worked up into a lather. He grinned again, enjoying their discomfiture.

It wasn't that he disliked them, although he knew Molly Carr for a sour-faced gossip who hadn't a good word for most folk. And Fiona Herron spoke as if she had marbles in her mouth and thought she was a cut above the rest. Howling Gail, the minister's wife, he *did* like. She was a friendly big woman, quick to offer a helping hand, and she'd a terrific voice, both in the church choir and at the regular ceilidhs in the village hall. Alec didn't know why she had got involved with the society, because the argument over the Haldane plan had split the community, polarising the *fors* and the *againsts*. That wasn't Gail's way. John Dean, her husband, had kept firmly out of it. He was a nice enough fellow in a quiet sort of way who went about his business, gave short, if boring and unfiery, sermons, and was good at visiting the sick. Everybody knew, or assumed they knew, he had a problem in the fatherhood department, but nobody thought the less of him for that.

The women's obvious frustration and ire, however, appealed to Alec's own sense of humour and his sense of fair play. They had got themselves worked up over nothing, and they were *still* worked up. He heard the high chattering sounds of women who made up in volume what they lacked in common sense – and some of them, perhaps, in humanity. He felt a warm glow of wicked pleasure.

'Daft bitches,' he finally said out loud.

Two young lads, passing by with a stepladder carried on their shoulders between them, looked at him askance. Alec just winked at them. When they had passed, he turned back to the scene inside. Molly Carr looked up from the papers and caught him staring in. Her mouth was still drawn down into an unpleasant curve, thinning her red lips.

Alec gave her a big smile and his glasses slipped down his nose. He shoved them back up with a cheeky forefinger and gave her a wave.

She glared back at him furiously.

'Are you going to cut the trees, Dad?'

Ben and Dorrie were sitting side by side. Duncan was at his usual seat at the head of the table, hunched over the three sheets of paper. He kept picking them up, scanning them and putting them back down again. He couldn't keep the smile off his face. Rose was at the other end, looking at him over the rim of her teacup, eyes sparkling.

'Sure am, son. Nothing to stop me now. Want to help?'

Ben shrugged. 'Maybe.'

'Some good wood there. Straight oak brings in a fair price. It's going to pay for half of what I'm building. Carman sawmill has offered top whack. If you're good I'll give you a shot of the cutter.'

The boy gave a weak smile. He looked less than enthusiastic. Duncan didn't notice, but Rose did. Her son had been very quiet these past few days. She knew he hadn't got over the fright they'd had in the forest. Dorothy seemed to have let it go, but she was a lot younger. She'd woken up crying in the middle of the night, but she'd gone back to sleep again. The younger children were, the quicker they forgot, at least consciously. They had the ability to shuck off scares and frights, because there were so many bewildering things in a child's life. Rose also knew that time was different for small children. Every day was a week long and every month was a year, and the summer holidays for Dorothy stretched into infinity. The episode in Fasach Wood had happened long enough in the past, even at a few days, to make it history to the seven-year-old.

Ben was different. He was older. After that frantic night and the

207

next, odd morning when he'd spoken about what he'd seen or *thought* he'd seen in the trees, he hadn't mentioned it. But he didn't go out to the front of the house where the valley dipped down towards the thick green wood. She'd sent him out with tea, or a sandwich for his father, but he hadn't stayed long. He'd come back, looking uneasy, and had gone through the house and out of the back door. It was as if he was keeping the house – and his mother – between himself and Fasach Wood. Rose didn't worry unduly. He'd had a fright, and he'd get over it. It was a lesson well learned. He wouldn't get lost in there again.

'Want to help your old dad?' Duncan was asking.

'If you like,' Ben said wanly.

He looked up earnestly at his father's face.

'Will you be cutting down the new ones?'

'New ones? Ha. They're all older than me, lad. Older even than your grandfather was. It was my old grandfather himself who put them in as seedlings.'

'No. I mean the *new* ones,' Ben said, stressing the word. 'The ones that weren't *there* before.'

Duncan looked over at Rose, and raised an eyebrow. She raised both of hers to let him know she hadn't a clue.

'New trees, Ben? Whereabouts would they be?' Duncan asked kindly, humouring his small son.

The boy wasn't fooled.

'I *saw* them, Dad. There's one down at the stream. And another. No, *two* more where you were cutting yesterday. And another along near the gate. They weren't there *before*.'

Duncan took a swallow of his tea, trying to hide his smile. Ben was getting agitated.

'What, they just walked up the hill, did they?'

Ben gave a visible start. Rose quickly stuck out her leg and tapped Duncan on the foot under the table. Trees were something Ben was taking very seriously at the moment.

'But I *saw* them, Dad. Last night when I woke up, they were there. Not where they were *supposed* to be.'

Rose looked from Duncan to Ben and down to Dorrie who was sitting, chin just above the level of the table. Her eyes were wide and her mouth was puckered, dimpling her chin as if she was going to burst into tears.

'That's enough, Ben,' Rose said, quite sharply. Ben turned quickly towards his mother and she saw the pinched, almost *scared* look on his face.

'Dorrie's getting upset with this nonsense.'

'But it's not—' Ben started.

'Your mother said that'll do, son.'

Ben's mouth shut like a trap.

Duncan reached over and ruffled his hair. The hand felt big and warm and strong, but it didn't help that much.

'Tell you what. After I've finished my tea, you and me will take a wee walk and have a chat, eh? Just you and me, man to man.'

That helped a bit, though Ben just wondered *where* they were going to walk.

His father was big and strong, the biggest man he knew. Ben loved him, even idolised him. He had always known his Dad would keep him safe, would protect him against anything.

But Ben had seen the *trees* down there. He had seen the bones *stuck* in the wood. He couldn't get it out of his head and he knew no one believed him. Dorrie seemed to have thrown the memory away, shucked it off and buried it. She just didn't want to talk about it, but Ben *knew* what he'd seen.

And while he loved his big strong father, his perception of the world had *changed*.

Before they had got lost in the forest, he had firmly believed that his Dad knew everything, could do anything.

But he didn't know now what manner of man could fight the trees.

For they were *monsters*. And they grabbed people and they killed them. They *squeezed* them to death.

19

Caitlin came awake slowly, swimming upwards through the lightening layers of dark. Her breathing was slow and laboured as if a weight was pressing down on her, locking her ribs. Her eyelids flicked open and Caitlin stared into two shining black eyes only inches from her face.

A cry of alarm escaped her, high and sharp. The eyes disappeared. There was a blurred black movement and the weight vanishe from her chest. A noise came from the far corner and Caitlin turned towards it, gasping in the aftershock of the fright. There was another liquid black movement and then her eyes focused. A big black cat sat on the top of the dresser. Beside it, an identical animal curled lethargically. Two sets of obsidian eyes pinned her.

Sheila Garvie opened the door and backed in carrying an ornate wooden tray. Caitlin started to shove herself up from the pillow, then stiffened, remembering her back and shoulders, but there wasn't so much as a twinge. The pain had disappeared completely as she slumbered.

'And how are you now?' the woman asked. 'I thought I heard a cry.'

'I got a fright. The cat was was sitting on my chest when I woke up. It scared me.'

'Oh, they're just watching over you.' Sheila laughed. 'They're good friends. I call them Night and Shade, for obvious reasons. Can hardly tell them apart. Don't worry, they're a pair of big softies. They'll look after you.'

Caitlin smiled wanly. The weight on her chest had caused her to panic. She wondered what would have happened if the big black cat had curled up over her face, and she shivered, recoiling at the thought.

'Anyway, how are you this morning?' Sheila asked.

'I can hardly believe I'm not hurting all over,' Caitlin said. She stretched her arms up and yawned widely, unable to stop once she'd started. Sheila Garvie beamed at her.

'I knew you'd be much better for the rest. Still want me to fetch the doctor? I can call on Hudson Gregor, if you think I should.'

'Oh no. Whatever you gave me worked wonders.' She twisted her head from side to side. By any standards, her neck should be flaring raw with every movement.

'Just a wee touch of mother nature. You can't best it,' Sheila told her. She came over to the side of the bed with the tray and held it with one hand while she flipped down four small carved legs.

As she did so, Caitlin noticed the odd shaped mole on the woman's forearm, black against the pale smooth skin, so clearly defined at first she thought it was a tattoo. It was like a tiny figure of eight. The shape sparked off a memory from sometime in the past, but then Sheila put the tray down on the bed and turned to the side. The fleeting memory disappeared. The woman reached for the platter. 'I made you something in case your appetite came back.'

She lifted the silver dome from a plate, immediately releasing a wonderfully appetising aroma. Caitlin felt the sides of her tongue twist in expectation. Suddenly, she was ravenously hungry.

'I'm starving,' she said. 'I could eat a horse.'

'If I catch one, you can have it,' Sheila said with a motherly chuckle. 'Until then you'll just have to bear with my cooking. I've made you some coffee. It's my own blend, but if you prefer tea, then that's not a problem.'

'No, coffee's fine. Anything at all.'

'Well, you just enjoy it. I'll be back upstairs in a while.'

Caitlin nodded her thanks and the older woman went out, closing the door softly behind her.

The smell was so tantalising that Caitlin started immediately. There was a plate of muesli cereal with pieces of fruit which had an odd but pleasant tart tang. It tickled her taste-buds and left a spicy afterburn. She poured a cup of coffee and drank it rick and dark, with two spoonfuls of jewelled sugar, then fell upon an enormous grill, consisting mostly of huge, apple-sized mushrooms which had a nutty flavour that Caitlin had never tasted before. The courgettes and onions were crisped and dusted with a savoury pepper. There was no meat. She ate it all and then cleaned the plate with a piece of thick-cut crusty bread that had chewy grain all through it and crunchy seeds on the outside. She was on her third coffee when she heard the clack of shoes on the stairs. Sheila came back into the room.

'Well, how did you do?'

'I'm afraid there was no finesse. I've wolfed the lot,' Caitlin admitted, a bit sheepishly. 'I didn't realise I was so hungry.'

'Ah, that's the healing process for you. It takes a lot of strength, and you have to put it back.'

Caitlin sat back, replete, stomach tight. The aftertaste was still savoury under her tongue. 'You could start a restaurant,' she said. 'That was truly wonderful. I've never tasted anything like it.'

'All home grown and picked,' Sheila informed her, with more than a hint of pride in her voice.

'You must have green fingers as well,' Caitlin said. Sheila laughed aloud, a jolly peal that brightened the room.

'Oh, you could say I have, but mostly it's from out there,' she said, indicating the front window. 'That's my garden too.'

'I don't understand.'

'Oh, except for the courgettes, the rest grows wild around here. The mushrooms are what I was picking yesterday. I had to go back for my basket.'

'They were huge. I've never seen them that size.'

'Oh, they're the baby ones at this time of the year. Wait till later. I'll make you a mushroom steak big as your plate that will really make your mouth water.'

'It did already,' Caitlin said. She leaned forward, pushing herself up from the soft pillows.

'I can't thank you enough. If it wasn't for you, I wouldn't—'

Sheila held her hand up. 'Now, we won't think about could-have-beens and might-have-beens, will we? That's all behind you now, and you're a lot better.'

'But—' Caitlin started. Sheila forestalled her with a mock serious look. 'Well, thanks. Thanks for *everything*.'

Sheila showed her perfect teeth again. 'It's *my* pleasure. I'm just pleased to help, and even more pleased to make a new friend. I don't see so many people these days. I'm glad to find I have such a pretty neighbour.'

Caitlin felt her words of thanks were weak and ineffectual. This woman had saved her life and taken away her pain. She had carried her – *carried her* – up the steep slope of the valley for God knew how far and she'd lifted her into her own bed and done *everything* for her. A warm wave of gratitude burst out from her.

'Would you sit for me?' she blurted out.

A puzzled look crossed the other woman's face. She obviously didn't know what the young woman meant.

'I mean sit for your picture. Let me do a portrait?'

Sheila looked at her and the light from the window caught the left side of her face, highlighting the fine cheekbones and the shining white hair. A hand came up to her mouth and fluttered there in feminine abashment, though she smiled with genuine pleasure.

'Oh, heavens, girl. Not me. There's enough pretty young women in the village who'd look lovely in a picture.'

'But you've got such a terrific face,' Caitlin said, quite honestly. 'Your hair's perfect, and you've got a complexion anybody would kill for.' Caitlin hesitated. 'Please. I'd love to paint your picture. I want to thank you properly.'

'Well, I'll think about it,' Sheila said, and another shy smile played about her mouth. 'But after you're completely better. You haven't seen the bruises yet, and you don't want to either. You're as black and blue as juniper in berry.'

'You will think about it?'

'Of course I will, Caitlin. Yes. I certainly will. As long as you promise to take this.' She held up a small polished wooden box that was carved with an intricate design.

'What is it, a jewellery case?'

'Oh no. It's what's inside. I've put in some of the mixture you had last night and this morning. It will keep the pain down and help build your strength. You can mix it with water, or tea. Even sprinkle it on your salads. Works a treat.'

She handed the box to Caitlin. The lid came up easily. Inside was a small woven bag tied with a braided piece of grass. It smelled like a pot-pourri.

'Oh, and for the bruising, rub this on where you can reach.' Sheila handed the girl a porcelain bottle with a neat little stopper which looked like a pixie mushroom, red and spotted with yellow. 'It smells a bit, not too pleasant, but it clears bruises like magic. I'll drop in so if you can't reach your back, don't worry. Believe me,

213

you'd think you'd been rolling in elderberries, if the season wasn't too early. It's like a tattoo from top to bottom.'

'I can imagine. Maybe it's just as well I can't see it,' Caitlin said. Sheila laughed again.

The problem of getting downstairs again was easily – and surprisingly – solved. Sheila drew the covers back for her and Caitlin saw that she'd been sleeping in a delicate cottony nightdress that was so fine it was almost transparent. Sheila bustled about in another room while she got dressed and then came through.

'Ready?'

Caitlin looked up and, in a single movement, the woman bent down, got an arm under her knees, another round her back, and lifted her straight off the bed. She carried Caitlin to the door and down the stairs. It looked as if she made no effort at all.

In the small living room Caitlin saw her wheelchair in front of an empty fireplace. It had been cleaned of the mud and leaves.

'Did you go back and get it?' she asked stupidly.

'Well, you surely couldn't, could you, girl?' Sheila retorted mischievously. 'Had to search a bit for it last night. It was snagged in a bush above the pool.'

'I saw it there before I took my flying lesson!' Caitlin exclaimed. She shivered at the memory. Sheila didn't seem to notice.

'You've still a sense of humour after all you've been through! I'm glad to find you're my neighbour.'

'Oh, I meant to tell you about the animal,' Caitlin said, suddenly remembering. She thought of Sheila coming down to the woods in the dark.

'What animal?'

'The one that attacked me. It was big. I didn't see it properly, but it growled and hit my chair and sent me flying into the trees.'

'Och, there's no big animals around here. Are you sure you saw it?'

'I only got a flash of the thing, but it was there.'

'Maybe a dog, nothing more,' Sheila insisted. 'There's nothing but a few deer and if they see you first you won't see them. There's some otters down by the river. I'll have to show you them some time. Mischievous little beggars.'

'I've never been in the forest before, at least not until yesterday. And that wasn't through choice.'

214

'Oh, you must let me take you there. It's beautiful. That's my real *garden*.' She waved a hand expansively from the front door. 'There's everything you need in there.'

Sheila offered to help Caitlin up the slope towards her cottage. She didn't feel strong enough for the incline but, more than that, she didn't want to be by herself on the straight stretch where *whatever it was* had attacked her. Sheila told her she was going up to the village anyway, she wouldn't be going out of her way.

When they got to the cottage, less than half a mile from the millhouse, Caitlin thought it strange that she'd never met her neighbour before. She hadn't even seen her passing by, though unless Sheila cut across the fields and through the trees, she would *have* to go past the front gate.

Caitlin offered the other woman a cup of tea but Sheila declined.

'I'll stop by and see you again, though,' she said. 'You have to make sure you get completely better. Remember to take my mixture, morning, noon and night. There's none better.'

Caitlin nodded. She had the box and the bottle in a small bag on her lap. 'I will. It's worked wonders so far.'

'And don't be worried about the bruises. In a day or two you'll be in the pink, so to speak,' Sheila said, laughing at her own pun. Caitlin went along with it, and sat at the gate while the older woman walked along the road, cutting an elegant figure in a light-green coat with a stylish hood, its skirts flapping as she walked briskly towards the village without looking back.

In the cottage Caitlin poured herself some lemonade and sat by the table. She took the small box from the bag and put it down. The lid opened smoothly and she drew out the neat sack. She teased loose the little circle of woven raffia until she could open the neck. A pungent fragrance rose from the small bag in an invisible cloud. It was so overpowering, sweet and flowery, yet with an underscent that was tart and spicy, that she immediately drew back wrinkling her nose, not in distaste but in sensory overload.

She dipped two fingers into the bag and took out a pinch of pepper-fine powder, brown as snuff. She put a few grains on her palm and bent to smell it again. This time the smell was less powerful and, strangely, in the heat of her hand, it began to *change*. She closed her eyes and drew in a slow breath. The kaleidoscope of mutating perfumes tingled in her nose and seemed to fill her head muggily. She smelled lavender and then the delicate fragrance of roses. They bloomed and were then overgrown by mint and thyme before transforming into a sharp, nutty smell that reminded her of an aromatic oil. Behind that there was something else, something subtle yet strong and possibly unpleasant that she couldn't identify. It slowly faded. She drew in another breath and the sweet liquorice of saxifrage pleasantly assailed her.

Caitlin kept her hand cupped and reached over the table to spill the small pinch of powder into her glass of lemonade. It dropped through the surface and bubbles immediately formed on the inside of the glass and trailed to the top where they sparkled and fizzed as they burst.

The powder was shot through with colour as it sank, turning from purple to mauve and then to a deep red. She lifted the glass and the motion was enough to stir the whole mixture to a delicate pink. She brought it towards her and took a small, wary sniff. This time the smell was wonderfully tantalising. She almost felt her taste-buds *crawl* with anticipation. It was as if every beautiful flower had blossomed and been squeezed and distilled.

Without thinking she lifted her mouth to the glass and took a sip.

The lemonade had been transformed. The taste exploded in her mouth in a wondrous rainbow of sensation. It was like nectar and honey. She felt it simultaneously burn and soothe as it swirled in her mouth. She swallowed reflexively, without volition, and a golden glow suffused her. It tingled inside, like a fine champagne starburst. Caitlin caught her breath, taken by surprise. Then she laughed, out loud, in a childlike reaction to the delicious pleasure that the pinch of powder in her drink had brought her. It was the laugh of a child who has been given a new and different sweet.

The glow spread, moving in slow rivers to her shoulders and back and down her arms, rewarding her with a sudden sense of *well-being*. It rose to her head and for a mere second she felt giddy. Then it passed, leaving her feeling warm and somehow delightfully *naughty*, as if she'd eaten forbidden fruit.

She put the glass down on the table, unaware of the slight tremor in her hand. The nagging pain in her shoulder and back, which had been starting to knuckle into her muscles again even as Sheila wheeled her chair up the road to her house, had been snuffed out.

'Whatever this is,' she told herself, 'it's worth a fortune.'

Tentatively, Caitlin lifted the glass again and took a small sip. This time the effect was not the sensory lightning of before, but it was still wonderful.

She took another, then another, then drained the glass.

She contemplated pouring a second glass. She looked at the small bag then regretfully shook her head. Carefully, she pulled on the drawstring and closed the neck. She replaced it in its box and found a home for it on the shelf beside the sink. Then she wheeled herself out of the kitchen to gather her paints and palette.

She set up the light easel next to the birch tree and brought out the painting she'd been working on the day before.

It was *still* good. There were one or two small details on the borders that she wanted to finish off before she put the painting in a frame.

In the cool shade of the silver birch, Caitlin looked again at what she'd done. The tall trees with their fudged grey bark and verdigris moss bisected in chevrons of deep shadow and beyond them the crowded forest and that alleyway of misty light to the dim shape beyond. Her eyes were drawn to the muted brush strokes where her hand had washed in diluted colours. The lines there, so faint they could hardly be made out, *did* resemble a distant dead tree. She wondered, as she mixed colours, thinning them down with drops of fresh linseed oil, if she should touch up that section. She decided against it and started dabbing in the details of the trailing net of blue-green needles of the closer larches.

As usual as she worked, her mind started to wander. The stand of trees on the board had brought back to her the nightmare tumble down the steep slope after the shocking attack by the animal. Immediately she recalled the dreadful growl as the thing had surged out from the hedgerow in a sudden black spurt.

Blood curdling. She had heard the phrase, read it, but she had never, until that moment, really understood what it really meant. It had felt as though her blood had *clotted* in her veins. The low, base rumble had vibrated through her with appalling threat. Every muscle had frozen into rigid immobility. It had bored itself into that primitive part of the brain where the fear of the predator in the dark lies huddled and the intense reaction had ricocheted through her body like a runaway bullet.

Then the thing had lunged at her. That black blur had struck like a snake and the jolt had thrown her head back, making her neck tendons scream.

Absently, she rubbed the skin just above her shoulders, under her hair. The whiplash had been agonising; now it was gone. Her other hand continued to make little stippling motions, catching the flavour of the needles on the conifers so well she could almost smell the resin.

Caitlin's thoughts went back to the tumble, jouncing and bouncing out of control as the rough trunks whizzed past her, sharp broken-off twigs sticking out at right angles, ready to snare and slash at her helpless body. She shivered as, in her mind, she went flying out of the wheelchair, arms in front of her face, through the oakleaves and then plummeting down, only aware of the fear and the sensation of falling. If the pool hadn't been there she'd have died, broken on the rocks or on some fallen tree. If Sheila Garvie hadn't been there she'd have drowned in the pool. If the animal hadn't been there, none of it would have happened. If she hadn't painted the picture that way, she would never have gone out to have a fresh look at the scene.

Too many *ifs*. Caitlin shook her head. It had just been a terrible happening, like a bad dream in real life. Even as she thought about it, she could feel herself tensing up, she tried to shove the visions from her mind.

Instead, she thought of Sheila Garvie. A woman she'd never seen before had been down near the river gathering early mushrooms. Unaided, she'd managed not only to haul Caitlin from the water, but also to carry her up to her house. Then she'd put Caitlin into her own bed and given her something to take the pain away and make her sleep.

She recalled waking sometime in the night, with hands smooth on her shoulders, and remembered how the pain had flowed out of her, drawn from her muscles and skin.

Sheila Garvie, whoever she was, was a remarkable woman. As she painted in the dappled light under the silent tree, Caitlin

218

decided she wanted to know more of Sheila Garvie and, most especially, she wanted to thank her properly for saving her life.

20

'Now what's all this, Ben?' Duncan Haldane asked his son. They were out beyond the old pig-pen which was now silent and bare, but still bore the unmistakable olfactory signature of its long-gone residents. Beyond them, and to the left, the field sloped down towards the stream and the border of the woods. Ben had studiously avoided looking over that way. Duncan had brought Ben out the back door and round by the front corner of the whitewashed farmhouse, keeping one big hand on the boy's shoulder.

He was concerned, but not worried. Ben had got a fright, he knew, and he also knew that he needed time to get over it. But he decided that he couldn't allow the boy to dwell on what he had imagined in the forest. Ben and his sister and Duncan himself had seen shadows in the dark of the crowded forest. Duncan had dismissed his imaginings as a trick of the shade. He wanted Ben to do the same. He wanted to sit his son down and get him to talk and then explain it for him. He knew what children's imaginations were like. He'd been a wee'un himself. He still remembered his childhood fears of the scurrying in the hay out in the barn and the scratching of long nails up in the loft. *The rasping sound of teeth gnawing on bones*. He'd been scared of a lot more things besides, and his father, on every occasion when his fears came to the surface, would sit him down and explain it away.

Up in the roof space, with his father holding an old Davey lamp, he saw the things which had scratched their way into his nightmares. No long skeletal fingers like the ones Ben had described, but a family of starlings nesting in a corner where the roof joists ran down to the eaves. Their claws had rasped on the gutterings as they squeezed themselves through a hole in the facing boards, with a scuttering sound that sent shivers down the boy Duncan on dark spring nights.

Further along in the roof space, the wasps' nest, a pretty paper lantern dangling from a slender stalk, was a pale, delicate glow in the dim light. Duncan had marvelled at its intricate construction and he'd watched as his father pointed out the worker wasps flattened on the old wooden joists, heads down on the wood, rasping tiny slivers to chew to make their nests. This was no gnawing on dead bones, it was life making life.

The scurryings in the hay were graphically explained on a summer morning when Duncan was led round to the barn, with his father's hand on his own shoulder, to be shown the row of dead rats. There had been six of them, without a mark on them, lying in a straight line, side by side, as if presented for inspection.

'Cat's done a good job, Dunky,' the old man had said. 'Best ratter we've had in years.'

The big black-and-white tomcat had sat beside its display, nonchalantly licking the fur on its shoulder, casually ignoring the humans.

'That's all they are, laddie,' the big, grizzled farmer had explained to his boy. 'Just wee rats keeping themselves warm. And the cat gets them as soon as they show themselves in the hay. Nothing for you to worry about, is there? I never heard of a man being bit by one of them, 'cept for when he picked it up in his hand and gave it a fright. They're just wee scared beasties that make a bit of noise and make a mess of the grain. Nothing to keep you awake at all, is there?'

Young Duncan Haldane had looked down at the pathetic line-up and shaken his head, abashed at his fears. The rats were all lying on their backs, paws dangling. Their black, beady eyes were open, but lifeless, and their mouths were opened far enough for him to see the gnawing incisors. They didn't look as if they could give anybody more than a nip. At the age of six, Duncan Haldane had done away with another terror.

Now, thirty-one years after that lesson, he wanted to do the same for his boy. He had shown them the starlings before Ben had noticed the noises in the loft. The wasps' nest was long gone, but there was an owl nesting in the outhouse and Duncan had found its pellets, little balls of regurgitated fur, and had picked out the dried skull-bones of mice and rats and voles, identifying each in turn for his boy. The barn was now empty of hay and the rats, too, had gone to seek warmer shelter and richer pickings elsewhere.

He sat himself down on the upturned cattle trough and shoved his cap onto the back of his head. He lit a cigarette and drew in a long drag. He patted the makeshift bench. It made a sound like a drum. Ben came and sat next to him, and his father put a big, heavy arm around his shoulders, bringing him closer.

'Right now, Ben,' Duncan said, keeping his voice soft. 'Tell me what's bothering you.'

Ben shrugged, a small movement that felt like a shiver against his father's ribs. He was in a spot. He wanted to talk to his father, needed to talk to someone, yet he was scared of being disbelieved, being thought stupid, and, worse, *childish*.

'Listen, I know you got a scare the other day,' Duncan said encouragingly. 'We all did. But that's gone now. Past. You don't have to worry about it any more.'

'Yes, but—' Ben said before he could stop himself, then wished his voice hadn't gone on without him.

'But what?'

There was a silence for a long minute. Duncan gave his boy a squeeze.

'Dad, I'm . . . I'm . . .' Ben faltered. He took in a deep breath that sounded like an inward sigh, then blurted. 'It's the trees. They're *coming*. I *saw* them.'

'How do you mean, son?'

'I saw them, Dad. Honest. There's two of them down by the cuttings. They weren't *there* before. They can move and they can get you. I saw them down in the woods. They caught people and they *killed* them.'

Duncan looked down at the boy. All he could see was the top of Ben's head, wavy hair cut short, shining clean. Ben gave a little movement and this time it was a shiver, a shudder that rippled through him and transmitted itself to his father.

'Dorrie didn't see anything like that. She told me she didn't know what she'd seen. It's dark down in those trees. And she didn't see anybody chasing her either.'

'But *I* saw it. It was there in the water and then it was made of leaves and it was trying to get us. And then, I saw those trees where they hadn't *been* before.'

Ben's words came tumbling out as the dam broke. Duncan waited it out.

'There were people down in the woods, on the island, and they were doing something and then one of them saw us. Then the thing came after us in the water and we ran and then we saw the big mushrooms and they swelled up like big balloons and they burst and some of the stuff got on us. It was like spiders' webs and it stung sore, worse than nettles. We were running as hard as we could and I was scared in case Dorrie let go of my hand in case she fell and it got her. Then I grabbed a branch and it wasn't a branch at all. It was a *hand* and it came off. I saw it, Dad, honest I did. And then I looked and all the leaves had joined together into a man with a horrible face and big hands and he came after us and then we saw you.'

'There, boy, be easy,' Duncan said. He could see himself how it had gone, with two small children down in a dark patch of unfamiliar territory. Three days after he'd found Ben and Dorrie panicking in the trees he'd taken a wander down beyond the stream and into Fasach Wood. The moon had been waning from full, though still white in the bright sky. He had strolled along the paths until he reached the stone wall close to where he'd come across the children. He clambered through the breach, eyes scanning the trees for anything at all that Ben might have supposed was something else. Here the trees stood closer, cutting out a lot of the light. There were shadows flickering as the leaves overhead shimmered in a breeze and it could have looked, to young eyes, as if the whole place was alive. He searched through until he came to the far wall, but found nothing. There were no corpses hanging from trees, no giant mushrooms or writhing branches. Nothing.

But. If the moon had been full, if Duncan Haldane had gone down to the woods a few evenings before, then he might have seen something very much different. And he might have believed his son. But that was an accident of timing. He saw nothing and because of that, he knew there was nothing *to* see.

'Now, what's all this about *new* trees? The only new ones are a couple of wee birches that have sprung up on the far side of the barn, and they're just a nuisance. They grow anywhere.'

'No. It's not them. I looked out of the window last night and saw them. Down by that big one you're cutting down. And there were other ones too. Then, when I looked out the window again this morning, they weren't there any more.'

223

'You must have been dreaming, Ben. There weren't any new ones when I was cutting yesterday afternoon.'

'But I *saw* them. I really did.'

'All right then, let's get this over with. You come and show me where you saw them.'

Duncan felt Ben give a little start, but he stood up anyway and took his son by the hand. He could feel the reluctance, but he gently tugged Ben to his feet.

'Come on, son. We'll go and take a look. After that I don't want you talking about the trees any more. You're getting your sister upset and your mother as well.'

Ben came with him, keeping close as they rounded the outhouse and followed the stone-chip path towards the front of the house. They crossed the main track and stepped onto the short grass that rose a few feet for several yards before dipping into the valley. Ben stopped but Duncan didn't let him stay. He tugged him along until they breasted the rise. On the level ground below, the remains of the beech tree lay in twelve-foot sections, massive logs with their cut ends cream white, drying to grey. Around them the earth was rutted and cross-hatched with tractor tyre slashes where Duncan had hauled the tangled branches away to a huge pile for burning.

'Show me,' Duncan said.

Ben was just behind him. Very slowly, he edged round by his father's hip, timidly, as if expecting something terrible to come leaping at him.

'Down there,' he said finally, pointing to where the giant root system angled towards the sky like a turkey-tail. A crow that had been pecking among the clods of earth that still clung to the fibres cawed and flew off on lumbering black wings to disappear into Fasach Wood on the far side of the stream.

'I don't see anything.'

'They were there last night.'

'All right. We'll take a proper look.'

Duncan started down the hill, his heavy workboots thudding on the short grass and arrowroot clumps. He went down a short distance and turned to look up at Ben who was still hesitating on the brow. The boy's face had that pinched, fearful look.

'Let's get this over with, son, and we can get some work done.'

Ben followed on slow feet.

Down at the crashed tree Duncan made Ben tell him exactly where the trees had been. He was determined to exorcise the ghost for the boy, to show him that what he thought he had seen was impossible, hoping to take the fear away from him.

Ben came round the tangled roots, averting his eyes from the dark green forest to the left. He pointed.

The grass on this side had been churned up as if a ploughshare had ripped and turned the turves. The earth was fresh and red. Puzzled, Duncan stepped forward and stood looking down at the gouged ground. Ben stole a small hand into his father's and held it tight.

'What's this then?'

He hunkered down and felt the earth. It was still soft and damp. The sun hadn't baked the soil into clumps.

The churned patch was about three yards wide. There were other cuts in the earth where the sods had been turned, leading off diagonally down the slope towards the stream.

It looked as if some large animal had clawed its way out of the forest and hauled itself up the hill.

Duncan shook his head. *Got me at it, now,* he thought.

'This is where they were, but they're not there now,' Ben said. Duncan hardly heard him. He was still looking at the odd slashes in the green where the turned earth was red as blood.

He walked across the broken ground, feeling it sink and settle under his boots, and leaned against the girth of the fallen beech. He took out a cigarette, flicked a match alight and took a long, slow draw.

Ben said nothing. He stood and waited.

Duncan bent down again and looked at the ruptured turf. The greensward had been ripped open. Grass and groundsel roots were turned over, exposed and drying in the morning sun. He walked round the patch of new earth and then followed the line of other diggings, scratching his head. It looked as if a hedge of bushes had been ripped up, but he knew that was impossible. There had been no hedge here. There was the green field, sloping to the stream. Until winter, the big beech tree and the elms further along where the cows had sheltered from the rains when he had cows. There had been no bush or bramble or bracken.

He came back to the sectioned logs where Ben waited and

looked at the boy. An instant of doubt flicked through his mind, then he shook his head again.

'There's a reason for this, Ben boy,' he said, 'and it's not the one you've got, neither.'

He scanned the patch again and then he saw it. Close to the big log the cloven imprints were clearly delineated in the soft earth. They followed a line, staying hard in at the lee of the beech where the ground was ripped and scadded. And on one of the warty knobs growing from the side there was a clump of dark, blue-black bristles caught on the rough.

'There you are, son. No trees, just a big pig, gone wild.' He beckoned Ben over to him. 'Look at that. That'll be John Lovatt's boar that went missing in the spring. Big bugger and all. See, there's his tracks. You remember that pig from when we brought him over year before last to see to the sow?'

Ben nodded. He looked far from convinced.

'He got out of Lovatt's sty a few months ago and he's never been seen since. Thought he'd gone right out of the glen, but he's still here, by the looks of it. That's another reason to stay out of those trees now, if you didn't have good reason before. Mean things, the boars. You stay well away from them.'

Ben looked at the footprints. He knew pig marks from the days when his father had kept their sleek bacon herd in the concrete sty. These prints were big and deep. The weight of the pig had stamped them eight or nine inches into the now-muddied ground.

'He's been rooting around here in the night. Came out of the trees and made his way up here,' Duncan was explaining. 'Great diggers, the pigs. Noses like shovels. Eat anything.'

He looked again at the messed area. It had fairly turned the earth over. *Must have been hungry.*

He'd never seen one pig root up such an expanse, but that was the only explanation for the patches of red earth leading up from the stream. Duncan was a practical man who could turn his hand to most things and give the rest of them a fair shot. It was the only explanation, so it must be the right one.

'Right now, Ben. You've either been dreaming or you've just seen shadows in the night. So I don't want to hear anything more about trees walking about.' He looked down at his son and again took his hand and ruffled his hair. 'Not on my land anyway. We need it to build the cabins on.'

Ben still said nothing, which his father took for acquiescence. Together they walked up the hill. When they got to the rise just before the farm track, Duncan looked down and saw even more clearly the diagonal line of dug earth that came out of the forest to the place where he'd been slicing the tree with the chain saw. That pig had really made a mess of the grass. It had used its nose and tusks to bulldoze a thirty-yard stretch which, from Duncan's vantage point, looked like giant claw-prints striding from the forest edge towards the farmhouse.

His son did not look back.

Craig Buist did not look back either, when Alec Stirling saw him on the Linn Road, limping down the slope and staying close to the hawthorn hedge. He was a stocky teenager set to gain his father's broad shoulders, but he had inherited his mother's temperament, a fact which was sure to keep him out of Drumbain Jail. His father had done two three-month stretches marking time to the *Drum* beat. The first was for drunken breach of the peace and malicious mischief when he'd taken a cobble-stone and hefted it through the big smoked-glass window of the Douglas Arms bar, narrowly missing barman Brendan Bain. He'd done another three-spot for an aggravated assault on Willie Adam, the sergeant who'd come up at a fast clip from Craigard after Ernie had exposed himself – inadvertently at first because he was taking a drunken piss against the balustrade of the Corrie Bridge – to three village matrons and two small girls. When they'd objected, he'd flaunted all he had and loudly offered the women a share. Willie Adam had arrived in the nick of time to protect Ernie from the attentions of a few of the workers off shift from Ardbeg distillery who had taken objection. Willie separated them all and in the mêlée, Ernie Buist had managed a lucky kick that had cracked two of the sergeant's ribs. He'd been strapped up for a fortnight and Ernie was up before the sheriff at Lochend on the Monday morning.

Ernie Buist's temper was legendary. His own father had passed it on like syphilis and stories were legion of old Geordie's fighting

227

days. The villagers – not the white settlers, but the *real* Linnvale folk – liked to recall over a beer in the Douglas how Geordie had single-handedly taken on Mick Ritchie and his five boys over a dispute about a bull which wasn't up to the mark. Legend had it that the old man, then well into his sixties, had dragged the unfortunate animal up the mile of road to the top end farm, rammed its head against the door of the byre and then given it a kick in what he described was its useless balls, and announced to the Ritchie clan that if they had balls better than the bull's they should come out and prove it.

The story went that old Geordie did all his fighting stone cold sober and only fought men, unlike his son Ernie who hadn't even tried to fight the bottle. His long-suffering wife had often been seen down at the corner shop with the brim of her old hat pulled over her face to hide the bruises. Even when young Craig was born down at Levenford General the doctor had been appalled at the tracery of bruises on her shoulders and arms. They reckoned two hard blows on the side of her belly had caused the complications which had brought her to the hospital in the first place over Ernie's protests that she should '*whelp*' at home, the way his mother had.

They gave her a Caesarean and kept her in for a week longer than they should and then they had to let her home again. She refused to say what had happened and there was nothing they could do about it. Tina Buist had died in a fall from the open stone stairs that led up to the old grain store hard by the small farm. Nobody was able to prove it was anything but a fall. Young Craig had been at school at the time. Folk whispered over their beers and behind their curtains, but whether Tina had fallen or been pushed was anybody's guess and most folk guessed the latter. Her death had no sobering effect on Ernie Buist. Young Craig stayed away from school when the bruises were fresh and managed to get himself an education the rest of the time and he spent much of that time hoping he'd wake up and find his father had died in his own vomit. John Lovatt, who ran the neighbouring farm, took him in when Ernie was hauled up to Drumbain for the third time, and this one for a year.

Ernie was beating the Drum because he'd taken a spade and nearly caved in the skull of a hillwalker who'd had the misfortune to cross the Buist scrubby land when the farmer had a hangover.

There were two of them, young students from Glasgow just out for a summer hike when they chose the wrong gate to open. Ernie had almost half a bottle of whisky in him and had heard his terriers barking as they did when anybody came within two hundred yards of the farm. He confronted the two hikers and told them in no uncertain terms to get off his land. One of them made the mistake of telling him there was no trespass law in Scotland (*a common misconception*) and that he had no right to put them off his land.

Their bad luck was compounded by the fact that young Craig had been clearing out a drainage ditch, one of the many chores he had to do around the farm in between schooling and beatings. The spade was leaning against the wall. Ernie proved his inalienable right of possession and eviction by swinging it down with such force on the first young man's head that he nearly dented the fellow's skull. The other student dropped his rucksack and broke his own sprinting record, hotly pursued by Ernie's four bad-tempered Scotch terriers. The year in jail gave Craig some peace, allowed his bruises to heal and, being a hard-working boy, whose ambition was to become a fighter pilot, he managed to catch up on the classes he'd missed and pass six of the seven ordinary level examinations he sat, much to everyone's surprise. He was almost fifteen.

Ernie Buist got out of Drumbain nine months later and everybody wondered how he'd got the time off. He was not a chastened man. Craig was immediately hauled back from the Lovatt farm and set to work while his father hit the bottle from his first day home, determined to make up for lost time.

It was three months after that when Alec Stirling met the boy on the road.

The postman had collected the mail from Shona Gibb, who was postmistress and corner-shop owner, and was on his way to Craigard late in the afternoon when he saw young Craig walking along, limping quite heavily, beside the hedgerow.

He passed by, then pulled up just ahead of the youngster, letting him catch up.

'Hey, young Buist, want a lift?'

The boy stopped and looked warily at him. He shook his head. Alec caught a glimpse of a mark on the lad's cheek, but Craig kept his face angled away.

'What's wrong with your leg?'

'Nothing. I hurt it.'

'Come on, hop in. I'm going up to Craigard. It'll save you a hike.'

'I'm not going there.' The boy had a determined look on his face. His voice was soft but Alec, who never missed anything, couldn't help but notice the serious tone.

He stopped the engine and got out of the van.

'Nice night for a walk, right enough,' he said amiably. 'Think I'll take a break myself.'

He strolled across to the verge and sat down on the grass. Craig Buist hesitated a moment then prepared to walk on.

'Hey, what's the rush? Come and have a smoke,' Alex said coaxingly. Normally he wouldn't have offered the boy a cigarette, but he could sense the boy was carrying more than the faded rucksack on his shoulders. Anyway, he'd spied young Craig and his pals smoking up behind the wall at MacKinnon's calor-gas store.

The boy glanced up and down the road, as if expecting to see someone coming after him. Finally he came over and sat down beside the postman. He took the cigarette and cupped his hands over the end while Alec lit it, then drew in heavily. This close, the bruise on Craig's cheek showed the clear outlines of knuckles. He'd been punched *hard*.

'Who did that to you?'

'I fell,' Craig said. 'Hit my face on the barn wall.'

Alec's glasses had slid down his nose. He looked at Craig over the top of the lenses and said nothing. Then with his forefinger he shoved the frames back up again.

'And what happened to your leg? One of the chickens kick you?'

The boy took a deep draw and blew it out again slowly. He looked up at Alec Stirling and, to the postman's surprise, he smiled a boyish grin which dispelled the troubled look in an instant and transformed the sullen-looking boy into a handsome young man. Alec was immediately reminded of the young Tina Buist who'd been a beauty in her time, before the years of living with Ernie had worn her thin and haggard.

'Aye, that's what happened. Fell over a straw and a hen kicked me. I have to watch where I'm going.'

230

'And where *are* you going, with a knapsack on your back and a bad leg?'

'Out of here.'

'Trouble at home?'

'There's never anything but trouble, Mr Stirling. Sure everybody knows that. He'd kill me if he knew I said that. But . . .'

The boy turned away. Alec put a hand to his shoulder and gently turned him back. He could feel the tremors under his fingers.

'He'll kill me one of these days anyway. I wish he'd *died* up in jail.'

Craig took another draw and hauled it into his lungs. He held it in, Alec sensed, to hold away the tears, but when he blew out again there was a shudder in his breath.

'Don't tell him you saw me, Mr Stirling, eh?'

'No, course I won't. And call me Alec, everybody else does.'

'I thought they called you Scoop.'

'Aye, that as well. And don't worry about me. What about yourself? Where are you going to go?'

The lad shrugged. 'Anywhere. Levenford maybe, even Glasgow. Somewhere he won't come looking.'

'Have you got a place to stay? Or any money?'

'I got ten pounds. I nicked it from the tin. He'll never notice. He'll think he spent it on drink. My mother had an auntie in Glasgow. I'll see if she can look after me. I want to do my higher exams and go to college. The old man can't even *read*.'

'Why don't you just go down to Willie Adam and report it. That leg looks as if it's in a right mess.'

'Aye, then they'll put him in for a few months and I'll go into a home and when he comes out again he'll take a shovel and cave *my* head in.'

Alec thought this was the most deadly, most *terrible* statement he'd ever heard from a youngster in his life. But it was probably terribly *true*. The thought saddened him deeply.

'Listen, you can stay with my sister up in Craigard. She's got plenty of room. She'll take you in until you get fixed.'

'You don't understand, Mr Stirling. He nearly broke my leg last night. He kicked me down the stairs at the feed store. I could have broken my neck. It's not going to happen again. Craigard's

231

too close. He'll find me, and honest, I'm really scared of what he'll do to me.'

Alec could see the deadly seriousness in the boy's eyes. He really *was* scared. He was about to reply when the stuttering roar of a tractor engine came bellowing from up the hill.

Craig Buist jumped to his feet like a cat, the blood suddenly draining from his face.

'It's *him*,' he managed to say. Alec heard the instant *fright* in the boy's voice and put a hand out to grab his shoulder. Craig twisted and hauled away. With one easy movement he grabbed his rucksack and, injured leg or not, he scampered across the road like a scared rabbit. Alec saw him vault the short-cropped hawthorn hedge, ignoring the thorns that snagged his patched jeans. The last he saw of the boy was his dark hair bobbing on the other side of the hedgerow, heading down through the thistles in the field towards the river and Fasach Wood. If Alec hadn't stopped the lad, he'd have been a mile or more down the road and would have run in another direction when he heard his father's old tractor lumbering down the road. It was an accident of time and place. Alec Stirling's good intentions could have sealed the boy's fate. Bad luck and good luck, however, were dancing hand in hand on that summer day. If Alec Stirling had not stopped to talk to the boy and give him a cigarette, then the key to what was happening in Fasach Wood might never have been turned, and what happened in the Glen might have turned out very differently.

Ernie Buist pulled the tractor up only an inch from the rear bumper of the post-van. It juddered and panted and there was a harsh metallic crash of gears then an animal gasp before the tractor stopped moving.

'Where the fuck did that wee bastard go?' Ernie snarled without preamble.

'Who?'

'You know who, Stirling. Don't come the smartarse with me. And shift that fucking van before I drive right over it.'

'That's Government property, Buist. You get five years in the Drum for that,' Alec said levelly. Ernie Buist was a scary man any day of the week, but Alec, never a fighting man at the best of times, was suddenly filled with *fury* at the man who liked to beat up women and hurt his own child.

232

'Are you trying to be funny?'

From somewhere, and for some reason, a response jumped straight into Alec's mouth and was out before he could stop it or even think about it.

'Is that your *own* face, or is it an arse with teeth in it?'

As soon as the words were out Alec realised it was probably a mistake. But that feeling was followed by the certainty that if he distracted Buist for long enough, the boy would make another mile and, who knew, even with a tenner in his pocket and his whole world in a tattered rucksack, he had to be better off than having this red-faced beast of a father running him down.

Ernie Buist's face was a purple picture of instant rage. In the late afternoon sunlight, Alec could see the colour rise up from a bull neck and flood the already-florid cheeks. The man's head appeared to be inflating like a balloon. Alec thought that if it kept expanding it would suddenly burst with a pop. Sudden wild laughter bubbled up inside the postman and came out in a huge guffaw. *An arse with teeth?* he thought. *Where the hell did that come from?*

'Oh, a funny fella, are you?' Buist roared.

He heaved himself out of the tractor seat, bustling in the way only the heavy, drunk and furious can manage. 'I'll show you what's fuckin' funny.'

Alec backed off, wondering what his next move should be. He was at the back end of the van, only feet away, as Buist landed with a crunch of tackety boots on the road. The man pulled his cap down over his forehead with an angry jerk, a gunslinger's motion, and came bulling forward. Alec bumped against the back door of the post-van then moved to the left, still backing. Buist's fists were two big hard bunches of knuckles.

The postman reached the van door, but it was far too late for him to wrench it open and drive away. Buist reached out a horny hand and grabbed him by the shoulder of his postman's jacket. Alec turned and, as he did so, his glasses which had slid down his nose slipped further and fell off. Immediately the world blurred. With the instinct of the short-sighted he immediately bent to catch them, thus saving himself from the effects of the powerful roundhouse punch which Ernie Buist swung at his head without any preamble.

There was a loud hollow *thonk* next to Alec's ear which left his head tingling with the bell-tone resonance. This was instantly followed by a bellow of pain and rage as Ernie Buist's knuckles collided with the side of the van. Buist had not expected Alec Stirling to duck – in truth, Alec hadn't actually *ducked* as such – and the big farmer's reflexes were too dulled with drink for him to pull the punch when he missed the side of the postman's head. His half-bottle of whisky was not enough, however, to dull the pain in his hand. Ernie Buist felt a crack on the knuckle of his middle finger and a pain like broken glass shot up the length of his forearm.

Alec's outstretched fingers found his glasses in the blur round his feet and he grabbed them, swinging them up and onto his face in a practised movement. Still unaware of exactly what had happened, but making a shrewd guess, he straightened up to see Buist doing a strange little dance, first raising his head and then ducking his whole body down, all the while clasping his right hand in at his belly.

'Shite. Oh you fu—,' gasped the farmer. 'You've broke my fuckin' *hand*, you—' He was rocking himself backwards and forwards as if the movement would take the pain away. Alec noticed a serious dent in the side panel of the van. But for the accident with his glasses, it could have been the side of his head.

'Just you wait till I get my hands on you, you *bastard*,' Buist bellowed. He didn't look as if he was going to put *that* hand on anybody for a day or two, maybe longer.

Alec stepped back and watched the other man doing his weird little war dance while his beefy red face worked itself into a variety of contortions and expressions.

The postman took in the scene for a few seconds, then he got another blast of the righteous anger he'd felt at a man who was known to have battered his wife on a regular basis and was now making life hell for his son.

Not only that, Alec told himself, he'd have felled the postman like an old tree if that punch had connected.

Alec Stirling was not a fighting man. He never went looking for trouble, and he had such a happy-go-lucky way about him that it rarely came looking for him. Nonetheless, his anger spilled over. Suddenly he was *furious* with Buist. The big man rocked backwards, still holding his hand as if it was broken. His face was screwed up and his eyes were tight closed as he rode the crest of another jagged wave of pain shooting up to his elbow.

The postman took two strides and swung his foot up *hard*.

His black service boot came up and his instep connected with Buist's crotch with a meaty *smack*. Through the leather toecap, Alec felt the fleshy connection and a wonderful surge of satisfaction swept through him. The farmer made an *ooof* sound and sank to his knees like an Aberdeen Angus bull down at the abattoir. He made another small, quite high-pitched sound from a mouth that was as round as a doughnut.

'You 're going to *what*?' Alec asked.

'*Ung.*'

'Sorry, I didn't quite catch that,' Alec said, still grinning, enormously pleased – and *surprised* – with himself.

Buist made a dry, retching noise and his florid face had gone very pale indeed. Alec toyed with the idea of giving him another one just for good measure, but then dismissed the notion. No doubt, on some dark night as he made his way home from the bar, Buist would come lunging out of a doorway and make him pay, but that was for another time.

He watched as Buist slowly got to his feet, eyes still glazed and both hands tucked into his crotch as if he was holding everything together. He took a couple of steps towards Alec and then his face twisted in evident pain and he staggered across the road and fell against the low hedge. He made a couple of grunting noises which at first Alec took to be moans, then he let out another bellow.

'*Bastard!*'

Alec thought he was the subject of Buist's address and was about to make a retort on the nature of illegitimacy when he realised the farmer wasn't talking to him at all.

Buist straightened up and raised a hand, pointing over the hedge.

'*I see you, get back here,*' he roared, surprisingly loudly since only a minute before he had been incapable of speech.

Alec looked over the hedgerow and saw, in the distance, down the slope of the field, young Craig's head bobbing up and down as he sped between the thistles and groundsel that had grown out of control since Bill Aitken had sold off the last of his cattle in the spring and had taken himself and his family elsewhere to find work.

Ernie Buist seemed to have forgotten all about the postman. He barged along the hedge until he found a place where it was low enough to climb over and simply thrust himself through, ignoring the hawthorn spines. He blundered into the field and took off after his fleeing son, one hand still clamped against his testicles. Alec grinned. At the rate his father could manage, the boy would make it to Glasgow with twenty miles to spare.

The postman stood and watched the progress of events. The big farmer, moving like an injured bull, crashed through the thistles and knapweed bellowing his fury. Way in the distance, close to the edge of Fasach Wood, the boy was moving like the wind. It was no contest.

A sudden blast of noise from close by startled Alec so much he almost jumped out of his boots. His mind had been so focused on the uneven chase that he hadn't noticed the gas tanker hauling its way up the Linn Road. The driver smacked the heel of his hand down on the horn again and the big Tautliner *honked* twice in succession.

'Haven't you got work to go to,' Jock Weir shouted, leaning out from his cab, 'or are you going to spend all day sightseeing?'

Alec gave the driver a wave. He was a drinking fellow from the Douglas Arms bar.

The white gas bowser gave an aggressive sneeze as Jock whacked on the air brakes. He threw open the door and stepped onto the plate.

'I can get past the van, but that tractor'll have to shift,' he said. 'That Buist pissed again?'

'I suppose he is. I'll try and move the thing.'

Alec climbed up into the metal pan seat and thumbed the starter. The tractor was so old it didn't even have a key. The engine spluttered then caught with a stuttering roar. Black smoke coughed from the high stack and Alec heaved the gear into reverse. He sat almost side saddle and eased the decaying hulk back up the road for about a hundred yards until he reached the gate at Buist's low field, a scraggy patch worn threadbare by massive farm tyres and overgrazing. He spun the wheel with an effort, backed the monster into the field and let the engine die.

236

Back down at the van he waved Jock forward. The airbrakes sneezed again and the tanker's powerful engine took the strain. Jock edged the machine up towards the van. There was a gap of no more than six inches, but the driver took his tanker up the Linn Road every day of the week to the MacKinnon storage depot. As he passed he leaned out of the cab again, making sure his tail end wouldn't clip the post van.

'That Buist should be back in jail. He's not the full shilling, you know.'

'Oh, I know that all right,' Alec told him. He was still savouring the meaty *thud* from when his shoe had connected.

Jock revved the engine and was gone in a powerful roar and a brief cloud of blue diesel fumes. Alec switched on his own engine and let the brake off, taking the van down the hill towards the Loch Shore Road and then up to Craigard.

On the way, he thought of the boy running from his brute of a father.

'Bloody shame,' he said aloud.

When Craig Buist had heard the familiar roar of his father's ancient tractor, his heart had leapt into his mouth, and *he* had leapt over the short hedge like a startled roebuck, despite the pain in the joint of his hip.

The old man had seemed even crazier than usual this afternoon. He'd tripped over a brush that Craig had left against the crumbling corner of the farmhouse after he'd swept the yard of chicken shit and that had been enough to send him into a blinding fury. He'd shouted his son's name at the top of his voice and as soon as Craig heard it, he'd cringed. He was up in the grain store where he used to play as a small boy, using his old daisy air pistol to pick off the rats that scuttled along the skirting where the wall met the wooden floor. Now he used the place as a sanctuary. The old man hated the idea of Craig getting an education, chiefly because Ernie Buist hadn't bothered with his own, assuming that farmers didn't need anything except a broad back, a knowledge of cows, and how to barter for livestock at the market.

Craig didn't want to be a farmer, especially not on the scrubby patch that had been the Buist holding since the turn of the century. He'd seen the pictures on the primary school wall, showing the valley looking green and lush, but he knew, as almost everybody else did, that farming was dead in the glen, and had been for the past ten years or more. Craig Buist had got up one cold, bright morning when he was only eleven years old, while his mother was still alive and a buffer between the boy and his father's worst excesses. He had seen two fighter planes come screaming up the glen, their wings almost clipping the tops of the tall trees at the edge of Fasach Wood and causing a majestic swirl in the silvered morning mist. He'd watched them travel at terrifying speed, deadly *beautiful* machines riding on a wave of thunder, and the hairs on the back of his head had crept and crawled in sudden realisation of destiny.

That was what he wanted. That power. That flight. That *freedom*. A week after that he'd hitched a ride in one of Aitkenbar's farm supply vans to Levenford and into the ATC office where a small man with a thin, fair moustache had told him that pilots needed to study maths and physics – things that Craig hadn't even *heard* of.

Most of all, the man in the uniform said, they needed to study a *lot* and get *top marks*.

In the following months his class teacher Miss Finn, known to everybody, quite affectionately, as *Old Huck*, had been amazed at the change in young Craig Buist. From being one of the handful content to sit at the back and swap comics and gaze out of the window, Craig had left his underachieving friends where they sat and moved himself to the front. In the space of four months he'd caught up with the rest of the class, not without difficulty, not without sweat and graft, and then he'd started to crawl ahead. He'd spent hours up in the grain store – from which his mother would fall *(or be pushed)* to her death in three short years – singing his multiplication tables until he could hear them in his sleep. He'd struggled with verbs and nouns and pronouns and finally got the hang of apostrophes, and when his exams had come round he'd come out third in the class. At Lochend High, despite his worrying absence record, he pushed himself hard and kept himself in the top five per cent. This year he had sat his ordinary levels, which would determine what highers he would qualify for, and while he expected good results – *especially in maths and physics* – he had borrowed the advance textbooks from a helpful and encouraging teacher to get himself ahead for when school went back.

He'd set up an old trestle table next to the window in the grain store and was struggling with complex algebraic functions when his father's almost incoherent bellow had rattled the rafters.

Craig froze at the sound. With the instinct acquired in the years of keeping out of his father's way, his mind automatically calculated the relative values of keeping quiet and hoping the old man would stump off and maybe forget about his son, or getting himself down the stairs as quickly as he could to get it over with quickly and keep the damage to maybe a backhander across the ear. Ernie Buist took the decision out of his hands. He bawled from the bottom of the stone stairs.

'I know you're up there, boy.' His voice was harsh with the drink. 'Bloody nancy-boy with your books. Get yourself down here *right now*.'

Craig scraped the three-legged stool back from the table and made for the door. He didn't know that his father was already clambering the stone steps. The boy appeared at the doorway and took a step out onto the open landing at the top just in time to catch a knuckle on the side of his face. Stars exploded and went into orbit and the boy's arms pinwheeled as he staggered, off balance. It was a twelve-foot drop from the ledge to the cobbled yard below. Craig started to topple. In that split second he visualised his mother's panic when she fell from the same spot more than a year before. Even then, in his dizziness and bewilderment, the black thought lunged at him: *he must have pushed her!*

Craig might have met the same fate but for the strangely fortunate fact of his own father's anger. He was teetering at the edge of the drop when a big hand clamped like a vice on the collar of his denim jacket and hauled him backwards. Ernie Buist had not intended to save his son from a broken neck. In fact, it had all happened so quickly that he didn't even realise the boy was falling off the top of the step. He only grabbed because that's what he always did when he was getting ready to give Craig a good hiding, and on this afternoon in summer, that is *exactly* what he intended to do.

The boy's feet missed every other step as his father dragged him down the stairs, hauled half out of his jacket.

'Teach you to laze about and leave tools all over the place,' he rasped when they'd got to the bottom, every syllable punctuated by a slap. Craig instinctively kept his head low. The beefy thuds caught him about the shoulders, painful, but not damaging. He let out a yell with every slap just to let his old man know he was feeling it. Long practice had taught him it was always best to mollify Ernie Buist.

'Nearly broke my damned leg on that brush. Could have crippled me and then where would we be, eh?'

His son did *not* tell him that the prospect of his father laid up and crippled would be like Christmas, New Year and pancake Tuesday all rolled into one. He kept yelling and telling his father he was sorry and he wouldn't ever do it again.

Finally Ernie Buist gave the boy a hard shake and let him go. Craig stumbled to the right and spun. His father aimed one of his big tackety boots at the boy's backside, but his aim was off and Craig was still spinning. The toecap caught him high on the thigh, right in at the hip joint, and suddenly a *bomb* went off under the muscle. A huge pain exploded in there and sent jagged pulses up into his waist and down to his knee. The leg gave way underneath him and Craig sprawled in the un-brushed-up chicken shit.

The pain was so exquisite, so all-consuming, that the boy was unable to cry out. It was as if the hurt had stopped his breathing – as indeed it had – and taken his voice away. He lay in the muck for several long seconds in a daze of pain where the world looped in and out of focus. Behind him Ernie Buist said something, but it sounded far away and faint and Craig was still riding the roller coaster so he didn't even instinctively jerk away. As it happened, his father did not aim a second kick at him. Instead, his footsteps crunched on the cobbles, fading as they reached the edge of the farmhouse. A few seconds later, the brush which he'd tripped over came clattering across the yard to scrape to a halt a few inches from his boy's face.

'When I tell you to sweep the yard, I mean put your *back* into it,' his father growled. He disappeared round the corner and was gone. Craig lay in the mire for another five minutes, oblivious to the muck and the smell, concentrating on the pain in his leg, trying to get a grip on it and hold it tight in case it got any bigger and twisted out of his control. Eventually, it began to fade away to something he could handle and still think at the same time. He got himself very slowly to his feet and made it to the wall, using the brush to support himself. He stood there for ten minutes, breathing hard with his mouth wide open. Tears streamed down his face, but he wouldn't give anyone, especially his father, the satisfaction of hearing him cry.

In that moment, Craig Buist made his decision to get himself away from the scrubby farm and the bully who called himself his father. The tears were for himself and for his mother. In that moment, Craig Buist, only fifteen years, knew with sudden clarity that his mother's fall had *not* been an accident. She'd been pushed off the top step, or more likely *punched* off, to fall and break her head on the basalt paving of the yard. For her, after years of living with an animal like Ernie Buist, it had probably been a release.

Now. *Now*. Craig Buist was scampering down the long field towards where the line of willows and tangled gorse bushes delineated the edge of the Corrie water, angling towards the junction with the south end of Fasach Wood.

Unspoken, he cursed Alec Stirling for stopping him on the Linn Road and persuading him to sit down and have a smoke. If he hadn't done that, he might have reached the Loch Shore Road and got a lift either north or south and been free and clear. Even as he thought it, he knew that was untrue. His father must have woken up and called for him less than ten minutes after Craig had bundled his good shirt and school jeans into the rucksack along with his maths and physics books and his only treasure, the finely illustrated colour edition on fighting planes, a book that was Craig's bible, the one he read at night in the dim light and used to transport himself to the cockpit of a jaguar fighter, roaring at Mach Two up over the glen, seeing the little farm white against the brown and green. Sometimes in those evening *waken* dreams he would see the white in a circle cross-hatched with aiming lines, and he'd feel his thumb on the red button on the joystick.

The few minutes spent with the postman had made little difference. In fact it might have saved him, for the Linn Road is a long, straggling country track with tight twists and turns as it makes its way down the glen. Despite the roar the tractor made, the bends could have masked the sound. His father might have caught up with him on a stretch where there was no place to run.

Craig scampered down the slope of the field, heading for the shelter of the forest, hoping his father had missed him.

Then he heard Ernie Buist bellow again from up at the roadside and the nerves down his spine shivered in sudden apprehension. Despite the creaking pain in his hip that drove a shard of glass into the joint with every stride, Craig did not stop. He was maybe three hundred yards in the lead. Once he got to the trees he could disappear for a couple of hours if he had to, then cross the Corrie at one of the shallow points, or up near the Witch's Cauldron, then head through the Douglas estates to get back to the road.

Meanwhile Ernie Buist's mind was filled with red rage. It sizzled with incoherent thoughts that sparked like shorted circuits. He'd just been kicked in the balls and his son had run away from him and he could see him down there in the field. The boy was *ignoring* him. He'd shouted to him and told him to come back and he had been completely *ignored*. The appalling *defiance* was such a huge thing in his mind that Ernie Buist was almost completely out of control. He'd bulled his way through the hedge and started off down the hill. The postman was almost completely forgotten, though the pain in his testicles pulsed through him with every heartbeat and, in a dark and festering section of his sparking brain, Buist planned an evil reckoning with Scoop Stirling.

The boy's head bobbed in the distance behind the high thistles and Ernie Buist lumbered in pursuit. He roared several times in the course of his downhill charge, but neither he, nor his son, nor Alec Stirling up at the roadside was aware of exactly what it was he said.

Up ahead Craig darted out of sight into the trees. A few minutes later his father, seething with wild rage, followed him into Fasach Wood.

Craig heard the rasping shout behind him and jinked to the left, angling towards the river. He was breathing heavily by now, but not hard. It was cool in among the trees and the air was still. A short distance away the sound of running water competed with the heartbeat in his ears. Craig ignored both of them. He'd known these woods since he was a toddler. He found an old, familiar deer track and followed it. Behind him he could hear the crackle of bushes as his father ignored them, simply ploughing them under his farm boots.

The boy left the track a hundred yards further along and angled off to the right where the undergrowth was thick. He came to a moss-covered dyke and scrambled over it into the dense forest. He ran for another fifty yards.

Then Craig Buist didn't know *where* he was.

Huge trees with gnarled, muscular roots crowded together in dense stands. Ahead of him he could see a cluster of big red and yellow mushrooms that were more than a foot high. He stopped and stood still, leaning with one hand against a tree while he got his breath back. Something skittered over his fingers and he looked up to see a centipede fully six inches long disappear into a hole in the rough bark. He jerked his hand back at once, sensing instinctively that something was *wrong*.

This was a part of Fasach Wood the boy had never *seen* before. There was an odd smell in the air, not the usual summer forest smell of resin and sap and green leaves and pollen. Here the air was filled with a thick, sweet odour that spoke of wild growth and fast decay.

Craig stood silently for a few seconds and, as he did, saw a mushroom not twenty feet away begin to expand eerily, as if filled with animal life. From underneath it a big toad, not brown but with brilliant yellow tiger stripes over its warty skin, hobbled out and blinked an amphibious golden eye. Above him an insect ratcheted by on whirring wings and under his hand he felt the tree suddenly *shiver*.

Perhaps it was Craig Buist's heightened sense of survival in the face of his father pursuing him that made him abruptly *aware* of the threat. He was instantly riveted with a sense of terrible *badness* which engulfed him totally. And the threat did not come from his father. It came from the *forest* itself.

He snatched his hand away from the tree, still feeling the aftertouch of that strange *breathing* ripple, and spun off to the right. He blundered between two trees, then shoved his way through a stand of strange, leathery, somehow succulent yard-long leaves and beyond them to the bole of an old hoary oak. He crept around it, keeping his body away from the hairy runners which tangled the scarred bark. He peered ahead.

There was nothing to be seen until a shape, a *pattern*, sprang into focus, in the way that the eyes suddenly spot the shape of a face in a jumble of lines and whorls. That was *exactly* what happened to Craig Buist. It was a *face* which abruptly and without warning snapped into his vision from the tangle of branches and leaves in front of him. It was white and oddly misshapen, but the white of bones and the dark of eye sockets caught his attention and froze him rigid. It was a human head, squeezed out, extruded from the surface of a tree, the cracked dome of the skull sparsely covered in long, fair rat-tails of hair. In that one dreadful second, Craig saw where the bark had turned outwards, like hard lips curving away from the dreadful head. Beyond, hanging limply on each side of the thick trunk, he could see the long bony arms, a heavy gold bracelet round one wrist.

The boy's breath backed up. Way behind him, as if in a dream, he heard his father bawl his name and a few other words, but it was as if somebody else was hearing that. Craig's attention was *nailed* on the awful sight of the body that had been swallowed by the tree.

The sense of danger that had squirmed and danced in the nerves in his spine suddenly screwed itself up so tightly inside him that he felt his very back arch with the force of it. Appalling dread swamped out the initial fear. Craig Buist could feel his eyes bulge in their sockets, his heartbeat thudding too fast against his ribs.

An overwhelming instinct told him to back off, get away, take himself out of this place.

The boy took a step backwards, forcing his paralysed foot to move. He dragged a third step before he was quite sure he was able to unlock his muscles and make them carry him away from this place. He retraced his steps, backing all the way, keeping his eyes locked on that dark and *unnatural* place in the forest. The hairs on the back of his head and the small fuzzy ones down the length of his back were prickling with a life of their own. The sense of sudden and terrible threat was *enormous*.

At last he was far enough away from that dreadful place to force himself to turn. He ran along the track until he reached the old drystane dyke once more and found a niche where years ago some of the boulders had toppled away. Without thinking he squeezed himself into the tight space, shoving his body hard against the slick damp, his face hidden in the shadows. He opened his mouth wide to take the rasp out of his breathing and willed his heart to slow.

His hands were still shaking and he clasped them together to still their motion. He cowered, shivering like a scared rabbit.

Three minutes later there was a thud and a metallic scrape on the rocks only a few feet from his head. A deeper shadow formed on the stones.

'Fuckin' nancy boy,' his father growled, though it was hard to make out the words. 'I'll kill the wee bastard.'

In that moment Craig Buist realised that his father was deadly serious. There was something very *wrong* inside the old man's head. Maybe Craig had lived with it so long that he hadn't recognised it. Maybe he'd taken his father's violent rages as the norm since birth. Now, in the stunning clarity of huge fright, he could see the madness from a distance and notice, with almost calm objectivity, the utter craziness that seethed within him. By this time young Craig Buist was very detached from the world. The intense terror that had swept through him in the dark glade in the forest, the utter horror of the supernatural, had come screwing itself in from some primitive part of his mind where the fear of the dark and the dread of claws in the night dwells within us all. Craig Buist was the first person in the whole of the Glen, with maybe the exception of young Ben Haldane, to accept completely and utterly that there was something about Fasach Wood that was completely and utterly *wrong*, completely and utterly *evil*.

Ernie Buist clambered down from his vantage point on the drystane dyke and crashed onwards into the dense trees, taking the rough direction his son had in his flight. Craig did not move a muscle. Even if his father had turned round then, he would possibly have failed to notice the boy crouched in the niche. Craig was as still as the stones which surrounded him.

The man swore loudly again and shoved his way between the trunks. Craig watched his bison-like progress with wide eyes. He saw his father move heavily through the edge of the odd green jungle-like fronds and head towards the mushroom patch.

From the dyke Craig had a clear view of what happened. His father stopped close by the old oak and, like his son before him, he put a hand on the trunk. Even at a distance Craig could hear the heavy panting as his father tried to catch his breath. The months in Drumbain had not improved the farmer's fitness. Drink had taken its toll.

A movement to his father's left caught Craig's attention, though the boy was still locked into immobility and at first he did not even risk swivelling his eyes. Ernie Buist cocked his head and half turned. Craig's eyes flicked to the motion and saw the same big toadstool, now swollen to twice its previous massive size, expand further. A series of contractions rippled up its slimy red and yellow parasol, as if muscles heaved and shuddered under the pustulent skin.

Get away. Getawaygetawaygetaway . . .

The urgent internal voice yammered inside the boy's head, but he did not move an inch. His fingers were dug so far into the moss that they were clenched on the cold stone underneath.

The toadstool gave a jerk. There was a loud pop, like a paper bag being burst between clapped hands, and silver dots spangled the air between the trees near where his father's bulk leaned against the tree. The boy saw his father's head jerk back slightly and the air was full of silver streamers. Little points of light spread out from the burst mushroom like fireworks, trailing delicate filaments that caught the few stray shards of light filtering though the leaves.

Craig heard his father grunt, then the dark figure, half-hidden in the shadows, made another jerking movement. This time his body twisted as if he'd been stung. There was another twitch and Ernie Buist took two quick steps backwards. His hands were raised as if he was trying to fend something off. Craig saw a little silvery nodule parachute onto his father's cheek and heard the old man yell aloud.

Ernie Buist did a little dance, beating at the air. His head snapped back and his flat cap flew off and rolled behind a tree. He roared again, this time louder. It was a bellow of pain and surprise and incomprehension. Craig squeezed himself further into the cleft among the tumbled stones. Eyes fixed on the scene some distance ahead, he watched as his father backed off. The threads were sticking to his hands like early morning gossamer on the hayfield. Ernie snapped a hand up to his eyes and he screamed. A shiver ran through his son. The boy had never heard a man scream before, never mind his *father*. The sheer immensity of it was sickening. Craig felt a big scream wind up within himself and that scared him terribly. He jammed his knuckles into his mouth and bit down *hard*. The flaring pain strangled his cry.

246

Ernie Buist staggered back from the oak tree, both hands clamped up against his eyes. His bellow had tailed off into a gurgling sound in his throat. Craig saw him stumble backwards, still keeping his feet, until he fetched up against a tall larch with a straight trunk that reached way above the broad-leaved canopy. There was a crack as his father's head connected with the ringed bark and the old man didn't even seem to notice.

The trunk of the larch tree darkened, as if it had suddenly become wet. In a matter of seconds, the whole girth of grey bark was flooded with sap which oozed out from the surface. It was reddish gold in colour and even from where he sat with his face pressed in against the fusty moss Craig caught a strong, over-powering waft of the clogging resin smell. He saw his father bend down, still clutching at his eyes. Long sticky trails of syrup had attached themselves to the back of his head. They seemed to yank him upright again, hauling him back against the trunk in an elastic *snap*. The man grunted again as his body hit the tree once more. He raised a hand to the back of his head. The boy saw the arm jerk again, but it seemed to be stuck in a weird salute. Resin dribbled in sticky rivers down Ernie Buist's head and face and onto his shoulders. The flow congealed where it stuck and more came down to cover it like molten wax. Sluggishly it oozed down the man's chest and arms, coating him in a honey-coloured lacquer. Craig watched, fascinated, *horrified*, as his father's movements slowed down. The arm, held fast to his head, ceased to twitch. The gurgling sound was cut off. The other hand remained fixed to the front of his face. Ernie's legs jittered and danced until the streams of resin finally encrusted them too.

The resin continued to flow out until Ernie Buist was a frozen amber statue in the dark patch of the forest. A big insect swooped down from the trees, maybe attracted by the thick, cloying pitch smell. It landed on Ernie's shoulder and stuck. There was a brief rattling of wings and then more sap oozed out and covered the creature, binding it like a fragile brooch to the dead man's coat. The forest went very quiet.

Craig Buist sat in his niche for fully fifteen minutes, mouth wide open, eyes staring at the contorted face under its jewelled glaze.

Up above, a zephyr of wind moved the topmost branches and the shards of sunlight winked in and out of existence. Craig saw movement in every shadow that appeared and disappeared. Still his fingers were clenched against the stone. He felt as if the whole forest was watching him, waiting for him to make a move. Strangely it wasn't the *fact* of his father's death, but the method that had shocked him to the core. It was the dreadful, alien, *unnatural* way of it that had put a cold hand on his heart and clenched with a ferocious grip. His breath came in panting gasps, as if he'd run a long way and his lungs hurt with the effort of it, but he was powerless to stop himself.

Then there was a movement, only a few feet away from him. It happened so slowly and innocuously that it was fully ten seconds before the reality – or *unreality* – impinged on the boy's frayed mind.

A small, quite pretty tendril of honeysuckle, a runner from the main shoot which was clambering up the narrow trunk of a rowan sapling, began to move. It was the leaves which snagged the boy's attention, growing in simple symmetry, two on either side of the stringy runner. At first Craig thought it was a butterfly, then he saw the second pair about six inches behind the first, then the third, and the fourth. They were moving very slowly, like moths in a line crawling over the dead leaves.

Craig's eyes swivelled. The honeysuckle tendril was thickening near the roots of the rowan, snaking forward as it grew, snaking *towards* him. At first it did not quite register. The movement was so gentle that there seemed to be no threat. In the space of a few slow seconds, the leading tip of the creeper lazily touched the toe of his boot and looped over it. The growing end flipped itself round and up the other side in a gentle coil, then continued its blind quest forward. It was only when the leading soft green bud touched the skin above his ankle that Craig jerked his foot back. The tendril suddenly tautened with remarkable force. He felt his foot drawn out from underneath him and, at the perimeter of his vision, he saw another runner writhe forward, not so innocently this time, but like a slender and deadly snake.

Craig heaved and felt the tendril contract pulling him away from the niche. He let out a high cry of pure fear. He rolled and kicked out savagely. The metal half-moon studs that he'd hammered into his boot-heels to cut down on wear snagged the honeysuckle creeper and sliced it in two. There was a rubbery twang as the strange growth flipped back in a whiplash towards its roots and the boy tumbled in the opposite direction.

He scrambled backwards up and over the tumbled stone wall and away from the dense, unnatural part of the forest. The pain in his hip was completely gone and he jinked like a hare between the trees. He reached the field where Alec Stirling had last seen him fleeing from his drunken father and crashed through thistles and burdock and knapweed without breaking stride. He went up the slope and through the hedge and darted into the gateway where his father's tractor stood, red and rusting in the sunlight. He made it to the farmhouse and crashed inside, pausing only to slam the old wooden door against its frame. He grabbed the big black key and snapped the lock home before collapsing down with his back to the door, unable to get the image of his dying father out of his mind.

For an hour he sat motionless. Finally he noticed the tendril of honeysuckle still wrapped around the toe of his boot so tightly it had squeezed the leather into grooves. Craig scrambled to his feet and dashed into the kitchen, spilling forks and spoons before he finally found the serrated bread knife. With two quick slashes he cut the thing from his boot. He used the kitchen tongs to pick them up, while with his free hand he hefted the cast-iron lid of the wood stove and slung the pieces inside. There was a sappy smell as the tendril sections sizzled on the hot coals.

Craig sat himself down at the kitchen table, put his head in his hands and, very softly, began to cry. He stayed there for some time, letting the tears trickle down his face, before finally getting up. He went upstairs and closed the shutters in every room and then came down and did the same in the small kitchen and living room. It was only after he'd secured the famhouse that he realised that he'd left his rucksack down in the forest. In it were his maths and physics books and his beloved edition on fighter planes. The tears flowed again. Craig Buist had not yet shed a tear over the loss of his father. He never would.

21

The Linnvale Preservation Society held their emergency committee meeting in the church hall on the night Ernie Buist came –
allow the pun – to his sticky end down in Fasach Wood.

Gail Dean waited until the women were seated and then
hesitated to let the rumble of chairs being adjusted fade away
before rapping a spoon on the jug of water. The bell-like tinkle
brought an immediate, expectant silence.

'Good evening, ladies. You all know why we're here,' Gail said,
lifting up the buff-coloured envelope with the official black print.
'The secretary of state has refused to call the planning application
in, which means that we've lost this round.'

There was a swell of muttering. Heads turned and bodies moved
closer as each woman told her closest neighbour her own thoughts
on the matter. Gail rapped the jug again and the whispering slowly
died.

'What exactly does it mean?' asked Fiona Herron, sitting
opposite Gail at the table.

'It means basically that the planning permission awarded by the
local authority stands. The Haldane plan can go ahead immediately, which allows him to clear ground and build.'

'Is there anything we can do? Maybe take out an injunction?'
This was from Molly Carr, the schoolteacher, whose thin face
was pinched and angry.

'We could try for an injunction, but we've been told there is
hardly any chance of success. Anyway, it would cost a fortune, and
we don't have the money. I'm afraid we will have to concede this
one.'

'We could hold a protest,' Agnes Gillon said. 'Maybe even stop
people getting up to the farm.'

'We could do that,' Gail said. She swept a hand through her
short hair. Everybody noticed there was now more gold in it than
silver, but nobody said anything.

'I don't think that would do much good,' Fiona Herron said. She was sitting with her elbows on the table, fingertips steepled together. The painful-looking swellings that had twisted her knuckle-joints had lessened considerably. The angry red skin had faded down to an almost-normal flesh colour. Gail looked at Fiona's hands, and smiled. The pain, always lessened in summer, must be almost gone by now, and she was glad to see that Fiona had disdained the fine black gloves she habitually wore to hide her disfigured fingers.

'He's going to build the cabins himself, mostly,' Fiona went on. 'A few of us with placards could hardly stop his deliveries, and I can't see any of the men helping us.'

'That's a fact,' Molly Carr broke in. 'They've been no use to us at all. They don't care.'

'Well, it seems there is little we can do now,' Gail said, and the muttering started again as each woman gave vent to her own view on the loss of the official battle.

'We might have lost officially,' Sheila Garvie said in a quiet voice from the far end of the hall. The words carried clearly. 'But it doesn't mean we have lost altogether.'

There was a strange silence in the hall. None of the women said a word.

'You all know how important this is, and we will not give up,' Sheila said. She walked slowly between the ranks of empty chairs left from the community council meeting the week before. 'We do not *ever* give up.'

She covered the distance slowly, letting her words sink in. The women watched her, tall and white-haired and elegantly dressed in a light green coat that had the sheen of silk. She wore no jewellery.

'But what can we do?' Molly Carr blurted.

'You *know* what we can do,' Sheila said. She reached the table and sat down on the one vacant chair, resting both hands on its wooden surface. 'You know what *I* can do. Each one of you knows.' She paused and the silence lengthened. She looked round the table and met them all eye to eye.

'You're looking well,' she said to Jean Fintry, the corner-shop owner. Jean's hair was now almost as black as it had been more than twenty years ago. Everyone had noticed in recent weeks how Jean, the jolly plump shopkeeper, had been losing weight. She looked ten, maybe fifteen, years younger than she had done two months ago. She no longer wore the tented one-piece dresses that had been her trademark for years. Today she'd even put on some make-up.

'Thanks, Sheila.' Jean beamed, then blushed.

'And Fiona, how pretty your hands look.'

Fiona Herron's eyes flicked down to her fingers then back up to Sheila Garvie's face. She brought her hands apart and slowly opened and closed them, flexing them in a way that would have been impossible in the spring of the year. She smiled at the other woman, but said nothing.

Sheila's eyes swept the group of women, then turned to Gail Dean.

'You all know me. *All of you*,' she said, softly and clearly. 'Each one of you has come to me, haven't you?'

Jean Finty nodded and blushed. Fiona Herron smiled widely. Molly Carr tried to keep her face straight, but there was a downward twitch at her lips which Fiona noticed and she wondered: *Just what did Sheila Garvie do for* you?

'You have all come to me. You have asked me for help and I've given you help,' Sheila went on. She turned and looked Gail straight in the eye. 'Some of you *will be* helped. All of you will get what you wish. You *know* that.'

Heads nodded, but nobody spoke.

'You have trusted me and I have kept faith with you. The Fasach Wood must *not* be desecrated. You need me and I need you all, remember that.'

The heads nodded again.

'Don't worry, the plans have been laid. The time is almost ripe. What we have done together is wonderful, and we cannot stop now. Trust me now, and you will all have what you want, and we will save the Fasach.'

Sheila's words trailed away to silence. Nobody spoke for a full minute.

Finally she resumed: 'Leave this to me for the moment. You should carry on with the rest of the business. Have you finalised the arrangements for the ceilidh?'

'Oh yes. Everything's ready. It should be a wonderful night,' Jean Fintry replied quickly, relieved at having something to say and an opportunity to say it.

The ceilidh was a tradition in the glen which went back further than anyone could remember. It was held every year and in days gone by it had always been held on midsummer night but, more recently, at least since before World War I, it took place on the closest Saturday. This year, by chance coincidence, the longest day of the year fell on the Saturday.

The women of the village and from the surrounding houses and hill farms always made a special effort, baking cakes and brewing cordials. The Douglas Arms always donated a couple of kegs of beer and Ardbeg Distillery were generous with a crate of their malt. Everybody who worked there was in the regular habit of syphoning off enough for their needs for any occasion.

This year, like the last and all those years before that going back beyond the days of Bonnie Prince Charlie, there would be a midsummer celebration in the Glen, the kind of thing that had been discouraged elsewhere before, during and after the reformation. There had been too much of a pagan ring to that kind of thing, but Linnvale, until very recent times, had been in fortunate enough isolation before the Loch Shore Road brought civilisation to this part of the country.

Whether this summer's gathering would be as spectacular as the previous ones – and you could always tell by the number of men who failed to get out of their beds to go to work or church the following morning – was a matter of speculation. Hector Ritchie's second eldest son Norrie was the best piper in the Glen and had been a star turn at the ceilidh since he was fifteen, playing jigs and reels and, later on, when enough drink had been taken, old laments which could even bring a tear, some said, to Molly Carr's eyes. Nobody expected Norrie to be playing this year. In mid-April, when the elderflowers were in full bloom and the leaves were just bursting forth on the trees at the edge of the woods, Norrie had disappeared. So had Donnie MacKinnon's wife Betty and people put two and two together quite rightly and came up with four. There had been whispered rumours about Hector's son and the relatively young wife of the former farmer who'd seen the potential of calor gas in the rural areas when the price of oil was getting out of hand and where the natural-gas pipelines were prohibitively expensive to lay. He'd got out of farming and had bought the disused quarry, from which most of the valley's houses had been built, to store his white tankers and he was now doing very well. He'd married Betty Dunn from Lochend in the early seventies, two years after he'd been widowed. He'd been forty-two and she'd been twenty-two and while tongues wagged for a while, the passage of time had dulled the spice of the age gap.

The age gap reared its head again in spring when the whispers started up about something between Betty MacKinnon and Hector's boy, who was only twenty-eight and had come back to the Glen, not to farm, but to work for the MacKinnon outfit as sales manager. They'd been seen having an indiscreet lunch in Callander, which was thirty miles away on the other side of the loch. One of the drivers had spotted Norrie's car and Betty's little four-by-four run-around parked nose to bumper on a side road that led down to the Corrie water, which was almost a declaration in anybody's language. He'd mentioned it to his wife who told somebody else and the rumour of the affair was well under way. The last man to find out that his tall, blonde and rangy wife was having it away behind his back with someone half his own age was Donnie MacKinnon himself, and that was only after they'd gone. He'd come back from a meeting with the suppliers in Glasgow one afternoon to find her missing, while her four-track was still parked in the gravel driveway. He'd assumed that Betty had taken a stroll down to the village on a fine spring morning and thought nothing of it. What did concern him was that Norrie Ritchie was nowhere around, though *his* car was parked in its usual space beyond the tankers' turning circle. Nobody knew, when he'd asked them, where the sales manager was. That was a nuisance because the two of them had things to discuss. Donnie had planned to open another yard across at Kirkland and his meeting with the suppliers had taken those plans a step further. He wanted to get right down to it and start planning the move that could double his business in two or three years.

Norrie Ritchie did not turn up by the time the yard gate at the entrance to the box-canyon rectangle of the store was closed at six o'clock. Donnie called old Hector, who told him he hadn't seen his son for a couple of days. The receptionist at the Douglas Arms said she didn't think he'd been in, but she'd check the bar. The only hint Donnie got was when he heard the tinny ripple of distant laughter a few seconds after the girl had put the receiver down on the desk. He'd heard muffled voices, and then two people, both girls, giggle with what sounded like embarrassed laughter. A few seconds later the receptionist came back to tell him that, no, Norrie Ritchie hadn't been seen all day.

Donnie was still so wrapped up in his plans and the new deal and his growing resentment at the absence of his sales manager that he hadn't really noticed that Betty was nowhere around. It finally dawned on him when he realised he was hungry and went into the kitchen. There was nothing on the hob, no smell of cooking from the oven. He raised his eyebrows and went outside, round the side of the house to the small paddock that was fenced off from the garden. Her bay gelding was munching contentedly at the grass. She hadn't gone riding.

It was at eleven o'clock that evening that, half-drunk, he'd called the police. Willie Adam checked up at Norrie's cottage on the other side of the village and got no response. The pair of them had gone. Finally somebody told Donnie of the rumours and MacKinnon spent a week making a manly attempt to consume the entire contents of his considerably well-stocked drinks cabinet. At the end of the week, he emerged, unshaven and looking his sixty-odd years, but he seemed to recover fairly well. Within two weeks he'd promoted his salesman to manager, hired another lad as a replacement, and went ahead with his plans. He was not seen in the Douglas Arms again and rarely went down to the village. Everybody accepted the simple fact that young Norrie and Betty MacKinnon had simply run off together. The women tutted and clucked, shaking their heads and commenting on the folly of older men and younger wives. The men simply decided that Norrie Ritchie was a lucky bastard and if any of them had the opportunity to run off with anybody, it would have been the rangy and *very sexy* young blonde wife of Donnie MacKinnon.

Their disappearance caused another problem for the ceilidh organisers. Betty MacKinnon had been a champion country dancer in her day and always organised the girls and the up-and-coming village youths in some dancing lessons. Her absence meant that more toes would be stood on this year than before.

Also missed would be John Byrne, the drystane dyker who hadn't been seen around for a couple of months, though that wasn't a great surprise. John, or his father, or his ancestors going back several generations, had been responsible for the lattice of fences that separated one farm from another, one croft from its neighbour. Dyking, building the walls with bare stones and no mortar, was a skilled craft, but a dying one. The big, bearded fellow, who had the broadest shoulders of any man in the glen, spent half his time in Linnvale and the rest of the time on other farms all over the area. He had a small caravan which he towed behind an ancient ex-army jeep and he lived in that when there was no room available on the particular farm whose walls he was building or repairing. John's caravan was still parked up against the hedge behind his tiny house at the top end of Linnvale on Hill Road. Sometimes it stayed there unused for months. Sometimes John himself wasn't seen for months. He always turned up, though this year it looked as if he would miss the ceilidh, and his harmonica would be missed by all. He often played it of a night down in the bar and could remember every tune he ever heard. The women liked to hear the reedy strains of the old highland airs, while John himself, despite his rumpled and raggedy appearance, liked to cup the harmonica in his big stone-calloused hands and play the blues.

Up in the church hall, the women's committee busied themselves with the arrangements, making lists of who had agreed to do what and who had promised which donation. The band, an accordion, fiddle and drums, was the same as last year, the two Wallace Boys and Danny Dunbar. Jean Fintry herself was baking pastries, while some of the older women were mixing their own ingredients for cakes and dumplings. Sheila Garvie herself had promised some home-made wine.

While the discussion was going on, every one of the women able to listen to three conversations at once while talking at the same time, Sheila took a gentle grip on Gail's sleeve and eased her away from the table. The minister's wife followed, quite unnoticed by any of the other women. She and Sheila walked behind the curtain on the small stage to a dusty anteroom.

'We won't have anything to worry about,' Sheila said.

'No. Things are going well. It should be a delightful occasion.'

'No. Not that. The other thing. *Your* thing. *Our* thing.'

Gail Dean opened her mouth to say something, but Sheila Garvie lifted her hand. 'You will get what you want. The time is almost ripe. *You* are almost ripe.'

She dropped her hand and slowly held it against Gail's abdomen. The minister's wife and Sheila Garvie were about the same height, both tall, though Gail was the more strongly built. She breathed in at the other woman's touch, almost a gasp, and her ample breasts heaved upwards slightly.

'Yes. *Almost* there. You are taking it properly?' Sheila asked with a slow smile. Her hand.pressed against the other woman's belly. Through the fine dress she could feel the softness of skin and the warmth.

'Yes, of course. Just as you said, every morning first thing, then last thing.at night. John gets it in his cocoa. He hasn't noticed a difference.'

'Nor should he,' Sheila said. Her smile faltered very slightly. 'There is another thing. There are patterns, you know.'

'What?'

'Patterns. Some things fit and some things have no place. I'm afraid John might not be in the pattern.'

'I don't understand,' Gail said in a small voice. A look of abrupt disappointment sagged her face.

'No, Gail dear. You have not to worry. I *told* you that,' Sheila said soothingly. 'It's just that I've examined what you brought me before. Your husband . . . I mean . . .'

She paused and looked at Gail with concern.

'What I'm saying is that this thing will work for *you*, but I'm afraid it will not work with *John*. I'm sorry.'

Gail looked as if the blood had drained from her face.

'Does this mean I can't . . . ?' The sentence trailed off.

'No, of course it doesn't. You *can*. And you *will*.'

'But if John can't . . . I don't understand.'

'You are almost *ripe*. *The* moment is close. Remember there is more than one power, and the ones we seek are the stronger. Eternal. You shall have your wish. You trust me, don't you?'

'Of course I do.'

'Look at yourself. Your hair is almost gold again. I am giving you back your youth. You will have a child. I will ensure it, and your husband will *never* know.'

'But I could never do that. I've *never* slept with anyone else since . . .' Her voice trailed away.

257

'Oh, Gail, dear. You *do* have some quaint notions, don't you? I can see my missionary work is not quite complete.'

Gail was about to respond when the older woman cut her off.

'Don't worry. Everything will be fine. You won't have to do anything you don't *want* to do,' Sheila said, with a light laugh. 'Remember you are my friend, and you are important to us all. There is more than one power, and *our* power is the older and the stronger. Trust in that and you will have your heart's desire.'

She gave Gail another wide smile, showing her perfect teeth. The minister's wife returned it slowly. Sheila pressed her hand hard against the woman, just below her navel, gently kneading the soft, feminine skin. Gail felt her flesh tingle and prickle at the touch, feeling the other woman's strength flow into her.

'I *do* trust, Sheila. I *do* believe.'

'And all will be well with us all,' Sheila Garvie said. She withdrew her hand and Gail Dean still felt the tingling warm sensation. 'I must go now. I have things to prepare. I'll see you at the ceilidh. I'm quite looking forward to it.'

'What about Duncan Haldane?'

'Oh, we've lost one battle, but there are other ways. Let me consider that. We'll win in the end, you know.'

Sheila gave the other woman a small wave and disappeared through the hanging green curtain. Gail Dean waited for a few moments before going back into the hall. For a second she felt an urgent *clench* deep inside her and then it faded. She reached the door and stepped into the hall. The women were still chattering away animatedly. Of Sheila Garvie there was no sign.

Martin Thornton's fingers rattled away at the keyboard. When the phone rang he picked up the receiver and jammed it under his chin while he continued typing. His deadline was only half an hour away and he had no time to waste.

Andrew Toye's voice spoke into his ear.

'Haven't seen the story yet, Martin. Anything wrong?'

'A million things, Andy. Possibly two.'

'Well, if you need more information—'

'Andy, I need *any* information. I need some facts. I didn't see anything and I won't persuade the Editor to use a story I can't back up. It would make the two of us look like fools.'

As soon as he said that, he regretted it. Andy was no fool, and he was also a decent fellow.

'Sorry, Andy,' he continued quickly. 'I'm up to my eyes in it for the next half-hour. Can I call you back?'

'You can buy me a beer.'

'Delighted.' Martin arranged a time and place and clattered the receiver down. During the brief conversation his hands hadn't stopped clicking the keys and he'd written four paragraphs since picking up the phone.

Andy Toye was sitting at the far end of the bar off Byres Road, one frequented by lecturers and students alike. He was reading a paper when Martin strolled in, but looked up when the younger man sat himself on a stool beside him and offered him a drink. Martin ordered two pints and a brace of toasted sandwiches after he discovered that Andrew hadn't eaten either.

'Sorry about earlier. I was up to my armpits in salmon droppings.'

'I thought you were writing a story.'

'I was. It happened to be about fish farms. Apparently salmon shit is bad for the environment.'

Andy raised his eyes sceptically.

'It's true. They have facts and figures to prove it. Which is more than we've got on the poltergeist affair.'

'Well, I have taken the thing a little further,' Andrew said. 'I had one of the electronics people test the videotape. Said it hadn't been wiped normally. He told me he reckoned it had been some sort of electromagnetic pulse.'

'And what would cause that?'

'Like I told you before, an atom bomb could do it.'

'The Editor would never wear that,' Martin said, and both men burst out laughing. Andy took a man-size bite of his toastie and spent some time chewing before he was able to speak.

'The technician said he couldn't think of anything under normal circumstances. But I do have an idea. On poltergeists, Fernwood in Tennessee made some very interesting experiments on several alleged cases. All of them involved young girls. He said that in all the cases his equipment detected a build-up of electromagnetic energy. There was no apparent source, although Fernwood himself suggests that for some reason the girls were actually *manufacturing* a series of energy pulses.'

'What would cause that?'

'If I find out, I'll win a Nobel Prize and confound every scientist in the West.'

'What about the sound tape?'

'For the most part nothing but snores. Then a couple of bumps and small noises, then louder noises. I've timed them and they fit the time when the girls were getting bounced around. You can hear them crying out, at least the younger one. It's difficult to hear because this is the point where we get a lot of static.'

'So, in other words we don't have very much?'

'Not empiric, no.'

'Well, I can't write it. And frankly, I don't know if I *would* even if I could. Whatever happened up there scared the hell out of me. Things like that give me the heebie-jeebies. I didn't get to sleep for nights afterwards.'

'Oh, I thought you were a big tough newsman.'

'Very funny. We've all got our weak points. I just discovered mine. I don't feel comfortable with this supernatural stuff.'

'Does that mean you *believe* something happened?'

'I don't know *what* I believe. I was close to something I don't understand, and I didn't like it very much.'

'That's the mistake most people make. They label things *supernatural* and *paranormal* when there's probably a very *natural* explanation behind everything.'

'Look at who's talking. You're a *professor* of the paranormal.'

'No, I'm a professor of Celtic Mythology. The paranormal is only a sideline. I'm more a debunker or, better still, a seeker after knowledge. I don't believe in ghosties and ghoulies. I just believe there are things that we don't understand yet. You show a TV to a tribesman in New Guinea and he'll tell the folk back home that he saw ghosts in a box. We know differently, but we're not that far removed from them. That's why every newspaper, including your own, has an astrology column, and why the Von Danniken books sell in every airport.'

Andrew took a long pull on his beer, put the glass down and wiped his mouth with the back of his hand. The bar was beginning to fill up with students, with a few academics down at the far end, crowded together.

'Come on,' Andy said. 'Let's go up to the flat. I've a few things to show you.'

'No more poltergeist hunts?'

'Actually, there hasn't been a recurrence. The girl had her first period and the whole thing seems to have stopped. I think that tends to indicate a more human source than supernatural. The mind is a wonderful organ.'

They got to Andy's flat overlooking the river and the professor put some pork chops under the grill. He busied himself about in the kitchen and wandered through with a glass of wine for Martin. He handed him a book, a fairly old and tattered publication.

'Have a read through that,' he said.

Martin had switched on the television. He picked up the book and opened it at the flyleaf. Some quiz show ended and a children's programme came on. Martin read the inscription. *Ley Lines and the Power of the Druids*. A picture of the author, J. R. Friel, a thin man with wire-frame spectacles, was printed underneath.

Andrew had stuck a bookmark between the pages, about halfway in. Martin turned the book and it fell open at the marked page. He sipped his wine and read.

Gleann Linn, which has been known since the late nineteenth century as Linnvale, is recognised to have been the centre of Druidic culture since pre-Roman times. It is thought that prior to the Irish immigration of Celts, the Scottii, the glen was a centre of worship for the Pictish peoples. Five cup-and-ring stones mark the directions of the ley lines which, up until modern times, were believed to intersect in the stand of trees known as the Fasach, just below the old lade.

Whilst little is known of Pictish rituals, the folk legends of the area up until the late-eighteenth century reported the central figure of the Druidic hierarchy of the area was known as the Seilach Garbh-aidh. When translated from the Gaelic this means Wild Willow, possibly a reference to the healing nature of the plant and its significance in Celtic culture. The Seilach was the guardian of the ley – or dragon or fairy – lines which the Celtic and Druidic folk understood to be the veins of the planet, where the pulses of energy flow (see also Glastonbury, Stonehenge, Callanish). The lines were sealed to encapsulate the powers, with the ability to open them being devolved to the Seilach who was a high priest of the Druids. Where those lines intersected, the power was greatly concentrated, nowhere more so than at Gleann Linn where the five lines form an exact pentangle, a five-pointed star.

In addition to the Pictish cup-and-ring stones, which may have been used for ritual blood sacrifices, there are a considerable number of Celtic monoliths. These include several megalithic standing stones bearing a number of examples of pictogram sculpture, with figures of entwined snakes predominant, along with a rare early image of Cernunnos, the stag-antlered god, otherwise known as Herne the Hunter, whose most famous representation is on the acclaimed Gundestrup Cauldron. It is unfortunate that several of the stones were misguidely removed in the seventeeth century, though there are a number of woodcut depictions of several of the carvings in the Kelvingrove Museum.

Andrew was whistling as he worked in the kitchen while a tantalising aroma of pork seeped through to where Martin sat with the book on his lap. He wasn't particularly interested in Celtic or Druidic culture, but something about the book had caught his attention, if only as something to share with Caitlin Brook when he next drove up the Loch Shore Road. He intended to keep his promise to alter her kitchen to make it easier to use from a wheelchair. He knew himself that it was merely an excuse. He *did* want to do a story, a real piece on how Caitlin had overcome the odds, but, aside from that, there was something about the red-haired girl that tugged at him. There was something between them. Had been since the first night he had seen her. He didn't know what it was and he wasn't sure what he planned to do about it, but he did know he wanted to see her again. The fact that she was in a wheelchair he hadn't even begun to deal with.

The television was still on, playing some distracting tune. Martin shifted in his seat, put the still-open book face down on the arm of the chair and got up to turn it off. Just as he reached his hand out the picture changed and Martin's heart did a little *flip*.

The beady eye of a teddy bear, close up to the camera, twinkled blackly at him.

Quite reflexively, Martin jerked his hand away, as if he'd been stung. Immediately the image of that other stuffed toy, seen on the video monitor in the darkened house and in the boot of Andrew's car, came looping back to his memory.

The camera panned and then drew back. A young, quite trendy girl with a nasal voice grasped the teddy bear's stubby outstretched arms, making it perform an unnatural, bouncing walk. She was singing 'The Teddy Bears' Picnic', warning young viewers that if they went down to the woods today they were in for a big surprise.

Martin watched for several seconds, then shook his head. It was only a stuffed toy. The other one had only been a stuffed toy too.

Then how did it get into the car boot? the voice inside his head asked. He shucked the thought away. He didn't know how the toy had got there. Didn't *want* to know. He was a realist. A foot-in-the-door, feet-on-the-ground newspaperman and he did not like to be involved in things he didn't understand. With an impatient, almost urgent stab of his finger, he hit the control. The teddy bear flickered, dwindled to a small dot in the dead screen and disappeared.

Andrew came in with a tray. 'I thought we'd just eat in here, if that's all right.'

Martin turned.

'What's up?' Andrew asked.

'Nothing.' Martin shook his head and went back to his seat. 'I was just turning the television off.'

'Hardly watch it myself. Just for the news and anything David Attenborough brings out,' Andrew said amiably. 'Pork chops and apple sauce do?'

Martin nodded. He flicked away the visual memory of the teddy bear, annoyed with himself for letting something as innocent as that upset his equilibrium.

'Great, I'm starving,' he said. Andrew beamed with pleasure.

They ate at the table next to the window. The pork was delicious. Andrew had sprinkled a pinch of cinnamon over the meat which combined wonderfully well with the apple sauce.

'Fascinating book, eh?'

'Interesting. Ley lines. Where did they go to?'

'Anybody's guess. The Celts thought they were the way in and out of the underworld. There's a place at Creggan down the Clydeside where there was a ring of stones with the same reputation. There was some sort of accident there a couple of years ago. Some fellow's house caved into them.'

'I remember it. Corrie, or Crombie, a name like that?'

'I think so. Local folk said it was the curse on a ring of standing stones somebody had dug up to build a house. Can't remember the details, but Friel mentions the ring in his book. Great ones for contacting the underworld, the Celts. Picts were just as bad.'

'What about now? Nobody believes in that sort of thing, do they?'

'Of course they do. It's a multi-million pound industry, the occult. Pays a good fraction of my salary here, buys my equipment and lets me spend time on my hobby. Bookshops are full of that sort of thing. It's today's culture. There's too much pressure, too much of the mundane. People see wars and repression and poverty every night on their television screens. They want to get back to a more peaceful and simpler time when you could find a husband by washing your face in the morning dew.'

'What about you?'

'I've an open mind on everything. Scientists have discovered the magnetic lines of the earth. They've even found that the polarity poles switched from north to south every now and again. Who can say what other connections of power there are. They say pigeons fly home because they have a compass in their heads to detect the magnetic lines. Physicists are still trying to work out the strong and weak nuclear forces. Maybe there are other ones which we just don't know about yet.'

'So you do believe in them?'

'*People* believe in them. I don't believe in *anything* yet. I stress the *yet*.' He dealt himself another spoonful of sauce and invited Martin to more green beans. 'But *you* believe more than me, no matter what you say.'

'Don't be daft.'

'I saw you the other night. You know what happened in that room. You've got it down in your mind to ghosts and spirits. I think there's a much better explanation, a more *human* explanation. You, on the other hand, were scared *witless*, if you don't mind my saying so.'

'No, carry on,' Martin said with heavy sarcasm. 'Don't sit on the fence. Tell me the truth. Hold nothing back.'

'Oh, come off your high horse. We've been friends long enough.'

Martin allowed that they had. He smiled sheepishly.

'All right. I admit it. I got the fright of my life and I've seen some frightening things in my time. It must have been a traumatic experience in childhood, or something that I can't remember. It just gave me the willies. I didn't *like* it.'

'I find that with many sceptics. They'd rather say something didn't exist than admit to being scared of it. Fear is a wonderful emotion. That's what's kept us at the top of the evolutionary ladder. But generally there's a neat explanation, if you look hard enough.' Andrew pointed his fork at Martin. 'You take last year when you asked me about your policewoman friend. Something definitely happened to you. It was *real* and ever since then you've been trying to ignore it.'

'Maybe I have. I didn't ask for it to happen.'

'But you've been *scared* of it. You never sat down to work out the possibility that since the human brain works on electrical impulses, it just *might* be conceivable that one brain could pick up signals from another, like radio waves. Maybe if the signal was strong enough, and I imagine the circumstances of being shot in the back and blasted to hell from a building might just be such an occasion, actual telepathy, or tel-*empathy*, might happen, even future prediction. Many animals have an ability to sense danger ahead of time. Why not us? It could be a natural survival function. But, you want to run away from it, rather than looking at it as a fascinating idea. You're not the first, and you won't be the last.'

'So what are you trying to tell me?'

'Nothing, really. But I do think there's a good story in the poltergeist thing. It wouldn't hurt me at all if you got it in your column.'

Martin suddenly burst out laughing.

'You insult me and expect me to do you a favour?'

'Of course. That's what friends are for, isn't it?' Andrew said with a mischievous smirk.

Martin shook his head, still laughing.

'All right, I'll think about it, just for you. It's a strange world. Half of them want to keep stories out and the rest of them are twisting my arm to get them in. I can never win.'

'And you can also impress your lady friend with your new-found local knowledge.'

Martin laughed again.

Later, as he drove down the Levenford bypass, Martin realised he was humming the annoyingly insistent tune he'd heard on the television. From some long-locked mental cupboard the words to the song had tumbled out. As soon as his conscious mind made the mental leap to grasp what he was unconsciously singing, the picture of the teddy bear came alive in his mind once more. Immediately he was back in that room again, with the pale-faced girl kneeling on the bed, shoulders shivering.

'*She's drowning. She's in the water and she can't swim. Her legs won't move and she's drowning.*'

Martin could see again the wide, dark eyes, blind to everything, and the hands crawling in the air, making those slow swimming movements. In his memory he heard the harsh, rasping, *drowning* cough.

'*A brook. A river. A tree. A willow. She's drowning. She can't breathe and the water is cold. The willow will take her, but she is still dying.*'

Those black eyes, locked on his, swallowing him completely.

'*There's still life. Still life. Life and death. Life in death.*'

The blare of a horn spun Martin out of the memory and he came back to the present in the flick of an eye, just in time to wrench the wheel to bring the car back to the lane from which he'd wandered. A truck driver snarled silently from his cab and tapped the side of his head, showing Martin what he thought of his driving. He exhaled shakily and took his foot from the accelerator, letting the truck gain distance.

It was a Saturday morning and Martin had organised a long weekend off work. He didn't have to go back to the office until Tuesday. He'd spent most of the night at Andrew's place going over the tape recording and Martin's interview notes with the parents, the girls and the priest. He'd told Andrew he would cobble a piece together, but an open-ended one, and strictly for use in the weekend feature pages. Andrew seemed happy with that. They'd had a few more wines and then the professor switched to brandy. Martin declined. He'd been a whisky man until he'd decided drink was getting to be less of a friend than it once had been. He took an expensive taxi-ride home and woke up with a headache.

He'd picked up his Land-Rover after several cups of coffee and then headed for the old bungalow in Levenford to pick up the tools he needed. The workroom, built on to the wooden garage his father had built when Martin was only ten, was redolent of the woodworker's trade. Dry shavings still littered the floor, planed from a block of pine and still smelling of strong resin. Martin had stood and looked around at his father's tools, neatly hung or lined on shelves, old saws with handles smoothed and worn from use, an ancient brace and bit, the quirky little spokeshave with which Martin had carved a fine bow from a yew branch. He remembered his father, bent over the bench, showing him how to mitre a joint, strong fingers delicately manoeuvring the fine chisel and the sudden punch with the heel of his hand to take a cube of wood away from a plank with the deftness of fine craft. His father had wanted him to use the tools, to follow in the trade, but Martin had gone his own way and the old man had shrugged, maybe a mite sadly, and let him go. The tools were still there. His father, now in his sixties, was out fishing in the boat he'd built and was now puttering along with the aid of the outboard Martin had bought him. When his son had phoned him, he'd been delighted that he was picking up the tools and told him to do a good job and keep his thumbs away from the plane-edge. He'd been saying that since Martin was a boy. In the workroom Martin had savoured the old scent of red cedar and parana pine underlaid with linseed oil. He'd opened the wooden tool-box and started to load it, each tool friendly and familiar in his hands.

Caitlin Brook looked up in surprise when he wandered round the side of the house. The hot, early summer weather was stretching out to a heat-wave. She was sitting in the shade of the birch tree and the sound of the stream was muted to a trickle, shrunken by the dry spell. A warm breath of wind shivered the leaves and the shadow dappled her painting, giving it motion as well as life. For a second Caitlin seemed confused, as if she'd expected someone else, then she recognised him and flashed him a wide smile.

'Hi, stranger,' she called across.

'Hello yourself,' he called back, returning her smile. He was lugging a big brown box with leather handles, not without some effort.

'What, no wine this time?'

'Workers get fed on the job,' he retorted. 'You can supply the wine.'

'What's in the box?' Caitlin took a small piece of cloth and twisted it round the bristles on her brush, pulling the thin shaft backwards to clean it. This done, she dropped the brush into a small jar of white spirit. Traces of dark green paint oozed in a fine cloud, darkening the clear liquid.

'Tools. I said I would fix up your kitchen, didn't I?'

'I thought that was just a ploy.'

'Ploy or not, I've brought them now. Any chance of a coffee?'

Caitlin turned to him and her red hair swung with the movement, catching and scattering the light.

'I suppose so.'

She wheeled herself away from the easel and Martin stood for a moment looking at the picture, a forest scene with trees at the right and left borders, striped with disruptive summer shadows. In the centre a clearing showed red russet fallen leaves and, at its far edge, deep in the centre, a massive tree, maybe an oak, with gnarled limbs. The blocky trunk dominated the picture. It seemed to force itself from the distance into the foreground. Martin saw how skilfully her brushwork had painted the slanted shadows which drew the eye into the middle of the scene. The painting looked so *alive* he could almost imagine the fallen leaves turning in the breeze and the needles of the nearby larches swinging softly. Even the great bare oak in the centre seemed taut with life. He bent and looked closely. There were no leaves on that tree. It was a forest giant which had died there in the woods, but when he peered closely he saw the tiny dots which looked as if they'd been dabbed in with a single bristle. They resembled minute buds preparing to open.

'Come on then,' Caitlin called over her shoulder. Martin drew his eyes away from the scene and bent to lift the heavy box. He followed her into the cool of the kitchen.

Caitlin let him put the kettle on while she spun the chair around and fished out a biscuit barrel.

'Are you staying for lunch?'

You bet. And dinner too. This is going to take all day, maybe some of tomorrow too.'

'Oh. I haven't got anything in.'

'Then you can take me up to the Douglas Arms. I don't mind.'

'Maybe you newsmen are loaded with money. Us struggling artists can't afford that.'

Martin turned back from the stove. As he did so, he caught sight of the cheque, still angled up against a cookery book on the low shelf.

'Haven't you cashed that yet?'

No. I told you I don't want it,' she said evenly.

'Well, if you had you could afford at least one decent night out on the town.'

'I told you, I'm not interested in having another story about me in the paper.'

'And I told you that's got nothing to do with it. I might talk you into it, and then again I might not bother, but that's for another time. Cash the damned thing and buy yourself some new paintbrushes.'

'I don't need any,' she said, but she was smiling.

'Well, use it to put an engine on that damned thing,' he said, indicating the wheelchair. 'I prefer fast women.'

Caitlin laughed girlishly and shook her head. Martin made two cups of instant and sat down beside her. He took a biscuit, dunked it in his coffee, then shoved it all in his mouth. She wrinkled her nose.

'Right. First of all, I want to see you move around the place, to see what's most comfortable.' He tapped on the table and told her to lean on it. She had to raise her elbows slightly. 'I'll drop this about three inches for a start.' He pointed at the sink, set into a modern unit. 'You're in luck. I brought my pipe cutter and a couple of yorkie joints for the plumbing. If I take the plinth off that sink unit, you'll have no bother. Ever think about a dishwasher?'

'Only in my dreams,' Caitlin said.

'Well, put that in the bank and get one. You'll have girl's hands forever.'

He stood and took a tape measure from the pocket of a tattered old leather jacket that had seen plenty of better days but hung comfortably on his shoulders. She watched as he quickly took measurements, talking to himself as he did so.

'Stove's all right. It can stay where it is. Wall cupboards useless. Down three feet. Dresser: top come off?' He took hold of the glassed cupboard that sat on the drawers. It shifted slightly. After about fifteen minutes he came back and sat down.

269

'You'd best make some sandwiches for lunch. This place will be out of bounds all day.'

Caitlin interrupted him for a snack just after two in the afternoon. He refused to let her into the kitchen, insisting that they ate out in the garden, and wasted no time devouring the salad sandwiches before going back to work. She noticed the sawdust in his hair and, when he reached for the salad dressing, she smelled the dry wood mixed with man-sweat. It was not unpleasant. She told him about her disastrous tumble down the slope and into the river, recounting the story of the animal that had charged her and how she had tumbled through the tree and into the pool. He sat in the shade and listened to her as she told him how she thought she was going to die and then explained how she had met Sheila Garvie. In turn he told her about the episode with Andrew Toye in the tower block in Blackhale and she laughed when he revealed how scared he'd been.

'I thought you reporters never got scared,' she jibed.

'That's just a story we put about. Good for street cred,' he added, with an almost embarrassed grin.

Later he went back to work and the sounds of hammering and sawing punctuated the still afternoon air. Caitlin worked on the fine detail of the painting that she'd *thought* she'd completed days before, but which drew her back again and again. She was hardly even aware of how the tree, at first a shadow, barely perceptible in the misty swirls just above the centre of the canvas, had become more clearly defined until it dominated the scene. With each brush stroke and stipple, her hand worked automatically, deftly dabbing and stroking, while the centrepiece waxed dominant.

It was close to five in the afternoon when Sheila Garvie came silently up the flagstone path.

'Hello, dear,' she called softly and Caitlin spun round.

'Oh, it's you,' she said, favouring the older woman with a smile. 'I didn't hear you.'

'Not over that racket. Sounds like they're rebuilding your house.'

'Just the kitchen. It's a . . . a friend of mine. He's trying to make it easier for me to use.'

'Good for him,' Sheila said. Just then Martin came out of the back door with a plank of wood over his shoulder. He set it up against the wall and turned, noticing the other woman for the first time. He walked over. There was a trickle of sweat on the side of his face. He rubbed it away on the sleeve of his old workshirt.

'Martin, this is Sheila Garvie. I told you about her.'

Sheila held out her hand and he wiped his on the backside of his jeans before shaking it. Her touch was warm and soft, but firm. He noticed her perfect teeth and bright black eyes.

'Nice to meet you. Caitlin tells me you saved her life.'

'Oh, I was just in the right place at the right time,' Sheila said. 'She was in a sorry state.' She turned to Caitlin. 'And how are you today?'

'Wonderful. The bruises are all gone.'

'And are you still taking the mixture?'

'Of course.'

'Good. I was just passing and thought I'd drop by.' She looked over Caitlin's shoulder and stood with a hand on her chin, examining the painting. 'It's getting better all the time. It's really wonderful. I'd like the first option on it when you come to sell it.'

Caitlin laughed. 'My first advance commission. You're on.'

But even as she said it, she had a twinge of regret at her own enthusiasm. This painting was so good, the best she'd ever done. She wasn't sure that she would *want* to part with it.

Sheila chatted for a few moments while Martin went back to work and then left Caitlin at her painting. The girl was bent over the easel when Sheila Garvie stopped and turned to look back at her. A small smile played on her face as she watched, in silence, from under the trailing virginia creeper. Then the sounds of hammering from the kitchen interrupted the moment. She frowned, turned, and was gone.

An hour later, Martin let Caitlin back into the kitchen. She wheeled herself down the path and then jumped the wheels up over the sill as she always did. It was only once she was over the threshold that she realised that movement wouldn't be necessary any more. Martin had built a short double ramp which allowed her to rise smoothly over the short step and roll right into the house. There was a smell of burning.

'It's not quite finished, but it's nearly there. I'll have to plaster the holes where the wall cupboards were and maybe give the place a lick of paint, but it should be easier. I had to cut and solder the pipes and I've scorched the back of the unit with the blowlamp, but the smell will go away in an hour or so.'

Caitlin looked around. The scent of sawdust overlaid the burned-wood odour. There were odd, bleached marks on the walls which had been hidden before. The whole place looked *different* and it took her a moment to realise just how transformed it was.

The work surfaces had been lowered to a height just above her waist as she sat in the wheelchair. Four small cubes of wood sat on the table and it took Caitlin a moment before she realised they were the cut ends of its legs. The sawn edges were straight and smooth. The sink and taps had been reduced in height by the removal of their plinths and Martin had cut and shaped a backboard to fit the space under the window and it merged in with the rest of the wooden surfaces. The eye-level cupboards, which had remained unused since she moved into the cottage, were now on a line on the wall beside the table, all within easy reach. The masterpiece was the top section of the Welsh dresser which was now on the wall next to the door. Martin had lined her glasses on every shelf where she could reach them with ease.

'I can't believe you've done all this,' Caitlin said in a voice filled with delight and wonder. She wheeled herself across to the sink and reached to turn on the tap. Cold water jetted down and, instead of raising herself up on the arm of her chair, Caitlin could actually bend *down* to get her hands in the sink.

'Me neither. It was easier than I thought,' Martin said. 'If you want you can hang a couple of pictures over the holes in the walls until I get some plaster.'

'It's marvellous,' Caitlin told him, a wide smile creasing her face. She spun the chair and came scooting towards him. She took his hand and squeezed it tightly.

'My pleasure,' Martin said, feeling a warm glow at her delight. 'Now, if I can have a shower and get this dust washed off, you can take me to dinner.'

'Gladly,' Caitlin said, favouring him with the smile that hadn't faded since she'd seen the transformation. 'Except I don't have a shower. I can't get into one.'

'One problem at a time,' Martin said. 'You do have a bath?'

Martin scrubbed himself clean in lukewarm water and changed

into a clean pair of casual slacks. In her room Caitlin spent some time brushing her hair and putting on some enhancing but lately unaccustomed make-up.

'Your treat or mine?' he asked when he came through, hair combed back from his forehead and looking clean.

'Mine, of course.'

'I'll only accept if you cash the cheque,' he said, looking at the rectangle of paper which he'd put on top of the dresser.

'All right, I will,' she said, feigning resignation. 'And I might even let you do a story.'

'Maybe later. Let's eat first.'

They went out through the front door. Martin asked if they should use his Land-Rover but Caitlin said it was such a nice night she'd rather walk. When she said that Martin gave her a quick look.

'It's just a phrase,' she said. 'If I said I'd rather "chair" it would be accurate, but it wouldn't sound right.'

They went along the flat road, caught in the evening sunlight as they passed out of the shade of the trees lining the way. At some point Martin, quite naturally and without forethought, put his hand on the back of the wheelchair. Caitlin noticed, but said nothing. A few moments later both his hands were on the pushbar and both of hers were in her lap. She smiled to herself without letting him see it.

The fresh smoked trout in the Douglas Arms was remarkably good. They washed it down with a dry white wine and Martin insisted that Caitlin indulge herself in the sweet trolley. He waved down her protests and ordered her a Drambuie and then they sat, on either side of the small table in the almost empty restaurant, talking as the shadows lengthened.

He discovered she'd been a nurse in the Western Infirmary before joining the experimental *cop-angel* scheme in the city's rough housing estates. For more than a year she'd been teamed up with beat policemen, ready to cope with the wife-beatings, the child abuse, all the casual violence that deprivation spawns.

She discovered that he'd been in newspapers since he was eighteen, starting on the *Kirkland Herald* then slowly progressing to the nationals. He told her he'd been thinking of getting out of the trade for some time because, as he put it, the business had

273

changed. It was no fun any more. All the papers, he said, were now owned by megalomaniacs who were only interested in money and few editors had the brains they were born with or the guts to stand up to the owners. She asked if he was getting cynical and he told her to come and work in the press sometime. She detected the twinge of late regret that he *hadn't* followed in his father's footsteps and had therefore disappointed a man whom he admired and loved. As they spoke, she noticed the way his eyebrows knitted down over blue eyes when he was serious and the quick parenthesis of laughter lines on either side of his mouth when he grinned at something funny. She felt herself warming to him again and wondered if that was a good idea. She shrugged the thought away. Caitlin was *enjoying* herself. This was the first meal out she'd had in a year. It was *nice*. Too nice to worry about anything, even if she *was* paying.

He watched as she wrote a cheque for considerably less than she thought the meal would cost and then they went out to the front of the hotel and on to the Linn Road. They stopped at the side of the bridge, watching the late sunlight catch the water as it tumbled over the rocks. Then they made their way down towards the bungalow.

Halfway there Martin offered to race her to the gate and Caitlin, without a word, shoved downwards on her wheels, scooting ahead of him. He watched her red hair catch the glow of the fading light before following on. He let her win, they both knew, but they laughed all the same. At the front door, she told him there was some wine in the fridge, but he said he'd reached his driving limit. There was somebody he had to see in Glasgow the following day and he asked if he could leave his tools and finish the job when he came back. She was in the shadow of the doorway and he didn't catch the regretful look that flicked over her face.

He opened the door for her and, just as she was about to propel herself inside, he put a hand on the back of the wheelchair and quickly bent to kiss her cheek. Just at that moment, she looked up quickly and their lips met briefly.

'Thanks for a wonderful night,' she said softly.

'My pleasure,' he said in a low voice, then changed tone to break the moment. 'You paid.'

'Cheeky bugger,' she shot back, but there was laughter in her voice.

'True.'

He backed off, clanging the gate behind him as he went. She watched him walk towards the Land-Rover and was about to turn to go into her cottage when a thought struck her.

'Martin?' she called out. He stopped and came back to the gate.

'Yeah?'

'Want to go to a ceilidh on Saturday?'

'If that's a pass, I accept. Where and when?'

'Church hall, eight o'clock.'

'Do I have to wear a kilt? My legs are too thin.'

'Don't be daft. Just come any way you like.'

'All right. Saturday. You've got a date.'

He strolled off whistling. Caitlin went into the house, smiling to herself. She'd decided she *did* like Martin Thornton. There was much more to him that his jaded manner wanted to admit. She hadn't planned to ask him to take her to the ceilidh but she was glad she had. She wheeled herself into the transformed kitchen and looked around. He'd done a really good job. The place was *perfect*. She sat back for a moment, recalling the expression on his face when he realised she was asking him out, then remembered the set of his shoulders as he strolled towards his beat-up jeep. He'd been whistling something. A familiar tune. After a few moments, she realised it had been the children's song, '*The Teddy Bears' Picnic*'. Caitlin laughed aloud at that. Some hard-bitten reporter, Martin Thornton was. Before she turned off the light in the kitchen she went across and lifted the cheque from the dresser. The signature was a flourish of black ink. She slipped it into her handbag, the decision made.

22

Caitlin Brook mixed some of the powder Sheila Garvie had given her into a glass of water and drank it all in one delicious swallow. The tingling *warmth* spread out along her arms. The wine had made her giggly and she smiled to herself as she did her arm exercises on the pulley frame and then massaged her legs, kneading the muscles to help her circulation. The skin under her fingers was warm and smooth, though it felt nothing as she worked her fingertips into the muscles. She swung herself out of the wheelchair and manoeuvred herself with her elbows into a comfortable position before pulling the eiderdown up to her waist. She lay in the deepening dark for a few minutes, thinking of the enjoyment of the night, and slowly slipped into sleep.

She was running again, along by the road and then down into the forest, feeling the energy in her body bursting to be free. Exhilaration soared within her. Her legs powered her smoothly along and her feet padded a soft drumbeat on the earthen track. Trees blurred by and she moved like a summer wind. The forest was dark but there was a light mist which caught the rays of the moon and spread the beams. Caitlin moved with ease and grace. She could hear her own breath, light and strong, and there was a warmth in her thighs as the big muscles contracted and expanded. Her heartbeat was a pulse she could feel in her veins.

In this dream she was completely *alive*, replete to bursting with wild vigour. She sensed her body rhythm *sing* with joy and she gave herself to it, building up speed, running like a deer down the path and deep into the forest. She came to the part where the trail branched and she took the left fork, skipping between two trees which stood close together and brushed aside fronds of dark honeysuckle that swung themselves over the track, smelling their heady scent as she passed. Her feet never missed a step. No roots entangled her, no thorns snatched at her. She was running in the magical forest, feeling the pull of it inside her, drawing her deep into its core.

She breasted a small, moss-covered rise then scampered down

the slope, nimbly skipping over the old fallen line of stones of the ancient wall. She swept past the tall tangle of succulent, tropical plantain leaves and swung herself at an angle, leaping over the massive, fairy-tale toadstools crowding the narrowing track and sprinted for the river. The water-roar became louder as she approached until finally she was running on the bank. The path curved, following the course of the silvered water, then it ended abruptly on the flat riverside. Caitlin did not stop. In her dream she knew where the stepping stones were. A long stride carried her to the first smooth rock and her momentum swung her to the next, never missing a beat, taking just five paces to cross the water. The trail resumed as if it had never been cut by the flow and she raced along it, breath now high and fast, anticipation burgeoning in her chest. She could *feel* the power of the forest. The night air was scented with a thousand tantalising smells. Finally she was through the trees and into the clearing and she *saw* it.

The massive oak stood with its branches spread like arms reaching to a velvet sky. It was stark and colossal, a wooden monument, a giant. Its leafless limbs spread upwards from an immense sweeping bole. Gnarled roots thick as a man's chest tangled round themselves and curved into the earth. Caitlin felt herself slow. Under her feet she could feel a shivering *beat* like giant footsteps, like a monstrous heart pounding under the surface of the world.

She stopped and stared at the tree. It stood alone, a dark ponderous work of nature drawing her towards it. All around there was movement, unseen, almost unheard. It was as if the whole *forest* shivered with anticipation at this strange meeting in the darkened clearing.

Caitlin felt no fear. It was as if she *belonged* in this place that she'd never seen in her waking life. She walked slowly towards the tree and the earth-beat became stronger, a deep seismic rhythm transmitting itself to her own heart. Finally she stopped and stood like an acolyte in front of the old oak. Its bark was stripped in places where it had fallen away from the hard wood. The cleared surface was smooth and whorled, like skin. The trunk, wider than her arms could span, reared up above her and then split into two tremendous limbs which soared high into the night. There were no leaves on this tree, but she could feel the *life* pressing within it. She stepped forward again, hands outstretched to touch the giant. Her fingers were splayed, only inches from the whorled wood, when she heard an urgent whisper.

'*Caitlin*!'

She turned and felt another shiver spread like a ripple through the trees on the far side of the clearing.

Her body turned around to face the shadows. There was no one there.

'Caitlin! *Caitlin*!'

She felt another pull and began to drift away from the tree, from the centre of the clearing. The subterranean heartbeat faded from her dreaming consciousness.

Now she was travelling back the way she had come, but she was not running, she was *floating* like a cloud. Behind her Caitlin felt the magnetism of the tree's great presence, but there was something else pulling at her and she could not resist. She let herself go, smoothly flying over the water, gliding past the toadstools and the strange leafy fronds, then drifting, accelerating, over the tumbled rocks of the old wall. Here the forest was more open and her feet finally touched solid ground again.

A man was standing on the green verge. She went towards Martin Thornton and he opened his arms. Without a thought she fell into them. Their mouths met and her heart soared. A warmth tingled up and down her spine, jittering and sizzling through her veins.

Caitlin Brook woke up in her own bed just as she soared towards orgasm.

The intense *clench* inside her burst asunder and swept her up on a tidal wave of agonising pleasure. Her hands jerked back once, twice, and her hips shuddered. The intensity of the feeling was overwhelming, indescribable. Caitlin's eyes flicked open and the room blurred as her vision clouded then sprung back into sharp focus. She let out a small gasp, then a loud cry as the feeling surged through her again, taking her up to a pinnacle of pleasure then bursting within her like an exquisite fruit.

Very slowly she floated down from on high and gave a low, shuddering sigh. Immediately tears flooded her eyes and they were not tears of pain or sadness.

*

Martin Thornton almost died less than five minutes after he left Caitlin Brook's cottage, whistling that annoyingly repetitive tune as he walked towards the Land-Rover. He turned the key, the big diesel engine coughed to life and he swung away from the kerb.

As he rounded the first bend, he wondered what he was going to do. Martin had felt the attraction to Caitlin Brook the minute he'd walked around the corner and into her garden, seeing her painting in the tree shade. She was quite startlingly pretty, possibly even beautiful.

But he hadn't come to Linnvale to give her a line. It hadn't been that way at all. There had been something that snagged his consciousness and his conscience. There had been something *between* the two of them since two minutes after he'd admired her well-turned ankles as she walked briskly and innocently towards the tragedy that would break her back and condemn her to a wheelchair.

No, he hadn't come to take anything from her, to make any demands on her, but as he drove round the next bend his mind was a whirl of thoughts and feelings and emotions. They'd kissed, albeit briefly, and he'd felt a hunger behind the kiss. That was something he'd have to sit down and think about before he did anything else.

He hauled the wheel to the right at the turn which skirted the edge of the trees.

Something big and black came bulleting out from the side of the road and slammed against the driver's door with a thump which rocked the jeep on its springs.

Martin got the fright of his life. He instinctively jerked himself away from the black shape at the window and the Land-Rover veered to the other side of the road. He tried to compensate as the front nearside tyre dug its way into the soft earth at the edge of the trees, then the thing leapt at him again. There was a shattering creak and the glass seemed to bulge inwards.

Martin got a glimpse of a red mouth and white teeth and then he felt the jeep tip. It happened so quickly that he didn't know what was happening. One second he was sitting in the driver's seat, hands on the wheel, heart suddenly pulsing in his throat, the next he was in the footwell under the wheel. There was a high-pitched whine as the engine revved much faster than it should and then a lurch. Martin was thrown to the side and his shoulder came off the accelerator. The whining died and the engine spluttered and stopped. The fourtrack was sitting at a slant, its nose pointing down.

For a few seconds Martin was completely disorientated and slightly dazed. He reached up slowly and took a hold of the steering wheel, clasping it hard enough to heave himself up out of the awkward slump and, gasping for breath, he crawled onto the seat. Very slowly and apprehensively he raised his head above the ledge of the window and looked out. He could see nothing *moving*, but that meant little because there was a tree only inches from the window.

A jagged line ran up the glass and branched into a delta of cracks. Martin didn't know if that was a result of hitting the tree or whether the thing, *whatever it was*, had hit hard enough to almost shatter the toughened glass. Gingerly, all his senses alert, he clambered into the back seat and peered out. Nothing big and black came leaping out from the undergrowth.

'What the *hell* was that?' he breathed. He hadn't really seen the thing. It had come charging in from nowhere, without any sign or warning. It might not even have been an animal, although that, he told himself, was unlikely. It had been fast and dark and was able to leap high enough to hit the window right next to his face *twice*. It was powerful enough to have almost knocked the jeep on its side and, when it hit, the side of the car had boomed like a bass drum.

It took him another few minutes before his hands stopped shaking and he plucked up enough courage to gently open the passenger door. The driver's side wouldn't creak more than two inches before banging against the tree that bracketed it. Very carefully, he pushed the handle. The lock gave a loud click and he froze. Still nothing moved. There was no sudden slavering growl, no black shape launching itself from the tangled brambles close to where he crouched. He took another breath and opened the door, hoping it wouldn't creak. It didn't.

He eased himself out and cast his eyes around. There was a thick branch lying on top of a log. He bent quickly and hefted it. It was hard and stout and maybe a yard long. What he could have done with it if something *did* jump out of the bushes he wasn't really sure, but he felt better anyway. He crept round the front of the jeep. The tyres were hard up against another deadwood log. Just beyond it, only five feet from where he'd stopped, the bank gave way to a steep drop towards the river. He could hear the water, though the flow itself was obscured by leaves.

He made his way to the back of the Land-Rover. Another branch had wedged itself under the axle. He had to put his own stave down to work it free and eventually it came loose suddenly, dumping him on his backside on the dry leaves. The jeep wasn't badly damaged. There was a scrape along one side which merged with the older ones which he'd never bothered about, and a slight dent in the driver's door. The vehicle was tilted at an odd angle, but he couldn't see any major obstacles. Finally, still apprehensive, he climbed back into the cab and started the engine. He slammed into reverse and let the clutch ease out. The wheels spun on the lose leaf litter and the jeep rocked a little, but there wasn't enough traction to ease him up the slope. He tried it again, using all four wheels, but the angle was too great and the ground too soft. Just then the sinking sun dipped behind the Dumbuie Hills and the forest grew a whole lot darker.

Martin pondered his next move. He could either wait until morning, which he relished not one bit, or he could go up to the road and try to flag down a passing car, which seemed to be stretching his expectations of luck. Eventually he decided he'd go up to the road anyway. He got out, searched about in the gathering gloom for the stout piece of wood and, when he found it, began to make his way cautiously up the slope. He reached the roadside with no accidents except for a couple of bramble-thorn scrapes. He looked right and left and right again, not from his long-ingrained sense of pedestrian safety, but searching for any black shape which might be lurking behind tree or bush. Finally, as satisfied as he could be – and still very apprehensive – he started walking back in the direction he'd come from. It took only five minutes to reach Caitlin's house. He opened the gate, went up the path and knocked gently on her door.

There was no reply. The cottage was in darkness.

'Probably gone to bed,' he said to himself.

He knocked again, several times, with no response. Finally he bent down and forced a finger onto the letterbox flap and held it open. He put his face close to the narrow slot and called her name into the darkened hallway.

Along the hall in the first room on the left, Caitlin was asleep and dreaming. She was raising her hand to the tree when she heard someone call her name and then, very soon, the wonderful wave came and swamped her. Outside, kneeling on her front doorstep, Martin heard her cry out in her sleep.

There was no further reply. Martin debated knocking on her bedroom window, then thought better of it. It might give her a fright. He pondered for a few moments, then went back out through the gate, picking up the stick as he went. It was less than half a mile to the Douglas Arms, but to Martin it was the longest few hundred yards he'd ever walked. The shadows were deepening and he kept seeing movement at the edge of his vision. Several times he turned round, holding the stick out in front of him, ready to ward off an attack. He imagined something squat and fierce creeping along behind the willowherb and brambles, getting ready to pounce. When the lights of the village hove into view, he let out a sigh of relief, but he held on to the stick until he got to the hotel. It was closed but the receptionist was in the darkened bar having a nightcap with the barman and a couple of regulars who stayed after closing time. She let him have a room for the night and when he'd signed in he went straight to the bar and ordered a large brandy which he swallowed in one gulp. He had to stop himself from asking for another.

That same night Craig Buist had spent in his bedroom, alone in the quiet farmhouse. He did not sleep until the early hours of the morning when the sky was just beginning to turn pink in the east. Even then, he lay crouched on the old peeling sofa with a blanket around his shoulders and dozed fitfully. His dreams were of trees which moved and plants which crawled and of a twitching golden statue, eyes magnified behind the amber glaze, feebly struggling for life.

The boy awoke with a start, shivering with cold, eyes red-rimmed. He sat in the gloom of the darkened room for some time, then made his way slowly towards the shuttered window. He slid the bolt and gingerly opened one of the wooden screens. Summer sunlight stabbed in at him and he blinked hard when his eyes immediately flooded. Out there, out in the yard, the world looked fresh and clean. But from where he stood, young Craig could see the edge of Fasach Wood. Like little Ben Haldane, he'd developed an immediate and all-consuming aversion to that alien, murderous forest.

Young Craig Buist was as close to a complete breakdown as anyone can get and remain sane. But he was a strong boy, and a bright one. Having sat out the night, and after only a couple of bad hours sleep, he got up and opened the shutters and then went down the stairs. There were chickens in the yard, two old cows in the field next to the byre and potatoes in the shed. He had enough to live on for quite a while, he told himself, without going anywhere. For the moment, Craig Buist did not want to put one foot outside the farm perimeter. There were trees and bushes there, brambles and hawthorns. He did not trust *any of them*.

The fifteen-year-old boy, now completely alone in the world, went into the kitchen and made an inventory. There were three tins of beans and some corned beef. There were four loaves in the freezer and not much else.

Before he went out, very warily, to milk the cows and feed the chickens, Craig went into the shed and put a few things into the old rusted barrow. One of them he hefted with much effort. It was a ten-gallon drum of powerful systemic weedkiller. Craig wheeled that round to the side of the house and opened the cap on the drum, inserting the hose of the stirrup pump. For the next hour he sprayed the clematis and virginia creeper which grew up the sunny side of the old farmhouse. His mother had planted the pretty creepers when Craig had been a baby and now they covered the entire wall, sending fine tendrils along the gutterings to hang down over her bedroom window. Craig recalled how she'd loved to see the clematis bloom and the virginia bracts turn red in the autumn. It was with a very heavy heart that he sprayed the killer chemical on them. Within the hour, their leaves had started to wilt and wither. It was powerful stuff.

That done, he worked on the hawthorn hedge that ran alongside the paddock, then shifted his attention to the other hedgerow that all but ringed the farm. Next he took his father's big single-bladed axe and cut down the stand of stray ash and birch saplings which had sprung up next to the gate in the past couple of years. They were still green and slender. They fell quickly.

It was only when he heard the cows moaning with the distress of full udders that he put the axe down beside the farmhouse door, leaving it where he could grab it quickly. He took a bucket and headed for the byre. By that time, there was not a living plant, weed, tree or bush, except a couple of lettuce in the old garden, within forty yards of the farm.

Craig Buist had set up his perimeter. Any plant that shoved its way out of the ground within that circle, he was determined to destroy.

That same night, up at the manse, Gail Dean sat in the small dressing room adjacent to the bedroom, facing the mirror. She had drunk the odd, bitter mixture, as she had every night for the past two months. The light above the glass showed up the golden highlights in her hair and she ran a hand through the short waves. Even the texture was different. Her hair was softer now, somehow *younger*. She held her face up, noting that the rounding under her chin had tautened, giving her back the face she'd had ten years before. There were slight hollows in her cheeks where only weeks before they had been quite full, not unpleasantly so, but almost matronly. If her husband John had realised, he hadn't said anything. He probably hadn't noticed at all.

They had been married for twenty years this year. She had been drawn to the tall, ascetic young man who had just gained his divinity degree and together they were almost perfect in contrast. She had been tall and quite startlingly good-looking, with a sunny, outgoing nature. He had been quiet, distant and quite serious. She had not quite been a virgin when they met, not even religious, while he most certainly was. They had met at a university debate, on opposite sides of the table, and had gone out for a year, he quite shyly at first. They had married in the same year as he had taken his first charge, a country church in the border country, and Gail had slowly adjusted herself to the life of a minister's wife.

After five years, the children she'd wanted hadn't come. Gail had tests which showed an underproduction of eggs. Pregnancy, the doctors told her, was not impossible, or even improbable, given time. They had wanted her husband to give a sample, but John, highly embarrassed and religiously opposed to the method of obtaining such a sample, refused.

Gail sat there in the dressing room, her arms crossed over her breasts, her hands resting lightly on her shoulders. She listened to the soft snores of her husband as he lay, mouth open, on the bed. He was not a mean man, not a *bad* man. But inside her, despite her good-natured exterior, she harboured a resentment against him for refusing to recognise the urgency of her need. In the past ten years, sex had become more infrequent. He had never been strongly driven even at the beginning, and seemed to have lost interest almost entirely.

She turned her head, admiring her profile in the mirror, taking in the now well-defined bones in her cheeks and her chin. Her hands slowly dropped from her shoulders, caressing the skin under the silk of her nightdress. Her fingers moved over the swell of her substantial breasts, sending a small shiver through her. They seemed firmer, more sensitive than they had been. A year ago they were conceding to gravity, but now they had reversed the process. Her hands continued downwards to meet on her belly. The skin tingled at her own touch. She pressed quite firmly against the muscle wall and inside her she felt the *pull*, the little pang of burgeoning need. Life was about to stir there. She could feel her body prepare itself.

John gave a little snort and turned over in his sleep. Gail hadn't put the mixture in his cocoa tonight, but he hadn't noticed any difference. In the last two weeks she had expected, even *prayed for*, a change, but there was nothing. John was distantly companionable, almost brotherly, but even when she had carefully snuggled up beside him he seldom noticed her need.

Gail's biological engine had started to falter in the last year or so. She had seen the fine hatching of what she jokingly referred to as laughter lines around her eyes. There had been stretch-marks on her breasts. Her menstrual cycle was no longer that, just an intermittent, haphazard occurrence.

But Sheila Garvie had told her everything would be fine. Gail smiled to herself. Her even teeth caught the light in the mirror.

'*There is more than one power, but all is one.*' Gail hadn't told John of her conversion, hadn't told him anything of what the women's circle did, because he wouldn't understand. It wasn't such a conversion really. It was merely a *change* in viewpoint. God, *her God*, would manifest Himself not only in church, at the eucharist, but through His whole creation. Sheila Garvie said He had created the world and the plants and had left man to husband them. There was power in the plants and the trees. Sheila Garvie had demonstrated that to them all. The birthmark, a purple, pear-shaped splash on Gail's calf, a constant source of embarrassment to her in her younger days, had vanished in two weeks with the application of the pungent cream Sheila had given her. There was no trace of it now.

Now, as she sat by the mirror, alone with her thoughts, she could feel the engine rev itself up and hum smoothly, picking up speed. She smiled to herself and felt the pulse of maternal want within her.

'*It will happen. It will,*' she told herself.

Also that night Jean Fintry was in bed reading a glossy magazine. She had spent some time brushing her now black and shining hair and had taken her new dressing gown from the box. It had arrived only that morning, special delivery from a fashion house in London. It fitted perfectly. She had stood at the tall mirror – another new addition to the house – and admired herself at length, in both senses of the word. Now, she sat and looked at the pictures of the leggy models and smiled to herself. After years of being just Fat Jean, she was shedding pounds at a remarkable rate. Her ruddy cheeks had lost their country-woman's glow and she had started to wear lipstick. She had taken out all those tent dresses with their hideous floral patterns and had great pleasure in burning them in a bonfire in her back garden. She lay back and envisioned herself on the catwalk, hearing in her mind the cheers and the whistles. She saw the pop-flash of cameras and smiled to herself.

Fiona Herron was sitting at her kitchen table, hands steeped in a prettily-decorated earthenware bowl filled to the brim with a black, almost tarry liquid which smelt of greenery and bitter fruit.

286

The fluid was warm and she kept her fingers moving slowly, setting up ripples on the viscous surface. She had done this every night for the past two months and the fire had slowly drained from her ugly fingers. Now there was hardly an ache. The contorted, hideously-swollen joints had regained shape. Her hooked, claw-like fingers had straightened to look like normal hands and not the scabrous witch-talons that had throbbed constantly with grinding pain. After a while, she withdrew her hands and watched the thick liquid drain off them. It ran slowly, in an oozing film, but completely, leaving her hands pink and smooth. Even the ache was gone now. She flexed her fingers, revelling in the smooth motion. She closed her eyes and blessed her good fortune to have become friends with Sheila Garvie. At that moment, she would have done *anything* for her.

Molly Carr had gone walking her dog just before sunset. She'd taken the Linn Road out of the village heading in the rough direction of Dumbuie Hill, letting the little spaniel snuffle and sniff at the hedgerow. She had felt the need build up in her all day and a warm buzz of excitement tingled under her skin.

Molly was thin and had an angular, flat-chested frame. Her hair was dark, almost black, and she kept it pulled back from her face and rolled into a severe bun which, she thought, made her look more intellectual, more *serious*. She had never married. At teacher's training college she'd had one or two boyfriends, but the relationships hadn't lasted long. She had been too demanding, too imperious. She'd been no *fun*. Then, she'd dreamed of being pretty and meeting a handsome young man who would lust after her, but it never happened. She seemed to have a reverse magnetism which repelled them.

She came strolling down the road, keeping the dog on its leash, and turned up towards her house. There had been a small group of young folk standing at the corner, teenagers whom she'd taught in school when they were small. One or two of the girls said hello, though the three boys in scuffed leather jackets looked at her sullenly. She deigned to give them a curt nod. When she walked past she heard one of them mutter – Peter Bain, probably, in her estimation a ne'er-do-well since childhood. One of the girls giggled and Molly felt a brief flash of anger.

She was tense now. The demand within her was tugging at her, twisting away deep inside. She felt hot and flushed and soon her hands began to tremble slightly in anticipation. She turned at the corner and almost bumped into a man coming the opposite way along the narrow street which led to her home.

'Oh, sorry, Miss Carr,' the fellow said, stepping out of the way. She smiled to herself. *Miss Carr*. She'd taught this man as a boy. She stood back and looked at him.

'Ah, hello, Thomas,' she said. 'Haven't seen you for some time. Still working?'

Tom Cannon had been one of the less able pupils, as she remembered. In primary school he'd been big and sturdy, an amiable boy destined for mediocrity.

'Yeah, I'm driving Aitkenbar's trucks. The money's all right.'

'Glad to hear it.' She stood back and looked at him. He was a head taller than she and he had filled out. He had the shoulders and forearms of a trucker. She could smell beer on his breath.

'Listen, Thomas, could you do me a favour? I've a light bulb needing changed and I can't reach it. Do you think you could . . .?'

'Aw, sure, Miss Carr,' the big fellow said. 'No problem.'

'I'm not keeping you from anything?' she asked, taking him by the elbow and walking slowly towards her house. She could already feel the quivering of the nerves in her legs. She felt sure he would detect the tremor in her voice.

'No. I was just down for a pint. I'm up early in the morning.'

'Oh good. It's such a nuisance when a bulb goes. Always gives me a fright.'

Tommy laughed. The possibility of *anything* giving his old teacher a fright was hard to imagine. She had scared the hell out of everybody when he'd been small. He strode up the road with Molly Carr beside him while she almost dragged the little spaniel behind her.

She opened the front door and went in while he stood hesitantly on the doorstep.

'Well, come on in, Thomas,' she ordered. He wiped his feet and entered, his bulk darkening the hallway. She switched the light on and went through to a back room with the dog. He heard a door open and close and she came back out, without her coat and without the spaniel.

'I don't have any beer in, but if you'd like a whisky?' Molly said.

'No, it's all right, Miss Carr.'

'Oh, don't be silly. If you do me a favour, you deserve a reward. Didn't I always teach you that?'

The big fellow nodded.

'Right, then. Come with me.' She led him into the kitchen and took a decanter down from the shelf. 'I don't often myself, but it's bad manners to let you drink on your own.'

She smiled through thin lips which pulled back over uneven teeth. Inside her body was *twisting* with tension. She poured a substantial measure for each of them and handed one to Tommy. As she did so, her finger brushed against his and she felt a jolt run through her.

Tommy looked on in surprise as she quaffed the drink in one swallow.

'Come on then, Thomas, drink up.' He put the glass to his lips and threw the whisky over. It was a strong malt. He felt the burn down his throat and then the spread of heat in his chest. There was a peculiar aftertaste, not unpleasant, like a hint of cinnamon which did nothing to spoil the tang. He smacked his lips and let out a sign of pleasure.

'Oh, all right. Call me an old fool. Have another one,' Molly said. Before he could react, she had filled the tumbler again. He thanked her again and lifted the glass, taking half of it in one swallow.

'Go on, don't disappoint me. Finish it off.' Tommy took the rest in a gulp and drained the glass.

'Good lad.'

'Where's the light?' Tommy asked. He could feel the spreading heat rushing through him and he wondered what kind of whisky it had been. The aftertaste was spicy and already he could feel the headiness of the drink. For a brief moment, his vision blurred and then refocused.

'This way,' Molly Carr said. 'Follow me.'

He followed. She walked out of the kitchen and along the hall, her heels tapping on the wooden floor. She had long, quite skinny legs, he noticed, a tight, quite severe black skirt and a white, schoolmarmish blouse. From behind, the bun in her hair looked solid. Another brief wave of dizziness washed through him and he shook his head. Tommy told himself he'd taken the whisky too quickly.

Molly Carr turned at the stairs and started to walk up quite quickly. He came after her, holding on to the bannister, and as he did so he saw her dip her hands in under the waistband at the back of her skirt and begin to tug at the blouse. He had gone three steps when she made a quick movement and hauled the thing over her head, without missing a stride. She just let it drop to the steps. He hardly even realised she'd done it until he stepped on the thin white cotton. He looked up in confusion, then the heat suffused his head like a fever. His vision wavered again, cleared and he took another two steps. Molly Carr reached both hands behind her, moving them up her long, thin back, and snicked open the white strap of her brassière. He noted, quite distantly, how her ribs stood out like slats on either side.

'Oh, Miss Carr,' he tried to say, but the words wouldn't come. All of a sudden, his breath was hot and tight.

She stopped at the top of the stairs and looked down at him, now only wearing the skirt. He looked up and she give him a thin, hungry smile. Her small breasts were widely separated. The dark nipples stood out, puckered and taut.

'Come on, Thomas, quickly now,' she said curtly. She turned and walked into the first room. He followed dumbly, head spinning and heart thumping, unable to stop himself. Down below his waistband there was a swift swelling pressure. He reached the top of the stairs and followed her into the room just in time to see her step out of the black skirt. She bent swiftly, hooking her white panties down as she moved forward, simultaneously kicking her shoes off. One of them banged against a small table, rolled over and was still. He looked at her long, angular frame as her hands reached up to pull the pins from her hair. She gave a shake of her head and the bun uncoiled and fell into surprisingly long tresses. The swelling in his crotch was almost a pain. She turned and looked him up and down and gave him another tight smile. Her tongue slid out and licked her bottom lip, quickly, almost reptilian. She came striding towards him, a gaunt, now somehow *feral* woman. Without hesitation, she reached down and unzipped him. She dived both hands inside and, with her thumbs over the waistband, pulled his boxer shorts down. He felt warm hands on him and he gave a small gasp, head still reeling. It felt as if his skull was filled with hot fumes.

Molly Carr turned, not towards the bed. She made for the chair which faced the window where the wide-open curtains let in the moonlight.

'Now, Thomas. Do it now.'

He moved forward, unable to stop. She bent herself forwards over the back of the chair, hands grasping the stuffed arms. She widened her stance and in the dim light he could see the two white half-moons of her skinny backside. He reached her, shuffled in closer, felt himself touch. She wiggled for position then pressed back against him. He felt the slide into velvet warmth and then she bucked against him, her muscles clenching in a tight rhythmic grip.

She closed her eyes and the amazing *searing* pleasure started. She opened them again and stared at the moon while behind her the man moved and she grunted like an animal.

Everything spun away from her and all she could feel was the motion and the frantic clenching inside her. He put his hands on her hips, digging his fingers into the soft flesh under the bones, and gave a huge heave. She moaned aloud and felt her own clenching pulses synchronise with his and she shuddered with the force of it.

Finally he collapsed against her and she twisted away quickly. He groaned as he slumped down, spent, on to the arm of the chair. She crossed the floor and picked up her panties, stepping into them almost as quickly as she had shucked them off. She put her skirt back on again and took a blouse from her drawer, immediately starting to button it up. She had started to redo her hair when she seemed to remember he was still there. She turned towards him. He seemed oblivious, sitting awkwardly, exposed, with his trousers and boxer shorts below his knees.

'Thomas!' she said sharply.

'Yes, Miss Carr?' he muttered distantly.

'You will not remember what happened tonight, understand?'

'No, Miss Carr,' he said, almost sleepily.

'Good boy. Now get dressed and go home and go to sleep.' He nodded and stood up slowly, pulling his pants up like an awkward schoolboy. She led him downstairs and out of the door. He wandered off without a word. She smiled at his retreating back.

She could still feel the friction warmth inside her but the itch, the terrible urgent irritation, had gone.

She went back into the living room and picked up a book from the shelf, opened it at a marked page and began to write in her diary. When she had finished she flicked back a few pages and counted her tally. There were twenty-three names written down there.

'Not bad for an ugly spinster,' she whispered happily to herself.

Tom Cannon stumbled home in a daze. He woke his elderly mother when he hauled the door open and then slammed it behind him. He clattered up the stairs to his room, ignoring her call, and barged into his bedroom. He awoke at nine the following morning with the worst hangover he'd ever experienced and was an hour late for his shift at Aitkenbar. He wondered what on earth he'd been drinking the night before, but for the life of him he couldn't remember. His mother, who'd tried and failed to rouse him more than an hour previously, made him eat a wide platter of bacon and eggs. As soon as she left the kitchen he stumbled into the bathroom and was hugely and gratifyingly sick.

23

Just as Tom Cannon was leaving, still feeling like death, for work at Aitkenbar, Martin Thornton was down among the ferns on the steep slope at the side of Mill Lane. Alec Stirling had stopped Jock Weir on his way down the road with an empty bowser and the driver had been good enough to lend a hand. Because of the narrowness of the road and the angle of the Land-Rover they couldn't drag Martin's car directly back, but Jock suggested turning the towrope around a tree-trunk to haul the vehicle sideways. Martin hooked the loop on the towbar and the big tanker took the strain. The Land-Rover slowly eased back, found its level and came up over the lip with surprising simplicity. Once on flatter ground Martin started the engine and let it run for a few moments before jamming the gearstick into reverse. This time the wheels bit and he was able to steer, neck craned backwards, until he reached the road.

'That's a pint you owe both of us,' Alec said, although he'd only stood and watched.

'You surprise me,' Martin answered back, shaking his head ruefully. He thanked Jock Weir who told him to think nothing of it and climbed back into his cab. He disappeared in a cloud of blue diesel fumes.

Martin had told Alec about the black shape which had crashed against his window and caused him to veer, almost fatally, into the trees.

'Another five feet and I'd have been in the river. It's a fifty-foot drop there.'

'Aye, you came off lucky,' Alec agreed. He struck a match on the roof of his red mailvan and lit a cigarette. 'What was it, a dog or something?'

'I don't know. I didn't see it properly. But it came at me twice. It really scared the hell out of me.'

'I can imagine. Listen, it could have been John Lovatt's pig. That's been missing for a month or so. Reckon it's running loose in the forest. Duncan Haldane found its marks up at his place. As far as I remember it was a mean big bugger. Size of a pony and blacker than two yards up a chimney.'

'Can pigs jump?'

'Damned if I know. If that thing came after me, *I'd* soon jump, that's for certain.'

'The same thing happened to Caitlin Brook last week. Something came out of the hedge and knocked her off the road. She *did* end up in the river and nearly drowned.'

'She never did,' Alec protested. 'I never heard anything about that.'

'So you don't know everything. Big deal.'

'And how did she get out, for sure, the girl can't walk.'

'Some woman. I met her yesterday. Sheila something. She fished her out of the water and got her home again.'

'Sheila Garvie. The white witch.'

'The what?'

'Och, that's just what the boys in the pub call her. She's into faith healing and the herbal stuff. In the Green Party and whatnot. Wants to save the whales and the forest. Some folk reckon she's at the back of this thing with Dunky Haldane, but she's probably harmless.'

'I remember you told me that before. She seemed all right to me. She's been a looker in her day.'

'A bit long in the tooth for my taste,' Alec disparaged without malice. 'She's an odd one, though. I'm never away from her door with parcels from all over. India and Bolivia and places like that. She grows plants and things. Never lets you in the door, never a cup of tea for your trouble. I had a look in her window one time when she wasn't in and the place was like a chemist's shop, full of bottles and beakers and what have you. She came right up behind me and tapped me on the shoulder and I nearly jumped a mile. I dropped the parcel and it caught on one of them rockery stones and burst. Out comes this pile of withered old roots and the smell would have taken the nose off you.' Alec wrinkled his face in recollection. 'She drew me a right dirty look and made me pick them all up, and I never got so much as a thank you. And then on the way out, that cat of hers, biggest tom cat I've ever seen, was sitting on the fence post. It hooked out its paw and

294

took a swipe at me. Would have taken my eye out if I hadn't seen it coming.'

'She can't be all bad. She did a lot for Caitlin. She'd have been killed if it hadn't been for her.'

'Oh, I'm not saying she's *bad*. But she's *weird*. I see the women coming down here every other day. I heard they get pills and potions for their women's things, you know, *complaints*. All this herbal mumbo jumbo. I hear tell there's a few men getting things put in their tea. Some to keep them off and some to get them on, if you catch my meaning.'

Martin laughed. 'I get the picture,' he said. 'There's nothing unusual in that. There's shops like that all over the place doing big business in all that organic stuff. I blame the Tories. If they hadn't run down the health service, folk wouldn't be looking for alternatives.'

Martin promised he'd buy Alec a pint at the ceilidh on the Saturday night. The postman said he'd hold him to it and volunteered he'd welcome the sight of the reporter coping with a strip-the-willow after a few drinks. Martin toyed with the idea of dropping in on Caitlin, but then thought better of it. He remembered her kiss from last night. He wanted to think about it before he saw her again. Instead he drove down to the end of Linn Road and turned right, heading for Lochend and then Glasgow. Alec took the left turn to Craigard.

It was only when he got home that Martin remembered the book Andrew Toye had lent him. He had a full day ahead of him. He'd planned to put together the poltergeist piece and simply hand it in to the office for the Editor's attention. What kind of reception it would get he wasn't sure, but he'd told Andrew he'd at least give it a try. The little professor was trying to get more funding and wanted all the publicity he could get. Martin was all for the quid pro quo. Andrew had given him a good few stories in his time.

He went through his notes carefully, marking the ones most relevant, and finally started typing. As he did so he remembered the crawling sense of fear that had shaken him up in the Blackhale flat and shook his head. Now, in the light of a summer's afternoon, that seemed distant and foolish. Andrew was right, of course. There was a logical explanation for everything. Martin just didn't know what that explanation was. He switched on his Amstrad and began to type.

Later in the afternoon, once he'd finished what he considered to be a fairly balanced piece, leaving out the names and addresses as requested, he reckoned it was interesting enough to make a Saturday piece in the features section. He went through to the kitchen and brewed up a coffee. When he came back to his cluttered study he picked up the old red book. It fell open again where Andrew had left the bookmark.

Martin took a drink of coffee, grimacing at the bitterness, and began to read:

In 1513 the Lord Lennox and the chief of the Colquhouns lent their names to a petition to the Archbishop to purge the pagan blasphemies, as the seasonal ceremonies were described. The provost and armed men marched into Gleann Linn accompanied by the Abbot of Inchmurrin and held an inquest. The people of the village put up a show of passive resistance, claiming not to have heard about any rituals. Houses and farms were searched and certain images carved from wood were discovered which depicted strange animals and stunted creatures, some with the hind legs of a deer and bearing antlers. Those properties where such artefacts were discovered were put to the torch and their fields scorched. The inhabitants were locked inside their homes and perished in the flames.

The Seilach Garbh-aidh, or leader of the cult, was thought to have fled into the nearby forest of Fasach which was ringed around by a stone dyke. Men were despatched to bring this person to the Abbot, but after two days they returned and reported that there was no one to be found in the wood. Of the people of Gleann Linn, numbering three hundred and twenty, fifty-six were put to death. Five soldiers, who had been searching the forest, did not return to their posts. The provost believed they had deserted, but the Abbot believed that the blasphemers had conspired to lure them to their deaths. In his further inquisition four men died when put to the question and two women were drowned. The Abbot was able to report to his archbishop that he had purged the village and the surrounding lands and advocated the construction of a Christian church on ground that he had blessed for the purpose. Assent was given, and the chapel was built at a cost of three hundred Merks, half of which was a bequest from the Lennox purse. Extract from Accounts of the Estate of Lennox, 1823.

Martin flicked a few pages further. Despite the chapel and the evangelising zeal of a succession of pastors the glen seemed to fall back on pagan ways. In 1720, two hundred years after the massacre, a certain Bailie Crawford presided over hearings in a case of alleged witchcraft at Linnvale, as it was now known as more and more people forsook their natural Gaelic for the lowland English. As Martin read he noted a very obvious similarity between that judicial event and the seventeenth-century Salem witch trials. In Linnvale five children claimed to have been involved in strange rituals in the woods. They said that a hooded figure whom they named the Garbh-aidh had made them drink potions and had summoned up demons in a clearing. These demons, they said, had cavorted wildly and changed their shape and done indecent things to the children and to each other. When asked to identify the Garbh-aidh they could not do so, only claiming that it was an old woman. They said the woman had told them of the Forest Lord, the supreme spirit who would come in all his glory at her summons. The inquest extended. Fingers were pointed. An old woman, in her eighties, a toothless, half-deaf widow whose mind had been wandering since a fever twenty years before, was brought before the inquiry. It was quite clear, reading the report of the trial, that she hadn't been aware of what was going on. She had cackled and nodded and slavered almost on cue and then she had been lowered into the mill lade. The villagers had watched as her old white head had disappeared under the water and saw her hands wave above the surface before the tiltseat had been lowered further. Her death proclaimed her innocence, and panic over who would be next flashed like a brushfire through the small community. A mother of five, who was probably an epileptic, was said to have spoken in tongues while in a fit. She was probed for witch marks and drowned in the morning. Bailie Crawford's men heeded every rumour and accusation. Finally they brought in a woman who lived in a tumbledown stone cottage near the mill. She was known as Meg Moine and was not a native of the glen but had lived in her grandmother's house since the old woman's death ten years before. The bailie pounced on the fact that the woman was known to frequent the woods to collect mushrooms and herbs. When the men arrived she appeared in the garden – from nowhere, they said – with a rustic broom. She refused to answer any questions, treating the bailie, who had the power of a magistrate, with haughty contempt. She did not flinch when they probed with pins the devil's mark on her arm, a black mole, and she showed no emotion when they strapped her into the chair and lowered her into the black waters of the lade. At that moment, so the report went, there was a great wind which blew up and whipped the waters to a frenzy and almost blew the watchers into the deep pool. The pole bearing the chair swung this way and that and then there was a thrashing below the surface. The pole snapped and Meg Moine was lost to sight. The men used hooks from the blacksmith's bothy to drag the pool and finally snagged the chair. The straps were still intact but there was no sign of Meg Moine. The bailie was able to report that he had been successful in rooting out the witch and that she had died under the waters and been summoned back by the father of all demons to the nether pits of hell. That neatly wrapped up the case. He shed not a tear for the innocent women who had drowned. In those days, that was just an incidental expense.

Martin closed the book with a snap. He'd been reading for nearly an hour without noticing the passage of time. He told himself he'd have to remember the stories from the old book when he went back to Linnvale on Saturday for the ceilidh. It would give Alec Stirling a laugh. As far as the postman was concerned, half the women in the village were witches. The other half, if Alec's tales were anything to go by, were fair game.

Caitlin awoke to the sound of knocking on her door. She eased herself into the chair, using the pulleys positioned above her bed which also served as her excerciser. At the front doorstep Sheila Garvie beamed good morning and handed her a freshly-cut spray of lilies.

Sheila had come to Caitlin's cottage every morning since their dramatic first meeting, each day bringing a small gift, some mushrooms one day, walnuts and hazelnuts softened in a marinade another. And each day she made sure Caitlin put a spoonful of the powder into a glass of water and watched her drink it. The taste was still delicious and Sheila promised her it was good for all sorts of ailments. Caitlin agreed that she must be right. She felt better than she had for years, and last night – *last night* she'd experienced a wonderful thing she thought she'd lost forever. Over the week, Sheila told her some of her own history, how she'd come back to live in the glen where she'd been born. She'd travelled the world, studying botany, was a member of Friends of the Earth and a supporter of the Gaia theory that all life and the planet were inextricably linked. She was working, she told Caitlin, on a book on herbs and remedies, a practical guide to their use. She told Caitlin that forests all over the world were only now yielding secrets that had long been lost to modern man. The old folk, she said, had known all about the power of the plants.

Sheila shared a light breakfast and waited until Caitlin got ready, then the two of them went out together.

'I thought I'd show you my forest today,' Sheila said. 'It's always fresh and bright in the mornings. You can smell the primroses everywhere.'

Caitlin told her she'd love to, though she confessed a small apprehension about the animal that had charged at her.

'Nonsense. I've been wandering these woods for a long time. There's nothing in there that could harm us.'

She took hold of Caitlin's pushbar and swung the chair around to cross the road. There was a path leading down a gentle incline. On either side, tall larches stretched grey pillars towards the sky. As soon as they passed the edge of the forest and got under the canopy, the air became still and cool. Caitlin could smell the pollen in the air. Up above, myriad insects droned lazily.

'This is what we want to protect,' Sheila said. 'It's the most marvellous place. Look,' she pointed. 'That's primrose. It grows on the wet banks. And those dandelions we passed. They're good for curing warts.'

As they followed the forest trail – which was less rugged than Caitlin had imagined – Sheila pointed out this tree and that shrub, giving their colloquial names. They came close to the river where some low-lying parts of the ground were marshy. She stopped to tell Caitlin about the infusion from marigolds that helped sore eyes, and horsetail that was good for helping bones to mend.

'That mixture I gave you, it's got all sorts of things in it. Like damiana and vervain, valerian and crampbark. They're the best for nerves. They relax and stimulate and restore. It's a very old recipe. That's why you're feeling better in yourself.'

Caitlin smiled. 'It tastes wonderful. I could become addicted.'

'Ah, that's because I put a few other things in it too. If you had a taste of those plants on their own, you'd never swallow a drop.'

They walked on in the cool morning air, Sheila pushing the chair and chatting away, astounding Caitlin with her knowledge of forest lore. After a while they came to a fork in the path. Caitlin let out a small gasp.

'Anything wrong, my dear? You're not cold, are you?'

Caitlin pointed, her face a portrait of surprise. 'This place. I've *been* here before. I've *seen* this.'

'Have you? I thought—'

'No. I haven't *really* seen it,' Caitlin interrupted. 'It's just that . . .'

'Just what?'

'I've *dreamed* I was here. It's amazing. It's *exactly* the same. I don't *believe* it.'

Sheila chuckled throatily. 'Why can't you believe it?'

'Because I've never been here before. Not ever, even as a child.'

'And don't you believe in the power of dreams?'

'I'm not kidding, Sheila. I've dreamed it lots of times. I've been running down here in the trees and when I come to this part I take one of the paths.'

'And which one do you take?'

'That one,' Caitlin said, indicating the left path which went straight down into a dark part of the forest.

'And then what do you see?'

'It's different there, not like a real forest. It's more like a jungle. It's warmer and the plants are strange. Bigger, with wide leaves. It feels damper. I remember – *oh, it's so vivid!* – there are giant mushrooms and spiders' webs that stretch between the trees. It feels so real in the dream. Even the air smells different, more moist and *hot*. Then I come to a river.'

Once she'd started Caitlin couldn't stop. It was as if she was running through the forest again. She closed her eyes in concentration, recalling the dreams. 'There are stepping stones across the river. I think it's an island and there's a tree there, standing alone. It looks dead, but I feel drawn towards it.'

'Interesting dream. How long have you been having it?'

'I've had running dreams since the accident. I don't mind them. It's the next best thing. But it's only in the last week that I've gone down that path towards the river. When I saw the two tracks, it all suddenly came back to me.' She looked up at Sheila. 'What's it like down there? *Is* there an island?'

Sheila smiled. 'There are many things down that path. There are many paths and many tracks. All of them lead somewhere, and some of them lead to the centre of the forest. I'll have to show you sometime. You'll like it.'

'But the island. Is there one just like my dream?'

'You'll find out,' Sheila said mysteriously. 'I promise you that.'

'I've never experienced anything like this before.'

'You should be proud of it. Few folk have the gift of future-dreaming. There's a tribe in the desert of Mexico who live their whole lives through their dreams. They believe that the dreams are real and the rest of life is a dream. The people of Australia, the ones who still live a natural way of life, believe the same thing. That's because they are so close to the earth. They know the one-ness of all life. That is what we have to get back to, I believe. That's why it's important to save this forest. It's the last remnant of the great wood, you know, and if it is lost, then a wonderful force of nature will die.'

'Do you believe in dreams coming true?'

'Of course I do. There are many paths, and dreams are only one. They are our road to what's to come. They show us where to go.' Sheila patted her on the shoulder. 'They're very important. You should believe in them, for they come true.'

'I wish,' Caitlin said ruefully.

'Oh, they will, my dear. They will.' Sheila turned the chair around and started to walk back the way they had come, away from the dark and shaded part of the forest, along the path that led to the road. In the distance Caitlin heard the *rat-a-tat* of a woodpecker on a hollow tree.

When they got back to the cottage Sheila insisted on making herb tea. While the water boiled she took a small satchel from the bulky woven handbag she carried and refilled the carved box she'd given Caitlin.

'I don't think I need any more,' Caitlin told her. 'The bruises are all gone and there's hardly a trace of the scratches.'

'Of course they are. There's nothing stronger than the sap from the right plants, if you know which ones to pick. This is something different. This will *really* help you.'

'How?'

'It's very powerful. It will make you sleep, and your dreams

301

might be more vivid, *more real*, but . . .' She paused, as if choosing her words.

'But what?'

'Do you want to run again?'

Caitlin had been spreading cottage cheese on some biscuits and she stopped instantly as if struck by a sudden blow.

'What did you say?'

'I asked you if you want to run again.'

'I thought that's what you said.' Caitlin's face had gone very pale. 'I don't think that's very fair.'

'Why?'

'Because I'll never walk again. I'll never run again. The doctors showed me the X-ray plates. What I have is permanent. I'm not allowed to hope or wish. They told me that. It's the first thing you learn when you break your back. It's gone, forever.'

Sheila was instantly contrite. She looked as if Caitlin had slapped her face. 'Oh, my dear, please. I didn't mean—'

'I don't know what you meant. I don't *care* what you meant. You don't know what it's like being in this thing, with these damned legs. Look,' she said, agitated, taking her hand from the table and squeezing her thigh viciously between finger and thumb. 'Nothing. They don't feel and they don't work, and they never will. They told me if I don't convince myself of that, then I'll have a breakdown. Hope is a word nobody uses. You can't hope because there is *no* hope.'

Suddenly Caitlin burst into tears, rocked by the emotional outburst. Sheila immediately pulled her chair towards the stricken girl and put her arm around her shoulder. Caitlin shrugged hard.

'Don't,' she wailed.

Sheila ignored her. She pulled herself closer and, in doing so, brought Caitlin's head towards her bosom. She dug her fingers into the thick red waves and held on tightly, feeling the sobs rack the young woman.

'I'm so sorry, Caitlin,' she finally said when the heaving shoulders subsided to an irregular twitch. 'I really didn't mean to hurt or upset you. Please forgive me.'

Caitlin said nothing.

'Please. I wouldn't do anything to hurt you. Not for anything,' she continued, still holding tight, and using her left hand to gently pat Caitlin's back in a motherly way.

'You don't know what it's like,' Caitlin finally said. 'You *can't* know.'

'Maybe not, but I can try, and I *do* know some things,' Sheila said softly, persuasively. She kept Caitlin close and gently kneaded her shoulder. 'Remember how quickly your cuts and bruises healed, how the hurt went away?'

Caitlin was silent for a moment, but finally she nodded. Sheila felt the motion against her shoulder-blade.

'Maybe I *can't* cure what ails you, but believe me, what I *can* do can help.' She gave Caitlin a quick, encouraging hug. 'I wouldn't hurt you, but I can help you in many ways. Hm?'

She let the girl's shoulder go and reached with her hand to take a pinch of the fine peppery powder and drop it into a glass on the table. Deftly she poured water from the jug and watched the colour swirl to a deep red-wine hue.

'Here. Drink this up and you'll feel better,' she said, keeping her voice low, the way a mother would speak to a distressed child.

In a moment of two, she felt the tension ease from Caitlin's shoulders and the young woman began to uncoil from her hunched position. She reached into a pocket for a tissue and blew her nose loudly. She dabbed her eyes and looked at Sheila, blinking.

'I'm sorry too. I shouldn't have gone at you like that. You've done so much for me.'

'Not enough yet,' Sheila said and smiled widely at her.

'It's just that . . . .' the girl faltered. 'I'm not allowed to think of that, you know. It's *bad* for me.'

'Well, we shall just have to do what's right for you. Come on, drink your medicine.'

She handed the glass which Caitlin took in both hands. The drink was darker than the previous infusions that she'd taken night and day since her fall into the river.

'What's this for?'

'It's to make you feel better in all sorts of ways.'

Caitlin sniffed at it. A strong aromatic flavour swept up from the surface.

She bent her head and tasted it. Immediately the flavour, even stronger than before, suffused her. It tingled at the sides of her tongue and even though she tried to hold the cool liquid in her mouth, she couldn't prevent an automatic, almost reflexive swallow. A warmth cascaded down her throat and, as before but this time more powerfully, the heat raced through her in a sparkling tide. Instantly an irresistible feeling of wellbeing flooded her, banishing her tight anguish. Without hesitation she took another drink, raising the glass and letting the liquid flow, not stopping until it was empty.

'That's better, hm?'

Caitlin swallowed a gasp, then nodded.

'Much better. That's truly wonderful, it really is.'

Sheila reached forward to pat her lightly on her hand. Her fingers clasped the young woman's and gripped them firmly.

'Still friends?'

'Of course. And I'm sorry.'

'No. I'm the sorry one. It was silly of me. Please forgive me.'

'Honest, Sheila. It's me. Sometimes it gets to me. I shouldn't have shouted at you, not after you saved my life.'

'And glad I am that I did,' Sheila said, her smile widening. 'It's good to have a new friend.'

Caitlin nodded, then reached forward to hug the woman closely. 'Yes. We *are* friends,' she said.

Sheila left the new herbal mixture on the table. There was enough to almost fill the box and she told Caitlin to take a pinch three times a day.

'Trust me. It will make you feel a lot better,' she said as she left. 'And if there's anything at all that you need, remember I'm just along at the millhouse. Come any time.'

Later in the afternoon Caitlin *was* feeling better. The anguish and sudden despair had fled. She bustled about the kitchen, as much as anyone in a wheelchair *could* bustle, and delighted in the new sense of freedom and capability that the simple matter of lowering the work surfaces gave her. Martin Thornton had done a splendid job of it. She felt at home here now, as if, for the first time, she'd found a place that fitted her exactly. In the afternoon she left the major painting and did some sketches. The sensation of wellbeing still suffused her and she felt an unaccustomed vigour. She took her box of charcoals and began to boldly etch strong lines on the paper, drawing from memory the fork in the path in the forest. Her hands moved quickly, scoring decisive lines of definition and then flattening the charcoal to rough in shade. She thought she'd use this for her next painting. When the sketch was finished she selected another sheet from the folder, expecting it to be blank. It was a sketch of Martin Thornton she'd done the day after his first visit. She held it up, then leaned it against the slanted wooden drawing board. She'd caught the likeness well, but it was very rough. Working quickly, she filled in the shoulders, getting his old leather jerkin to hang just *right*, gaving him a turning stance, an ambiguous pose, swivelling towards the viewer or perhaps just taking his leaned. In fact, Caitlin thought, that was exactly right for Martin Thornton. He was a stranger, someone who turned up for a short while and then left again.

Her thoughts travelled back to the night before when they'd kissed. Caitlin smiled to herself, and even though she was alone, she felt her colour rise.

While she reminisced, her right hand worked quickly on the sketch. She'd caught his expression just right. He had that half-quizzical look on his face, an exact hybrid of light cynicism and mischievous humour. She used a finger to lighten down the creases on either side of his mouth, still leaving them visible, but soft and not stern.

She thought of her dream, how she'd passed the fork in the forest, then seen the very spot in real life today. Sheila had told her there was more to dreams than people realised and she wondered at that.

'*Dreams can come true,*' that's what Sheila said.

And then Caitlin truly blushed. For as soon as she thought of that, she recalled the sensation of the night before, just on the point of waking. She had been with Martin Thornton. She had walked into his arms and her whole body had rocked on that stupendous wave of pleasure. Just thinking about it sent a another wave through her, this time an abashed flood of discomfiture.

Now that *had* been a miracle. She felt the hot blood redden her face, and the flush stole down her neck.

Before the accident she wouldn't have believed such a rush of pleasure was possible. It was even harder to believe that it had happened *now*.

The first few weeks after her fall she'd been swamped by an

almost-suicidal depression which the doctors, very matter-of-factly, but with gentle consideration, said was normal. They were gentle and brutal at the same time, making her realise that it was vital for her to understand exactly what had happened and to accept it. That way she could begin to *live* with it. The neurologist had sat at her bedside, the pain of the lesions almost gone, and he'd answered her questions directly.

No. You won't walk again..

That was the *big* answer. The one that towered over all the rest like an impenetrable, un-climbable range of mountains. Beside it, the other answers were gentle slopes.

Dr MacDonald – call me Clive, he'd insisted – told her that the itching and tingling sensation she felt now would pass. Immediately after the fall, there had been no feeling at all, but he explained it was a residual *parenthesis*, a sensation along the lost sidings of nerve roots, phantoms that would disappear in time. He couldn't tell her how long that would take. Dr MacDonald carefully told her that everyone with spinal lesions experienced the parenthesis and often mistook it for recovery.

'You will get muscle spasms, and you'll think we've been wrong, but our camera does not lie. That's another residual effect. The nerves send the wrong messages to the muscles, and the spasms can be quite severe. If they happen, simply tap your knee. There will be no reflexes and that's the *real* sign. I know it's hard, but it's something you must learn to do.'

The doctor had shown her the big plates on the lightboard. It took Caitlin a second or two to realise that she was looking at her own spine. She hadn't realised just how massive the breaks were. The fall must have been catastrophic.

'Here we have before and after pictures,' he'd said. 'Before the operation and after, I mean, because you can't see the damage behind the splints.' He pointed a long finger. 'Here, you can see the *lumbar* vertebrae. There are five of them. Two of yours were crushed. There, on the other plate, you can see where we've put in one of our own to stabilise the bones. That stays in there. You're now *bionic*,' he said, dredging a smile from Caitlin. 'If you look carefully you can see the cord lesion. We injected a small amount of radio-opaque fluid. The ends are severed. It does not regenerate, no matter what you read in science magazines. Rats and some other rodents have that ability, as do some amphibians and reptiles.' He turned and looked directly at her. His eyes were kindly, but serious. 'We don't.'

The words fell like thuds. Caitlin absorbed only some of the impact then.

'What are these white dots?' she asked, trying to get away from *that* part of the lesson. There were three of them, below the break, set in a triangle.

'They're white because it's a negative. Actually they're black, and they have to stay because they're too deep. We took fifteen pellets out of your back, but these three are lodged in at the *sacral* vertebrae. Now, at the moment, we don't know exactly what effect they will have, because you're still swollen inside and some of the functions you've lost may return.'

'I don't understand,' Caitlin said honestly.

'Well,' Dr MacDonald continued patiently, 'you must have noticed we've had to catheterise you?'

Caitlin looked blank.

'To help you urinate. You can't do that without some assistance at the moment. We're hoping you've been lucky, that the ability will return. The pellets might not have caused any damage.'

'Lucky?' Caitlin asked. It was easy for the doctors to talk about luck when they were walking and talking.

'My choice of words might surprise you, but it's something you may appreciate later. The sacral area of the cord controls bowel and bladder function while at the top end, along with the lower part of the lumbar area, motor function in the legs and sensation in the genital area is controlled. Now, there have been many more people in your position than you might imagine. We've done some detailed research and they all want the same thing. Top of the list is normal leg movement. They want to walk again. Believe it or not, the next one is bladder and bowels. Sometimes that's even in first place. We're hoping you have been lucky. It makes a big difference.'

'What's next on the list?'

'Sexual function always comes last, surprisingly enough, but a good thing too. That's almost a certain loss in any complete lesion in any part of the spine. I hate to say it but I'm afraid that's something you will have to consider,' Dr MacDonald said gently.

'There are other ways of looking at it. If your body had landed a few inches over, you could have lost arm movement along with the rest. Further up, your breathing would have been affected. Your injury will allow you to lead a fulfilled and mobile life. It will be restricted, but you will not be helpless.'

In the course of that hard lesson and in subsequent ones Caitlin learned about the other things she had to cope with. The therapists warned her about temperature regulation, pointing out that her muscles couldn't shiver. She would not feel cold or heat and she had to take care to ensure those muscles were exercised, using the pulley system, to ensure that the blood flow was maintained and to prevent the calcium of her bones from being reabsorbed. She was told about hyperaesthesias, an increased, almost compensatory sensitivity on the unaffected parts of her body, and discovered this to be true. Sometimes, if she rubbed the skin of her forearms gently, she would get a sensual tickling sensation which was quite pleasant. Later, she discovered an acute sensitivity on other parts of her body. Sometimes, lying in bed, the soft material of her nightdress would rub over her breasts and they would instantly tingle with a powerful sensation that was almost as strong as the few orgasms she remembered.

The therapists made her learn her own body maintenance programme and coached her on skin care and damage limitation. The lesson they drilled into her was that pain is a message that something is wrong, and where there was no sensation, no possibility of pain, then damage, cuts, burns and bruises might go unnoticed until too late.

As she sat, remembering those hard lessons, Caitlin also recalled the assistant neurologist, a small oriental woman with the kindliest face Caitlin had ever seen, explaining about the loss of her menstrual cycle, which, she was assured would – and did – return.

Dr Lei, who had a girlish lisp, also told her that a phantom orgasm was also possible, and orgasmic imagery in dreams as vivid as the reality.

Caitlin hadn't believed her then. She'd never had such a thing in a dream before.

Now she realised what Dr Lei had been talking about. Last night had been *vivid*. In fact, as sensations went, it was multi-chromatic vistavision with wraparound sound and laser lights. It had been a *supernova*.

She gently rubbed in some shading on the sketch of the man whose dream image had coincided with the internal seismic wave and smiled to herself. He didn't even *know* what he'd done. Caitlin wondered how he'd react if he did.

Martin Thornton, standing half-turned, as if about to leave, or maybe as if he'd been called back, gazed back at her with a half-smile. He *looked* as if he might have an inkling.

While Caitlin Brook sketched and let her mind ramble, Duncan Haldane was down at the stand of oaks. The loader from the mill had come for the beech trunk sections and Duncan had called Ben down to watch the grab arm come down like some metal monster and snatch the massive logs up onto the back bed. Each time it dropped a log in position there was a loud *boom* and Ben felt the ground shiver under his feet.

He hadn't objected when his father had called him down to the front field, because he'd promised him he would be good and not scare Dorrie any more. She seemed to have forgotten what happened, but Ben knew that was because she was small, and she hadn't seen what *he'd* seen. Ben knew what he'd seen. It had not been a dream. It had not been his imagination.

The leaf man haunted him.

It was a brown ghost that rustled in his dreams and came crunching and scraping after him, twig fingers outstretched and acorn eyes rolling crazily in the sockets.

At night, before he went to sleep, Ben carefully closed the cupboard and tidied everything away, all his toys and his books and his football, so that there was nothing, no shadow, that would catch his eye. His room was now almost bare, and that's just the way he liked it. The night after the dreadful experience, he'd leapt up with a start, shaking with fear, while his heart welled so big in the back of his throat that he thought he'd never breathe again. There was a shadow in the corner, tall and oddly humped. He'd sat there, eyes wide and bulging, covers drawn up to his neck, trying to cry out, but unable to. A few moments later, the cloud which had obscured the moon moved off and the light on the curtains swelled enough to let him see that the monster standing in the corner was only his summer jacket hanging, not in the wardrobe

309

where his mother kept telling him to put it, but carelessly slung over the wooden bow Ben had made from an ash branch, and standing in the corner. From that night on, Ben hung the jacket away. The corner was shadow-free.

The timberman took less than an hour to load his truck and he made a wide arc on the bottom field before engaging gear and hauling the ponderous weight up the hill. The loader groaned and wheezed and finally made it to the top, like a tired old man. The driver had waved down at Ben and then swung the big wheel and angled the truck carefully through the gate, with only an inch to spare on either side. Ben wished he was on the truck, heading out of the glen.

Where the beech tree had come down, the ground was gouged and scarred where the branches of the falling giant had forced their way through the turf in the aftermath of the blowdown. The other scars, the odd ones where Ben had thought he'd seen the small trees standing that shadowed night, were still there, but now, with the fallen tree gone, except for a few lopped off branches that had been hauled into a bonfire pile, they didn't look so noticeable.

Ben had agreed with him. He'd said everything was all right now, and Duncan had accepted it. But inside Ben, the doubt loomed large. Maybe he *had* imagined the trees, standing in places where they had never been before. Maybe he had – *though he didn't really think so* – but he was still scared. He *had* seen the leaf man, and he *had* seen the bones in the forest. He knew there was something badly wrong with Fasach Wood and he never wanted to go near there again. In the Haldane household, the joy at winning the battle to build on the land was not shared by young Ben. He couldn't have said, *wouldn't* have said, but he would have been a lot happier if his father had lost the battle, and if they'd had to sell up and move out of the valley.

Ben didn't want to stay here any more. That forest over there – and he kept his eyes diverted from it, no matter how much it tugged at him with persuasive, *demanding* insistence – lay like a shadowed threat, spreading over the bottom of the valley. It would not go away.

'Want to try the cutter, Ben?' his father called up. The boy still seemed quiet and reserved but the big farmer didn't worry too much. He knew that given time, Ben would be right as rain, and when the cabins were built, he'd be able to afford some of the things they'd had to forego in the past disastrous year, like a new mountain bike for his son that would give him more freedom, and get him out of the house.

Ben came slowly down the incline to where his father stood at the edge of the coppice. Here were the hundred or so oaks and elms planted nearly a century ago by Ben's great grandfather. On the far side, over the hill lane, the stand of straight larch trees that had shot to full maturity in the past ten years was now a bare patch of scrub. The tree-trunks had been lying further up the hill in neat piled rows for the past twelve months as they dried and seasoned. These were the ones which would be used to form the outer walls of the cabins in the Lapplander design. The rod-straight lengths of timber were perfect. Only some of the oaks would be cut, and they would go straight to the sawmill. This was Duncan Haldane's bank for his investment. Fifty of the mature trees would bring in enough to pay for the first phase of the operation.

Duncan pulled the safety goggles away from his face and eased the stretch-band from the back of his head. He let Ben put them on himself. They were too big, even at the tightest adjustment, but they stayed on without slipping too far for protection. Duncan pulled the skip of his cap down over his eyes and bent to lift the chain saw. It took three tugs at the cord before the thing racketed into fierce life. The teeth spun in a blur. Duncan raised his right elbow and Ben came in under his arm. He put his hands, small and pale beside his father's big strong fingers, on the bars. The vibration tingled up his arms and rattled his teeth. Duncan Haldane eased the blade forward and the teeth chewed into the thick bark. Dark chips sprayed out, then lighter ones as the chain saw bit its way into the hardwood a foot or so up the trunk. Ben heard the change in pitch as the powerful saw laboured. He wasn't really using the machine, though it felt as though he was. His father's powerful frame shifted behind him, easing the whirling blade out and then back against the tree at an angle. Sawdust spewed and a wedge-shaped piece of oak flew off to the left, tumbling as it went. Duncan moved to the right, to start the main cut, and the white gap in the tree grinned like a mouth. He bent in again, pressing Ben forward.

The leading edge sank itself into the oak and then Ben's heart gave a sickening double thud.

Out from the sawline, thick syrupy blood began to ooze.

It was not sap, not resin. It was *blood*. It pulsed sluggishly, as if pumped to the surface by a great slow heart. It welled out over the blade and the sawdust which was spraying out was as red as raw minced beef. Ben cried out in fright, but the noise of the saw was so loud in their ears that even *he* didn't hear his own wail. If Duncan Haldane felt his son jerk backwards, he gave no sign of having noticed. His eyes were fixed on the line where the saw was buried in the oak trunk.

Ben watched in horror and disgust as the blood continued to flow in a viscous upwelling. It blurted from the edge of the sawline and thickly ran into the crosshatched clefts in the bark below. It flowed down to the roots and began to puddle about Ben's feet. The thick, cloying smell caught in the back of his throat. He'd smelled that odour before, down at Craigard slaughterhouse when his father had taken the last of their dwindling herd of bullocks to the abattoir. The air had been hot with the stench of the blood which ran like rivers into the drains. Now, as the gory scent wafted up, clogging his nose, a wave of dizziness made Ben's vision waver.

He was trapped.

He couldn't move. In front of him the tree was *bleeding*, pumping the impossible fluid out through the gash in its side. His father, leaning in to the work, carefully arched over the boy so that Ben could get his hands on the machine while Duncan guided the saw, continued working. His bulk and embrace prevented Ben from moving backwards.

Duncan moved his arms to angle the saw and the red gobbets of sawdust flew in towards them. Something hot and wet splashed on the boy's face, trickled down over his lips. He immediately clamped his mouth shut, but not before the warm coppery taste had invaded his mouth. There was another spray and Ben felt heavy splashes on the front of his summer shirt. He jerked his head down, seeing everything fuzzed through the protective glasses, and saw the red splotches spread on the white material. He began to panic then.

The tree was alive. It was *bleeding*.

Suddenly Ben had to get away. He took a step backwards, a cringing, frightened step. His hands came off the bars. Duncan Haldane didn't seem to notice. The machine was heavy and he had to lock his own elbow joints to prevent the torque from spinning it out of the trunk.

Then Ben felt the throbbing vibration under his feet. It shivered up through him just at the same time as another pulsation of blood welled out in a thick splurge. The ground shook. Ben half-turned and saw a movement just beside his father's foot. The thin grass was humping upwards as a gnarled root, moss-camouflaged and warty, slowly shoved its way out from the ground. He felt himself gasp in greater alarm. Duncan Haldane shifted again, bearing both of them to the left, eyes fixed on the saw's bite. His heel caught on the root. Because Ben was between his arms, his balance went awry. He tried to compensate, failed and began to keel over. The chainsaw twisted in his hands and bucked wildly as the weight forced the blade down. It came spanging out of the gap, suddenly out of control. A splash spat out and covered the safety glasses, turning Ben's world a sickening red.

The heel of Duncan's boot was still snagged under the loop of root. As he struggled for balance he tried to hold the screaming saw away from his son. A sharp pain stabbed at the back of his knee as his weight twisted the joint. Even as he was falling, he swung himself away, arching his back, to hold the chain saw out and up over Ben's head. The boy slipped out from under his arms and rolled onto the grass. Ben could feel the slippery blood under his knees. He tried to crawl away, but his hands, knees and feet scrabbled, gaining no purchase like in a nightmare chase. He kept slipping backwards.

His father fell with a thump to the ground. The saw bucked madly again and his left hand lost its grip. Duncan gave a yell of alarm as the machine flipped over. The blade came arcing down.

'*Ben!*'

His father's roar, even louder than the racketing of the chain saw, made Ben turn his head. As he did, his hands, slipping on the oily surface, went out from under him. His shoulder came down and hit the ground and he rolled over onto his back. The chain saw blade came shrieking down and chewed into the turf just where Ben's neck had been a second before. The goggles slipped down

313

from his eyes and he saw the grass and small stones whipped up out of the earth. The thing was only inches from his eyes and, as he watched, he saw the machine jerk as it hit something solid several inches underground and the blade came whirring out with a tortured squeal towards him.

Then his father's hands came flashing in front of his face. One of them grabbed the bar and the other hit the off switch with a hammer-blow sound. The shriek died instantly. A few droplets of soil arced into the air and the blade stopped its blurred motion. The teeth were brown with dirt. The rest of the metal plate was as red as the grass Ben lay in.

Duncan Haldane let out a heavy, shuddering sigh. Ben loked up at him and saw the horror still written on his father's face. The ruddy, weather-beaten skin looked grey.

'Oh, son,' Duncan murmured when he finally got his breath. He reached down and picked Ben up, holding him tight against his old jacket. 'That was damned silly of me, boy. God's sake, I nearly . . .'

Ben *knew* what had nearly happened. His mind was a whirl of fear and relief and his stomach was clenching on itself in the aftermath of a very close brush with death. Yet all he could think of was the blood that was rubbing off from his shirt onto his father's jacket. Duncan hugged him hard and Ben could feel his father shaking. After a minute or two, he released his grip and gently lowered the boy to the ground.

'I think we'll have a break for a moment, lad,' he said. 'Look at you, you're all covered in mud.'

At first Ben thought his father had said *blood*, and he looked down at his shirt where the red splashes had smeared. The coppery taste was still thick and warm. At his feet, the pool of blood that had flowed from the tree was already congealing. He could see a stalk of couch-grass slowly sink under the weight of a slick, ropey clot.

Duncan walked forward and hefted the chain saw. As it swung up from the ground, saliva-like strings of drying blood dripped back onto the grass. One of them flipped round and splattered Duncan's hand.

'Need to clean the mud off before we use it again,' he said.

Mud. That's what his father had said. *Mud* not *blood*.

The realisation struck Ben like a heavy weight.

He doesn't see it.

As if to emphasise his blindness to the monstrous, *impossible* river that was now pulsing more slowly from the gash in the tree, Duncan reached forward and put his hand right into the slit. Ben saw his fingers disappear into the viscous upwelling in the space where the segment had been. He had an instant of terror at the thought that the *mouth* would shut with a snap and take his father's hand. He felt a big yell get ready to blurt out from him, but then Duncan brought his hand out. It dripped red onto the grass, but he didn't wipe his fingers, didn't seem to notice the flood or the smell.

'Don't know what happened there, but we were lucky, *damned* lucky,' he said.

He turned round to where his foot had snagged on the upthrust root, but there was nothing to be seen above the surface.

'Thing must have jammed on a knot. I'd better finish the rest off myself. Give me the goggles, Ben.'

The boy took them off and handed them to his father, his hand still trembling. Duncan noticed it, but said nothing. In his mind's eye he saw the shrieking sawblade ripping the earth inches from his son's head and he felt himself shiver.

'You go on up to the house and get a drink of juice. Your mother'll have a fit when she sees all that mud.'

Mud again, Ben thought, and that worried him more than anything. The tree had been *alive*.

It had snaked out a root to trip his father. It had tried to kill *him. And still his father did not see it.*

He backed away, eyes on the tree, hesitating.

'Go on, lad. You take a break and get cleaned up. Just tell your mum it was muddy down here, but don't tell her we had an accident. I'll explain that to her myself.'

Ben wanted to tell his father that he had to stop cutting the tree. He wanted to show him the pool of blood and the red flow down the gnarled bark. But he couldn't. His father couldn't see it. Only Ben could. For the first time the boy wondered if there was something wrong with *himself*. Then the smell of the abattoir clogged his throat again and he *knew* he was not imagining it. The forest was talking to *him*. That day when he was lost with Dorrie, it had shown him part of itself that was alien, frighteningly strange. Now it was showing him it really *was* alive. And it wanted to *kill* him.

Ben backed off again, suddenly sure, and suddenly more scared. He could not bring himself to tell his father. He knew Duncan would not see it. He would not believe him. He would not *listen*.

Ben was very afraid for his father in that moment and yet he felt powerless. Slowly he turned and walked up the slope towards the house. Just as he got to the door he heard the whine of the chain saw again. In his mind's eye he saw the blade bite and the blood flow. Misery settled round him like a cold blanket.

In the kitchen, his mother took one look at him and told him to take the shirt off.

'Looks like you've been rolling in the mire,' she said. 'That shirt should have lasted you two days in this weather, Ben. You'll have to be more careful.'

She couldn't see it either. Ben's misery deepened.

24

Nothing much happened in Linnvale in the week leading up to the ceilidh. Ernie Buist's rusty tractor still remained jammed against the hedge close to the road. Alec Stirling passed it every morning. He'd seen neither father nor son. He wished the boy well.

Sheila Garvie visited Caitlin every afternoon and spent an hour or so with her, talking while Caitlin painted, or taking her for walks in the forest. The girl took her sketch pad with her and did skilful drawings of the plants which Sheila plucked from the side of the path. She marvelled at the older woman's knowledge. She seemed to know where to find every flower, every root. And every day Sheila encouraged the girl to take more of the powder she'd prepared. Caitlin listened as Sheila told her of her belief in the healing force of *Gaia*, mother earth, and the power that was in every growing thing. As each day went on, Caitlin felt herself become more and more convinced of Sheila's beliefs. She felt sheepish guilt at her outburst of a few days previously. Now she felt healthier than ever before. In the mornings she would wake early and use the pulley to haul herself out of bed and immediately do her exercise before enjoying a warm bath. She felt full of energy and the sense of wellbeing only seemed to increase.

Two days before the ceilidh Caitlin had been wheeling herself into the kitchen when there was a sharp knock on the door. She turned swiftly and banged her knee sharply against the table leg. Caitlin backed away then propelled herself down the hall to the front door. Alec Stirling was standing under the porch with a bundle of letters in his hand. It was only later that she tried to recall the moment. She was lying in bed, carefully applying a cold compress to the bruise, as she did for every knock and bump. She remembered the accident and seemed to recall a brief flare of pain. She shook her head. It was her memory playing tricks on her again. She hadn't felt pain in her legs for eighteen months. Just before she went to sleep, she took another glass of Sheila's mixture. In the morning, the bruise was gone. She had *never* healed so quickly.

Up at the farm Duncan Haldane used the days leading up to the ceilidh to cut down ten of the oaks and dress out their branches, hauling them all in a tangled pile to the rocky scrubland at the edge of the forest. If anything gouted from the trunks, he did not see it. He worked well on his own, without having to worry about Ben. Every time he recalled the near-catastrophe, his heart sank, so he tried not to think about it. During the week, the sawmill lorry came back for the oak trunks and Duncan added another tranche to his investment account. Bob McCourt was still in the Western Infirmary, very slowly recovering from his brush with death, occasionally awaking from dreadful nightmares in which he saw bodies hanging from trees, hanging *within* trees.

Every night, long after midnight, figures could be seen walking quickly and quietly, singly and in pairs, as the village slept. They gathered down near the old mill and then together, in a group, they walked into the forest. Some time later, if anyone had been down beyond the fallen dyke that marked the boundary of the original Fasach Wood, they might have heard women's voices, raised in a chant. But there was no one else to hear.

In that deep part of the forest that could only be reached along one of the shadowy paths that angled in towards the dark heart, some time before dawn the soft chanting would stop and, later on, figures would be seen walking back up towards the houses, singly and in pairs, while the village continued sleeping.

Saturday finally came and Martin Thornton was late. He'd had to work on to make changes in a story and by the time he got home, showered and shaved, he was running tardy. He put on a light tweed jacket which was smart enough without making him overdressed, bundled some casual clothes in a holdall in the back of the jeep and once past Levenford, on the quiet country road, he floored the pedal, trying to make up time.

Beyond Levenford there's a straight road towards Lochend, which, as its name implies, sits at the south end of Loch Corran, straddling the river which meanders down its nine-mile stretch to empty itself out into the Clyde's tidal waters at Levenford's castle rock. North of Lochend, the road follows almost exactly the line of the shore, twisting and turning to the vagaries of the bedrock. Occasionally it heads inland to avoid some stony headland that the glaciers had failed to move, before returning to the banks. At this time of the year, and this time of the night, the waters were still, reflecting the blue of a light summer evening's sky. Far out, a speedboat cut a white line on the glassy surface. Here and there, a trout rose for a nymph and made dappled magic rings. Further north, where the broad waters narrowed and deepened, turning blue-black no matter how calm or sunny the day, the wild swooping slopes were covered in oak trees which seemed to march down to the waterside.

As he drove along the tree-lined road, Martin Thornton got a glimpse every now and then, when there was a break in the tree cover, of the spectacular scenery on the far side. In two years' time, there would be an almighty row over a plan to quarry into the steep slope to build a terminal to hold the oil that seismic studies would find three miles under the placid waters. That battle would make Duncan Haldane's difference of opinion with the Linnvale Preservation Society seem like a friendly exchange of pleasantries. That, however, was in the future. For now the waters were placid.

Martin drove as quickly as the aged diesel engine would allow. The Land-Rover was ancient and battle-scarred and bounced about on protesting springs, but he'd had the thing for seven years, and treated it like an old, if temperamental friend.

A mile past Ardoch, a small collection of houses beyond the old Colquhoun estates, the road took a left turn, then a sharp right before coming back to a straight stretch with trees on one side. The entrance to Linnvale's glen was flanked on either side by tall lime trees which roughly paralleled the course of the Corrie water as a trailing adjunct to Fasach Wood.

Martin sped on for about a quarter of a mile, watching out for the signpost which he'd seen close to the trees on the verge. It was only when the road became a series of zig-zag swings following the contours of the shoreline that he realised he might have missed it. A few yards on, the Land-Rover swept up and over the bridge which spanned the Corrie. He decided he *had* shot past the Linn Road. Muttering to himself, he stopped at the first farm gate, reversed, then retraced his route. Out of the twists and on to the straight, he slowed down. The loch was on his left and he scanned the right side for the entrance. The tall trees crowded close together. There was no break. There was no signpost. He travelled to the far end of the straight and spent five confused minutes before he could find

319

a place to turn the jeep. Facing back north again, he shook his head.

Like any lochside road in Scotland, one part can often resemble another, especially to travellers who have driven the route infrequently. Martin cast his mind back to a week before, when he'd visited the valley for the second time. He didn't remember having any difficulty. He tried to reconstruct in his mind the pull-in to the Linn Road, visualising the serpentine bends before the straight part. He gave up. The more he thought about it, the less sure he was. He now couldn't say for certain that the Linn Road was before or *after* the Corrie Bridge.

He pulled on the wheel, angling the nose out of the farm-track he'd backed into, and was about to move forward when a blare of noise made him stamp on the brakes. There was a flash of headlamps, pale in daylight, then a big white tanker with the name *MacKinnon* bold and black along its flank roared past him. Martin saw a hand wave from the cab as it swept up the Loch Shore Road, but he couldn't tell if it was a friendly gesture or an irate sign of the driver's annoyance. After it had gone past, travelling at speed and creating a bow-wave of pressure strong enough to rock the jeep where it stood, Martin realised that the big truck would be heading for the Linnvale depot.

He slotted the gearstick forward and got out of the track and onto the road, changing up as quickly as he could to catch up to the bowser. He went through the series of bends again and was onto the straight before he caught a glimpse of the big white back end in the distance. He floored the pedal and soon saw a twinkling of red and orange that told him the tanker was slowing. It turned and disappeared into the trees. Martin followed, maybe a quarter of a mile distant. When he reached the spot he slowed to a crawl, frowning. At first he couldn't see anything but unbroken verge. He eased forward, puzzled, then, all of a sudden, his wheels were on the tarmac of the Linn Road. The branches of the big lime trees, now thick with leaves, were close enough to intertwine, providing an almost complete barrier. The road was effectively hidden. Martin cast his mind back again. They hadn't seemed so close before, he thought. He swung the wheel to follow the road and then, for the first time, he saw the signpost with its blue arrow pointing into the space between the trees. Thick ivy had grown up the post and sent out bottle-green sprays of waxy leaves to hang down over the words.

Martin smiled to himself. He drove in between the trees. The trailing branches scraped the top of the jeep, rapping like knuckles on the roof. He imagined the tanker driver, much higher in his cab, having to force his big machine through the foliage. He thought it might be a good idea if they hired a tree surgeon to trim the branches back, otherwise the road to Linnvale might become completely overgrown.

He caught up with the tanker halfway to Linnvale and thought no more about it.

Caitlin was ready and waiting for him when he finally knocked on her door. She didn't mention his lateness, favouring him instead with a bright smile.

'You look very smart,' she said. 'Smart but casual. Just right.'

He took her hand and lowered himself down onto the arm of the easy chair so she wouldn't have to crane up to him.

'And you. You look terrific.'

Caitlin had put on a green silky top which matched her eyes perfectly and set off her cascading flaming waves of hair. Around her neck a string of amber beads spangled honey light. She accepted his compliment.

'Now, do we drive, or do we race again?'

'Neither. We stroll elegantly.'

She let him push the chair along the road and, as she did, pointed out the flowers in the hedgerow, telling Martin of her walks in the forest with Sheila Garvie.

'You'll meet her again tonight,' she said. 'She's made some wine. Everybody says it's strong enough to take the top of your head off.'

'Sounds like my kind of woman.'

'Just remember you're taking me home tonight,' Caitlin said. As she did, she recalled the end of her dream and suddenly, very girlishly, she blushed. She kept her head facing forward so he wouldn't see it.

As Martin pushed the chair along the lane, neither of them knew that, quite instinctively, the other kept a wary eye on the hedgerow. Martin hadn't told Caitlin of how he'd come off the road and almost tumbled the jeep into the river. He didn't

321

want to scare her again, though he thought he'd better warn her later about coming along here by herself. Caitlin, despite Sheila Garvie's dismissal, could not forget the deep threatening growl and the savage lurch of her wheelchair as the black animal had smashed into it.

Finally, they came to the bridge, crossed over, and were away from the hedgerows. Having interviewed Gail Dean, Martin did not need directions to the church hall. When they got there, the music was loud enough to rattle the slates on the roof.

For the most part it was the best night either of them had enjoyed in a long time.

Alec Stirling was collecting the tickets at the door. He welcomed both of them with the delighted bonhomie of a man who's already had some to drink and planned to spend a lot of time improving his condition.

'All strictly off the record, boss,' he told Martin. 'No notebooks tonight and if you see me dancing with somebody I shouldn't, I don't want to read about it.' He turned to Caitlin. 'You take the brakes of that bogey and we'll show them how to boogie,' he said unashamedly. Alec had few reservations at any time. A couple of pints of the Douglas Arms' best heavy beer had swept those few away entirely, but he was the kind of man who could say whatever came into his head without giving offence.

'You'll never keep up with me,' Caitlin retorted with a laugh. 'You're halfway to falling over as it is.'

'Well, when I do, you can lend me your wheels and see that I get home all right, unless I can get some of the women to give me a fireman's carry.'

Alec ushered them through and, when they were gone, reached under the ticket table and pulled forth his pint of beer. He was in the middle of a long swallow when Molly Carr and Fiona Herron came in through the front door. He almost choked in his effort to hide the evidence.

The hall was crowded. Caitlin waved to a few couples sitting in the corner. Martin stood behind her, feeling slightly awkward because he recognised very few faces. Finally he noticed Duncan Haldane and his wife beside another couple close to the entrance. He gave them a wave and got a cheerful acknowledgement in return. Rose Haldane looked a great deal less careworn than she had the last time he'd seen her. He made a mental note to congratulate them both on their victory, though he automatically warned himself to make it discreet. Caitlin had friends on both sides of the divide.

They sat at a table close to a group of younger couples who made a space for them and Caitlin introduced Martin to them all. Caroline Petrie and Melanie Cuthbert were friends of Caitlin's. The three young women helped organise the summerplay for the smaller children in the glen. He shook hands and one of the men with them offered him a beer which he was delighted to accept. It was already hot in the hall and the temperature was rising. Three young lads in white shirts and bow ties were playing passably on piano, accordion and drums as the evening got off to a fine start. Now and then a gust of childish laughter would come from the anteroom where the children were being entertained at their own party and out from under their parents' feet. The teenage section was in the annexe built during World War II as a billet for the servicemen who guarded the fuel dump in the quarry which forty years later would become MacKinnon's calor depot. They were having their own disco under the watchful eyes of two kirk elders who were posted sentry to guard against the impulsiveness of youth and to ensure that nobody made use of the store-rooms for any purpose whatsoever.

Martin's beer went down a treat. Caitlin had a glass of Sheila Garvie's wine and declared it marvellous. One of the young men produced a stone jar from his wife's big handbag and proceeded to pour everyone a dram of liquid so dark it looked like caramel. Martin hadn't the heart to tell him he'd sworn off whisky. He only took a small sip. It tasted of heady malt, and immediately Martin felt a sudden desire to quaff the lot. The young man confided, with a conspiratorial wink, that it had matured in oak under Dumbuie hill for five years and that there were another five barrels getting old with quiet dignity in the same place, where, he assured Martin, the custom's men had never looked, despite regular searches going back two hundred years. Whatever its provenance the whisky had a rosy glow and the after-kick of an angry bull. Martin pushed his glass out of arm's reach and harm's way. He'd spent too much time looking at the bottom of a bottle.

Sheila Garvie came to join them for a moment and poured

Caitlin another wine. As she reached a slender arm, Martin noticed the little birthmark close to the crook of her elbow, black against the smooth skin. For a second, the shape seemed familiar, then Caitlin interrupted his train of thought, offering him her glass. Martin took a sip, but after the whisky it was too fruity for him. Sheila tasted from Martin's glass and wrinkled her nose.

'Too much peat,' she said. She reached into her bag and pulled out a small hip flask worked in silver. Before he could protest, she poured a small amount of clear liquid into the whisky.

'Here. Try it now.'

Martin could do nothing but take the glass. The dark colour had faded to the amber of real whisky. He put the tumbler to his lips and sipped. Instantly the glow spread down the back of his throat. Whatever Sheila had put into the spirit, it had smoothed the taste perfectly.

'Now *that's* a whisky,' he said. 'You're definitely in the wrong trade.' Sheila gave him a slow smile. Martin took another sip and the heady tang spread under his ribs.

A piper came on and the music livened up. Somebody called for a strip-the-willow and some of the younger guests took their places on the dance floor. The pipes skirled up and away and the four formations started to whirl. Beside Martin Caitlin started to clap her hands enthusiastically in time to the beat of the music. With each gesture her flaming hair bounced, catching the light like hot embers. Martin watched her and a shadow passed over his face. Caitlin was smiling, almost unaware of the fact that the young couples enthusiastically throwing each other about were doing something she could not dream of. All of a sudden he wanted to take her hand and pull her from the seat, somehow *willing* her injury to be gone. As he watched he realised, not without a twinge of disquiet, that he could seriously fall for this woman.

When the dance ended and the partners separated to come back to their tables, foreheads glistening with sweat, a big man with bull-like shoulders came on and sat himself down on the small stage. He produced a small, rustic-looking flute from the pocket of his trousers and started to play a slow lilt. Most people in the hall sat and listened in silence. One or two couples got up and started dancing slowly, most just swaying in time to the music. The wife of the man with the never-ending supply of whisky asked Martin if he

324

wanted to dance. Caitlin jerked her head at him, silently ordering him onto the floor.

The night progressed and the room got hotter. Martin took his jacket off early in the proceedings, then his tie. He opened his shirt down two or three buttons. Every now and then Sheila Garvie gave him a drop of her clear liquor when she came across to pour Caitlin more wine. Despite himself, Martin had finished the first glass. After the couple of beers and the first taste of whisky in a long time, his control ebbed away. He drank without thinking.

Somebody announced a two-step just as Martin was speaking to Gail Dean. She'd remembered him from the interview and had come across to tell him his story had been balanced, even if they had lost the battle. Gail was slightly flushed from the heat and her cheeks were rosy from the exertion of the last dashing white sergeant, into which she had thrown herself with girlish glee.

'Can you do this one?' she asked.

'If I can remember my Boy Scout days,' Martin said, hesitantly.

'Good. I was in the Guides.'

'I tried to get in, but the torchlight in the tent gave me away. They threw me out.'

'Mischievous beggar, I'll bet,' Gail said, giving him a wide smile.

She took his hand and led him onto the floor. He extended his right arm and she stepped in towards him, coming close. She was almost as tall as he was, with a comely, well-formed face which tended to dimple when she smiled. She had deep-blue eyes which sparkled when the dimples showed. Her hair was golden fair. Aside from Caitlin, Martin thought, she was the best-looking woman in the room.

They danced slowly round the floor as the music played. Alec Stirling came in just as they were passing the door, pint in hand, and a mite unsteady on his feet.

'Hey, twinkle-toes,' he shouted raucously at the top of his voice. 'Give it a passa-dobley!' He lifted his glass and took a long pull. When he brought it down there was a froth of beer under his nose. 'Come on, Howling Gail, let's see you shimmy.'

All the men laughed, while some of the women tittered, embarrassed.

'They think I'm a little overenthusiastic but, as the young ones say, if you enjoy it, go for it.'

She laughed and Martin felt the ripples move against him. Maybe it was the movement of her laughter, but he thought he felt her hand tighten on his back, pulling him a little closer. He could feel the heat of her body through his shirt.

They danced once more round the crowded floor. Somebody bumped into Martin and he stumbled forward, feeling himself forced against the minister's wife. Again, her arm pulled and squeezed him closer. Then, to his surprise, she *twisted* against him, dragging her breasts quite hard across his chest. He could feel the slight feminine bulge of her belly against his. At first Martin thought the motion had been accidental but, even as that notion came to him, she did it again, and this time, through the thin summer material of her dress and the fine brassière, he felt the unmistakable sensation of nipples pressing against his chest.

Immediately he felt a flush suffuse his face. He was dancing with the *minister's* wife. All of a sudden he felt like an awkward schoolboy. He was man of the world enough not to be fazed by any woman's attentions, but not here, in the middle of a roomful of strangers, with Caitlin Brook looking on—

Just at that moment the dance came to an end. Gail Dean was talking to him, though he never heard the words. The accordionist called out the name of a dance which he also missed, while the music immediately changed to a faster beat. Gail pulled away from him, grabbed his hand and then they were off again, round the floor, doing a skipping sort of jig. Martin felt instant relief. After the first turn round the floor, as the perspiration started to run down his temples, he told himself he had imagined it. He'd given the woman no encouragement.

They turned at the top end and he caught Caitlin's eye. She was clapping in time to the music and flashed him a big, bright smile of encouragement. Alec Stirling whooped and did a little jig all of his own as they passed. He was standing with a beer in one hand and his arm around a plump, dark-haired young woman who, in that fleeting moment, seemed to welcome his embrace.

The music creaked up another gear and he spun with the minister's wife. She said something which he couldn't hear over the din and then, all of a sudden, the beat slowed. The music took

326

on a curious double-tone, as if his ears were picking up the sounds a fraction of a second apart. The accordion's note went from a high tremolo down, in the space of a few seconds, to a burbling bass, as if somebody had turned a switch and the record had started to glide to a halt. The overhead lights flared in his eyes and then changed their colour from fluorescent white down through orange and then took on a pinkish hue.

'What the hell . . .?' Martin started to think.

The dancers around them moved as though through treacle. Martin and Gail sailed smoothly past them. They passed a woman and Martin saw the slow evolution of a smile on her face as she leaned into her partner. Off to the left, Alec Stirling jerked slowly. The beer slopped from his glass and took an age to fall in a wavering thick river silently to the floor. They came round the far side of the room. Caitlin's smile was still wide. Martin's eyes locked with hers. They looked dark brown under the odd colour of the lights. He saw her hands come together and move apart then come together again. He heard the double-boom of his heart beating in his temples. Caitlin did a lethargic handclap and another movement caught his eye. Her right foot was slowly tapping on the footplate of her wheelchair in time with her hands.

The dance turned and Gail and Martin moved on. Beside him he heard a woman laugh, yet he only knew it was a woman because he saw her. The noise was a low warble, scarcely audible. He *felt* the vibration in the bones of his head.

Then Gail spoke.

'Oh, it's so hot.'

Her voice was slow and low, but not like the rest. It sounded natural.

'I think I need a cool drink,' she said, smiling at him. Her cheeks were infused with colour. Her dimples dark rosy hollows on either side of her mouth. Her eyes sparkled under the red glow of the lights. She turned, with one hand in the small of Martin's back, and walked him straight into a side room. The pounding in Martin's ears was like a sluggish, underwater pulse.

Martin followed in the weird red light, feeling dizziness begin to spin his vision. The room was empty. Gail went to the sink and poured water into a glass. She slipped her hand into a decorative pocket in her dress and, from a tiny bottle, dropped a clear liquid into the glass. The drink, already pink in Martin's clouding vision, went instantly dark.

Gail took a long draught, half the glassful. She smacked her lips and handed it to Martin.

'Drink this. It should cool you down.'

Martin reached for the glass and, as he took it, their fingers touched. He felt a physical jerk as energy leapt between them. Without thinking he lifted the glass and drank.

Stars popped into existence in front of his eyes and a bitter taste made the buds on the sides of his tongue burn with sudden heat.

Gail moved behind him as he drank. He heard a dull thud. The room swam in front of him and his lungs laboured for breath. For a second he thought he was going to faint. The woman moved up beside him, took the glass from his fingers and laid it down on the metal board next to the sink. It made a sound like a footfall. Martin turned. She was doing something and at first he couldn't make it out. The heat in his head was oozing down into his chest and belly. His skin felt oddly numb yet tingling at the same time.

With one slow, deft movement, Gail Dean pulled her dress over her head and laid it on the table. She turned and gave him a delighted smile.

'It's time,' she said softly, beaming all the while like an excited schoolgirl.

Martin tried to say something, but the words wouldn't come. He just stood there, a bewildered statue. She shucked off her brassière and her large, firm breasts sprung out as the flimsy material pulled away. Her skin was smooth as silk, tinged pink under the strange light. She bent and slipped a pair of silk pants off, delicately raising each knee in turn. She laid them beside her clothes and came towards him.

'It's time,' she said. '*Now, John.*'

'But I'm not—' Martin tried to say but she clamped her mouth on his. Her tongue forced his lips apart. Stars exploded behind his eyelids as he felt her warmth against him. Hands scrabbled urgently with his clothing and he was *gone*.

All thought went as the heady fumes filled his head. She pulled, keeping him pressed against her. She reached the table and arched herself backwards. Her legs came up and Martin Thornton was lost in the heat and the thumping of the pulse behind his ears and the pounding of her heart against his chest. At some point she cried out, low and demanding, but he heard nothing.

Caitlin saw Martin spin past her and clapped loudly, watching him being whirled around by Gail Dean. She thought he looked helpless against her robust enthusiasm. Gail was saying something to him, which he obviously didn't hear. He looked at her as they turned and their eyes locked. His face was suffused with red and she could see the glisten of sweat on his temple. She clapped with the music and they danced away from her.

The reel played on and on. Somebody said something at her side and she turned, still clapping.

'Wonderful fun,' Sheila Garvie said. She too was swaying to the music. Her eyes followed the dancers.

'They're having a ball,' Caitlin said. She'd had several glasses of Sheila's wine and was feeling warm and flushed.

'You'll join them,' Sheila said, eyes sparkling. There was a mischievous smile on her face. 'I'll see you dance, little Caitlin,' she murmured, just loud enough to be heard over the music.

'What—?'

Sheila put a finger to Caitlin's lip. She inclined her head and, with her own eyes, drew Caitlin's gaze downwards.

Caitlin followed and then her green eyes widened in shock.

Her foot was tapping out the rhythm.

It was *moving*. Just a little up-and-down motion, but enough to show that it wasn't being caused by the vibration of the dancing feet on the floor.

She turned, her mouth a round oval of disbelief.

Sheila quickly put her finger to the young woman's lips again.

'Not now, *seedling*,' she said quickly.

Caitlin's mind whirled dizzily. It was *impossible*. It was utterly, completely *inconceivable*.

A terrible fear surged into her mind. *She must be going mad.* She had to be *hallucinating*. She looked down again. The movement had slowed to a twitch, but it was still *movement*, something the doctors had told her could *never* happen.

'What's happening, Sheila? What's *happening* to me?' she asked, too loudly. Across the table her two friends turned their heads and looked at her before going back to their conversation.

329

'Trust me, Caitlin. There's more power in the plants than you know.'

The girl looked at her blankly. Inside her, hope surged and dismayed her. She was not *allowed* to hope. It was against all the rules.

'No, you're not going mad,' Sheila said, close to her ear. She reached and took both of Caitlin's hands in hers.

'No matter what they say, there is *always* hope. Where there is death, still there is *life*. You will be yourself again, Caitlin, if you trust me. And you will be *perfect*.'

She squeezed Caitlin's hands and held them until the tremor in the fingers died away.

Martin Thornton awoke on the back seat of his Land-Rover. The sun was high and, when he opened his eyes, daggers of pain stabbed him and he squeezed them shut tight again. Very slowly he heaved himself up to a sitting position and opened his eyes again, keeping them averted from the glare. The movement sent loops of nausea rolling up from below. He leaned on the doorhandle, swung it open and leaned out, retching drily. A heavy pounding in his head announced a devastating hangover.

He couldn't recall getting into the car. In fact his memory of the night before was a *foggy*, impenetrable haze. He clambered out to stand on the short grass that tangled up from the roadside beyond the hedge just past Caitlin's home where he'd parked the previous night. Every movement was purgatory. The pounding in his head felt like hammerblows. He groaned to himself and tried to remember. Nothing much came, a drink with Alec Stirling and Jock Weir, buying them the pints he'd promised, dancing with one or two people, but he'd spent most of the night sitting with Caitlin enjoying the music.

How he had ended up in the Land-Rover, fully clothed but minus his jacket, he hadn't a clue.

Martin reached forward and pushed the gate open. It squeaked sharply and he winced as the noise drilled into him. It took twelve steps to reach the front door, every one of them a thudding punishment in his temples, and he wondered how he was going to make it through the ordeal of actually knocking on the oak surface. As expected, the rapping noise jacked up the pounding a few more degrees. He screwed his eyes shut and waited for the pain to pass.

He heard movement inside the house. The door opened. Caitlin looked up at him.

'Where on earth did you get to?' she asked, crossly and very loudly.

He held his hands up in mute protest, bringing one finger up to his mouth to indicate that less noise would be greatly appreciated.

'You damned well left me at the ceilidh and went off with Alec Stirling and his drinking partners, didn't you?'

Martin shook his head and then wished he hadn't.

'I don't know what the hell happened,' he said in a voice full of gravel. 'I must have slept in the Rover. Oh God, my head.'

'Well, it serves you right, getting yourself drunk. The last I saw you were dancing with Gail Dean and then you disappeared,' Caitlin said, eyes still blazing.

Gail Dean. The name sparked behind the throbbing. Gail Dean. There was something he should *remember*. He made a weak grab for the significance, but it easily eluded him. For some reason, a shadow of guilt, or maybe embarrassment, flickered over his thoughts before fading. He didn't have the mental acuity to work it out.

'Can I come in?' he whispered hoarsely.

'I don't know if I should let you. Sheila Garvie and some of the women had to see me home last night. It was dreadfully embarrassing.'

'Look. I'm sorry,' he said as loudly as he could, and every word cost him. 'I didn't mean to get drunk. I was having a good time . . . I think. I just don't know what happened.'

She sat in silence while he stood with both hands on the doorposts. His face was haggard and grey. His eyes were red and ratty. He looked exactly like a drunk suffering a monumental hangover. He took her silence for refusal. He shrugged painfully, then turned to walk away.

She let him reach the gate, heard the loud squeal of the hinges and saw him wince, then called him back.

'Oh, don't be so damned silly. Come in and have some coffee.'

He turned slowly and, by the time he was facing the door again, she had spun the chair and gone back into the house. He reached the door before it swung shut.

The coffee was the best drink he had ever tasted in his entire life. He took a big mug and scooped four spoons of sugar into it then lifted it to his mouth. It was sweet and strong and his throat gulped it down, despite the heat, as if desperate. As soon as he finished it, Caitlin poured him another.

'You look terrible, and it serves you right.'

'I feel terrible, and it probably does. What the hell was I drinking last night?'

'You had a few beers. Then some whisky. Then God knows what else in the bar with Alec Stirling.'

'But I don't drink whisky.'

'You did last night.'

'I really thought I was doing quite well.'

'Alec and the boys took you home. You were being sick in the sink. God, I was embarrassed.'

Martin felt himself flush with colour.

'Oh. Was I really sick?'

'So they told me. They took you home. I thought you'd gone to Alec's place.'

'Apparently not. I just woke up in the back of the car. I've lost my jacket.'

Caitlin looked at him sternly, then her expression softened.

'You're really not feeling very well, are you?'

'Frankly, I feel like death.'

'You look it. Why don't you lie down for the rest of the morning and try to recover.'

That idea sounded just fine and dandy to Martin Thornton. He finished his third coffee, swallowed the aspirin tablets she thrust into his hand and allowed her to show him to her bed. He lay down on top of the blankets and in five minutes was sound asleep. Sometime before noon, he dreamed he was at the Ceilidh, dancing with Gail Dean. Hands were clapping as she whirled him off the floor towards the anteroom at the far end. Just as he turned away from the crowd he saw Sheila Garvie smiling. There was a hungry, triumphant look in her eyes. He got an instant image of a shotgun, double barrels aiming at his heart.

Then Gail opened the door and they stepped into the trees. The smell of pollen was thick in the air. She said something to him, and he saw it was Caitlin, standing beside him, but the words were whispered and faint. She was looking across the river and he followed her gaze to the island. A mist hung low over the water, making the trees on the far side indistinct. She wanted to go there, he knew, but he felt oppressed by that thought. He turned back at her touch and found himself standing beside a sapling that stood tall and green. There were lines and whorls on its green bark and as he looked they twisted and resolved themselves into a face. Two eyes opened and gazed green on him. There was a rasp of sound and a slit in the bark formed a mouth and he heard Caitlin's voice from within the tree and terror grabbed him by the throat.

He woke up in a sweat, a cry of fear caught in his lungs.

Caitlin was shaking him gently.

'Huh?' he asked stupidly, trying to find his bearings, while the image of the dream fragmented and dissolved. 'What time is it?'

'Lunchtime. You've had three hours,' she said. 'How do you feel?'

He swung his legs over the side of the bed. There was a dry taste in his mouth and he put his head in his hands for a moment, trying to reorientate himself.

'Fine, I think. Headache's gone.'

'Good. Though I still think you deserved it.'

'Listen. I *am* sorry about last night. I just can't remember a thing about it.'

'Forget it. I could tell that as soon as I saw you this morning.'

'I feel really bad about leaving you on your own.'

'Oh. I wasn't. I knew everybody there. There were a few casualties. Old Hector Ritchie had to be carried out. Even the minister was a bit unsteady on his feet.'

'Well, I was in good company.'

She laughed, reaching a hand up to ruffle his hair, as if telling a mischievous boy that his punishment was over and he was forgiven.

'Come on. I've made lunch. I hope you can eat.'

Martin thought about it for a moment. The hangover was gone. Suddenly he was very hungry.

'I could eat a horse,' he said.

He followed her through to the bright kitchen and watched

while she laid out a ploughman's, then fell to with enthusiasm. He cleared his plate and used a kerb of crusty bread to mop up the salad dressing. The lunch killed his hangover completely. He felt human again.

He cleared the plates, still trying to make up lost points with her, and in the afternoon they went for a walk. Caitlin, who bundled her sketch pad into a satchel which hung over the back of the chair, told him she wanted to go to the old churchyard. That was fine for him. It was a lazy, blue-sky day, ripe for doing nothing.

The graveyard was just behind the small church and could be reached by a curving path which led to an old wrought-iron gate. Near the entrance the headstones were quite recent, but as they proceeded, where the yew trees swept bottle-green branches over the old slate monuments, they got progressively older. In the far corner the shadow was cool and filled with the smell of resin. Caitlin took her pad and began to draw firm lines, quickly delineating the corner wall with its tumble of ivy and an old, slanted gravestone that caught the light through the trees. Martin wandered around, looking at the epitaphs. Some of them were so ancient that the carved words had been almost worn smooth. Others were obscured by moss which he scraped away with a twig. Most of the decayed ones were in a mixture of Latin and Gaelic. Even some of the names were difficult to translate.

'They had big families in those days,' he said, almost to himself, but Caitlin heard him in the quiet of the cemetery.

'Nine or ten children were common.'

'Most of them didn't make it.' Martin was looking at a stone which listed eleven children, each of whom had died in infancy. Two had a fever, one drowned and the rest of them, according to the stone, had simply died.

He wandered on, stopping here and there. One stone, set against the wall, caught his eye.

'Here's an odd one,' he called over. 'Says a farmer called MacFarlane was killed by his own bull.'

'I know about that. Sheila told me her mother tried to fix him up, but it was too late.'

Martin bent to look at the stone.

'Must have been somebody else,' he called out. 'This one was way back in 1720. MacFarlane of Ardbeg Farm.'

'Yes, that's the one,' Caitlin called back. 'Her mother was some sort of healer. You must be reading it wrong.'

He squatted down and hooked a small piece of lichen from the figure seven carved in the stone, to make sure it was not a nine. It was clearly delineated.

'Nope. Definitely 1720. Nearly three hundred years ago.'

'History must have repeated itself.'

He straightened up. There were other MacFarlane stones, all from Ardbeg Farm. The dead man's son had eight children, only two of whom, a son and a daughter, survived. That son had three daughters, both of whom lived to ripe ages. The eldest married a man called MacPhail who came to work Ardbeg. The MacFarlane line petered out.

'There aren't any more MacFarlanes,' Martin protested. 'That was the one. She must have got the date wrong.'

'Impossible. She was there herself.'

'Well, she's a few years older than she looks,' Martin called back. Caitlin's laugh came tinkling through the graveyard.

She sketched on, enjoying the warmth of the sun on her cheek, while he explored. A rabbit came hopping between the stones, sat up and eyed him, nose twitching, before turning quickly. He got a flash of its tail as it disappeared into a rhododendron bush.

He came to the far wall where an old metal gate was rusting on its hinges. He pushed it open, ignoring the metallic protest, and found another small part of the cemetery which was separate from the rest. Here, under the spreading yew branches, was a small collection of tumbled stones.

Here, where the sunlight could not reach, it was damp and musty. A spider's web, still damp with dew, stretched between two of the stones. None of them stood upright. They lay at slanted angles, old and crumbled. He hunkered down in front of one of the slate slabs and peeled away the moss with his fingers.

The carved letters were almost worn flat into the surface. He couldn't make out more than a few of them. One date, he thought, might have been sixteen something, though he couldn't be sure. Underneath it was a name so indistinct that the letters had all but disappeared. He tried to trace it with his finger.

Finally he joined them together in his head. *Seilach*. The name was familiar. Hadn't he read it recently? There was something familiar about it. He searched his memory and recalled the name from the book Andrew Toye had given him. He bent down to the stone once more and looked again at the headstone. The lines were obscure. He shook his head. He'd probably read it wrongly. Alongside was one less worn. Martin hunkered down in front of it, trying to translate the old stilted language into English. This grave was dedicated to a man called Corrie, a farmer. He had died two weeks after being married, according to the stone, to one Seila Moine. Whatever became of the bride, the carvings did not elaborate, though most of the headstones in the other section gave a complete history of the families of the dead, often down the generations. Martin wandered between the slanted stones. All of the graves, as far as he could make out, were the burial-places of men. He wondered vaguely what happened to their women.

Caitlin was finishing her sketch when he came back into the main churchyard. Martin looked over her shoulder and watched as her finger smudged the charcoal into shadows. The black-and-white drawing had captured the corner of the churchyard perfectly.

'You'll have to write an elegy to go with that,' he said. 'It's damned good.'

'Yes. Maybe I'll do a painting. Put in some more sunlight to make it less sombre. People don't want pictures of shadowy graveyards on their living-room walls.'

They went down through the gate and back onto the road. He put an arm on the back of the chair and pushed lightly, allowing her to put her hands back in her lap.

'How's your head?' she asked, turning to look up at him.

'All the better for not being reminded of my shame and sorrow,' he said.

'Oh, don't worry. You're forgiven. I'm in a great mood.'

'Any reason?'

'I'll show you when we get back,' she said. He saw the smile at the corner of her mouth and didn't push it.

Instead of going in the front door, she angled the chair round the side of the house and up to the back garden. The smell of alyssum was heavy in the air. Just beyond the lawn, the stream burbled lazily. Caitlin swung her chair round. Martin sat down on the garden bench.

336

She looked at him in a strange, concentrating way, as if trying to read him, then she spoke.

'I'm going to see if this works again, but you must promise me you won't tell anybody. Not a soul. Promise?'

He looked at her, puzzled.

'What do you mean?'

'Just promise me, Martin, otherwise I won't even try.'

'All right. I promise I won't tell a soul.'

She stared into his eyes, probing again.

'I believe you,' she said, quietly. She held onto the arms of the chair and her brow furrowed. Her eyes were closed.

'Now watch carefully.'

'Watch *what*?'

'My *feet*,' she said, through gritted teeth.

He looked, and nothing happened.

'I can't see anything,' he said, perplexed. Caitlin opened her eyes and immediately bent to slip off her shoes. She straightened and resumed her pose of concentration again. He heard her breathing quicken, tight in her throat, as if she was making a great physical effort. He looked at her face, screwed up and tight, hair falling over her brow in a cascade of red. Then he let his eyes drop. He followed the length of her body, down to her knees, her calves and then her small, bare feet resting on the plate.

She made a small noise, as if holding her breath with some difficulty, and, as he watched, a tremor ran under the skin of her calf, a small ripple which shivered the pale curve at the side of her ankle.

Then the toes of her right foot *moved*.

It was a small, delicate motion. Not more than a twitch, hardly perceptible.

'See it?' she gasped.

He looked again and the toes moved up and down, just a fraction of an inch, all together. Her left foot moved slightly, lifting a millimetre or two up from the plate, before falling back again.

'Can you *see* it?' Caitlin gritted and then, as if all her energy was spent, she let her breath out in one violent exhalation.

'I saw it. Your toes jiggled a bit,' Martin said, unable to comprehend the enormity of the moment.

'I knew I wasn't imagining things,' Caitlin said. She suddenly burst into delighted laughter. 'They *moved*, Martin. That's the first time they've done that in almost two years. And I *felt* it. I *made* them move.'

'But I thought the doctors said—'

'Yes, they did,' Caitlin interrupted. 'They said that. They showed me the X-rays and told me it could never happen. But Sheila Garvie, she's been giving me some stuff. It's made from herbs. And it's *working*.'

'I don't understand,' Martin said flatly. He could see she was excited, and her exuberance was infectious, but he couldn't figure out what she was saying.

'She's a *healer*. I've been taking these herbs in a powder. She makes them up from plants and things. It tastes wonderful and makes me feel really good. When I fell into the river, all my cuts and bruises healed up in no time. She told me to keep taking it and it would make me better. I mean *really* better. I didn't believe her and I got angry, but last night at the ceilidh I looked down and my feet were moving in time to the music. I hadn't even *noticed*. At first I thought it must be the drink. I thought I was imagining it and it stopped. But then today, I remembered banging my knee on the table-leg. I didn't notice at the time, but now I remember *feeling* something when I did it.'

Her torrent of words stopped and she drew a breath.

'I *felt* it, Martin. I mean I felt something in my leg. And now my toes can move. It's a miracle.'

'I still don't understand,' Martin said honestly.

She shook her head, impatient with his ignorance.

'Listen, silly. When I fell onto that wall, I broke my back. It was my spine, down here.' She twisted and jabbed a thumb down at the base of her back. 'The nerve was cut completely. That meant I had no feeling from there down. No sensation, no movement. There is no cure known to medical science. This,' she said, hitting the arm of the chair for emphasis, 'is for life.' She stopped, holding him with her eyes. They were wide and luminous green. 'And now I felt touch.' She rapped her knuckles on her knee and screwed her face up again in concentration. 'It's distant, like a feather touch, but I can *feel* it.'

She gave a wild laugh. 'And today, that makes three things.

338

You saw it wasn't just my imagination. My feet moved, didn't they?'

He nodded. 'Yes. There was something. A twitch.' He looked up into her smiling eyes.

'And what was the third thing?'

'It was the other night when I—' she started, then stopped. Her face was suddenly flooded in a blush almost deep enough to match her hair.

'Hm?' he asked.

'Nothing,' she said, dropping her eyes. Embarrassment consumed her.

'Come on. It must have been something.'

She shook her head again. There was a silence for a few moments. Finally she lifted her head.

'Remember I told you there was no sensation from here down?' she said, jabbing the base of her spine with her thumb again.

He nodded.

'Well. It's true. No sensation from there to my feet. You know what I mean?'

He nodded his head dumbly, failing to catch her meaning.

She gave him a tight smile.

'If you were completely numb from your hips down, what might you miss most?'

The blank look annoyed her.

'Oh, think about it, Martin. You're a man, aren't you?'

Light dawned.

'Oh,' he said. 'You mean . . .?'

She nodded slowly. 'Exactly. Nothing. *Forever*.'

'Christ, I didn't realise. Oh, that's awful.'

'Well, it is. Believe me.'

It was Martin's turn to be embarrassed.

'So . . .' he started.

'I was having a dream. You were in it,' she said, with a lopsided smile. 'I woke up, and I felt . . . something.'

'What do you mean?'

'Oh, for God's sake, Martin. I had a damned *orgasm*,' Caitlin said, almost angrily.

She swung her green eyes on him. He was sitting there on the bench and she saw the colour creep up from his collar into his face. He was blushing furiously.

As soon as she saw that, she laughed out loud, a throaty, delighted chuckle.

'Oh, don't worry about it. It was wonderful.'

Finally the colour subsided. He grinned sheepishly.

'And how was it for me?' he asked her.

The pair of them suddenly burst into giggles simultaneously. Caitlin's shoulders were shaking with the gales of laughter. Martin was holding his stomach. She reached for him and put her arms around his neck. He could feel her jiggling against him, helpless under the force of the laughter. Eventually the fit subsided. Her head was in at his shoulder, his face buried in her hair. She pulled herself back and he looked into the green of her eyes. Slowly she closed them and brought her face forward. He kissed her, softly at first and then brought his hand up and pulled her tighter. She made a small, moaning sound and leaned herself into him.

25

Susan Herron's blonde good looks were indirectly to cause the grief that befell Paul Thomson. There were a few factors besides that, but the fact that at sixteen Susan was set to be as tall as her mother and had a dazzling smile in a pretty, heart-shaped face put her in the top flight as far as available teenagers in Linnvale were concerned. Paul Thomson was eighteen and lived in Lochend, a town-boy by comparison to the village youths. Susan had plenty of admirers. She wore tight jeans to show off her coltish walk and, whilst she was aware of her appeal, she was a fairly level-headed and sunny-natured girl. Paul was a student at Glasgow University. He was just a shade taller than she, with dark hair and brown eyes and an easy, self-confident manner. Compared with the Linnvale boys of his age, he seemed worldly and educated.

Not long after Martin Thornton had crawled into the back of his Land-Rover and lapsed into a stupor and an hour or so after Caitlin Brook had been overwhelmed by the fact of her toes tapping on the footplate, Paul and Susan had walked, from the disco hand in hand. Although Paul was old enough to drink, he'd contented himself with a lemonade while Susan had sipped coke. The music had been loud and repetitive rap, not to his taste at all, but they had enjoyed dancing together. It was after eleven when the hall committee had called a halt. The flashing, multi-coloured lights had been finally switched off and the youngsters piled out, mostly in giggling groups. The pair had walked, with their ears still ringing and crackling from the three-hour din, down towards the Corrie Hotel.

Susan knew her mother was still at the ceilidh and might not be home for another two hours. There was a lane just off the Linn Road which was hedged on both sides by tall privets and then, further along, past the houses, widened a little before petering out into a footpath. Susan and Paul ambled down, still hand in hand, to a spot where a stile bridged the field wall and he sat himself down on the wooden step. Without a word, she came and sat on his knee. They would have spent the next half an hour kissing in the shadows before Paul took the long hike down to the Loch Shore Road to hitch a lift down to Lochend. Normally he'd only have to stick out his thumb for a few minutes before somebody would slow down and open the passenger door.

She leaned towards him and their lips touched. Susan settled herself against him and sighed. He could smell the perfume he'd given her and the faint sweetness of perspiration.

'Well, well,' a voice came from the darkness.

A light flared very close by and the struck match flickered, partly illuminating a face which leant into it to light a cigarette.

'What's all this then? Love in the open air?'

Paul groaned to himself. The last thing he needed was to be disturbed by the locals.

'What do you want, Peter Bain?' Susan snorted irritably.

'What *he's* getting,' came another voice from the right. The glow of a cigarette brightened, a red pinpoint in the dark beside the ash tree which overhung the spot. The first youth laughed.

'*He's* getting out of here,' Peter Bain said. 'Isn't that right, mastermind?'

He walked forward, still shadowed. His boots crunched the stones on the pathway.

'Always the same, isn't it? Coming up here, taking our women. Think we're just a bunch of hicks.'

'Come on, guys,' Paul said, shifting his position, easing the girl from his knee. He'd had a spot of bother before, just some namecalling, the odd shoulder barging against him as he walked the narrow pavement to Susan's house. He'd seen the three of them hanging around at the gable end of the hotel. In fact, Peter Bain and his two cronies had been among the youngsters Molly Carr had passed on the night she'd been walking her dog. If any of them had been alone, they would have done just as well as Tom Cannon had.

'Come on where?' The solid fellow stopped in front of them, feet planted apart. He took a long draw of his cigarette while he pondered the notion. '*We're* not going anywhere. We *live* here.'

'And so do I,' Susan piped up. Paul put a hand on her arm.

'But lover-boy doesn't. He's from Lochend, isn't he? And we don't like his kind around here, messing with our women.'

'I'm not *your* woman,' Susan retorted angrily.

'Aye. We can see that. Not good enough for the likes of you. You have to bring them in, eh?'

'Listen. I don't want any trouble,' Paul said. He wasn't really afraid, but there were three of them and one of him.

'Oh very good,' came another voice off to the left.

'I don't want any trouble,' the third youth mimicked.

The three others began to slowly come together until they stood shoulder to shoulder. Paul eased himself off the step of the stile and stood up. He was about the same size as any of them, but Pete Bain was solid and thickset. His hands were jammed into the pockets of a biker's jacket. The studs reflected the distant lights of the main road in the village. His hair was cut short in an aggressive spike.

'No trouble, man, just as long as you get your arse out of here.'

'He's not going anywhere,' Susan cried out. 'Just leave us alone.'

Pete Bain turned to her.

'No telling what he'll do to you down a dark lane if we left you alone.'

'We weren't doing anything.'

'Aye, nothing you would do with a Linnvale boy. But the Lochenders, they're *special*. What have they got that we haven't?'

'Brains,' Susan spat back. 'And *manners*.'

The three of them laughed, taking Pete Bain's lead.

'Got no fuckin' brains coming up to Linnvale, has he? And no fuckin' manners taking little miss tight-arse down here to get his hand up her skirt.'

Paul stood up.

'That's enough,' he said angrily. He could feel his hands begin to shake as the adrenalin started to flow, preparing him for fight or flight. This was beginning to look ugly. He gauged the distance between them, measuring the set of their shoulders, alert for any movement. He reached down and took the girl's arm, pulling her insistently to her feet.

'Come on, Susan, I'll take you home.' He held her away from the other three and shoved his way past. Rory McIntyre, a gangly boy with a straggly fair moustache, leaned into him aggressively. Paul ignored it and managed to get past them. Pete Bain put a hand on Rory's arm.

Susan and Paul made it to the end of the path and onto the lit street. He could feel his heart beating quickly and felt a little shaky. By the time they reached her house he was calmer, but he didn't spend too long kissing on the doorstep. They said goodnight and she went in, closing the door behind her. He turned and followed the road down past the church hall. The ceilidh was still in full swing. Somebody was singing and the sound of the accordion, from outside, sounded thin and reedy.

Paul walked fast along Linn Road, slowing down warily where it branched into the path where he'd walked with Susan. Nobody jumped from the shadows. He let his breath out and walked on. He only got a hundred yards along the road when he heard footsteps behind him and turned quickly. Somebody was following him, making no attempt at stealth.

'Shit,' he said to himself, and increased speed. The footsteps picked up, gritty on the road surface. Paul got past the tall birches crowding the road where it took a slight bend and then froze. Two figures ambled out from the side of the road.

'Well met in the moonlight, prize tit,' Pete Bain said in a lazy drawl. 'That's Shakespeare.' Beside him Tam Donald giggled. 'Told you he'd be back this way.'

Pete lit another cigarette. The smell of sulphur drifted towards Paul. The match flickered in an arc as the other fellow threw it to the side. It guttered out and left the roadside in gloom.

'And he hasn't got Miss Crazylegs to protect him either.'

Behind Paul, footsteps crunched and he jerked to the side. Rory McIntyre sniggered.

'Aw, you *scared* him,' Tam said with heavy sarcasm.

'We'll do more than scare him,' Pete Bain declared. His voice, low and quite soft, was coldly threatening.

'Look, you guys. I just want to go home.'

'Aye, so do we. We want you out of here, and we don't want to see you back.'

'You can't—' Paul started to say. Pete Bain took three quick steps and lunged his hands forward, grabbing Paul's jacket lapels and hauling him with such a jerk that the words were instantly cut off.

'I can't *what*?' he demanded. 'You can't tell me what the fuck I can't do. Not up here. This is our place. And we don't like you bastards coming up here to piss about with our women.

Suddenly Paul was very frightened. He could smell beer on Pete Bain's breath, and the sour overlay of whisky. Behind him feet crunched the road metal. He half turned and Pete Bain nodded his head forward in a fast strike. His forehead caught Paul hard on the cheek and the blow knocked him to the side. Pain flared on the bone and a dizzy, sick feeling rolled inside his head. Pete Bain released his jacket and he tried to call out but a fist came up and hit him straight on the mouth. He felt something give, then the salt taste of blood. The blow threw him to the right and he spun against the hedge.

'Get the bastard,' somebody shouted behind him. He heard the boots grate on the road and instinctively jinked away. The pain in his head was like a migraine and his lips felt huge and blubbery. The prospect of more of the same galvanised him into action. His quick movement saved him from catching a heavy boot on his thigh. Tam Donald swung it with considerable force, missed his moving target, and the leg continued its motion as his other foot slipped on the grass at the side of the road. He went down, landing on his backside with a jarring thud which snapped his jaw shut on his tongue. Like the fleeing Paul Thomson, he too tasted the coppery flow.

'Come on,' Pete Bain rasped. He was rubbing his forehead where it had connected with the other boy's cheek. If the boy hadn't turned, he'd have split his nose wide open. Instead, his brow had connected with hard bone and, while Paul Thomson had come off second best, Pete Bain's forehead would have a bruise the width of an apple the next morning.

Paul raced down the road. He heard the shouts behind him and they were enough to lend a spurt of speed. The big tackety boots crunched on the road, seeming too close. He reached the bend and threw himself round it. Here the road made a tight, almost right-angled turn. Paul gauged his chances. It was a long run with three maniacs chasing him right down to the Loch Shore road. Ahead of him, just on the turn, a five-bar gate stood out against the dark. Instead of following the road, he launched himself at the horizontal bars. His foot purchased, his other leg came up and he threw himself over. The hand that broke his fall landed in something soft and smelly, but that was the least of his problems. He scrambled to his feet and ran across the field, feeling the burdock snatch at his trousers.

He skidded to a halt, looking right and left. In the untended pasture, away from the lights of Linnvale, it was dark. About forty yards behind, the gate rattled as three bodies hit it simultaneously. He heard an oath, then, heart racing and breath panting, he veered to the right. Ahead of him loomed the deeper darkness of trees. He ran towards it, hoping to find someplace to stop and get his breath back. In seconds the deep shadow swallowed him.

Paul crept into the yawning dark. He kept his hands up protectively in front of his face, walking blind. Behind him he could hear the muffled thuds of boots on the grass. He walked in between the trees and then cut to the right, banging his shoulder twice against trunks as he passed deeper into the forest. Out at the edge somebody shouted hoarsely, an angry voice lancing through the darkened trees, and Paul froze in alarm. He was not a country boy and he knew his progress over the fallen pine needles and dead branches could be heard for some distance, but still he kept on. After a while, the sounds of pursuit faded away.

He reached a tall tree and crept round the far side; the roots were like buttresses, standing out to form high, spreading grooves between them. He felt his way into a cleft and hunkered down, waiting. His breath sounded loud in his ears, loud enough to be heard by anybody following him. He tried to breathe with his mouth open to diminish the rasping sound, but it didn't seem to work. Against each of the three chasing him, he felt he could give a good account of himself, though he was not a fighter, but at the present odds he knew he could be badly beaten up. He huddled close to the tree, all of his senses suddenly very alert. He was badly frightened. He imagined a hand coming out of the darkness and grabbing him, and his heart started to beat faster.

Off in the distance somebody barked a curse. There was answering laughter, mocking in the darkness. His pursuers were not afraid of the dark, and Paul realised he might have made a bad mistake. He was a town boy, at home on streets paved with concrete. The three others were raised here and they'd probably played in the forest as kids. To them, the tracks might be like familiar streets. Suddenly he was certain they would find him, huddled against a tree. They would drag him out and then . . . He didn't want to think about *then*. They were in the dark forest.

They could do what they liked and leave him here in the dark. They could leave him half dead. His heart sank as a cold thought oozed through him. They were a pretty vicious lot. They could leave him *dead*.

He closed his eyes and wished they would go away. Off to the right, a branch snapped. There was the crackle of dead twigs crushed underfoot. Pete Bain's voice carried down to the hidden young man.

'Waste of bloody time. We'll get him again. Don't worry about that.'

The sounds of progress moved off to the right then began to dwindle. Paul gave a very slow sigh of relief. All he had to do now was wait for a while until they'd forgotten about him. He could get back onto the road and down to the Loch Shore. He might not get a lift now, but that was the least of his worries. A long walk home would not trouble him at all tonight.

He sat motionless for half an hour and was just about to move when it happened.

At first he thought he'd become wedged between the roots. He pushed himself away and a cramp in his leg caused him to fall back again. Paul massaged the muscle of his calf and then he felt a motion on his shoulder. He thought his jacket had snagged on the tree and tried to shift position, but his shoulder wouldn't move. Still unalarmed, he twisted his body, thinking he was wedged in between the buttress roots.

Then something shoved *hard* on his shoulder-blade while something equally strong squeezed on his opposite collarbone.

He tried to heave himself back, but he was stuck fast. In the dark, unaware of what was happening, the young man squirmed against the force which now squeezed him from both sides. He managed to turn his head and got a hand up onto the edge of the groove where he'd been hiding.

Then, a convulsion rippled violently under his hand. The wood contracted momentarily, then expanded towards him. He felt the crack in his shoulder-blade just as an enormous pain launched its way right across his neck. Bones ground together as the tree's massive stanchioned roots flexed, pinning him between them. The wood rippled again in a monstrous jerk and his ribs creaked under the pressure.

He screamed in pure agony. He'd never screamed before, not at any time in his life. The pain did not stop. Instead, it screeched inside him and his scream went on and on and on, girlishly high, reverberating in the woods. There was another squeeze on his ribs and, quite distantly, still surging on the crest of the unbelievable hurt, Paul Thomson heard them give completely. There was a shocking, hollow sound as back and front ribs were forced together. The sharp ends of broken bones came together like tongs, gripping his heart and his lungs and then ripping through them.

Paul Thomson's scream stopped instantly. From the narrow dark space there was a wet, grinding sound for a few moments, then utter silence. A stream of blood flowed out from between the roots and formed a pool which was quickly soaked into the ground. Down below the surface, thread-like rootlets sensed the flood of nutrient. They twitched in anticipation and then, in the dark, they thirstily drank the new life.

Up at the road, beside the gate, Pete Bain and his cronies waited, smoking cigarettes and joking aggressively. They were hoping that the outsider would come wandering out of the forest to where they could ambush him. After half an hour there was no sign of him, but none of them were interested in clambering through the dark undergrowth of Fasach Wood. Bain took a last draw of his cigarette and flicked it over the gate, watching the tiny red light arc out in the darkness.

'Come on, fellas, this is a waste of time,' he muttered. 'He'll be back.'

He turned away just as the thin, wavering scream came soaring up from the forest below.

The sound startled them for a brief moment and they all turned to look down at the amorphous black mass at the bottom of the field.

'What the fuck was that?' Tam Donald asked. 'A wildcat?'

'Naw,' Pete Bain said. He gave a throaty chuckle. 'It's the city boy. He's either shit-scared of the dark, or he's fell and broke his leg.' He snorted again. 'Nice one. Saves us the trouble.'

He jammed his hands into the pockets of his jacket and sauntered up the road towards Linnvale. Tam and Rory followed him, laughing together.

'That'll teach him,' Rory McIntyre said. 'You going to have a go at wee Suzy then?' he asked.

'I'll think about it.'

'Better watch out for old claw-hands,' Tam warned, and they all snorted derisive laughter. Everybody was aware of why Fiona Herron kept her hands in her gloves. 'If she gives you a swipe, she'll take the face off you.'

'Maybe that would be worth it,' Pete said, and they all guffawed again.

It is possible that if Paul Thomson's parents had not been in Spain on holiday that summer, then his disappearance would have been noted earlier, and perhaps a search would have been launched which might have answered one or two mysteries which were exercising the minds of the Linnvale gossips that June. Unfortunately, the only person who missed him was young Suzy Herron. At first she was worried about the lack of contact, thinking he might have had an accident. She remembered the confrontation with Bain and the others and thought he might really be too frightened to come back up the Linn Road. She called his home and got no reply. Later that week she went down to Lochend to find his house deserted. She told her mother, but Fiona Herron didn't seem terribly interested. After all, her daughter was only sixteen. There would be many other boys in her life over the next few years.

So, for some time, Paul Thomson's disappearance went un-reported. Suzy was approached by Pete Bain one evening when she was going to a friend's house. He asked her, in sarcastic, disparaging tones, about her towny-boy. She slapped his face and he merely laughed arrogantly. At the weekend, after she'd helped organise games for the small children at the summerplay, she was invited to a party at Lochend where she met another boy who was quite good-looking. She thought of Paul, decided she wasn't interested in somebody who would be scared off so easily, and, during the party, in one of the bedrooms she let the new boy kiss her and even went so far as to allow him to briefly fondle her breasts. This young man could borrow his father's car. He wouldn't have to walk the Linn Road.

*

Three hours after Paul Thomson's agonising scream rent the air around Fasach Wood, lights appeared on one of the five paths which arrowed in from the edges of the forest. The small group, walking almost in step, passed quite close to the place where the roots were thirstily soaking up his blood, bloating under the damp earth. They moved silently, each holding a small light that threw just enough illumination to send muted shadows behind the nearest trees. They followed the line until they reached the fallen tree over the river, the big beech, wide as the path itself, which formed a natural bridge. They crossed, still staying close, and on the far side they continued to the clearing. Then on the warm dark evening they spread out to encircle the great tree.

There was an air of expectancy, hushed anticipation.

'Sisters,' a voice called out clearly.

'We are together, and we are one. We are one with ourselves and with the forest. It is our *soul*.'

The surrounding figures listened intently. The lights they carried lit their faces and threw a glow on the base of the tree, highlighting the pale wood. They stood still, each of them wrapped in what looked like a dark robe.

'It is almost time. It is *growing*. The power of the forest is ours and it is a wondrous power. It will give us what we need and it will make us *strong*.'

The speaker pulled back the hood of her robe and her white hair shone in the light.

'You, each of you, have had one gift of many.' She passed around the circle, taking one woman's hands in hers, feeling the soft skin, the straight fingers. She passed on, raising her arms to clasp another, drawing her hands down a lithe frame. She stopped and embraced a third, feeling the urgent tension shivering in the other's body. At a fourth she paused and put her hand out to gently stroke the tall woman's abdomen.

'*Life*,' she whispered. 'Your gift.'

She passed on, round the circle, feeling the concentrated power of them all, sensing their hungers.

'It is nearly time. I have found the perfect one. She is being prepared for us. *For this*. We will awaken the power of the forest and we will have what our hearts desire.'

She turned to face the tree.

350

'Look,' she called softly, raising her hand to point. They all followed with their eyes. There, on a knobbly burr that stood out on the gnarled trunk, a small twiglet bore a bud. It was half-opened.

'Life returns,' she said. 'The *Garbh-aidh* returns to his glory.'

26

Martin Thornton was thinking about what Caitlin had told him. He'd seen her feet move, very slightly and with great effort, and he pondered the implications. She'd told him about the effects of a break on her spinal column: no sensation, no movement. She'd said all the doctors had told her there was no chance of a cure. He was prepared to believe that. Few people who went into a wheelchair ever got out of it again, even at the Lourdes grotto. That left two options. The doctors had been wrong, which Caitlin insisted they hadn't been – she'd seen the plates herself – or something very momentous had happened. With the instinct of many years in newspapers, he realised that this was something he should look into. There could be something of great importance in the twitching of Caitlin Brook's toes.

On the night after the ceilidh he was making dinner for them both, partly because he enjoyed cooking and because he wanted to thole his assize for getting monumentally, if inadvertently, drunk the night before.

Caitlin was enjoying a bath. He could hear her humming a tune in the little bathroom down the hallway. Every now and again, there would be a splash and the sound of water pouring. He wondered how she managed to get in and out of the tub.

The kitchen surfaces were on the low side for him as he stood, though he knew they were perfect for someone in a wheelchair. He mixed the tomatoes with onions and garlic then stirred them into the minced meat. There was a tall tube near the window, holding stalks of dry spaghetti. He reached for it and selected enough for two of them, letting the pale straws soften as they sank into the boiling water. The smell of the meat filled the kitchen while the pasta pot simmered steamily.

The implication of even a slight movement in Caitlin's feet and her claim that her sense of touch was re-awakening could, he knew, be enormous. She'd told him about the mixture of herbs Sheila Garvie had given her to drink with water. Vaguely he recalled the woman giving him something to drink at the dance, but couldn't remember much of the details. Alec Stirling had told him he delivered packages to her from all over the world, and he had done enough stories about the destruction of the rainforest to have heard a thousand claims about the healing properties of plants.

The small wooden box was on a low shelf just beside the stove. He lifted it, and looked at the wooden carvings. They were intricate intertwined circles etched cleanly in the polished wood. The lid flipped up easily, and a strong, spicy smell billowed out when he took out the small woven pouch. He loosened the drawstring at the neck and shook some dust out onto his hand. It was fine-grained and brownish, with lighter specks scattered at random in the small mound of powder in his palm. He bent to sniff it and his nose was assailed by a strong mixture of odours. It was like a spoonful of all-spice, but stronger, more pungent, and under the spice there was a tart bitterness. He sniffed again, bending closer, and some of the powder was drawn into his nostrils. Instantly the bitterness made his eyes water. Little spikes of sensation itched on the membranes and he sneezed suddenly. He spun away from where he was standing by the oven, and as he moved, his hands jerked. The powder spilled out. Martin reached blindly for a tissue, feeling another sneeze build itself up. He drew in breath and the itch in his nose faded. He wiped his eyes and then used the soft paper to pipe up the dusting of brown powder close to the pasta pot. As he did so, he noticed that some of it must have fallen into the saucepan. The water had turned a light, purplish brown. He wondered what to do about it, but when he leaned over the pot, into the steam, it smelled quite pleasant. With the spices in the meat and the generous helping of chopped garlic, nobody would notice.

He put the lid on, edging the pan away from the heat to let it simmer slowly, and went back to the table. Caitlin had left her art-case leaned against the wall and he opened it up, pulling out the sketches she'd made in the cemetery. She had a fine, deft hand, catching shape and perspective quite naturally. The sunlight gave the picture focus and depth. He put the drawing down and looked at another, this time a woodland scene, again in charcoal, showing the tall trees marching into the distance. In the foreground light flowers seemed to shiver in a carpet. Even in monochrome, he had the idea they were yellow.

The next one surprised him. He flicked the tissue away and saw himself looking out from the paper. He had a half smile on his face, and his body was turned three-quarters to the viewer, his jacket slung over his shoulder. It was a remarkable likeness, obviously done from memory. Martin felt a tickle of pleasure. He was flattered that she'd taken the time to draw him, and wondered if she'd let him have it. The drawing, quite stark in its simplicity, was just how he saw himself, lived-in, capable, and a pretty all right sort of fellow.

'How's dinner coming along?' Caitlin called from the bathroom. Martin jumped. He looked up, sniffed, and smelled the garlic.

'Coming along a treat,' he called back. 'You'll love it.' The sound of water draining away echoed from the bathroom.

'Good. I'm starving,' Caitlin shouted back, her voice barely muffled by the sounds or the bathroom door.

Martin put the drawings back in the folder and went across to the stove. When he lifted the lid on the meat pot, he was treated to the mouth-watering aroma of the ground beef in its sauce. He gave it a quick stir to make sure it wasn't welding itself to the bottom of the pan. The garlic was strong and tantalising. He clanged the heavy lid back down and, selecting a clean wooden spoon, absently lifted the lighter lid on the pasta saucepan.

Inside the pot, a mass of creamy white pasta heaved and wriggled. He started back, surprised at the unexpected motion. For a split second he thought the stove was too high.

Then something long and sinewy looped out over the rim. The flat-cut end swung from side to side in a worm-like, searching motion. Martin's mouth opened in amazement. It happened so smoothly that at first his brain couldn't comprehend what his eyes were seeing. Another thin, serpentine piece slithered over the rim. This one moved like a slender snake, rippling from side to side. It oozed over his wrist, hot enough to make the skin pucker. He jerked his hand back, gritting his teeth. The winding movement continued. Tiny ripples, like muscular contractions, ran down the length of the stringy pasta. Another segment, thin as a worm, nosed along the handle. A fourth looped its way over the edge.

354

Completely bewildered, and suddenly riven with eerie alarm, Martin could only stare at the heaving mass. He reached, automatically, to take the pan off the stove. As his hand clamped on the black handle, the creamy worm crawling along it reared up. The flat end swelled to a round knob. A slit appeared to bisect it, and just as Martin's hand clenched the protruding handle it dipped down and fastened itself on his finger. Without thinking, his left hand came up and grasped the thing, pulling it away. It broke into three parts in his hand, each of which wriggled robustly, winding themselves around his fingers. He shook them off with a startled, almost panicked motion and grabbed the top piece again. He felt a pulling sensation on the skin of his finger, then an audible pop as it came away. A small pain flared, like cold vinegar on grazed skin, and as he pulled the thing off he saw a tiny red circle between his knuckle and the first joint of his finger.

'Jesus Christ,' he said aloud.

'What's that?' Caitlin called from the bathroom. He could hear the sound of the hair-dryer whine down as she switched it off.

'Nothing,' he called back. His mind was whirling, but even in the middle of his utter unnerving astonishment he knew it would be pointless to tell her he was holding a pot-full of living spaghetti that writhed and bit like a pallid mass of blind snakes.

He was about to set the pot back on the stove to grab the lid and cover the lot when a whole writhing *rope* of the wriggling stuff braided its way over the lip and coiled around his arm. He felt the sucking mouths fasten on him and he jerked his whole body back. The pot went flying. It tumbled to the floor and the contents spilled out, wriggling and humping like a slithering migration of eels.

Caitlin called something which he didn't hear. Without thinking he took a step forward and stamped down hard. Under his foot it felt as if the floor was moving. The crawling, serpentine sensation was alien and revolting. He heard things squash between his sole and the tiled floor. Cut ends coiled upwards and tried to twist round his ankles, and he gasped in fright.

For a moment he thought he'd gone mad, that maybe he was imagining all this. Then he felt the sucking rasp on the skin of his ankle. He brought his other foot up and stamped it down, scraping the white worms off, and squashing another section of the mass.

'What's happening?' Caitlin called again.

'Just dropped a pot. It's all right,' Martin bawled, hoping she would hear nothing else in his voice. All the time, the white mass was slithering on the floor in all directions. Despite the impossibility of it, the sight filled Martin with a sudden loathing. He drew his foot back, leaving a flattened pale print. He turned quickly, eyes darting all around, until he saw the metal dustpan hanging on a hook beside the door. He grabbed it quickly and started to scrabble the wormy pasta into it with fast flicks. One long strand, moving with the sinewy motion of an adder, was trying to get under the table. Martin saw the tiny blob which swelled at the tip, blanched and somehow *repulsive*. He snatched out with the small brush and flicked it backwards. Like an eel, it looped back on itself and tried to get away. He reversed the brush, turning the bristles upwards, then brought it down sharply to hit the thing with the wooden stock. There was a splattering sound. The elverine shape arched upwards, gave a small shiver, then flopped to the floor.

A few more scrapes and Martin had forced all of the stuff into the dustpan. He got to his feet, holding the thing at an angle to prevent them flopping out, opened the back door and hurried out into the garden. He waded through the flower beds, leaving man-sized footprints of crushed primula. At the far side, he reached the stream and with a punching motion jerked the pan forward. The pasta whirled out in all directions to land in the water. He stood there, breathing heavily. For a second, a messy, discarded plateful of spaghetti began to sink. Then, as he watched, the piece began to twitch. One of them wriggled under a stone as if seeking cover. Others shivered their way downstream. Two small trout which had fled for shelter came back out into the open. One of them approached a small maggoty piece and darted in. The fish took one end in its mouth and the other end came looping round to fasten itself in the small trout's eye. Martin watched in amazement and shivering disgust as the little fish wriggled desperately. There was a small splash as its tail came out of the water. Another piece of pasta latched on to its side, and then another. For a few moments it thrashed frantically and then it went suddenly still. The current carried it down to a patch of reeds at the bottom of the pool and it disappeared from view.

Martin drew his eyes away and stared at the water nearest him.

The wriggling things were gone. The stones and duckweed hid them from view. Martin shivered, completely confused and baffled, and not a little frightened. He stood for a few moments, wondering what it was all about. He'd seen something which he *knew* was impossible. He'd seen something so utterly mundane and familiar suddenly transform itself into a loathsome, utterly alien *abomination*. Something in him shivered, and he felt greasily sick. Finally, assured that it had all disappeared – somewhere, but out of sight – he turned and went back to the house. His legs and hands were shaking. Back in the kitchen, he carefully lifted the pot, making sure he'd got it all, then sat down at the table, wondering what the hell was happening.

From down the hallway, he heard Caitlin making normal, domestic sounds, opening drawers and rattling coat-hangers, while he sat there, thinking about the sheer preposterous absurdity of inanimate spaghetti pasta coming to life.

After some time, he crossed the kitchen and carefuly lifted the little box, pulling out the canvas bag. He opened it and then searched in the drawer for a container. He found a small cellophane bag and with a teaspoon he took a small quantity of the powder. Another rummage in the drawer found him a flexible, paper-covered wire which he turned and twisted tightly round the top of the bag to seal it. He dropped the sample into his jacket pocket and went back to sit at the table. He'd come to a decision.

A few moments later, Caitlin came wheeling through, face fresh and pink from the heat of the bath.

'All right, masterchef. It smells good. When do we eat?'

'Change of plan, I'm afraid,' he said, hoping she wouldn't detect the odd tightness in his voice. She did, but she later took it for embarrassment.

'I dropped the pasta. It's ruined.'

'Oh no,' she groaned. 'I'm really hungry.'

'Fancy another go at the Douglas Arms?'

'Only if you let me pay again.'

'Come on then. We'll argue over the bill later.'

A few minutes later, he was strolling behind the wheelchair. Again, as he walked, he kept a wary eye on the hedgerow as they passed. All the time, he felt an odd prickling under his scalp. It was the kind of feeling he got when he knew he was being watched. All the way up to the village he had the same uncomfortable sense of covert *threat*. Caitlin chatted amiably. She seemed to have forgiven his trespass of the night before, and she did not seem to notice anything amiss.

Martin made a few telephone calls from the office on the Monday morning. He checked his own diary for anything urgent which he might have forgotten, but there was nothing major that early in the week. Anyway his mind was not on work. He called in at the Mitchell Library and spent half an hour in the medical section, leafing through a book on spinal injuries, checking off the facts against what Caitlin had told him. Nothing he read contradicted anything she'd said. From there it was only half a mile to the regional analyst's department. Over the past few years, he'd done enough stories on drug dealers to have visited the place a few times with certain substances. Most newspapermen had done the same.

Tony Cassidy, who was one of the young analysts, held the small package up to the light. The powder looked like fine brown sand. 'Not hash, heroin or crack,' the young man said. 'What is it, a new compost?'

'Don't really know,' Martin said. He'd dealt with Tony before. 'Some sort of herbal remedy thing I'm having a look at. I'd just like to find out what's in it.'

'Could take a week, maybe more,' the chemist said. He transferred the powder into a small plastic container with a screw lid. He spent a few moments writing something on a label before wrapping it round the vial.

'Get a few of these in. Baldness cures. Diet additives. All crap. This one will be too, I guarantee. Listen, I'll try to rush it through, but the environmental health boys have got us snowed under and the drug squad have got off their backsides for a change. It's like ICI in here.'

'If you could sneak it through, I'd be grateful.'

'Oh, I'll see what I can do. Checking pies for additives gets boring.'

Martin thanked him. He went back to the office and found he'd been scheduled to cover a tedious press conference at the Scottish Office. He got back later that evening and called Caitlin. The phone rang for a while before she answered, sounding breathless.

'Been exercising,' she explained. 'On the pulley.'

For a moment Martin wondered what she was talking about, then he remembered the set of handles on the frame which swung over the bed. She'd told him how she had to keep muscles and bones in trim, despite the fact that they didn't actually *work*.

'Been overdoing it, by the sound of it.'

'No. I'm feeling good. Really I am. Listen, I'm . . .' She paused, sounding unsure of herself. 'What I mean is, I had a great weekend.'

'Me too. The bits I remember anyway.'

'Oh, don't keep beating yourself over the head about that. I'll put it down to youthful exuberance. Anyway, you more than made up for it, though I was looking forward to the bolognese,' she said. Her laughter tinkled in his ear. 'I converted it into chilli and had it for dinner.'

Martin instantly had a visual rerun of the wormlike slivers creeping and looping from the pot. His eyes darted to his right forefinger. There was a minute dark circle where the skin had been abraded. It looked like a small burn.

'Oh, the Douglas Arms was better than anything I could make,' he told her. 'We'll have to do it again. And I promise to stay sober this time.'

'I'd like that,' she said. He let the words hang in the air.

Finally he asked her about her legs, trying to keep his voice light. He didn't want to say anything until he knew what was in the powder. If it was repairing the spinal damage, it would be nothing short of miraculous. But still he couldn't shake the memory of dropping a small amount into the pasta pot and then seeing that scary transformation. There was a serious possibility that one sniff of the stuff had made him hallucinate it. If that was the case, then he *should* warn Caitlin.

'I moved them again,' she said, sounding wonderfully pleased with herself. 'It took a lot of effort, but they *moved*. You can't believe what a simple little thing like that feels like,' she said laughing, 'though I can't really feel it. My legs are pretty numb, but I'm sure I can sense *something*.'

'Have you told Sheila?'

'I didn't have to tell her. She was the one who pointed it out at the ceilidh when you were—' Caitlin cut herself off before she said anything undiplomatic. 'When you were dancing. She came round today and I showed her again. She doesn't seem very surprised about it all. The woman's an angel. She gave me something else, which tastes horrible, like pine needles. She says it's good for building muscles.'

'Listen, do you think you should really take anything else? We don't know what's in it.'

'I don't care what's in it,' Caitlin said. Her voice was suddenly flat and very definite. 'I *trust* her. Sheila's an expert. All the women go to her for help. Jean Fintry's lost about three stone in the last few weeks and Fiona Herron's hands, you should have seen them. She had terrible arthritis, and now it's nearly gone.'

There was another silence. Martin was in a dilemma. There was something about the whole issue that didn't sit comfortably with him. Maybe there *was* a miracle cure, a herbal remedy. He'd heard a thousand similar claims in the past. But the odd, frightening scene in the kitchen kept coming back to him. Finally he said nothing.

'Anyway. I'm feeling terrific,' Caitlin pursued. 'There's no harm in that, is there?'

'No,' Martin said, trying to get his voice to sound light again. 'No, not at all.'

He changed the subject.

'I might be down your way at the weekend.'

'Oh? Another story?'

'No, just visiting a friend.'

'Anybody I know?'

'A gorgeous redhead,' Martin replied.

'Flattery works with me, Thornton,' Caitlin shot back at him. 'Just tell me when and I'll have dinner ready.'

'Saturday, unless there's an emergency at the office. I'll call you on Friday.'

She told him she'd like that and he was about to hang up when a thought came to him.

'Will you sell me the picture?'

'Which one?'

'The one that makes me look like a film star.'

She went silent for a moment, then her laugh came tinkling in the receiver again.

'Oh, you nosy bugger. You've been through my portfolio. Typical tabloid journalist, aren't you?'

'Is that a yes?'

'Oh, you can *have* it. We'll call it quits for the cheque.'

'Fair enough.'

'Done,' she said, still laughing. 'And I think you have been.'

She hung up first. Martin let the receiver fall and leant back in his chair. He didn't get a chance to ponder the conversation. One of the sub-editors needed clarification of a point in a story and it was back to business for the present.

Back in Linnvale, Paul Thomson's disappearance went unnoticed by anyone except Suzy Herron.

Alec Stirling made his regular runs up and down to Craigard, drinking tea in every other house and picking up the gossip from everybody. Ernie Buist's tractor was still gathering rust. A couple of times when he'd passed the croft lane, Alec had seen it jammed in against the hawthorn hedge where he'd left it. Early in the week, somebody had lit a bonfire up at the Buist croft. There was a pillar of smoke reaching up behind the little tumbledown house and Alec fancied he saw a lick of flames in the black cloud. Of Ernie Buist or his son, there had been no sign.

Towards the end of the week old Hector Ritchie, whose son Norrie had done a runner with Donnie MacKinnon's wife, mentioned over a coffee laced with whisky that he'd spotted the Buist boy a day or two previously.

'Don't think so, Hec,' Alec told him. 'Lad's moved out. Couldn't take Ernie's temper any more. Can't blame the poor wee bugger.'

'No,' Hector interrupted, holding his hand up. 'My eyesight's as good as it ever was. I was coming down with the dogs just at the boundary when I saw the smoke. Smelled it first, as a matter of fact. I took a daunder down by the hedge and had a wee look. It wasn't that madman Buist neither. Haven't seen him in a week or more, and that suits me just fine.'

Hector took a sip of his drink. He was just turned seventy, white-haired and wiry, with a face lined into creases by a life of winters on the Dumbuie hills. He'd been mightily annoyed by the lack of diplomacy his son had shown in running off with a neighbour's wife, but family was family. He'd gone down to the front of the church on the following Sunday with the rest of his sons in a show of solidarity and he'd kept his head high. He'd known MacKinnon's wife, a high-stepping, high-arsed woman in his opinion, but if he'd have been forty years younger he knew he could well have done the same thing. Despite that, he knew that if Norrie came back to the glen with his tail between his legs, seventy years or not he'd take a boot to his backside and kick him round the yard.

'No, it was definitely the young fella. He was making himself a bonfire. I smelled diesel oil in the smoke and all. Don't think that lickpenny Buist would be too happy about wasting tractor fuel.'

Alec told him about the incident when Ernie Buist had come roaring down the road in the old tractor and gone charging after his son on the field down at the Corrie.

'Had to shift the tractor to let Jock Weir past. It's been lying there ever since.'

'Well, I've seen no sign of Buist. He's either fell and broke his neck or he's lying drunk somewhere.'

Alec hoped it was the former. In any small village there were always one or two uncouth bullies, and the problem with village life, especially a tucked-away place like Linnvale with one good road in and only hill tracks out, there was no getting away from them. You just had to put up with them. Over the years, Ernie Buist had been hard to put up with. For the boy it must have been pure murder.

Over the next few days, the postman thought about what Hector had told him. The lad's aeroplane magazine, which came once a month, was waiting for him down at the post office. Craig Buist had been getting the glossy publication for the past year or so. Right at the start, he'd made arrangements with Shona Gibb at the little post office that he'd come down and collect it. He didn't want it delivered to the Buist holding and Shona knew why. His old man would have thrown it in the fire and taken a stick to the boy for his high-falutin' nancy-boy ideas.

Alec hesitated for a while before taking the magazine out of its pigeonhole and slipping it into his bag. Despite Ernie Buist's threat – and the postman had been keeping a wary eye out for the big, bull-necked farmer – he decided to take a wander up to the steading. Alec was simply curious. It was a trait he couldn't fight against at all.

He left his van down at the far end of the lane and walked up towards the house, still slightly apprehensive. He kept himself close to the hedge so that he couldn't be seen from a distance. It was only when he got to the end of the rutted track that he noticed that the hawthorn on either side was shrivelled and brown. The grass growing in among the roots and twisted runners and the bramble shoots were yellowed. Their leaves hung limp and dead. He walked further and saw the farmhouse itself. The south-facing wall, which at this time of the year was normally a swathe of green ivy and creeper, was a dirty grey colour. The ivy had been torn down. Alec hesitated at the corner of the house. He decided against knocking on the front door. Instead he went across to the disused grain store and walked around it. On the far side, the field hedge was withered away and a small stand of saplings stood gaunt and leafless. In the hollow beside the manure pit there was a blackened patch where a fire had recently been lit.

Alec came back round and, as he did so, he saw a movement close by the dilapidated byre. There was a squeal of rusty hinges and a soft thud as the door closed. He walked as quietly as he could to the low window and peered inside. It was gloomy in there and the dust and cobwebs on the cracked glass obscured the interior. He leaned up close against the pane, blocking the reflection with his shadow, and tried to make out details in the gloom. The boy was at the end stall, sitting on a stool, absorbed in milking one of the two scrawny cows.

The postman moved away from the window and went round the corner of the byre. He was heading for the door when he noticed the two-gallon can of diesel standing at the side of the grain store opposite. There was another next to the byre, and two right at the front door of the house. He tried to make no sound as he went towards the byre door, still apprehensive lest Ernie Buist should come charging out of the house. Alec gauged the distance between the kitchen and the byre and compared it to the yardage he'd have to cross to get down the lane.

He opened the door with a grinding squeal of dry hinges. A

shaft of light fell on the dirty floor in front of him. There was a scuffling sound far at the back. Then a thunderous roar crashed out from the gloom.

A blinding flash of light stabbed at his eyes. The door slammed back against his hand with such force it jarred his arm up to the shoulder. Splinters flew in all directions. Alec yelled with fright, dropped his bag, turned to run and fell over it, sprawling headlong in the muck outside of the byre.

Young Craig Buist had got the fright of his life when the door of the byre suddenly screeched open. He'd been sitting with his head against the cow's flank, alternately squeezing and pulling at the udders while the cow calmly munched the hay in the trough. The noise had startled him so much that he'd come off the stool like a cat and grabbed the shotgun angled on its butt against the stall wall. He'd hefted it, turned and saw a tall, dark shape lumbering in towards him.

Terror simply exploded inside him. In the fraction of a second it took for him to reach the gun he saw the image of his father, dead and covered in resin, come lumbering towards him. Still spinning, he'd slipped on a soft patch of cowpat and started to fall. His finger jerked the trigger and both barrels went off almost simultaneously. The gun bucked in his hands, spinning him right off balance. He slid into the slurry runnel and the gun went flying out of his hands to land with a clatter.

The roar of the gun was so deafening that he didn't even hear the yell.

As the boy slipped, off balance, the figure in the doorway went staggering away. Craig didn't know what it was, but he knew he had shot it. He scrambled forward, ignoring the hot, acid stench of the slurry, and snatched the gun up. He fumbled jerkily in his pocket and grabbed two more shells, at the same time breaking the gun. The spent cartridges jumped out and, without a pause, he thumbed the fresh ones into the barrels, snapped the gun closed and very warily walked forward.

He got to the door and poked the barrel out.

There was a moan from the yard. Carefully, Craig poked his head out.

Alec Stirling was lying on the dirty cobbles. His glasses had skittered three yards away and he was blindly groping around him.

He saw a shape loom towards him and yelled: 'For Christ's sake don't shoot!'

Craig's hands were shaking. He scanned the prostrate postman for signs of injury, but there was no blood. He stood there, dumbstruck for several moments, unsure of what to do.

'Oh, Mr Stirling. I'm sorry. I didn't mean it.'

Then the boy burst into tears. The nerves jittering behind his knees seemed to sap all his strength and he slowly sank down to the cobbles. The gun fell away and Craig Buist put his head in his hands and let the tears flow.

'Jesus bloody *Christ*, boy,' Alec spluttered. His scrabbling fingers found his glasses and after a couple of unsuccessful attempts he managed to sit them on his nose. He peered at the youngster through the smeared lenses and then swore comprehensively and without repetition for several minutes. His voice was shaking all the while, but not so much as his hands. They fluttered like bird's wings.

He managed to get to his feet, vaguely conscious of the fact that he smelled very strongly of fresh and very runny manure and not caring much about it. He peered at Craig Buist who was sitting in the mire close by.

'What the *hell* are you playing at?'

'I didn't *know*!' Craig bawled. 'I thought it was . . .'

'Thought *what*, for God's sake?'

Craig tried to answer. His mouth opened a couple of times but nothing more than a choked sob managed to come out. Then the tears started to flow again. The boy's shoulders hitched up and down with the force of his fear and misery. Finally Alex moved towards him. He kicked the gun away from them and hunkered down beside the lad. He put his arm around his shoulders and gave him the kind of hug he thought seemed appropriate.

'Jesus, boy, you nearly gave me a heart attack,' he said. He looked over at the byre door. The central planks had been blown out completely. He shuddered at the thought of what he'd have looked like if he'd caught the full blast.

'I didn't mean to shoot,' the boy said, hiccuping from the hitching in his chest. 'Honest. I slipped.'

Alec helped the boy to his feet.

'Well, at least you *can* hit a barn door,' he said. Sudden euphoria at still being alive when he could have been stone dead made his head feel light. When he was sure the boy was steady he picked up his mailbag and, as an afterthought, grabbed the shotgun, then he led Craig Buist towards the house.

'All right, young fella. Let's get into the house and get ourselves cleaned up of all this shit,' he said. His hands were still shaking violently.

An hour later, Alec Stirling was standing with his back to the fire he'd made in the living room, trying to dry the muck off the backside of his blue serge trousers. He asked the boy if his father was at home.

'No,' the boy said flatly. 'He's dead.'

'Oh, Jesus,' Alec gasped. 'You didn't . . .' His eyes travelled to the shotgun.

The boy shook his head. 'It was something . . . *else*.'

Under the circumstances, the best thing to do was make a cup of tea for them both. As he stood in front of the log fire drinking, Alec Stirling listened to Craig Buist's bizarre story. The boy told him of his flight into the forest with his father roaring behind him and threatening all sorts of dire punishments – most of which Craig had experienced at some time in his life – then he described seeing the skeleton in the trees.

Alec listened, not believing a word of it.

Craig told him how he'd hidden in the hollow of the old tumbled wall and saw his father back up against the tree, then get stuck like a fly in the thick resin glue. He described the scene in detail, graphically relating how the old man had tried to free himself before the syrupy flow had covered his eyes and his mouth and frozen him in death against the trunk.

'And what have you been doing since then?' asked Alec carefully.

'I've been *here*.'

'Did you have a bonfire the other day?'

The boy nodded.

'And what happened to all the hedges?'

'I killed them. I don't want them near me. I would have used the tractor to pull them up but I don't want to go down there. It's too close to the hedges.'

366

'So why did you do all that then?'

The boy looked up at him, face screwed up in exasperation.

'It's the *trees*. They're *alive*. I think they're *all* alive. I don't want them to get me like they got my old man. I've been watching them. I've been watching them *all the time*.'

Alec looked down at the boy. It was clear he believed everything he said. Alec didn't know what to believe, but he knew there was something really not right about the whole business. Young Craig Buist's eyes were wide and staring. He looked as if he hadn't washed in a week, nor slept for twice that time. He'd almost killed Alec with both barrels of the shotgun, and he believed the trees were coming to get him. This, thought Alec, was a very disturbed boy. Alec didn't know *what* had happened down in Fasach Wood, but he thought that maybe Ernie Buist had taken his bullying one step too far. He was probably lying down there with his head caved in by a stout branch or a heavy rock.

The boy pleaded with him not to go down and fetch Sergeant Adam and Alec went along with it. He told Craig Buist he'd be back with somebody to speak to and Craig nodded warily.

The postman went back to his own house and put a call through to Martin Thornton.

Throughout the week following the ceilidh Ben Haldane was beset with nightmares which tore their way into his sleep. In his dreams he saw the blood spurting from the cut tree, splattering on his father's hands. He was too frightened to tell anybody about it. He wandered listlessly about the house and his mother began to get worried. She spoke to Duncan about taking him to the doctor in Lochend, but he didn't think there was too much to worry about, thinking his son would eventually get over what was bothering him.

Duncan Haldane spent the week down at the stand of oaks, working his way in from the edges. Ben didn't go down there. In his mind's eye, he saw the bare patch where the grove had been, puddled with the blood from the toppled trees. At night, the clematis on the front of the house swung in the breeze, scratched on the glass, and sent cold fingers into the frightened boy's dreams.

As Duncan Haldane's grandfather's oaks fell one by one Caitlin could feel her strength returning. Sheila Garvie came round to her house every morning and, each time, she made Caitlin move her toes. The effort was less now and the movement was conversely greater. After four days, Caitlin lifted her foot from the plate and a savage joy soared within her. The muscles in her legs twitched spasmodically and she could *feel* them move, although she had no control over the jittering motion under the skin.

The barriers against hope, built slowly and at great cost as a counter to despair, were tumbling down. She was now drinking Sheila's mixture every waking hour and, with every drink, she could feel herself come more and more *alive*.

Sheila had made a lotion which she massaged into the girl's legs and, at night, she'd return to help Caitlin with her exercises on the pulley. The mechanism was a simple arrangement of wires and slings which Caitlin used twice a day. She would hook the straps on her feet and then alternately haul with her hands, systematically building strength into her arms while keeping the blood circulating in her legs to prevent the atrophy of the muscles. Now, under Sheila's coaching, she began to feel the pressure of the straps against her soles and, reflexively, involuntarily, her legs started to react, exerting a small pressure against the pull of the ropes.

Caitlin had developed an utter, unquestioning faith in the older woman. Their friendship had blossomed since that first meeting, when Caitlin had awoken in a strange bed after her terrifyingly close encounter with death. Now, she clung to the friendship in the same desperate way she had struggled against the current in the black river pool. Sheila Garvie was the answer to her wildest dream.

During the day, they would go for walks in the forest. On the third day, when they reached the fork in the path, Sheila turned the wheelchair and took the left-hand track which angled straight into the dark heart. The pathway led to an old tumble of moss-covered stones, which Sheila explained had been the edge of the forest many years before.

There was a break in the wall and the path continued straight through. Beyond it, the trees crowded so closely and densely that it would have been difficult to get the wheels through the tangle. Here, the forest was dark and gloomy. The trees soared above their heads, and there was a damp smell of permanent moisture. Yet it all seemed familiar to Caitlin. Her dreams had been so vivid that even the scent of wet vegetation and decaying leaves underfoot had assailed her in her sleep. Now she was experiencing it for *real*. As they went, Sheila kept up her running commentary of how she had studied plants and their essences since childhood. She believed that the forests of the world held the cure for every ailment. By this time Caitlin believed her implicitly.

At night, Sheila would rub her oils into Caitlin's calves and thighs, kneading the muscles under her strong yet delicate fingers. Then she would mix a drink, insisting that Caitlin drank every drop. The young woman was by now used to the increased bitterness of the infusion. It was a heady mixture, tart and biting under her tongue, but gradually mellowing. It made her sleepy and, as she began to drowse, Sheila would keep talking to her in a low, insistent voice until Caitlin fell asleep.

In her dreams the voice beckoned her and she ran and ran like a deer through the forest, down the dells and up the rises, leaping over the roots and fern clumps, running like the wind down the path and through the break in the wall, not hesitating even at the river, but leaping from stone to stone until she reached the other side. The voice would urge her on, insistently, encouraging. She would race through the trees and into the clearing and only then would she check speed as she approached the massive tree. On each night, she would slow to a walk and then, unsure, but urged by the whispered voice, she would ease herself forward. The tree was now beginning to bud, after years of standing dead, and in her dream it seemed so *right*. The words in her head told her to go forward, to *touch*. She would raise her hands to the hard trunk and when she pressed her palms against the wood, she could feel the pulsing of a massive heart.

In her night journeys Caitlin would lean against the gargantuan oak and press herself to its rough skin, feeling the slow, ponderous beat vibrate through her own body. She could sense the life surge within the wood just as she felt it burgeon within herself.

Then she would awake in the night. Sheila Garvie would be gone. In the morning Caitlin would test herself again and wonder at the strength now fast returning to her paralysed legs.

27

Tony Cassidy, the assistant analyst, completed his tests eleven
days later. Martin had been forced to cancel his planned Saturday
with Caitlin at very short notice. A fishing smack working south of
Shetland had bagged yet another nuclear submarine and lost the
subsequent tug of war. It went down with all hands. Martin was
the only man available at the time and, on the Friday evening, he
found himself on a rackety twelve-seater plane with a motley crew
of assorted reporters, dismally pondering the task of asking
questions of dead men's families. It was something he had neither
stomach nor talent for. At the end of a miserable six days he left
the northern outpost and took the same plane back to Glasgow.
He was in the office only an hour and a half when the call came
from the analyst's department.

'How did it go?' Martin asked without preamble.

'Worked all week, day and night. That's how long this one
took. You gave me a real headache. What the hell *is* this stuff
for?'

'What's in it?'

'What's *not* in it is more like it. It'll take me too long to explain
but I've got a print-out. Come up at lunchtime and you can have it.
And don't tell anybody what you're here for. I'll get my backside
kicked if they find out how much time I spent on this.'

It was just after noon when Martin got to the regional
laboratory. Tony Cassidy came down the stairs, white coat
flapping. He shoved his glasses up on top of his head and sat down,
looking a little furtive. Martin noticed his unease and invited the
young scientist across the road to a pub which served bar meals.
He had to wait half an hour until Tony got off for lunch. When the
other fellow arrived he ordered a pint of beer for each of them and
stretched to two steak pies. Cassidy devoured one with relish.
Martin left most of his. He was too busy reading.

The report came to eight pages of computer print-out. Martin
didn't understand a word of it.

'It's no cure for baldness, that's for sure,' Tony said. 'It's more like a toxic dump.'

'You'll have to translate this for me,' Martin told him. Tony gulped a large swallow of beer and took the folded sheets from Martin's hands. He slipped his glasses on and scanned the print.

'Everything but the kitchen sink. Some of it really pretty volatile. Dangerous too. They're pretty concentrated in that mixture.' He took a finger and went down the list. 'Sugars, fructose and glucose, they're fine. Get them in every kind of fruit. Then you've a whole string of large-molecule proteins and alkaloids, digitoxins and narcotics. It's mostly plant material. There's chlorophyll and tannins, pollen, haemoglobin, volatile oils.'

Tony stopped and took another drink of his beer.

'That's just the half of it. I still didn't have time to identify some of the rest. There's stuff in there that isn't in any of our books.'

'Break it down for me. What does what?' Martin asked.

Tony flicked the sheets until he got to four or five down the sheaf.

'Here's most of what I can identify, and possible sources. For some of the glycosides and alkaloids there's a number of different plants which yield them in greater or lesser quantities. Some of them are native, others introduced, and there are plenty more that only grow in the tropics.'

He ran his finger down the list. Martin's eyes followed, scanning the plant names. Beside them there was a list of long, Latin names like the ones he'd read on the first sheet.

'Belladonna,' he said, pointing. 'I've heard of that.'

'Nightshade. It gives you atropine, hyosyamine and a few other alkaloids as well. Causes visual disturbances, coma, hallucinations and heart failure.' Tony moved his finger. 'Here's foxglove. That yields digitalis. They use that in heart treatment. It slows the heart and eases circulation. Too much stops it completely. Celandine here gives you chelidonine, another alkaloid which acts as an antispasmic. It stops messages passing through the nerves. Too much causes paralysis.'

Tony looked at Martin. 'You'll have to give me a clue on this. The more I worked on it, the weirder it became.'

'I'll tell you sometime,' Martin said, though he was sure he wouldn't.

'Well, I wouldn't recommend anybody using the mixture. That colchicine comes from a crocus-type plant. It disrupts cell division. I hear they use that in genetic manipulation. And there's aconitine, from the monkshood plant. Extremely virulent.' He drew his finger right down the page. 'But they're mild compared with some of the hard stuff. Here we've got traces of inocybe, amanita, and gyromitra.'

'Terrific. I only got two years of Latin. Can you talk English and tell me what they are?'

'They're the deadliest mushrooms you can get. Kill you just looking at them.'

Martin raised his eyebrows.

'Just kidding, but pretty close to it, believe me,' Tony said. 'Some of the rest, those I've been able to identify, that is, are pretty straightforward. You can get most of them in a health shop.' He read them off. 'Damiana, skullcap, vervain, valerian. All well-known nerve agents. I read a paper that they're doing tests on their extracts for nervous system injuries and motor neuron disease. Oh, and here's a thing. On the protein side, there's some really complex molecular structures. It took me a night and a half to get to the bottom of some of them. Finally I got a clear reading on the gas chromatograph. There's amphibian nervous tissue, reptilian secretions, mammalian blood platelets, and a fair amount of insectivorous cells. You've a right witch's brew here.'

Martin looked at him.

'What do you mean?'

'Eye of newt, toe of rat, something from insect larvae and about forty poisonous plants. This,' he said, tapping his finger on the sheaf of paper, 'will never get a licence, not unless you're into chemical warfare.'

Tony finished his beer. 'I'll leave that with you, but remember, not a word to a soul.'

Martin shook his head.

'You won't tell me what it's for?' Tony asked again.

'Not yet.'

'But can I keep the rest of the stuff? There's a lot more work to be done.'

'Sure,' Martin said. 'But the same applies to you. Not a word.'

'Count on it. I could get a paper out of this some day.'

Tony picked up his jacket and was about to leave. Martin put a restraining hand on his arm. 'Hang on. How would that stuff affect somebody?'

'You mean physically?'

Martin nodded.

'Damned if I know. Some of the stuff in there can stop your heart in seconds. Others are a bit like snake poisons. They break down tissue and disrupt the nerve impulses. The fungaloids, like destroying angel and death cap, they're *mean* buggers. Some of their toxins can burst cell walls if you take them in large enough amounts, but it's difficult to say how they will catalyse with each other.'

'How do you mean?'

'Basically, it's a chemical cocktail. Some of the constituents will cancel others out. Compounds can react to others to form intermediaries which can have different effects. Like sodium and chlorine, two deadly poisons which bond to make common salt. I couldn't say how your powder will combine exactly, but I wouldn't recommend putting it on your skin.'

'What about swallowing it?'

Tony looked at him and laughed out loud.

'You have to be pulling my chain, eh?'

Martin met him eye to eye, giving nothing away.

'Listen, I wouldn't recommend that at all. Seriously. I don't know what that stuff is supposed to be for, but if they're selling it to kids at discos, then there's going to be one almighty mess. It's a hell of a concoction, and that's just the stuff I've been able to identify. There's some long chains in there that have me beat so far. Now I'm fixed up for some time on a mainframe diagnostic programme at the University. It might cast a light on the rest of the mixture, but I'm betting it will be just as powerful as the more common substances.'

Cassidy finally stood up and put his jacket on. 'Listen, man, if you have any more of that stuff, don't go testing it on yourself. Not if you want to wake up tomorrow.'

He took his empty glass over to the bar and waved to Martin as he left. Martin finished his pint and ordered another. He sat for another hour leafing through the print-out. Finally, he decided on a second opinion.

On the night Martin Thornton showed the report to Andrew Toye and asked him for help, Duncan Haldane shot Morag, his old border collie.

Duncan had had a hard fortnight cutting the oaks for the lumberyard. The chain saw buzz rang in his ears long after he finished work each day. It had been tough going. The greenwood was hard and difficult to cut and then he'd had to dress the trunks, stripping off the branches and hauling them off to the side to make them manageable for the loader's grab-arm. He hadn't asked Ben to come down to help him. The memory of his near disaster kept springing into his mind as he worked, and each time he thought of it he got a cold shiver, despite the sweat-work. He was glad the boy was staying up at the house. It kept him out of harm's way.

The last of the tall oak trunks had been loaded and carted off, leaving the cleared section with a naked, stubbly look. The bare boles of the trees stood out white against the green. They would all have to be hauled out by the roots and dragged off and that would take another fortnight.

Duncan ate a hearty dinner and let the dog out before soaking himself in a hot bath, feeling the tightness in his shoulder muscles gradually ease. He came down in his dressing gown and Rose poured him a welcome cold beer which he sat savouring in the overstuffed chair next to the fireplace. Ben and Dorrie were up in their beds though it was still light on the long evenings following midsummer.

Rosie was knitting a school sweater for Ben for the autumn, absently watching a long-running serial on television, while Duncan sat back comfortably enjoying a beer and a cigarette. He thought about the amount of work he'd managed to get through and the huge amount still facing him. It was a daunting task, but the sooner he got the ground cleared, the sooner he could start, and it was always best to get the building work done in the summer. It was close to ten at night when Rose's programme finished and the weatherman came on to say that the hot spell of weather was about to change, which came as no surprise to a farmer like Duncan. This part of the country never had a hot spell for long. Rain was heading in from the west which would make the

374

hauling more difficult for the tractor, but it wouldn't be such a sweat using the chain saw. Duncan didn't care.

It was ten minutes or so before he noticed that Morag hadn't come back. Normally she wandered around for half an hour and then came scratching and whining at the back door, demanding her accustomed place on the rug in front of the summer-empty fireplace. Duncan wasn't concerned about her lateness. Sometimes she might go sniffing up at the rabbit warrens on the hill and take her time coming back. She always knew the road home.

It was half past ten when the two of them looked up. Rose's needles stopped their staccato clicking. Duncan put his beer glass down on the slate mantelpiece.

The noise came again, a harsh, metallic shriek. It sounded like a stone saw working on granite.

'What the hell's that?' Duncan asked.

There was a high yipping sound, like a wavering howl, and Duncan exlaimed: 'That's the dog!' For some reason. He felt the hairs on the back of his head creep.

'What, Morag? Doesn't sound like her.'

'Aye, it's her. Something's upset her.'

Duncan got up from the chair and looked around for his trousers. He'd left them on the back of the chair but Rose had folded them and taken them through to the bedroom.

'You're not going out again after your bath,' she said.

Just then the high yelping came again, followed by an agonised whine. Morag barked frantically. There was a crashing sound and then a series of angry grunts. The dog barked loudly, but it was in fright, not an angry yap.

'She's fighting,' Duncan said grimly. 'Something's hurt her. Where's my boots?'

Rose looked up at him. He had that look on his face that said nobody was going to argue with him.

'They're under the kitchen table. Your trousers are on the bed. There's a shirt in the wardrobe.' Duncan nodded. He went up the stairs two at a time and was down in two minutes, fully dressed. His flat cap was pulled down over his eyes instead of sitting back with its peak aslant, farmer-style. He *really* meant business. He told her he'd be back in a minute. Outside, the grunting and yipping was still loud in the air.

Rose heard the rattle of the lock on the tall gun cabinet beside the front door where Duncan kept his prized over-and-under twelve-bore and the cartridge belt Rose had bought him two Christmases before when the farm was still a going concern and they'd had some money to spare. She listened for the snap of the barrel lock then heard the snick of cartridges entering the chamber. There was a final loud metallic click. The front door opened then closed with a slam.

Upstairs the cacophony startled Ben Haldane from a light, fitful slumber. He'd been half-dreaming, seeing the visions that had haunted him for weeks. He and Dorrie had been down in the forest. She'd been crying and he'd been scared, but he knew he had to be brave for her. The darkness had closed in around him and the mushrooms had glowed poisonously. He had pulled her along behind him, trying to find a way out of the dark heart of Fasach Wood, but he couldn't find the wall. In his dream he knew that *this* part of the forest was not *real*. It looked real and it felt real, but it was *wrong*, as if it didn't belong in the world that Ben Haldane knew. It was like a mysterious, *evil* place that only came into being when it *wanted* to exist, when small boys were lost in the forest. That other time, he'd stumbled through the gap in the drystane dyke and found himself in a place that was more like a jungle, rotting and wet and filled with odd sounds and smells. Here in the dream, it was the same. There was something creepy and festering and horribly *alive*, and he couldn't find his way back to the tumbledown stones that would lead him out of there. In his half-sleep his breath quickened. He tossed on the bed, getting tangled in the sheet.

The trees came alive. He saw their scabrous, wooden fingers stretch out to grab at Dorrie and he dragged her onwards. They passed the virulent, luminescent mushrooms which were already swelling with the disease inside them and he skirted round them, feeling his skin crawl. The roots underfoot were bulging out of the ground, trying to trap the children's feet the way the root had tripped his dad when the tree tried to *kill* him. Then a movement to the right caught his eye. A long, thick twist of ivy creeper was sinuously snaking its way down the trunk of a tree, moving like an shaggy python, ready to strike.

Dorrie screeched and he turned and his heart almost exploded in shock.

It was not Dorrie. It *was not Dorrie!*

Cold, twiggy fingers grasped his own. He was holding the hand of the *leaf man*.

The forest began to spin around him and suddenly Ben couldn't breathe. His heart felt as if it had swelled and burst. There was no beat. His throat wouldn't open and the scream wouldn't come.

The creature in front of him turned its head towards him. He could see the individual leaves that made up its face. They were compressed together, solid and dry. There were two hollows where oak apples, shiny with impossible life, gleamed madly. There was a scrapy rasping sound and a mouth opened just inches from his face. Holly leaf lips opened, venomously barbed, and behind them blackthorn spines, set in serrated rows, began to spring apart in a demonic gape. From that yawning mouth came an arid rustle of laughter like wind in tall grass. A hand with chestnut leaves for fingers and sycamore knuckles came and clamped itself on his face. It squeezed and he felt the desiccated veins scrape on his skin. It gripped hard, with sudden power, closing over his mouth.

He screamed in his dream, high and wavering, and came instantly awake, struggling against the claustrophobic bindings of the sheet that had wrapped itself around him. His whole body was shaking with the terrible dream-fear. His lungs unlocked and he sucked in frantic breaths and the screams went on and on and on.

It took several long moments, sitting shivering in the dark of his bedroom, before Ben realised he was breathing and that the screams were not his own. They were coming from outside the house.

At first he was rocked rigid by the thought that it was Dorrie, that she had somehow got out of the house and gone down through the blood-puddled field and into the trees. Then the tone of the screech changed and he knew it was their dog. Morag's squeal came again, high and agonised. And behind that whine of pain, Ben heard the low, snuffling grunt, like the snort of a lion in a bush.

Ben struggled to free himself from his covers and stumbled across to the window. He pulled the curtain aside and the near-full moon glowed in the sky. He opened his window, too intent in the dog's plight to recoil from the clematis tendrils hanging across the pane, and leaned out.

377

Morag's howl came from further up the road, close to where his father had been cutting the oaks. Near the path there was a shadow. He shielded his eyes with one hand against the glare of the moon in the clear sky and peered out. The white of Morag's breast flashed silver. Then something big and black moved forwards and blotted it out. The dark shape was twice the dog's size, maybe even bigger. The collie snarled desperately and turned. Ben saw her spin, roll on her belly as if kicked and then get to her feet again. She backed away and then launched herself at the black bulky shape. There was a savage grunt and the dog went flying outwards. She landed on her back, twisted and got to her feet again to face the attacker.

Ben tried to call out to her to run away, but the words wouldn't come. The black shape lumbered forward, in a strange undulating yet *powerful* motion. Morag jinked, turned and then dived under it. There was another shuddering growl and Morag screamed again.

The front door opened and light spilled out onto the flagstones. There was a shadow on the path and then Duncan Haldane strode out, gun held up high.

'Morag?' he called loudly. 'Where are you, girl?'

The dog howled. From where he leaned out of his window Ben saw the white of the collie's fur stand out like a pale flag against the dark ground. The shape was moving away at speed, bobbing up and down in an ungainly motion, jet black and indistinct. Ben heard it snort and the drum of hard feet on turves as it reached the cleared oak plantation. He got an impression of a powerful head and humped shoulders and then the shape seemed to change, beginning to move more fluidly, until it merged with the shadows. The trees swallowed it up, as if deliberately crowding round to welcome it into the blackness.

His father ran up the road towards where the dog lay. He knelt down and Ben saw him put the gun on the ground. Then he heard his father say a word the boy had never heard him say before. He said it several times before he straightened. Something glinted just beside the animal lying on the pathway. Moonlight reflected from a growing pool of deeper dark that spread from where the dog sprawled, panting hoarsely.

Ben watched his father pick up the gun then lean over Morag.

The shotgun roared once and the collie's head flopped to the ground.

The report rolled up the hill like thunder. Duncan Haldane stood, head bowed, with the long-barrelled gun hanging in the crook of his arm. Ben's eyes filled with tears as he listened to the sound rumbling and echoing from the face of the cliff on the Douglas Hills. The noise seemed to go on for ever, rolling up and down over the bracken and heather, a long epitaph on the dog's life and death.

Down below, his mother came out of the house and stood in the pool of light. She looked up the farm track and saw Duncan standing there. She called something, but her voice was lost in the distant roar that continued to boom from up on the hill above her husband.

Three hundred yards upslope from where Duncan Haldane stood lay the tall, straight larch trunks he'd felled and stripped for the walls of four, maybe even five, cabins. They had been lying up there, drying out and seasoning into quality timber, built up into pyramids of good timber across waste bearing logs to keep them off the damp earth, solid for a year and a half.

As the echo of the twelve-bore reverberated around the valley the twisted, unprofitable trunks which Duncan Haldane had used as the pallets for the bulk of his timber began to move. The knots and whorls where the chain saw had stripped off side branches began to twist and swell. The trunks stretched and from the knot-holes limbs budded, growing out quickly and bending with muscular *alien* strength, seeking out the ground beneath them. The tips dug unto the earth which rippled and humped as the new branches probed irresistibly. Then the branches *flexed*, shoving the logs they bore upwards in a violent jerk, all heaving together in a monstrous, insectile jolt. The ends of the load-bearers pushed up from the ground with a ripping noise and, as they did, the piles lying above shifted backwards, crashing against the light wooden stanchions which held them in place. The weight was too much for the softwood planks. They had been built only to steady the pyramid piles of wood, not to take their weight. There was a sudden crack, then another and a third, then a whole series as the wooden pickets gave way and the long piles of logs started to slip.

Ben Haldane heard the noise first. The thunder *seemed* to be coming from up the hill. He craned out of his window as far as he could, recoiling against the soft touch of the clematis tendrils on the back of his head. He could just make out the upper slope. Something moved there in the dark.

Ben saw a long grey shape shift against the dark background. It tumbled down the hill and a faint tremor ran up through the house, rattling the glass in the window. He stared at the motion. It was something long and thin and Ben couldn't imagine what it could be.

Then he saw it hit a bump. One end came up. Another shape hit against it with a rasping crack and suddenly Ben knew *exactly* what it was.

Duncan Haldane was on the point of turning when Ben yelled, his voice almost a scream.

'Dad. *Daddy!*'

His father turned.

'*Daddy, run! It's the trees!*'

Ben almost fell out of the window with the force of his frantic outburst.

Duncan looked towards the house and then something seemed to catch his attention. His whole body jerked as if he'd been hit. Some distance up the hill, the outrunner of the avalanche of timber bounced out of the gloom and hit the ground with a jarring thud. The rumble suddenly became a roar. Duncan Haldane looked as if his feet had been nailed to the ground.

'Dad, *please, run!*' Ben screamed.

It might have been Ben's desperate cry, but whatever it was Duncan unfroze. He spun away and simply ran for it, haring down the track towards the farmhouse. Above the now deafening thunder, he shouted to his wife.

'Get in! *Get in the house!*'

He got about ten feet when the first of the massive larch trunks came bouncing out of the gloom, a caber thrown by a mythical giant, tumbling end over end. It hit the ground just above the path and somersaulted clean over Duncan Haldane's head. Behind it another trunk crashed right onto the path, only feet away from the farmer, digging a two-foot crater in the hardpack.

Ben watched, eyes wide, as his father sprinted towards him. The gun fell from his hands and Duncan put his head down and threw himself down the path.

From behind the house there was an almighty crash as the old outhouse behind the haybarn was simply smashed into match-wood and, immediately after that, a clang like the toll of a giant bell as the corrugated side of the barn was stove in. The chicken coop with the last of the Haldane livestock was sheared in two. One chicken managed to get eight feet into the air on whirring wings and was immediately battered by a tumbling tree-trunk which hit it with such force that it flew on, every bone in its body broken, and dead as a doorstop, for another forty feet before landing, a bloody rag, in the herb garden.

Duncan Haldane made it to the lee of the byre just as the main mass of the wooden avalanche hit the south side, tearing away the fence as it went. Over the roaring thunder which shook the ground like an earthquake there was an odd popping sound as the fence posts were hauled out, one after the other, by the drag on the tough strands of wire. They came free of the earth like a giant zip being opened.

The pile of logs rolled in a deadly grey mass down across the path, spanging and clapping against each other, twisting and tumbling as they descended the slope below the farm track towards the flat area where Duncan had culled the oaks. The noise reached a crescendo as they piled themselves up, thudding and hammering together against the stumps which still stuck up from the ground. Eventually the noise died away and a strange silence fell over the farm.

Ben leapt back from the widow and ran from his bedroom. He took the stairs two at a time and got to the bottom just as his father came barging inside.

Duncan Haldane stood in the hallway, panting for breath. Rose threw herself at him and Ben followed suit. They stood there, in the little lobby, holding on to each other for a long moment.

Finally there was a noise at the top of the stairs. Duncan Haldane looked up and Rose and Ben followed his eyes. Dorrie stood there on the top step, still in her pyjamas. She was yawning and rubbing her eyes, still half asleep, her teddy bear clamped under her arm.

'What's happening?' she asked.

In the morning after the night of thunder, as soon as it was light,

Duncan Haldane went out to inspect the damage. The outhouse was completely demolished. The dry stones which had formed the walls and had stood for more than two hundred years had simply exploded apart, littering the short grass for fifty feet all around. The roof of the chicken coop had sailed up into the air and landed on the pitched slates of the byre, sitting swaying in the morning breeze. The red barn was repairable but, in the following day, as Duncan cleared up the debris, it took him three hours to remove the great larch spears which pierced the sides. They had hit end-on, three of them, with such force that they had stabbed themselves right through the metal. Duncan's gun had miraculously escaped damage, but during his morning inspection he found what was left of Morag. The little dog which he'd shot in the gloaming darkness had been terribly injured in a fight with something. Even in the gloom, Duncan Haldane had seen the cloven tracks of the boar which had turned up his turves only a fortnight before. The collie had been razored in great scores down her flanks. Blood had been pumping from a gash in her belly from which dark wet intestines had been pushing themselves into the night air. The following morning Duncan found the body several yards from where he'd left her, the black-and-white carcase squashed flat by one of the rolling trunks. Nonetheless, his first job early that morning was to fetch his spade and bury the bloody scrap in the field.

Duncan's next task was to haul every one of the logs from down in the valley, and the others which had stopped rolling while still up on the high pasture, on to the level. It took him three days of hard graft and he had to steel himself for the work. Here, he let his head rule his heart to an extent. Really what he wanted to do was get into the trees, track down John Lovatt's old boar which was running wild down there, and put two barrels of ball shot into its brain. In the few moments that he'd had before the devastating avalanche of logs had come thundering down the hill towards him, he'd had a chance to look at the damage done to the dog. When he was a youngster, when his own father had bred pigs, he'd seen the same marks on the flanks of a stray dog which had been stupid enough to jump the fence of the enclosure, mistaking the pigs for the easy meal the sheep had proved.

On the day after the devastation, he'd taken a walk up to

Lovatt's farm. John had sympathised, even said he'd come and help Duncan find the beast whenever he was ready, but there was not much else he could do about it. The boar had broken out months before, and he'd had a real good search for it himself, seeing it cost two thousand pounds in sterling, worth more pound for pound in its own weight, on its short hooves.

While Duncan worked, he told Ben and Dorrie to stay at home, and neither of them had any objection to that. Duncan, who'd already had a scare when the chain saw had whipped out of his hands and nearly taken his son's head off, was concerned in case the animal might return during the day. If it could tear a dog to shreds with its short, vicious tusks, a boy or a small girl would have no defence at all.

28

Dr George Watt, who held the seat in clinical pharmacology, was one of Andrew Toye's many friends. He'd been lecturing to a huddle of students in the Western Infirmary and was on his way to his rooms in the evening when Andrew collared him and invited him over for a drink. He was a small, bald man with ruddy cheeks and a dry wit. Andrew introduced Martin.

'Wondered if you'd care to have a look at this?' Andrew said after pouring whiskies for two and a small beer for Martin Thornton.

'Ah, I knew it wasn't a social invite,' George said, but he took the whisky anyway. 'By the way, I read that piece on poltergeists. Fascinating, if you're into that sort of thing. Fortunately we've come a long way since we put all our aches and pains down to curses and evil spirits. Why don't you get a *real* job, Andrew?'

The professor beamed over the edge of his glass. 'I've *got* a real job. I don't get to swan around with a stethoscope and hordes of idolising white-coated bimbos.'

'Wrong profession, old boy,' the other professor retorted jovially. 'I'm in pharmacology, not pathology. They're the ladykillers.'

Andrew handed over the computer print-out. George scanned it quickly. His lips moving as he read. The other two could hear him mumbling as he rhymed off the list of substances.

'All natural compounds. Interesting mix,' he finally said.

'That's what Martin thought,' Andrew said encouragingly. 'It's from the regional analyst.'

Martin shot him a look of dismay. Andrew raised his eyes.

'So what's it for?' George asked, appearing not to have heard.

'That's what we'd ask you.'

'Well, on first glance, it's pretty heavily weighted towards the alkaloids. There's a fair spread of hallucinogenics too. Mostly plant substances. You've got everything but the kitchen sink in here,' he said, unconsciously repeating the lab technician's summing-up. 'What is it, some new sort of drug?'

'I honestly don't know yet. I hoped you could tell me,' Martin answered.

'Well, I wouldn't recommend it, that's for sure. It's a pretty deadly cocktail. It's got traces of some of the most powerful naturally-occurring toxins. This will give you more than a hangover. There's psilocybin here, a well-known mind-altering drug. Comes from mushrooms. The effects are very long lasting, sometimes permanent.'

'If you took a mixture like that, what would happen?'

'Probably kill you straight off,' George said, then he laughed. 'Or perhaps it would take a little longer. No, seriously, it's hard to say. I'd have to spend some time on it, maybe test it on a few rats, but on the face of it I'd say it was fairly lethal. Some of the ingredients will stop your heart. Others will cause pathological changes in nerve and muscle tissue.' He scanned down the list. 'Here's an odd thing.'

The other two sat forward.

'Most of the compounds are of plant origin, but here's some animal protein.' He rhymed off the Latin taxonomy, then sat back, eyes raised to the ceiling in concentration.

'There's a connection here,' he said finally.

'What do you mean?'

'Well, there's amphibious nervous tissue, rodent haemoglobin and juvenile insect cells, not to mention haemotoxins and neurotoxins from snake venom. The odd thing is that there's a link between these very different animal orders.'

'Go on,' Andrew urged, as interested as Martin.

'Well,' George pursued. 'All three have unique properties of regeneration. Both rats' and amphibian cells have special free-roaming trigger hormones which, if necessary, begin the process of rebuilding in the event of major damage. It causes them to regrow destroyed nerves and severed limbs.'

Martin remembered Caitlin's feet, slowly tapping on the footplate. Her nerves had been severed, her limbs useless, and now they were beginning to *move*. Martin thought back to the farcical scene in the kitchen when he'd dropped the pot of writhing pasta. *Had* it come alive, or had the hallucinogens in the mixture just made him see the impossible? If the herbal potion could regenerate destroyed nerves, make the paralysed walk again, then it was an absolute world-beating *record* of a leap for medical science. It would make an incredible story.

Yet there was something *wrong* about the whole thing that tugged and pulled insistently at Martin's mind.

'Could that work on people?' he asked George. 'I mean nerve regeneration, new arms and legs?'

'Davidson in Edinburgh has been working on research in that field, using polypeptides and extracts from rat nervous tissue. He thinks it might conceivably be possible to synthesize the substance and apply it in cases of human amputation.'

'And what about the insect cells?'

'Similar, to an extent. These are juvenile cells from the larval, or early pupal, stage. When certain hormones are activated, a major regeneration process is initiated. The living cells are absorbed and broken down and the dormant cells are triggered into enormous growth. They re-form the entire animal in metamorphosis at an astounding rate. That's what happens when an insect larva becomes an imago.'

'What's that?'

'An adult, the higher stage, equipped to breed. For example, a caterpillar emerges as a butterfly, ready to take flight. Its whole structure has been completely altered into what some people would say is a higher, purer state.'

'So what would that kind of cell be used for?'

'Well, it's great for changing insects, that's about all. There is *no* higher state for man; not until you get to the hereafter, the existence of which Andrew is doing his damnedest to disprove.'

Andrew grinned amiably but Martin ignored the light gibe.

'What about the snake poison?'

'Oh, the venom? Very complex protein compounds. Neuro- and haemotoxins. One destroys nerve function and the other breaks down body tissues in a way not dissimilar to the way in which larval cells are disassembled into constituent organic soup before being used as building blocks for the adult cells.'

'And the whole mixture?'

'Well, I'd like to run some experiments, if I may. It looks like something out of the Middle Ages. The old alchemists used to make all sorts of compounds from plants and herbs and bits of animals. Some of their mixtures worked very well for some things, but I'm afraid their treatments killed as many as they cured. I'm also reminded of the South American Indians. They've achieved some remarkable treatments with plant extracts, some of which we use today. There's a fear that if the rainforests are destroyed, we'll miss out on some of the most powerful natural antidotes for all kinds of illnesses, maybe even cancer.'

He stopped for another sip of whisky before summing up professionally.

'The ingredients here are quite simply like something from the dark ages. There's a remarkable concentration of toxins and narcotics. Whoever made it up certainly knows botany. They've picked some of the most dangerous plants there are. I'd say that under no circumstances should this be ingested, or even applied to the skin.'

Martin heard him speak and his mind immediately conjured up a picture of Caitlin taking a spoonful of the mixture, morning, noon and night. Suddenly he was very concerned.

'Best person to ask about the plants is old Carmyllie in Celtic Mythology,' the professor advised. 'He's got tons of gen on the old sorcery stuff. In the meantime if you can get me a sample I'd be pleased to run a few tests on it, whatever it's for.'

Martin said he would do his best to get him some of the mixture, and the professor did not push him further about its source or potential use. George had another whisky and chatted to Andrew about the poltergeist story, mostly in disparaging terms, but light-heartedly enough. When he had gone Martin sat down opposite his friend and picked up the sheets of print-out.

'There's something very strange about this,' he said.

'You'd better tell me what it's all about, before I rope in the whole campus,' Andrew told him. 'We'll go see Finlay Carmyllie later.'

Martin sat back and, after getting Andrew's solemn assurance that this was just between the two of them, recounted the whole story of his night at the ceilidh and its aftermath. There was little to tell, except that he'd got very drunk and had the impression he'd done something wrong before he woke with a catastrophic hangover. He described Caitlin's injuries and then those small movements of her toes and the faint but definite sensation that had been nonexistent before.

'And she's been taking this?' Andrew asked.

'Yes. She mixes it in water. She hasn't had any ill effects, as far as I can see.'

He went on to tell Andrew about the spaghetti and how he'd seen it slither and writhe out of the pot.

'I don't know whether I imagined it or not. I sniffed some of the powder and then that started to happen.'

'Did you see anything else?'

'That was enough.'

'No, I'm trying to find out if it was a general or specific event. You rarely get hallucinations which are quite so particular. You'd expect to have seen other odd things.'

'That was all I saw. Scared the hell out of me.'

'Just like the poltergeist?' Andrew asked him with a mischievous smile.

Finlay Carmyllie was in his seventies, a tall, stooped man with a doleful, wrinkled face. He looked every inch the crusty old professor, but his looks belied his manner. He was childishly enthusiastic and his hands waved continuously as he spoke, emphasising the fascination his work still held for him after a lifetime of study. The old man was delighted to see his fellow academic, for they had interests in common. Both men were devotees of Celtic culture, though they looked at it from different perspectives, and Andrew's other specialty, in paranormal studies, was paralleled in Finlay's field of mythology.

He looked at the sheets of paper, poring through them, using a finger to follow the lines.

'Know nothing of chemicals, young feller. Medicine's not my field. Never was. Leave that to the sawbones and headshrinkers. They're hoping I'll pop off soon so they can let the young Burkes and Hares cut me up and see what makes me tick. *Ha.* I can save them the bother. Good brandy and cigars.'

He was talking nonstop as his eyes followed the finger down the list.

'It's a real witch's brew you got here,' Carmyllie said. Again Martin recognised Tony Cassidy's words. He sat up, instantly alert.

'That reminds me, Andrew,' the old man went on. 'Where's

388

my copy of *Friel*? Didn't I give it to you months ago?'

Andrew pretended not to hear and Carmyllie went back to reading. Finally he looked up from the pages, shaking his head.

'There's enough in here to start an apothecary shop. All powerful stuff too. Haven't seen the likes of this in a while. You're not into black magic, are you?'

Martin shook his head. 'It's just something I'm researching.'

'It's what I've been researching all my life,' he said raising his glasses on top of his head. 'The herbs on this list were powerful ingredients of charms from pre-Roman times right up until the early Middle Ages and beyond. They could come straight out of any of the old works on Druids. Mistletoe, for instance, was sacred to the old *shamans*. They used to mix an infusion of the leaves with mushrooms. Gave them visions. The mistletoe was to slow the heart and sedate them, while the mushrooms gave them the gift of prophecy when they were in a trance. Aconite, that's monkshood, was deadly poisonous, as was hemlock, but they used extracts from them in their ceremonies. O'Connor says they believed the potency of the plants gave them the power to see into other people's minds and influence their actions. Friel's early work spoke of using some of these plants in the same way as the Mesquite Indians. They believed that the whole earth and everybody on it, including the animals and plants, were part of a great oneness. They would take deadly mixtures to get themselves in a trance state which would allow their souls to travel the low roads.'

'What low roads?'

'We'd call them ley lines. The Druids believed they were lines of power which led to the nexus which joined all the worlds together.'

'That's in that book you lent me,' Martin said to Andrew and his friend almost spluttered into his coffee cup.

'Oh, you scoundrel,' Carmyllie said accusingly. 'I *knew* I'd lent you *Friel*.' Andrew's face went red but the crusty academic turned back to Martin.

'Some of the other plants here,' he went on. 'Cuckoopint, lily of the valley, black bryony, they were used on special occasions, like the summer solstices, the equinoxes and, at certain times in the lunar cycle, to call up the spirits of the dead, or the spirits of the forest.'

He eased himself slowly out of his high-backed leather chair and turned to the bookshelves which lined the walls right up to the ceiling. Some of the volumes looked old. Many were layered with dust. He searched along the shelves before darting out a hand to ease one from where it was jammed tight. He brought the book back to the desk and opened it, riffling carefully through the pages.

'Here's a representation of a fragment of hide parchment. Dates back to pre-Roman times, maybe 2000 BC.' He turned the book round to let Martin see it. 'It's known to be a recipe for a special enchantment.'

Martin looked at the old, primitive drawing. There was a clear outline of a tree and around it, drawn in like astrological signs, was a halo of finely detailed etchings of plants. Wavering lines stretched out from the tree like spokes and, on the surface of the bark, a face seemed to be emerging from the trunk. Above the face, the branches jutted like antlers. In front of the tree, a cloaked figure, tiny by comparison, stood with arms raised. Other figures, crudely drawn in motion, appeared to be dancing in a circle around the tree.

'This was found in an old beaker somewhere in the west. Can't remember the place. Remarkable preservation, but even more remarkable detail. The botany boys were able to identify every plant from the drawings because they were so faithfully represented.' He turned the book back, scanning the accompanying text. 'Yes. Here we are. Black bryony, cowbane, wolfbane, milkweed and thornapple. You've got them all in that list. Plus the mushrooms, death cap and destroying angel. Heap big magic, as they say,' Carmyllie added, with a smile.

Martin's eyes remained on the stylised image.

'And what was that for?'

'Oh, that was the most powerful of all. It's the recipe for summoning *Cerunnos*.'

'What's that?'

'The spirit of the forest,' Andrew butted in. '*Herne the hunter*.'

'Well remembered, Andrew. You should come to more of my lectures,' Carmyllie said drily.

'I don't understand,' Martin said blankly.

'Cerunnos was the most powerful of the Celtic spirits. There

390

were parallels in Greek and Nordic mythologies, the horned god of the woodland. They believed that Cerunnos, or Herne as he was latterly known, was the force which kept the forest alive, and at that time the whole of Britain, especially Scotland, was covered in forest. One of the Celtic or even *pre*-Celtic beliefs was that in times of need Cerunnos could be summoned from the nexus of the ley lines by ritual and sacrifice.'

'What sort of sacrifice?'

'Oh, human, of course. He was a masculine god, antlers and hooves, that sort of thing. The sacrifice would have to be young, female, and a virgin. They'd let her blood into wooden cups and pour it onto the ring-stones to let it drain into the ground. It was a sort of fertility thing. They would give the sacrifice to the forest god and he would reward the summoners. Give them more powers, longer life, better crops, that sort of thing. Some people still believe in the old magic. That's why you get the hippies at Stonehenge on midsummer's night. It's all pretty harmless stuff.'

'This stuff doesn't look harmless,' Martin said.

'I couldn't tell you about that. Speak to George Watt in pharmacology.'

'I'll do that,' Martin said before Andrew had a chance to say that they'd already spoken to Professor Watt. He looked over the desk at the old man. 'Do people still believe that this sort of potion can work?'

'Some folk have never *stopped* believing. To them Christianity is only a transient newcomer. Look at Aleister Crowley at Boleskin on Loch Ness. He'd quite a cult following a few decades back. Called himself *"The Beast"*. Spent most of his time trying to raise the devil, which is the modern equivalent of Cerunnos. There's been plenty more like him.'

The old professor heaved himself up from his seat again and went back to the bookshelves. He pondered for a few minutes, mumbling to himself, and then selected another volume. 'Have a look at this. There's a lot about Crowley in it, and others who've been doing similar things like trying to raise demons. Can't say what success they had, but they seemed to have fun.' He shoved both books across the table to Martin. 'Have a read through these. Might recruit you for my classes. Oh, and don't give them to Andrew here. I'll never get them back.'

The professor offered them both a brandy, which Andrew accepted readily. His face was still flushed with the two whiskies he'd had previously, but he didn't seem to care. He was enjoying himself.

'This *Cerunnos*,' Martin said, 'what was he supposed to be?'

'He was the very essence of the wildwood. Remember, at that time the forest was as important to folk here as the rainforests are to the Amerindians. There's a very good representation of him on the Gundestrup Cauldron, which is almost identical to that drawing on the old vellum. He was believed to come forth from the heart of an oak tree where the ley lines met, at the juncture between the earth and the underworld. Powerful totem for the old shamans. He's the *Green Man* of legend, if you remember your Arthurian sagas. Once summoned, he had to be paid in blood or else he would make the earth tremble with his anger. The Druids believed that he would make the forest come alive and destroy them. They reckoned every tree had its own individual resident spirit, all of them ruled by the Forest God.'

Something in that statement jarred on Martin's memory. He snatched for it, but it eluded him.

Later, as they walked back through the campus towards Andrew's place next to the sluggish river where Martin had left his Land-Rover, his friend said: 'Curiouser and curiouser.'

'Hm?' Martin mumbled, his mind on other things.

'What Alice said after eating the mushrooms. The whole thing strikes me as a bit odd. I think you should do some checking on this Sheila Garvie.'

'My thoughts exactly,' Martin said.

When he got home Martin called Caitlin, unsure of what exactly he was going to say. The line was engaged and, though he called several times, it remained so for more than an hour. Later he tried again and there was no reply. He got a can of cold lager from his fridge, popped the ring-pull then sipped as he leafed through the books.

As a newspaperman Martin had never had much time for mythology. His stock in trade was facts, quotes, comment and, to a great extent, current and documented events. In this respect none of what he read made him any the wiser. Friel's book on ley lines, of which he'd read extracts at Andrew's flat, was a tattered twenties edition, written in a pedantic style. It had old plates of standing stones, carved megaliths and stone tables. There were maps with dotted lines showing the directions of the leys. It described the lines as rivers of force and it all seemed far-fetched to Martin Thornton.

Farrell's *Evolution of Magic* was a more interesting read. It gave a history of the occult from prehistory up until the recent past. It went into Celtic beliefs, shamanism of the Nordic and Lapp tribes, and even had biblical quotations. Farrell's later chapters dealt with the more modern alchemists including Cagliostro, John Dee, who claimed to have transmuted base metals into gold, and, from the twentieth century, Aleister Crowley himself, pictured with a group of people at Boleskin House on the shores of Loch Ness. They all sounded like charlatans to Martin, but he persevered as the evening grew dark and kept on reading. Farrell mentioned the *ley lines* in his work, and in one section went into a detailed account of the Celtic forest lore, referring to the forestal as the *Seilach Garbh-aidh*.

Martin flicked back to Friel and found the same name. It described the cup-and-ring marked stones and their suspected use as runnels for sacrificial blood. Friel explained the nature of the *leys* as power conduits where forces of good or evil passed through the polarity between the underworld and the physical plane.

He moved on to O'Connor's old book on Druidry which went into more detail of the religious ideology of the ancient pagans. O'Connor had been involved in the translation of the old western vellum pictograph which Finlay Carmyllie had shown them in his study. His was the most scholarly work, drawing on evidence from archaeological digs in the British Isles and parts of the continent, including northern Spain. In a long treatise he listed the special herbs which the *shamans*, their medicine men, had used to achieve various states. Many of them matched the ones in the now dog-eared sheaf of papers Martin had been given by Tony Cassidy. Then, again towards the end of his book, Martin found a description of Cerunnos, the horned god of the forest, and how the *Seilach Garbh-aidh* would offer sacrifices to raise the power of the forest spirit, mixing the blood of victims with special potions, to ensure fertility for the coming year. O'Connor said that there was a rumour of a ritual to not only evoke the power of the horned god but, in special times, to summon him from the world under the roots to offer him special sacrifices and gain rewards of supernatural powers and longevity.

When Martin finally put O'Connor's book down it was after three in the morning. He hadn't realised it was so late. His eyes were strained and he felt a pressure headache building up. He was still unable to decide whether anything that he'd read had any relevance. He dragged himself off to his room, forced himself to undress and threw himself onto the bed, drawing the duvet up. He was asleep in minutes.

Alarm bells were clanging in his head. He was in a dream where he and Caitlin Brook were running. He had her by the wrist and they raced through shadows. He didn't pause to consider the fact that she was not in a wheelchair. He only knew he had to get her away. It was the one *certainty* in the dream.

The bells were ringing in his ears and something black was closing in behind them. Caitlin struggled against his grip, twisting her wrist, trying to shake him loose, but he kept pulling her and, all the while, behind them the darkness spread and grew like a disease. He bawled at her, feeling the panic tighten his chest and clamp his breath. Still running he turned and saw the looming wave of darkness behind her, a baneful, *malevolent* tide. He jerked her, pivoting himself so that she spun away from it, whirling round in front of him. As he turned back, her grip came loose and she went flying over the old dry-stone wall. Martin leapt after her, landing precariously on top of the stone, arms pinwheeling for balance.

He was no longer on the low wall. He was on the balcony ledge, teetering at the brink of a dead drop. Caitlin was below him, facing him, *falling*. Her arms clawed the air in frantic helplessness. Her green eyes were wide open, blazing their terror into him. Her mouth opened in a silent scream and she fell. He reached out to grab her but she was beyond his reach. She plummeted backwards. Below her he could see the hard concrete and the low bannister wall. Caitlin hit it with the pulpy crack of a pomegranate under a hammer. He saw her contort, spine *impossibly* twisted and bent, then she flopped to the ground below. From the height of the balcony he saw the deadly shivering vibrate her body so that it twitched and jerked as she lay on the wet pavement.

Martin screamed her name and, as he did so, he felt the cold blackness enfold him, smothering him in suffocating coils.

He woke with a start, lungs hauling for air. The bells were still ringing and for a moment Martin was completely disorientated. He freed himself from the tangled sheet and dragged himself out of bed, stumbling towards the telephone.

He snatched it up and held it to his ear, pain throbbing behind his eyes.

'Yeah?' he said breathlessly.

'Hey, boss.' It was Alec Stirling.

'Hi,' Martin said groggily. 'What's up? What time is it?'

'After nine. Did I wake you up?'

Something was tugging insistently behind Martin's consciousness. He made a mental effort to shrug it away, to listen to what Alec Stirling had to say.

'Yes, Alec, what is it?'

'Could have another story for you,' Alec said brightly. The postman had been awake for hours. He began to speak while Martin tried to hang on to what was being said against the insistent clamouring of his own mind.

'I might have a murder for you,' Alec said, sounding quite pleased with himself. 'Down in Fasach Wood. I think the Buist boy's done his old man in. Lad's nuttier than a fruit scone.'

'Whoa. Hold on a minute. What're you talking about?'

'Ernie Buist. Remember you saw him that night in the Douglas Arms?'

Martin shook his head. The pain thumped against his temples and he groaned. Then he realised Alec couldn't see him. 'No. Can't say I remember him.'

'Big bugger. Tartan nose. All shoulders and red-raw temper. Anyway, I think he's been murdered. I saw him chase his boy into the forest nearly two weeks ago. He hasn't been seen since and the boy's up at the steading with a good going case of galloping paranoia.'

Alec waited for a response and, when none came, went on.

'And here's another thing. Remember you were telling me about the wee Haldane boy? How he got lost in the forest and came home with a weird story about the trees chasing him or something?'

'Yes, I remember that,' Martin said, while his mind was telling him to get off the phone and *think*.

'Well, young Buist was telling me the same story. He says the bloody *trees* got his old man. He's holed up in the shack and he's cut down every bush and shrub for forty yards around the place. He thinks the trees are coming up to *get* him.'

As Alec spoke, something went *click* inside Martin's head and a blurred pattern that had been coalescing in his mind while he slept suddenly twisted into a kind of focus, the way a jumble of squiggles will congeal into a recognisable face. The mental alarm bells stepped up their clangour and he had to squeeze his eyes shut to fade them out.

'Listen, Alec, can I call you back?'

'Sorry, did I interrupt something? You got a female there?'

'No. There's something I have to do. I'll get back to you soon as I can. At your place?'

'Sure. Are you interested in the story?'

'More than you'd believe, Scoop. I want to speak to that boy. But I have to go now. I'll get back to you *pronto*.'

Alec said that would be fine although there was a trace of puzzlement and disappointment in his tone. Martin didn't notice.

He hung up and went into the kitchen to put on the kettle. He needed some hot coffee. Black.

While the kettle was building up to a boil he got Finlay Carmyllie's books out and put them on the kitchen table. The pattern had interlocked and formed a part of a picture while he slept, while he *ran* with Caitlin Brook. Martin held onto the small portion that had snapped into definition, because he knew he was on the edge of something, a *bigger* picture.

He opened Farrell's *Evolution of Magic* and flicked through the pages in a quick riffle. There was something he had seen and missed the night before, but his subconscious had caught it, stored and analysed it, and given it to him in the symbology of a dream.

He found it more than halfway through. The familiar, brutish face of Aleister Crowley stared out from the group. Head shots from the picture had been used in features in every newspaper whenever a story on witchcraft made the rounds during the summer silly season.

Crowley had called himself 'The Beast 666'. He'd been one of the Masonic inner circle and he had practised the black arts. At Boleskin House he'd tried to raise the devil, laying river sand at the entrance to his remote mansion to catch the demon's footprints. The story had been that he had succeeded and preserved the cloven prints of a massive two-legged being. The picture had been taken in the early twenties and had that grainy flat look of the old-style plates. There were seven people in the group, Crowley in the centre. Around him were an unnamed group of men and women, acolytes, according to the caption. Off to one side, a woman sat in a chair. She was not looking at the camera. Her eyes, fixed forever in the print, were staring straight at Crowley, her expression one of acute concentration. Her hair was white and caught up in a bun, showing a slender neck, finely curved jawline and high cheekbones.

The photograph had been shot, in the flat glare of a magnesium flash, more than seventy years before. The woman was wearing a light summer dress which looked translucent in the flash glare. Her arm was crossed over her body, hand laid on her thigh. On her forearm there was a black mark, close to the crook of her elbow.

It was Sheila Garvie.

Martin's mind automatically selected a memory of Sheila Garvie reaching to pour him a drink from her flask. He'd seen the mark on her arm, up close. It looked almost exactly like a black figure eight. It had not been a tattoo. Unbidden, an image loomed into memory. The black eight of the double-barrel shotgun he'd seen in the vision on the night Caitlin Brook had broken her back. For some reason, the mark on the woman's arm was just as deadly.

The woman was staring, *glaring* at the man in the centre, with almost palpable intensity, though whether it was anger, or something else, Martin couldn't tell. His eyes flicked to the caption. *Aleister Crowley, self-styled Beast, with acolytes in mysticism at Boleskin House, June 1922.*

Then, in a rush, the whole hidden memory of the drunken ceilidh came back to him in a sudden flush of hot embarrassment. He'd tried and failed before to remember how he'd got back to his car, and, in the grogginess of the hangover, had been unable recall anything. Now, as he sat at his kitchen table, he remembered, in sudden shocking detail, Gail Dean pushing herself against him. He remembered the heat of her body and the stud-like insistent buds pressing against his chest. Her hands had been soft on his skin when she pulled his shirt up and ran her fingers on his back. She'd called a name, not his, but another name, and she had fastened her mouth on his, kissing him hard, while leaning herself back on the table, drawing him into her sudden warmth. He now remembered the heat surround him. Her legs had come up to grasp him and he had plunged headlong into oblivion.

The memory stopped there. There had been nothing after that. Nothing at all until he had woken up.

The flush of embarrassment surged through him. Martin shoved himself back from the table and crossed to where the kettle was now bubbling, keen to have something to do to take his mind off the memory. He poured himself a big mug of black coffee and *click-click-click*, like the fast shutters of a camera, the pattern of focus sharpened. Sheila Garvie had poured something into his drink. It had tasted *wonderful*. And then, a few minutes later, his head had started to spin and he had followed Gail Dean into the anteroom and he had let her pull her into him, heedless of anything but the surge of heat and his own dizzy desire.

It had been the drink. *Another of her concoctions . . .*

Martin shook his head, ignoring the pounding behind his eyes. He picked up the cup and poured hot coffee, loaded with sugar, down his throat, ignoring the painful burn. He immediately poured another and sat still for a moment, trying to settle his mind into a state of calm. Finally he opened the drawer on the table, pulled out a spiral-bound notebook and flicked it open. He stared at the blank page for a moment and began to write down notes in a scribbled, fast longhand:

Sheila Garvie – Aleister Crowley – black magic 1922.
Caitlin – paralysed/moving – powder – Gail Dean??
Ley lines – Linnvale – cup stones – blood.
Cerunnos? Herne? – forest – tree – painting.
MacFarlane farmer – bull – 1720. Sheila Garvie?
Teddy bears – picnic – woods – Caitlin – river????
Haldane – animals – trees – boy?

He sat back and stared at his list. After a few moments, he leaned forward and drew curving lines with arrow points at either end, joining some of the words together until the whole page was crocheted with interconnections.

The pattern got clearer. The picture in his mind expanded.

It centred around Sheila Garvie. He remembered his first night in Linnvale. Her name had been mentioned then, in connection with the Preservation Society and the opposition to Duncan Haldane's felling and building. Someone had joked about her herbal remedies, something about wives using it on reluctant husbands. She had poured something into his drink and he'd been smothered in a haze of red, urgent heat. There had been a sudden and quite irresistible absence of reluctance.

And Caitlin. She was paralysed beyond all hope of recovery. *For life*. Yet now her legs were moving and she could *feel* again where there had been only flaccid numbness. Sheila Garvie had given her a powder *loaded* with toxins and poisons and instead of killing her it had brought life – quite impossibly – back to what had been dead. That same powder had transmuted the spaghetti into a wriggling, creepily *alive* tangle of worms. Martin recalled how they had looped and squirmed when he'd thrown them into the river. He'd thought he might have been hallucinating, but now he thought the absurdly *impossible* might have been *real*, that the powder had conferred some sort of vile life to an innocent, commonplace pot of pasta.

He'd drawn the lines between the dates, barbs pulling the numbers together. Was there a connection between 1922 and 1720? The old plate in the book which was still open on the table was unmistakably Sheila Garvie, perhaps a year or two younger than she looked now, but not – *no, definitely not* – more than fifty years younger. Caitlin had said the woman had been a girl when the farmer was crushed against the byre wall by his own bull, and yet the tombstone, moss-covered and worn with age, showed the man had died nearly three hundred years ago. The MacFarlane line in Linnvale – *Gleann Linn* – had died out in two generations. Had Sheila Garvie just been telling a story? *Had she*?

Or was there something *else*?

Martin ran a finger through his hair in a quick, exasperated sweep.

He tried to find the connection between the powder Caitlin had been drinking and the plants drawn on the old piece of wrinkled leather some archaeologist had found in a pot that had lain hidden for God knew how many thousands of years. The pharmacologist had told him some of the compounds were lethally toxic. The old Druid priests had used some of them in their ceremonies in the forest. Yet there were other things in the bittersweet mixture. Animal blood. Cells from insects and frogs. Snake poisons.

He thought hard while he drank his third cup. There was a connection somewhere. There was something he'd been told that he couldn't grab hold of. He shucked the thought away and went back to the scrawl on the paper.

He'd drawn the arrows between *trees* and *painting*. Another connection. He went back to the first book and riffled the pages until he found the reproduction of the ancient pictogram. There were the plants surrounding the massive tree. There was a small figure in front of it, arms raised. Other people were depicted in a circle around the trunk, drawn in a primitive absence of perspective. He stared at it and at the face growing out from the trunk. There was something familiar about the scene, something repulsive. His eyes scanned the picture, then he caught it. The central figure, directly in front of the monstrous, animalistic face, was not raising hands in the air. *There were* no *hands*. The arms stopped short at the wrists. Martin leaned forward to get a closer look. It was hard to make out among what were obviously wrinkles in the leather, but it looked as if the figure's hands were shoved *into* the tree, pressing *beneath* the bark. It could have been a simple artist's mistake, but there was something about the oddity that sent a small shiver of unease rippling under the skin on Martin's back.

He closed his eyes and concentrated. There was something about the *tree*, something tantalisingly *familiar*.

He looked at his scribbled notes, words drawn in columns, then his eyes flicked to the old drawing and it hit him with a sudden snap of recognition.

It was the tree from Caitlin's painting.

The cold prickling intensified, like nails scraping down between his shoulder-blades.

The massive dead oak that had started as a faint misty shadow had been redefined, over and over again until it dominated

Caitlin's picture. Martin closed his eyes again, recreating the visual memory. It had stood in the clearing, a colossal image of a forest giant. The trunk had been gnarled and massive and, high up, it bifurcated into a pair of cumbrous limbs, knotted and twisted. He opened his eyes and looked at the picture. It was another dead tree, though the ancient artist had drawn in stylised buds on the ends of the branches. It had two huge branches splitting from the colossal trunk, dwarfing the figure in front.

There were just too many coincidences, Martin told himself. The thought that came hard on the heels of that was: *There's something badly* wrong *here.*

There was something *seriously* out of kilter. He didn't know yet what it was, but he was determined to find out. There were so many things that he did not understand, words on his list that were interconnected in some way that he intuitively knew but could not explain.

Teddy bears. He had written that without even being aware of it. The image had popped into his mind and his hand had automatically scribbled the words. That tune was infuriating and banal, but when he was driving along in his Land-Rover he would find himself whistling it, or humming it, until he caught himself short and tried to think of another tune to sing.

The teddy bear, that creepy memory from the night up in the flat in Blackhale when the video monitor had started to fizz and crackle. There had been something eerily *alive* about that glittering eye staring from the flickering screen. He remembered, with another creepy shiver, the skinny girl sitting up on the bed, black eyes blank and sightless.

'*She's drowning,*' the flat drone came back to him. 'The forest. *There's still life.* Still life!'

And then the odd little stuffed toy had popped up in the back of Andrew's car, scaring him half to death.

He crossed the room to the sideboard where he kept his diary. It was just a slim pocket book which had arrived with many others at the office last Christmas. He flicked it open, trying to decipher his almost illegible scrawl, a legacy from a lifetime of taking shorthand notes. He'd been run off the road by a sudden, terrifying black shape two weeks before. A similar thing had happened to Caitlin two weeks before that. He did a back calculation to the Friday when it must have happened, according to Caitlin's story. The date popped into his head and he crackled the pages in his haste to find the entry.

He turned the last fine leaf, and there it was, written in quite neatly: *Ghostbusting. Andy Toye. Blackhale. Crazy, eh?*

He recalled writing the words, smirking as he did so, convinced that the poltergeist episode was a figment of someone's imagination, water gurgling in pipes, or just a stunt to get some money from the newspaper.

He hadn't been prepared for the sudden, mindless *dread* that had flooded him, the scrabbling shivers of cold twisting the muscles of his spine and making his blood feel as if it was congealing in the big arteries under his jawline.

The girl's dead words had been spoken on the same night that Caitlin Brook had been attacked and had tumbled into the black pool on the River Corrie.

She had been *drowning*.

Martin sat for a moment, eyes unfocused, remembering the pale girl, while his heart thudded almost painfully against his ribs.

She *had* been speaking to *him*. She *had* been *warning* him of something. Warning him that Caitlin was drowning. And warning him about something *else*. The teddy bear. Somehow his attention had been riveted on that unnerving little toy and the song had been going round in his head for weeks.

He had been *warned*. Not just about Caitlin Brook. It went deeper than that.

The little girl, in the seconds before she bled onto the sheets, had been connected to something, plugged in to some *power*. It had been like the momentary terrifying connection that had locked Martin into Caitlin Brook's mind almost two years before, just as she plummeted from the balcony onto the back-breaking wall.

Whatever source of prescience the girl had been tapped into, she had *known* Caitlin was on the point of death. And she had *known* there was danger for Martin Thornton.

She was telling him not to go down to the woods.

The *woods*.

That tune again. The woods. Where you're sure of a big *surprise*. Where you'll never believe your *eyes*.

It, whatever *It* was, was in Fasach Woods. Where Sheila Garvie took Caitlin for walks almost every day.

Martin had heard of cold sweat. Now, for the first time, he experienced it. A damp perspiration suddenly clammed his forehead and he could feel a trickle of ice down at the base of his spine. His stomach clenched in an involuntary spasm and he had to hold on to the edge of the table for several seconds until the moment passed.

He was now sure that Caitlin Brook was in danger. He didn't know yet exactly what kind of danger, but he knew for certain, clearly and absolutely, that she was in awful *peril*.

Martin squeezed his eyes shut and took several deep breaths, ventilating hard. When he opened them again his vision wavered on the brief crest of an oxygen high. He marshalled his thoughts, deciding on what he must do, before shoving his chair back and crossing the room to the phone. He dialled the number and, when the reply came, he asked for the Department of Celtic Mythology. The extension number rang for more than half a minute while he waited, jittering with impatience.

Finally the other receiver was lifted and a familiar voice came on the line.

'Who?' Finlay Carmyllie asked.

'Martin Thornton. I met you yesterday with Andrew Toye.'

'Oh yes, young fellow. Can't forget you've got my books. Don't give them to that absent-minded spook-hunter.'

Martin assured him he wouldn't then asked if the old professor could help him some more.

'There's a name that keeps cropping up,' he said. 'I'm not sure what it means.'

'Fire away, old boy.'

'The *Garbh-aidh*.'

'Never heard of it,' the professor told him flatly.

'It's in the three books. It's a Celtic name.'

Martin repeated it and then spelled it out.

Immediately there was a throaty chuckle of laughter.

'And you're a Scotsman, eh?' the professor managed to get out through the laughter. 'That's *Gaelic*. Language of the Gods. You should be ashamed.'

Martin clenched his teeth together and *willed* him to get to the point.

'It's pronounced *Garv-ay*. Roughly translated it means *wildness*, or *wilderness*. The haunt of wild spirits.'

The name clicked with a jolt in Martin's mind.

'And there's another name. I read it in Friel's book. It says the *Seilach Garv-ay*.' He tried to get the pronunciation of the second word correct this time and got another burst of laughter for his pains.

'That's a *name*, silly boy. An old one and a modern one. Really, you should spend some time in the Western Isles and pick up some of your native tongue.'

At the moment Martin felt like grabbing the jovial old academic and using pliers on *his* tongue.

'It's not *Seilach*,' Finlay went on, 'it's *Sheila*. All the druid high priests took the names of trees. Sheila means *willow*. Seilach Garbh-aidh would mean *willow-of-the-wilderness*. Probably had some symbolic connotation with the healing powers of the willow. They've been known for thousands of years.'

Something else *clicked* in Martin's mind.

'And the high priests,' he went on, realising he was speaking too quickly. 'Could they be female, or were they all men?'

'Either. Didn't have gender divisions in the Celtic culture. Natural egalitarians, old boy. Even the women went to war as a matter of honour.'

'And the high priests,' Martin interjected, running over the old man's words. 'When they used those plants and the cup-and-ring stones, what were they trying to do?'

'Oh, raise the power of Cerunnos. Bring him to life.'

'And the person in front of the tree in the old drawing?'

'That was the sacrifice. They tied a virgin to a tree on the night of the full moon and Cerunnos took her to the underworld. It was a kind of marriage which made the land fertile and gave the priests power.'

'And did it work?' Martin asked without thinking, immediately realising how stupid *that* sounded.

But the professor didn't seem to notice.

'*They* believed that it did. There's some folk believe Merlin is still trapped in a crystal cave. People now believe in the Holy Trinity and flying saucers. I'd hate to judge, but I'd like to think that it *did* work. There's too little magic in today's boring old world.'

404

Martin tried to get his jumbled thoughts in order. The professor's voice crackled tinnily from the receiver. Martin vaguely caught something about the Celts being a very ecological society who believed that all living life was joined and inter-connected and, furthermore, connected to the dead places of the underworld.

He let the old man talk on for a few minutes more, before thanking him and promising to get the books back to him soon. He put the phone down and stood still for a few moments, holding his breath.

The pattern was almost there. Almost complete.

He picked it up again and dialled a longer number. The phone burred in his ear. He let it ring nearly thirty times, but there was no reply. He pressed the clicker with his finger and punched in a series that only differed from the first by two digits.

Alec Stirling answered on the third ring. He was eating something and his voice sounded momentarily muffled.

'Alec? Martin.'

'Hey, boss. Thought you'd lost interest.'

'No. I'm coming down to Linnvale. That boy you mentioned . . .?'

'Craig Buist. I reckon he's done in his daddy.'

'Aye, maybe. I want to speak to him.'

'Have you got a bulletproof vest?'

'What?'

'Only kidding. The boy's a bundle of nerves. Nearly took my head off with two barrels of w.f. shot.'

'I have to talk to him.'

'That's what I thought you said,' Alec said, with some resignation.

'I'll be down in an hour. I'll see you at your place.'

'This will cost you plenty.'

'Nothing changes,' Martin said, managing a small smile.

But he knew that things *were* changing, and so quickly he could barely comprehend them.

He now had some idea of what *might* be happening down in Linnvale. He hoped he was wrong but, inside himself, in the cold shiver that still chased up and down his spine, he feared he was not.

He had to get to the glen quickly. And he had to see Caitlin Brook.

405

29

Sheila Garvie was talking in a low voice, almost a whisper. Her words came in a sing-song cadence, a lulling chant. Caitlin Brook sat opposite her on a rush mat on the floor. The girl was sitting with her legs crossed, both arms stretched in front of her, each one clasped by Sheila's own.

The basement room was dark and shadowed. The only light came from an oil lamp on top of an old wooden dresser whose surface had been intricately carved to resemble leaves. In the flickering light, the leaves and vine-shoots seemed to have life of their own. Sheila's deep-set eyes were dark yet luminous in her pale face. Caitlin's own eyes were closed.

Caitlin had come down to Sheila's house in her wheelchair. She had closed the gate behind her and swivelled round to face down the slope of the lane and eased herself forward with slow pushes on the rims. Just as she passed the end of the privet hedge she thought she heard a bell ringing and stopped, head cocked to the side. A curlew piped up on the hill and down at the edge of the stand of saplings a blackbird warbled liquid music. Caitlin waited impatiently until both sounds died down then listened intently again. The ringing sound was very faint but she recognised it finally as her telephone. Martin hadn't called her in several days. He'd promised to come down almost two weeks before, but then he'd called from Shetland to say he'd been covering a story and would have to cancel. Since then she'd heard nothing and had been more disappointed than concerned. She wasn't quite sure how she felt about Martin Thornton though she *was* sure she wanted to see him again.

Caitlin hauled back on the right wheel while pushing forward on the left, expertly spinning the chair to face back the way she'd come. She was about twenty yards from the gate and powered herself fast up the slope, easily taking the strain on her shoulders and arms. The latch on the inside was awkward to grasp and Caitlin cursed under her breath as she jiggled with the paint-encrusted catch while the telephone trilled insistently. She finally got the metal to move and it snapped open, allowing the wooden gate to swing back against the hedge while Caitlin drove herself onto the flagstones of the path. At the door she had to stop and fish in the pocket of her jeans for her key. She found it and reached up to turn it in the Yale lock. Just as the door opened, the phone abruptly stopped ringing. Silence descended on the cottage.

Caitlin sat there for several moments on the threshold, hoping it would start again. But the moment stretched on and the telephone remained silent.

'Damn,' she said aloud. With a quick jerk, she slammed the door shut and went back down the path, itching with exasperation.

In Glasgow Martin Thornton slapped the receiver onto the cradle and made his call to Alec Stirling. When he'd done that, he let himself out of the flat and went down the stairs to the Land-Rover. He stopped twice in Glasgow to pick up a couple of things before driving west once more.

At the old millhouse Sheila Garvie welcomed Caitlin with a bright smile. ˜

'I thought you'd got lost,' she said. She opened the door and allowed Caitlin to propel herself inside. Before closing it again she stood on the doorstep, looking up and down the road. There was no one there.

She turned to the girl in the wheelchair.

'And how are you today?'

'Wonderful,' Caitlin replied. 'Getting better by the hour. I just can't believe it.'

'But we're as well to keep it to ourselves for the time being, hmm?'

'Of course.'

'You've not told anyone?'

'No, I haven't,' Caitlin said quickly. Immediately she remembered the excitement of showing Martin the tiny movements in her toes. But that had been a fortnight ago. Now he just wouldn't believe what was happening to her.

'So, show me!' Sheila commanded.

Caitlin looked at her for a long moment. She kept her green eyes locked on Sheila's and gripped the arms of the chair. Her knuckles stood out white as she pulled herself forward. Her feet slowly slipped from the plate and she braced them on the floor.

Then she raised herself to her feet.

Sheila nodded, unable to keep the smile of satisfaction from her face. Caitlin gave a little laugh of sheer exuberance. She straightened up and then walked towards the other woman, keeping her eyes locked on hers. There was no shakiness any more. Her step was careful, but sure. It took her eight steps to cross the room.

'There,' Sheila said. 'What did I tell you? And there's better to come, I *promise*.'

'I believe you,' Caitlin said earnestly. 'I do, really.'

'Of course you should. Come on. I take it you can make it to the kitchen. I've made dinner for us both. And I've got more medicine for you. We've got one more thing to do then you'll be running like the wind.'

The very thought of it made Caitlin's heart leap.

In ten days, since the night of the *ceilidh*, she'd seen her whole life take another somersault, and this time she had landed, quite literally, on her feet again.

Since showing Martin the movement in her toes the sense of *touch* had slowly returned to her legs. It had started as numb tingling where before there had been *nothing*. On the third day she could lift her foot an inch or two from the plate before the effort became too great and dragged it back down again. Then her legs had started to itch under the skin. The muscles had twisted and jumped and trembled as if they had life of their own. Then, on the following morning, the jittering sensation had died down. Real feeling was returning so quickly she could hardly comprehend it. On the seventh day, under Sheila's direction and having agreed to say nothing to anyone about the miracle, she had levered herself up from the chair to stand, tottering, arms waving wildly for balance, for a few moments before Sheila caught her and eased her back down onto the seat.

After that night Sheila Garvie had been an almost constant presence. She made Caitlin take ever-increasing amounts of her mixture and Caitlin herself noticed that the concentration of the infusions was ever stronger. Where at the start the liquid had been sweet and deliciously perfumed, the taste had now gradually altered to a bitter, astringent sourness, with an oily, viscous texture. While Caitlin noticed the difference, it had happened so gradually that it did not seem unpleasant, and even if it *had* she wouldn't have cared. She knew it was working a miracle within her own body, making nerve endings grow again, strengthening dead and flaccid muscles, giving her *life*.

And each might she came down to Sheila Garvie's quaint old millhouse beside the black stream to sit on a straw mat down in the cavernous basement while Sheila would first of all rub pungent oils into the skin of her back and her legs and then, holding hands with the younger woman, she would begin the low, slow chant that would make Caitlin's body sway and her eyelids droop until there was nothing but darkness and the sound of the song as she drifted off into the world of the dream.

But now the dream was *different*. She was no longer running.

She was *there* in the middle of the forest clearing. All around was darkness and the rustling sounds of growth. In front of her was the tree, massive and gaunt, wider than the span of her out-stretched arms. She was dressed in white, a soft flowing material that felt like silken gauze. Her arms were bare and there was no breeze to stir the red fire of her hair. There were people there, around her, in a circle, but out of focus. Her eyes were intent, fixed on the tree. Already buds were forcing themselves from the surface of the bare branches and she could feel burgeoning life expanding with irresistible force within. It was the tree of her painting, the tree in her running dreams. It was the tree that had been drawing her towards it for weeks. Sheila was beside her, unseen, willing her onwards.

She walked – or *floated*, she couldn't tell which – towards it and touched the bark. Immediately there was a tremor, as if something had swelled under the dragon's-skin surface, as if a muscle had twitched in response to the gossamer touch.

The bark rippled and knotted with a life of its own, but Caitlin was unsurprised. Part of her wanted to go forward to the tree, to press against it until she was at one with its life.

Yet another faraway part of her mind was *afraid*.

In the curious world of the dream she felt the conflict within her. Beside and behind, Sheila was urging her onwards. She could sense the other shadowed people around her *willing* her forward.

Something held her back. The bark of the tree writhed expectantly, almost sensuously. Within the wood she could hear tiny creaks and groans. Under her feet the ground trembled as roots pulsed and squirmed.

Yet there was something *wrong*. She couldn't move forward and couldn't step backwards. Sheila whispered something in her ear and she half turned and then, quite suddenly, from the far side of the clearing, a man's voice called her name.

'Caitlin. *Stop!*'

She turned and looked at Sheila Garvie. The smile on her face was fixed, frozen. Her eyes had gone black as hot tar.

'*Go on*,' the other woman ordered in a whisper that was a hiss of breath. '*Go to him!*'

Caitlin half turned back to the tree. She could hear the wood straining and twisting under the pressure of its own movement. She sensed the life within it, tugging and pulling at her.

Then again the man's voice came, calling her name, faint but clear in the distance, beyond the far side of the clearing.

She felt her legs begin to buckle, as if the new strength in them had drained away. The trees in the night clearing blurred and swayed in the still air. Sheila Garvie came towards her, eyes drilling into hers with such intensity it looked like fury.

And then Caitlin was falling. The world spun, just as it had done on her first, terrifying visit to the forest when she had tumbled from her wheelchair and catapulted through the trees and down into the water.

Then she woke with such a start she toppled forwards.

Sheila caught her as she slipped sideways, out of balance, mind floundering to keep a grip on the dream.

'What's . . .?' she started to say.

'Hush, girl. You're safe here,' Sheila whispered gently.

'I was . . .' Caitlin started again. She was *what*? She searched for the word, holding tight to the other woman's shoulders. The odd dream had broken into fragments and scattered on the point of wakening. It flickered and faded and fled. She tried to catch the fleeting remnants, but it was no use. The dream was *gone*.

The oil lamp fluttered behind the glass and the smell of the burning herbs was thick in the air.

'Almost ready,' Sheila said softly. 'But *you* have to decide.'

'Decide what?'

'Whether you want to be *whole* again. It must be your choice. You have to *wish* it.'

'What do you mean, *whole*?'

'Complete. As you were before. You have to want to *run*!'

'Oh,' Caitlin said, 'I *do*.'

'You will have to do something for me.'

'Anything. You've done so much for me. I'll never be able to pay you back.'

'Oh yes, you will, my dear,' Sheila said, and her eyes crinkled up in the corners. 'You will, believe me.'

Martin Thornton drove fast along the Loch Shore Road. The sense of ominous foreboding sat heavy on his shoulders and the muscles below his ribs were tight with anxiety. Over and over in his mind he heard the flat words of the Reid girl's eerie warning.

Still life.

Sometime between going to bed and his early breakfast, he'd become a convert. He had sat and written down everything he knew on a torn sheet of his shorthand notebook and the pattern had *clicked*. It was like putting the pieces of a big jigsaw together, seeing the picture take shape.

He was dreadfully worried for Caitlin Brook. She was in danger. He knew that for a fact. Worse, might be too late to do anything about it. His stomach muscles clenched and unclenched in a series of spasmodic grips.

Sheila Garvie was using Cartlin. She had filled her up with toxins and poisons and God knew what else, and she planned to use Caitlin in some *prehistoric* pagan ritual. He recalled the night of the ceilidh and remembered the look of smug triumph on the woman's face. He remembered when he'd first met her, how he'd felt her cold eyes on him, her cool rebuff.

Martin was not quite ready to believe that the ritual Sheila Garvie had planned would actually *work*. That thought hadn't entered his head. But he had read enough and discovered enough to know that Garvie herself probably believed it. She meant to take Caitlin into the woods and sacrifice her to a dead tree. The books had told him what would happen. Her blood would be poured onto the cup-and-ring stones to drain into the earth. Still drugged with whatever poisons Garvie had fed her, she would be lashed to the big oak tree for the final sacrifice.

Another spasm of anxiety gripped him when he thought of that. He stamped down on the accelerator and gunned the jeep forward, swerving out to rattle past a slow-moving saloon car filled with wide-mouthed tourists waxing lyrical over the stunning beauty of the hills on the far side of Loch Corran. Martin saw none of that. His mind was fixed on the road. Way ahead the early-morning sky was darkening with clouds rolling in from the west. Already there was a chill in the air and a tightness of low pressure that carried the threat of thunderstorms. The long hot spell of weather was beginning to crack.

He got to the series of bends which had confused him before and counted them off again. He slowed reluctantly and again overshot the turning. The sign was so overgrown with ivy that it looked more like the stump of a dead tree.

He skidded to a halt, big tyres churning up the small stones at the edge of the road, and slammed the gear into reverse. The Land-Rover juddered and shot backwards several yards. A loud blare hard by Martin's elbow made him physically jump in his seat. The car he had passed earlier fishtailed as the driver fought to keep the wheels straight on the road. Martin got an impression of a white face in the passenger seat and realised that his sudden reversing had steered him right into the tourists' path. He watched, breathing hard, as the saloon's wheels ground into the verge, then let out a sigh as the car steadied and got back onto the road. There was a flash of brake lights and then the other car continued on its way. Martin knew its driver would be cursing him comprehensively and that his hands would be shaking on the wheel as much as his own. The saloon disappeared round a bend and Martin sat at the wheel of the jeep for a moment before he hauled the wheel to the left and headed up the Linnvale road.

If he hadn't known about it, he would have sworn there was *no* road here. He cast his mind back to a fortnight – *was it only two weeks?* – before, when he had missed the turn. Then the tree branches had been reaching down, badly in need of cutting back. Now they almost hid the road completely. They trailed right down to less than six feet from the road surface, heavy with broad leaves. Even the verge was overgrown with wild hawthorn and privet. Bramble runners stretched a quarter of the way across from each side, scratching at the side steps on the jeep. Martin could hear the crackle as they were crushed under the tyres. The Linn Road looked as if it hadn't been used for years.

It looked like a road to nowhere.

30

Caitlin's heart was beating fast with the surge of anticipation.

Sheila took the girl's hands from her shoulders and rose to her feet. She moved across the room to the table covered with tall, dusty jars containing liquids and powders. She brought a small bottle with a glass stopper and sat down again on the rush mat in front of Caitlin.

She removed the cap with a small popping sound and immediately the air was suffused with a pungent smell. Caitlin's nostrils wrinkled as the scent wafted towards her.

'This is very strong. The most powerful so far. We are almost at the end.'

Caitlin simply nodded.

'You must drink it all,' Sheila added.

The girl said nothing. She reached forward with both hands and took the bottle eagerly.

'All of it,' Sheila said.

Caitlin raised the small, dark bottle to her lips. The smell was almost overpowering, but she ignored it. She tilted her head back and poured the liquid down her throat in one swift motion.

As soon as the thick liquid hit the back of her throat she tried to scream, but the pain was too intense. Her mouth and neck were clamped in a hand of fire. The burning was so fierce that she felt herself rocking backwards and forwards, mouth agape, desperately trying to shake it away.

'Forget the pain. That is the price you pay. It will be gone soon,' Sheila's voice came through the fire from far away. The scream was still backed up inside Caitlin, but she couldn't get rid of it. The river of fire drilled and twisted its way into her belly and then expanded through her veins. White heat sleeted along her arms and down into her legs, sizzling as it went, like acid.

She fell back with a thump against the wooden floor, eyes tight shut and lips pulled back in a rictus of agony. All she could think of was the dreadful suffering hurtling like an agony express through her. Her whole body writhed in an attempt to escape it and she knew, if she could only scream, some of the terrible pressure might go away. But her throat was locked tight – *burned away,* came the dreadful thought – and the pressure filled her head and she felt her consciousness soar up and out.

'*I'm dying,*' she thought dumbly.

Darkness closed in on her and then she was gone.

There were no dreams here in the dead place. Images came to swim close to her, eerie, ghostly faces that zoomed in to her mind's view.

Her mother's face coalesced out of a grey cloud and snapped into focus. She was saying something but Caitlin couldn't hear it. The image began to fragment and she tried to call out to her to come back, but the face was turning away from her even as it changed back into smoke again and was blown away.

Out from the dark Martin Thornton came running towards her, arms outstretched, trying to catch her as she fell, but she could see he was running too slowly. His mouth was working frantically in the dread silence of this dark place. She knew he was shouting her name but still no sound came. The wall came up towards her as she swooped and she felt the snap of her back and the tearing of the muscles and then she too was breaking up. Her mind soared off, back to the days of her childhood, to this valley where the sun shone on summer days and her grandfather would take her up to the Corrie Linn where they would fish until the sun dipped behind the Dumbuie Hills and then they'd take the winding path down the slope again towards the cottage. Ahead of them Fasach Wood was wide and dark, a blanket of night rumpled at the base of the valley in the gloaming.

'*You stay out of those trees, girl,*' a voice spoke into her mind, and she didn't know if it was her grandfather or somebody else. The scene flipped and she was in the hospital, lying on her front, straddling the table. Urgent voices were to right and left. There was a bleeping noise from a machine, an insistent pulse of information. Something was making her breathe, forcing its way into her mouth and down her throat, pumping oxygen into her. There were hands on her back and nagging pains in her arms where they'd stuck the tubes.

'Vertical incision,' a voice droned, so low it was like a tape played slowly. Something touched her skin and she felt the pain as the skin parted.

'They're *operating* on me.' She heard her own voice inside her head.

The scalpel cut in and drew a line through muscle and a new pain erupted.

Something dug into her back. She could feel the jagged ends of fractured bones grind together, like broken teeth. The agony was colossal.

'*Drill*,' the sonorous voice took an age to say. Way in the distance there was a low buzzing sound, like a hive of bees turned out to swarm under the trees. Something touched her low down on her spine and the previous pain faded to a tickle by comparison. The drill bit chewed into her bones like a mad corkscrew and Caitlin still couldn't move, or blink, or *scream*. The pain went on and on and on, ripping into her, tearing her apart. Her whole world was a screaming *hurt*.

Vibration juddered through her. She felt the table underneath her shiver with the force of it and then she was falling.

The drill was still inside her bones, grinding away, boring into her as she slipped to the side and began to topple from the bench.

'It's all right now,' a slow voice echoed.

And Caitlin came back again.

There was still fire in her throat. A sharp pain pulsed between her hips, but it was nothing to the pain she had experienced before.

She gave a little gasp and then flopped forward again, cheek banging heavily against the cold floor.

'Oh, *God*,' she groaned. 'What's happening to me?' Her voice was husky and ragged.

'We're almost there, child,' Sheila's voice came through the aching mist. 'And your God has nothing to do with it,' she said.

Caitlin lay there, eyes still closed, while the other woman gave a low chuckle.

Finally she raised her head up from the floor and used her arms to push herself round until she reclined on her hip. Every little movement caused her to grunt with exertion.

'The pain will go soon. You'll see. It was something that had to be done.'

'What on earth happened to me?' Caitlin managed to gasp.

Sheila said nothing. Her dark eyes were dancing. She held up her hand and opened it. A metallic insect nestled on her palm, glinting in the light. There was blood on its shiny surface.

'What's that?' Caitlin asked, though there was something about the shape of it that was eerily familiar. Her mind searched for the memory. She felt nausea rise in her aching throat.

Finally it dawned. She had seen the shape before, on the light-cabinet on the hospital wall, when Dr MacDonald had explained to her exactly what they'd had to do to her, to keep her from falling apart.

'*But that's* . . .'

Sheila grinned, nodding. Satisfaction was written large on her face.

The insectile shape was in two segments, a metal thorax and abdomen. Curved legs hooked out from either side in little claws. The two metal plates had fitted the curve of her broken backbone perfectly. The claws on either side were where they had clamped themselves on the battered vertebrae. There were little holes where the pure metal screws had been fixed into the hard calcium.

It was the brace the surgeons had fitted inside her to keep her spine together. Now it nestled in Sheila's hand, still gleaming in the light of the oil lamp.

'This can't be *real*,' Caitlin finally managed to say. She could not comprehend what had happened. It was *impossible*.

'Oh, it is real. Believe me,' Sheila said, voice shaking with the intensity of triumph. 'Now you are *whole* again. It had to be done, and now the pain is over. Tomorrow you will run like the wind.'

The fire still burned in Caitlin's throat and the ache still pulsed in her back, but they were fading slowly. Caitlin sat up gingerly, bewildered. She reached behind her and ran her fingers down the bumps in her spine. She came to the place, just below the level of her hips, where the scars of the operation ridged themselves out from the smooth surface.

But the scars were gone.

Her skin was unblemished all the way down.

She turned to Sheila, eyes wide.

'No. Not a miracle,' Sheila said solemnly. 'That's the *power*.'

*

A big weeping ash branch smacked against the windscreen, leaving a green smear and startling Martin into slowing down. There was a lush, wet smell in the air, the kind of thick, damp odour he'd smelled in the hothouse in the botanical gardens up near the university. Wild, unfettered growth.

He eased the jeep forward, hearing the twigs and leaves of the overhanging branches scrape along the roof. Maybe it was his imagination, but they seemed to crowd the road more closely, as if they had moved themselves to form a barrier against intrusion. Whatever it was, the Linn Road was narrower and harder than ever to negotiate. It wouldn't take much for the lane to be completely hidden from view, impassable to anything without all-weather tyres and four-wheel drive.

Martin kept his window rolled up to prevent the branches whipping into the cab as he passed, but the green smell and the musky scent of pollen oozed through the vents to catch in the back of his throat. He levered the gearstick into third and took the three bends slowly, pushing his way along the narrowing road until he saw sunlight ahead. He broke through the lochside belt of trees into the open glen and allowed the jeep to gain speed on the climb to Linnvale. Even here, beyond the trailing and crowded foliage, there was a change in the place. Two weeks before, the hawthorn hedges that lined the road had been trimmed back to form even walls of tight bush. Now, fresh growth was shooting out in all directions for three feet on either side. He noticed that some of the branches had been snapped backwards by passing tractors or trucks, probably the big bowsers from the MacKinnon calor depot.

On the breast of the hill he got a clear view of the lower valley. He slowed down before the turn, just at the point where Alec Stirling had stopped to talk to the Buist boy. The field on the left, which swept down towards the river, was a riot of high thistles and dockens. Already the thistle-heads were white with silk as the seeds swelled, ready to burst and scatter. The field was a spiky mass entangled in spider gossamer. In the early morning light, with the big clouds building up from the west, it looked eerie and foreign. He drove on.

All the way down from Glasgow Martin had been thinking about what he was going to say to Caitlin. He knew he couldn't just blurt out that Sheila Garvie was feeding her a load of poison and planned to take her into the woods and drain her blood into the ground. She would look at him as if he was mad.

There was no answer to his heavy rap on the old wooden door. He leaned up to the window and held a hand over his eyes to cut down reflection and peered inside. The small living room was dark and shadowed behind the half-closed curtains. There was a magazine lying on the floor and a nightdress casually slung over the back of the small lounger, but there was no one there. He shoved himself away from the window and went round the side, walking on the flagstones and trying to avoid crushing the colourful tangles of orange-trumpeted nasturtium flowers.

The garden was empty. He stood at the corner, the way he had done on his first visit, and surveyed the scene. The early summer sunlight from the east spangled through the saplings at the edge of the stream and planted dots of glimmer on the flowers and the lawn, but the quality of the light had that weakened lustre of impending rain.

He tried the back door, found it unlocked and, after a moment's hesitation, let himself in.

The cottage was quiet and still. He stood in the doorway for a minute, feet angled on the little ramp he'd made for Caitlin, and surveyed the kitchen. She had put the sketch of him into a light pine frame and hung it beside the table. Martin looked at himself looking back over his shoulder and smiled wryly. He didn't look worried in the sketch, but it was more than a month since she'd drawn those lines. He'd had nothing much to worry about then.

There was still warmth on the stove. Martin put his hand over the flat plate and felt the residual heat. The nagging cold in the back of his spine eased a little. She had been here very recently. He walked through to Caitlin's bedroom. As soon as he opened the door, he smelled her light perfume and the calid closeness of a room where a woman had slept the night. The light eiderdown had been rolled down to the foot of the bed and the thin sheet she'd pulled over herself in the sultry night was lying rumpled and thrown back. His anxiety relaxed another notch.

Caitlin's excerciser dangled from the frame at the edge of the bed. It looked like an instrument of torture. Beyond it, angled on the dresser against the wall, a paint-streaked flannel covered a rectangular shape. Martin gently pulled it back and saw her painting.

For a second he was completely thrown off balance. His breath drew in tight and locked and immediately the fingers of cold unease started their scrabble on his spine.

The scene had *changed*.

The conifers seemed to have edged back from the picture, almost a mere frame for the dominance of the mighty tree that stood athwart the centre, a study in bleak power.

The ancient oak stood swollen and gnarled, trunk bulging, bark peeled and rugged. It forked into ponderous boughs which branched ever smaller as they reached for the unseen sky. There was a stark bareness about the tree, but the thick branches had the hint of green buds pushing their way out from the surface, as if new life was swelling within.

Yet that was not what caught Martin's eye and made his breath stay hitched and locked for a long moment.

It was the surface of the trunk itself, bark cross-hatched and rutted. The paint had been slashed on with hard, bold strokes, layer upon layer, almost making the tree stand out in relief on the canvas. Clearly this part had been painted over and over again. It was shadowed and lichen-green, and the way the shades mixed and merged made the trunk seem to have life of its own. And there was something else. Martin's eyes, riveted to the pattern of shadows and hollows, brought a kind of mad order to the chaos of dirty colours.

It was like recognising the bawling mad face in the craters of the full moon on a summer's night.

Here was the hollow of a cheek, there the jut of a jawline. Above them, a furrowed, frowning brow. The eyes were black holes and the ridges on the bark were like teeth in a mouth pulled back in a rictus of effort or anger. It looked as if the face was *shoving* its way from the tortured wood, ramming its way into the clearing.

With a sudden jerk Martin drew his hand away. The oily rag fell down to cover the painting once more. It was as if someone had thrown a switch on a film projector, cutting off the light. The oppressive sense of menace was instantly dissipated.

Martin shivered in the warm air of the bedroom. There was a cold trickle low down on his back and he realised it was sweat.

420

Martin backed out of the room. His hip nudged the doorframe and he stepped into the corridor, drawing the door closed. It shut with a thud that was suddenly all too loud in the empty house.

Back in the kitchen, where the sun managed to shine through the saplings and in through the window, giving a semblance of daylight normality, he lowered himself onto one of the chairs and put his elbows on the table.

His mind was jumping around, trying to latch itself on to the rush of thoughts yelling for his attention. He gave his head a shake and tried to concentrate.

The tree. That had thrown him, and not just because of the chilling sense of threat that had come off the canvas in palpable waves. No, it was much more than that.

It was the tree that he'd seen in the photograph of the old pictogram in the book. It was the one that had been surrounded by the crudely-drawn stick people. The shape was there, the same massive trunk and the heavy forked boughs. There had been a figure in front of the tree and, above its head, there had been a feral face glaring down.

Caitlin's tree was the *same*. It was bursting with the threat of life and the face, only a pattern of shadows and hollows, was alive with sinister power.

Where had she got the image from?

Did she know about the old drawing? Or was there something more?

He remembered seeing the painting for the first time, when he had admired the delicate touches of the fine sable brush which brought to life the fine larch bristles and the chestnut leaves. But now they had been overshadowed by the heavy slashes that had been used to flesh ou. – *an odd choice of phrase,* Martin told himself – the tree at the centre of the clearing. It looked as if it had been painted in anger, maybe even in haste, as if the artist had been *driven*.

Whatever the reason for the grotesque and unnerving evolution on the canvas, it worried Martin Thornton.

Martin wasn't ready to believe there was any substance in the old Druidic rituals. All he knew was that the mysterious Sheila Garvie was feeding people poisons and toxins and mind-altering potions and that she was planning to go one step further. Caitlin

421

Brook, he believed he knew for certain, was involved in that next step. Martin Thornton knew he would have to stop it.

He sat for a few moments more, considering what to do, then shoved his chair back. It made a loud noise in the empty room. He went to the door, then stopped. Quickly he took his notebook from his pocket, the one that he'd used that morning to write his fragmentary list of words, and tore out a clean sheet. He bent over the table and wrote a note to Caitlin, then left it propped up against the salt cellar on the table. He'd written the note in bold capitals. It simply told her that he'd be back and that she *must* wait for him.

Back at the front of the cottage Martin clambered back into the Land-Rover and turned the engine over. It came to life with a rackety diesel clatter. As he swung away from the gate he saw the clouds piling up thick and dark over the Dumbuie peaks. They looked heavy and thunderous and full of rain.

Alec Stirling opened the door of his house at the end of the short terrace. He was still in his postman's blue trousers and was wearing a natty pair of non-regulation braces. His glasses as usual had slid down the ski-slope of his nose and the gangly man peered over the top of the rims.

'You took your time,' he said. 'I'm in the middle of my dinner.'

'Sorry. I got held up.'

'I thought you'd lost your nerve after the arse you made of yourself at the ceilidh. You reporters are supposed to be able to hold your drink.'

'You postmen certainly seem able to manage,' Martin shot back half-heartedly. He was in no mood for banter, but Alec was irrepressible.

'How's that bird of yours?'

'That's what I wanted to ask you,' Martin said. 'I've tried to call her, but she's never in.'

'Oh, I see her every morning, haring along in that hot rod of hers. Looks fine to me. Nice face, shame about the legs.' Martin shot him a look. 'Oh, no offence, boss. Just doesn't seem right for a bonny girl like that to be stuck in a wheelchair. Seems like an awful waste.'

'Yeah, I suppose you're right,' Martin allowed. Alec was such a straightforward talker that he couldn't take offence with him. In all the years the postman had been his stringer for this part of the west, he'd never heard him speak real malice of anyone.

Alec led him through to the living room and offered him a beer. Martin shook his head and asked for coffee instead. When the cup finally came he put three spoons of sugar in it and took a big drink, feeling it melt the chill inside him.

'This boy you were talking about?'

'Young Craig Buist. I reckon he's done in his old man. Couldn't happen to a nicer fellow, I have to tell you.'

'Have you told anybody else?'

'And lose my payment? You're kidding. If the bugger's dead, he's in no hurry. It's the boy I'm concerned about anyway. He looks as if he's not the full shilling. Nearly put a hole the size of a plate through me with that big shotgun Ernie Buist used to have on his wall. Said it was an accident, and I kind of believe him, but it was pretty bloody close. Sure cured my constipation, I can tell you.'

Martin grinned at the thought. It was the first time he'd smiled in two days.

'So what makes you think he's killed this farmer?'

'Well, I saw old Ernie chase after the boy down the field next to the Corrie. I had to shift his tractor out of the way to let Jock Weir past in his tanker and I've not seen hide nor hair of him since then. That was more than a fortnight ago. Ernie's a bad bugger. Mean as a stoat and worse in drink, and he'd had a few that day. He came at me as well and I accidentally kneed him in the balls, so it took a fair bit of bottle for me to go back up to his farm afterwards.' Alec gave Martin his biggest grin. 'But you know me. Can't keep my nose out of everybody's business.'

'So what happened?'

'They went off into the Fasach. The boy was streets ahead, faster than a ferret up a roanpipe, and the old man was coming after him like a Sherman tank. They both went into the trees and old Buist never came out. The funny thing is, the boy said the trees got him and I reckon that's probably true. I think young Craig picked up a branch and gave it to the old bastard on the back of the head. He's probably riddled with maggots by now. There was a lot of eating on old Ernie.' Alec screwed up his face at the thought. 'You can probably smell him from the edge of the woods, especially in this hot weather.'

'Delightful,' Martin told him. 'But what did the *boy* say again?'

'That's the funny part. I got up to their tumbledown only the other day and the wee bugger took a pot-shot at me. Oh, I told you that before, didn't I?' Martin nodded. 'It kind of sticks in my mind a lot.'

'It would,' Martin agreed.

'Well, then he starts to tell me how his father got stuck in the trees.'

'How do you mean *stuck*?'

'Well, stuck. How else do you say it?'

'I mean, caught in the branches? Snagged by the thorns? What?'

'No. Stuck. Like glue. The wee fella said old Ernie saw the bodies hanging from the branches. There was something about toadstools swelling up and exploding or some other rubbish . . .'

Something snagged Martin's memory. Little Ben Haldane had talked about mushrooms growing like balloons and then bursting, sending *stingers* out at him and his sister.

'. . . then he backed up against a tree and some kind of sap came out,' Alec was saying. 'Like pine resin. He said the old man got caught in it and was smothered. More likely smacked his father's head up against a pine tree.'

'What bodies?' Martin asked suddenly, as if he'd just heard them mentioned.

'The bodies in the branches,' Alec said matter-of-factly. 'At least that's what he told me.'

'What does that mean?'

'Damned if I know, boss. I'm telling you, the poor lad's away with the fairies.'

'I'd better have a word with him. Would you come up with me?'

'If I don't, you're liable to get a bellyful of lead shot. I was damned lucky.'

Martin finished his sweet coffee with one gulp and waited for Alec to haul himself into his jacket.

It took them only five minutes to get up the farm lane to the edge of the little yard. The smell of old ash still hung in the air, alongside another astringent odour that nipped their nostrils like

424

acid. At the edge of the yard where the old muddy cobbles gave way to the paddock, the grass was scorched black. The hedge was a tangle of leafless thorns and the wood was shrivelled and dead.

'He's been killing the weeds, poor bugger. Thinks they're coming to get him.'

Something in Alec's statement jarred again at Martin. The image had a surreal quality, yet it seemed to fit with what he'd learned in the last two days.

'Hey, young Craig,' Alec bawled at the top of his voice, startling Martin with the sudden noise in the quiet yard. 'Craig. It's me. Alec. The postman,' he shouted again, enunciating his words clearly.

There was a noise over by the byre. Both men swivelled towards it. The door was wide open. Alec pointed to it.

'There's where I nearly got two full barrels. See those holes in the door?' Martin nodded. 'That could have been me. Scared the living shite out of me.'

Just then there was a movement at the door. Martin watched as the shadow in the darkened byre resolved itself. A young boy of maybe fifteen edged warily outwards, a big double-barrel shotgun gripped in both hands.

'Hey, young fella. No shooting now,' Alec said with great sincerity.

'It's all right, Mr Stirling. I didn't mean it last time.'

Craig's eyes shifted to Martin.

'Who's that?'

'It's a friend of mine. He wants to have a word with you.'

'Is he the police?'

'No. I'm a friend of Alec's,' Martin called across. He began to walk slowly towards the boy, hands in his pockets. For a moment, the lad's eyes flicked left and right, gauging whether he should run or stay. Martin saw his knuckles whiten on the gun barrel and he felt his own heart start to pound.

'I'm not here to hurt you, son. I'm trying to help a friend of mine who might be in a bit of bother. I think maybe you could help me.'

'Who's that?' the boy asked. His face was dirty and he looked like a breath of wind might blow him away. His hair stood up in corkscrews as if he'd just awoken and, from a distance of several yards, Martin could see pieces of straw lodged in the tangles.

425

'Caitlin Brook. You know her?'

'Aye, mister. She helped me with my art exams. She's good.'

'Aye. I think so too.'

'I gave her flowers,' the boy added. The way he said it made him sound almost simple, but there was something behind his voice that told Martin otherwise. The way he stood, clutching the big gun, with all the colour drained out of his face, made Martin think he was a very frightened young boy indeed.

'You mind if we go inside?' Alec asked gently.

The boy's shoulders suddenly slumped, as if he was unable to hold out against whatever was straining inside of him. Martin saw his knees buckle just a little before he managed to gather himself again. He walked forward quickly, and put his arm around Craig Buist's shoulders and hooked a hand under the lad's armpit, taking the weight.

'Come on, Craig. Just lean on me and we'll get inside.'

Alec quite wisely kept himself on the other side, away from the business end of the old side-by-side gun.

They got into the house. It smelled damp and musty. The kitchen table was a mess of dirty plates. Alec put the kettle on and rummaged around until he found a few teabags lying at the bottom of a caddy. There was a pail of milk with a dirty muslin cloth draped over it. Alec wrinkled his nose, leaned over the bucket and sniffed. It was fresh enough. He shrugged and ladled some of the milk into a jug.

Martin sat the boy down and gently eased the gun out of his hands. It was heavy and solid and looked as if it could stop an elephant. He rested it in a corner, unsure of how to make it safe.

While Alec pottered over by the stove, Martin spoke to the boy, keeping his voice low.

'Craig. My friend Caitlin has a bit of a problem, and I think you've had some trouble yourself.'

The youngster nodded, sniffed, then wiped his nose with his sleeve.

'Something to do with the trees?'

'Aye, mister.'

'It's Martin. Okay?'

Craig nodded again.

'Can you tell me what happened?'

426

'The trees got him. They got those other people as well. They're dead. Like *skeletons*.'

'I don't understand, Craig. Tell me all of it, from the beginning.'

'It was down in Fasach Wood. My dad, he was chasing me. He'd been on the drink and he was pretty fearsome. I was dead scared. I kept on running 'cause I thought he was going to kill me. I really did. *Honest*.'

Martin nodded and kept silent.

'He was coming after me and I kept going until I got to the old dyke. But it was *different* there. Different from before.'

'What do you mean?'

'Like a different *place*. I've caught rabbits in those trees since I was wee. There's a bit in the middle that's like an old wall that's all fallen down. It goes round in a circle, where the big trees are. But this time it was not the same. It was *bigger*. And the trees were different too. It was like a jungle.'

Martin was about to ask something, but Craig just blurted on.

'It gave me the creeps. There was something wrong about it. There was big mushrooms like a yard high and beasties flying around. Like dragonflies, they were, but they were *so* big.' Craig held his hands out more than a foot apart, like an angler. 'Then I saw the bodies hanging on the tree. Jesus, mister . . . Martin . . . I was awfully scared. But my Da was coming right behind and I was scared to go back an 'all.'

'So then what?'

'I got into a hole in the wall and hunkered down and he came right past me. If he'd have turned then I'd have been . . .' Craig stopped and his eyes focused themselves in the distance, re-running the past, seeing for himself the *might-have-been*. A moment or two later, he gave a little start, swooping back to the present.

'My old man stopped right over there and he saw the bodies as well. There was an arm hanging down. All bones. It had a bracelet on it that was making a chinking noise and—'

Suddenly the boy's face went even paler. Martin watched him and saw it happen. The lad's eyes opened wide and the blood seemed to drain right away, making him look ghostly.

'I *know* who it was!' he exclaimed. 'I've *seen it before*!'

'Seen what, son?' Alec asked. He had a tray in his hands and

427

three steaming cups. He put them down on the floor between them, lifted one of the cups and passed it to Craig Buist. 'Get some of that down you, Craig. Do you the world of good.'

The boy's fingers hooked round the handle of the mug, but he appeared not even to have noticed it. Martin saw the ripples shivering on the surface of the tea, showing the palsied shake of Craig's hand.

'The bracelet. It was Mrs MacKinnon. You know, the one that went missing with Norrie Ritchie.'

'Betty MacKinnon?' Alec asked. 'Couldn't have been her, son. Sure, she ran off *months* ago.'

'It *was* her, Mr Stirling. It was the bracelet. I remember it now. A big gold thing with a green stone on it. I remember her showing it to my mother before she . . . before she . . .'

Craig's voice faltered. Alec reached a hand over and gripped the lad's shoulder.

'I remember it too. It was a wee green Buddha. Made of jade. And the gold on the bracelet must have weighed a ton. She was fair proud of it, I remember.'

'That's what I saw. And he saw the bodies up in the branches too and he stepped back and then he stuck to the tree. All this juice came out and ran all over him. It was like that airfix glue you get for model planes. It came out of the tree and went all over him. He was yelling and screaming. Oh, *God*,' he said shakily. 'I never heard my Da scream like that before, even the time he took the top of his finger off on the woodsaw. It kept on covering him and it got in his mouth and he couldn't breathe. I couldn't *do* anything. I was too *scared*.'

Craig gave another shiver, a whole body motion that shuddered him from head to toe and made him spill a splash of tea onto the old worn rug.

'Here, drink up some of that before it gets cold,' Alec said, giving the boy a gentle nudge. Craig took a swallow of the tea without seeming even to be aware of it.

'And then the trees started coming for me. One of them dropped its branches right down. And then the creepers . . . Jesus, they were like snakes. One of them nearly got me round my boot, but I got it off and then I started to run.'

'And then what did you do?'

'I came up here and waited.'

'And what happened to the hedges?' Alec asked.

'I killed them. I burned some of them and I put weedkiller on the rest. It was stuff my Da had for killing the bracken and brambles. It killed them.'

'Why?' Martin asked.

Craig looked at him the way an adult might look at a stupid child.

'Because they're *alive*, mister. They're alive and they *kill* people. But they won't get me.'

The boy looked Martin straight in the eye and Martin saw the fevered look of madness there. But it was not *insanity*. It was wild fear, stark and naked.

'No. They're not getting me,' the boy said. 'I'll burn them all first.'

31

Rose Haldane came down from putting the children to bed to find Duncan cleaning his gun. It was an an over-and-under twelve-bore, just like the one which had blasted Caitlin Brook into a wheelchair. He had spread newspapers out over the broad table and carefully held the weapon over them while he worked.

'John Lovatt said he'd come down with me tomorrow,' he told Rose.

'Only the two of you?' she asked. 'Is that enough?'

'I hope so. He's got a handful of terriers to help us root the bugger out. We can't afford to have it hanging around here, not after what happened to the dog.'

Duncan gritted his teeth and pulled the wire brush up through the right barrel, twisting it as it came.

Dorrie was going to the summerplay picnic the next day with the rest of the wee ones from the village. Ben hadn't shown any inclination to join in, although it had been a month since his foray into the forest. Since the night Morag had been killed and the avalanche of logs had almost swept their farmhouse away, he'd shown even less enthusiasm for leaving the yard. That was fine with Duncan. If John Lovatt's pig had gone feral, anywhere else was dangerous.

'We'll be out most of the morning, and probably the afternoon as well,' he said.

'I'll make you some sandwiches and a flask in the morning.'

Duncan nodded, eyes intent on oiling the gun.

'Pity Bob McCourt's still in the hospital. He knows the woods better than anybody, and he's got a good team of dogs.'

'I'm surprised he hasn't seen the pig before, if it's been running loose since the spring,' Rose said.

'It's a big chunk of forest,' Duncan told her. 'But we'll find it all right.'

He snapped the barrels closed and raised the gun to sight along the top barrel. In his mind's eye he saw John Lovatt's big boar standing in a forest clearing. He squeezed the trigger and felt the pin snap forward to strike hollowly on the empty chamber.

Martin Thornton left Alec Stirling's place around seven. The postman had made the boy eat a huge fry-up and then had ordered him into a hot bath. When Craig Buist was upstairs, he came and sat down next to the reporter.

'I still think he did him in,' Alec said.

'No. I don't think so. There's something wrong here.' Martin was in an agony of anxiety. 'I have to get down to Caitlin's place. But before I go, I have to know about Sheila Garvie.'

'What? That old witch? What's the score with her?'

'She's got Caitlin involved in something.'

'Her and half the women in Linnvale,' Alex said disparagingly. 'They're just a bunch of old nosy parkers and do-gooders. She's got them into saving the lentil and drinking herb tea. They near enough ruined Duncan Haldane and I'm glad they got their come-uppance on that one.'

'But there's more to it than that.'

'Like what?'

'I can't tell you that right now. But this Sheila Garvie. I want to know where she's from.'

'I dunno,' Alec said honestly. 'I mean, they reckon she was born here. Her old grandmother had the millhouse until she died about five years ago. Real old dear she was. Well into her nineties. The Garvie woman came last year and took the place over. She's got all the women's heads filled up with herbal remedies for warts and wrinkles. They've all taken to colouring their hair. I never miss a trick. There's a fair procession of them down at the millhouse every other night. What they're doing down there beats me, but they say some of the fellows are getting fed a few things in their tea to make them perform a wee bit better, if you know what I mean.'

'I know what you mean,' Martin conceded, 'but does anybody *know* anything about her?'

Alec shook his head. 'Who cares? She keeps herself pretty much to herself. Apart from all those women looking for cures and potions, she doesn't mix very much. Then she's in and out of that forest like a peep of gas. Always has a basket full of stuff. I reckon she's just an old hippie.' Alec looked at Martin. 'What's with Sheila Garvie? That's got nothing do with young Buist.'

431

'You'd be surprised.' Martin got his jacket and slung it on. 'I'll take a run down to Caitlin's and see if I can catch her in. If I don't get back tonight I'll give you a call in the morning.'

Alec grinned. 'Planning to strike it lucky?'

'Oh, give me a break,' Martin said, but couldn't help returning Alec's mischievous grin.

As he reached the door Alec called him back.

'What about the youngster?' he asked, jerking his thumb back towards the stairs.

'Better let him stay the night. He looks as if he could use a good sleep.'

Martin climbed into the Land-Rover and set off for the cottage by the river. The clouds had now covered almost the whole of the valley, casting a sombre shadow over the Dumbuie Hills to the west and hanging heavy over the glen.

For the second time that day he pushed open Caitlin's garden gate. As he did so there was a rustling in the hedge and he got a glimpse of a dark shadow moving swiftly towards him among the dockens and brambles at the base of the bushes. He remembered the black shape that had sprung at his car and his whole body tensed. The shape was still about twenty yards away, moving with ponderous speed. He could hear the crackle of the twigs and stems breaking as it pushed its way through.

'Shit!' he said aloud and made off round the side of the house, still listening to the snapping of the undergrowth and, above that, the harsh *snuffling* sound of a large animal.

He made it round the back of the house, swung open the door, then banged it shut behind him. Caitlin stood there, her face a picture of surprise and delight. She put her arms around his shoulders and, with no hesitation, leaned forward and kissed Martin on the lips.

'What—?' he started to say, then realised what he was doing. His momentary fright over the animal in the bushes evaporated. He leaned forward and returned the kiss. It was only a small peck, but Caitlin held on to him and pressed herself forward. The peck became a kiss, a *real* kiss. He could feel the strong warmth of her against him, and the delicate perfume he'd smelled in her bedroom that morning. His hands reached into the thick fiery curls of her hair and held tight.

432

They broke away, each savouring the other's taste.

'Oh, I've missed you.'

'Me too,' Martin said stupidly.

Something was nagging at his mind, clamouring for his attention, while the rest of him was still enfolded in the warm aftertaste of the girl.

There was something *wrong*. Mental alarm bells clanged, demanding urgent attention. Martin stood there, his hands still clasped on Caitlin's shoulders, when it struck him like a blow on the forehead.

Her wheelchair.

She wasn't *in* it.

Quite instinctively he grabbed her tight to prevent her from falling. In his haste to get indoors, away from the black animal shadow in the bushes, he hadn't even realised that she was *standing* there when he came through the door.

'Jesus! You'll kill yourself,' he said. He was holding her tight against him, her head so close to his own that her hair brushed his cheek.

'I won't get the chance,' she mumbled, voice muffled under the pressure of his embrace. 'You'll choke me to death first.'

'What?'

'Oh, Martin, put me down. I'm not going to fall,' she said, her voice filled with laughter, and immediately he could feel her shaking against him.

Caitlin pushed him back and he reluctantly allowed the distance between them. Finally she broke free and stood there, green eyes sparkling at him. She was tall, only an inch or two shorter than himself. He'd only seen her on her feet once, minutes before her fall from the balcony. Since then, she had always been seated.

She looked a completely different person.

Martin stood there, mouth gaping. It was too much for him to take in. He tried to speak and found the words wouldn't come.

Caitlin stood, legs limber and straight, planted wide apart. She had her hands fisted on her hips, leaning herself back slightly to take in the range of expressions that trailed each other in rapid succession on his face.

'But . . .' he managed.

433

'But what?' she said, and began to laugh again, this time a wonderful, delighted laugh of innocent joy.

'Don't worry,' she said finally. 'I can hardly believe it either. But it's true.'

'But how on earth—?' Martin started. He stopped, stared, gathered himself together and finally exploded.

'Bloody hell, woman, you're *walking*!'

'Oh, you noticed, did you?' Caitlin took two steps forward and threw her arms around him. 'Does this mean we can have a dance at the next ceilidh?'

She finally allowed Martin to sit down. When he did so, he slumped to the seat, completely drained. Too many things had happened to him and this last was just too much for him to take in.

Caitlin did the decent thing. She made a cup of strong tea and made him drink it. Finally she sat down beside him, lowering herself easily, with an almost athletic litheness, into the kitchen chair opposite.

'You look just like your picture,' she said, pointing to the framed sketch. 'You've got that bewildered little boy look again. It's cute.'

Martin shook his head.

'I don't know what's going on here,' he finally said wearily.

She told him. It didn't take long.

She started with the infusions that Sheila Garvie had given her and how she'd begun to get sensation back in her legs and how every day since then she'd found her strength returning. She told him how Sheila had rubbed oils into her skin and finally taken her for walks into the forest. As she spoke, another piece of the jigsaw clicked in Martin's mind. The pattern almost became complete.

Finally he told her what *he* had done.

'I was dead worried about you,' he confessed. 'I sniffed some of that powder and I started to hallucinate. I saw the pasta crawling out of the pot. I dropped the thing and threw the whole lot into the stream.'

'Oh, that's what happened to my spaghetti?' Caitlin said, smothering a giggle. 'I wondered why you looked so pale. I thought it was the wine.'

'But there's more,' Martin persisted. 'I took some of the powder for analysis.'

434

'You did what?' Caitlin's expression changed immediately to one of disbelief. 'But you promised you wouldn't tell—'

'I *didn't*!' Martin insisted vehemently. 'I never told a soul. But I had to find out what you were taking, and I *did* find out.'

He leaned across the table and took her by the shoulder in earnest emphasis.

'It's poisonous. All of it. I've got a list and just about everything in there could kill you.'

Caitlin's face took on a stony look.

'I don't care. Sheila's an expert. She would never give me anything that would hurt me.'

'Christ, Caitlin. There's snake venom and deadly mushrooms and other things in there. I've got a print-out. The top pharmacologist said there's enough in there to kill a dozen folk.'

'There might well be, but I really don't give a damn.'

Caitlin glared at him. She shrugged off his hand.

'Look at me,' she said tightly. '*Look at me!*'

She shoved her chair back and stood up. Without a pause, she walked across the kitchen and turned to face him, moving like a ballerina.

'I don't *care*,' she said, eyes flashing again, this time with hurt or anger. He couldn't tell which. 'You might call it poison. It doesn't matter. It's given me back my legs. It's given me back my *life*. You can't begin to imagine what it's like for me to be able to walk. To be able to *run*. It's a miracle, and I don't care what's caused it. I just want it.'

She came back to the table and leaned on it. For the first time, he had to look up to see her face. There was an awesome beauty in her anger.

'You shouldn't have done it, Martin. I trusted you.'

'But I did it because I was concerned. I was worried. That stuff made me hallucinate. She gave me a drink at the ceilidh and I—' He faltered. He wasn't quite prepared to tell Caitlin Brook what he'd done with Gail Dean in the anteroom of the church hall. 'Never mind. I was just worried, because I . . .' He halted again. 'Because I *care* about you.'

He looked up at her, matching her glare for glare.

'I *still* care about you. And I'm *still* worried. I've cared about you since before you took that shotgun in the back. Christ knows why, for I sure as hell don't. I knew you were in danger then, and I've got this God-awful feeling that you're in danger now and, believe me, Caitlin, I'm just about shitting myself.'

Caitlin stared at him, conflicting expressions fighting for mastery. Finally laughter won out and she dissolved into a fit of high, girlish giggles. Martin sat and watched her, completely baffled.

'Oh, Mr Thornton. You're such a romantic, silver-tongued bastard.'

She went off into a peal of laughter again and let it run until she almost choked. When she got her breath back she turned to him, green eyes glazed with tears.

'"Shitting myself"? You *really* know the way to charm a girl, huh?'

She came round to his side of the table and pushed him back, turning herself so that she could sit on his knee. She settled against him and put her hands up to both sides of his face, holding him firmly.

'All right, Martin. I understand why you did it. I still don't think you should have done it, but you've said the magic words. You told me you care for me and that's very special. I was hoping you'd say something like that.'

She pulled herself back from him, gazing into his eyes, trying to gauge his reaction. Martin stared back, unable to make himself move.

She broke first.

'Oh God, I've missed you these last couple of weeks,' she said and, without a pause, she leaned forward into him and kissed him again, hard and urgently.

Some time after that she eased herself away. He held tight onto her shoulders, reluctant to let her go. His mind was a whirl of conflicting emotions, all of them centred around Caitlin Brook.

No matter *what* had happened, no matter that she was walking on her own two feet, nothing had changed his mind about the danger she was in. His only problem was in deciding what to do about it.

Down in the village, Susan Herron was in the church hall with Caitlin's friends, Caroline Petrie and Melanie Cuthbert, who both helped organise the summerplay. They were busy making up the hampers for the children's picnic the following day. Susan was spreading butter on slice after slice of white bread while the others put in the fillings. Caroline had seen the clouds beginning to pile up in a thundery barricade and hoped the weather would stay dry for the next twenty-four hours, though she knew it might be asking too much. The long hot spell had lasted only a month or so but that was almost a record in this part of the country. There was a distinct possibility the picnic might have to be cancelled, but she'd prepared for that. The youngsters could all come back to the church hall if it was wet.

Susan's mother, Fiona Herron, had been crocheting a cardigan when her daughter left the house in the late afternoon. Since the miraculous cure of her arthritis, Fiona had taken up the craft with a liberated delight. Her fingers moved rhythmically as the hooks jabbed and pulled, working deftly yet delicately with the wool. Later that evening Susan saw Fiona pass by the church hall, presumably on her way to the Preservation Society meeting. Personally she thought the women of the almost exclusive club were mostly a bunch of busybodies. She wished her mother hadn't become involved.

In fact Fiona, together with most of the women in the Society, was making her way down the Mill Road, past Caitlin Brook's cottage, towards Sheila Garvie's old millhouse by the stream.

Gail Dean left her husband going over his sermon for the following Sunday. He had accepted the news of her pregnancy with some surprise, but quiet aplomb. He'd long given up any plans for a family and now, in his late forties, he wondered how he would cope with a small child in the manse. Gail, on the other hand, was in the full bloom of expectant motherhood. She looked maybe ten years younger than her true age, her skin had a pearly, *girlish*, glow and her short hair was now strikingly fair. It was around nine in the evening when Gail made her way down the Mill Road, smiling to herself. Already she imagined the life stirring within her and allowed herself a warm surge of pride.

Molly Carr had gained some weight and looked much the better for it. She glanced at herself in the mirror, noticing how she was beginning to fill the well-cut light leather jacket, and smiled at her reflection. She'd got her new contact lenses the week before, asking the optician to give them a lilac tint. They made her eyes look bigger, more youthful. She'd taken her skirt up an inch or two and had put on her red shoes, with the slightly higher heels. In the tote bag she carried another pair of walking shows.

Molly was later than the rest, and for good reason. She'd been getting her living room redecorated. Rab McGraw, who drove Ardbeg's whisky haulers and had a reputation in the village for wallpapering, had given her a good price. He could only work at night, which suited Molly fine. She'd watched him strip the walls with the ease of long practice and had sat in the kitchen with the door open observing his progress.

A familiar warmth had begun to spread through her as she watched him slap the paste on with deft sweeps. He had wide hands and strong fingers. As the sultry, storm-threatening evening wore on, he opened the buttons of his overalls one by one until she could see the hair on his chest. There were sweat rings under his armpits and Molly's heightened senses picked up the *man-smell* even from the distance of the other room.

She waited until he was finished before offering him a drink. He asked for a beer, but gladly accepted the whisky. She poured him a large measure and a smaller one for herself. When she passed the glass to him, she let her fingers touch his and felt the wonderful connective *jolt*, the warmth like a fire within her.

'I have to go upstairs for a moment. If you could just rearrange the furniture for me, and I'll get your money,' she said, giving him her best smile. Unconsciously, her tongue slipped out and licked her bottom lip.

Rab sipped his whisky as he cleaned his pasting table and emptied the bucket. He hauled the furniture from where he'd crowded it in the centre of the room and looked at his handiwork. The expensive wallpaper showed not a seam. He sat on the arm of the settee and finished his drink. Molly Carr was still upstairs. He heard the sound of water running and went to the door of the living room, shyly peeking round. There was no sign of her. An opportunist at heart, Rab quickly unscrewed the top of the bottle and poured himself another large one, telling himself she would never notice. He drank it with relish and waited another few minutes.

Almost immediately the effects of the drink took hold. All of a sudden the room seemed to tilt, much as it had for Tom Cannon only two weeks previously. Rab blinked and shook his head. The whisky was burning nicely in his chest and his head was filling with a hot, misty glow.

'Strong stuff, that,' he mumbled to himself, looking round for the schoolteacher. He remembered her walking away from him and recalled that she had done something to improve herself. In Rab's view she had always been a sour-faced slat-ribbed woman with a disposition to match. But then the heady buzz started inside his head and he remembered the look on her face as she told him she would get his money. Her tongue had snaked out and dragged itself across her lip in a hungry, almost predatory way. As soon as the image came to him, he felt the pulse quicken at his temples.

Less than half a minute later, he was standing on the stair landing, completely unaware of how he had got there and caring less. The sound of running water whispered from the bathroom and a light cloud of steam billowed out through the open door.

He made it up the next six steps, now *fizzing* with anticipation. Rab stumbled to the doorway and stood there, looking in.

Molly Carr was in the shower with the curtain drawn back. Her back was to him and she was lathering herself with soap. Her black hair was piled high on her head, giving her a strangely exotic look, quite unlike the prim schoolteacher the whole village knew. As he watched, she bent down to soap her legs and the pressure within him surged wildly.

'What are you waiting for?' she asked, without even looking round.

Rab McGraw hauled at his boiler suit, slipping it off his shoulders to let it fall to the floor.

She turned round in the shower to face him, eyes wide and hungry, lips parted over her uneven teeth. She raised her foot and stepped out of the shower, keeping her eyes fixed on him.

Half an hour later, Rab McGraw found himself standing at the gable end of the Douglas Arms, bucket and pasting tray in hand. He had no idea how he had got there. The last thing he remembered was admiring his own handiwork and sipping a very nice whisky. Now he had a crushing headache.

Molly Carr climbed back into her skirt, a wide grin of supreme satisfaction on her face. She then slipped on her walking shoes before following Gail Dean and Fiona Herron down the Mill Road to Sheila Garvie's old millhouse.

32

There was nobody on the mill road to see the shadowed shapes slowly cross to the verge then pass into the trees. The sky was unseasonally dark, the full moon hidden behind the black clouds that loomed over the glen. There was a warmth in the evening air, a damp, clammy heat in the night, and no wind yet to ruffle the tops of the trees or to shiver the silvery aspens on the slope down to the valley.

They were dressed in black from head to foot and they walked in single file along the pathways, stopping only when they got to the breach in the old wall. Beyond that the tracks split five ways and the shadowed walkers dispersed in twos and threes, each small group following one of the divergent forest paths. At the end of the radiating tracks they each stopped beside the cup-stones which were carved with the powerful rings. From under their black cloaks they took stone bottles and poured the contents into the cups, letting them drain down the ring carvings until the liquid reached the earth, where it was instantly soaked up. The pungent spice and bitter tang of the fluid evaporating on the stone filled the air around them, adding its scent to the sappy smell of the dense forest.

This done, they retraced their steps to where the paths had met before, but now the doors of the old forest had opened themselves. The paths no longer intersected in the centre. Instead they reached into that part that was hidden, the wild *heart* of the wood that was closed to the rest of the world, except for the times of power when the moon rose bloated and white in the night sky and the opening rituals had been completed.

Now the centre of the forest stretched alien and mythical on either side of the paths. Strange smells of rampant growth filled the air. Night insects chittered and screamed and their wings clattered in papery, whirring passes close to the heads of the walkers. The night was dark on the straight trail which led to the black river, but there was light to see by. There were bloated fireflies, incandescent heads poking out from boreholes in the trunks, waiting with spread pincers to trap the night fliers. Under the spreading trunks, the swollen mushrooms gave off a pulsating, purulent glow.

The slow walkers finally gathered together at the place where the dried-out and maggot-ridden bodies hung like grotesque puppets from the trees, the first sacrifices to the *Fasach*, then they moved deeper into the heart.

They came to where the black river swirled round the island and crossed on the immense tree-bridge to the shrouded flat land. They followed their leader to the clearing. There was no light there. There were no sounds of life in the trees. No owl hooted and no bat sent out its echo call.

Yet the tree was visible, monstrous and pale, warped roots dug into the couch grass and thick moss.

The tall shape in the lead walked forward and the rest of them encircled the tree, standing silent, watching as pale hands reached towards the enormous, twisted trunk.

As soon as the fingers touched the bark a judder rippled through the earth beneath their feet in seismic waves. The trunk bulged outwards in a slow spasm, as if the tree had suddenly drawn a vast breath, and, under the earth, in the aftermath of the shock, came a deep vibration, like the slow beat of a mighty heart pulsing blood through colossal veins.

The pulse *thrummed* through them all.

Gail Dean felt it and sensed the life quicken within her, the life that should have been *impossible* but was now burgeoning in her womb. She felt the surge of the forest's heart and felt her own heart pound in response.

Fiona Herron felt the vibration ripple up through her feet and legs and shiver down towards her hands. She held them up, pale in the darkness, and saw her fingers flutter with quick life. They were warm and tingling, strong and delicate, no longer the grotesque claws that had caused her to hide them from the rest of the world.

Jean Fintry felt the pulse and her new body responded to it. Under her black robe she was naked. She could feel the material slide sensually across her smooth skin. Her belly was flat and her breasts were tight and firm where before they had drooped in doughy pendulousness. She felt young and alive. She savoured the

442

sense of her own new-found shapeliness after a lifetime of shame at her corpulent, dumpy form.

Molly Carr felt the pulse and smiled cat-like in the dark. She too was naked under her robe and felt even more strongly the beat of the forest heart and the touch of the coarse material on her skin. Between her hips she was aflame with wanton desire, even though she had slaked that hot thirst only an hour before. After a lifetime of repugnance, she had been given the pleasure of her own body. The physical revulsion for men that she'd had since childhood had been transformed into an intense *hunger*. She revelled in the heat and demand of her body, the urgent, feral, coupling, and the triumphant *rapture* of wild pleasure. With every sonorous pulse under her feet, she could feel the heat build up deliciously inside her until her whole body was shaking with the overwhelming desire. In front of her the tree writhed. The wood groaned as it twisted against itself and a small groan escaped from the school-teacher's mouth. She could not drag her eyes away from the powerful contractions and contortions on the surface of the ancient tree. They mirrored what was happening inside her own body. All of a sudden, she had a mad urge to run forward and press herself against the motion, to feel it for herself, to become *one* with it.

But something held her back.

It was not quite fear, but it was close to it.

What she had been given could be taken away again. And now that Molly Carr had discovered her gift, she knew she could not live without it. She forced her feet to stay still, allowing the beat to rumble through her. She dragged her eyes away from the motion and fixed them on Sheila Garvie who stood in front of the tree, hands planted on the moving surface, neck arched back so that her face pointed up towards the massive fork where the immense boughs diverged.

Sheila was breathing heavily. The women who surrounded her could hear the deep gasps as she hauled air into her lungs. She had untied her hair from its customary tight and elegant roll. It now hung down in a long mist of finest silver.

Then she started to speak in the kind of sing-song chant that Caitlin Brook would have recognised.

'Hear us, Lord of the Fasach, heart of the wilderness. Hear your

443

Wild Willow, the *Seilach Garbh-aidh*. The *seedling* is prepared for your planting. The awakening is upon you. The earth is ready for the might of your power. Your daughters thank you for the gifts of your hand. We will repay you, Lord *Cerunnos*, with life for our lives, with power for our power.'

The tree shuddered violently, almost throwing Sheila Garvie's hands from the surface, but it was not a rejection. It was as if a monstrous pulse had ripped up through the roots to swell the tortured wood. Knot holes opened and yawned darkly before closing again. Above, the branches twisted and turned as if shaken by a violent wind.

And as they watched, their eyes now accustomed to the dark, they saw the pulses ripple along the branches in an impossible series of peristaltic twitches. The ends of the branches, which until now had looked dead and dry, were swelling. Buds forced themselves from the wood, expanding like green warts at first. There was a small, popping sound as the first one burst open. A tight leaf uncurled and began to straighten and bloat with quick life. Another bud cracked open in a spray of sticky sap and another leaf began its throbbing distension. Then another and another until the branches above were writhing with the sudden upsurge of growth.

The smell of sap was sweet and thick in the forest air. They drank in the powerful scent, feeling it catch and tickle at the back of their throats.

Sheila Garvie pulled her hands back from the trunk and watched the movement slowly die down to immobility.

'He senses the imminence of life and sends it up from the earth,' she said. She turned to the others, her back to the tree. Her face was white and triumphant. Her eyes were black coals.

'One more ritual, sisters, and we will have our hearts' desire.'

With a triumphant smile she walked through their midst and strode along the path to the edge of the clearing. The women followed behind her, still aware of the presence of the massive tree at their backs. As Sheila reached the band of trees, she gestured into the shadows. A dark shape came low and sinuous towards her then settled at her side, keeping pace with her fast stride. It was like a liquid shadow, moving without a sound.

They crossed the river, a group of silent women, each lost in her own thoughts. They came through the dense lush forest that was hidden from the rest of the world until the special nights when the moon was high and then, in a line, they crossed through the breach on the wall. Once beyond, Sheila Garvie turned and made a gesture with her hand. The women heard her speak in a language that they had heard before but could not comprehend. It was as if their vision blurred momentarily. There was a strange *twist* in the shadowed darkness beyond the break in the dry-stone dyke. When the flicker stopped, the forest had returned to the way it had always been.

33

If she dreamed, she did not remember it when she woke up in the grey light of early morning.

Martin was lying on his side, hair tousled, his face in repose making him look more boyish than ever. She reached over and brushed a strand of hair from his forehead and his eyebrows twitched. Caitlin smiled and held the warm feeling into herself.

He had been so cautious, so careful with her, and it had still hurt, for a brief pang.

And the rest of it – *oh, the rest of it* – after nearly two years of numb lifelessness. That had been *wonderful*. It was as if he had been the last piece of the magic to bring her completely to life.

She lay back, careful not to disturb him, and thought about the night they'd had, running it through her memory, savouring the recollection of his touch, their skin and the heat of their perspiration. They had fit together so perfectly she felt that they had become one, body and mind merged with such intensity that she could sense *his* pleasure, while having her own reflected and magnified to her through *him*.

It had never been like that with anybody else. It had been mystical and it had been magical and it had been *perfect*. She remembered taking him by the hand, pausing only to kiss him gently. He had seemed reluctant, almost shy, but he had not refused her. They had sat on the thick rug in her snug front room, sharing a bottle of wine that she'd had in the fridge in anticipation of his last cancelled visit.

She'd explained to him every step of her miraculous journey with Sheila Garvie out of her wheelchair. She told it with open-eyed wonder and pure, unalloyed joy.

'You can't begin to believe what it feels like to be dead and then come alive again. I can *run*, Martin. I can hardly believe it, but it's true. I've dreamed about running, and my dreams have become reality.'

He listened to her intently, but there was a gravity in his

look that she could sense as well as see. He let her talk on.

'After the first time, at the ceilidh, when my feet began to move, I couldn't let myself hope. I thought it was just the nerves playing tricks on me. They've done something like that before, though not for a long time. Sometimes the muscles spasm if I haven't done enough exercises to keep the blood flowing, but I've always been pretty careful.

'It was Sheila who told me. She showed me the movement at the dance. I hadn't even noticed it. She told me about the healing powers of the plants. I remember getting very angry with her when she said I could walk again. The psychologists at the hospital drummed it into me for months that I couldn't afford to hope. I couldn't *allow* myself a single glimmer. They schooled me against optimism and complete acceptance. And they were right. There was no cure, not in their medicine.

'But Sheila told me about the power of the plants. She gave me the powder and made me drink it, at least three times a day, and with every glass of the stuff I could feel the sensation returning. I don't know what makes it work, but it *does* work, Martin. I'm the living proof of it.'

Martin just looked at her, keeping his face as blank as possible. He had things to tell her, but he wanted her to run on first, to say it all.

'She's a member of the Gaia movement. They're dedicated to preserving the earth. They're against pollution and the destruction of the rainforests because so much of the wealth of the world is tied up in growing things. All right, I know she's a bit airy-fairy. She likes to pray to the forest and I don't mind going along with it. It gave me back my legs and all the doctors in the world couldn't do that. Sheila really believes there is an earth power that's every bit as powerful as . . . well, God.'

'Do you believe that?'

'I can run again, Martin. There must be *something*. Oh, I don't mean a *conscious* power, even if Sheila does ramble on about the beliefs the old Druids had. They believed there was a god of the forest who gave the life back to the land and fertility back to the people.'

'Does she believe it?'

'I think she believes in the power of plants, and with good

reason. She's collected specimens from all over the world and made them grow here. That's where she gets her medicines from. Everybody around here comes to Sheila for help, and she gives it freely. She asks for nothing in return.'

'But what about side effects?'

'What side effects?'

'That's what I mean. How do people know there aren't any?' Caitlin shrugged her shoulders.

'I haven't had any. I got a bit dizzy at first, but that's gone.' She reached over for the wine bottle and poured for both of them. 'Not as much as I get from this stuff,' she said with a smile.

'Have you ever wondered about how you met her?'

'I don't understand,' Caitlin said, genuinely puzzled.

'I mean the strange coincidence of her being in the right place at the right time.'

'Oh, you can't fault her for that. She saved my *life*.'

'I know,' Martin said, soothingly. He wanted to keep this as even as possible. 'It's just that she was the only one who happened to be there. I'm thinking about the fact that *you* happened to be there. You didn't go into the forest deliberately. Something *forced* you in there. Have you considered that?'

'I've thought about it. Of course. It was an animal. Sheila thought it must have been a dog. There's a lot of them about on the farms.'

'Yes. Like the animal that jumped at my Rover and turned me off the road. Something came at me and I nearly went over the drop down to the river. It tried to kill me. But it never followed through. Maybe it was a warning or something, but I don't believe it was a dog. I don't know what the hell it was but, looking back, there seems to have been a purpose.'

'What purpose?'

'To get rid of me.'

'And to kill me too?'

'No. I think it might have been to *fetch* you.'

'This is all getting very mysterious.'

'No more so than the fact that you can walk again, after being sentenced to life in a wheelchair,' Martin said. Caitlin conceded that with a shrug. 'Does she have any animals?' Martin asked.

'Only two cats,' Caitlin said. She remembered waking up on the bed with the dark shadow wavering in front of her eyes, finally resolving itself into a cat. She recalled the slitted eyes transfixing her.

'Nothing bigger?'

'No. Martin, what is all this leading to?'

He sat for a moment, seeming to gather his thoughts, then leaned forward, earnestly holding her eyes with his.

'I think there's a few things this woman hasn't told you. Remember I told you I had the powder analysed?' She nodded. 'Well, first of all, as I told you, I discovered that it is full of toxins. Things like alkaloids and digitoxins, atropine and colchicine, along with some very nasty neurotoxins and haemotoxins.'

'You've said a mouthful. I didn't understand any of it.'

'Neither did I, but I do now. They're some of the most virulent naturally-occurring poisons known to man. You get them from plants and toadstools and snake venom and the like. Each of them can kill you even if you only take a little of it. That's what you've been filling yourself up with.'

'But it hasn't *harmed* me. For God's sake, Martin, it's *cured* me.'

'There's more. The analyst could only tell me what was in the stuff, but he couldn't say why. Neither could George Watt, who's the professor of clinical pharmacology. He could tell me where the stuff came from, the plant and animal species, and he told me it was like a recipe from a witch's brew. All he could say was that some of the stuff there was used in old medicines. The ones that killed more people than they cured. He sent me off to another expert, this time not a medical man. He's the top of his field in Celtic mythology.'

Martin stopped for a moment, still holding Caitlin's eyes.

'Have you ever heard of *Cerunnos*?'

'Yes. He's the Forest God. Sheila told me all about the old myths. She thinks they're wonderful.'

'I'll bet she does.'

'What does that mean?'

'Well, let me tell you about Finlay Carmyllie. He showed me a book with a picture in it. It was a drawing made on leather thousands of years ago showing a ceremony dedicated to the horned god. They used it in a fertility rite or some kind of ritual. The amazing coincidence is that all of the plants they used in their magic potion are included in the list of ingredients in yours.'

'So?' Caitlin asked, a trifle truculently.

'The magic mixture was used in a ceremony. A sacrifice. They had to kill a virgin.'

'And you think I might be the one?'

Martin nodded his head gravely, aware of how idiotic it might sound, but he meant what he said. Caitlin could read *that* in his eyes. Martin was deadly serious.

Despite that, she let out an involuntary giggle. 'That rules me out then. Sorry to disappoint you, but I graduated from that state a while back.'

'I don't know whether to be pleased, or annoyed over that,' Martin said, lightening a little. Caitlin gave him a wide smile and told him she was pleased he cared.

'Of course I care,' he said, serious again. 'I wouldn't be telling you this if I didn't. Remember the story she told you about the farmer who was crushed by the bull? She said her mother tried to fix him up, but he died anyway. That was nearly three hundred years ago. There's a gravestone in the churchyard which tells about a MacFarlane who was killed by his own bull.'

'Yes, I remember his name,' Caitlin agreed.

'He died in 1720. The MacFarlanes haven't farmed in the glen for nearly two hundred years according to both the gravestones and Alec Stirling who knows everything about the place. That means she was either lying or she's a lot older than she looks.'

'Oh, that's nonsense,' Caitlin said with an incredulous laugh.

'Is it? Well, try this. Up at the churchyard there's a walled-off section. There are five graves in it, spaced about a hundred years apart in time. All the men's names are different. There's a MacPhail and a Colquhoun and a couple of others. Each of them was married to a Sheila. Maybe this is stretching coincidence too far but, unlike all the other gravestones, there's nobody else buried in the graves. There's no mention of the wife dying at all.'

'They could have remarried.'

'Yes, true, but how about this?' Martin said, almost triumphantly. He reached into the pocket of his leather jacket which hung on the back of the chair and drew out a wad of papers. He separated the computer print-outs and found what he was looking for. The photocopier in the office hadn't made a great job of reproducing the old plate from the *Farrell* book. The edges were blurred and stretched where the page had curved onto the glass, but the picture was clear enough.

'Who's this then?' he asked. Caitlin's brow furrowed as she scanned the unfolded paper.

'It looks like Sheila,' she admitted.

'I thought so too. Look at that birthmark or whatever it is on her arm.'

The photocopy had picked up the small mark, but with none of the clarity of the original plate. It looked like a smudge.

'What about it?' she asked. 'I know Sheila's got a mark, but you can't tell it from this.'

'Well, I had a look at that under a magnifying glass. It's *exactly* the same figure of eight. And it's in precisely the same place. I saw it at the ceilidh.'

'Was that before or after you got drunk?' Caitlin came back with gentle sarcasm.

'Touché. Not that it matters. That picture was taken at Boleskin House in 1922. The madman in the front is Aleister Crowley. He called himself "The Beast 666" and spent his life trying to raise the devil.'

'And that's what you think Sheila's trying to do?'

'I think she *believes* she can. I don't give a damn about what she believes. It's all mumbo jumbo to me. But it's *how* she plans to do it.'

'You mean the sacrifice of a virgin?'

'Something like that.'

'She's never mentioned anything like that to me.'

'Now there's a surprise.'

'You'll have to forgive me, Martin. But I have to take all this with a pinch of salt,' Caitlin said. She leaned over and gave him an apologetic kiss, trying to make it easier.

'I can accept that. I had problems too. I didn't believe in anything, but now I know that *some* things are possible. Like the night you were shot. I was *there*. I saw it happen. And then, on the night you nearly drowned in the forest, I got another warning.'

'What, telepathy again?'

'Not quite,' Martin said. He told her about the strange night up in Blackhale with Andy Toye and the girl on the bed. When he described in detail the unnerving sight of the girl kneeling bolt upright on the rumpled bed while the wind whooshed and whirled through the window, whipping the curtains to flap against the ceiling, she gave a shiver. He repeated the girl's words. Caitlin shivered again.

'That would have scared me to death,' she said.

'Didn't do my nerves any good, I can tell you. But the point is, this happened at exactly the same time as you were drowning in the river. I checked my diary. She was warning me about *you*.'

Caitlin stared at him. 'You really believe that?'

'It's taken me a while, but I do. If I didn't, I'd feel like a real idiot sitting here telling you this. I really would.'

She sat silent for a while, eyes flicking to his, searching. All she could see was earnest concern. Martin *meant* what he said, no matter how fanciful, no matter how incredible, it was.

Caitlin was not ready to believe any of it, but his anxiety was so evident that her heart went out to him.

'So what do you want me to do?'

'I really want you to get out of here. The sooner the better. I want you to stop taking those poisons, and really I don't want you anywhere near Sheila Garvie. No matter what she believes, she can't do anything if you're not here.'

'I can't,' Caitlin said blankly.

'What do you mean?'

'I can't stop taking the medicine.'

'But it's *toxic*, for God's sake.'

'I don't care if it's radioactive,' Caitlin shot back fiercely. 'Can't you understand?' She shook her head. 'No. Of course you can't. You've never been in a wheelchair, have you? You just don't know what it's like to be trapped in that thing with no life in your legs and no sensation from the waist down. People treat you like an idiot, like a vegetable. Half the time you believe they're right.' She raised her eyes and glared green at him. 'You're only half a person. You see the world from a different point of view, and it's not pleasant. That stuff I've been taking, that *poison*, has given me my world back. Given me my *life*.'

Caitlin looked at him with bleak accusation.

452

'You want me to give that up?' For a moment Martin was unable to say anything. He hadn't thought of that aspect of it. His mind whirled with the dilemma.

'No, I don't want you to give up *walking*,' he finally said, letting his pent-up breath out slowly in a kind of sigh. 'I just want you to be safe and I'm trying very hard to show you that you're in some kind of danger.'

'Well, I'll do a deal with you,' she said, lightening a little. The fierceness melted as her eyes softened. She moved close to him and he could have drowned in the green depths. 'I'll come away with you tomorrow and stay for a while, if that will make you feel better.'

A look of surprised relief instantly changed Martin's expression.

'I'll settle for that,' he said slowly.

Caitlin edged even closer and brought her hands up to his shoulders. She leaned into him, eyes glistening like forest pools.

'Come here, you,' she said, insistently pulling him forward to kiss him again. Her lips parted and they lost themselves in each other for a while.

How they ended up in bed together Martin wasn't quite sure. He had a vague memory of her telling him that she couldn't go away with somebody she didn't know. He recalled her leading him by the hand and remembered how he'd suddenly felt like an awkward schoolboy. She had unbuttoned his cotton shirt slowly and then pressed herself to his chest. Her coppery waves had tumbled to her shoulders and onto his skin, trailing like feathers.

She had been perfect.

They had lain side by side, saying nothing, just drinking each other in, and then she had run her fingers through the short hairs on the back of his neck and the touch had been like an electrical contact, as if sparks had leapt between them. He had leaned down and placed his mouth on hers and she had let the hand trail slowly down his shoulder and then it pressed hard against his back as she pulled him to her.

He had been scared of hurting her, but Caitlin Brook had had no such concerns. In the heat of the sultry night she had been like a pent-up dam suddenly burst in an irrepressible torrent. Her tongue was pressing on his and she dragged her breasts across his chest, trying to feel all of him at once, trying to make the contact complete. She had pulled him on to her, hungrily insistent, obeying her own demands. He had hesitated at that final moment, scared to hurt her, but she had clenched him down. There was a hot touch and then a tearing pain inside her. A high cry escaped from her and he stopped immediately.

'What's wrong?' he asked in the darkness. Tears stung her eyes. He tried to pull away but she held him tight. The pain flared again and she felt a trickle of blood.

'It's all right, Martin. Don't stop now.'

She held him tight and thrust herself very slowly against him. The pleasure swamped the dying pain and she lost herself in it.

34

In the morning, when he awoke, she was gone.

Martin came awake slowly, swimming up from a dream where the teddy bear speared him with its beady eye and then turned towards him, changing as it did into something *else*, a rustling thing with a face as dry and papery as a wasps' nest. He woke then with a start, breath hitched and tight, startled from sleep by the sudden sense of hideous threat.

He twisted in the bed, disorientated, still half in the dream, unsure in the brief confusion of where he was.

He reached over and felt the other side of the bed. It was rumpled and cooling. The trailing memory of the dream fragmented and faded and he sat upright, rubbing his eyes, abruptly aware of not only where he was, but why.

The recollection of the previous night came back to him in a rush of conflicting emotions. He reached to feel the place where she had lain again. There was a streak of blood on the sheet, forming a pattern like a leaf, and a twinge of guilt squeezed at him. Martin reached for his watch, discovered he was still wearing it and checked the time. It was after nine. The house was silent and the room dark behind drawn curtains. Outside on the roof a crow rasped the morning air with its call. There was no sound from the kitchen, no smell of warm coffee.

He eased himself from the bed and found his clothes in a heap where they'd been dropped. Martin pulled on his jeans, aware of the slight stiffness in his upper arms and shoulders from taking his weight. He shook his head ruefully, chiding himself in the cold light of the morning for taking advantage. Behind his self-accusation, however, he could not deny the wonderful warm sense of discovery.

Sometime in the dark, in the course of the night, she had held him close, her body hot and slick with their effort and she'd told him she loved him. He had responded immediately in like manner, spontaneously, not considering his words.

Now, with her side of the bed cool and empty, he realised that he *had* meant it. He had said it without thought, without question, because it was *true*.

It didn't matter that he hadn't known her, *really* known her at all. What had happened the night before was just the final key turning, the final physical joining to match the mysterious mental bond that had lashed them together since the first awful night. Now he realised what his fear and anxiety had been all about. There was no escaping the fact that his mind had somehow been locked on to Caitlin Brook without him being aware of it. Maybe the girl in the darkened room in the tower block in Blackhale had not been making a prophecy at all. Maybe she had been picking up his *own* unconscious telepathy.

Martin smiled to himself for having worked that out by himself. His body might be stiff and aching, but inside he felt *good*.

He jammed his feet into the casual walking shoes without loosening the laces, bending the heels down as he did so and automatically making a silent apology to the memory of his mother who'd spent too long teaching him not to ruin his shoes that way. He tucked his shirt into the jeans and came along the hall towards the living room.

Caitlin was not there. There was some sunlight, but it was dim and watery, coming through the kitchen window. He went to the stove and found the kettle cold. Martin turned the gas up underneath it. Beside the sink there was an empty glass. He raised it and sniffed.

The stench was awesome. His nose wrinkled in disgust as the oily perfume assailed his nostrils. It smelled of fetid, decomposing meat, underlain by the noisome stink of rotting vegetation.

He felt his palate try to squeeze itself shut against the nausea rising in his throat, souring him with hot bile. He gagged, mouth agape, desperately trying to swallow it down. His vision swam as his eyes watered. The glass slipped from his hands and tumbled to the floor, bounced on the mat and rolled in a semi-circle, still intact. The foul smell still hung around in the air, tainting his breath. He moved to the back door, swung it open and went outside as quickly as he could. When he was beyond the first of the flower beds, he opened his mouth and let his lungs swoop in clean air.

Martin cursed expansively and with feeling. When his ribs stopped heaving with the effort of breathing and swearing, he got himself to the garden bench and sat down heavily. The physical revulsion was fading a little, but still lingered in an oily afterscent, as if the sensitive membranes inside his nose had been abraded by it.

He recalled the taste of the first diluted mixture that Caitlin had drunk. He'd sipped a little and the taste had been extraordinarily pleasant. That had been the mixture he'd taken for analysis and it had turned out to be loaded with poisons.

He thought of Caitlin drinking this new mixture whose mere smell had made him almost vomit, and wondered what on earth it contained.

It *reeked* deadly and poisonous.

He waited until his head cleared properly and walked back down the path. The sky to the east was still light and summery, but above and to the west it was bruised and blackened. There was a tense quality to the air, as if it was charged, ready to fizz with lightning.

In the kitchen, Martin tried to breathe through his mouth to spare his nose. There was no sign that Caitlin had made breakfast. She was simply gone. She had taken a drink of the foul liquid and had disappeared.

That thought hit him like a sandbag. She was gone. But *where*?

There was only one place he could think of and his heart sank. She couldn't have taken in any of what he'd told her the night before. She must have been humouring him, pretending to him that she would leave the glen and come away with him, at least until he thought it would be safe to come back. Now she had left him lying asleep and had gone.

To Sheila Garvie, who else?

'Damn!' Martin said, for want of a better expletive.

He reached to the back of the sofa and grabbed his scuffed leather jacket, shrugging it on as quickly as he could, while taking quick steps towards the door. He jumped into the Land-Rover, not knowing that the woman lived less than four hundred yards down the road. He could have walked the distance more quickly but instead he reversed the jeep, did a three-point turn and scooted down the hill, door mirror scraping against the hedge as he took the tight turn.

There was a widening in the road just past the millhouse, leading into a kind of natural lay-by. Martin swung the wheel hard and brought the jeep right off the road, angling the nose between two saplings on the slight slope which led down to the stream, now shallow and sluggish from the long, dry spell. He stamped on the brake, felt the tyres dig into the soft earth, and stopped with a jerk.

What he intended to do was completely unrehearsed and unplanned. He hadn't even thought about it on the way down the road. All he could think of was his rising sense of panic. Caitlin had gone to Sheila Garvie and *something* was about to happen. Perhaps it was the weird connection that linked them together, the peculiar bond that had been there since the first time he'd seen her, but now his whole *self* was twitching with the sense of threat. He could feel the hairs on the back of his neck stand on end in a prickling crawl. The clammy sweat was trickling between his kidneys.

He got out of the cab and slammed the door shut without thinking, then realised he should be more careful. Martin stopped at the garden hedge and peered over the top. The old millhouse was angled away from the garden, its east side overhanging the steep rocky stream bank where the wheel had once turned under the weir. The roof was swaybacked and the stone was old and grey. The windows were small and, beyond them, there was only darkness. There was no smoke from the chimney but at this time of the year that was hardly a surprise.

Martin wondered what to do. Should he go up and rap on the door and demand entry? Should he skulk around first to find out which room they were in?

Slowly he opened the wrought-iron gate, pressing it hard against the hedge which tried to spring it back against his thighs. He walked forward then turned quickly to grab the gate just before it clanged shut. Already he could feel his heart beating faster. The clammy feeling of menace squirmed the muscles between his shoulders.

He crossed the garden to the window, like a burglar, keeping low, then edged forward to peer cautiously in. The room was dark. He glimpsed a movement just a few inches away and he heard himself gasp in alarm. Then he realised the movement was his own reflection.

'Get a grip on yourself, Thornton,' he muttered under his breath. He was behaving like a scared child.

He turned away from the window and was about to cross the path at the front door and look in the other small frame when a rumbling growl stopped him in his tracks.

Martin spun in a panic, his heart leaping into his throat. Something big and black streaked towards him in a blur. He jerked back instinctively and the thing stopped moving. One second it was yards away at the gate then it moved and then it stopped, faster than his eye could follow.

It stood, squat and broad, four thick and heavily muscled legs planted apart. Its short fur was jet black, with the iridescent gleam of crude oil. It had a broad face that reminded him of a pit-bull terrier, yet was cat-like and fierce. Black eyes, even blacker than the liquid fur, glared at him with deadly intent. The creature was the size of a dog, but looked as powerful as ten. It took a step forward and he heard the scrape of claws on the flagstone.

Then the freezing rumble came again, too loud in the quiet garden, like a tiger in a cave. Martin stepped backwards.

There was a movement behind him, sensed rather than seen. He stumbled against the step at the front door, lost balance and fell back just as the door opened. He toppled through and landed heavily in the front hall.

'Ah, visitors,' a woman's voice said softly. 'No. Just one visitor.'

Martin was sprawled on the polished wood of the hallway floor. He turned and saw Sheila Garvie standing there at the bottom of the stairs, one slim hand delicately draped on the newel post. She was smiling broadly.

It was the coldest smile Martin Thornton had ever seen.

'Now that you're here, I suppose I should invite you inside, even if you have taken the opportunity to invite yourself,' she said. Her voice was creamy and confident, yet to Martin it had the quality of fingernails scraping on marble.

She swivelled her gaze to the doorway and said something in an odd tongue, as if she was clearing her throat. Martin followed her gaze and looked at the thing that squatted, blacker than night, sides heaving as it grunted for breath, on the pathway. He had no sooner set his eyes on it than it flicked to one side and was gone.

'I see you've met my friend again?' she asked.

'Again?' Martin asked dumbly. His mind was in a commotion.

'Oh yes, you two have met before. His name is *Dorchadas*. It means *darkness*. *Nightshade*. He . . .' She paused, searching for the word. 'He *obeys* me. If it hadn't been for your damned luck, you wouldn't be here now. But never mind, I'm gifted with fortune myself. I've had it a long time.'

Martin hauled himself up to his feet. He was taller than Sheila Garvie, but not by much. She looked magnificent in a long black cloak made from a coarse cloth. The dye looked natural and gave it a sheen of purple. Black eyes in a pale skin seemed to bore through him. Her hair was pure white and was caught up high. It was as fine as dawn gossamer.

'How long?' Martin asked.

'Oh, you *have* been a clever boy.' She gave him in a smile of congratulation. To Martin it looked like a hungry rictus. 'You wouldn't believe me if I told you.'

She took her hand down from the balustrade and put it against her chin, as if considering.

'Since your forefathers dressed in skins. Since they boiled the yellow woad and painted themselves purple. Since *my* people took quartz crystals and ground out the cups and rings on the stones. That's how long.'

'I don't believe that,' Martin said, though there was something yammering at the back of his mind, telling him that this new impossibility was *true*.

'That's fair. You don't have to. You're not the first to suspect me and you will not be the last. As you young folk have a habit of saying, I've been around a long time. I can tell you this, because *you* won't be.'

She said that last sentence so flatly and calmly that it sent a cold shiver through Martin.

'Oh, don't worry, I may have uses for you. I've had uses for others. And I laid them all to rest in the old churchyard. My family have taken that *unhallowed* ground to themselves since before your family existed.'

'So I *was* right,' Martin said. 'There was a connection between the names?'

'The name, young man. I am the *Seilach*, the willow. My name never changes. To every one of them a daughter, to keep this place for me until I have to return. Fortunately for them, and for me, I pass on longevity.'

She stopped and drilled him with the black eyes again.

'Do you think you will give me a daughter? I think perhaps you will. Would your little friend be sorrowful if she knew you have given Gail Dean a *son*?'

She laughed then, loud and clear, a real laugh of pure pleasure. Martin felt the sound of it scraping on the inside of his skull. He was standing in the hallway, unsure of what to do. He sensed she was toying with him. He wondered what she would do if he just strode forward and took her by the throat. The thought gave him a momentary, savage pleasure.

'Yes. The cycle will go on, thanks to your little Caitlin, my *seedling*. That's what her name means in the old language, and it is perfect. *She* is perfect. It was not my grandmother who held this place in trust for me. It was my daughter. And the next will do the same, long after you are gone, long after your Caitlin has given herself.'

'What do you mean, *given* herself?'

She stared at him, a small smile playing about her lips, then she turned.

'Come with me,' she said imperiously. Martin debated whether to follow or maybe even just raise his fist and smack her on the back of the head and ransack the place until he found Caitlin.

Just as he thought that, she made the cat-like hawking sound again. Martin was suddenly aware of a presence behind him. The oily squat thing that was sometimes like a cat and sometimes like nothing on earth made the low growl that rumbled up from the depths to shake the air.

Martin followed Sheila Garvie into the room.

'Don't worry, he won't eat you, not unless I tell him. You've heard of a *familiar*, have you? From the old fairy tales? The witch's cat? Nightshade is one of mine. He travels between the worlds. He travels for me.'

She sat elegantly on the settee and patted the seat next to her.

'Come and sit down. Let me tell you about myself.'

'I don't know that I want to hear it.'

'Oh, you do. You've been checking on me. I can read that in your face. You cannot live as long as I have and not develop some talents. You're not the first to suspect. The Colquhoun suspected me. His priests prodded me and cut me to find the witchmarks. But I have the power of the forest, the power of healing. The pain was nothing to me. The blood a mere drop. And they *drowned* me in the river. Ha. They *thought* they'd drowned me. Fools.'

She turned to him and her eyes sucked the light from the room.

'They cannot kill me. And neither can you.'

'What are you going to do?'

'I think you know something, but you don't want to believe the rest. You folk today,' she shook her head sadly. 'All technology and computers. But that makes it easier for me, of course.'

She grinned.

'I am going to pay homage to my lord and master. He gives me life and I give him life. While you spend your time on your knees praying to a Lord you have never seen, I worship a *Lord* who repays.'

'And you're going to use Caitlin?'

'She will go willingly. His power has given her life. It has made her complete. She will give the power back with herself, and the tree will grow again. It will fruit and I will drink the life for another five generations. The Lord *Cerunnos* will take her to himself, to his world.'

'And then what?'

'Then he will return to protect his earth from you people.'

'You're mad,' Martin said heatedly, then instantly regretted it for being a line straight out of a third-rate movie.

'Me? Mad?' She laughed again with a snort of derision. 'Look at the world. I have walked all over its surface. You people have almost destroyed it. You have raped and robbed it in your hunt for wealth. You have cut down the forests, even here, in the heart of the old wood which stretched from the islands to Siberia when the land bridge was intact and from there across the Americas. Now the forests are gone. You have poisoned the air and made it reek with your stench and your filth.'

Sheila Garvie's face twisted with the strength of her emotion.

'In your atheism – your disbelief – you have plundered the Earth in the name of your gods and your money. You call me *mad*? What is the few drops of blood I have spilt and will spill to save this world? I will bring the power of the earth back to this place. He will be born from the tree and he will stalk the earth like thunder and make you pay the price. His power will be irresistible and behind him will come the old ones to reclaim their right.'

She stopped, eyes like burning pits.

'Then,' she said, '*then* you will see the face of madness. And maybe I will spare you that. Maybe I will spare you that and let your seed live on. Perhaps we will go a-planting on the fertile ground, you and I.'

Martin shook his head.

'No chance,' he said slowly. 'You're off your head. Seriously. You should be locked up.'

'But I won't be,' she shot back. 'And you won't be telling the story either. Not in your newspaper, not to *anyone*.'

Martin stood up quickly. There was a small, intricately-carved coffee table between them standing on a thick leg which branched into three feet. He reached and snatched it up as a defence against the creature in the hallway. His left hand scrabbled in the pocket of his jacket.

From outside the door there was a monstrous growl, so loud that the door actually vibrated against the jamb.

Martin turned his head towards the sound and Sheila Garvie came at him with the speed of a snake. She reached up her hand and his face was taken in the grip of a clawed vice. The force of it was unbelievable. He felt his cheekbones creak under the pressure.

'Foolish boy,' she grated. He tried to swing the coffee table up but she jerked her arm and forced his face towards her, almost tearing the tendons in his neck. She loomed towards him, eyes searing black.

Then Sheila Garvie opened her mouth and spat at him. With an open-throated coughing sound a dark liquid jetted forward and splattered across his face. His skin seemed to shrivel as the mucus burned across it and there was a dreadful putrid stink. He gasped, trying not to breathe, but she held him tight. His fingers went numb and the small table clattered to the floor.

Sheila Garvie laughed and, as his vision wavered, her face seemed to turn into a grinning skull with black eye sockets and long clenched teeth. He felt his legs give way, then a darkness came and swallowed him up. He fell into it and it felt as if he was falling forever.

35

Caitlin Brook came back from her early-morning run to find Martin Thornton gone. She had lain beside him in the early hours, when the sun was just on the rise behind the Douglas Hills, sending a pearly glow into the east sky. He'd been breathing heavily, lying on his side with one hand tucked under the pillow.

She had softly moved the curl of hair off his brow, resisting the temptation to touch him again. The memory of the night was still a warm glow and she smiled to herself at the recollection. She watched for a few more minutes, then slowly eased herself from the bed, trying not to disturb him. He half-turned in his sleep when she drew the cover back over him, then his breathing settled. Caitlin went into the kitchen, picking her clothes up as she went, skin puckering into gooseflesh in the cool morning air. She took her jogging suit from the airing cupboard and dressed quickly before taking the wooden box from the shelf. Sheila had filled it again two days previously. The drawstring on the sachet opened at a light tug and she scooped a tablespoonful of the powder into the tall glass.

She drank it down in one long swallow, feeling the hot burn in her belly, then the glow of fire as it spread, kicking her whole body with energy.

The kitchen door creaked as she opened it, but it closed without a sound. She got through the front gate, darting her eyes left and right to make sure she was unobserved. Sheila Garvie had made her promise to tell no one about the change in her, at least for the time being. She'd broken that promise by telling Martin Thornton, but she owed him that. She crossed to the edge of the trees where a walkers' track angled round the edge of the coppice and then became a pasture path bounded by tall hedges. She increased her pace, feeling the wonderful energy spangle within her, and a few yards further on she started to run.

Her steps made soft padding sounds on the dew-damp earth as she ran lightly along the path, savouring the expanding bubble of exhilaration. She was suddenly *alive*.

Sheila Garvie had been right, she told herself. There *was* a magic in the plants of the forests. She had promised her she would run again and here was the living proof. Caitlin didn't question it. It was enough that the nerves had knitted themselves together and made the muscles move and feel again. Last night – the thought caused a hot flush of pleasure to redden her cheeks – she had felt *everything*. It had been as miraculous as the astonishing fact of reborn sensation.

Caitlin moved smoothly along the path, relishing the memory, unable to keep the smile from her face.

It had been right and it had been good. Sometime in the hot night she had told him she loved him and, in the cool of the morning, she knew that was true. She couldn't explain it any more than she could explain the sudden need to give herself to him. She recalled the sharp pain and the trickle of blood and laughed aloud. Whatever else Sheila Garvie's *mélange* had done, it had accomplished *another* impossibility. Caitlin had felt the stretching sensation and then the ripping pain as her hymen had torn. She had immediately recognised it for what it was, because it was the *second* time in her life that the momentary sear had caused her to cry out. The first time it had happened, more years ago than she cared to recall, the panting boy had ignored it and drilled himself into her in frenzied thrusts while she cried aloud and tried to push him off. Martin Thornton had been different. He had stopped, eyes filled with concern, and tried to pull back. It had been Caitlin, aware of what had happened, who had held him close.

Caitlin ran lightly, not pushing herself, though already she knew that her muscles were strong enough to carry her racing along the track. She was thinking about Martin Thornton and what he had said to her. He was obviously concerned and she could accept that. What she could not – and did not – accept was his insistence that she stop taking Sheila's herbal remedy. That law laid down, she was prepared to agree to anything else. She *would* go with him if it stopped him from worrying. But it was difficult for her to identify with his fears.

Sheila Garvie had saved her life. She had given her back the joy of motion. Caitlin could see no danger in that. Sure, the older woman was mysterious, perhaps a bit *fey*. She didn't seem to mix in the normal life of the village. She might spend her life gathering plants and making old-fashioned remedies, but Caitlin could see no danger in that. She had read enough to know of some poisons like *digitalis* and *curare* which were deadly but also used as medicines throughout the world. They had worked the miracle, they had made her run again.

It was an hour before she got back to the cottage, running slowly and then walking. As soon as she got to the edge of the coppice she noticed Martin's Land-Rover was gone and a pang of disappointment tugged at her. In the kitchen she searched for a note, but there was nothing. She checked the bed. He'd folded the duvet down and she saw the leaf of dried blood. The bed was still warm. He must, she realised, have woken, found her gone and left.

But where? Probably up to the village for some milk or rolls, she thought, more in hope than in certainty. She was sure he'd have left a note if he'd decided to leave the glen, especially after what he'd said the night before, especially after what they'd *done* the night before. She didn't believe he'd suddenly got scared and cut and run.

Just as Caitlin turned to go into the living room, something on the floor caught her eye. It was the tall glass that she'd used to take the infusion of herbs. Curious, she bent to pick it up. She was sure she'd left it on the work surface beside the stove. She put it back there and walked away thoughtfully.

Duncan Haldane waited until nine o'clock for John Lovatt to turn up with his dogs. The farmer, who still had a few head of hill sheep and a full sty of pigs on the far side of the glen, was late. Eventually Duncan pulled on his boots and his torn walking jacket and unlocked the gun cabinet. The twelve-bore was sleek and gleaming from his careful cleaning the night before.

The children were having their breakfast in the kitchen. Rosie had decked Dorrie out in a yellow summer frock over the girl's strongly expressed objections. Dorothy had wanted to wear her jeans and told her mother she'd feel a *cissy* in a dress. Duncan had laughed at that and Rose had shot him a look. She told her daughter that all the other girls would be wearing dresses to the summerplay picnic and she wouldn't want to be the odd one out. Dorrie countered by telling her that dresses were no good against stinging nettles. Rose told her to stay away from nettles, thistles and anything else. She also told her it might be a good idea to leave the teddy bear at home, but Dorrie kept it firmly tucked under her arm. It hadn't left her side since the day they'd been lost in the forest. The mother-and-daughter war of words went on. Duncan let them get on with it.

Ben was staying at home. He'd hardly been out of the farmyard in a month and spent his days in the yard, kicking a ball against the old byre wall, or up in his room making model aeroplanes. Duncan thought it was a complete waste of a summer holiday but any time he mentioned it Rose hushed him. She knew Ben would take his own good time getting over what was troubling him. She thought forcing him would just prolong it. Anyway Duncan felt easier if the children didn't wander too far. Once he'd killed the boar that attacked Morag, he told himself, it would be different. Maybe he'd take the boy down to the Loch shore and do a spot of fishing, get the lad out of himself, so to speak.

John Lovatt's arrival was heralded by the high-pitched yapping of his terriers. Ben heard the commotion outside and went to the window. He'd seen his father oiling the shotgun the night before but hadn't given it much thought.

'What's happening?' he called from the far side of the room. 'Mr Lovatt's here with his dogs.'

'We're going to get the beast that got our Morag,' Duncan told him. 'It was John's pig. He's come to help me catch it.'

'Where are you going?'

Duncan came across to the window where Ben was kneeling on the seat, arms hooked over the back, peering out. He bent down close to the boy and pointed out to the left beyond the path to where the land sloped down to the stream and to the Fasach Wood.

'We'll start off high and drive down by the river. If it stays on our side, it'll be a lot easier,' he said.

'You're going into the trees?' Ben's face was suddenly wide with alarm.

'Well, if we don't, there's a chance it could come out again and do some more damage.' Duncan didn't say exactly what damage he thought the pig could do. In his mind's eye he was not thinking about farmyard dogs but of children.

'But, Dad,' Ben protested, pale-faced. Duncan had turned away, adjusting his thornproof coat. 'Dad, please.'

'What is it, son?'

'It's the forest, Dad. It's *bad* in there. Please don't go.'

Duncan gave his son a wry grin. The big man looked down at the small boy. He took off his hat and planted it on Ben's head. It swamped the nine-year-old, drooping right down to cover his eyes, the peak aslant. Ben smelled the warm *father* smell. It did not help him.

'You keep that warm till I get back. It looks as if it'll rain. I'll take the waterproof.'

'Dad, please,' Ben begged, his voice crackling and close to tears. 'The trees *move* down there. They'll *get* you.'

'Nonsense, lad. Look at this,' Duncan said, hefting the shotgun. He was wearing the big cartridge belt that Rose had bought him a Christmas or two back. It was lined with bright yellow shells filled with heavy ballshot. 'This could stop an elephant. There's nothing down there but badgers and foxes and maybe one big bad bugger of a pig. Don't you worry about me, wee man, I'll be back for tea, and we'll have fresh ham to go with it.'

Duncan flipped the peak of the cap back from Ben's eyes and gently flicked his son's nose.

'Once I come back, you and me, we'll have a wee talk and we'll organise a couple of days' fishing.'

Ben nodded slowly, almost sleepily. He wasn't listening. In his mind's eye his memory reran the scene from his race through the jungly forest and then flicked forward to the blood pouring from the cut roots down in the coppice and the deadly racket of the chain saw spinning out of control, whirling teeth arcing towards his head.

The forest was *alive*. He knew it and nobody could understand him. His father was going down there and Ben was *dreadfully* afraid.

Duncan cupped his big hand round his son's chin and held it for a moment before he went into the kitchen to tell Rose he was heading off now. She had packed some sandwiches in tin foil in his haversack, along with a flask of coffee. Little Dorrie beamed up at him, bright and summery in her frock.

'My goodness, you almost look like a girl today,' Duncan said.

He bent down and kissed the top of her head. He told her to enjoy herself and then asked Rose to keep an eye on Ben. She told him she'd be taking him into the village when Dorothy went to the summerplay picnic.

Duncan went out of the house with the shotgun over his shoulder. John Lovatt was waiting in the yard with four wiry terriers yipping at his heels. From the window, Ben watched them angle across the road and start to walk down the hill. Inside, his stomach was roiling with anxiety. A great grey weight of foreboding settled on his shoulders as he saw the two men go down the hill. In a few steps his father had disappeared from view, heading for the stream and Fasach Wood.

Susan Herron welcomed Dorrie Haldane at the church hall with a big friendly hug. Most of the small children were already gathered there, most in their summer best, though a couple of mothers had looked at the lowering skies with weather eyes and been more practical. One or two of the boys were in jeans and boots and a couple of them had thin nylon overjackets crumpled in their pockets.

Rose Haldane took Ben to the coffee shop for an ice cream. Meg Balfron was not at her usual place behind the counter, which was loaded as always with delicate cakes and pastries. Her niece, a dark-haired heavy-set girl with pretty blue eyes, was standing in for her.

In the church hall Susan, along with Melanie Cuthbert and Caroline Petrie, who ran the summerplay project with funds from the community council, were handing out plastic bags filled with sweets. Some of the men had been press-ganged into carrying the hampers down to the field next to the Corrie earlier that morning. They'd also taken a scythe to some of the weeds to leave a clear space for the children's races.

'Right, children,' Caroline called out. 'Are we all set?'

They all affirmed in unison, high children's voices, excited and expectant.

'Right, then. Let's go and have a picnic,' Caroline yelled. She clapped her hands and the children filed out, most of the girls hand in hand, some of the boys with arms round each other's shoulders, the way only small boys do and grown men can't.

Susan held Dorrie and another small girl with each hand and

they skipped together with the rest of them down by the corner, close to where Tom Cannon had come, bewildered, to his senses on the night he'd gone to change a lightbulb in Molly Carr's living room. He was one of the men who'd helped clear the area down by the river and still had no recollection of the events of that night.

The group of adults and children were singing '*Mhairi's Wedding*', walking in step to the cadence of the tune as they made their way past the row of shops. Many of the villagers waved from their windows or from shop doorways. Rose Haldane had chosen a window seat in the coffee shop, where she was having a pot of tea while Ben shoved his ice cream listlessly around on his plate. She gave her daughter a cheery wave as the little girl skipped by, a huge smile of childish happiness on her face, teddy clutched in a hug.

In a few moments, they were gone along the top road and heading for the first bend, everyone staying close to the edge in case of traffic, although everybody in the glen knew about the children's picnic and would have been ultra-careful.

They passed the place where Craig Buist had fled from his father while Alec Stirling watched the chase down the slope, and they skipped on, still singing, as they turned the corner and came to the spot where Susan Herron and her ex-boyfriend Paul Thomson had been surprised in the moonlight by the three village toughs. The sky was still light in the east and the day warming up, though the pall of clouds stacked over the Dumbuie Hills was swelling thick and dark. Susan hoped the rain would stay away for just one more day, until the picnic was over. Everybody had put a lot of work into it and she would hate to see the children disappointed at missing out on the high spot of the summer.

The crowd of them, girls in bright frocks, pigtails and ponytails, crossed the stile, the smaller ones being lifted over by the three young women, and then they scrambled down the hill towards the shallow part of the meandering river. Off to the right, some three hundred yards away, the edge of Fasach Wood loomed darkly, shading the Corrie River as it tumbled out into the open.

Peter Bain tossed back the dregs of a can of lager as he watched the procession from his vantage point on the rocky outcrop at the far

470

end of the slope. Beside him Rory McIntyre passed him a joint, breathing out the blue smoke wheezily.

'Isn't that Susie the Stork?' he asked, sniggering.

'Crazy-legs Herron sure enough,' Tam Donald said. He was sitting on the stump of an old tree that had been hit by a bolt of lightning three years before and was now almost completely overgrown with moss.

'Give her one, so I would,' Rory ventured.

'And I'd give her the rest,' Tam said, grinning at his own wit. He turned to Peter Bain. 'Hey, Pete, didn't you give it to her?'

'Nah. Couldn't be bothered. Didn't want that city slicker's slippery seconds. I'd just make him look bad anyway.'

'We made him *feel* bad, right enough,' Rory came in. 'We showed him. Bastard's never been back.'

The three of them had been on the outcrop for more than an hour. Tam Donald had hiked a six-pack of his brother's lager from the fridge. There were four boys in the house and he reckoned he'd probably be able to pin the blame on the others. Peter Bain was supposed to be helping his father lay in field drains, but had sneaked away. He'd probably get a thick ear when he went home, but by then most of the hard work would be done. He and the others had chipped in for a cube of poor-quality hash at a disco in Lochend the week before and were trying to convince each other that they were getting a huge buzz out of it.

Pete watched Susan Herron stroll down the field, long, coltish legs taking easy strides. She was wearing tight white jeans and her fair hair streamed behind her. He felt a momentary tightness in his own jeans and a bitter taste of sullen envy. No matter his bravado, she wouldn't look the road he was on, and he knew it.

'Fucking high-arsed bitch,' he muttered.

They watched as the children reached the flat part of the field where the river meandered round in a loop, leaving a grassy peninsula which was ideal for the picnic. Here the river was slow-moving and shallow. It had sandy banks where sandmartins had pecked their nest-holes and in the easy current sticklebacks and small trout darted.

Caroline, Melanie and Susan started laying out the canvas groundsheets for everyone to sit on. One of them had brought a

471

big tape player and the tinny sound of children's music floated up the hill.

'Right, children,' Caroline called out, gathering them round. A couple of the small boys had already shucked off their shoes and were getting ready to paddle in the river. 'First of all, we'll have a drink of juice and a piece of cake,' she told them. Shrill cries of approval chorused. 'Then, we'll have some games and races. Anybody who's brought a swimming costume can have a dip, but you have to stay with Susan and Melanie. No running off. Later, we'll have a treasure hunt, and there's *big* prizes for everybody.'

More hoots of pleasure followed this announcement and the children got down to the serious business of demolishing the cakes from the hampers.

The three idlers watched from the distance, drinking and smoking as the clouds rolled in further from the west. The children competed in the usual sack races and egg-and-spoon events, using hard-boiled ones which later went into the sandwiches. The sound of childish laughter floated up the hill towards them.

'Bloody kids' stuff,' Tam Donald said with a derisory sneer. 'Never had that when we were that age.'

'All we got was a boot up the arse and sent out to clean the shit out of the yard.'

Just then one of the MacKinnon tankers drove by in a low-gear roar as it climbed the hill. The driver hit the horn and sent a two-toned flat bellow of acknowledgement down the field to the children.

'Jesus, *fuck*!' Pete said, choking on his lager. 'Nearly gave me a bloody heart attack.' The other two laughed uproariously as he wiped the froth from the front of his stained T-shirt.

'Can't hold your beer, man,' Rory remarked.

'I'll get a hold of your bloody throat,' Pete spat back.

Down in the flatland, the children waved up at the tanker as it rounded the corner and disappeared up the hill.

Even at noon there was sunlight down at the Corrie, though by this time the clouds had lowered and edged towards Linnvale, casting a shadow over the village.

Pete Bain and his cronies finished another can and had a belching competition.

'Wouldn't mind a shot on one of those tankers,' Tam ventured. 'Nobody messes with those bastards.'

472

'I'm going to see old Donnie about a job,' Rory said.

'Don't be daft. You have to pass your test first and then get your heavy goods ticket. It would take you ten years,' Pete jumped in. 'I wouldn't bother with it. You'll be rolling barrels along with the rest of them down at Ardbeg. They pay peanuts, but you get as much whisky as you can drink.'

Just then, Tam let out a low whistle.

'Look at that *body*,' he breathed.

Down by the river Susan Herron had stepped out of her jeans. She was standing with a small group of children who were in bathing costumes. From that distance they couldn't hear what was being said but there was no mistaking the girl's lithe frame in a brief two-piece outfit.

'Christ, that toffee-nosed bastard had that all to himself,' Rory said enviously.

Over to the left, in the shade of a small willow, Caroline Petrie was taking her clothes off, with her back to the children, and hidden from their view by a low gorse bush. She was entirely unaware of the audience up on the outcrop. She shrugged out of her shirt and then quickly undid her bra, slipping it off with a quick flick.

Rory heard Pete's sharp intake of breath as the young woman's breasts erupted into view, standing proud and firm.

'Holy shite,' Pete muttered. 'Would you look at—'

Just then, Caroline shrugged her white summer slacks down, taking everything else with them as well. The three layabouts sat stock-still, eyes wide and disbelieving.

'Fuck me, you can see her . . .' Rory started and then trailed off.

Still unaware, Caroline stretched and lifted her hands to her hair, catching it up with a clasp, still completely naked. She strode forward several steps, bent to a towel roll and pulled out a swimsuit. She stepped into it and drew it up over her body.

'What a woman,' Tam said. Rory nodded dumbly.

'I'm going to have her,' Pete said. He was absently rubbing his crotch with the half-empty can of lager.

Down on the flat, Caroline, still unaware she'd been observed, picked up her clothes and went back to the crowd of children.

Half an hour later the clouds held back no longer. The big low pressure that had been building up beyond the Dumbuie Hills shifted to the east, rolling dark over the village and blotting out the sun. The rain started with none of the usual spitting drizzle that was normal for these parts. The skies opened and simply *deluged* the valley.

Up on the outcrop, accompanied by a selection of oaths and curses, Pete Bain and his sidekicks hauled their jackets over their heads and made for the shelter of a big chestnut tree whose branches swept down to only feet from the ground at the side of the road. It took them twenty-five seconds to make it to shelter, by which time they were soaked through.

Down at the river Susan and Caroline were laughing with a mixture of pleasure and disappointment. One minute they had been splashing in the shallows with the children, corralling them in close to the bank. The next, they were standing in a downpour of huge drops of rain. The rainfall was so heavy that the slow-moving surface of the river seemed to come alive with ripples and silver spinning-coin splashes. The children squealed in delight while, on the flat grass, Melanie rushed around, trying to gather clothes and hampers.

Susan and Caroline shepherded the children to the bank while everybody tried to wipe the streaming rain from their faces.

'What do we do now?' Susan asked, shouting over the loud hiss of rainfall.

'Let's get to the trees,' Caroline said. 'We can dry off there and then have the treasure hunt. It's only a spot of rain.'

'Feels more like the flood to me,' said Susan, laughing.

They helped gather the clothes and picnic gear together and then they all ran, with the children racing ahead, towards Fasach Wood.

Above, the sky was blue-black. Ahead, the forest was dark and shadowed.

Up on the hill, the three youths watched the flight with derisive laughter. They had three cans of lager left. Pete sprung the pull and the beer hissed in a frothy arc, covering Tam's jacket.

'What'll we do now?' Rory wanted to know.

'I'm for staying here until the rain goes off.'

'Me too,' Tam said. 'I want to see her putting her clothes on again.'

'You're just a dirty bastard,' Pete accused. What he didn't mention was that he'd been thinking the same thing.

36

The first time he had woken, head spinning and temples pounding, he was lying on a cold floor.

He turned slightly and felt the rasp of stone under him. He tried to move, but his body could only respond lethargically.

It was not dark, but it took several moments for his vision to clear. He felt as if he was lying at the bottom of a rectangular pit whose walls soared high into the distance, narrowing towards each other as they climbed. He blinked, shook his head, and the throbbing pain thudded on the inside of his skull. The walls were lined with shelves crammed with bottles and jars, each of them elongated into tall tubes in his distorted vision. Gradually his eyes righted themselves. The walls shrunk down, widened out. He realised he was lying in a cellar. There was a musty smell in the place, an old, cobwebby, damp smell. Martin tried to recall how he had got here, but his memory was fuzzy and indistinct. He wondered if he was dreaming.

Then, behind him, Sheila Garvie spoke and the memory rushed back to him.

'Welcome back,' she said. Her voice was light and mirthfully sarcastic.

Martin twisted himself around, ignoring the thumping behind his forehead. He remembered she had hawked something up from her throat and spat at him. Then he had fallen.

'Oh, don't bother getting up,' she said. 'You won't be able to.'

Martin pondered this for a moment. He shoved himself upwards with his elbows until he was in a sitting position, then tried to bend his legs under him. They refused to move.

'What—?' he mumbled, puzzled. He shifted position and tried again, grunting with the effort. Nothing happened. There was no feeling in his legs.

Sudden fear swelled.

'*I'm paralysed.*' The panicked thought jumped into his mind and flashed there in big black letters. His legs wouldn't move and he couldn't stand up or crawl. He was helpless. A vision of a wheelchair froze him.

'Interesting,' Sheila Garvie said. 'Your Caitlin has got her legs back, and you've lost yours. How does it feel?'

'What have you done to me?' Martin blurted out, fighting down the bubble of dread.

'Oh, don't worry. It's just my little joke,' Sheila Garvie said. She came round from behind him and he followed her with his eyes. She stood looking down at him disdainfully. 'I shan't leave you like that. I only chose the strong. And you *will* be. I can guarantee that.'

She lowered herself to a wooden seat that stood a couple of yards away beside the broad table.

'I can do what I want with you. But first, I want you to *believe*.'

'Believe what?' The words had to fight their way past the tightness in his throat.

'Here, let me help you,' she said, rising and walking towards him. She bent and got her hands under his armpits and lifted him with surprising strength until he was upright. His legs trailed limp underneath him. His arms were weak and felt boneless. She pulled him roughly to the table and sat him on it, then simply let him flop back to the surface. His head hit the wood with a jarring thump and stars spangled in front of his eyes. One arm flopped over the side of the table and when his vision cleared he realised how vulnerable he was. His legs were splayed and dangling almost to the floor. He was wide open.

She leaned over him and smiled.

'Where shall we begin?' she said in a storyteller's whisper.

She reached for a bottle on a shelf and plucked out the glass stopper. Green liquid sloshed turbidly. She dipped a finger in up to the first knuckle. When she withdrew it the finger was coated in a gelatinous substance. She reached forward and took him by the face again, squeezing until his mouth opened, then she plunged her finger right inside, smearing the fluid on the inside of his cheek.

There was no taste, no expected acid burn, but almost instantly his muscles spasmed in a violent jolt. His spine arched from the surface of the table and his arms flexed by themselves, hooking up into the air, fingers clawed rigidly. An uncontrollable shiver ran through him and then a wave of heat raced under his skin, as if his whole body was on fire. There was a crackling in his ears and his vision blanked out for a third time. The fire raced down his ams and legs and then gathered in the centre of his body. An enormous swelling pressure expanded in his groin. It continued to swell and stretch and the pain of it overwhelmed his confusion. Sheila Garvie reached a hand between his legs and touched him where the pain was greatest. He felt as if he was about to burst. The light contact sent a shiver of agony through him. He heard himself cry out.

'Oh, yes. I can make you do what I want,' she gloated. 'Anything at all.'

Despite the pain and the crackling in his ears, he could sense the quickening of her breath.

She drew her hand slowly down the painful length of him, then squeezed. The pain bucked like a wild animal.

'I could do it *now*,' she hissed. 'Now, while it's *hot*.'

She leaned over him and speared him again with her black eyes. 'Do you feel the heat? Do you *feel* it?'

It was like a white furnace. Her fingers squeezed and he felt as if he was being ripped at the roots. He cried out again and Sheila Garvie laughed.

'Something to cool your ardour, I think. I can wait for you, and you can wait for me too.'

She reached beyond his vision and brought her hand round to the front of his face. She opened her palm and blew on it. Tiny motes of golden dust spangled the air, catching the glint from a lamp behind him. He tried to turn his face away, but couldn't help breathing it in. His throat caught and the fire in his crotch instantly died. The release was unimaginable. Instant coolness doused the raging fire and the agonising stretching of his tissues collapsed. He let out a groan of relief.

'Now dream, my lovely,' she said in a soft voice. She reached again and came back with another palm full of dust. He couldn't tell whether it was the same or not. She blew a cloud into his face again. Without warning, the whole room spun. He turned, mouth agape, expression frozen. Sheila Garvie's eyes were laughing at him. She was moving away, *floating* away from him down a long, dark corridor. Her laughter, at first loud, was diminishing with the distance. She disappeared and the world went black.

Martin Thornton awoke lying on his back on soft earth.

Above him leaves rustled. Under his back, something moved beneath the ground. He rolled over, scrambled to his feet. A root came poking out of the brown soil in a sinuous, snaky motion. He stumbled back. A branch reached down and snatched at him. Martin whirled. Wooden eyes opened in the rough bark of a tree and glared blindly at him. He tried to turn away but something held him and the terror of the dream began.

Duncan Haldane and John Lovatt had come down from the top end of the valley. John was unhappy about Duncan bringing his gun. If the pig actually was his escaped boar then it was worth more alive than dead. He'd brought a stave with a wire loop attached to the end and told Duncan that if the terriers managed to corner the animal, he had a fair chance of catching it and bringing it back to cover the sows in his sty.

'Not if I see it first,' Duncan had said. 'If you'd seen the mess that thing made of our Morag you'd be carrying a gun as well. If yon beast comes out of the bushes, I'd advise you to head for the nearest tree. Without the gun I'd be doing the same.'

The dogs were ranging through the undergrowth. Duncan had led them to the churned area where he'd been cutting logs and let them sniff around. They were small sleek terriers, with short, muscular legs and an aggressive, broad-chested stance. They had yipped excitedly and then had followed the scent to the stumps of the coppice before angling down to the stream and into the trees.

They were good dogs. Once inside Fasach Wood, they had worked tirelessly, ranging about, calling to each other with their shrill barks. Duncan and John had quartered the top end of the woods by lunchtime, but as yet there was still no sign of the boar.

It was just around noon when they stopped at the old dry-stone dyke. Duncan put his gun up against the stones then sat down to open his haversack. He poured coffee for them both while John gave the dogs a few biscuits to fight over. The men ate their sandwiches and savoured the coffee. Down in the forest it was dark. Over to the west a rumble rolled across the sky and the texture of the air thickened.

'Looks like rain,' John said.

'Looked it this morning. Maybe it'll hold off,' Duncan said.

Just as he did the first huge droplets hit the top canopy of the trees and in seconds the forest was drumming with the pelting rain. It took a while for the water to filter through the leaf cover. It pattered down to the litter underfoot and splashed on the moss on the stones. In a few minutes the forest floor was sodden. Duncan got up and hefted his gun.

'More shelter over there,' he said, pointing beyond the wall to where the trees crowded closely. John followed him, scrambling over the tumbled stones. Behind him the little dogs stood, all in a line, sniffing the air. One of them whined uncomfortably and the rest of them took it up in sympathy.

'Come on,' John said, emphasising his command with a low whistle.

The terriers milled around, moving up to the wall, then sniffing the air, before quickly turning to retreat for a few yards.

'What's got into them?' Lovatt muttered. He walked back several paces and called to them again. 'Get across here. Come on.' He whistled again.

One of the dogs whimpered and took a few steps forward. It snuffled, uncertainly, then started to scuttle over the stones. It reached its master and immediately huddled close to his feet, bob-tail trying to tuck itself away. The others hesitated then followed reluctantly. John made his way to where Duncan sat under the bole of a big beech and found a convenient root under a thick bough which offered more shelter from the drumming rain. The dogs were no longer barking. They whined plaintively, like lost puppies, and their aggressive stance had changed to a cowering, fearful crouch as they huddled close to their master.

'Skitterish craturs,' John said. 'Must be the thunder.'

Duncan poured the last of the coffee into the two screw-on plastic cups and they drank it, finishing their lunch and talking just loud enough to hear each other over the incessant drumming of the rain. When they had finished, Duncan hefted his gun and John took his rustic stave-snare and they walked on through the trees. In a short time they came to a track. John shooed the dogs away, telling then to go-seek, but they refused to move away from him, walking so close he almost tripped. Thunder strode the dark sky and beneath the thick canopy the sizzling flickers of lightning etched the outlines of branches and trunks on their eyes. They

479

walked on in the now tight and charged atmosphere into the lush depths of the wood.

On the far side of the forest, Susan Herron and Caroline Petrie were shrugging themselves into their clothes on top of their wet costumes. Melanie Cuthbert was glad she hadn't gone into the water. She couldn't swim in any case but at least she was drier than the other two. The women helped the children out of their wet things and into clothing that was only damp. They had all scampered towards the forest, clutching everything in their arms, while the rain hammered down in solid rods of water. Then they'd had to spend some time sorting all the clothes out. The children had been laughing on the brief dash, not caring about the warm rain, until the first clap of thunder reverberated down from the hills and the spike of lightning had stabbed down from the bruised sky. Some of the smaller ones had squealed in sudden fright. One wee girl was holding onto Susan's legs so tightly she could feel tiny fingers digging into her thigh through her damp white jeans.

'Come on, children, into the shelter,' Melanie had called to them. She knew that in a thunderstorm it was best to stay away from trees, but she decided that it was even better to get in from the open. She turned round to herd them along and looked out from under the spreading branches. The rain was coming down straight and so heavily that the river was lost in a haze. Caroline and Susan were just at the edge of the forest. For a brief second they were silhouetted in the flare of lightning. Orange *woman* shapes danced in her eyes before they faded to purple and then broke up. The three of them gathered the children and moved deeper into the forest. They found a spreading sycamore tree with a mass of palmate leaves which formed a barrier to much of the downpour and huddled under it. Caroline did a head count. There were twenty-two children plus themselves, all present and correct.

'Well, children. I think it's story time, and then we'll have our treasure hunt.' At the back of the group, two boys seemed more interested in climbing the tree and Caroline ordered them down to earth. 'We all have to stay together. I don't want you wandering off.'

She sat down with her back to the tree. Susan and Melanie gathered the smaller children who were still frightened of the thunder and held them close. The dark-haired young woman, whose body had so impressed the three roustabouts on the outcrop, gathered her thoughts for a moment, then started to improvise a story. As she spoke, the little ones quietened down. Most of the children sat wide-eyed, enjoying the excitement of the storm and the thrill of the fairytale.

A little way into the story, Billy Lovatt, John Lovatt's nephew, eased himself round the base of the sycamore tree where they were sitting. Neil McKinnon, old Donnie's grandson, crept after him and they wormed themselves past a tangle of ferns towards where a brightly-coloured cock-pleasant was pecking at the ground. Its beak made the leaves fly up in a brown shower a few inches from the ground. Then it walked maybe ten steps away from them. They followed like Indian scouts. None of the women noticed them go.

Alec Stirling ran from the post office van, holding his canvas mailsack over his head, towards the door of his house at the corner end of Hill Terrace. He'd driven up the Linn Road with his wipers going at double speed and even then he'd had to peer through the windscreen, nose only inches from the glass, to see where he was going. He did his rounds as quickly as he could and it was when he was down Mill Lane, returning from his delivery at the Douglas estates, that he passed a large green shape at the side of the road near the millhouse. The rain was too heavy for him to get a real look at it and he kept his eyes firmly on the road ahead while he negotiated the bend close to the old millhouse which was just a brown smudge in the corner of his vision. He drove on to drop two letters at Caitlin Brook's house. He knocked on the doors, both back and front, and peered in the windows, getting only a cold drip of rainwater down the back of his neck for his trouble.

When Alec burst in to his own place, the dripping empty sack draped over his shoulders, Craig Buist was sitting on the couch wearing one of the postman's old baggy jumpers. The television was on, while Craig sat blank-eyed. Alec couldn't tell if he was watching it or not. The boy seemed lost within himself.

Alec made beans and sausages for them both and watched Craig push the food around his plate. Outside, the rain hammered on the roof and every now and again lightning would flash the window into a white rectangle.

It was only halfway though his second piece of toast that Alec realised what he'd seen on the way back from Douglas Estates. The green shape angled in against the millhouse ash grove had been Martin Thornton's Land-Rover.

He stopped in mid bite and wondered. Martin had left the previous night, heading for Caitlin Brook's house. He'd been asking questions about Sheila Garvie, though he wouldn't say why. His Land-Rover hadn't been at Caitlin's house and Martin had promised to come back to see Alec that morning.

He wondered a bit more, chewing a chunk of sausage slowly as he did so. He thought again about the boy's story of what had happened in the woods. Alec had been convinced that Ernie Buist was lying in some thicket with a fair-sized dent in the back of his skull, and he, for one, would have lost not a blink of sleep over that. But Martin had acted oddly when he'd heard the tale. He had questioned the boy as if he *believed* something had happened, as if maybe he was prepared to *accept* at least a part of it. Alec had known Martin a long time. He'd been feeding him stories for more than ten years. He thought Martin was a bit long in tooth and trade to believe any of it.

Yes something nagged at him.

Something funny was going on. Maybe something *not* funny. There were one or two things that had struck him as odd in the last couple of days, not least Craig Buist's tale of trees with an aggressive bent. That very afternoon, heading along the Loch Shore Road in the sudden vicious downpour, he'd overshot the Linnvale turn. It had never happened to him in his life before and he'd lived in these parts a good long while. He'd had to reverse back again, wiping the rain-misted driver's window with his elbow, then had to roll it down altogether. When he did that, the road appeared as if by magic through the drizzle. Then when he'd angled the van into the turn he'd almost had to ram the thing through the overhanging leaves. It was as if the downpour, after the long hot spell, had spurred the trees and the bushes at the side of the road into instant growth. Some of the bramble runners were stretched right across the tarmac like thick horny ropes.

There was something else tugging at the back of his mind, but he couldn't catch it. He slowly finished his lunch in thoughtful mood. At the end of it he decided he'd go and find Martin Thornton.

*

Up at the Haldane holding, Ben sat up on the ledge of the window in his bedroom and looked out through the rain-frosted glass. His mother was downstairs. He could hear the whine of the vacuum cleaner and it brought back a shuddery reminder of the chain saw in his father's hands.

The world on the other side of the glass was warped and indistinct, but he could make out the dark swathe of the forest. It was the first time he had looked at it for any length of time in more than a month. The memory of his run under its terrifying branches was still clear, right up at the front of his mind.

Nobody believed him. Even Dorrie seemed to have forgotten. But he knew what he had seen and he knew it was *real*. Ben Haldane had just a little bit of the gift that Martin Thornton had begun to realise in himself. He had the ability to see *beyond* the mask of reality, to where the daytime nightmares lurked. He was nine years old and he had run from a demon in the forest. A special part of his mind, a little corner that only a very few possessed, was tuned out of step with the rest of the world and into somewhere that was dark and shadowed, but none the less *real*.

Ben stared out over the dark mass that was just a low shape in the mist of rain and shivered.

His father was in there and Ben could do nothing about it. His dad hadn't seen the blood pulse from the wound in the tree when the chain saw had bit. He wondered if it was possible for him to see *anything* of what Ben had seen. Miserably he rubbed the steamed-up window and watched the raindrops run down the pane, growing darker where they crossed his sightline to trickle down past the image of the forest. Thunder crashed overhead and Ben flinched as a simultaneous blaze of lightning danced across the valley. The glass rattled with the shudder of the air.

Ben thought of his father down in the woods and a dreadful black foreboding stole into him.

37

Caitlin Brook was running through the forest of her dreams.

She ran like the wind. She ran like a roe fawn along the tracks the deer used. All around her the forest was alive with the pounding of the rain high in the shaded leaves. Ahead of her, to the right, the stream roared, swollen by the thunderstorm as it cascaded into the deep dark pool.

She ran with the joy of *life* down the track and through the breach in the old wall, feeling the insistent and powerful tugging within her, drawing her forwards along the soft path. She had never been much beyond this point before, except in her dreams. When she passed through the break in the old dyke, the texture of the air changed. It became thick and *tight*. Above her the thunder rolled and the rain hammered at the broad leaves, while the scent of musky pollen drifted down from wood anemones and forest primrose flowers to mix with the earthy scent of wet leaves and soil.

The character of the forest changed, though Caitlin Brook noticed nothing. All she was aware of was the speed and the pull that drew her onwards, along the straight path. The trees crowded together. Further in, they were covered in wet ferns and ivy creepers, thick and strangling on warted trunks. Great fronds of strange leaves dripped water. At her feet, huge, swollen mushrooms drank in the moisture and swelled.

Caitlin was not completely awake. She had waited for a while, hoping that Martin Thornton would return. She put on the kettle and waited for it to boil. She made tea, let it grow cold, and felt the regret grow. Perhaps he was scared of commitment. Maybe there was someone else. Caitlin dismissed all those thoughts. Somehow she *knew* there was no one else. Somehow she was *certain* that he had made a commitment and that he intended to keep it. She couldn't have said why she knew, but in Caitlin Brook there was a little of the magic in the odd connection of synapses and dendrites within her brain, tuned into the *other* reality, binding her in an invisible thread to Martin Thornton. While she sat a vague sense of unease stole into her. She did not know why. She tidied the teapot away, washed her cup out, dried it and put it in a cupboard. She was suddenly restless, needing to be busy, needing to do something to swerve her mind away from the queer track of concern that it was idling along.

Just then there was a knock at the back door. Immediately her expression changed and a smile spread across it. She crossed quickly and opened it with a wrench.

Sheila Garvie stood there, her long cloak-like coat dripping with rain. Caitlin's smile faded.

'Not much of a welcome, my dear,' Sheila said.

'Oh . . .' Caitlin was flummoxed for a moment. 'Sorry, Sheila. I was expecting someone else.'

'And not an old woman like me, I'm sure,' Sheila said, smiling disarmingly.

'No. I mean, it's all right. Come on in. I'll just put the kettle on.'

'Oh, I'm just passing. I don't want to disturb you. I just wanted to make sure you were taking your medicine.'

Caitlin halted in mid turn. It was the *medicine* that Martin had been so concerned about. He'd told her it was loaded with poisons. Some of the night's conversation rushed back to her. She tried to shrug it away, but it hovered, just at the edge of mental reach.

'Yes. I had some this morning.'

'Well, as the best doctors say, you have to complete the course. I've brought you the last of it. Once you've taken that, it's the end.'

'Good,' Caitlin said.

Sheila raised her eyebrows in question.

'I mean, I won't have to take it with me,' Caitlin explained quickly. 'It's just that I'll be going away.'

Sheila flashed her another winning smile.

'With the person you were expecting to come knocking on your door, hum? The young reporter?'

Caitlin nodded, feeling as if she might have slighted the older woman, but Sheila's smile never wavered.

'Good. That's as it should be. And I'm going away myself. I have business elsewhere and I'll be gone for quite a while, so it suits us both.'

She came forward and put her bag on the table. She reached inside and brought out a sachet identical to the one in the box. It bulged heavily, as if it was filled with gold dust.

'This is the final mixture, the one that binds the cure. It means that there is no going back, you understand?'

Caitlin wondered at the curious choice of words, but she nodded anyway.

'Well, I'll make sure you take the medicine, then I'll be off and let you wait for your young man.'

Sheila fetched the tall glass and filled it with water from the tap. She took a large and delicately carved wooden spoon from her bag, scooped a heaped tablespoonful of powder from the sachet and quickly stirred it in. The water immediately purpled.

'Now drink this in one swallow. It may smell a little, but it's the vital one.'

Caitlin took the glass and held it up. Already the bitter smell had spread out, wrinkling the inside of her nose. She remembered what Martin had said. Toxins. Poisons. *Snake venom*. She thought about it, then she thought about the fact that she was able to walk again, to *run* again.

She closed her eyes, raised the glass to her lips and poured it down. It surged like bitter fire inside her, through her. Caitlin's eyes sparked with sudden tears. She turned. Sheila took the glass from her fingers then gently eased her, unprotesting, to a chair.

The whole world was fading in and out in Caitlin's vision. Her heart was pounding fast, fluttering in her chest. The fire spread right to her extremities, then a cool numbness followed. Sheila was speaking, but her voice sounded far away, as if from the inside of a cave or along a dark tunnel. The words were distant and they didn't seem like proper words at all. The velvety dark came to swamp her and she had no more thoughts at all. But the voice continued, slowly, in a sing-song chant, until it too faded out, leaving her in a world of soft darkness.

Caitlin's head began to droop. Sheila Garvie took her by the shoulders and slowly let the girl slump forward across the table.

'Wait there, *seedling*,' she said, a feral smile of triumph on her face. 'Wait for the summons.'

Then Sheila Garvie went out through the back door, closing it lightly behind her, and strode away through the misty torrent of rain.

Martin Thornton stumbled down the stairs, the old umbrella held forward like a bayonet.

The black animal was no longer cat-like. It squirmed on the coat-hooks that held its punctured skin out on its back in torn tent spines. He kept himself close to the wall and it arched its neck back, mouth agape, tongue lolling out blood-red between a jagged array of ripping teeth.

It made a coughing sound, much like the noise Sheila Garvie had made when she had hawked to spit her awful phlegm at him, and lunged, jaw yawning then clamping shut with the sound of a gin-trap sprung in the night. Its claws scrabbled the wooden backboard, tearing lines down the grain as it tried to clamber off the hooks. It was stuck fast. It snarled and screeched, spitting blood on the wall. The hairs on Martin's neck stood to attention, hackles of fright and plain cold creeps.

His hip bumped against the door and he groped for the handle, unable and unwilling to take his eyes off the squirming thing on the coatstand. It had made a terrific thump when it had sprung for him, missed and slammed onto the hooks. But for that accident, when he'd slipped and the thing had leapt for him with liquid black speed, he knew he'd be dead by now.

Martin slammed the door open and stepped back into the basement room. He had to get out of the house, but there was something else he knew he must do first.

He allowed himself to take his eyes off the thing that cater-wauled its hatred at him from the wall and looked around.

The room was *alive*.

The jelly-like fungus had spread over the walls. Knotholes in the skirting board had swelled and sent out runners, growing them out at floor level in twisted rootlets. The insectile seeds that had sprouted legs had rooted themselves in cracks between stone flags and before his eyes tiny shoots were forcing themselves upwards, pallid and poisonous-looking in the dim light. Tender stalks and burgeoning leaf heads quickly distended, opening out, curved spines on their edges. The leaves yawned like venus fly-traps and Martin stood frozen in a kind of repugnant awe as they snapped shut again with tiny leathery clapping sounds. Away to the side of the table, a dirty reed mat was slowly untangling its weave, raffia ends lazily uncoiling. He reversed the umbrella. It had a heavy handle carved into the shape of some animal. He didn't bother to look. Instead, he strode across the floor, ignoring the writhing of the carpet and the tiny snapping sounds of the green mouths growing from the floor. He swung his whole body around, bringing the heavy handle arcing with him.

Glass bottles exploded under the impact.

He raked his improvised club in swift swipes, pounding and beating at jugs and jars, smashing and cracking them where they stood. He cleared one shelf, then another. A noxious stench, oily and bitter, sweet and sour, filled the air as the powders and grains of herb-dust mingled. He caught his breath and held it for as long as he could as he continued his destructive rampage through the well-stocked shelves. Glass and plants and seeds crushed and cracked under his shoes. He shifted to another bank of containers and smashed everything that stood there. The air turned chalky with the fine motes that billowed out after each swing. Eventually he could hold his breath no longer. He turned and fumbled his way out of the door, banging it closed.

On the coathooks the creature was still writhing madly. He saw the black fur was beginning to shrivel. It seemed to be drying out and crumbling on the animal's back. The head was still arched back and the black eyes fixed him with such venom he could feel the poison of it. As he watched, the fur was flaking, turning scaly and losing the depths of darkness, becoming brown and scabrous. He took a step up the stairway, then another, keeping the spike of the umbrella pointed at the thing just in case.

A piece of the beast's skin, the size of a hand, flaked off and fell in a fluttering swing to land gently on the floor. Another followed it, light brown and dry. Then another and another. The animal seemed to be turning to paper as it agonised. Its movements were slowing and the hollow rasp of its roar was fading, becoming thin and rustly. Martin backed away, got halfway up, when sudden recognition stopped him in his tracks.

The way the skin was falling, in drifting, pendulous motions.

More pieces slowly fell, tumbling lazily to the ground, before the recognition suddenly clarified in his mind.

It was the motion of falling *leaves*.

Something else urgently screeched for attention. Some memory trying to force its way through. It came in an instant.

The leaf man.

That's what young Ben Haldane had called it the night Duncan had carried him in, ashen-faced and tear-streaked, from the forest.

He had told his father that he and his little sister had been chased by a creature made from leaves. Martin got an immediate picture of the small boy on his father's knee while the girl sat snuffling in her mother's arms.

The leaf man. The thing on the wall was dripping *leaves* to the floor. They were falling off in an autumnal rain, dry and veined with ridges. He watched and recognised a hand-shaped sycamore leaf. Then an oak. Then a chestnut.

His heart nearly stopped in his chest, then came to life with a massive *thump*.

It was *escaping* from where it was impaled.

It was *made* out of leaves. It was manufactured from the *forest*. Sheila Garvie had called it her familiar.

A sudden realisation of her power dawned on him.

He had not thought it through. He had not taken it far enough. He had not believed it *possible*.

But now he was seeing the impossible. Ben Haldane had seen it. Craig Buist had seen it. They had seen the forest come alive. And if that could happen . . .

What Sheila Garvie was planning to do was not just the weird, crazy plan of a madwoman.

The dawning had taken a long time but now the sun was up and over the hills in Martin Thornton's mind. Bright daylight hit him hard and in that moment he became a believer. He watched for a few seconds more as the torrent of leaves tumbled to the floor, gathering in a small pile. The snarling had stopped and the only sound was the rustle of leaves falling to the floor. From beyond the heavy wooden basement door came a humping, slithery noise that chilled Martin's blood. He didn't even want to *think* about what might be going on in there.

He backed cautiously up the stairs and got to the third from the top. He took another look at what was happening below and his heart did its high kick again. The pile of leaves was beginning to stir. It was about four feet high, like the kind of brown mounds you see in gardens on October afternoons. It looked as if a wind had stirred the heap, swirling the leaves in a will-o'-the-wisp eddy.

Martin turned and ran. He made it to the top and scrabbled for the handle. Behind him the rustling increased. The leafstack was *moving*.

The door finally opened. He dashed outside, blinking in the daylight though it was far from bright under the tumbling clouds. He jinked to the right and ran through the gate and along the road. Over to the left, low thunder and lightning crashed together in heavenly ballet, searing his eyes with dancing after-images. He ran on along the hedgerow, digging amongst the coins and odds and ends in his pockets for the keys. He fished them out as he reached the Land-Rover and instead of opening the driver's door he twisted one in the lock of the tailgate. It swung open with a slight squeal and he leaned inside. The toolbox was angled against the back seat. He bent in further just as the susurrant rustle of dry leaves reached him.

He cursed aloud and hooked the box towards him. There was a hasp, but no padlock. He flipped its lid and shoved aside tools, slicing his finger almost to the bone on the teeth of a crosscut saw, but never noticed. Under the vice the calor blowtorch spout stuck up a few inches beyond an unruly pile of screwdrivers and chisels. He'd used it when he'd cut Caitlin's water-pipes to lower the sink unit and had to solder a joint on the cut ends. He grabbed and hauled it out. Behind him came the papery whisper, faint but deafening. His right hand scrambled in his pocket as he turned. Outside the millhouse gate a pile of leaves billowed onto the road as if swept by a broom. They swirled around each other, bound by their own gravity. Before his eyes the pile elongated, stretched, became a pyramid, a cylinder, a standing shape. Arms made of leaves grew out. Brown parchment legs parted.

A head from hell tilted up. It looked at him.

Martin held the blowtorch and twisted the black screw above the handle. Gas hissed.

'Right, come on then, you torn-faced bastard,' he shouted at the top of his voice. Fear was flowing away under the force of his fury. He'd reached the end of his rope.

The leaf man took a step towards him.

He held the blowtorch in one hand, letting it hiss like a firework. The flat smell of calor filled his nose. He ignored it.

'Come on,' he said, jerking his hand like a drunken street-fighter. Martin heard himself and a sudden silly giggle escaped him as one part of his mind caught the ridiculous picture of himself talking this way to a bunch of leaves.

The leaf man flowed towards him, its feet not leaving the surface of the road. It gained speed. Leaves flew off, spun and then were drawn back into the mass of it. Jagged holly lips opened. Shiny acorn eyes glared deadly at him. It closed the distance in mere seconds.

Martin brought the blowlamp up. He held the lighter in front of the spitting invisible stream and flicked. There was no hesitation. The spouting gas flared bright yellow-red and then immediately became a roaring blue lance of flame.

Brown arms with hooked thorn claws at the end of twigged fingers were reaching for him. The flame hit it right in its impossible face with a *whoosh*.

The leaf man was unable to stop. Martin stepped to the right as it passed, swivelling the knife-edge blue flame. In less than a second he was watching a dancing bonfire in the middle of Mill Lane.

The hideous leaf man roared as it danced, but it was the roar of flames. Despite the rain, the fire licked up and scorched it instantly. Burning leaves fell off or floated up from it. There was a slight hiss as the rain made contact with the individual blackened leaves, but on the thing itself the heat was so intense that the rain could not douse it. Martin followed it with the flame, jabbing it into the shape for good measure, but the fire was consuming it, alive with its own hot power.

From inside the moving pyre there was a dry rattle, like dying breath. The thing spun away from him, a flickering orange monstrosity, angled back in the direction it had come, gaining speed, seeming desperate to flee. Martin followed but he was not fast enough. The thing flew the few yards to the gate and he could see the brightness of flames through the thick hedge as it raced up the path and disappeared back inside the house.

Martin stopped. The blowlamp was still spitting blue fire in his hand. He turned the screw and the flame shrank instantly, made a *phut* sound and died. He slowly walked to the gate and looked up the path into Sheila Garvie's old millhouse through the open front door. The leaf man had gone downstairs. He could see the flickering glow on the walls. He watched for half a minute, seeing the glow get brighter. He knew then that he'd killed the thing, if it ever was *really* alive.

He turned slowly and went back to the jeep. He put the blowlamp into the old haversack lying next to the toolbox and selected his two sharpest chisels and a metal stanley knife with a retracting blade. He slung the bag into the passenger seat and started the engine. It coughed into life first time.

But when he tried to reverse, the jeep didn't move. Its engine whined and protested, but the heavy rains had softened the earth so much that the big tyres simply dug themselves into the ground, where they spun uselessly.

Martin tried it again, revving the engine high and hard, though he knew that there was no four-wheel drive in reverse and he was too close to the bank to risk going any further forward. The tyres screamed again as they spun in the mud.

'Shite,' Martin snarled, slamming his hands down on the wheel in angry frustration.

Just then there was a screech as the doorhandle was jerked down. The door swung open. Martin's heart vaulted into the back of his throat and sat trembling. Before he had time to turn, a hand reached in and grasped his arm.

The shock was so great that Martin nearly fainted. A pale face swam into view through the open doorspace.

'Hey, boss, need a hand?' Alec Stirling said.

It took Martin nearly thirty seconds to get his breath back, though his heart still bounced around out of control under his ribs for some time after that. Then it was Alec's turn to start back as Martin grabbed him by the lapel of his sodden jacket and cursed him so roundly that he didn't repeat himself once in the space of a minute.

Finally he stopped. Alec flicked his lapels huffily as Martin got out of the Land-Rover.

'What's got into you?' he asked, shoving his glasses back up on his nose.

'You nearly gave me a bloody heart attack, that's what,' Martin said, then, to Alec's surprise, he burst into almost hysterical laughter. He leaned against the jeep, holding on to his stomach until the uncontrollable gales lessened and he got himself under control.

'Are you all right?' the postman asked, with some concern.

'I am now. Christ!'

'What?'

'Something came at me. You wouldn't believe me if I told you. I got it with the blowtorch. Then when you opened the door, I thought it had come back.'

'What was it?'

'I told you. You'd never believe it. That crazy Garvie bitch sent it after me. She's not just a lunatic, she's fucking malignant. I've got to get out of here.'

'Will I get Jock Weir again?'

'No time. Where's your van?'

Alec pointed along the lane a distance. It was parked just beyond Sheila Garvie's house.

'Right. I have to get to Caitlin's, and I want you to get that Buist boy back up to his farm.'

'What for?'

'He's not mad either. He was *right*. He saw the same thing as the Haldane youngster and he wasn't hallucinating either. It would take too long to explain, but I want you to take him up there and get all the weedkiller he's got. If you can find something to spray it with, that'll be handy.'

'But why?' Alec demanded.

'Because if I'm right, we're going to gave to kill a few plants.'

Alec looked at him as if Martin had gone crazy, but Martin stared back with such intensity that the postman finally shrugged.

'You're the boss,' he said.

They climbed into the van, Alec shoved the gearstick forward and the car lurched off the verge. He drove it past the gate at Sheila Garvie's millhouse. As they passed, Martin looked through the gap in the hedge and saw the front door still open. A flickering glow of fire threw an orange glare against the walls.

Martin got out at Caitlin's house. He went straight round the back and into the kitchen, his haversack banging against his hip. He went through the house quickly, calling her name. There was another glass on the kitchen table, a different one. He saw the brown dregs in the bottom and realised she'd taken more of Sheila Garvie's poisonous mixture. He stood for a moment, debating what to do. She'd obviously come back then gone out again. On the kitchen floor, just inside the door, there were a couple of muddy footprints on the vinyl. He bent to look at them. They were zigzagged, with three little circles, the kind of marks running shoes would make.

He stood up, still thinking, and went back out of the cottage. Round the front, beyond the gate, he stood in the lane, looking right and left, as if practising his kerb drill, while the rain poured down incessantly. Martin debated going up to the Buist farm, but something made him cross the road to the stand of saplings that edged the lane. He couldn't explain what made him do it but he followed the instinct anyway. At the edge of the grove there was a narrow track in the grass. The rain had made the brown earth slick and greasy. He walked along it for a few yards then stopped.

There on the soft mud was a footprint. He didn't have to crouch down to see the wavy lines and the small intertwined circles.

His heart sank like a stone.

Caitlin had gone into the forest. Martin stood for a few moments, taking deep breaths to try to calm himself. She had gone into the forest with Sheila Garvie. Whatever the witch planned was happening *now*. Martin walked further along the path to where the grove gave way to the big trees of the Fasach Wood. Inside him he was trying to batten down the dread that increased with every step. He walked quickly under the spreading boughs of the first big tree and then the jolt hit him.

It was that inside-out vertiginous sensation he'd experienced before. He'd felt it as a small boy in the middle of the night when his dreams had taken that off-centre spin on the edge of a nightmare. He'd had something similar on a few occasions in the early hours of the morning when he was still drinking heavily, a sick, lurching mental stagger that scared him numb.

And it had come to him in a brutal mind-slam only seconds before the appalling electric connection between himself and Caitlin Brook on the night she'd taken the blast of a shot-gun in her back and plummeted from the balcony.

He stopped still and braced himself, eyes tight closed.

The blast followed instantly and his whole *being* rocked with the intensity. It came blaring into his brain, a vast, formless sense of extreme *danger*. It flooded him in a black cold tide. He stood there, feet rooted in the damp earth, and shook with the force of the sensation. It did not pass but, after a while, he found he was able to withstand it.

The sense of menace and peril clenched him and he gritted his teeth, holding himself still, trying to get it under control. Finally he was able to move. He took two tentative steps forward, then speeded up until he was running along the track. With every step the threat swelled darker. He followed the dreadful compass arrow deep into the forest.

It was some time later when he came to the old dyke. Without hesitation he followed the pull and went through the gap into the most terrifying place he'd ever seen in his life.

The rain dripped from the high branches which formed an almost impregnable canopy, blotting out what little light was left in the sky. In the Fasach Wood it was darker than dusk.

Martin shoved his way past a luxuriant frond of thick, rubbery leaves. His suddenly acute senses identified the smells in the thick air. There was growth, rampant and unfettered, underlain by noisome decay. Underfoot, strange flowers blossomed. Even as he moved he could see them open their petals, flaunting sharp colours which jarred the eye. The dripping trees were festooned with hoary ferns which uncurled their spongy heads like octopus tentacles. He moved on, quickly skirting a rubbery field of mushrooms painted in poisonous hues, mindful of Ben Haldane's tale of how they'd swelled and exploded. Above him, insects clattered, razoring the air with helicopter wings. Behind the dripping of the rain and the drumming in the leaves high in the canopy, there was the scraping sound of insectile jaws chewing leaves and wood.

As he ran through the nightmare forest a memory came back of a story he'd done years before in Creggan, twenty miles away as the crow flies, on the peninsula between two sea lochs. A young boy had disappeared and then been found under the flat table stone of an old Celtic monument. Martin searched his memory for the name. Roderick? Roger? Something like that. The boy had been horribly disfigured. The doctors said it looked as if he'd been bitten, stung, poisoned, acid-burned and infected with tropical fungus. He'd said it looked as if the lad had been dumped in an Amazon rainforest. The mystery had never been resolved. It had taken the youngster a year to recover physically from the terrible wounds and infections, but even then he had never been *right*. His parents had told Martin Thornton that all he would speak about were the trees. And in the nights after he'd got out of hospital he'd wake up screaming and bawling, hysterical with fear, incoherently screaming about the trees that were coming to get him.

Martin Thornton hadn't understood it then, but now he had an inkling of the nightmare that young boy from Creggan peninsula had suffered. He'd gone to hell and come back again, not quite whole.

Martin Thornton was now running through it.

Something landed on his cheek and he felt the sharp sting of insect jaws. He slapped hard and his hand came away bloody. A crushed insect the size of his finger fell away, but his cheek continued to pulse in an acid burn. Something else fluttered close to him and he knocked it from the air with a quick swipe of his hand and kept on running.

Inside him the black alarm was clanging with dreadful urgency.

38

Caitlin ran, oblivious to her surroundings. Nothing flew at her, no vines entangled her feet, no thorns snatched at her clothes as she passed. She was aware of nothing but the insistent imperative that spurred her on. It was a tug at her heart, a drag in her soul, reeling her onwards to the depths of of the forest. Inside her, there was only the need to follow that urgent pull. She ran without missing a step, feet padding on the leaves. Around her flowers blazed malignant, unearthly colours and tendrils of choking ivy crawled up the trunks and branches with slow and deadly menace. She ran on and the implacable drag on her soul tugged her ever onwards.

She reached the edge of the black river where the mighty tree had fallen to span the flow. She nimbly clambered up the ladder of huge roots and onto the flat trunk, balancing easily while she crossed over to the island. She leapt down, landing lightly on both feet, knees bent, then ran onwards, following the straight path.

Finally she came to the clearing and began to slow down. Here the insistent pull was like the beat of a giant heart. It pulsed through her in powerful waves, blotting out everything but the need to respond to its summons.

She walked from the edge of the trees into the clearing. In this part of the forest the rain had stopped, but overhead the eye of the storm swirled in a spiral.

All she could see was the tree, gaunt and overwhelming. Even the figures around it did not immediately impinge on her consciousness, for since she had woken, slumped over the kitchen table, she had *had* no consciousness of her own, only the irresistible urge to run and run and run towards the summons.

She halted, eyes fixed on the forest giant. Her chest heaved under the light running suit. She stood, feet planted apart, head thrown back, hair a mass of curled flame hanging down below her shoulders.

Caitlin Brook had no mind of her own at that moment. Her body had moved of a volition that was not her own. She had been filled with an intense *desire* which had grown to a *hunger* as she got closer to her destination. Now her body was consumed with it. She *needed* to answer the call. She could not resist the pull in her soul.

Yet underneath that febrile intensity was a small part of Caitlin Brook that was hers, the tiny corner of her mind that she herself was completely unaware of. And it was dreadfully *afraid*. That part of her self tried to break through the overwhelming control that had taken possession of Caitlin's soul. It yammered a warning but it could not make her respond.

Far away, at the edge of the wood, that unheard cry was picked up, like a stray radio signal glancing off the only receiver tuned to that frequency. Martin Thornton felt it hit him like a blow.

The women watched her emerge from the side of the clearing.

They were standing in a wide circle, each of them dressed in a long cloak woven from a coarse material that was not wool. Closer to the tree Sheila Garvie stood stock-still, tall and slender, her white hair untied and hanging to her waist in silken strands. She looked magnificent, but Caitlin had eyes only for the immense tree which dominated the whole clearing.

Sheila watched the girl, black eyes smouldering in triumph and anticipation. Beneath her feet, she could feel the pulse of the earth quicken in readiness. The moment was almost there. She walked forward and stopped in front of the girl, who stood swaying slightly, eyes wide and dreamily green. She reached forward and unzipped the running jacket, slipping it down Caitlin's arms. There was no response. Sheila Garvie removed the brassière, then bent to turn the leggings down. Obedient, docile, Caitlin lifted each foot in turn, almost childlike. Finally, she stood, naked on the grass.

Sheila Garvie turned away from her, flicked the wooden brooch which served as a catch on her cloak, raised her arms, and let the dark robe fall to the ground. Around the tree, the gathered women did the same.

For several silent minutes they stood there, pale figures under the thundery sky, arms raised to the tree.

Sheila Garvie started the chant in a language none of them understood, but every one of the women felt the power of it. Above them the giant cauldron of the thunderstorm spiralled into the black drain-hole in the sky. Silent lightning forked down and flash-danced over the tops of the trees. The air was instantly charged with tension as the forces of the sky and the earth were conjoined. From under the ground the beating rhythm pulsed, sending vibrations through them all.

Molly Carr felt her body riven by the power. Within her she felt the flare of her tight desire.

Gail Dean kept her arms upraised, her prominent breasts high and her flat belly as yet showing no signs of motherhood. But there was a *twist* within her as the new growth responded to the pulsating charge.

Fiona Herron felt the dynamic energy arc from one perfect hand to another. Her fingers were outspread, like receivers, drawing the potency from the air.

Jean Fintry felt the ripples shudder up through the earth and spread throughout her slim and elegant length.

The other women stood there, experiencing their own special gifts. The time when their wishes would be crystallised and made permanent was upon them.

Sheila Garvie drank in the power. She could feel it whine in the air between sky and forest and sensed the imminence of fruition. Her black eyes blazed with a light of their own as she stood, slender as the willow for which she was named, white as the sap that poured from its bark, a conduit for the power. The ground shivered violently once more in a seismic rumble which shook the tops of the trees and made the giant oak *thrum* in sympathetic resonance.

Caitlin Brook took a step forward.

Duncan Haldane and John Lovatt had crossed the dyke on the north side with the dogs staying close, whining their worry. They had moved through the place where the trees crowded together like old men in a huddle, then passed into the humid, damp luxuriance of the deepwood.

'Never seen this bit before,' Lovatt said, his voice quiet, almost a whisper. He was unconsciously holding his snare out in front of him like a weapon.

'Odd,' Duncan Haldane agreed. 'Smells funny and all.'

'Like a bloody jungle. I did my service in Borneo. Where the hell *are* we?'

Duncan shrugged his shoulders. They moved through a stand of succulent fronds with leaves almost a yard long. Where the big green spears met on the stalk, pools of silver water had gathered. Duncan saw small things squirming under the surface. The two men pushed their way through the rubbery foliage and out to where oddly-angled trees like ferns with trunks stood hairy and overgrown. As they moved through the grove, something trailed across Duncan's face and stuck there. He pulled back and a thin white thread stretched before it snapped with a soft twang. He turned, in time to see a spider the size of a mouse scuttle along a woven web that spanned the path, moving away from a silken pouch which dangled, twirling, from the spoked spiderweb. The pouch wriggled and, as Duncan passed it, he got the impression of a small animal twitching within the spider's cocoon, trying to break free. He shuddered and a feeling of apprehension started to build up inside him.

Beyond the fern trees huge draped oaks and overgrown elms crowded round a flat part where the brown leaves were thick and mushy and wet, stretching in a russet carpet under the spreading boughs.

Duncan stopped and John caught up with him.

'This place gives me the creeps,' John said flatly. 'I don't like it. Did you see the size of that spider?'

Duncan nodded. The hairs on his arms were prickling with tension though he could not explain why.

One of the dogs pressed itself against the side of Lovatt's calf, seeking comfort. He could feel the little body shiver, matching the tautness winding up inside him.

'I reckon we get the hell out of here,' John said. Duncan was about to agree, when there was a movement in the cleared space in front of them. It started at the edge of the leaf cover. Something twitched and rustled. Duncan swung towards it. His eyes scanned the far side but saw nothing.

'What is it?' John whispered.

'Dunno. I heard something.' Duncan held up his hand, listening intently. The tension abruptly twisted up tight and the vague sense of threat narrowed down to a fine focus.

At the far side the leaves twitched and humped up from the ground. Duncan swung the gun over in that direction. Nothing happened for a moment of two, then the pile moved forward in an eerie wave. At first Duncan couldn't make it out. It was as if a mound of leaves was slowly crawling forward of its own volition. Then he realised what was happening. There was something *under* the leaf litter. It was burrowing towards them, and the pile of leaves was the bow wave of its progress. He stared, uneasily fascinated. The mound swelled as it neared them.

Whatever it was, it was something *big*.

At his feet the dogs whimpered high and fearful. They sounded terrified. Both men stood, unable to draw their eyes away from the approaching bore of leaves.

The movement stopped. John was about to say something when the pile erupted, right in the middle of the cleared space. Dead leaves shot into the air in a sorrel, rustling fountain. A shape emerged from the tumbling scatter and a dreadful grunt, so deep its vibrations could be *felt*, rolled out from the centre of the dell.

'Christ on a . . .' John blurted, and then his voice died.

The boar stood facing them on the cleared space. It was black and squat, shoulders humped and heavily muscled. A spiky mane of bristles, thick as porcupine quills, quivered erect on its neck and down its back. Tiny black eyes glittered.

It stood stock-still, sides heaving, hooves planted in the leaves. Its flat, leathery nose twitched and drew back, snuffling the air. On either side of its mouth, yellow tusks, flat as knives, curved up and out.

'That's not my fuckin' pig,' John said in a fast whisper. 'I don't know *what* in Christ's name that thing is.'

Duncan swung his gun up and in that moment the animal moved. It charged at them without warning, grunting and snorting as it came, a black monstrosity, ugly and deadly.

Duncan's finger hooked round the trigger. He lowered the barrels and centred them on the thing's warty skull, keeping the barrel steady, ignoring the bobbing motion of the boar's head as it loped in ungainly strides towards them. He began the squeeze, now at the centre of a cold concentration where every perception was drawn out in slow motion.

Then one of the dogs barged against his leg with enough force to knock him off-balance. The gun roared and a puff of leaves just beside the boar scattered into the air. Duncan toppled sideways and the dogs streaked towards the charging animal. Even as he fell, Duncan marvelled at their courage. The little barrel-chested terriers had stopped whining. Now they were snarling their anger in defence of their master. The lead dog streaked forward, a white and tan blur, straight for the boar's head, then instinctively jinked to the side, going for the flank. The beast twisted its head almost casually. Its left tusk hooked the little dog in its side and caught under its thigh. There was a squeal as the boar's snout flicked up and the dog came with it, cartwheeling through the air over the brute's back, now a red and white blur as blood sprayed in a fountain. It landed, twitching, on the leaves.

The second dog went for the throat, snarling high and fierce. Its teeth clamped on the bristly neck and the animal shook its head from side to side. Another dog scurried round to the rear, going for the tail, and the thing whirled, appallingly fast. There was a crunch and the third dog suddenly spun away squealing. As Duncan twisted and got to his knees he watched aghast, the whole world still slowed down under the surge of adrenalin that was pumping hot and fast through his veins. From the corner of his eye he saw John Lovatt take slow, lumbering steps forward, the stave out in front of him with the wire noose dangling stiff at the far end. The third dog was cartwheeling away from the animal and Duncan realised with chill horror that it was only the front *half* of the little terrier. The back legs and tail, still joined at the pelvis, were twitching and scrabbling on the ground a few yards from where he knelt.

He heard himself bawl at John to get back, but either his neighbour didn't hear him or simply ignored him. The second terrier was still worrying at the beast's throat while the last dog stood in front of it, snarling and yapping, trying to find a vantage. Its own hackles were raised in a miniature parody of the ogrous bristles on the muscular humped back. In the blink of an eye, the thing shot forward and pinned the little bitch to the ground. The massive head came down and swung from side to side in swift deadly arcs.

The terrier screamed, a keen ululating agony as the tusks gored it right and left, razoring it in vicious slashes. The beast spun on its haunches and the dog at its throat was swung out far enough for the boar to get a snap at it. The tusks flashed yellow. There was a sickening crunch and the small dog instantly flopped limp.

John was yelling something but, in Duncan's speeded perception, the words were so low they were just a rumble in the air. He powered himself forward and dabbed his noose over the thing's neck.

The wire tightened and John hauled back on it. The animal took off in the opposite direction, dragging the farmer with it. The man dug his heels in, but they skittered on the leaves and he was dragged along for twenty yards, looking for all the world like a dry-land water skier. The beast made it halfway across the cleared space then spun. John was yanked right off his feet. He managed to keep a hold of the stave and, as the beast turned, so did he, his feet several inches off the ground.

The brute's strength was phenomenal. It whirled in a complete circle and John Lovatt defined a larger concentric one, swinging through the air back in the direction he'd come. At that point, the wire noose snapped and John went flying right past Duncan to crash into the lush undergrowth beyond. The pole spun away and landed in a bush. John twisted and rolled. Duncan tried to get up and slipped on the wet leaves. The grotesque animal shook its head, snorted gutturally and came charging towards them. Duncan raised the gun, much too late. The head dipped and he flinched away.

That movement saved his life. The tusks came down, a blur of yellow, and took him on the outside of his thigh. A fraction of a second before and it would have unseamed him from neck to groin in one searing slash. There was no pain right then, only a hard thud on his leg. The creature barged past him and Duncan got a whiff of pungent musk. He levered himself up with his elbows in time to see the blood drench his torn moleskin trousers in a sudden flood.

Beyond him, John Lovatt had got to his feet and was off and running.

He took off down the path, boots kicking up the forest litter, hammering down the track. Duncan tried to swing the gun round but the barrel jarred on the juniper bush he'd fallen against. The black boar raced after the fleeing farmer, its tail straight up in the air like a pennant. All Duncan could hear was the thud of John's heavy boots on the track and the snuffling grunt of the pursuing creature. In seconds, both disappeared from sight. Duncan hauled himself up to a sitting position. Very close to him, the severed hind half of the small terrier was still twitching on the ground, both paws trying to run in empty air. The other three were scattered around the dell, lifeless and bloody. He bent forward and pulled aside the rent in his trousers. It was a neat, straight cut. Below it the skin of his thigh was opened in a fleshy parallel. The pain had started scissoring as the severed nerves sent out pulses of alarm. He had nothing to staunch the flow with, so he quickly slid his belt out of its loops and lashed it tightly round his leg, not knowing whether he'd severed an artery or not. The sudden escalation of the pain as he cinched the leather made him wince, but he pulled hard, hoping the razored edges of skin and muscle would hold together.

Not long after that he heard the scream.

As soon as John had seen the black beast erupt from the leaves, he knew he'd made a terrible mistake. He'd seen his bloodied and broken brave little dogs fly out from the mêlée and something had snapped inside him. He had not wanted to catch the ugly animal. He'd wanted to throttle it, choke it to death. He'd dashed forward without thinking, yelling as he went, and seconds later he was flying around the dell like a weight on a string.

When the wire had snapped and he'd gone flying past Duncan Haldane, his courage had simply failed him. He'd landed with a thump, scrambled to his feet and after that there had been only one thought in his mind, pure and shining. He had to get away from that thing before it killed him.

He went haring down the forest path, oblivious to the bushes that snatched at his face and whipped his cheeks, caring nothing for the nettles and bramble runners. All he could think of was flight.

Then behind him he heard the snuffling grunt.

A cold surge of fright burst within him and he wailed in panic. He jinked sideways, off the path, crashing through the low undergrowth and dodging between the oddly slender trunks of saplings that stood in a clump, trying to get some obstacle, *any barrier*, between himself and the thing snorting at his heels.

He leapt between the saplings, grabbing one of them to swing him to the right, and a stringy rope of ivy uncurled itself from a tree and looped itself round his waist.

Even as it happened, John Lovatt didn't take it in. His

momentum carried him forward for three steps more and then the ivy runner tautened and sprang back. His feet went from under him, swooping up to waist height, and he crashed to the ground with a gasp.

He scrambled to his knees and tried to get to his feet. Something snagged at his foot, tightened and pulled. John was rolled sideways onto his back. Beyond the ferns and brambles he saw the dark shape battering its way through. He scrabbled backwards with his left heel digging into the soft earth. Something coiled round his hand and pulled it off to the side. He twisted his head in disbelief and saw a braid of bindweed forming a living bracelet on his wrist.

He tried to snatch his hand back but the stem wouldn't break. He was pinioned, one arm tugged out above shoulder height, the opposite leg stretched straight.

The black beast rammed through the bushes and came barging towards him, head jerking up and down. It did not hesitate. It came straight at him. He saw the snout dive down. Tusks flicked right and left.

The shrill unearthly scream of the dying man came reverberating through the forest and Duncan Haldane came limping along the track moments later. He neared the stand of pale saplings and skirted the bushes. Beyond them there was a thrashing as bracken stalks shattered and tore. The animal was grunting madly. The scream rose higher and was suddenly cut off. A sickening gurgle followed. Duncan lurched out from the saplings and raised the gun.

He could see John Lovatt's outstretched body, the boar's head down on him. The man's eyes were open, wide and staring, but Duncan couldn't tell if he was alive or dead. The beast kept ramming its head into him. The ground and leaves all around were dripping red. It was so intent on its savage attack on the prostrate man that Duncan was able to get himself right up behind it. He jammed the gun into the side of its neck, below the bristling hackles, squeezed the trigger and let it have the full load.

The hog dropped.

All the life went out of it in one flashing roar. It fell straight forward on top of John Lovatt, not even twitching. Duncan hauled the thing aside.

The farmer was lying on his back. His throat was working as if he was trying to swallow. His mouth opened twice, quite wide, but no sound came out. The eyes stared into infinity, then all movement stopped. Duncan turned away and was sick.

He spent some time at it until he could retch no more. He turned back to the dead man and, as he did so, a movement to the side caught his eye. The black boar shape was crumbling, losing colour, turning brown. Papery skin was tumbling from it.

Duncan backed away, limping very badly. His vision swam and he realised he'd lost a lot of blood. Nonetheless, he kept on going, trying to find his way back to the wall.

His son had told him, had *warned* him, not to come to the forest. His son had been terrified by what he had called the *leaf man*.

Suddenly Duncan Haldane was very much afraid.

A screech of a child in pain or fear came ripping through the trees.

Caroline Petrie had been getting to the end of her story, while the children gathered round, listening attentively. The sudden sound made everyone start in alarm. One of the girls sitting close to Susan burst into tears.

'What was that?' Melanie asked, instantly on her feet. Above them the rain was drumming on the leaves, but under the massive sycamore it was still dry and quite warm.

Susan came alongside her while Caroline gathered the children together.

'Right, who's missing?' she demanded.

They did a head count. There were two short.

'Anybody seen Billy Lovatt? And where's Neil MacKinnon?' she asked them. The children at the front shook their heads. Beyond, in the trees, further into the forest, the screech had stopped as quickly as it began.

'Okay, everybody settle down. We'll find them,' Caroline said calmly. 'Susan, you come with me. Everybody stay here with Melanie.'

Caroline was not surprised that the two boys had sneaked away, though she berated herself for not noticing it. She had been too intent on her story. Probably one of them had fallen and cut himself. Maybe he'd even got stung by a bee. It had been a shriek of pain or fright, but it hadn't lasted long.

She called Billy's name in a loud, clear voice. Way over where the trees were thick there was an answering cry which she couldn't make out.

'Damn them,' Caroline said, surprising Susan who had never heard the young woman lose her poise before. She walked forward quickly, with the girl two steps behind. They came to a low wall and clambered over it. Caroline called again and heard another high cry. It seemed to have moved. They followed it, barging their way through the thick vegetation.

They came into a clear area and found Neil MacKinnon lying on the ground. His whole body was shaking. There was no sign of Billy Lovatt.

'What's happened, Neil?' Caroline asked crossly. It was only then that Susan noticed the big mushroom standing beside the prone youngster. Its top was covered in ragged holes, as if it had burst. Beside it another one stood bloated. Just as she looked away, a motion dragged her eyes back. The big fairy-tale spots on its surface were beginning to expand visibly. She turned to Caroline and was about to say something when she saw what had happened to Neil MacKinnon.

Silver filaments like glass fibres criss-crossed his face. Where they touched, the skin was puckered and red. There were sparkling, pinpoints of light on the end of each thread. Some of them hung, tangled in the rest. Others had buried themselves into the freckled skin of the small boy's cheeks and forehead. Where they dug, the flesh was swollen into massive lumps. Neil was not even crying by this time. In the few moments since they had found him his face had become unrecognisable under the silver tangle. The boy's skin seemed to be rotting away as they watched.

Caroline reached a hand to snatch at the mass of threads and abruptly let out a yell. The young woman snatched her hand away, turned it palm upwards and saw the criss-cross lines like acid burns on her own skin. Despite the pain, Caroline bravely reached forward once more. Her fingers grasped the skein again and this time Susan *heard* the hiss as they burned into flesh. Caroline ignored it. Her breath gasped out, but she kept her hold and pulled the thing away from the stricken boy. She rolled to the side, squirming in agony, and dived her hand into the cool earth, scraping the stuff from her hand. She was moaning loudly. Susan knelt in front of the boy. One eye was sagged inwards, as if it had imploded. The flesh around it was puckered and grotesque.

'Neil. Where's Billy?' Susan asked urgently.

The boy made a little moan. His one blue eye rolled around as if he didn't know where he was, but then it seemed to focus on her. She asked him again, pleading with him. Finally the boy lifted a scarred hand and pointed upwards to the tree branches. He made a coughing sound, trying to speak, then his whole body spasmed, back arching impossibly, before collapsing again, completely still. The life drained away from the staring eye.

Caroline backed away, her whole body shaking. Her breath came in hitching gasps as she fought to control herself. She turned, face screwed up as the burn tore into her fingers, her eyes scanning the trees in the direction the boy had pointed. Susan got to her feet, unwilling to leave the dead youngster, unsure of what to do next. Slowly she followed Caroline, who cautiously edged through the trees, breath now whistling through grated teeth.

A few minutes later they found Billy Lovatt. There was no question that he was dead.

His small body was hanging upside down, about ten feet from the ground. His feet were tangled in the branches of a thick, thorny tree. Around his neck a straggling climbing rose runner, saw-toothed with hooked thorns, was wrapped so tightly it had squeezed the flesh to the thickness of a woman's wrist. The boy's face was black and his tongue stuck out from between swollen lips. The rambling rose barbs had torn his throat open.

As the two women watched, the last droplets of blood from his drained body dripped a gentle rhythm. They could hear the quiet plopping sound in the sudden silence of the forest. Susan's eyes followed the drops as they fell and landed in a small hollow on the flat stone that stood up from the undergrowth. Little ripples of red spread out with each drop and the cup slowly overflowed into the rings carved in stone parallels and then dribbled down the runnels to the ground.

Where the boy's blood soaked into the earth, Susan could see movement. There were plants uncurling there, forcing themselves from the ground, visibly rising and stretching as they soaked up sustenance.

Caroline tried to say something, but the words wouldn't come

508

out. Susan clutched her arm and felt her own shivering mirrored. Caroline turned to her, the two of them mesmerised by the drip drip drip of the falling droplets.

Then another scream rent the air. Both women jumped.

'Oh, no!' Caroline moaned. Susan could hear the instant dread in her voice. She turned herself away from the sight of Billy Lovatt dangling from the tree and started to retrace her footsteps.

'What about Billy?' Susan cried out.

'Oh, Susan, I don't *know*,' Caroline said, her voice loaded with shock and despair. She hesitated, eyes flicking from Susan to the dead boy. She was standing only a few yards from the other small crumpled form in the ferns. Again a screech of terror or pain, soaring so high it almost went beyond the range of human hearing, came lancing between the trees.

Caroline's hesitation broke. She whirled and ran. Susan followed and they dashed through the trees. Another scream shattered the air, then a cacophony of shrieks. They whizzed past the stand of swollen toadstools. In peripheral vision, Susan saw one of the yellow heads balloon and then burst open. Silver threads arced outwards. She raised her hand instinctively, fending them off. Nettle-stings burned into the skin of her arm then sizzled like acid. She gasped but kept running.

They raced down the track like hares towards where the children had sat to listen to the fairytale. By now, the forest was riven with the screaming of children. They pounded past the old oaks, barged through juniper and over clumps of forest ferns until they came to the old sycamore.

Caroline skidded to a halt, face white despite the exertion, mouth wide open to haul breath.

The children were *gone*.

Yet all around them the girl and the young woman could hear the screaming of small children in pain.

'What's happening?' Susan asked, her voice ready to break into sobs.

'I don't know,' Caroline responded. Her eyes were darting this way and that, trying to pinpoint the source of the crying. It seemed to surround them.

'Melanie!' she bawled. 'Melanie, where *are* you?'

From beyond the junipers where Billy and Neil had first spotted the cock pheasant, a loud moan came drifting eerily out of the shadows. Caroline angled towards it, feet kicking up leaves.

They found Melanie Cuthbert lying spreadeagled in a stand of ferns. She was twitching and writhing. Susan bent over her and then the blood seemed to drain out of her head. Her knees buckled and the forest swam in her vision. Caroline caught her just before the girl slid to the ground.

Moments after Caroline and Susan had run off into the woods Bobby Tomlinson swung up into the tree. Everybody turned when they heard the rustling leaves. At first Dorrie thought Bobby had jumped up to swing on one of the low branches. It was the kind of thing boys and trees did when they got together. Before the summer, Ben had always been up some tree or another, at least until they had got lost in the forest. That memory was just a hazy recollection in Dorrie's mind, like a distant bad dream.

Melanie called out to him sharply. She gathered all the children around her and turned her head to see Bobby swinging on the branch. 'Come down,' she cried.

'I can't,' Bobby shouted. 'I'm stuck. I'm—'

Then he screamed. The sound started off high and then soared up to a piercing howl.

Melanie scrambled to her feet and shifted her stance to look up at the boy. The scream went on and on. Bobby was moving around up there, half-hidden by the foliage. She could see flashes of his yellow T-shirt between the leaves as he moved with phenomenal speed, getting higher and higher in the tree.

'Bobby,' she called out sharply again.

Then she saw the boy pass a space in the foliage and her mouth opened into a perfect circle as the realisation dawned on her.

The boy was not climbing, not swinging from branch to branch.

As she watched she saw the branches bend and turn towards each other. Twigs spread then closed around the boy's legs and arms and at one stage fastened themselves on his head.

The branches were like arms with hard, twiggy fingers. They moved in concert, with dreadful mechanical smoothness, as the tree-hands passed the struggling screaming boy like a parcel. He reached the outermost branches where the sycamore edged

510

towards a beech tree. To Melanie's horror, the great beech *bent* a branch outwards. Twig fingers opened, grabbed and drew the squirming shape into itself and the whole process started again. Bobby Tomlinson was passed through the beech, handed over to an oak and beyond that to a shivering ash tree. It happened so quickly and smoothly that in seconds he was out of sight.

Melanie heard his screams fade in the distance. She wanted to press her fingers to her ears to cut the awful sound out. Her whole mind had gone numb, as if she'd been struck a sickening blow on the back of her head. Around her, the small children were screeching in panic. Melanie spun, trying to speak, trying to *think*, but for a long moment nothing came. It was as if she had simply stopped functioning, stunned into imbecility by the horror of what she had seen.

One of the small children grabbed her leg and held on so tightly her nails almost punctured the denim of her jeans.

'I want to go home,' a fair-haired little boy wailed girlishly and emphasised it with a stamp of his foot.

Just then a branch came looping down and snatched five-year-old Monica Walsh by her head. The tiny girl flew upwards into the air and disappeared. She didn't even have time to cry out.

Pandemonium erupted. The children, who had been standing stock-still, frozen with fright, suddenly scattered. A group of them ran out in the direction Caroline and Susan had gone. Others went the opposite way. Two small boys tried to scramble though the gap between two trees, each of them hauling on the other, trying to be first. A thin rope of ivy peeled itself from its hold on the side of a Scots pine and came striking like a snake. It wrapped itself around the hindmost boy's chest and contracted, swinging him up and out of sight. The lead boy never even saw it but he *sensed* it. One second, George Welsh was hauling at his collar, trying to drag him back, and the next, he was gone. Wee Davy Currie screeched and jumped forward, completely unaware of the fact that his bowels had opened in one quick venting into his jeans. He would not have cared if he *had* known, such was his terror.

Dorrie Haldane ran blindly through the tangled junipers, too scared to cry out. Behind her she heard the dry rustle of leaves and the creak of twigs moving and she lost every notion but flight. She ran and ran, hearing the crackle of branches behind her, not knowing that it was the sound of two other girls who had followed her lead. She ran on blindly, holding her hands up to protect her eyes from the whipping needle-leaves, until she came to the clear space where the spreading roots stood out from the tree. Without thinking, she dived for the shelter the roots afforded and squeezed herself in to where the roots parted. The other girls tumbled in beside her, huddling so close Dorrie could hardly breathe.

Melanie unfroze, grabbed the small boy next to her and held him. He kicked and squirmed. The other small shapes were darting through the undergrowth in all directions, the air shrill with their shrieks. Melanie called to them, telling them to stay with her, but they didn't hear, or chose not to.

She backed away from the trunk, clutching the boy by the arm. He was crying desperately and struggling to get away. At that moment, something happened up above them. The tree shook as if a sudden gust of wind had moved its topmost branches. Melanie looked up and saw a swarm of insects fluttering down from the leaves.

She cried aloud and dragged the boy away. Something flickered green beside her and fell to the ground. Another of the fluttering things landed on her shoulder. Another one alighted on the boy's head. Melanie snatched it away, then realised it was not an insect. It was a sycamore seed, its single moth-wing curving out from the head. The seeds were helicoptering down from the tree in a butterfly shower, whirling rapidly in the still forest air. Melanie's heart started beating again.

She let her breath out and, still holding tight to the boy, quickly walked towards where she had last seen a group of the children. Just out from the lee of the sycamore, where the seeds were flickering in their thousands to land gently on the ground, Melanie pushed her way though the clump of ferns.

She did not see the fern frond uncurl like a paper party hooter. She was only aware of it when she fell headlong, her ankle snagged. The boy fell with her and immediately clambered to his feet. Melanie dragged at her leg, but it refused to budge. She saw the tight coil of green just above her shoe and tight panic clenched her stomach. Another fern unrolled with blurring speed and whiplashed round her wrist. She jerked back and felt the bite on her skin as it tightened. The seven-year-old's eyes opened so wide they looked as if they might pop out and roll down his pale cheeks. Melanie let him go.

'Run,' she bawled. 'Run away, Colin. *Get out of here.*'

The boy started back as if struck. Melanie swung her free hand at him. A dreadful realisation was dawning on her. She was caught in this mad forest where the trees had suddenly come to deadly life. A cold chill of certainty swamped her.

'Go on, Colin. *Run!*'

He stood staring for a moment then scampered away. She saw his white T-shirt flash beyond the ferns, then one of the plant shoots snagged her hair and drew her head down with such a snap it hit the ground with a sickening thud. Another looped around her leg, close to where the first one had her in its grip. Fluttering sycamore seeds came whirling down like paper flies. One of them landed on her neck. A second, on her bare arm. They stuck where they touched. In a few moments, there were dozens on the prostrate woman.

Then Melanie felt the tiny, probing touch as the seeds sent out hair-thin shoots. There was no pain as the first one wormed its way into a pore on her skin, only a cool numbness radiating from the point of contact. The seed twisted, came upright and then broke in two. A small shoot, bright green and tender, swelled, opened two tiny leaves and began to grow.

Melanie watched it happen in the space of five seconds. The numbness spread up her arm as the other seeds twisted and swelled. There was a coldness in her neck. Under her skin she could feel the rootlets grow along her capillaries and fill up her small blood vessels, seeking her veins. The coldness spread inside her, filling her with a strange torpor. She saw a stalk growing on her bare leg just above her short sock. Two green leaves expanded and uncurled, two tiny, perfectly-formed sycamore leaves.

By the time Susan and Caroline found her, Melanie's body was a mass of writhing plants. She was still alive, though it was a tiny flicker of life. She saw Susan lean over her, hazy and indistinct. The girl turned away and then Caroline's face loomed into view.

Melanie tried to speak. Caroline knelt close just in time to hear the gasping word.

'Run,' Melanie whispered, so faintly it was almost a sigh.

Caroline got to her feet. Susan was standing only a yard away, her face blank. It looked as if all the life had been sucked out of her.

'Where are the children?' Caroline asked, eyes darting here and there.

Susan stood completely oblivious to the rest of the world. Caroline stepped forward and grabbed her by the shoulders.

'Susan! *Susan!*' she said sharply.

The fair-haired girl seemed to come sleepily awake.

'The *children*! We have to find them,' Caroline yelled. Her voice echoed through the trees.

Susan nodded silently. It could have meant anything. Caroline shook her again, hard enough to whiplash her head back and forth, and Susan's eyes suddenly focused. She was back.

'I hear something over there,' she said, pointing beyond the ferns. 'There's more that way.'

Susan followed her finger to where the juniper bushes crowded darkly.

'Go and find them and get them out of here. I mean it, Susan, get these kids to *hell* out of this bloody forest.'

Caroline spun round and scampered beyond the ferns, following the sound of panicked children. Susan backed away from the green-covered body of Melanie Cuthbert before she too turned and headed off quickly through the junipers, every nerve in her body twitching in shock.

A few minutes later she found Dorrie Haldane and the two other small girls. Without a pause she hauled them from their shelter between the roots and dragged them along with her until she came to the dry-stone wall. The children hadn't seen the mouldering corpse jammed on the other side of the tree where the roots had clamped together with enough force to crush bone, but Susan had seen it. The sight had almost made her sick. The distorted skull had leered at her. A fly buzzed out from a rotted socket. It was fortunate for Susan that she did not recognise the corpse of Paul Thomson whom she had kissed on the night of the ceilidh up at the stile.

Dragging the children behind her, it took her another fifteen nightmare minutes to find the edge of the forest and get out into the field below the village. She never saw Caroline Petrie again.

39

Sheila Garvie felt the *change*.

Her whole being was resonating with the pulse of the forest and she sensed the instantaneous tension as the vibration altered.

The time was *now*. The cups were full and brimming red and the forest was drinking the first of the sacrifices. Her body tingled in tune to the throbbing resonance of the stirrings of new life, the vibrant song of the *old* power.

She closed her eyes slowly and let it throb through her. The moment was imminent. Her entire *self* sizzled with hungry anticipation. Everything she had done was coming to fruition.

Fruition. An apt word. She smiled, showing perfect teeth. Underfoot, the ground thrummed, a deep base rhythm, too low to be heard.

Caitlin Brook stood naked in front of the tree, arms by her sides, her breathing slow. Her eyes were open, but they were unfocused. She looked as if she might be asleep.

The tension twisted higher, crackling the air. Overhead, the cauldron stirred and lightning ripped electric gashes in the maelstrom. Thunder cracked across the swaying tops of the trees as the forces of earth and sky once more came together at the forest nexus where ley lines met and worlds conjoined.

Sheila Garvie opened her eyes and saw the first movement in the tree.

A loud creak emanated from the surface as the bark high on the trunk puckered and bulged.

A huge joy swept her.

'*Now*,' she cried out.

The other women stood stock-still, every eye fixed on the vast oak.

The hoary surface rippled as if vast forces inside were pushing outwards. Overhead, a massive branch shivered and creaked raspingly. The ripples on the surface strengthened, like a powerful tide. Corrugations furrowed the flaky grey bark and

from within there was a powerful, grinding sound of wo...
ripping apart.

The front of the tree *stretched* outwards. About twelve ...
from the ground, just below the fork where it split into m...
boughs, the tissue pushed forwards. With a tortured so...
ripping timber a gash yawned above Caitlin's head. One ...
great branches twisted in the air then another followed su...
of them heaving slowly, turning downwards. The trunk s...
further and a vast snort of breath whooshed out fro...
cavernous opening that had widened to more than a yar...
whooped back in with the sound of a hurricane bla...
expansion continued, a formless mass extruding itself fr...
tree with ponderous slowness.

The huge branch swept down, angling as it did. The ...
rippled as knotted muscular heavings torqued within. Th...
branches shrunk themselves down, subsumed into the bul...
wood until they turned into great horny hands. Fingers ...
and closed, gripping the air over the women's upturned fa...

Above them the tall branches, now growing apart fr...
mighty arms, stretched out and down, bare against the bla...

Yet on them shoots were beginning to form. Buds ...
themselves out like green bubbles and expanded quickly ...
ing tender green leaves. At the ends of the branches, fin...
elongated, pliant and budding.

Sheila Garvie's eyes flicked from the powerful bulge tl...
stretching the trunk out of shape. She saw the swelling in ...
branch-ends. The tree was fruiting.

Fierce joy leapt within her. Her reward was comi...
renewal, her own rebirth, was at hand.

Golden flowers burst into luminescent, dazzling bloo...
petals widened and danced on the stalks, then immediate...
started to tumble in an incandescent shower to the floo...
clearing. Where they had been, round fruits expanded ou...
as golden lustrous as the blossoms had been, swelling qu...
the size of apples, then grew even larger. They pulsed wit...
of their own. The fruits grew so quickly that their weight ...
fine boughs bend slowly until the swollen, shining glob...
dangling down like crystals on a chandelier. They conti...
sink very slowly towards the waiting women.

516

Sheila's eyes went back to the tree. The surface of the trunk was now wildly distorted. Up near the fork where the muscular tree arms flexed and twisted something was taking shape. An immense snout was poking outwards just above the slash. A vast moan, like an animal grunting with exertion, came juddering out of the hole in the bark. Below it a colossal chest heaved, bark-covered ribs expanded. A shoulder appeared.

There was another horrendous *rending* and the snout elongated, formed a jaw. A wrinkled forehead stretched out. Branches curved themselves into a spread of antlers. The grey bark twitched and wrinkled and a gargantuan eye creaked open. It stared blindly, its dull wooden surface impervious to light. There was a flick sideways, as a nictitating membrane curtained it then drew back. Now the eye could see.

It turned in its knotted socket and fixed itself on Caitlin Brook.

The girl stood perfectly still, as if unaware of what was happening. She was transfixed in the space between the worlds, paralysed with the power, her mind held in the thrall of the creature birthing itself from the surface of the tree. Yet in that little corner that was connected tenuously to this world, and even more tenuously to another *mind*, a panicked voice was telling her to turn and flee, turn and run.

Caitlin Brook's body did not respond to the voice.

Above her the neck arched outwards and the great head lowered. Eyes as brown as mahogany shone with other-worldly life. The skin of the face was creased in the criss-cross hatchings of old oak bark. The brows were drawn down, great ridges bearing the tremendous spread of curved antlers. The snout was hooked, with flaring nostrils which quivered as the thing snorted with exertion. Hoary growth spread under the neck right down the powerful rippling body. It heaved forwards, using its thick corded arms to lever itself from the tree as it emerged, a grotesque, horned giant, into the world of men.

The women looked on in fear and awe. They had expected something to happen but they had been unable to picture it in their minds. They stared in fascination at the emergence of the antlered tree-man. Below the body the bark writhed and a knee shoved itself outwards, while all the time the golden fruits swelled, their own weight bearing them down towards the encircling group.

The giant speared Caitlin with its eyes. Below its belly, the bark started to twist and bulge. The thing's nostrils flared and it drew in a tempestuous breath. At the base of the antlers, ears like bat wings came forward. The mouth widened into a hungry grimace, almost a grin.

One of the golden pendulous fruits slowly dropped down to within two feet of Sheila Garvie's head. She reached up her bare arms and clasped it. The golden light shone through her fingers. She gave a small tug and the fruit came away, a luminescent apple-shaped globe in her hands. The smell of honey and nectar drifted up pungently, full of promise.

The other women were reaching to pluck the fruits, as they had been told. This was their reward, the gift that would *fix* for always what they had already been granted. Gail Dean clasped hers to her belly, feeling the life within respond to the closeness of the miracle. Fiona Herron held hers in her hands, feeling her fingers stroke the smooth texture. The women were reaching and plucking greedily, while the creature growing from within the tree forced its way from the trunk.

The antlered thing was impatient. It had eyes only for the sacrifice which stood ready. It was not yet fully into the world of men when it started to reach forward, great arms flexing and joints creaking, hands opened wide and horny fingers spread.

With ponderous slowness the hands stretched down and out towards the girl. Sheila Garvie watched in fascination as they groped in the air, still stiff and uncoordinated, for its gift.

The hands were within a yard of the girl's flaming hair. She waited for the touch, the claim.

Then a voice came from the far side of the clearing.

'*No!*' a man bellowed.

40

He had run along the track, not knowing where he was going, heading where instinct told him he *must* go.

The forest was strange to him, a deep and shadowed place, but he ran on with the urgent, wordless call ringing inside his head. His mental lodestone had locked on to Caitlin Brook and drew him onward. As he ran he said a prayer of thanks for whatever had made him cut out the nights of hard drinking that had dismayed his father and earned him a reputation he did not want or need. Now he was leaner and fitter than he had been for five, maybe ten, years. He ran the way Caitlin Brook had done, easily striding along the wet path, feet padding on the soft tilth.

He came to the tumble of moss-covered stones and stopped, head swinging left and right. Then the magnet pulled him straight ahead. He went through the breach and onto the track where the trees formed a barricade of ivy-strangled trunks. He noticed the *change* as he passed through, as if the world had taken a sudden almost imperceptible *twist* out of true. His senses picked up the alteration and he realised that he had entered a place that was *not right*.

Yet he kept running. Twisting anxiety tugged him along.

On one level he was aware of the physical strangeness of the forest he was passing though. The tree ferns that draped leathery green spears conjured a picture in his mind of illustrations in dinosaur books he'd read as a youngster. This part of Fasach Wood seemed to have flipped over into *Jurassic* times. The air was warm and heavy, laden with scents that were redolent of green growth or rampant putrefaction. The forest seemed suddenly *alive* around him. He did not stop. He brushed past trees festooned with bromeliads clamped on their sides, parasitising the thick sap. Hideous, misshapen blooms that resembled dragon's heads stuck out from the bunches, dripping slavers of nectar.

The mental clamour ricocheting around in his head dragged him on. At his side the haversack bumped on his hip. The small bottles tinkled together in his jacket pocket. Things moved in peripheral vision, but he kept his eyes straight ahead, not *wanting* to see what was moving in this alien forest

Martin came to where the old tree had fallen to bridge the river. He clambered up the roots and onto the trunk, slowing to a walk. The bark was slippery from the rain. He made his way across carefully.

Below him the Corrie flowed, sluggish and black. It was unlike the part of the river he had seen up at the bridge a month ago, though that day felt like a *long* time in the past. There, the water had been clear and tumbling fresh from the Linn high on the hill. Here it was twisted with eddies, sluggish and viscid, sleepily dangerous. The water reflected little light. Odd ripples, up-wellings from below, sent turbulence across the surface. Things were moving down there that Martin couldn't see. He didn't look for them, but he sensed their presence. He got the impression they would be things found in no other forest river. The Corrie looked and smelled as if it had travelled a thousand miles through a blighted land. On either side, ugly, contorted willows dipped bulbous tangles of roots into the blackness and drank.

He came to the other side and entered the island trees. The path led almost straight. Above him leaves rustled and made the hairs on his neck prickle with warning, but he kept going. On for thirty paces, the path skirted a thick, bushy tree. As he passed by, something caught his eye and involuntarily he turned his head.

The skull stared at him from black holes. The mouth was open in a silent scream. The flesh had caved in, eaten away from within by a thousand maggots. Still, a cloud of black and bloated flies buzzed around it. The corpse was dripping and wet, though it looked as if it had been dry for a long time. Martin dragged his eyes away, wondering what had happened to the poor devil dead in the tree. He forced the image from his mind and ran on.

Ahead there was light, pale, but brighter than in the dim shade of the tangled forest. He slowed.

Ahead of him there was sound. A creaking sound of protesting timber. He slowed further to a walk then moved cautiously forward. At the edge of the trees, he crouched behind a plant with pale green palmate leaves, like a docken grown monstrous and distorted.

He peered out onto the clearing and saw the face of the monster.

It was vast, and it was grotesque. The sheer horror of its utter *alienness* rocked him backwards.

It was like a moving *gargoyle*, its face at once man-like yet animal. It radiated a primal hunger, from the depths of its polished mahogany eyes. The nostrils on the sharp snout flared open and closed. The great antlers rooted in the massive brow ridge swept the air as the neck arched and the head swung down. Both hands were slowly reaching forward, great twisted muscular arms knotted and rippling with malevolent power.

The glade was torn with the screeching wrench of wood stressed beyond breaking point. A monstrous leg was dragging itself from the trunk, stamping the earth with a thud which shook the earth. The foot had a huge brown splayed hoof as polished as the dully-gleaming eye. The leg was oddly jointed, the hoary knee high up close to the rippling torso, the heel where knee height should have been, like on the fauns of Greek myth. The earth shook with the force of the massive footstep, but Martin hardly felt it.

His eyes were riveted on the goblin face, the monstrous, nightmarish head crowned with a vast spread of antlers.

He had seen that face before, in the picture in the old book on *Druidry*.

But before that he had seen that face in his childhood nightmares. It was the face every child saw in the shadows in the dusk. It was a nightmare come true out of the tree. It was death come to life.

There was a movement below the thing. Martin's eyes flicked downwards and then his heart socked against his ribs with such force it felt as if it was tearing apart.

He'd been so riveted by the awesome sight of the monster tearing itself out from the centre of the tree that he hadn't seen the pale figures below and around it. They were women and they were all naked, arms raised, reaching for the golden globes that swung down, heavy and pendulous, from the sagging branches.

And Caitlin Brook stood alone. Her back was to him, but there was no mistaking her lithe shape and the fiery cascade of hair. Stock-still, legs planted slightly apart, arms down by her sides, she looked as if she was passively waiting.

The thing stretched out thick arms. Massive horned fingers spread wide. It was moving slowly, as if its own timescale was out of synchrony with the real world. It was reaching hungrily for Caitlin Brook and she stood there, waiting.

Martin's heart kicked again and hot blood surged into his head. He got to his feet, diving one hand into his pocket. He threw himself forward, crashing over the misshapen dockens and out into the clearing.

The hands were reaching slowly, stretching out from the grotesque tree-beast. Martin scrabbled with the bottle in his hand. He got halfway there, when the hands were only feet away from Caitlin's head, when the cry came barrelling up from his lungs and he bellowed his alarm across the dell at the top of his voice.

Suddenly all motion stopped.

Caitlin Brook did not move but the women turned their heads in unison. Sheila Garvie twisted round and saw Martin come crashing across the grass towards them. She turned towards the tree. The hands were still moving slowly but the beast's head was beginning to turn away from the girl.

'Take her,' she rasped. 'Take her *now*!'

'*No*!' Martin bawled again. He was bulleting towards them like a madman. 'Take your fucking hands *off her.*'

The head turned and speared him with its glittering eyes. The nictitating membrane flicked across the shiny surfaces from side to side. The nostrils flared. The mouth opened and a gale of breath was sucked in, then came back out again in a roar that shook the whole glade with its force. The mouth yawned and Martin saw a row of jagged teeth stretching round in a horseshoe behind the thick bifurcated lips.

'Get away from her, you ugly big *bastard*,' Martin yelled as he ran.

'*Take her!*' Sheila Garvie screeched again. 'She's *yours*!'

The head continued to swing ponderously, roaring its fury like thunder. It was the sound of a chain saw, rocks being crushed to powder, wood being torn and pulverised.

Even as she screeched, Sheila Garvie reached up and grabbed another of the golden fruits close to her head. She bent down and stuffed it with the other one in a woven bag which was lying at her naked feet where she'd put Caitlin's clothes.

She straightened and turned to Martin who was approaching at a sprint.

'Too late. Too late. You cannot stop this. She is *gone*.'

'Not if I can help it, bitch,' Martin rasped.

He pulled his hand from his jacket pocket and held up a small white plastic bottle with an oddly familiar label. He was unscrewing the dark cap as he ran the last few yards.

On the tree the beast roared fury. It leaned forward, trying to pull the rest of itself out of the oak. The free mammoth cloven hoof pawed the ground for leverage, sending up clumps of dirt. Its eyes rolled madly.

Sheila Garvie planted herself in front of Martin and held up her hands. Around her, the naked women just watched. The running man did not pause. He swung his arm in a short jerk and sent a splash of clear liquid into her face.

The effect was instantaneous. Sheila Garvie screamed as if she'd been burned. Where the liquid had splashed on her arms and face, the skin puckered and shrivelled. There was a line down the hair on the top of her head where droplets had spattered. It curled up as if under a flame and fell out, leaving a narrow pink parting. She squealed like a pig dragged into an abattoir and spun in an ungainly, frantic dance, both hands up against her face.

Martin didn't pause. He ran right past her towards Caitlin Brook. The great hands recommenced their slow downward motion, one of them reaching for the girl and the other swinging out towards Martin Thornton. He jinked past the spread fingers that spanned a yard and lunged forward, throwing his arm up. The liquid shot from the bottle in a clear arc, right into the creature's shiny brown eye.

The head jerked back with the sound of a rent branch. The mouth opened in an appalling gape and a sound like a jet engine roared up into the sky. The great eye seemed to melt and run. Bubbles formed on the surface. Down the hoary cheek, the barky skin suddenly lost its tension and began to flake like dry rot. Martin jumped back, his arm still raised, and then fingers clamped on his wrist with the force of a vice. He felt the bones grind together and a pain shot up into his shoulder. His hand jerked spastically and a splash jetted from the bottle as it squeezed. The liquid landed on the horny fingers and sizzled. The hand instantly jerked open and Martin dropped back onto his haunches. Fiery rivers of pain were shooting from his arm to his elbow as if he too had been burned. He got to his feet, turned, grabbed Caitlin by the waist and hauled her away just as the terrible hand came closing down on the space where she'd been standing.

Beside the tree there was a scream of rage. One of the women came dashing towards Martin, arms outstretched, red fingernails hooked. He kept hauling Caitlin away but the woman followed, whirling and screeching like a cat. He swang a wild fist and punched her on the jaw, the first time in his life he'd ever hit a woman. His knuckle rang with the force of it. She dropped like a sack.

Molly Carr made a grab for him but he shouldered her out of the way and she tripped over her woven bag, landing with a splat on the swollen fruit, which burst with a watery sound and sent golden juice spraying all over the grass. Gail Dean lunged too and he lashed out, slapping her with the back of his hand. Blood spurted from her nose.

Martin turned and held up the bottle, waving it in front of him.

'Nobody move or I'll use this,' he shouted hoarsely. Up against the mighty forest giant the creature was roaring in pain and fury, its head twisting from side to side as it tried to escape the acid burn that was eating away the side of its face. Sheila Garvie was still whirling, blinded. The women stopped still. Martin backed away. Caitlin had said nothing. She did not seem to be aware of anything at all. Her eyes were wide open, blind and green. Martin shook her, keeping a wary eye on the rest of the women. They stood, undecided. He could see anger and frustration twisting their faces.

He lowered Caitlin onto the grass. She lay there placidly, flopped and limp.

'Come on. Come *on*!' he yelled, shaking her shoulders. There was not so much as a flicker. She seemed in a deep trance.

Martin quickly screwed the top back on the first bottle and brought out a similar one. He hadn't been sure the first concoction would work but something had made him go to a little shop in the centre of Glasgow and make two purchases. It had been an instinctive thing.

He grasped Caitlin by the jaw, jamming his fingers into the skin of her cheek to force her jaws open.

'Now drink, damn you,' he bawled feverishly, twisting of the second bottle's lid. He jammed the neck of the white, green-labelled container upended between her teeth and squeezed *hard*.

Caitlin choked. Her eyes screwed up, closed, then flashed open wide. Martin kept squeezing on the bottle, forcing the liquid down her throat. She gagged, coughed and suddenly came to life.

'Oh, get *off*,' she cried, eyes streaming, though the words were completely incomprehensible. Martin hauled the bottle back and she coughed again.

'What on earth are you—' she began, then she seemed to realise where she was.

'What's happening?' she asked, bewildered. She turned her head and Martin heard her breath hitch back in a gasp when her eyes took in the monstrosity that writhed stuck half in and half out of the tree.

'They were feeding you to *that*,' he said.

Caitlin's mouth fell open and a look of revulsion swept across her.

He dragged her to her feet. She was naked and beautiful in the pallid light of the clearing, but Martin didn't notice that. He had only one thought, to get himself and Caitlin Brook as far away from that forest, as far away from the valley, as he could go.

They reached the edge of the clearing and Martin shoved his way through a patch of blackthorn. Behind him, Caitlin gasped and he turned. The inch-long spines had ripped three long gashes in her thigh. In his haste to get her away from the monster and the mad women who had raised it, he had forgotten she was naked. If he dragged her through Fasach Wood she'd be cut to shreds.

He turned, eyes watering from the pain in his arm, and gritted his teeth.

'Your clothes. Where are they?'

Caitlin looked at him, eyes wide and confused, as if she was still dreaming.

He shook her hard; her head rocked backwards.

'Come on. Your clothes!'

She raised a hand and pointed back into the clearing. He moved past her quickly, still gripping her hand. Out there, the tree was writhing and jerking. Screams, terrible screams, shredded the air. Martin ignored all of that.

'Show me,' he ordered. Caitlin pointed to where Sheila Garvie had been standing. The leg of her jogging suit trailed out of a bag on the ground.

He dropped her other hand and darted forward. He bent and scooped up the bag. Something cracked close to his ear. To his left, something heavy fell to the ground with a meaty thud. He didn't wait to look. He spun and raced back to where she stood and hauled her into the trees again, this time avoiding the blackthorn spikes. When he thought they were deep enough into the trees, he stopped and pulled her clothes from the bag. As he did so, he saw the sheen of gold from two of the big fruits in the bottom of the bag. He handed the bundle to Caitlin. By now she seemed to be completely awake. Her eyes were wide and bright with fear, but she did not fumble. In a few seconds she was dressed. She slung the bag over her shoulder and they were off and running. It took them minutes to reach the tree bridge. They skittered over it, jumped down on the far side and sprinted into the forest.

Behind them, something terrible was happening in the forest clearing. The grotesque tree-man, tree-*beast*, roared in frustration. The fruit on the tree reversed their process, shrivelling on the trailing branches. A shiver ran through monster, trunk and branches. The drooping stalks whipped back and forth, sweeping out for dozens of yards beyond the trunks, probing the air. One of them touched Sheila Garvie. The massive head swung round and glared at her with its one eye. The whip-like branch stroked down her body. Another curled around Gail Dean's belly and squeezed. Molly Carr saw a stalk flick towards her and moved back, too slowly. It caught her by the leg and traced its way upwards in a quick slash. All round the tree the searching branches found their targets.

Sheila Garvie aged dreadfully in a matter of seconds, almost quicker than the eye could follow. Her hair fell away from her shrivelling skull. Her breasts sagged like wrinkled toffee. Her whole body shrank in on itself as her back hunched and the bones within started to crumble. She sank to the ground, her shrieks now a whimpering mewl. Her face was a caved-in ruin.

Gail Dean pulled away from the thing round her belly. It tugged once, twice, and she was drawn forward for more than a yard. The life inside her died instantly. There was a terrible *wrench* and her body bucked with the enormous jolt of pain riding through her. Something inside swelled and burst. Muscles convulsed, pushed down, and a hot torrent gushed. Gail Dean experienced the deadly drain and sank to her knees. The flow went on and on until she slid to the ground, eyes glazed and staring.

Fiona Herron was still holding a golden fruit, like a basket-ball player going for the shot. The branch swung almost lazily and the fruit tumbled to the ground. The leaves trailed over the woman's hands. Twigs twisted and caught. Thorns sprung from the tendrils, flicking out like needles into the woman's skin. The tendrils *squeezed* and instant white surged into the knuckles. Raw ends of bone rasped against each other. The woman twisted and turned, trying to free herself. Finally she ripped them out of the branch, skin peeling back in flaps where the thorns held.

Her mouth fell open and her eyes stared in disbelief at the hands she held up in front of her face. They were no longer *hands*. The fingers were curved into rigid hooks, the knuckles horrendously swollen and raw-red with poison. But for the colour, they looked as if they were formed from twisted, distorted twigs. Worse, the inflammation flowed visibly upwards beyond her wrists in a crawling tide of red. Where it flowed, the joints crumbled and swelled. Her right hand was turned back on itself as the tendons shrank. Her elbows ballooned as the collagen was sucked out of them and the calcium started to crumble. Her shoulders were swamped in the tide of venom burning up under her skin. She turned and her whole body creaked. In the space of twenty heartbeats, Fiona Herron's spine began to sag down on itself as the chalky bone was crushed under its own weight. Her jaw, wide open now as she screamed with the hideous, all-consuming *hurt*, distended as even those joints swelled grotesquely. The bones in her knees pulverised each other like grindstones. They could no longer bear her weight and she too crumpled to the ground.

Jean Fintry felt the immediate effect of the poisonous touch as the branches whipped round her and hooked their barbs into her skin, pulsing the deadly sap into her bloodstreamn, infecting her with the malignant *forfeit*. She felt her body bloat as the tissue underneath seemed to fill itself with lumpy dough. Her fine black hair became straggly and thin and lost its colour, turning a drab grey. Her slim body puffed up as the skin stretched under the internal pressure of fat cells expanding with relentless speed. Fatty tissue bloated her cheeks, distending her face and squeezing her eyes into piggy slits. Ripples of cellulite sagged on her buttocks and thighs and visibly billowed. She gave a little moan and her red nails fluttered in front of her face, borne on ugly sausage fingers. Under the pressure of the ghastly distension, her heart started to pound painfully as it stressed and heaved to force blood through her narrowing arteries and veins. Her knees buckled under her own weight and she sagged to the ground, landing with a flaccid thump. Jean Fintry kept inflating, her skin like dirty dough. The internal pressure continued and her heart laboured until it could labour no longer. Her left ventricle gave one final heave and then it ripped under its own vast compression. The prone woman made a gurgling sound and then was silent, a grey mound on the trampled grass.

Molly Carr felt the heat build up inside her. The branches had whipped around her, gripping her in a murderous embrace, and pumped their *other* magic. Instantly she felt the burn, the hot flush flare in her core. Sudden desire flooded her and her breath quickened to rapid shallow gasps. Then the flush became an itch. It needled inside her as the heat flamed and spread, while at the same time her new-found feminine roundness started to deflate and decay. Her breasts were sucked dry until they dangled like flaps on her slatted chest. Her spine poked out in reptilian knobs on her back and her long legs narrowed to skinny, varicose-mapped shanks. Inside her the itch became a fire. She tried to scratch, nails clawing at the tops of her thighs, at her belly, and below. But the burning raged and could not be cooled. She felt herself consumed by the heat of her own flesh. She whirled and twisted, trying to escape, and her wail wavered across the clearing. She fell, still clawing at herself as the heat consumed her. It spread upwards, through her gaunt frame. It rushed into her head and sizzled like a fever. Her eyes felt as if they were boiling in her head as her body temperature rose so high that her skin turned fiery red. Twenty seconds later her nervous system, unable to cope with the fever, simply stopped working. Molly Carr's spindly body twitched and danced on the ground, tangled in the grip of the branches, but that was only the overloaded nerves jerking. She was already dead.

The tree snatched and clawed at the other women who had stood expectantly around the tree, waiting for the fruits to swell and crystallise the gifts they'd been bestowed. Now the great tree which had burst into bud in the clearing and from which monstrous life had emerged, roaring into the world, reclaimed the gifts and more, reversing the process beyond the beginning, wresting everything from the women who had summoned the life, turning their dreams into nightmares and death.

As Martin and Caitlin scampered over the tree-bridge, the monster, one eye still puckered closed, twisted its head to survey the scene. Its gargoyle face was twisted with fury. Around him, bodies lay strewn and contorted, some still twitching, some still alive, all of them befouled. It gave a mighty roar, a jet engine blast that seared the trees around the clearing and made the branches whip backwards under the force of the bellow. Then it started to back away. Its colossal hoof came up off the ground and stepped backwards. It merged itself into the tree with a crackling sound of protesting wood. The chest sank back and the bark rippled over it. The mighty arms raised, swelled, became thick bifurcated branches standing up from the trunk. At last, slowly, the face was subsumed into the trunk of the tree. The one shiny eye glared out, then slowly creaked shut. The gnarled trunk twisted and writhed and then was still. The leaves shrivelled, curled, turned brown and started to tumble in an fluttering ochre hail. The stalks dried out, broke off, fell twig-like to the ground. Above, the black galaxy of the storm swirled. A mighty bolt of lightning speared out from the centre in one apocalyptic stroke and hit the tree in a devastating blast of power. Shards of wood flew up into the air from the epicentre of the strike, whirling deadly slivers for hundreds of yards around. The mighty limbs split away from the trunk and crashed to the ground, where they snapped to powdery cordwood. The force of the lightning bolt had speared through the trunk and into the ground, blasting the very roots out of the soil. The shattered trunk toppled and fell with a thump which vibrated the ground as far as the river. The dust settled on a scene of appalling devastation. Above, the storm began to dissipate as the clouds fragmented and drifted in the swelling breeze over the Douglas Hills.

*

That would have been the end of the story. It *should* have been the end of the tragedy that laid its curse on Linnvale and the people who lived there that summer.

It would have been the end of it, had it not been for the fact that Martin Thornton – though he could not really be held to blame – had not blowtorched the leaf-creature that had come stalking him on rustling feet. It had fled, crackling fire, back into the house and down into the cellar where Martin had smashed every vial and jar that crowded the shelves in Sheila Garvie's bewitched basement. The incandescent thing had stumbled and rolled down the stairs to the basement and rolled about on the floor. Burning leaves had floated off. One of them caught the curtains and flame ate its way upwards. Some of the liquids that had been spilt caught fire and they in turn ignited the dust-filled air in an explosion which was so powerful it blasted the window right out of its frame to land forty yards away in a tree, simultaneously snuffing out the fire which had caused the explosion in the first place.

Powder from the shattered jars spewed out into the air and was carried on the breeze across the road and dispersed in a dirty cloud, drifting right across the valley. Where it landed, life of a kind began to sprout.

That too would have been the end, but for the three layabouts who had been on the rocky outcrop drinking their superlarger and smoking joints when the rain had started and were now huddled under the shelter of the broad chestnut tree next to the road. In a way, Pete Bain, Rory McIntyre and Tam Donald were responsible for saving many of the lives that remained in Linnvale. But that was purely by accident.

41

Martin and Caitlin fled through the alien forest, crashing their way through thick wet foliage, crushing hideous orchid blooms underfoot and trampling fat succulent plants as they raced from the river. He still had her hand in his, keeping a desperate grip on her, scared to let her go. She ran beside him where the path was wide enough and behind him when it narrowed. Martin's other hand was throbbing intensely where the beast in the tree had gripped him. Shards of pain were shooting up to his elbow but he ran on.

The forest was alive with movement. The trees were shivering with motion and a rain of green leaves was tumbling to the forest floor. Thick-stemmed plants with fat fronds waved sluggishly towards them and swollen, spiny runners uncurled lethargically, reaching to rake them with saw-toothed thorns, but they were slowing down, as if the vitality was draining out of them.

Caitlin was tiring. She had run through the forest once before, mind blank and drugged with the liquor Sheila Garvie had made her drink, and she had been within an inch of being taken into the horny embrace of the monster that had extruded itself out of the tree. Now she could feel the strength drain from her legs. Ordinarily, at least before her catastrophic injury, she could have outrun Martin Thornton. Now she let him drag her along behind, grateful for his strength.

Branches dipped down at them and Martin batted them away with his hurting hand. They ploughed through a stand of shrubs and over the place where the grotesque toadstools had been swelling their poison heads, but now they were gone, shrivelled to oily decaying lumps emitting a stench of putrefaction. Even as they ran they could see leaves visibly wilt and shrivel, twitching with foul yet dying life as they barged past.

They reached a wider section of the path and Caitlin pulled up, gasping for breath. Martin jittered anxiously, itching to be out of the trees. He stood against a trunk while she bent down, hands to her knees, hauling the greasy air into her lungs. Martin put his hand against the tree to steady himself and his fingers pushed right through the bark. It was peeling and flaking, soft as wet rot. Fetid liquid poured from where his fingers had pressed. He snatched them back in disgust. Caitlin was straightening. He grabbed her hand.

'Come on. We have to keep moving.'

'It's my legs,' she quavered. 'They're giving out on me.'

'It's not far now,' Martin lied. He didn't *know* how far they had to go. He was lost. But he knew they had to keep going. He had a dreadful fear that the rot that was rampaging through the forest might infect them too.

The wall came into view only a few moments later. They were running across a flat space under spreading, *wilting* trees. Caitlin saw the drystane dyke and they accelerated in a last effort. But as they approached, the wall seemed to *recede*, as if the whole perspective of the place had altered. They stumbled forward, pushing past rubbery saplings that listed in front of them, trampled through hoary ferns that had not been visible at a distance, then suddenly they were through the gap in the wall.

There was a *twist* in the air. It wavered like a mirage. They passed through the break and Martin's ears popped.

They were out of the mystical forest. The very character of the atmosphere changed. Here, the air smelled dry and *normal*. Ahead of them, broadwood trees stood tall; under them tiny mushrooms sent up their colours. Wood anemones shivered in the ripple of breeze. Caitlin let out a sigh of relief as she moved though behind him, then she stumbled. He twisted, caught her by the waist and got her to her feet, never breaking his stride. Martin said nothing, he had no breath to spare. They staggered onwards together, lungs aching, until they saw real daylight ahead.

It took them what seemed like forever to make it to the edge of the wood. They broke through into the cool air and Martin kept going, half carrying Caitlin, right into the middle of the field above the Corrie River. Three hundred yards further on he collapsed with exhaustion and pain and Caitlin slumped to the ground. The world whirled around him as he slowly toppled to the grass, his vision fading. The last thing he heard before the world winked out was Caitlin's voice. The words echoed hollowly in his mind as he slipped into a daze.

'My legs,' she gasped raggedly. 'I'm losing them again.'

Though it felt as if an infinity had passed, Martin's consciousness returned only moments later. His lungs were bellowing for breath. The pain in his arm was now a squealing anger biting through his muscles. Caitlin was lying awkwardly on her side behind him, shaking him roughly.

'Wake up, Martin,' she pleaded.

He opened his eyes, wincing. He didn't want to waken up. His strength had gone. He wanted to lie still. She shook him insistently.

'Come *on*!' she yelled, an edge of panic rough in her voice. He shook his head, trying to clear the fuzz, trying to ignore the pain. His vision cleared.

'Look,' she ordered, pointing back in the direction they'd fled. He looked and saw nothing.

'There!' she insisted, finger pointing directly at the forest edge. He stared. Something moved, but his eyes couldn't focus.

Then realisation hit him with a punch.

The edge of the forest was *expanding*, stretching out towards them in a slow crawl. He sat up sharply, staring intently. The trees were not marching up the hill. They were *growing* up it, at an unbelievable, *impossible* rate. Martin rubbed his eyes with his good hand, like someone who thinks he is dreaming. He looked again and saw the spurt of growth. Small shoots were poking through the ground and swelling and stretching as they squeezed themselves upwards, leaves budding and uncurling. The whole forest edge seemed to be dancing as the growth progressed, seedlings twisting upwards to become saplings, then creaking and expanding to become small trees, and then continuing to stretch skywards, while all the time, ahead of them in the clear space of the field, new rampant life seeded, took root and grew.

'Oh bugger,' Martin said. He was drained of truly meaningful expletives.

'We have to move,' Caitlin said. Martin nodded. He wondered how far they would get, where it would all end. In the back of his mind a thought nagged at him, something he should remember, but it danced away from his tired brain.

He started to get to his feet, pushing down with his good hand, when his eye caught the left one and he froze.

'Oh my—' he began, before his mouth clamped shut as another twist of hurt corkscrewed up his arm.

Caitlin turned, looked at his eyes, followed their direction, then she started back visibly, her mouth falling slackly open.

Martin's hand was grotesquely swollen and the skin was puckered and scaled. It looked like a reptile's claw, wrinkled and brown.

He reached with his right and scraped back the sleeve of his jacket. The whole of his forearm was thickly rutted, to where it disappeared under the sleeve. He tried to move his fingers but they creaked slowly, his knuckles gnarled and swollen.

'What's happening?' Caitlin finally gasped, her face a picture of dumb revulsion.

'That thing. It touched me,' Martin said, voice shuddering at the pain lancing through him as he tried to open his hand. 'I don't know what it's done to me.'

He said that, but he knew what was happening. As soon as he'd touched his arm, he'd felt the hardness of his skin, the barky texture. His fingers seemed longer and ridged with wrinkled knots and whorls. The beast from the tree had touched him, infecting him with its *self*.

Martin's arm was turning to dead wood.

He sagged back in despair. Just then a movement below caught his eye. It was only a small flicker of white, but it dragged his attention away. Caitlin turned with him. There, at the dancing edge of the forest, was a small motion. She raised a hand over her eyes and peered forward. A child's hand reached through the leaves. Caitlin caught a glimpse of pale hair, then the little figure disappeared from view. A small cry of fear came piping up from the trees.

'There's somebody in there,' Caitlin breathed, her horror at the disfigured growth on Martin's skin momentarily shunted aside.

Just beside the first movement they glimpsed a flicker of red. Martin got to his knees, ignoring the agonising pulses. There was another child fighting through the writhing plants at the edge of Fasach Wood.

'Oh, for God's sake. Will this *never* stop?' he groaned. Caitlin forced herself to her own feet and stood swaying unsteadily.

'Stay here,' he said firmly. He turned and stumbled wearily back down the hill towards where the rampant growth was crawling with deadly menace up the field.

By the time he was close to the saplings, rootlets were crunching and squirming under his feet. They twisted and coiled, trying to snare his progress, but he kicked his way through, fear now gone. It had been replaced by a sudden emptiness. He had looked at his arm as he walked towards the rampant growth and the dead space within him had yawned. He was a walking dead man. He was a moving corpse. Vast and cold regret washed through him, but he kept on moving.

He might be dying from the poison touch of the beast from the tree but there were children in there, fighting to get out. He had nothing now to lose. Just as he forced himself between the vibrating saplings, he thought of what he might have had with Caitlin Brook and a sadness took his heart in a cold grip. He shouldered his way past grappling branches, tearing them away from him. Ahead of them he could see the two little girls and behind them, clasping them close, a teenager with torn clothing and a scraped and bloodied face. She was gamely trying to battle her way clear of the clawing growth.

Martin tore a path, ripping the newly grown branches when they snatched at his face and impeded his path. His left hand had gone hard as beechwood. He used it like a club, chopping down where growth impeded his progress, caring nothing for the thorns tearing at his clothes and skin. It seemed to go on for a long time, but he fought closer and closer until he reached the three terrified youngsters.

The girl looked at him as if he was a miracle. Her eyes flicked to his ruined hand and dismay crossed her face. She looked away quickly.

'Come on, then,' Martin said, grabbing up little Dorrie Haldane. Though he didn't recognise the farmer's daughter, something in her hands caught his eye.

It was a small brown teddy bear, with black beady eyes.

He stood staring at it for a long moment, then suddenly burst into laughter. The teddy bear glittered back at him, while the little girl looked at him in frightened puzzlement. The ironic laughter shook him like hysteria. He would die here if he stayed, he would die if he didn't.

But he *had* gone down to the woods.

'Follow me,' he finally managed to say when the laughter died. 'Stay close, and hold on if you have to.'

He turned and started to barge his way back through the path he'd forced through the uncontrolled growth. In the space of only those few moments new plants had squirmed up from the ground, trying to close the gap. But they were still green and reedy and he crushed them underfoot.

He led the little group to freedom. They reached Caitlin and together started to trudge up the hill. She had to stop every few steps and a few yards further on she was down to all fours.

'It's my legs. They're going again. I'm losing them,' she gasped. She rolled on to her face and smashed the grass with her first in a gesture of despair.

'No,' Martin said. The memory he'd been reaching for suddenly loomed out and blazed like a neon light in the forefront of his mind.

Down in that hellish clearing, when the creature had groped for Caitlin, the women had been reaching for the fruits from the tree. There had been something about the fruits, Martin remembered. Sheila Garvie had told him about it before she blew the dust in his face and sent him on his nightmare journey to hell.

The fruits were a *reward*. They were what *bound* the enchantments.

Martin urged the girl and the two children up the hill. They walked on up a grassy knoll, then stopped, exhausted, waiting for him. He scrambled for the bag that was still snagged over Caitlin's shoulder and pulled the neck open. By now his left hand was solid. The bark-like skin was cracking and creasing like old wood. Even as he moved, he could feel his fingers drawn to the ground, mindlessly trying to force themselves into the dirt. A part of him felt an urgent need for the soil and he had to fight against it. He reached in and pulled out two of the golden globes. They had the velvet texture of peaches and the shape of rounded apples, swollen with juice. They glowed with a rich light of their own.

He didn't pause, but instead grabbed Caitlin roughly and turned her over. She gave a little squeal as a jagged pain crunched in the small of her back where the plate had held the bones together. He grabbed the fruit in both hands, dug his fingers into the pulpy skin. Bright incandescent droplets of juice spurted and a wonderful tang of nectar filled the air. He held the dripping fruit over Caitlin's mouth and squeezed. Golden liquid dribbled from his hand into her open mouth.

She choked, coughed a glittering spray, then swallowed.

Immediately an astonishing glow rippled through her, like electricity racing down her nerves, miraculous energy gushing through her veins, pumping into her muscles. She gulped again as he squeezed more of the juice, gasping in as much as she could with every swallow. Her body tingled with it. She felt strength swell within her on a wave of well-being. Caitlin closed her eyes and lay back, letting the energy swell and expand. For a full minute she lay still, breathing deeply. Finally she opened her eyes again. They blazed green at Martin. She smiled at him and his heart did a little flip.

'They're back,' she whispered. 'I'm whole.'

She pushed herself up with her elbows, face flushed and rosy, hair tumbling flame over her shoulders.

'Now you,' she commanded. She took a piece of fruit from his hands and forced it against his mouth. Juice trickled between his teeth. The succulent taste hit his palate and his throat responded. The juice flowed down his throat. Pain pulsed in his dead hand. The warmth crept through him, expanding out from his chest, down his legs and down his arm, but it stopped at his left shoulder. Below there was only fire.

'It's not working,' he thought, and the words were out before he knew it.

Caitlin stared at him. She saw the look of cold despair on his face.

'If it worked for me, it must for you,' she said. 'It *must*.'

Then, something cool flowed inside his shoulder, slowly trickling beneath the skin. The muscle-fire began to abate. The incandescence turned to an icy coldness that pushed back the flames eating into him. He felt them doused relentlessly in a slow cessation of pain, like lava draining away. He pressed his mouth forward into the pulp of the fruit, forcing it into himself. The heady scent filled his head, making his vision blur then come sharply back into focus with extreme clarity.

The searing flames in his arm guttered and died. The muscles in his forearm twitched, as if nerve endings had reconnected themselves, but the movement was *normal*. It was human again. He dared look and saw the bark-like skin lose its ochre shade, beginning to smooth itself out. His fingers opened creakily and closed again. The swollen twig-like knots were deflating. He raised his arm, marvelling at the incredible return and the soothing of pain. Caitlin mistook his intent.

She came into his embrace and hugged him tightly.

Above them the girl and the two small children watched, bewildered.

Finally she pulled away from him and looked into his eyes. Again he felt the jolt as they *connected*.

'That stuff you gave me down there,' she said. 'What was it?'

'An old magic potion,' he said, unable to keep from grinning. 'I checked up on plants. There's a flower called rue that's supposed to hinder witches. And then there's oil of evening primrose, which they've used as a healer for centuries. They both seemed to work. I didn't know if they would, but it was all I could think of.'

'I thought you didn't believe in all that,' Caitlin said.

'I didn't, but I've been *starting* to believe for a while now.'

'And where did you get it?'

'Body Shop,' Martin said, still smiling. 'It's the only place I knew.'

Caitlin let out a giggle. She came back into his arms and held him tight again. When they finally parted, he took her hand and walked slowly towards the waiting group. Behind them, the unnatural new growth continued its relentless crawl up the hillside. Martin reached the grassy knoll and put his other hand out towards the little girl.

She tucked her teddy bear under her other armpit and was reaching up for him when something big and black came soaring through the air straight towards them.

When Alec and Martin had fetched Craig Buist from his house the boy had been reluctant to leave. He balked even more at the idea of going back to the tumbledown homestead. The postman told him they were going for weedkiller and Craig asked why.

'I don't know,' Alec said. 'Martin said we'll need it. He told me to tell you he believes you, though I can't see why.'

The boy looked up at him searchingly. Alec shoved his glasses back up his nose and stared back.

'Is that true?' Craig asked.

'Dead true. He wants us to fill things with weedkiller. That's why I need you to come with me. I don't have a clue. I'm just a postman.'

Craig reluctantly agreed, though with great misgivings. If Martin Thornton *had* believed him, and if he needed weedkiller, then something *bad* was happening. Craig didn't want to think about that.

Up at the Haldane spread Ben sat at his window for most of the afternoon, waiting for his father to come home. He was filled with a deadly feeling of foreboding. The lightning danced across the trees in time to the rolling drums of thunder. Downstairs, his mother was working about the house.

It was late in the afternoon when he saw the final massive, rending bolt stab down into the heart of the wood. The flash was so intense that it left a jagged imprint on his retina. Very much later, there was a dim rumble of thunder. It sounded as if it was very far off in the distance, though the lightning had seemed much closer. The swirling whirlpool of cloud slowly broke up and drifted away, leaving a damp smell of ozone in the air. Ben continued his vigil.

A little more than an hour later he sat bolt upright.

There was a movement at the edge of the forest. He saw branches moving, close to the ground. At first he thought it was someone making their way through the thick brambles and ferns. Yet no one emerged and the thrashing movement continued. Ben opened his breath-fogged window and warm air drifted in from outside. A far-off rustling sound came floating up the valley from close to the stream. He leaned out, puzzled.

Then he saw what was happening.

The forest was creeping towards him.

Memory came back in a jolt. He'd looked out of the same window, when the moon was high, and had seen the branches of trees shimmering in the evening breeze, just beyond the felled beech. And the next day, he and his father had seen the ground churned up. His father had said it was a pig, rooting up the turves, but Ben had never believed that.

The boy stared, mouth agape, willing his eyes to deny what they were seeing. But they refused. Twisted green stems were forcing themselves up from the ground by the stream. As he watched they gained a foot, a yard, swelling and stretching as the forest expanded like mould.

He backed away from the window, breath caught in his throat, and banged into the edge of the bed. He got such a fright that he jumped back and squealed. The really frightening thing was that he heard the screech in his head, but no sound came out of his mouth.

He forced himself to the door, *knowing* it wouldn't open, that he'd be stuck here, struck dumb, while the forest crawled and clambered up the hill towards his house and grew right over it. He twisted the handle and it opened easily. The relief was so great that Ben's throat unglued itself and he bawled for his mother, taking the stairs two at a time.

Rose was not in the mood to listen. She'd fed the remaining few chickens which kept the family – only just – in speckled eggs. She'd done a monstrous pile of ironing and she'd just put the kettle on for a well-deserved cup of tea.

Her son came skittering into the kitchen, his face creamy-pale, and barged into the pile of freshly pressed clothes. It tumbled to the floor.

'Ben,' she cried crossly, 'for goodness sake, watch where you're going.'

'Mum—' he started. His throat tried to tie itself closed again. He took a great big gulp of air. 'Mum. *Mum! It's the trees.*'

'Oh, get out of here! Look at the mess. I'll have to wash Dorrie's blouse again.'

Rose Haldane was suddenly furious. Her son had been hanging around for weeks, pale and withdrawn, refusing to go anywhere. He'd sat upstairs moping while his sister was out having a good time and while she herself was stuck over a hot steam iron. Her patience finally snapped.

'I've a good mind to give you a leathering, Ben. I think that's what you're needing.'

'But, Mum,' he pleaded, jittering from foot to foot in his anxiety.

'Don't but me, Ben Haldane. Just get back up to your room this minute.'

She turned to the tumbled pile of clothes. She was suddenly so mad she could cry.

'*No, Mum! Please, Mum*!' Ben bawled. He twisted round and swept his hand right into the rest of the clothes. They went flying in all directions across her kitchen. Rose stopped dead. Her mouth opened in a perfect circle.

The realisation of what he had done hit her like a shock and then on the heels of that came the jolt of sudden righteous anger.

'You just wait . . .' she cried, stepping over the clothes. She raised her hand to slap him for the first time in his life. Ben ducked, twisted away and ran into the hallway. She was so furious she came right after him.

He scampered towards the front door, now suddenly *glad* that she was chasing him. He snatched it open, dashed outside and went straight across the gravel pathway to the grassy lip that stretched for a few yards before the dip down into the valley. He stopped when he saw the green shivering down at the forest's edge. The stream had gone. The riotous growth had spread over it and was on to their side of the valley. Ben turned. His mother came across the path at a fast, angry walk. She reached out a hand to grab him by the front of his T-shirt when he yelled at the top of his voice.

'There, Mum!'

He was pointing backwards, his face a mask of urgency. Rose's left hand was raised to cuff his ear. It froze in mid swing.

'Oh my God, what's *that*?'

'It's the trees, Mum. They're *coming*.'

Rose took a step back, hand up in a kind of salute. Then all the fight went out of her. Ben ran in to her, flinging his arms around her waist.

'Please. We have to get out of here. We have to go *now*.'

Just as he said it, his sixth sense kicked in again with such an electrifying jolt that his legs almost gave way. Danger slammed into him with such force that his vision blacked out for a second. He stood, rigid as a fence post, every nerve in his body jangling raw. Finally he gave a little start.

'Ben, are you all right?' he heard his mother ask, from some distance, though she stood right beside him.

'Oh . . .' he moaned. He looked at his mother and she flinched back from the dreadful stricken look on his face.

'*Dorrie!*' he screeched. His cry cut across the valley and soared down to the crawling edge of Fasach Wood, where it was swallowed by the creepy rustling of frenzied growth.

But Ben was off down the road, running as if his life depended on it, heading for the edge of the village, in the rough direction that the mental blast had come from.

A few seconds later Rose Haldane followed her son, running as fast as her legs could carry her.

Down in the field on the far side of the wood Pete Bain and his cronies noticed the growth very late on, but that had something to do with the cans of strong lager they had drunk and the several joints they'd smoked.

They sheltered under the big chestnut, sitting close to the trunk, not in any hurry to move on. The children disappeared into the forest, leaving their hampers on the flat grassy spot, when the rain came on. For a while all was silent and then Pete, Rory and Tam had heard the children's squeals coming from deep inside the trees. There was always a treasure hunt at the kids' summer picnic. They'd attended something very similar ten years before, though now they sneered at the kids' stuff. The three of them took the screeches for childish laughter.

'Wonder if there's anything to eat?' Tam mused.

'There's always cakes and stuff,' Rory chimed in. 'Be plenty left. What you think, Pete?'

The dark-haired youth in the biker's jacket seemed deep in thought for a moment.

'I could eat a horse,' he finally said. He got to his feet and sauntered out from under the tree. The rain had stopped after that final blast of lightning. Now the sky was clearing. It wouldn't be long, he knew, before the three women and the little kids would be coming out from the shelter of the forest. The other two followed him quickly down the field of thistles towards the hampers. They reached the picnic spot and helped themselves to the sandwiches and cakes that were left. Pete upturned one of the hampers, scattering the remains of the food over the grass. Rory kicked the other such a blow with his high-toed farmer's boots that it sailed into the air and fell with a splash into the Corrie, where it spun a couple of times then started to drift with the current.

'What a goal,' he bawled.

Tam giggled gleefully. Pete jammed a cake into his mouth while the others wolfed the food they'd raided. They sauntered back up the hill. There was a rustling sound at the edge of the forest and Pete bent to a crouch, keeping himself low behind the high, downy thistles that overgrew the top half of the field now the cattle which used to crop them had been sold.

'They're coming back,' he hissed, sniggering.

Rory was ahead of the other two. He started to run up the hill. He got about twenty paces when one very tall thistle, with unusually spiky leaves and a vivid orange seedhead unlike the purple ones which crowded the field, swayed away from him. He turned at the movement. It came whipping back and hit him like a snake. The jagged spines, thistle spikes *much* larger than the others, drove right into his eyes, bursting through his pupils. Rory gave a little low cry and went down as if his tendons had been cut. Blood and bile frothed from his mouth, strangling the horrible moan that was trying to get out. His head whipped from side to side and his teeth gnashed together with a spine-chilling grinding sound.

'What's up?' Tam grunted. He'd been behind Pete Bain and hadn't seen a thing. 'Is that eejit throwing a fit or is he just drunk, or what?'

Pete shook his head numbly.

He'd seen it happen. The movement had caught his attention. The thistle had lashed forward like a . . . like a *triffid*. He'd heard the pulpy smack as it hit Rory right in the face. His sidekick had turned, as if punched on the chin, body already going limp. The eyes were gone. A purple blotch was tattooed from his forehead to his cheeks. Before Rory McIntyre hit the ground the purple had flooded right down to his chin.

'Oh, Christ,' Pete whispered.

'Come on, leave the drunk. They're coming,' Tam urged.

He tried to push past Pete, but the dark-haired boy grabbed him by the arm and that's what saved Tam's life. The thistle swayed back again lethargically and, as it did, its tight seedhead opened with a *click*. A halo of deadly spikes sprung out on the outside edges. The head flicked forward, an orange blur, and missed Tam by six inches.

He staggered back.

'What in the name of *fuck* . . .?' he shouted.

Pete Bain grabbed him by the shoulder and dragged him backwards, away from the plant. The thistle swayed like a cobra. He whirled round, scanning the field for other strange growths. There was another vivid plant ten feet away, its head swelling. They skirted it warily, each of them unable to comprehend what exactly had happened, but now aware that they were in terrible danger. They moved up the hill as fast as they could go, keeping themselves as far away from *any* plants as they could. They got to the fence at the top, clambered over and got onto the road. By this time, Tam was gibbering with fright and Pete Bain was shaking all over. They started up the road where the hedgerow now stretched in unruly growth out from the sides. There was a shiver of movement beside a tangle of hawthorn and Pete caught sight of another tall, deadly growth.

He stopped dead and then a huge blare of noise just behind him scared him so badly that he almost fainted. He spun round, expecting some monster to be creeping up on him.

Jock Weir's big white tanker was toiling up the hill with a throaty whine of diesel power. He had seen the two boys on the road, standing with their backs to him, and rather than slow down on the hill and change down three, maybe four, gears he had hit the horn, sending out a flat bray of sound. The kids ahead had jumped a foot in the air but it had cleared the road. He roared past them in a cloud of fumes, grinning to himself. He didn't see Pete and Tam at the ladder on the side of the bowser, each trying to clamber over the other in their haste to get aboard and away from the plants. They were hanging on Jock's side of the tanker. If he'd have looked in the mirror, he would have seen them, but he didn't.

Rab McGraw did, and almost too late. He was coming down from Ardbeg distillery with a full load, twenty-five hogsheads of sixteen-year-old Ardbeg whisky – all of it forty over proof – on its way to finally become one of the best-known export blends in the world. His articulated lorry was carrying more than a thousand gallons in the hard oak casks. Rab had picked up speed after the bends and was now on the straight run down the hill.

There was a curve halfway along the stretch and the truck came barrelling down there like a freight train. Ordinarily he could have passed the gas tanker without difficulty. But as soon as he rounded the bend he saw the two people hanging onto the ladder, swinging across to his side of the road.

Rab stamped on the pedal and heaved the wheel to the left, pulling the nose to the inside of the road, trying to get as far away from the tanker as he could. The airbrakes spat and the outside wheels juddered as the pads clenched the discs. The trailer and its big load swung sharply, pushed forward by its own weight. The wheels screeched in protest. The inside tyre hit the verge and twisted the steering wheel out of Rab's hand. Then the back wheels lost their grip on the warm, rain-slicked road and began to swing.

Jock Weir, hauling uphill and only doing not much more than thirty with his full liquid load, saw the rear section of the whisky lorry swing out as the juggernaut began to jackknife. Rab McGraw's face was a white blur behind the windscreen. The full load of whisky barrels came wheeling round, side-on to the road, straight towards his cab, a mountain of oakwood and steel. He pulled to the nearside automatically. The tanker veered off the road, crashed through the tangle of hawthorn hedge and went ploughing towards the outcrop at the brow of the hill. His left headlamp blew inwards as it cracked against a stout ash tree, then the tree itself snapped at its base and went flying off and behind as the big bowser carved its way through the straggly thicket.

Rab McGraw snatched at the wheel just as the whisky lorry's cab tipped. He heard the screech of rubber as the rear trailer tyres came swinging edge-on to the road and then he felt the rig topple. A branch smashed through his window and impaled his hat, scoring a groove right across his bald scalp.

Hanging grimly to the tanker ladder, Pete Bain and Tam Donald had been screaming without break since the whisky lorry hove into view, bearing down on them on a road that was just wide enough for two big carriers to pass with only an inch between their wing mirrors. Pete had tried to scramble *over* his friend in a bid to get himself out of the way before the lorry squashed them like summer gnats against the sides of the bowser. Tam lost his grip with one hand, screamed even louder and hooked his fingers, quite by accident, into the pocket of Pete's jacket. Pete felt the drag and panicked. He stamped his foot down, catching Tam right on the cheek. For a second, his pal's head was twisted to the side, face clamped so hard between Pete's boot and the rung of the stair he thought his whole face would burst like a squeezed grape.

Pete saw the load of whisky barrels shift, then come swinging round towards them. His scream rose several octaves and he managed to get up one more step, when the whole tanker veered. Branches whipped at them as they went crashing through the tangled saplings at the side of the road.

They burst through, Jock Weir at the wheel, eyes wide, mouth wider. At the top of the rocky outcrop, the great white tanker went roaring onwards. The land fell away sharply in its swoop down the hill towards Fasach Wood. There was a twenty-foot drop before the slope. Jock saw it coming and gave up trying to control the tanker. He opened the cab door and heaved himself onto the plate just as the offside wheel hit a knob of rock and flipped his vehicle up into the air, separating the chassis from the gas cylinder. He was flipped with it, spinning head over heels to land face down beyond the rocks in a thicket of nettles with such force that he stove in two ribs, broke his collar bone, lost two teeth and completely winded himself. Worse, every nettle in the clump seemed to have taken their revenge on him when he crushed them into the soft earth. When he finally emerged, wheezing for breath, his face was swollen to almost twice its normal size. The only other piece of good luck he had was in the fact that one of the ugly orange thistle plants had taken root only a couple of yards from the nettles. It swayed towards him, spikes beginning to flick out, but Jock didn't even see them. He had hauled himself to his feet, completely dazed and bewildered, and stumbled off, not even knowing where he was going. It was his great luck that he walked the other way from the trembling plant.

Pete Pain and Tam Donald were still hanging on to the side of the trailer, Tam by only one hand, when they were dragged, squealing, through the grove of saplings and bushes. The front wheel hit the rock and the side of the tanker swatted them off like flies, each still attached to the other, over the tops of the trees. Tam came down on Pete's face with such force that the tough boy's jaw was broken in three places, and Tam himself shattered both knees and his back. He ended up in a wheelchair very like Caitlin Brook's, which was a great misfortune in one way, because both of the ne'er-do-wells were instrumental in what happened next in Linnvale. Tam, on the other hand, managed to get on a course after he came out of hospital and developed an interest in computers, finally breaking out of his small-town layabout mode and eventually starting his own technology business. That was all for much later.

Right at that moment, as the four peole who had been in or on the out-of-control lorries were lying unconscious, dazed, or winded, the loads were still moving.

The gas tanker had hit a stony outcrop, twisted in the air, broken apart and the back section had flown over the drop, a huge white pivoting cylinder. It landed on its back tyres, which blew out instantly, and then went tumbling and bounding down the hill.

The lorry trailer hit the road with a crunch of tortured metal and the barrels simply bounced in the direction they were headed, which was over the hawthorn hedge and into the field, forty fat oaken casks tumbling and rolling at high speed towards the woods.

Martin Thornton grabbed little Dorrie Haldane and yelled an incomprehensible warning as the first of the barrels came flying from over the shoulder of the hill. He had snatched the girl, teddy bear and all, dragged her to the side and rolled, making sure he didn't land on top of her. Beside him Caitlin Brook had followed with the other child and the tall, fair-haired teenager had jerked like a frightened rabbit and dived off to the side. The barrel had come bouncing between them, hitting the earth with such a thud that it shook beneath their feet. It crashed on down the field. Another followed, then another, all of them bouncing and twirling in a lethal ballet as they raced for the forest. One of them hit a stone and crashed open, curved barrel staves erupting outwards. A metal hoop spanged away and whisky sprayed over the grass in a cloud of amber fumes.

The avalanche thundered past them in seconds. Martin looked around and found that they were all unhurt. He hoisted Dorrie to her feet and started up the hill just as the white monster came sliding over the shoulder fifty feet away. At first Martin thought it was heading straight for him and his heart sank. He had reached the end of his rope. But it slid away, bounding on the steep part

where a little gully had been worn out of the field by spring run-off.
He saw the tanker pirouette then somersault as it careered with a
thundering roar down to where the valley swept towards Fasach
Wood. There was a tremendous *thump* and a hollow boom as the
side hit a submerged moss-covered rock. Instantly a pure white
cloud spewed from the side as the liquid calor gas shot out under
pressure and vaporised in the early evening air. If the rock had not
been covered with water and a thick carpet of wet sphagnum
which prevented a spark at the moment of impact, then all of them
would have died instantly in the explosion.

Martin watched as the cloud spilled out, formed a blanket
around the tanker, then simply started to *flow*, following the
contours of the hill, right into Fasach Wood.

For several moments his mind was numb. He sat and watched in
bewildered fascination until the smell of gas and whisky was
carried up to him on an eddy of wind.

The realisation of what the white cloud was hit him with a
sudden shock.

'Everybody, *come on*,' he shouted, leaping with surprising
agility to his feet. Caitlin turned to look at him, saw the expression
on his face, and asked no questions. Martin got Dorrie Haldane,
grabbed Susan Herron by the wrist and started moving. They
made it up over the brow of the hill in twenty seconds flat.

From there it was only forty yards to the stile where Susan
Herron had kissed Paul Thomson on the night of the ceilidh. Two
of the boys who had chased him into the forest and to his death
were lying moaning on the ground close to the bushes beyond the
outcrop unseen by the fleeing group.

Martin helped the children across the stile, urging them to move
quickly, and handing them over to Caitlin on the far side. He
hustled the blonde girl with an ungentlemanly shove. There was
no time for gallantry. They headed uphill to the turn and met Alec
Stirling coming down with young Craig Buist. As soon as Alec saw
them, his glasses slipped down his nose and he stared goggle-eyed
at the tattered group panting their way up the hill.

'Stay away from the bushes,' Alec bawled. He was wearing
something on his back and Craig Buist seemed to be attached to
him by a black umbilicus.

'Look,' Alec bellowed again. 'Watch out.' He came running

forward and Craig placed a sturdy metal contraption next to him on the road. In at the hedge, a spiky green plant was worming its way above the brambles. It waved from side to side as it rapidly grew and then a seedhead began to swell with alarming speed. Alec turned towards it, keeping his distance. Craig stuck his foot in the metal contraption and started to pedal up and down with great vigour. A fine spray jetted from the nozzle Alec held in his free hand, right into the clump of brambles. Immediately the spiky plant shrank back, withering to brown.

Alec turned to Martin.

'You were right about the weed-killer, boss. There's dozens of these things. Killed the young fellow's cows. Thought the old stirrup pump would do the job.'

'Not for much longer,' Martin said breathlessly. 'Got to get up the hill. There's a gas tanker down there.'

'That's no good. Need this chemical stuff.'

'No,' Martin said, gasping for breath. 'It's burst. There's calor gas all over the place.'

Alec looked at him blankly and Martin had to grab him by the shoulder and drag him back down the road a little way to the stile. He pointed.

The snowy cloud was spreading down the slope, about six foot high and so thick it was completely opaque just in from the trailing edges. Tendrils of the mist snaked along the runnels and hollows as the gas flowed right into the trees. Even from where they stood they could see the hoar frost forming on the trunks and leaves as the liquid gas, cooling with amazing speed as it expanded, froze the forest wherever it touched. Down there, the edge of Fasach Wood was glistening like an ice-sculpture. The frantic growth had stopped dead.

As they watched, wide-mouthed, there was a movement further to the east, only fifty feet from where the far edge of the gas cloud was curling rapidly round the tall trees beyond the gully. There was a crackle of bracken and a figure dragged itself through the creeping foliage.

It was a man. He barged through the edge of the undergrowth, kicking and pulling at runners that twined themselves around him. Martin heard him let out a cry of desperation as he tore himself free and staggered on, then beside him a small voice yelled in alarm.

'*Daddy!*'

Little Dorrie Haldane had come down to the stile, following the man who had saved her from the forest. As soon as she saw the tattered man at the edge of the wood she threw herself at the stile and had scampered to the top, when Martin shot out a hand and grabbed her by the back of her dress, flipping the child backwards like a rag doll.

'Get her out of here,' he snapped, bundling her roughly towards Alec.

The postman took the girl without thinking, then stood, wondering what to do with the squirming, bawling child.

Martin climbed the steps again. He stood on the flat platform at the top and yelled down the valley.

'Come on, man. *Run for it!*' Martin was waving his hands in the air, trying to catch the staggering man's attention.

Duncan Haldane looked up and saw the group. Martin pointed, making exaggerated movements. The white face stared back, obviously uncomprehending, then finally the head turned.

The man saw the pearlescent cloud roll across the ground towards him. Where it touched, the leaves and runners and bark went pure white. There was a crackling as delicate, iced leaves tinkled against each other, frozen to glass. He took a few steps forward, slipped, got to his feet and started to clamber up the hill, all the time looking back over his shoulder, not at the cloud, but back into the forest, in the direction he'd come. In seconds the mist had flowed over the place where he'd stood, blistering it white.

The big farmer, clothes torn and ruined, started to climb. He was clearly exhausted. Despite his own tiredness, Martin went back down and met him halfway. Duncan was slick with blood from thigh to ankle and obviously at the far end of a frayed tether. Martin got his arm round the man and helped him make it up the steep part of the slope to the stile. When he got there, little Dorrie Haldane jumped over, dropping her teddy bear in her rush. She threw herself forward, thumping right into her father at waist level and hung tight. The big farmer was so fatigued after his terrifying flight from the thing in the forest that he couldn't even take her weight. He toppled to the ground, while his daughter held on to him in a desperate grip. Martin had to drag both of them to their feet and shove them over the stile.

Duncan Haldane was halfway up the step when he turned and looked over Martin's shoulder. His mouth dropped open and his whole body stiffened. Martin instinctively turned. Down at the edge of the wood, a little way from where the gas cloud was frosting the tangled plants, a shadow moved out low and snakelike.

Martin put a hand above his eyes and peered down at the indistinct mass.

'What the hell is that?' he asked.

'Nothing I ever want to see again,' Duncan Haldane said in a voice that was drained of emotion. 'Come on. Let's get these people away.'

The shape, long and sinuous, streamed out of the shadows into the open. It was brown and elongated, flattened to the ground. As it moved, its form changed. It bunched up and then spread out, as if unable to hold together.

In a flash, Martin realised what it was made of.

'Is there anybody in there?' he asked Duncan Haldane.

The big man looked at him blankly, as if he didn't have the capacity even to *think*.

'Come on, man. Is there anybody in those trees?'

Duncan shook his head slowly.

Susan Herron stepped forward.

'There's no one left. They're all dead. All of them. All the wee ones. It killed them.' Her voice trailed away.

Martin looked at the two little girls. They were beyond the stile and couldn't see the creeping thing that was now scrabbling up the hill.

'No one? Honestly?'

They both shook their heads, faces slack with the horror they'd seen when the trees in Fasach Wood had come alive.

'Right. All of you. Up the road.'

They stood stock-still.

'I mean *now*,' he bawled.

The children flinched back. Alec started to say something, then saw Martin's expression and shut his mouth. Caitlin looked puzzled.

'You too,' he told her. 'Get them out of here. Fast as you can.' He slid the knapsack from his shoulder. It clanked as it hit the road. The rest of the group were moving away, Alec and the boy searching the hedgerow for signs of movement.

'What are you doing?' Caitlin asked.

He drew out the old blowtorch from the bag. It was heavy and full in his hands.

'Go on,' he said. She stood her ground.

He lifted the weighty blue cylinder with its scorched nozzle and looked into her green eyes, and she saw the deadly weariness in his face.

'Look, Caitlin. Get out of here, will you? I don't want you around for this.'

She stared at him for a second, then came forward and hugged him very quickly. Her lips brushed his cheek.

'Don't waste time. I'll be waiting,' she said, close to his ear. Then she turned and went with the rest of them on up the hill.

Martin moved from the stile, unhitching the belt at his waist as he walked. To the left, the rocky promontory was a flat plateau leading away from the fence. He followed the ridge to the edge and looked down the drop, then swept his eyes down the far slope. The tanker was shrouded in the mist, a hard regular white shape against the expanding snowy blanket. The cloud was flowing outwards still under great pressure and spread like floodwater into the trees. One of the whisky barrels which hadn't quite made it to the forest stood out black against the white. The silence was eerie. No birds sang. No wind blew. The mist simply spread white through the trees, heavier than air, menacing in its purity. Beyond its far edge, the dark shape crept upwards, bunching and flattening. Martin could hear the dry rustle of its progress.

He slipped the end of his leather through the handle of the blowtorch, fed it through the buckle and pulled the noose tight. He swung the thing, hefting it, then laid it down to unscrew the black ridged valve and the canister hissed furiously. He fumbled in his pocket and found his lighter under his car keys, drew it out and flicked it just in front of the nozzle.

A spark jumped and blue flames roared. He let the heat build up, unscrewing the valve back to full throttle. The flame spewed out two feet from the end, tight and searing.

Martin Thornton did not hesitate. He stood up and planted his legs apart, took the end of the leather and let the torch dangle. It

552

spun on the end of the belt. A blast of flame seared his denim briefly, then Martin swung it once, twice, around his head, hearing the angry *whoosh* of the gas flame. He let it go at the apex of the spin and the torch soared upwards, spitting a blue arc as it rose, then descended. It dropped, whirling, and landed on the mass of moving, rustling leaves. Instantly the shape reacted, exploding upwards, drawing itself in. A shape began to form, first broad and squat, then tall and spindly, in a wild metamorphosis. Then flames simply *exploded* through it. The mass lost all cohesion. Pieces of burning leaves flew up and out. The mass of the scuttering thing wheeled and whirled and then it spun in a wide circle as the fire flared upwards.

Martin watched as it rolled, out of control, back down the hill, heading straight for the white cloud-bank.

Realisation smacked into him. He did not wait to watch. It was twenty yards from the pallid mist when Martin turned and ran for cover. He got halfway to the stile, hidden from the scene below by the rocky outcrop, when the world exploded in one devastating blast.

The sound rolled up the valley, along with the first shock of flame, blasting the hedgerows and saplings and then crisping their leaves to cinders. The field of thistles died in a scorching flash.

But that was just the thin gas at the edge of the wood.

Inside Fasach Wood, the cloud had pooled in the depressions and dells under the trees. All growth had stopped, all movement was dead. The gas had flowed as far as the Corrie River. Here and there, stuck in thickets and tangles, the thirty-nine remaining barrels of overproof whisky lay on their sides and on their ends.

The blowtorch ignited the edge of the gas cloud and simply blasted through the forest. In that split second, the whole of Fasach Wood became an incandescent field of flame. Lakes of fire flooded the forest from end to end. Torrents of flame cascaded down on the surface of the Corrie. Trees were blasted from the ground. Others were incinerated in seconds. Every plant in the forest, from towering beech to ancient oak and to crawling bindweed, shrivelled and burned in the first few seconds and then gave themselves to feed the inferno of pure white heat. The whisky inside the barrels evaporated and they too exploded in a series of thunderous blasts that shook the valley from end to end.

As the flames covered the whole spread of the forest, the heat scorched the valley for five hundred yards on either side of where Fasach Wood had stood for thousands of years, killing off every plant, including the foul growths that had sprung from Sheila Garvie's cellar. The rising heat drew air in from the cooler upslopes, bellowing oxygen into the raging forest until the flames reached two hundred feet into the sky. The pall of smoke was seen from John O'Groats two hundred miles to the north and was even picked up in the infra-red camera of a passing weather satellite in orbit.

Martin Thornton got to his feet, keeping low, and making sure the outcrop of rock was between himself and the hell-fire that was raging down the slope. Even then, the heat singed the hairs on the back of his neck and caused the threads on his jacket to smoulder. The firestorm's backdraught, dragging powerful winds down from the Dumbuie Hills, almost threw him off his feet and for one terrible moment he thought he'd be flung off the outcrop and down into the searing cauldron below. He made it to the fence, tumbled over it, reached the road and ran, coughing hot air from his lungs.

When he had got far enough away, he turned to watch the incredible destruction of one of the last remaining stretches of the old Caledonia Forest. He felt no remorse.

As the flames towered high, even at that distance reddening his cheeks, he smiled a tight smile and turned to walk up the hill towards where Caitlin Brook was waiting.